No, Amy thought, this was much better. This was her alternative. She rode the inrush of desire, of sudden wild wish that her own words produced in her. "George," she said, "I know I'm a bitch in a lot of ways. But I still want to be your wife. In every way."

"Ame. Ame." He was kissing her. But not in a tough or angry way. He was cradling her in his arms in his usual tender style...

Was she winning or losing? Amy wondered dazedly as he undressed her. Didn't he *hear* what she had said to him about excitement? ...she still wanted the spirit of lust, of comrade-in-armsmanship, of daring mockery of rules and respectability. She wanted combat thrusts, not sentimental strokes. She wanted sybaritic extravagance, not ladylike satisfaction. She wanted outrageous proposals, not murmurs of renewed affection.

She would have to find her excitement elsewhere

By Thomas Fleming

FICTION

The Officers' Wives
Promises to Keep
Rulers of the City
Liberty Tavern
The Good Shepherd
The Sandbox Tree
Romans Countrymen Lovers
A Cry of Whiteness
King of the Hill
The God of Love
All Good Men

NONFICTION

1775: Year of Illusions
The Forgotten Victory
The Man Who Dared the Lightning
The Man from Monticello
West Point
One Small Candle
Beat the Last Drum
Now We Are Enemies

*Published by
WARNER BOOKS

The Officers' Wives

Thomas Fleming

WARNER BOOKS

A Warner Communications Company

The names of most Army posts and units mentioned in this book are invented. This has been done to underscore the author's avowal that this is a work of fiction and any resemblance to actual persons, living or dead (except where historical or living persons are mentioned in passing), is purely coincidental.

Grateful acknowledgment is made for permission to quote from the following: "In Crisis" from *Collected Poems* by Lawrence Durrell. Copyright 1940, © 1980 by Lawrence Durrell. Reprinted by permission of Viking Penguin, Inc. *Legends of Hawaii* by Padraic Colum. Yale University Press, 1937. "Solomon and the Witch" from *Collected Poems* by William Butler Yeats. Copyright 1924 by Macmillan Publishing Co., Inc., renewed 1952 by Bertha Georgie Yeats. *Zen Buddhism* by D. T. Suzuki. Hutchinson Publishing Group ltd., London. Excerpts from *The Zen Koan* by Isshu Miura and Ruth Fuller Sasaki are reprinted by permission of Harcourt Brace Jovanovich, Inc., copyright © 1965 by Ruth Fuller Sasaki. *Anthology of Japanese Literature* by Donald Keene. Reprinted by permission of Grove Press, Inc. Copyright © 1955 by Grove, Inc. *Collected Poems* of Thomas Merton. Copyright 1944 by Our Lady of Gethsemane Monastery. Reprinted by permission of New Directions. "Abel" by Demetrios Capetanakis from *A New Anthology of Modern Poetry*. New Writing and Daylight, London. "Soldier" by C. T. Lanham. Copyright © 1933 by *Harper's* magazine. All rights reserved. Reprinted from the August 1933 issue.

WARNER BOOKS EDITION

This Warner Books Edition is published by arrangement with Doubleday & Company, Inc., 245 Park Avenue, New York, N.Y. 10017.

Cover design by Gene Light

Cover art by Jim Dietz

Warner Books, Inc., 75 Rockefeller Plaza, New York N.Y. 10019

 A Warner Communications Company

Printed in the United States of America

First Printing: March, 1982

10 9 8 7 6 5 4 3 2 1

To Alice

The Army wife . . . is equally at home in a cabin or a mansion, a fine hotel, a transport. She is a good mother and rears her family, generally, under conditions which would seem impossible to her civilian sisters. . . . Her sense of Duty, Honor and Country are those of the Army itself.

The Officers' Guide

Maybe the bride-bed brings despair,
For each an imagined image brings
And finds a real image there;
Yet the world ends when these two things,
Though several, are a single light.

William Butler Yeats

If the Army wanted you to have a wife, they would have issued one.

Old soldiers' saying

CHAIN OF COMMAND
U.S. ARMY

 GENERAL OF THE ARMY

 **GENERAL**

 LIEUTENANT GENERAL

 MAJOR GENERAL

 BRIGADIER GENERAL

 COLONEL

(silver) **LT COLONEL**

(gold) **MAJOR**

 CAPTAIN

(silver) **1st LIEUTENANT**

(gold) **2nd LIEUTENANT**

BOOK
ONE

I

Swish click, swish click went the windshield wipers. Rain pattered on the roof of the olive-drab Chevrolet. They were crossing the Tappan Zee Bridge. The Hudson was shrouded in November mist. Neither bank was visible. The bridge's huge steel girders loomed eerily around them. They might have been travelers in a spaceship, gliding down to dock on earth after a long voyage to distant, dangerous worlds. There was some validity to the metaphor, Joanna thought. But she preferred reality. She was grateful for the familiar sounds, the wipers, the tires slicking on the wet concrete, reinforcing reality. She was grateful for the uniformed man sitting beside her in the back seat, the stars of a major general gleaming dully on his shoulders. He did more than reinforce reality. He made it preferable to the dismal world of time passed, the shadowy jungle ruled by memory, that had once tempted her.

"Could we go up 9W?" Joanna said. "It's more interesting even if we can't see the river."

"Are you in a hurry, Captain?" Sam Hardin asked. A general was always sensitive about borrowing another general's aide.

"No, sir," said Captain Carl Collins of the class of 1969. He told the blond private at the wheel how to get to 9W.

Captain Collins was black. He was also a model West Pointer, a veritable paradigm of squared shoulders and ramrod back, emanating the controlled intensity of a man on familiar terms with violence. Even more of this intensity emanated from Major General Samuel S.

13

Hardin. West Point, the Command and General Staff School, the National War College, Korea, Vietnam, had trained him to organize the chaos of a battlefield, to orchestrate rifle and grenade, artillery and rockets, helicopters and fighter-bombers, to produce impersonal death on a scale beyond imagination.

Yet Joanna loved him. The day before yesterday she had kissed this man and said: "I love you." She was certain it was not a Judas kiss, the embrace of lying Joanna, the woman known only to herself and the dead. With this man's help, she had banished that game forever.

They were riding toward West Point, where Joanna's knowledge of violence had begun, to mourn the death of a friend. At least, that was what the general thought he was doing. For Joanna the journey had a different, darker aspect. Gray sadness crept into her lungs, her blood. She fought it, wondering if her will had any more power to banish it than it had to clear the mist enveloping the Hudson.

Captain Collins stretched one arm along the back of the seat so he could chat with the general and his wife in a relaxed way. He had obviously mastered one of the essentials of being a successful aide, the ability to make small but not insignificant talk. He and the general discussed the dolorous state of West Point's football team. He asked the general if it was true that the Army was planning to dismantle the Airmobile divisions. The general was inclined to think so. Heat-seeking missiles had made the helicopters too vulnerable.

Joanna found it impossible to follow the conversation. The sight of the West Point ring glistening on Captain Collins' black finger stirred elegiac emotion in her mind and body. *That reminds me of the time the first black lieutenant . . .* But a general's wife did not reminisce like an old soldier. At least not when the general was around. Better to think of the ring without the black finger. Think calmly, quietly of an equally murky fall day in 1949 when a smiling cadet had slipped a miniature version of that ring on her own finger.

Prehistoric was what her son called that year, when the only wars worth remembering were the two big ones, so misleadingly called World, as if they alone had engulfed the lives of the men who fought them. Joanna found it impossible to explain to her son that 1949 was

14

equally prehistoric to her. Yet contemporary. So achingly, savagely, sadly contemporary.

That smiling cadet—and the courageous soldier he became—was dead. So was the dreamy yearning girl who let him draw her lips against his young mouth in the shadows beside Cullum Hall. That girl had been as annihilated by time as the men whose Korean foxholes had taken direct hits from Communist artillery, the others who had plunged in their burning helicopters into Vietnam's triple-canopy rain forests.

Yet the girl still existed in timepassed, the treacherous jungle world where the guerrilla army of memory lurked. She was there just below them in the mist, riding the long-defunct West Shore Railroad, letting the *click-click-click* of the iron wheels say I-love-you-I-love-you-I-love-you-I-love-you until doubt, hesitation, was obliterated from her mind, until her flesh became wish, gift, an idea without will, a sentence without a verb.

"How do the girls get to the Academy these days?" Joanna asked Captain Collins.

"Mostly in cars, their own or the cadets'," he said.

The general asked the captain how the Academy was coping with the expansion of the cadet corps from two thousand to four thousand men. The captain, sounding like a Disgruntled Old Grad usually shortened to D.O.G.—confessed to profound doubts. There were men in the same class who did not even know each other's names. What would happen to the Army if the Corps became a collection of strangers?

Joanna barely listened to these intimations of doom. She was with the ghost of her twenty-one-year-old self, riding that abandoned train to her rendezvous with love in that most unlikely place, the gray Gothic-battlemented world of West Point. There she sat on the dusty green cushions, her small red suitcase on the rack above her, plump in her timeless black box jacket suit, with the large white bow at her chin. All the styles had been black and white that year. Not that Joanna Adrian Welsh was particularly interested in fashion. In her intensely Catholic, proudly intellectual soul, fashion had been something to be dismissed, one of the things of this world, a possible barrier to happiness, holiness. The two words had been interchangeable in her mind.

Now? That suit would swim on her. Gone was the baby fat. Gone too was the complacent religious fat that had encased her mind. For a moment she struggled not to hate—and for another moment not to envy—that self-satisfied girl on the invisible train. She had earned the right to do neither—to see her with the clarity created by pain.

"Too bad about Colonel Thayer," Captain Collins said. "It was pretty sudden, I guess."

"Yes," General Hardin said.

"He taught a course up here in my first-class year. You were deputy commandant of cadets that year, weren't you, General?"

"That's right."

"I didn't take the course. Guys said it was a mind-bender."

"I bet it was. He was the brightest man in the class of '50, by far."

"I hear he got into some sort of trouble at the Pentagon."

"Among other places," General Hardin said. "Adam Thayer was his own worst enemy."

Stop, Joanna wanted to cry. *There were other enemies and you know it. You were one of them. I was another one. Then there was General Stupidity and General Coveryourass and General Ticketpuncher.* They were all his enemies.

But she said nothing because she knew that General Hardin was right. Adam had been his own worst enemy. She had learned that opposite truths can coexist. They do not cancel each other out.

"The funeral service will be at ten," Captain Collins was telling General Hardin. "I'll have this car in front of the Hotel Thayer at nine-thirty."

General Hardin nodded. "I hope we can hang on to the car. We've got a noon plane to catch out of Stewart. The 106th is jumping in that mock assault on Puerto Rico at the end of the week. We're in the final planning stages. I've got to get back to work."

"The car is yours for as long as you want it, sir," Captain Collins said.

"Good."

"That's a big exercise, I hear. What's it called?"

"Doorstep," the general said.

"Are we trying to send Castro a signal?" Captain Collins said.

"Maybe," the general said.

For the third or fourth time, Joanna wondered why he had tried to use the Doorstep maneuvers as an excuse to avoid attending Adam Thayer's funeral. It was the closest they had come to an argument in their three years of marriage. When Joanna refused to accept the excuse, he had had his aide tell her that there were no available seats on any Air Force plane. Joanna had routed the conspiracy by telling the aide to book them on a commercial flight from Atlanta. That was why they were driving from New York, instead of from Stewart Field, where most VIP military visitors to West Point landed. The Commandant of West Point, another 1950 classmate, Brigadier General Victor Kinsolving, had sent his aide, Captain Collins, to meet them at Kennedy Airport.

While the general and the captain discussed how many divisions the Army would need to take Cuba, Joanna puzzled over why her husband had been so reluctant to go to the funeral. She knew the part he had played in giving the coup de grace to Adam Thayer's career. She did not think it troubled his conscience. Was jealousy the answer? Did he know what she had really meant when she told him two days ago: "I loved him. I loved Adam." Even his wife was never sure what a general knew. He had access to all kinds of secret files on everyone.

The car slowed. Joanna looked up and saw they were approaching a traffic circle. WEST POINT, proclaimed a huge green-and-white highway sign. In another five minutes they were passing the familiar roadhouses and motels and finally the abbreviated main street of Highland Falls with its random assortment of banks, supermarkets, souvenir shops and cheap restaurants. They slowed again at the West Point gate, where the white-helmeted military policeman smartly saluted the car. Along Thayer Road they wound past the comfortable red brick houses of the faculty colonels to the gray stone Gothic cluster of administration buildings and classrooms.

Cadets hurried past, each saluting the car, each salute returned by the captain and the general.

"They're so young," Joanna said.

"Look like a bunch of hives to me," the general said, using the 1950 slang word for studious types. "No wonder they can't field a winning football team."

"Maybe they can field a winning Army," Joanna said.

Was that Adam speaking? She must not, she could not let him have access to her soul. The general grunted. He was not amused.

They turned right, then left along Cullum Road, skirting the Plain, where the cadet corps passed in review. General George Patton's ugly larger-than-life-sized statue gazed at them. Past Cullum Hall, where they had danced beneath the carved names of famous battles and plaques to those who had died in them, they slicked through the puddles to Trophy Point. There a battery of Civil War cannons thrust their muzzles at the Hudson as the great river curved around the point of land that had given the Academy its public name.

"Remember the last hop, June week, Ruth on that goddamn cannon?" the general said.

Memory. Like a change of scene in a slide show, the gray light, the mist vanished from the river. It was deepest night, stars gleaming on the velvet water. Joanna Welsh was there beside the cannon in her blue taffeta evening dress. Amy Kemble, dressed like a Spanish princess. Honor Prescott in organdy, straight out of Richmond circa 1898. Ruth Parrott in telltale red, the wayward Daughter of the Regiment.

Memory.

It was blazing white day now. They still stood there, inanely smiling, with their cadets, their soon-to-be husbands, beside them, grinning in their gray uniforms. They were caught in the enormous flash of Memory. Not the wily guerrilla who roamed the midnight hours. But the main-force army of Memory, attacking with ultimate weapons. Joanna shuddered away from the car window, her eyes closed. She did not want to see it. Did not want to see the flesh shrivel from those innocent young faces. Did not want to watch the insouciant uniforms, the bright gowns shred in the nuclear firestorm.

Dimly she heard Sam's voice, felt his strong arm around her. "Honey—are you okay?"

She heard her own breath struggling to deny the death in her heart.

"I knew we shouldn't have come," General Hardin said to Captain Collins. "I knew it was going to upset the hell out of her."

Joanna opened her eyes. The gray light of reality was on the river again. The old cannons sat sullenly in the drizzle.

"No," she said. "I'm all right. I promise you I'll be all right."

She had chosen. She had thrown down the gauntlet and Memory had accepted the challenge. To meet it she would need all the strength and all the guile she possessed. In the name of what? Victory in spite of all the losses, deaths, defeats? Joanna looked into General Hardin's troubled eyes.

No. In the name of love.

Old love for the dead.

New love for the living.

II

Question, as Adam Thayer would say when he wanted to madden an opponent in an argument. How many June weeks were there at West Point in 1950?

One, you idiot. How can there be more than one June week? It ran from Friday to Tuesday and included marches, parades and concerts, baseball, tennis and lacrosse games, dances, receptions and finally graduation. Then weddings.

Wrong. There were many June weeks.

There was the June week of the Army, five days in which the Old Grads came back to worship at West Point's shrines and the brass and their political friends came up from Washington to approve the latest anointed ones, and to declare to a dubious press that a West Point education was better than ever.

There was the June week of the cadets, for the first class five days of exultant disbelief that the four years had fled so fast, of amazement that they had survived the ordeal. A time for wild practical jokes, often thinly disguised revenge on enemies and tactical officers (frequently synonymous), for the final acceptance of their fates, the branch of the service which they had chosen, if their class standing was good enough, or to which they were assigned, if academic mediocrity had been their lot. For the Cows, the second-classmen, it was the impatient expectation of reaching that summit of West Point social topography, first-classmen, rulers of the Corps. For the yearlings, the third-classmen, it was a sullen acknowledgment that progress of sorts did exist, something they had begun to doubt. For the fourth-classmen, the plebes, it was a gurgling struggle through one more week, often the worst week, of abuse and humiliation before they were recognized by the upperclassmen as members of the Corps.

There was the June week of the brides, five days that saw shade trees shimmering in matchless sunshine, the surrounding hills in their green glory. White sails skimmed the river. Everywhere light poured down on perfection. The cadets never looked more handsome, more masculine, in their spotless summer uniforms, the Corps never marched with such perfection, two thousand white legs striding in spectacular unison, guns, visors, shoes gleaming, flags billowing for them. The brides. The June week of romance.

Question: Which June week was real?
All of them.
Very good. You are learning. Slowly, to be sure. But learning.

They had watched the Army's June week, largely as tolerant, sometimes as admiring spectators. The Old Grads, no doubt including the usual percentage of Disgruntleds, opened the show. On Monday, June 5, the oldest of them, spare Major General Henry C. Hodges, Jr., class of 1881, led the traditional march to the statue of Colonel Sylvanus Thayer, "father of the Academy," on the edge of the Plain. Joanna found it difficult to feel much reverence for Sylvanus, because Adam Thayer had made him one of his running jokes. Adam called him "Great-granduncle Sylvie" and referred to

Thayer Road, Thayer Hall, the Hotel Thayer, and the Superintendent's quarters, which Colonel Thayer had built in 1820, as "ours." His fellow cadets had retaliated by nicknaming Adam "Supe."

It was the procession, not Sylvanus, that produced something akin to reverence on that June Monday in 1950. Behind General Hodges in cheap rumpled business suits, often with coats that did not match the pants (most brides' first glimpse of Army officers' indifference to civilian clothes), came the old men who had led regiments in the Spanish-American War and divisions in World War I. After them came the triumphant uniformed warriors of World War II, so many with general's stars or colonel's eagles on their shoulders. The cadets of 1950 eyed them with an ambivalent mixture of respect and envy. Their war had won them fame, rank and abiding glory, and simultaneously seemed to have eliminated the possibility of future wars. The new graduates faced careers in a peacetime Army, with its slow promotions, made even more glacial by the "hump" of World War II veterans who had already advanced to major and colonel.

The men of '50 and their fiancées retreated to Boodler's, the cadet soda fountain, to discuss this dismal prospect. "We could be lieutenants for the next fifteen years," Pete Burke told Joanna. "It'll be like the Army after the Civil War."

"Wuss, Old Shell Fragment," Adam said. "T'won't be no redskins to fight."

"I'm not worried about it," Joanna said. "Neither is Honor."

Adam gave them a look that ten generations of Maine forebears had perfected. It combined derision, suspicion and tolerant superiority in precisely equal parts. Never had Joanna seen a more Yankee face and frame. There was not an ounce of superfluous flesh anywhere. The deep-socketed eyes were as gray and cold as seawater in a rocky pool; but they could become flecked with laughter, seemingly by an act of the will. The proud nose descended to a dour mouth that could also produce without warning a smile of startling charm.

Turning his hat around and reversing his chair, Adam started rocking back and forth as if he were riding a horse across the prairie. "Lissen, Old Tatterdemalion," he said to Pete. "Every time I try to talk sense to m'squaw, Old Virginia Sue here, I find out she's been

21

listenin' to that squaw of yourn, Old Cincinnati Sal. She's got some real crazy notions from that Old White Father you two worship. Whattya call'm? The Poop?''

"Watch the blasphemy, wise guy," Pete Burke said, inclining his massive frame menacingly toward his roommate. Pete's blue eyes had a sunny good-humored light in them, belying his threat. There was an ageless quality to Adam's face. Boyish innocence was the dominant motif of Pete's features, in spite of his huge size.

"They're *not* crazy notions," Joanna said. She began trying to explain, once more, why she looked foward to trying to live on a second lieutenant's salary. Her enthusiasm was produced by a movement that attracted many American Catholic intellectuals in 1950—an attempt to sanctify the laity by persuading them to practice the Christian virtue of poverty. "It's the endless pursuit of things, possessions, that makes most Americans unhappy," Joanna said. "I'm glad we're escaping the rat race."

"I am too," Honor Prescott said with an emphatic shake of her sheen of red hair. "Almost every fight my momma and daddy ever had was about money."

Adam whinnied like a horse and shook his head. "As Old Sittin' Bull said when I shoved a pound of buffalo dung down his throat—"

"What character is he playing now?" Amy Kemble asked as she and her fiancé George Rosser, joined them at the table.

"Post-Civil War Army," Joanna said. "When everyone was called Old this or that, although most of them were under thirty."

Already she was a historian of Adam's routines.

During the past year, Amy and Honor Prescott and Joanna had evolved into roommates at the Hotel Thayer, the towering stone pile just inside the main gate where the cadet corps's female guests stayed on social weekends. Amy was virtually a prototype of what Joanna had imagined a Vassar girl would be—slim, compact, with thick dark hair worn close to her head, perfect taste in clothes and an expression that played between amusement and disdain. Life seemed to have no surprises for her, an unnerving idea to Joanna, who felt the reverse. When Joanna and Honor discovered Amy was dating George Rosser, a stocky Californian who roomed next to Pete and

22

Adam in the North Barracks, and was a fellow member of H Company, they decided fate had ordained them a threesome.

"Until our resident genius slipped into a time warp," Joanna said, "we were talking very sensibly about the class of '50's dismal prospects for promotion."

"Oh, that," Amy said.

"Those of us who callously pursue heiresses don't have to worry about it," Adam said.

Amy wrinkled her small aristocratic nose. "Any calluses George has acquired so far have been on utterly harmless parts of his anatomy."

Adam laughed. He liked Amy's sophistication. She liked to display it when he was around. For a while Joanna had wondered if Amy was trying to make Honor Prescott jealous. It was hard to penetrate Amy's Philadelphia Main Line manners to find out what she really thought or felt about George Rosser. She was not effusive about her affections, like Honor, who babbled constantly about how crazy she was about Adam. Joanna had eventually dismissed the jealousy idea. Amy seemed satisfied with George, whose smooth temperament seemed a perfect match for her own cool style. Anyway, how could she hope to match Honor's glowing red hair, perfect legs and eye-catching figure? The cadet magazine, *The Pointer*, for which Adam often wrote, had displayed Honor on its cover as "Queen of the '50 Femmes."

Sam Hardin, George Rosser's Texas roommate, and his fiancée, thin, gangly Ruth Parrott, joined them. Sam specialized in being good-natured and chipper. Ruth had a more scathing style. She worked hard at being a character. Her father was a master sergeant in the West Point garrison and Ruth had some rather nasty but interesting opinions about the Army.

"I thought Eisenhower was supposed to be here for the D.O.G. march," she said.

"He called to say he was too busy planning the invasion of Belgium," Adam said. "I told him they already were members of NATO and he got very upset."

"That sounds like him," Ruth said as Sam Hardin handed her a

Coke. "My old man says he's so dumb he couldn't invade Central Park."

"I can't believe Ike is stupid," Honor said. "How'd we win the war?"

"Show me a general who isn't stupid," Ruth said.

"Watch closely," Adam said. "One is about to materialize in front of you."

He stood up, his hand inside his tunic, à la Napoleon.

"Brains like you don't get to be generals," Ruth said.

"That's what I keep telling him," Pete said.

"Who does get to be generals?" Honor said. She put too much stock in Ruth's insider pretensions.

"The bastards and the phonies, no one else," Ruth said.

"That makes me overqualified, but what about Sam?" Adam said. "He's Mr. Nice Guy."

"He'll be a bastard by the time I'm through with him," Ruth said.

Everyone laughed. It wasn't really funny, but Ruth was a character.

On, brave old Army girl. What did you talk about in the room at the Thayer?

You. The other girls. Bands, movies, books, clothes. Do I have to supply a complete list?

Concentrate on what mattered, later.

"I had a letter from my cousin Johnny, in Japan," Amy said as she rubbed cold cream on her face to remove her makeup. "He thinks George is smart to stay in armor. It's the branch of the future. Engineers get stuck with a lot of boring jobs, like dredging rivers in Arkansas."

Amy was the only one who discussed branch choices and their probable effect on careers. George Rosser's marks were good enough to get him into the engineers, which was also Adam's choice. But Amy, with the help of several relatives who apparently knew the Army well, had nudged George into armor—tanks.

"Who's this cousin Johnny you're always talkin' about?" Honor asked.

There may have been a certain malice in the question. An undercurrent of hostility between Amy and Honor sometimes flickered into view. Joanna gradually realized that Amy had been on the defensive from the moment she saw Honor's face and figure. Honor in turn found it hard to endure Amy's offhand assumption of superiority. Charlesville, the small Virginia town from which Honor came, was no match for Philadelphia's Main Line, and Honor's college, Norwood, lacked Vassar's prestige. In a catty moment, Amy had told Joanna that Norwood was little more than a finishing school.

"John Stapleton," Amy said. "He graduated last year."

"Were you sweet on him once?"

"No," Amy said, whirling to glare at Honor. "Where did you get that idea?"

Honor shrugged. "Somethin' about the way you say his name. I've got a cousin the same age as me. He came that close to seducin' me one night."

"Another one?" Amy said. "Your love life in Virginia sounds more and more like the Perils of Pauline."

Honor let the barb go unanswered. Later she told Joanna that Adam had described John Stapleton as one of the fastest cadets who had ever graduated from the Academy. "Interestin', don't you think?" Honor said. Joanna earnestly rejected the implication. Thinking of her own deep affection for her brother, who had been killed in World War II, she told Honor that an only child like Amy could easily become very close to a cousin, without the least suggestion of immorality. Honor had listened to this little sermon with growing impatience. "Joanna," she said, "you're a dear girl but you don't know *nothin'* about men."

At first it was simply curiosity about the West Point system, then awe at its rigor. Then the pursuit began. The wanting. That was what Joanna remembered most—the first kiss, the explosive rib-crushing intensity of it, the awareness of his hands, those remarkably thick, powerful fingers, moving convulsively against the back of her dress. This man-boy boy-man engulfed her with a maleness she had never encountered in casual good-night kisses with high school dates. One kiss, perhaps two, was as far as she had gone with anyone. She had never been a necker, light or heavy. For the first time the formless, sacrificial gift-of-herself vision of love acquired dimension, reality.

Joanna never forgot, never doubted that Pete Burke's love for her began with this physical wish. It had both frightened and pleased her. She had never thought of herself as attractive. She had good legs and a nice face, acceptable hair when she worked at brushing it. But in between was a set of hips and shoulders that disqualified her for competition in the Betty Grable–Rita Hayworth league. She had also, in her dreaming intellectual self, subtly scorned the physical. Her marriage would be a union of the spirit, she had told herself. It was a shock to find herself thrilled, intrigued by a man's direct wanting. There was a sense of discovery, adventure in it that profoundly excited her. A meeting of minds and spirits was something that could be maneuvered, arranged, negotiated (so she thought). But physical attraction was a given, it was either there or it wasn't there.

Amazing how Hollywood and advertising had sold that idea to American women. You either had sex appeal or you didn't and Joanna had been resigned (and within the resignation defiantly proud) that she did not have it. The discovery that she had the power to compel frantic need from this huge male was an earthshaking discovery, a source of wonder and elation. It never occurred to her that after four celibate years at West Point, the same reaction could have been inspired by almost anyone, even anything, wearing long hair and perfume.

No, too crude. That's your voice speaking again. Ruthless reductionist of all exaltation, all pleasure, including your own. You wanted to own me, run me, just as much as Pete, for a different reason.

Maybe. But don't stop. I'm enjoying this meditation on inevitability.

Why did Peter MacArthur Burke get involved with this tall hefty brunette who had been handed to him by West Point's hostess, the Mother of the Corps, when he put his name on the list of cadets who did not have a date for the 1948 fall hop? Why did any of them pursue a particular drag? Was there any reason beyond sexual desperation and the wish to relieve it as soon as possible after graduation? For Cadet Burke, it was Joanna's Catholicism, the discovery that she was also a daily communicant. For Pete this practice meant the sacrifice of a half hour of precious sleep each day and in the winter a dash across West Point's freezing parade ground at 6 A.M. to reach the Catholic Chapel. For Joanna daily communion was more a habit than a sacrifice. Everyone at the College of Mount St. Monica was required to attend daily Mass and only a lazy or rebellious few refused to stroll to the altar each day.

On the worldly side, Pete had been impressed (he later told her) by Joanna's stylish clothes, which she bought in consultation with Mother at Pogue's and Gidding-Jenny, Cincinnati's best stores. At least as important was her knowledge of sports. Trying to replace the sports-loving son her father had lost on Omaha Beach, Joanna had acquired male-level expertise in baseball and football. Her father's response had been tepid. But a casual display of her athletic information had had a dramatic effect on Pete Burke. Before Joanna, talking to girls had been torture for him. Here was a girl who knew the name of Notre Dame's quarterback and could knowledgeably discuss his passing. Who listened with understanding, instead of with smiling, ooh-ahing incomprehension, when he talked about the dangers of blitzing too often against a team with a breakaway runner, who knew (or seemed to know) how he felt when he told her that he had really wanted to play fullback but Coach Blaik had decreed his career as "the Rock"—the mainstay of the West Point defensive line.

"It's my favorite picture," Honor said, gazing fondly at the photo on the cover of *The Pointer*. "Do you like it?

"It's lovely," Joanna said.

On the cover, only Honor's head and shoulders were visible. She gazed upward at some vision above and beyond the camera's lens, her eyes wide, her smile shy and ethereal. It was not the Honor Prescott that Joanna knew. That girl often came striding into their room at the Hotel Thayer, flipped her suitcase on a chair and boogied around the beds, saying: "Ohhhh, do I feel like *dancin'*." She frequently complained about the stodgy West Point rules that forbade cadets to jitterbug. The lindy was Honor's favorite dance. After the Army–Notre Dame game, she and Adam and Pete and Joanna had slipped out of the victory dance in the Hotel Astor's ballroom and gone downstairs to a private party thrown by the wealthy father of one of the cadets. The music was provided by a six-piece jazz band. Honor and Adam had done a lindy wilder than anything Joanna had ever seen in Cincinnati or at the staid dances at the College of Mount St. Monica. It was a hip-swiveling, head-spinning, foot-stamping celebration of youth. By the time they finished, the rest of the party had encircled them, clapping and cheering. The party's host, a little drunk, had pounded Adam on the back and said: "How did a skinny guy like you get a date like that?"

"She's not my date," Adam said. "She's my fiancée."

He took a West Point miniature out of his pocket and put it on Honor's finger. She started to cry. Pete had given Joanna her miniature a month ago.

"He's finally made up his mind," Pete said. "I don't know what took him so long."

They were at the spring hop. The band was taking a break. Adam was teasing Amy about her money again. "Tell us the truth. What does your father do for a living?"

"He sails," Amy said. "Occasionally he shoots. Frequently he just drinks."

"You may convince me that Karl Marx was right, after all," Adam said.

"Nonsense," Amy said. "Wealth is in the genes. It has nothing to do with the social system."

"A novel idea. Prove it," Adam said.

"Who's your earliest American ancestor?" Amy asked. "Skip the guff about Great-granduncle Sylvanus."

"Well now," Adam said, relapsing into his Maine accent. "We go back aways befer that'n. All the ways back to Miles Standish, in fact."

"Seriously?" Amy said.

"That's what the family genealogist says."

"We go back to Priscilla Mullins and John Alden," Amy said. "So we both started off at the same time in the same place. Plymouth, 1620. With about the same amount of money. Two hundred years later the Kembles were rich. What else explains it but superior brains and energy?"

"You went to Philadelphia and we went to Maine. You turned Republican and we stayed Democrats. You turned greedy and we stayed pure," Adam said, pounding the table and rolling his eyes like a fanatic preacher.

"I think you mean poor," George Rosser said.

Pete shook Amy's hand. "It's the first time I've ever seen anyone win an argument with Supermouth."

"I allus knew y'shoulda stayed away from that John Alden feller, Priscilla," Adam muttered in his Maine accent. "Y'poor little ignorant hussy, how was you t'know you was marryin' the fust Republican?"

Joanna was on the dance floor with Adam at the Christmas hop. He had just finished telling her why he no longer ranked number one in the class academically. He had cut back on the time he allotted to the regular West Point curriculum, with its heavy emphasis on math and science, and concentrated on giving himself a liberal education.

"The average Army private probably knows more history and literature than your typical West Point graduate," he said.

"Isn't that a slight exaggeration?"

"You should have seen Peter the Great trying to make sense out of those poems you sent him."

Joanna had published three poems in the fall issue of her college magazine, *The Monican*. She had sent them to Pete, who had replied with warm words of admiration. "I told him what to write," Adam said. "Anything to help the course of true love. But—"

"What?" Joanna said, growing more and more annoyed.

"In the faint hope that you may have some real talent, I will tell you the honest truth. You ought to stop imitating T. S. Eliot and that converted fruitcake Thomas Merton and try to write some real poetry. Say what you really think and feel about things."

"Thank God you're not going to be a teacher," Joanna said. "A little of your honesty would discourage every young person you met.''

"Hey, you're not so young anymore. Twenty-two years old, if Big Peter has his stats straight. My grandmother had two kids by the time she was twenty-two."

"Thomas Merton is not a fruitcake and T. S. Eliot is a great poet. I don't see why a young person''—she almost choked on the word—"shouldn't imitate them.''

"Nuts. Have you read Merton's 'For My Brother Missing in Action'?''

"Yes.''

Mockingly, Adam recited one of the interior stanzas.

> *"Where in what desolate and smokey country*
> *Lies your poor body, lost and dead*
> *And in what landscape of disaster*
> *Has your unhappy spirit lost its road?*

"The guy's dead. His plane is down or he's been scattered all over the countryside by an artillery hit—''

"You wouldn't think—feel—that way if you had a brother who—who died in the war.''

"Did you?''

"Yes. My brother was killed on D Day.''

"Do you think his unhappy spirit has lost its road?''

"No! He's just—just dead.''

"That's the point. You've got to make poetry out of that. The brute fact. Have you read any of Demetrios Capetanakis?''

Again, typical Adam. Joanna had never even heard of this strange Greek, who, she eventually learned, had written a series of remarkable poems in English before dying in London in 1944. Adam urged her to read his poem "Abel," in which the victim narrates his murder by Cain. Eyes closed, while the band played some inane popular song, Adam whispered in Joanna's ear:

> *"My brother Cain, the wounded, liked to sit*
> *Brushing my shoulder by the staring water*
> *Of life, or death, in cinemas half lit*
> *By scenes of peace that always turned to slaughter.''*

30

"WE ARE OUTNUMBERED BY OUR MOST DANGEROUS ANTAGONIST."

Secretary of the Army Frank Pace's words resounded beneath the steel-girdered roof of the West Point field house. Outside the June sun beat ferociously. It was 86 degrees, a record. It felt like 98 in the field house.

The Secretary of the Army did not name their most dangerous antagonist. It was official government policy to avoid challenging the Russians. What did being outnumbered mean? the Secretary asked his perspiring audience of 670 graduating cadets and 2,000 civilians. It meant they must intensify their research and development efforts to equip American troops with sophisticated weapons that would enable them to overcome the numerical advantage of their enemy. The Secretary talked of the danger of Western Europe being overrun by a surprise attack and declared that "masses of mechanized ground forces" could only be repelled by "highly scientific ground troops with revolutionary new weapons." After mentioning a few possibilities, such as a super bazooka, the Secretary went on to warn the cadets that national security now involved interlocking military and economic considerations. They would have to be "not only military scientists but students of political, social, and psychological factors on an international scale."

Military scientists.

Scientific ground troops.

Revolutionary weapons.

Students of political factors.

Lovely, soothing phrases that made it sound like the Americans, if they ever fought another war, would be nowhere near the battlefield. They would be miles away, zapping the enemy with Buck Rogers-like death rays and rockets, meanwhile discussing the profound political implications of it all. It was immensely reassuring to hear the confidence in the Secretary's voice, confidence in America's technological wizardry, shared by almost everyone in the audience. If anyone doubted, there sat bulky, bearlike Lieutenant General Leslie Groves, class of 1918, commander of the Manhattan Project, the man who had brought Japan to her knees with two atomic bombs, less than five years ago.

31

For the brides and their about-to-be second lieutenants, this graduation sermon was their first encounter with official stupidity, the amazing ability of the men in power in Washington, D.C., their civilian commanders, to look at reality and refuse to see what was there. Even as the Secretary spoke, artillery was being emplaced, troops and tanks were being massed above the thirty-eighth degree of latitude on an obscure Asian peninsula named Korea. Warnings had been drifting into Washington for weeks. No one listened. Officially, the Secretary of State had declared that Korea was outside America's sphere of interest. That made the warnings even easier to dismiss.

A cheap shot. Remember what President Truman said about hindsight?
Every ten-year-old's hindsight is worth a President's foresight? Very good. You are learning.

"Was that the truth, what you told Adam? Your father doesn't have a job?" Honor asked. "He's never worked?

"More or less," Amy said. "He was a broker for a while, investing the family money. When he lost about two thirds of it in 1929, they put a stop to that."

Honor found it hard to grasp the reality of being that rich. "My daddy worked so hard. He was a dentist. He'd come home at night and have one two three four double bourbons in a row. Washin' down the day, he called it. He told me once that he wished he'd stayed in the Army after World War I, even if it didn't pay much. But his daddy said the Army was a bum's life and made him come home and go to dental school."

"I'm in favor of steady jobs," Amy said. "Growing up, I was lucky if I saw my father four months out of the year. He was always hunting in Africa or sailing in the Caribbean. Leaving me home with Mother. I'm frankly looking forward to having a husband around full time. That's one good thing about the peacetime Army."

Joanna saw they were talking past each other, each trying to correct in her own way the marital mistakes of her parents. And Joanna? What was she trying to correct? Nothing. Her parents were happily married. True, she was a little uncomfortable when the parent talk turned to her and Amy neatly extracted the seldom admitted fact that the Welsh's prosperity originated from Mother's inheritance and not from her father's prowess as a Cadillac dealer. Amy had actually been impressed to learn that there was old money in Cincinnati, even if it was German. Mother's money was only an occasional shadow on her parents' marriage. Joanna was not trying to correct anything when she proclaimed her eagerness to live on an Army salary. Mother did more or less run the family, but it had nothing to do with money, it was her German blood, "the Kaiser in her," as her father jokingly called it. Joanna was confident that her love for Pete transcended petty realities like money. It even transcended him, his minor foibles and limitations. It was a commitment to, a sublime confidence in, love itself.

This half-religious, half-sexual mixture of emotion and faith enabled Joanna to hear evidence of love's fragility, its failure, without fear, without thought.

"It was one of those silent New England divorces," Adam said.

They were on the dance floor again. When? Where? Philadelphia. The victory dance after the Army–Navy game. Adam explained that he was going to leave them for an hour and take a cab to a nearby hotel to see his father, who had come down from New York for the game.

"It must have been—it must have hurt you," Joanna said.

"Yes, it was quite a shock." He switched to his Maine dialect. For the first time she saw how he used humor to conceal his feelings. "Yes, I cum down to get muh mornin' porridge. It'd snowed a mite outside, only six or eight feet, and I said, Maw, where's Paw? Skeedaddled, son, she says. Just put on his showshoes, hitched up the dog team and skeedaddled. Would yuh like some honey on yuh porridge?"

"Seriously—did he ask your mother to go with him?"

"Sure. She wouldn't even consider it. Her mother'd seen the rest of the country and it wasn't worth Sconnet's little toe."

"How old were you?"

"Ten."

"Oh, Adam."

"Don't 'Oh, Adam' me, you overcontented Catholic Trinitarian," he said, throwing her into a back-straining dip. "Don't you know that the one thing a Yankee can't stand is sympathy?"

They danced in silence for a moment. "Is—your father happy?" she asked.

"He didn't marry again, if that's what you mean," Adam said. "The question is irrelevant. Thayers—up until yours truly—weren't interested in happiness. Life was too serious. Besides, as the old judge—my grandfather—says, 'the puhsuit of happiness is too time-consumin'. And it don't pay nothin'.' "

"Why did your father leave—if it's not too—too private?" Joanna asked.

"Nothin' private or pussonal about it, gal. Just wuk up one mornin' and decided he couldn't take another day of Sconnet.

"That's my opinion, anyway," Adam said in a normal voice. "The way he tells it, the year was 1938, the Depression was getting worse again, and he decided it was time he did something about it. Time he made a contribution to the country. It wasn't enough, anymore, to make a contribution to Sconnet. To imitate his father, the old judge, and be the number-one lawyer in Knox County. What happened in Washington was decisive. He went down there and talked his way onto the Securities and Exchange Commission, with a little help from his congressman. He's been trying to keep the tycoons honest ever since."

"Has he succeeded?"

"He doesn't think so. He's pretty gloomy about the future of the country. He thinks we're going right back to the rampant capitalism of the twenties. Which will bring on another depression. This time I don't think the politicians will be able to keep the lid on. The Army may have to step in. It will be an interesting time to be a general."

You weren't very different from the rest of us, were you, for all your brains. Revealing just enough self-knowledge, passing just enough judgment on parents to seem wise—without possessing wisdom. Peering into the future and prophesying without possessing prophecy.

And all the time the future was gaining on us.

• • •

"Hello, Joey."

"Hello, Dad."

Only her father still called her by that almost forgotten tomboy name, applicable from the age of six to ten, when Joanna had tried to imitate her older brother in all things. It was Sunday night. She had just returned to the Hotel Thayer. Pete had not even tried to kiss her on the long walk from the Army Theater. She thought it meant he was feeling the same spiritual exaltation. He was probably thinking: *Two more nights. I can stand it for two more nights.* Her father said he and her mother and sister Beth and her grandmother were staying overnight in Philadelphia, as planned. They expected to arrive at the Hotel Thayer at 10 A.M. They had her wedding dress, which had been made to order at Gidding-Jenny. Joanna had had a final fitting during Easter vacation.

"How are things going?" her father said.

"Perfect. Everything's perfect. Even the weather. I just came from the Glee Club Concert. Oh, Dad, I never felt anything like it. It was so—so magnificent."

For Joanna-the-bride it had been the spiritual climax of June week. Massed on the stage of the Army Theater, the cadet glee club, in which Adam Thayer was a lead singer, had performed a generous sample of their repertoire—old West Point traditionals like "Benny Havens" and "Army Blue," medleys of World War I and World War II songs. They had closed with the greatest of all West Point songs, the one that summed up the mystique, "The Corps." Sitting beside Pete, her hand clasped in his, Joanna had felt the words lift her soul out of her body and unite her to this man beside her.

> *The Corps! Bareheaded salute it*
> *With eyes up, thanking our God*
> *That we of the Corps are treading*
> *Where they of the Corps have trod*
> *They are here in ghostly assemblage*
> *The men of the Corps long dead*
> *And our hearts are standing attention*

While we wait for their passing tread.
We sons of today, we salute you—
You sons of an earlier day
We follow close order behind you
Where you have pointed the way;
The long gray line of us stretches
Through the years of a century told
And the last man feels to his marrow
The grip of your far-off hold . . .

She had not the faintest idea that the massed voices were chanting a hymn to her future antagonist.

"Miss Welsh, your parents are here," the operator said.

Joanna was still feeling exalted. She was also somewhat light-headed from lack of sleep. She had risen at 7 A.M. to attend the 8 A.M. baccalaureate service in the Catholic Chapel, at the opposite end of the reservation. Down in the elevator Joanna floated to the lofty stone portico of the Hotel Thayer, where her father was helping a porter haul their bags out of the trunk of a gleaming white Cadillac convertible. As the owner of the largest Cadillac dealership in Ohio, Tom Welsh always drove one of his latest models. But this car was much sportier than his usual choice.

"What a beautiful car," Joanna said after exchanging ritual kisses with everyone.

"I'm glad you like it," her father had said. "It's your wedding present."

Joanna was tremendously moved. Ten months ago, when she had called her parents to tell them of her engagement, their reaction had been dismaying. Her mother said: "I knew I never should have let you go to school in that part of the country." Joanna understood exactly what she meant. If Joanna had stayed in Cincinnati, Mother would have steered her expertly into the arms of someone destined for the upper echelon of Procter and Gamble or one of the city's banks. Mother descanted on how shocked she was that her daughter would become engaged to a man before her parents had even had a chance to meet him. She recalled the solemnity with which Joanna's father had asked for permission to marry the very charming (and very rich) Miss Cecilia Sigel. Joanna almost told her that Grandfather Sigel was a family tyrant from whom she was glad death had delivered them, a decade ago. But she was not prepared to tangle with her mother, even as she announced her independence. She had humbly promised to bring Pete out to Cincinnati at Christmas. She had been even more dismayed by that weekend. No warmth had developed between her father and Pete, not even when they watched the bowl games on television. Their conversation had been a series of polite clichés.

To Joanna, the glistening convertible now seemed to be a statement of approval, of reconciliation. She kissed her father with violent enthusiasm and said: "I can't wait to show it to Pete."

An hour later, Joanna stood in the parking lot opposite the Hotel Thayer, tears streaming down her face. Pete, thoroughly appalled, stood on the other side of the white convertible, looking at her as if she were a lethal object that might explode at any moment.

"Joanna, so help me God, I never thought—I would have said something if I even dreamed—"

"They'll be so hurt, Pete. I can't believe it. I can't believe you won't accept it."

"Joanna, you know Captain Coulter, my tactical officer. He's given me a lot of good advice. Given all of us good advice. But especially me. He's been sort of an older brother. His father's a colonel. Captain Coulter was born in the Army. He's told me a hundred times, a junior officer, no matter how much money he has, *never* lives ostentatiously. And if he doesn't have a lot of money, he shouldn't pretend to have it by driving around in something—like this."

Joanna had met jut-jawed Captain Rodwell Coulter and his wife at several hops. She had even danced with him once and glowed when he told her: "You have a very fine soldier there, one of the finest in the Corps. He's going to go far in the Army, with a little luck and a little polish." But she had not liked Captain Coulter or his wife, Edna. Adam called them a pair of stiffs. That was too blunt but there was some truth to it. They were stiff in manner—and in attitude. They took it upon themselves to scrutinize the fiancées of the cadets in H Company and decide who would not make a good Army wife. To everyone's indignation, the Coulters had called in Sam Hardin and told him to jettison Ruth Parrott. Sam had refused and Ruth had counterattacked the Coulters by claiming that the captain often got drunk and beat up Edna.

Before Joanna could protest, she found herself sniffling in Captain Coulter's living room, examining a painting of one of the locks of the Panama Canal. The artist was Edna Coulter. The painting resembled her: severe, almost abstract, with a minimum of color. The Coulters had spent two years in Panama. Edna had also lived there as a child. Her father was a general in the engineers.

Mrs. Coulter served bitter coffee in blue Spode cups while a two-year-old boy in diapers toddled around them. She joined her husband in solemnly assuring Joanna that Pete was right, a second lieutenant could not own a white Cadillac convertible without inflicting fatal damage to his Army career. Joanna mournfully acquiesced and said she was more upset about explaining this to her father. She was sure Pete's refusal was going to hurt him terribly. Captain Coulter said he would be glad to talk to him, if that would help. He went out into the fierce sun with them and blinked at the beauty of the car, which Pete had parked in front of the Coulters' quarters. The captain wistfully (Joanna thought) ran his hand along the right front fender. "A beautiful machine," he said. "My mother has one."

Pete drove slowly down the winding road to the Plain. "I wonder if we should tell them now or wait till after the wedding?" Joanna said.

"Now," Pete said. "I'll explain it. I guarantee you not to hurt their feelings."

"How can you be so sure? You don't know them!"

"Jo. Calm down. I'll handle it."

Those words were her first glimpse of Peter MacArthur Burke's self-confidence. Its emergence took her by surprise. He had been so deferential, so full of admiration during their courtship, she had assumed that he saw her as superior in everything except physical strength. She had not the dimmest idea of how the West Point system worked, how it inculcated and reinforced an ability that other American schools ignored—leadership. Academically, Pete had stayed in the bottom third of his class. But he had been named cadet colonel of the 1st Regiment for his outstanding leadership.

At the Hotel Thayer, they found Adam pacing up and down the lobby. "Can I borrow your father's car to rescue my idiot mother-in-law-to-be?" he said. "She took a wrong turn and wound up in Newburgh. She's got the wedding dress and Honor's upstairs having hysterics."

"What's wrong with your Crosley?" Pete asked.

"They've still got the motor in a thousand pieces," Adam said. "Want to join me? I hate to drive alone."

Pete shook his head. "My family's arriving in ten or fifteen minutes. I've got to get my mother and father and brother settled here and then take my uncle over to the chaplain's quarters."

"How about you, Joanna?"

"Sure," Joanna said.

She was still angry at Pete and the Army about the convertible. It would serve him right, she thought, to get stuck with explaining it to her father and mother without any help from her. She was also glad to have an excuse to spend a few less hours with Pete's family. She did not like them very much. His father was singularly disappointing. When Pete had told her, "My father's a cop," she had pictured a prototypical Irish policeman, built along Pete's massive lines, with a reputation for fearless pursuit of wrongdoers blended with unfailing kindness to old ladies and small children. Instead, Arthur Burke was a dumpy balding man with sallow jowls and shadowy shifting eyes. He seemed more interested in local politics than police work. He was a district committeeman, proud of his ability to get out the vote, which apparently involved a nice mixture of threats and bribery.

The man whom Pete and his older brother, Arthur, Jr., resembled was their uncle, red-haired Monsignor William Clancy, magisterial pastor of one of the largest and wealthiest parishes in Hamilton, the northern New Jersey city the Burkes called home. Mrs. Burke also had the Clancy physique, without the height. She was almost as wide as she was tall. Unlike Joanna's mother, who was a college graduate, Mrs. Burke had barely gotten out of eighth grade. She was

39

what people in Cincinnati called a Western Hills type, with all their prejudices and limitations.

But you did not marry a family, you married a man, Joanna told herself, especially when you married an Army officer. Such reasonable reasoning enabled the dreaming bride to focus all her love, untroubled by doubts and hesitations, on the man she had chosen, the man who had chosen her.

> *"Done with indoor complaints, libraries, querulous*
> *criticisms*
> *Strong and content, I travel the open road."*

Adam was chanting Walt Whitman. The Cadillac convertible hurtled up Route 9W toward Newburgh.

"Now *that's* bad poetry," Joanna shouted into the hot wind that was raising havoc with her hair.

"It's so bad it's good," Adam said, determined, as always, never to lose an argument. "Why were you looking so down-in-the-mouth when you came into the hotel with the big mick?"

"Because of this car," Joanna said, and told him of the contretemps over the convertible, the visit to Captain Coulter.

"Mon capitaine is right," Adam said. "For the first and perhaps last time in his life. What about all that gas you've been giving Pete about the beauties of a life of poverty, which would seem to be our fate for the next decade or so? If Jesus were around today, I don't think he'd go Cadillac. Mostly Ford. Maybe an Oldsmobile for Palm Sunday. What the hell. By then he was entitled."

"Adam, I'm serious. You don't understand. You don't realize how much it's going to hurt my parents."

"I pride myself on understanding. I'm a seeker after truth, wisdom, like you. But I don't see you seeking truth here. I see you shrinking from it. Relapsing into middle-class sentimentality."

"I don't need that kind of advice."

"Yes, you do. You need a lot of advice. You need it almost as much as I do. If I was on God the Father's general staff, in charge of advice, you know what I'd do?"

"No," she said.

"I'd advise us to keep driving. Past Newburgh. Past Albany. Past

Boston. Past Sconnet to Nova Scotia. There's a little town just over the border, named Casey. It lies above a harbor so small it'd fit in the trunk of this car. The grass grows right down to the rocks and at this time of year it's full of goldenrod. You come in from a sail around four o'clock and you look up and catch the sun on those yellow flowers. I'll send the Superintendent a telegram, telling him I have momentarily taken leave of my senses and eloped but will return and explain everything. What do you say?''

Joanna heard her voice, almost lost in the hot wind. "Adam, that isn't funny.''

She knew he was serious. She knew, perhaps had always known, the furtive dance they had performed for the past ten months, the invisible dance within their real dancing, a spiritual dance of books exchanged, ideas argued, poetry discussed, pasts revealed. *Click-click-click* went the train wheels in Joanna's head but they did not say I-love-you-I-love-you-I-love-you.

"'Tain't funny?'' Adam drawled. "Wal I'll be dummed. I coulda sworn you'd be curled up laughin' by now. Ain't never failed me before. Hardly a girl in Sconnet ain't folded up like Grandpa's old accordion when I axed her to dump her fiancé and marry me on five minutes' notice.''

They drove in silence through the green glowing countryside. The hot wind beat at them. They passed a dairy farm, with clumps of cows standing beneath scattered shade trees. The heat, the brightness, the big white car, Adam's astonishing words, all contributed to create a sense of disbelief, of a special kind of dream, in which the dreamer knows she is dreaming. This man-boy in cadet gray was asking her to do something incredibly wild and daring. She did not think of herself that way. She was Joanna-the-older-sister. Joanna Mother's-good-girl. Joanna-who-studied-hard, who got such excellent marks, who always did her assignments on time. Joanna-the-sacrificer, always ready, in return for Mother's praise, to let little sister Beth, the tantrum thrower, have her way. Helpful Joanna, always ready to type someone else's term paper, to loan her evening dresses. Tenderhearted Joanna, who could not pass a beggar in New York without giving him money, above all holy Joanna, who taught catechism to handicapped children, who went to confession every

41

week and had to practically invent trivial sins like being inconsiderate to her roommate to have something to say to the priestly presence behind the screen.

"You've thought about it too," Adam said. "Admit it."

"I have *not*," she said. "I have never—I thought—I knew we were friends, that we—shared some interests. In books, ideas. But—"

"Jesus Christ." Adam jammed his palm on the Cadillac's horn. The tires screamed as he swung the car off 9W into a narrow macadam byroad that ran between two dairy farms. He slammed on the brakes and they sat there. Hot air wavered weirdly on the byroad, which ran straight ahead of them for a mile and disappeared over a hill. Adam was glaring at her. She thought he looked somewhat insane. "I'm telling you that I love you. Or to be more exact, that we could really love each other, if we spent enough time together. Nobody loves anybody right now. How could they? You've got to know a lot about somebody to love him. You've got to spend some time alone with him. The bubbleheads who run the Academy have made that impossible. The most you can do is predict on a scale of one to ten what the probability of a lifetime of happiness or love or whatever the hell you want to call it will be. I would put your chances with Pete at about five—if you work at it day and night. I don't think you will. There are too many other things that mean more to you. My chances with Honor are about the same—if I work at it day and night. Which I don't think I'll do. For the same reason."

If he had kissed her, if he had murmured anything even close to affection, passion—

But Adam only trusted, perhaps only really loved, even then, the mind. Feelings, hungers, were not important enough to merit consideration or demonstration. It gave Joanna time to control her astonishment, to subdue it and with it all unworthy unholy doubt.

"Adam. Have you and Honor had a fight?"

"No."

"She loves you, Adam. I know just how much she loves you. She's talked to me about it by the hour."

"I know."

"You can't turn your back on something like that. You shouldn't. And—she's so beautiful, Adam."

"I know just how beautiful she is. But I'm not sure I can stand thirty or forty years of talking to her. How about Pete? Do you think he's ever going to be interested in whether Yeats is better than Eliot? Or Mauriac's better than Graham Greene?"

"He'll—he'll be interested in what I think about that sort of thing."

"The hell he will. Not after the first year or two. When he's gotten everything he wants from your whatsis and you've had all you want of his whosis."

"Adam," Joanna said. "That's too crude. I think—I believe—it works the other way around. The physical—physical love—helps create a deeper spiritual love."

"That's standard Catholic doctrine, I suppose."

"Yes."

"Since the Pope and his friends have never tried it, how the hell do they know?"

The moment had passed. They were back in their roles as friendly debaters about Life, from the Congregationalist vs. Catholic, skeptic vs. believer point of view.

Adam turned the ignition key and the convertible's motor rumbled into eight-cylinder life. He began backing onto 9W. His head was turned toward her; his mouth was only inches from her lips; his eyes were on the highway. *Click-click-click* went the wheels in Joanna's head, but they still did not say I-love-you. *Now, whispered a voice from somewhere inside her body, now, kiss him, deny everything you just said, tell him you will take the risk, you will do the insane wild thing. Tell him you want to see the goldenrod from the sea.* No, Joanna, said another voice, that is your treacherous imagination speaking, the silly thing that feeds you unreal visions of yourself as a great poet-novelist. She heard her mother saying: *In Joanna I think we've gotten a perfect combination of the Irish and the German. So sensible and steady, yet she writes lovely poetry. Beth, on the other hand, is pure Irish. A handful!* Half-joking conversation with friends. Overheard, accepted, by Joanna-the-good-girl. So Adam's lips went

43

untouched, the car backed slowly onto 9W and they were on their way to the dull reality of Newburgh.

"You realize I have given you power of life and death over me, woman?" Adam asked as they drove back to West Point with the petulant Mrs. Prescott behind them in her 1950 Buick, with its dragon's-teeth grill.

"What do you mean?"

"I mean you can go back to the Thayer now and say to the behemoth you are about to marry: 'Wait till you hear what Adam tried on me.' " He mimicked a simpering female. "And I'll say—" He shifted to the squeaky voice of the stool pigeon pleading for mercy. " 'Pete old buddy, remember electrical engineerin', what I taught youse the night before the exam? And math, Pete. From Integral C to Analytic G. I mean it's the sun, Pete. In the convoitible with the top down. Or maybe it's d'time of d'munt. Dames get that way—screwloose.' " He shifted to Barrymore-like tragedian. "But it will do no good. They will find bits and pieces of my dismembered corpse below Nyack next year, caught in the shad nets."

"I'll never say a word. I'd be too embarrassed—for both of us," Joanna said, smiling.

"That's the most depressing thing you've said yet."

They dropped it. Adam spent the rest of the ride giving her an imitation of Mrs. Prescott's reaction when Honor told her that she was going to marry a cadet from Maine. "Ah mean, a West Pointer's bad enough. Army officers tend generally to be drunks. Rootless people. But a *Maine Yankee?* Honey, they're the ver' worst kind. I'm not prejudiced against northern people on the *whole*, mind you. They know how to make money, which is more than you can say for a lot of southun boys. But there's just extremes you shouldn't go to, y'all understand me?"

Pete was sitting with her father on one of the leather couches in the Hotel Thayer's lobby. Side by side like father and son, smiling, chatting. Joanna was stunned. She had expected tongue-tied Pete, annoyed Tom Welsh, frowning, fuming Mother.

"That's some car, isn't it?" her father said.

"Sir," said Adam as he handed her father the keys, "there are some things for which I would sell my right arm, others for which I would auction my left leg. But for that car, I would mortgage my soul. Thank God no one offered it to me."

Tom Welsh nodded, smiling. "Pete's been educating me on the peacetime Army. The hard lot of the shavetail. So we decided on a trade-in. The car for a piece of paper."

"What do you mean?" Joanna asked. She was disturbed, even a little hurt by the ease with which Pete had reached an understanding with her father, apparently with no consultation with Mother. It left her alone, peering wanly into a masculine world she was forbidden to enter.

"He wants to give us a check for the price of the car. I told him it was too much. But he's a hard man to resist," Pete said.

"Sir," said Adam, "for that kind of money, even half that kind of money, I can arrange a personal review of the Corps for you. If you can manage to be on the Plain at 4 A.M. tomorrow morning—"

"Yeah, lost a boy at Omaha Beach. Life's funny. I remember when I was in France—" Tom Welsh said.

"What division was you in?"

"Thirtieth."

"I was in the Rainbow. That's where Pete got his middle name. After old Mac. He was our C.-in-C. A hell of a general. I remembuh—"

The fathers talked about their war. Pete's older brother, Arthur Jr., who had followed his father onto the police force, told Joanna's sister, Beth, about World War II. He had been a marine lieutenant, fighting the Japanese in the Pacific. It was Monday night, June 5, 1950, wedding-graduation eve. They were sitting around a table in a private dining room at the Hotel Thayer, having finished the customary dinner given by the bridegroom's parents for the bride's family. Joanna was too tired to do more than listen. Earlier in the day, she had gotten her diploma from Mount St. Monica's and said goodbye to friends, particularly the chaplain, Father Denton Malone, who had persuaded her to put her name on the drag list for West Point. Father Malone had urged Monicans, who were only an hour's drive from

45

the Academy, to save Catholic cadets from "godless Vassar girls." By now she was aware that this was idiocy, but the daze of love in which she was living enabled her to look on everyone and everything with benevolence.

A few chairs away, Mrs. Burke was talking to Joanna's mother. "I sez to him, Pete, I can't get ova you marryin' a girl from Cincinnati. *Cincinnati!* Why, I hadda get out a road map to find it. He had a lotta home-town girls aftuh him. Bein' a football stah 'n' all that, y'know. But he just laughed and said, 'That's what happens when y'go to West Point, Mom.'"

Joanna's mother nodded, smiling politely, no doubt thanking God Cincinnati was a long way from Hamilton, New Jersey. Pete was different from his family, Joanna told herself. He did not even talk like them, he did not drop his *r*'s and slur his *g*'s. He had obviously profited from his West Point education, his exposure to a cross section of America. She thought of Amy Kemble from Philadelphia, Honor Prescott from Virginia, the other brides from South Dakota, California, Texas. It was exciting to be part of a cross section of America.

"I sez to Pete I on'y wanna know one thing. Is she a good Catlic? When he sez yes then I sez my mind's at ease."

"We felt the same way," Mrs. Welsh said.

"We hadda scrape to do it but we sent Artie and Pete to the Jesuits. St. Francis Prep. It was worth it."

"We felt the same way about Catholic education."

"We couldn'a done it without my brothuh the monsignor. Y'know, a cop's salary."

Joanna's eyes misted. She denounced herself as a snob. The Burkes were poor. They had endured the poverty that she talked about so blithely, while the Welshes relished the good life and even sold it with their Cadillacs. *Mea culpa.* It was another reason to love Pete, the son of these unassuming sacrificial people.

There was Monsignor Clancy in his magenta-trimmed cassock and white surplice, waiting for her at the end of the center aisle of West Point's Roman Catholic Chapel. Not as awe-inspiring as the Cadet Chapel, with its vaulted Gothic ceiling and dangling regimental standards, and its magnificent stained-glass window crowded with the military heroes of the Bible. That was a miniature cathedral. This was more like a country church, with its curved-beam ceiling, its cheerful red and gold decór, its modest stained glass. Charming but not awe-inspiring. The monsignor supplied the awe.

He was as tall as Pete or his brother Arthur, and immensely fat. A once rugged Irish chin and stern mouth peered from a sphere of excess flesh. Pete and Joanna had gone over to his parish church to meet him when Joanna made her weekend duty visit to the Burkes in late January. He had been geniality itself for the first half hour, telling jokes about crabby nuns and ambitious priests, splashing sherry into their glasses. Then, with no warning, he became solemn.

"I'm not going to talk to you about what you should do or shouldn't do. You've both had good Catholic educations, especially you, Joanna. But I just want to warn you. After a few years, you'll be having a hard time trying to raise two or three kids on a lieutenant's salary. That's when you'll be tempted to practice birth control. Tempted to take the easy way. I see it here all the time in the parish. It isn't the first two or even the first four that cause a problem. It's later. That's when you have to live up to your faith."

How ridiculous this man was, Joanna had thought. As if there was the slightest possibility of her yielding to such a temptation. He was typical of what was wrong with the American Catholic clergy. Obsessed with birth control and other variations on sexual morality while they and their parishioners did nothing for the poor, the Negro.

"You agree with that, Joanna?" the monsignor had asked, seeming to sense her wayward thoughts.

"Oh yes," she said.

"Good, good. We hear a lot about you Midwest Catholics being so liberal you want to elect the Pope by popular vote."

Not in Cincinnati. They're too busy making money, Joanna was going to say. But she only smiled and shook her head. Suddenly, again with no warning, the monsignor was raging. "When I look around me I don't see much hope for this country. The ones who aren't out satisfying their sexual appetites are trying to sell us

Communism in every movie, every newspaper you see. Washington, D.C., is infested with Communists—''

On he ranted for a half hour, quoting Senator Joseph McCarthy of Wisconsin, Columnist Westbrook Pegler. Listening to him, Joanna felt the first dim sense of contradiction between American Catholicism's attempt to be both part of America and alienated from it. The contradiction applied with special force to her and Pete, who were about to enter the service of the secularist, oversexed nation the monsignor was denouncing.

She had dismissed it then as no more than a shadow, an individual's idiosyncrasy. She dismissed it once more, now, as she walked toward Monsignor Clancy in bride's white to receive his blessing. At least as important were the six ushers waiting to raise their sabers high. Arm in arm with Pete forever, she would walk beneath that arch of shining steel to become an Army wife.

Still hiding it? Still afraid to remember?
How much do you want? I've remembered too much already.
You've got to remember it all. For everyone.
You hate me, don't you? I don't blame you—
Remember.

In their room at the Hotel Thayer, Amy and Honor and Joanna often talked about Ruth Parrott. By June week, they were inclined to agree with Captain Coulter that she was not prime material for an officer's wife. Her taste in clothes was atrocious. She tended to monopolize the conversation, almost always on the topic she knew best, the Army. Her scathing opinions of the brass, the government, had become monotonous. Honor often wondered aloud what Sam Hardin, so consistently cheerful and easygoing, saw in her. "Adam says he's a slave to his stomach. Until Ruth's father got transferred, Sam was down at the Parrotts' quarters at least once a week for a homecooked dinner."

"It's more complicated than that," Amy said.

"If you can tell us that much, you've got to tell the rest," Honor said.

"George told me—sort of by accident," Amy said. "He made me swear never to tell a soul."

"Sam's been sleeping with her, right?" Honor said.

Amy nodded. "He promised to marry her."

Joanna was as intrigued—but considerably more disturbed—than Honor by this revelation. Pete and Sam Hardin had both been assigned to Schofield Barracks in Hawaii. Joanna expected to spend much of the next year in Ruth's company. Ruth had assured Joanna Schofield was the best deal in the Army and hinted that her father had pulled a few strings to get Sam "the slot." Since this was virtually the only good thing Ruth had yet to say about the Army, the remark had the double effect of heightening Joanna's romantic anticipation of a year-long honeymoon in the storied islands and intensifying her desire to be broad-minded about Ruth, lest she spoil it. Thus they progressed to sharing a table with Ruth and Sam at the Graduation Hop.

The cadets had hired not one but two name bands—Carmen Cavallero and Tommy Tucker—which meant the dancing was continuous. With the temperature still in the eighties, Cullum Hall became unbearably hot. They wandered down to Trophy Point in search of relief. Ruth Parrott was rather drunk. Amy Kemble had brought a flask and had been sharing it with her, as well as with George and Adam.

Carmen Cavallero's music, with the Latin beat that was so popular that year, drifted after them. With no warning, Ruth Parrott announced she was going to sing a song. She ordered George Rosser and Sam Hardin to hoist her on top of the fattest cannon. From there she bawled in a raucous falsetto:

"THE OFFICERS' WIVES, THE OFFICERS' WIVES
THAT'S WHAT WE'LL BE FOR THE REST OF OUR LIVES."

"If that's the way you girls feel," Adam said, "we're ready to sign short-term contracts with any one or all of you. None of us wants to detain you one minute longer than you want to stay, provided you agree to a decent minimum. Say two weeks? How does that strike you, Miss Welsh? Do you think you could diminish the volcanic frustrations of Peter the Great Burke here in two weeks? If we factor in his Irish-Catholic inhibitions, I would say you could manage it in twenty days. I expect to be through fighting the Civil

War with Miss Prescott in about the same length of time. So perhaps we could meet to round out the contract."

"How about this?" asked Pete Burke, seizing Adam by the front of his tunic and placing his massive fist an inch from his lips. "How about this to round out your dirty mouth?"

"The man's impossible," Adam said, calmly extricating his tunic. "When he becomes General of the Armies after the great wars between the rich and poor, the blacks and whites, that are destined to shake the Republic, he'll make Cromwell look like a libertine. Our one hope will be my moderating presence as his chief of staff. You see what influence I have over him. Like Fay Wray with King Kong."

By now everyone was laughing. Adam segued into an earnest lecture on West Point sexuality. "It's really what we majored in," he said. "You thought it was mathematics and war. That's just camouflage to delude the unwary drag. It's sex, nothing but sex. All these guns are symbols. This school is a vast Freudian hoax."

"I sure hope you're right," Honor Prescott said, in her throatiest Virginia drawl.

That should have been the end of it. But they were all rather giddy without any help from Amy's flask. Maybe it was Adam's monologue on sex and the imminence of their wedding day. Honor started singing Ruth's song as they rode back to the Hotel Thayer in Amy Kemble's Chrysler. As they got off the elevator on the third floor, Honor persuaded Joanna and Amy to join her in a reprise.

"THE OFFICERS' WIVES, THE OFFICERS' WIVES
  THAT'S WHAT WE'LL BE FOR THE REST OF OUR LIVES."

To their amazement, Ruth Parrott burst into tears. "You poor dumb bitches," she said. "You don't know. You just don't know."

III

"Are you happy now, George?" Amy Kemble Rosser asked.

You bet I am. I graduated and got laid all in one day. That was probably what George thought. But as an officer and a gentleman, he just said: "Sure."

Amy enjoyed imagining the difference between what men said and what they thought. She knew it was a masculine habit. She knew how men talked when there were no women around. She had read Norman Mailer's *The Naked and the Dead,* in which every second word of dialogue was "fug." In Paris the previous summer, she had bought a copy of Henry Miller's *Tropic of Cancer* and revelled in his scatology. She liked dirty words. They echoed deep in her body when she read them. They echoed even deeper on the rare occasions when she had heard them.

"It was worth waiting for?"

"You bet."

For a moment Amy wondered if she could persuade George to whisper dirty words to her while they made love. She decided it did not go with his Methodist background. It would upset him. Like most men, he thought them but did *not* say them to women. Only to other men.

"I'm happy too, I think."

"Why the doubt?"

"I'm not used to it."

"Why weren't you happy before?"

"Take a good look at my family."

"They seem okay to me."

"George, sometimes I think you lack a certain subtlety when it comes to people—relationships. Did it ever occur to you to wonder why Mother is forty pounds overweight and talks too much? My father ignores her."

"Why? She's not a bad-looking woman."

"He's never forgiven himself for losing so much of her money—most of it was hers—in the Depression. Just looking at her makes him feel inadequate. She's never forgiven him, either, of course. But she won't admit it. Instead she yaks about the promising career as a singer that she gave up to marry him and have me."

"It must have been tough for you—growing up."

"It used to break my heart. Until I decided I wasn't going to let anything break my heart."

"And no one's done it?"

"No."

"No one even came close?"

"No," Amy said. "How about you?"

"You don't have much chance to get your heart broken at West Point."

"But in California? Tell me the truth now. About the orgies on the beaches, the wild parties in the mountains?"

"I've told you—Bakersfield isn't Hollywood."

"I liked your father. He has a nice sense of humor."

"He runs a good hardware store. Keeps the customers smiling."

"Your mother seemed sort of remote."

"If the show isn't being run by the Methodist Church, she's out of it. She's still sore at me for not becoming a minister. I was her last hope. After the two big shots failed her."

"Your older brothers."

"Yeah. Listen. It was a nice wedding, wasn't it?"

"Yes. It was perfect. Everything went perfectly."

"How about another celebration?"

"You second lieutenants are insatiable."

"You know how the song goes: 'On, brave Old Army team.'"

She opened her arms to him. A dozen floors below the Hotel Plaza's white-and-gold bridal suite, taxi horns beeped, voices echoed. New York City's million midnight eyes peered at their lovemaking in the shadowed room. To Amy Kemble Rosser it was still part of the public perfection of her wedding. She gave herself to her bridegroom with a fervor, an enthusiasm derived as much from her satisfaction with the whole day, even with all of June week, as from the sensations produced by this hard-muscled, hard-breathing young second lieutenant crushing her lips, caressing with apparent pleasure her unassuming breasts.

The wedding had been a triumph of military precision. Amy and George, along with the other brides and grooms, their maids of honor, best men and ushers, had been summoned to the Cadet Chapel early in June week and every step of the ceremony had been meticulously rehearsed. The ushers knew precisely when to draw their sabers as a couple left the altar, the couple knew exactly what pace to maintain going down the aisle to give the ushers time to slip out the side door and provide another arch of gleaming steel at the front door. Amy enjoyed every moment of it. She did not in the least mind that her wedding was a duplicate of ninety others that day and of several thousand previous West Point weddings. She liked being part of a tradition. She liked the Army's systematic way of planning events to achieve external perfection. She had no complaints about being "processed," as one bride had called it. She had no infantile middle-class fears of being swallowed by the system.

Everyone had been goggle-eyed at Amy's wedding dress, with its amazingly intricate pattern of Alençon lace. It had come down from her grandmother, bought when the Kembles were among the really rich, before the Depression had exploded her father's pretensions to being a shrewd investor. Amy had chosen her mother's dress—a dove-gray tulle, with appliquéd lace on the collar and sleeves and stiff flares near the hemline that shifted the eyes from the in-between bulges. Cousin Paula Stapleton, her only attendant, had also looked (for once) attractive in the dress Amy had selected for her, a blue silk chiffon with exquisite cutout work over a pale flesh-toned net.

Even Father had been on hand, in a role he was splendidly equipped to play. Teddy Kemble looked like he had been born in his cutaway. No one in Philadelphia wore dress clothes with more pleasure and more aplomb. A natural actor, he had lifted her veil and kissed her with such reverence, spectators could only assume they were watching the denouement of a tender family love story—instead of the parting of two semi-strangers. As Teddy stepped into the first pew, he even brushed away a seemingly authentic tear.

Amy's only disappointment was George's failure to win the

coveted first place in the drawings for the order in which they were married. DUSA, the Daughters of the U. S. Army, gave a reception for the first bride and she became the symbolic toast of West Point. Amy had suggested offering to buy the privilege from the cadet who had won. The offer had been savagely rejected. George had been upset and tried, largely in vain, to explain the Army's attitude toward money.

A minor pang. Everything else had been so perfect, including the presence of her smiling uncle, Paul Stapleton, who had given them introductions to a dozen Army friends in Europe, people he wanted them to meet on their honeymoon before George joined the 4th Armored Division in Nuremberg.

George's tongue roved Amy's mouth. Suddenly her heart pounded and it began to happen again, the memory of that other male tongue, so boldly, shockingly thrust into her mouth, while her father sat in a nearby living room conferring with his cousin, Paul Stapleton, on how Teddy might turn his wartime achievements as an OSS officer into a late-blooming career in politics.

Come on, cousin Amy, I know a set of hot pants when I see one, whispered Johnny Stapleton.

It had been four years ago, 1946, the first summer after the war, the first time they had driven from Philadelphia to northern New Jersey to visit their Stapleton cousins at New Grange Farm again. During the war three of the boys and their father, Paul, had been off fighting in Europe and in the Pacific. Amy had written polite letters to the sons at her mother's urging, to keep up their morale. They never bothered to answer. They thought of her as a child. Which she was.

But an only child, a precocious child. One of Amy's vivid memories was a prewar visit to New Grange Farm. The stated purpose was to get to know her cousin Paula, daughter of her mother's sister and Paul Stapleton's brother. The marriage was a troubled one, and the farm was selected as safer, more neutral ground. Amy had ignored Paula, a thin, solemn girl who only wanted to discuss books, and instead, hung greedily on the fringe of the male world of Paul Stapleton's sons. She had watched from her bedroom window their daily dawn routine, ferocious calisthenics in front of the barn, then a five-mile run. Always the winner, the one who could also do the most push-ups and chin-ups and jumping jacks, was Johnny Stapleton, the second son. He was taller, more powerfully built than his brothers and he had a swagger that they either lacked or eschewed. Paula disapproved of him; he was "wild" and had been expelled from a half dozen schools. Which only made Amy more interested.

That was where she had discovered the thrill of dirty words, the amazingly casual way that boys mouthed them. *Fucking son of a bitch*, snarled Mark Stapleton to John. *Up your ass*, was the reply. *Balls, prick, tits, cunt*, flew around as casually as they flung baseballs and footballs. Amy was fascinated. The language was a sort of code, binding them into an earthy solidarity totally different from the prim private girls' school world she had known. For the first time she sensed men as a group and women as separate, vulnerable because of their separateness. So violent too, this male world, with its explosions of punching, wrestling, tackling. So free, with its taunts, its derisive nicknames, its naked competition. She could not hear or see enough of it.

By 1946, that enclave of Stapleton maleness had vanished. None of the boys were home except Johnny, on a summer leave from West Point. He still had his swagger—and more reason for it. He was a war hero, a tanker, decorated in Sicily by General Patton himself. He had decided to make the Army a career and his father had gotten him into the Academy in 1945. He hated the place. As he explained it to Amy during the first part of their walk, it was the hazing, the tradition of indoctrinating new cadets by harassing and abusing them, that he especially disliked. Johnny had resisted it and earned numerous enemies among the upperclassmen. He was labeled a BJ, the derogatory term for plebes who acted as if they had been recognized before June. BJ's were usually challenged to fights by upperclassmen who outweighed them by twenty or thirty pounds, and beaten into cringing submission. But Johnny had flattened the best boxer in the first class with one punch and the hazers had decided to let him alone.

Strolling along the tree-lined path, Johnny surprised Amy by thanking her for her wartime letters, and apologizing for not answering them. "I guess I thought of you as a kid. It's always a shock for lugs like me to discover girls grow up." He started talking about how difficult it was to get to know American girls, compared to Europeans, especially Italians. He thought the American attitude toward sex was ridiculous. An American girl not only had to be seduced, she had to be reeducated, taught to relax, respond.

Suddenly Amy realized his arm was around her. He was turning her to him in the shadowy path. "How about you, cousin Amy? Are you interested in education?" She was in his arms, his tongue was in her mouth, he was whispering those startling words to her. *Hot pants?* No one had ever suggested such a notion to seventeen-year-old Amy Kemble, with her perfect manners and stylish clothes. "No," she had gasped, and burst out of John Stapleton's arms.

Nothing more was heard from cousin Johnny for a year and a half. In the middle of her sophomore year at Vassar, Amy got a cheery phone call. She was urged to come up to West Point to rescue a California cadet from chronic loneliness. George Rosser, Johnny explained, was a "yearling"—a third-classman, a good guy, a friend, who needed a date for a fall hop. "Don't worry, I didn't tell him about your hot pants," Johnny said.

She had accepted the date. Since Amy had seen cousin Johnny at his father's farm in New Jersey she had undergone a change in her attitude toward sex. It was largely through the influence of her Vassar roommate, Gloria Teitelbaum, the cool, very sophisticated daughter of a textile manufacturer from New Jersey. Gloria arrived at Vassar equipped with a diaphragm which she had obtained from her family doctor without the permission of her mother or father. Gloria justified her intentions with citations from the Kinsey Report, that land mine under American sexual morality. If three out of four men felt it was okay to have sex before marriage, why shouldn't a free, intelligent modern woman? Gloria and Amy discussed the sex lives of their parents and discovered they both had fathers who practiced the double standard—which justified their mutual contempt for their mothers.

When Gloria began a torrid love affair with a Yalie, while Amy went to insipid tea dances, she began to think she was a fool for having refused John Stapleton so abruptly. Amy went to West Point that first time, thinking not of her blind date, but of her cousin.

Johnny was escorting an overdeveloped blonde named Joyce, from the nearby Catholic college, Ladycliff. She was obviously in love and spent all her time gazing worshipfully at him, too stupefied even to converse. George Rosser told Amy that he and the rest of Johnny's friends were worried about him because he was sneaking off the post twice a week to see Joyce. If he got caught, expulsion was certain. George was afraid the Army was in danger of losing one of its future battle leaders. He spoke with awe and affection about Johnny's war record, his leadership in his class, the way he was trying to change the senseless bullying of the plebe system.

Later in the evening Johnny danced with Amy in the usual rotation of partners. "Why are you risking your career for that cow?" she said.

"Coz," Johnny said. "This place was designed for college kids. I'm twenty-six and I'm not used to being a monk."

"You knew I was in Poughkeepsie. Why didn't you call me?"

"Highland Falls is a lot closer than Poughkeepsie, coz."

"That's all it was, that night at the farm? Convenience?"

"As a matter of fact, no. I like your type. Hard to get started."

That remark made her determined to seduce him. He was a mistake in her past that she wanted to correct. As well as an opening into that male world which she had been so eager to enter. The fact that he was a cousin somehow made him doubly attractive. Perhaps he seemed safer.

"I can meet you any place you suggest, in my car."

"Tonight?"

"Why not?"

"It's a date. After you say good night to George, at the Thayer, wait fifteen minutes, then drive up Mills Road, the first left beyond the hotel. Turn off your lights and wait up there, behind the chapel. I'll meet you after bed check."

"Won't they notice that you're absent without leave?"

He laughed. "It so happens that my tactical officer was in my tank platoon. I saved his ass about six times in France."

As they left Cullum Hall, Amy was astonished to discover that each cadet was given a stipulated length of time to escort his date to her weekend residence. If the girl was staying at the Hotel Thayer, and the couple was walking, the allotted time was one hour. If she was staying on the post with an officer's family, there were forty-five- and thirty-minute zones. For those who drove to the Thayer, the time was shortest: fifteen minutes.

George Rosser rode back to the Hotel Thayer with Amy in her Chrysler coupe. As she parked he explained that he would like to kiss her, but Public Displays of Affection were taboo on the post. A cadet recently caught kissing a girl in a car had been slugged with one hundred demerits, forty-five hours of walking the area and a twenty-five-dollar fine. Amy said she understood and said good night to George at the hotel's front door. She went upstairs to her room, waited ten minutes and returned to her car. In exactly fifteen minutes by her watch, she was parked on Mills Road behind the chapel.

After about five minutes of mounting tension, a hand rapped on the right window. She lowered it and Johnny whispered: "Give me your trunk key." In ten seconds he handed the key back to her. He gave her directions to the Washington Gate, at the north end of the post. About a half mile beyond it was a byroad, opposite a gas station which would be closed. That was where she should stop.

Twenty minutes later, Johnny stepped from the trunk with a soft laugh and kissed her all in one flowing motion, lifting her off her feet. "Hot pants," he said. "I can always spot them."

"I don't know if I really qualify," Amy said. "This is my first time."

"I'm flattered, coz. I really am."

Johnny hurt her more than he pleased her that first night on the front seat of her Chrysler coupe. Her hymen, he muttered, was as tough as the armor plating on a German Tiger tank. But Amy dismissed the pain and the disappointment. When he came in her she was swept by a sense of triumph, of pride, that she had chosen this magnificent male to make her a woman, that he had acquiesced so readily. She wanted to enter him, possess him as boldly as he was entering her. She wrapped her arms around his brawny chest and whispered: "Do I get a passing mark, Professor?"

"Four point oh," he said.

"What does that mean?"

"Perfect—you can't go any higher."

"What's the next course?"

"Jesus," he said, sitting up. "I knew your father had the family wild streak. I didn't realize you inherited it."

It was astonishing, how much those words changed everything. She saw that his "hot pants" remark was just part of his line. She sensed her wildness made him wary. He thought it was all right for a man to be wild because he knew when to stop. Woman's wildness was different. It had to be controlled—by him. This pained, then angered her. Amy vowed to show him she could control her own wildness. At the same time she yearned to commingle it with his recklessness. She realized this was probably impossible. She foresaw that if she tried it, she might be very badly hurt.

But she could not resist the attempt. She told herself wariness would shield her. She let him tell himself—and her—that their subsequent meetings were simply additional lessons, part of her continuing education. Toward the end of that dangerous spring Johnny almost capitulated. "If I ever marry anybody, coz, it'll be someone like you. But it'll take me five or ten years to settle down." She heard him thinking about the unthinkable, actually marrying cousin Amy, in spite of her mediocre tits and cool, unmushy style. She also heard him estimating the likelihood of remaining faithful to her and finding it a very dubious bet. The pickings among the beauties like Honor Prescott and the well-stacked conveniences like Joyce were simply too good. That was when Amy began to realize just how much John Stapleton could hurt her. By then it was almost too late.

Meanwhile, Amy was fending off George Rosser. He sent her earnest letters, telling her how much he would like to see her again. She went to the spring hop with him and repeated the car-trunk routine with Johnny. That summer, Amy went to Europe with her mother, as usual. Johnny went to Texas to train with other cadets who had chosen armor for their Army careers. She wrote him two or three letters which he never bothered to answer. She got several letters from George Rosser, to which she responded in brisk chatty style.

In the fall of 1948, Amy met Johnny twice in New York. Both times it was so intense, so wild in every meaning of the word, that she was sure he was going to propose. Instead, at the end of the second session, he held her in his arms and told her it was time to stop. She almost wept, but she managed to control herself and say: "Back to Joyce? Convenience has triumphed?"

Johnny shook his head. "I've got to start beating the books or I'll flunk out of that damn military monastery. I can't disappoint the old man again."

Amy was dismayed to discover that she had been an emotional sideline. Why did fathers evoke such deep commitments from their sons and ask nothing from their daughters? Feeling doubly bereft, she went back to Vassar and found in her mailbox a letter from George Rosser, inviting her to the Christmas hop. She accepted. They sat with several members of his class. One was Adam Thayer, who kept everyone laughing with imitations of boneheaded tactical officers and instructors. Amy asked George if Johnny was at the dance and was told that he had turned hive. It only seemed to increase George's admiration for him.

Amy dated George a half dozen times in the next five months. She was surprised to discover that he was descended from Thomas Rosser, an 1861 graduate who had been a close friend of George Armstrong Custer. Rosser had become a brigadier general in the Confederate Army. George's father owned several letters and a diary of this long-departed great-grandfather.

Equally surprising was George's interest in Amy's disquisitions on bad taste, a topic which she had inherited from her father, and bolstered by majoring in art history at Vassar. She was almost as surprised by George's athletic prowess. He was a superb tennis player, one of the best on the West Point team, and equally good at lacrosse. He invited her to a lacrosse match with Cornell and she found it tremendously exciting. The crash of the sticks on wood and flesh, the gasping snarls of the competing players, the pounding feet on the grassy earth, the sweat gleaming on those sinewy male bodies, stirred memories of her Stapleton cousins at New Grange Farm.

Amy had gone to June week in 1949 as George's drag. That

Saturday, she saw her first review. She had seen the cadets march on movie screens, and once at a parade in Philadelphia. But this was different. The white and gray ranks, striding precisely across the green Plain, the bravura music of the blue-clad Army band, the fluttering flags and pennants, the swift salutes, stirred a satisfaction in her that she usually felt only when studying some perfect work of art, a painting by her Renaissance favorite, Botticelli, or her modern favorite, Mondrian. It was right to the last detail, there was nothing for the eye or the mind to fault. Like art, this perfection, this right order, was changeless. For a century and a half, almost as long as America itself had existed, cadets in white and gray had performed this ceremony. Remarkable.

That June, Amy did not dance with Johnny Stapleton or even see him at any of the hops. The first-classmen had classic Cullum Hall, the other cadets danced in the gymnasium. She asked George if Johnny was graduating and George hastened to assure her that he had made it. She asked if he was still going with Joyce. She was told that he now had some debutante from New York on the string. The debutante was not in view when Amy walked over to congratulate John after the graduation ceremony. She gave him a cousinly kiss on the cheek and he whispered: ''Glad to see you're still loyal to the Corps, coz.''

John shook hands with George and said: ''Hope I'll see you in a tank platoon some one of these years, Rosser.'' He turned to his father, Paul Stapleton, that spare stern-eyed man who had won medals in both world wars, and explained that Rosser was a hive but he was thinking of ''going armor too.'' Paul Stapleton smiled and shook George's hand and urged him to give serious consideration to armor. ''They could use a few guys with brains,'' he said. ''They've got plenty of shoot-'em-up types like this hotshot.'' He punched Johnny on the arm and they exchanged a look of intense affection that almost demoralized Amy. Again she felt the uneasy fear of never knowing or understanding the male world, with its suppressed but somehow more binding love.

Ridiculous, Amy told herself, in George Rosser's arms, in the bridal suite of the Hotel Plaza. Ridiculous. Why was she thinking about John Stapleton now? He was not the kind of man she wanted. But there he stood, in his cadet white and gray in the sunshine of last year, smiling at her.

No, worse than smiling at her. Strolling beside her toward the Central Area, the cadet barracks, while George turned away to congratulate other graduates, saying: "Take my advice and marry that guy, coz. He's nuts about you."

Infuriating. That July she had sailed to Europe with her mother. As usual, Father spent the summer as everyone's favorite house guest at Southampton, Newport and Bar Harbor. He went to Europe in the spring or fall to hunt and drink and sail and screw with the same dreary superficial crowd. Waiting at the Hotel Crillon when Amy and her mother arrived in Paris were ten letters from George. She did not even send him a postcard. He wrote more letters, minutely describing his duty in Beast Barracks, disciplining the latest cargo of plebes. Suddenly George was talking to her on the telephone from Idlewild Airport. He had borrowed money from his father and was using his summer leave to fly to see her.

Amy was both touched and troubled by this romantic gesture. It was fascinating to think that she was the global center of Cadet Rosser's attention. But the wariness she had learned from Johnny Stapleton made her disinclined to reward him. They strolled through the Bois de Boulogne. The green landscape was strewn with couples nuzzling, caressing in the August heat. George told her that he could not sleep, he could not eat, thinking, dreaming about her. They found a secluded, relatively cool hollow in the woods and Amy began to unpack the picnic basket the Crillon had made up for them. But George was not interested in food. He drew her to him with masculine authority. "I love you, Amy," he said. "I want to marry you."

Amy was amazed by how profoundly the words stirred her. She summoned wariness, reminded herself of the probable calculation in Cadet Rosser's passion. But she let him kiss her and she found herself returning the kiss with considerable enthusiasm.

Unbuttoning her blouse was another matter. "No," she said. She absolutely refused to go back to his hotel room with him, even when he offered to swear on his honor as a future officer of the U. S.

Army that he would marry her on graduation day. In his turmoil, Cadet Rosser made the mistake of revealing that other girls had yielded to this solemn guarantee—Ruth Parrott to his roommate, Sam Hardin, for instance. Amy was unimpressed.

They soul-kissed for an hour. But she stopped him again when he began to fondle her breasts. He yielded—regretfully, agonizingly. She found herself enjoying his agony and felt guilty. But she could not acquiesce, much as she found herself suddenly wishing he would overwhelm her. It was her way of proving to herself that Johnny had been a mistake, an aberration.

In the end, there was only one way to soothe poor George's distress. She kissed his pleading mouth once more and told him that she loved him and was ready to be his Army wife.

"Honey—are you with me?" George whispered.

Amy struggled to make the journey across space and time to join George as he came. She did not quite succeed but she felt virtuous, pleased, that she had made the effort, and even more pleased that he had wanted her there.

"I didn't feel—you seemed—"

"It's been such a long day. Wait till we get to Paris. I'll make it up to you. I'll even make up for being such a bitch last summer."

"It's okay. I had a great time. I was just afraid I'd hurt you or something."

"No," Amy said, touched. "It's my fault. For being such a softie. I have to get in training to be an Army wife."

IV

"Have a feel on me, Lucille
In my merry Crosmobile."

They were rolling north along the Hudson in Adam's blue Crosley, advertised as "America's only $1,000 car." Adam had instantly made it the automobile of his choice. It had, he said, "a Yankee price, even if it was made in Cincinnati." Honor Prescott Thayer didn't care if it was the smallest, silliest-looking car on the highway. She was happy to be sitting in it beside Adam, his wife. Yesterday, and the other days of June week, had been mythical. She had felt like she was in a movie and watching it at the same time. She had scarcely noticed her mother's carping about her failure to finish college. She ignored Mother's claim that Adam's father, who had drunk a great deal of champagne at the wedding reception, had put his hand on her knee under the table.

"If he did it," Adam said, "I'm proud of the old boy. But I can't believe he'd have the gumption." He suggested that her mother was having sexual fantasies, common among widows.

Adam warbled another verse to his Crosmobile and put his arm around Honor, slipping his hand under her brassiere to finger her right nipple. "Stop it," she said, slapping his hand away. "Whoever said Yankees were inhibited never met you."

"It's the novelty of it. Once I understand how it works, I'll lose interest."

"You better not!"

"What will you do when it happens? Have affairs?"

"I am never goin' to love anyone but you. I told you that a dozen times."

"I like that kind of loyalty," Adam said. "I don't deserve it but I like it."

He was always teasing her. Honor wondered sometimes if it was all fooling. Around Christmas, he had started calling her Little Red Riding Hood and warning her to stop trusting wolves with Yankee accents. He had suddenly asked her, while they danced at the Valentine hop, "What in hell do you see in me, anyway? Someone with your looks could have the First Captain. He's behind you practically drooling right now." She turned her head and saw First Captain John Murphy, a handsome black-haired Irishman, dancing a few feet away, talking earnestly to his drag. "Ah," Adam said. "You're interested? I'll introduce you to him." Struggling to be offhand, she told him she wasn't interested in anyone but him.

Listening to Adam argue with Joanna Welsh about books on philosophy or poetry that Honor had never even heard of, much less read, or with Amy Kemble about politics, in which Honor had no interest whatever, she would sometimes feel blindly, maliciously jealous and would be very bitchy to either or both of them when they all got back to the Hotel Thayer. Then she would hate herself and apologize.

Adam had not been her first date at West Point. Norwood College was only about twenty-five miles away, on the other side of the Hudson. Sometimes it seemed like half the six hundred girls in the place were dating cadets. They often needed three buses to transport the drags to a big hop. But Honor's previous draws on the blind-date list had been duds. She had begun to think West Pointers were a pretty dull bunch. Most men reacted to her looks either by blabbing or by drooling. So far the droolers, too tongue-tied to conduct a decent conversation, had been in the majority at the U. S. Military Academy.

When the cadet hostess in the leathery alcoved lounge at Grant Hall called her name, Honor had sauntered to the table with very little optimism to examine the latest prospect. Tall enough but much too skinny was her first impression. Then she noticed that he was blinking at her in the strangest way. He wrinkled his long nose and mouth into a total pucker and turned to the hostess. "Don't you have anything better than this?" he said.

"Cadet Thayer," the hostess replied. "I suggest you have your eyes checked."

He sighed. "Okay," he said. "But get it straight. The next time I want a decent blind date." Whereupon he groped toward her, saying: "You won't mind leading me around, will you?"

She liked him. He was not the cadet she was looking for but he was a welcome change from the tongue-tied droolers. She did not think she would ever love him, the way he clowned all through their first date. Honor had long since vowed that no one was going to get her unless she was in love with him. She had decided she was a one-man woman. She was like Melanie in *Gone With the Wind*, the only book she had ever read twice. She had seen the movie eight times. It did not bother her that she looked more like Scarlett. Honor knew that she had a touch of Scarlett in her. But she had no interest in the Rhetts of this world, men who regarded women as so much curvy flesh. Only to an Ashley would she give herself, forever.

On their second date, she discovered Adam was Ashley, underneath his craziness. He walked her down to Flirtation Path and worked the old gag on her at Kissing Rock. He had flung her back and told her that if a drag passed under it without a kiss, the rock would topple, possibly taking the entire Academy into the Hudson with it. "Well?" she had said. He kissed her in an interesting way, slowly, carefully, as if he was trying to learn something about her from it. They walked hand in hand for a while, passing other couples in similar embraces. No need to worry about Public Displays of Affection on Flirty.

Honor told him how much she admired the Academy because it was a school that taught ideals. Adam said he had come to West Point for the same reason—its ideals. He told her how he liked to visit the old Cadet Chapel down by the cemetery at twilight and meditate on the famous men who had worshipped there, Robert E. Lee, Stonewall Jackson, Ulysses Grant, William Tecumseh Sherman, John J. Pershing. West Point had a great past but Adam told her he was worried about its future. He felt the Academy should teach less science and more literature, history, philosophy. He said they were still in the grip of the old mercenary theory on which the school had been founded—to train soldiers for war and engineers for peace. Now they needed to know more than how to build bridges and fight battles. They had to think about mankind, what the world needed to prevent war. He poured out his vision of a world where America's ideals became realities. Honor listened and thought, *Ashley*. She loved him.

Later, when she heard him mock his own ideals, when he conceded some credit to Amy Kemble's narrow Republican nastiness toward everyone who wasn't from the Philadelphia Main Line, Honor saw Adam's churning brain as his enemy and possibly hers. He could argue on any side of any question. He told her once that he sometimes thought he was the reincarnation of the Greek philosopher Diogenes. He told her how Alexander the Great had met Diogenes and afterward said: "If I were not Alexander, I would be Diogenes."

"My problem," Adam said, "is I want to be both."

But all craziness, all doubt, all fear, had vanished last night. Adam had knelt beside her in the room at the Hotel Thayer, running his hands down her body, whispering: "Honor, Honor, you're so damn beautiful." And she had answered, "It's for you, no one else. Never for anyone else." She let him walk her to the full-length mirror and stand behind her, hands still roving. In the half light she had acknowledged her own beauty once more as a simple fact, relieved that at last she could do it without uneasiness, without hearing advice from friends and relatives about what "a girl with your looks" should do to make her fortune. Always there was a sickening suggestion of selling herself to the highest bidder. At times it had made her almost hate the mirror's long-legged supple body with the firm coned breasts that seemed to rise so naturally out of it, the glossy, dark red pubic hair, darker than the hair on her head, which had a sunnier sheen. It wasn't her, that body in the mirror. But now she could greet it as a friend, an ally.

While they drove, Adam had her read *The New York Times* to him. He said it was the only way he could justify the idiocy of going anywhere by car, which otherwise was the most moronic form of transportation devised by modern man. The *Times* reported that the Industrial College of the Armed Forces was holdng a conference on the cost of national defense. The College reported alarming U.S. shortages of raw materials and weapons. A colonel said if war came the United States would have to trust to its productive capacity and its moral and spiritual strength. Adam snorted derisively. On page 2, a reporter named James Reston described how optimism on peace prospects was growing. Western defenses were now strong enough to smash the Soviet Army if it attacked. The West was forging defensive weapons faster than the Russians were inventing offensive ones.

Honor was confused. "Do you think there'll be another war soon?"

"Not a chance," Adam said.

"But this Industrial College—"

"They're just trying to get the defense budget raised. The real reason is not Mr. Reston's balderdash about defensive weapons, either. It's Russia's casualties in World War II. Ten million men. They can't afford to start another war for at least a decade.''

"That's good," Honor said. "I want you around for every day of those ten years."

"Then I can go off and get killed? You'll be bored with me?"

"By then you'll be a colonel or maybe a general. They don't get killed."

"I'm flattered by your confidence in me. I wish you were in charge of the Army promotion system."

When Honor finished the *Times*, Adam turned on the radio and they listened to soap operas. Adam laughed at all of them, especially "Helen Trent, the story of a woman who sets out to prove what so many other women long to prove in their own lives, that romance can live on at thirty-five and even beyond." Adam knew this introduction by heart and recited it mockingly along with the announcer, as soon as the familiar ukulele refrain had ended. Honor was confused again. Her mother adored "Helen Trent," and Honor had listened to it on days when she stayed home from school with a cold or sore throat. Sometimes she and her mother cried together when Helen was in serious trouble, her daughter hopelessly lost in a fog of amnesia, Helen herself blindly trusting some skunk of a man.

In Boston, they stopped for lunch in Connolly's, a small tavern near the Common, where Adam used to eat with his father when he came to Boston on government business. Adam would come down on the train, have lunch with him and go back to Sconnet that afternoon.

Heading north along the shore into Maine, Adam turned on the Crosley's radio again. Now it was time for the kids' shows. Honor felt more comfortable laughing with Adam at the wheezy organ introducing "The Shadow" with the inevitable: "Who knows what evil lurks in the hearts of men?" Adam confessed to having been terrified by the Shadow at the age of ten. He had had fantasies about his father being a local Lamont Cranston, who had disappeared to fight evil in Sconnet. Honor said the Shadow had scared her too. Her favorite show was "Buck Rogers." She used to imagine herself as Wilma Deering, blasting off with Buck into the dark daring world of outer space.

"Now that I'm older and I've read the Kinsey Report," Adam said, "I wonder what went on in that rocket ship between Buck and Wilma while they were buzzing toward Venus for three or four weeks per trip? Or between Lamont Cranston and Margo Lane, for that matter. He was always meeting her in hotel rooms and apartments at 4 A.M. And the bastard was invisible."

"Do you think as many men play around as Kinsey says?"

"No."

"I hope you never do."

"You don't have a thing to worry about. I never do anything I can't rationalize. Why should I fool around when I've got the best-looking wife in the country?"

"Uh-uh. Remember Sue Anne Stackpole."

Sue Anne Stackpole had won the title of Miss Virginia in 1946. Honor had finished second, to the chagrin of her mother and friends. Their only consolation was Sue Anne's failure to win the Miss America title at Atlantic City. Adam used to tease Honor by asking for Sue Anne's address, telling her he was not a man who settled for second-best in anything.

"When I take command of Army Intelligence, you'll be in trouble. I'll assign every gumshoe in the organization to find Sue Anne."

"I hear she's gotten fat."

"Don't disillusion me, woman. A man has to have something to look forward to."

It was dark by the time they reached Sconnet. Adam insisted on driving down to the beach. He got out of the car and stood there, watching the waves foam whitely against some rocks offshore. The air was cold and thick with salt. He breathed it deeply. "That's my oxygen," he said. "That smell. I've got to have it every year or so, or my blood starts thickening. I start to age right in front of your eyes. But so fur, comin' back here reglur"—he slipped into his mock Maine accent—"uh've been hangin' on. Look pretty good for a hunnert and two, don't I?"

They drove slowly down the main street, with its drugstore, grocery and movie theater, which was showing Spencer Tracy in *Father of the Bride*. "Hey, look," Adam said. "They knew we were coming." Honor thought of her father and almost wept but Adam did not notice in the dark.

They turned right off Main Street and rolled down a tree-lined side street. Huge elms created a tunnel of almost total darkness. Through their drooping branches, house lights gleamed. A wind from the sea rustled the tops of the old trees. Adam slowed to a stop and helped Honor out of the Crosley. "I swear, this car should come equipped with a derrick," she said.

"Love me, love my car," Adam said.

A light came on above the front door and they mounted uneven wooden steps to a broad porch. Stepping into the hall, Honor found herself face to face with one of the biggest women she had ever seen. Mrs. Thayer was over six feet tall, with a round rather small face framed by bobbed gray hair. She was wearing a faded calico housedress with short sleeves. Her arms looked especially huge. Washerwoman's arms, Honor thought for some reason.

"Hello, my dear," she said, smiling broadly. Without waiting for Adam to introduce them, she swept Honor into her arms. For a moment Honor felt ten years old. Mrs. Thayer smelled musky, as if she had not bathed for several days.

"And Sonny."

She kissed Adam in the same way, with a bear-hug squeeze. "I hope you haven't eaten. I've got supper waiting for you in the kitchen."

Supper turned out to be Spam and baked beans, with some iced tea from a genuine icebox—not a refrigerator. Honor gazed at it in amazement, remembering a remark of her mother's about a woman friend who had a husband so cheap he would not buy her a refrigerator. When Honor asked for a slice of lemon for her iced tea, Mrs. Thayer made a production out of searching the kitchen and discovering she did not have a single lemon in the place. For dessert, Adam and Honor each got one scoop of vanilla ice cream and one cookie.

70

Mrs. Thayer wanted to know all about the wedding, but before Honor could tell her very much, she began explaining why she had not been able to come. She had to get the house ready for the summer visitors. In fact, her first guests of the season, a lovely family named Brady, who came up from Hartford every year around this time, were already upstairs. There had been some confusion about dates, and they had appeared a day early. This meant the master bedroom, with its view of the sea, was taken. In fact, she'd been so busy cleaning house that she hadn't had time to make up any other rooms. But Honor could sleep in with her, "in the spare bed," as Mrs. Thayer called it, and "Sonny" (Adam) could sleep in his old bed, which she always kept made up. It took Honor several minutes to realize that Mrs. Thayer had arranged matters so the newlyweds could not sleep together. Adam did not object. He simply smiled and said, "Sure, Mom."

"Oh my goodness," Mrs. Thayer said. "It's time for Bing Crosby. He's on Bob Hope's show tonight."

"Oh, you like Bing too? He's my momma's favorite. I can't stand him," Honor said.

"Honor grew up on Frankie boy," Adam said.

"That Italian? Oh well, I never did think much of young people's tastes. My mother used to say, the good taste of one generation leads to the bad taste of the next generation."

Honor helped wash the few dishes and they trooped into the living room, where Mrs. Thayer turned on a big dark brown Philco radio, with an unfortunate hole in one of the tan mesh triangles that covered the speaker. It wasn't a bad show. Bob Hope was funny, as usual, Bing Crosby wasn't a bad singer, not bad enough to turn him off. He just sang songs *about* people instead of songs *to* people, the way Sinatra did. Crosby didn't make you feel anything.

Mrs. Thayer started trying to tune in another favorite, "Welcome Traveler," when Bob Hope said good night. Adam suggested a walk on the beach. Honor accepted with alacrity. They strolled down to the shore in silence. Honor wished she could tell Adam that she liked his mother. But she did not want to start lying to her husband on the second night of their honeymoon.

"I never told you—or anyone else—that the old girl took in summer boarders," Adam said. "I guess I thought it didn't go with the picture of the officer and gentleman."

"It doesn't bother me, honey. I don't see why it should bother you."

"You don't? Can't you see the expression on Amy Rosser's face if she heard it?"

"She's a snob. Not everybody's that way. Would Pete Burke mind? Joanna?"

"I don't know. Anyway, the old girl's poor. You saw the size of those ice-cream portions. We'll have to send her some money."

"Doesn't your father—?"

"Sure. Every month. And every month she sends it back." Adam laughed harshly. "She's an artist at the guilt game. She's not going to let him off with a cash payment."

"You do whatever you feel's right. We'll manage."

Honor did not want to think about how they were going to send Mrs. Thayer any money out of a second lieutenant's salary of $180 a month. She wished Adam would say something about being separated on the second night of their honeymoon. But he seemed to have lost his sense of humor.

Back at the house, Mrs. Thayer snapped off the radio and led Adam and Honor upstairs to a small room decorated with dangling World War I airplanes that Adam had built from kits. On one wall were framed awards Adam had won at the local high school, and his diploma, testifying that he had graduated with highest honors. In a frame on another wall were a half dozen of his report cards, with A and A+ for every mark. On several shelves were a top, a baseball glove, a collection of marbles and other toys, including a lot of lead soldiers with blue Civil War uniforms. The room gave Honor a creepy feeling. It reminded her of a visit she had paid to a friend of her mother's, whose son had been killed on Iwo Jima. His room was like this one, full of mementos. Her mother said it was stupid, her motto was "Let the dead bury the dead." Honor had been furious, because she knew the remark was aimed at her father. But she also had to admit the woman was foolish. Pathetic but foolish.

In the bedroom with Mrs. Thayer, Honor felt very strange wearing the white satin nightgown and lacy ribbony white peignoir she had bought for her trousseau. "My goodness, you look like a Hollywood show girl," Mrs. Thayer said. She put on a floor-length, tight-necked cotton nightgown and knelt down beside the bed to say ten minutes of prayers. "Don't they say night prayers in Virginia?" she asked. "I thought Southerners were religious."

"We go to church, if that's what you mean," Honor said.

"What one?"

"Episcopal."

"Low Church, I hope. When Adam wanted to scare me, growing up, he used to say he was going to turn High Episcopal. Or Roman Catholic. We have a tribe of them here in Sconnet. French Canadian."

"I don't rightly know, Low or High," Honor said. "But we believe in God all right."

"I should hope so. I hope you know what you've gotten into, with Adam."

"I—I don't know what you mean."

"He's changeable, so changeable, like his father. He blows hot and cold on things, the same things. One minute he wanted to be a lawyer, next a doctor, next this crazy idea of going to West Point. He could have gotten a scholarship to the University of Maine. But it had to be West Point—or Annapolis. He took both examinations, they both wanted him. He tossed a coin and took West Point. Isn't that a terrible way to make up your mind? I never thought he'd stick out four years there. I was sure he'd be back here, changing his mind six times a month the way he was during high school. He's so brilliant, he talks himself into and out of things. No one has to do it for him. All you have to do is listen. I hope you're a good listener. Just let him talk and hope for the best. He doesn't really have any faith. That's what worries me. His father's fault, of course. How could a boy have faith when his father— But you probably know the story. Young people these days believe in telling each other every-thing. I never thought that way. I thought there should be a certain privacy, even between married couples. You probably don't agree. But let me tell you this much, you've got a friend here, someone who'll be ready to help, whenever Adam starts getting flighty.

Which he will. It's in the blood. I knew it was there when I married his father. The old man, the judge, ran away to join the Navy when they sank the *Maine,* in 1898. How old are you?"

"Twenty-three," Honor said.

"I was thirty-eight when I married. Everyone marries late up here. New England's a special place and we're special people. At least we think we are. Especially here in Maine. We like to think we're the last of the breed. The rest of New England's overrun with Irish Catholics and Portuguese and Italians and French Canadians and God knows what. Up here we've kept the ancestral stock pure, if you follow me. You have to listen closely to a New Englander, hear what he doesn't say as much as what he says. Do you follow me?"

"Yes," Honor said. "You don't have to worry, Mrs. Thayer. I love Adam."

"Love—" Mrs. Thayer said. The word hung there in the drab bedroom, not quite an echo, not quite a reply. Honor could hear it either way, as agreement or contempt. She could hear what was not said as well as what was said. She didn't like either one. But she was young enough and happy enough to ignore it. This woman was like her mother, half mourning, half hating a man she had once loved. She was old, her day had come and gone and nothing she had to say had much bearing on the future that Honor and Adam were moving toward. This unpleasant night was only a pause, a minor detour on the road to the happiness Honor knew was waiting for them. She slept well.

The next day they paid duty visits. The first was to Adam's maternal grandmother, about whom he made many jokes. She had traveled across the country to California on the transcontinental railroad in 1875 to marry a Maine man who had settled in San Francisco. He had died of cholera while she was en route and she had returned to Sconnet, contemptuous of California and the rest of the country. A large woman like her daughter, she sat in a rocker, her hair snow white, the back of her big hands almost black with liver spots. "Gamma," Adam said, "I want you to meet Honor, my wife."

"Honor," she said, with a bright smile. "What a beautiful name.

I should have named my daughter Honor. Instead, I called her Charity. But she had none. Now who are you?"

"I'm Adam, your grandson."

"Oh yes. The one who joined the Army. Do you think we'll ever win the war? They ought to fire that fellow Pershing. When I heard he was from Nebraska, I knew he was a fool."

Their next stop was the judge, Adam's paternal grandfather. At ninety-two, there was nothing wrong with his brain, or his eyes, for that matter. He gave Honor a long admiring look, and shook his head. "If this was the sort of southern womanhood General Lee and his friends were defendin'," he said, "I can see why they fut s'hard."

He was built along Adam's spare, bony lines. He insisted they join him in a glass of hard cider, which was very hard indeed. Honor felt her head spinning after two swallows. The judge flourished a letter he had just finished writing to President Truman, "your commander-in-chief," as he called him. He proceeded to read it to them.

"Dear Sir,
   Your policy vis-à-vis the conflict between the United States and World Communism contains a glaring fallacy. You claim to be pursuing what you call containment and I call playing with fire all around the Communist empire. You seem to forget that the Communists are a land-based power and have the advantage of interior lines of communication. They have numerous well-armed allies at various points on the rim of their empire. As General Albert Wedemeyer pointed out recently, our first team may be forced to fight their second or third teams, with much spilling of American blood in the process. My advice to you, sir, is to let the Communists have all they want on the Eurasian land mass, excepting, of course, the free states of Western Europe. They already have devoured more than they can possibly digest in the next fifty years. Let them figure out how to feed 600 million Chinese, 60 million Poles, etc. I would not even be averse to throwing in the

75

Japanese, so these dangerous economic competitors may also be hamstrung by the fallacies of socialism. I am prompted to write this letter not only from a concern for the nation's future, but because I have a grandson just graduated from the U. S. Military Academy, whose life may be at hazard because of your folly.

Sincerely yours,

Adam Thayer
Registered Democrat
Citizen of Maine''

Honor thought these last words might get Adam in trouble. But they were mild compared to what the old man called President Truman in conversation. The country was in peril, he said. But what could you expect when the President was ''an ignoramus from Missouri, the sort of fool who thought Lincoln started the Civil War.''

''Well, *didn't* he?'' Honor said. She smiled as soon as she said it, even though she was only half fooling.

''I can see you have a lot of educating to do, son. Good luck,'' Grandfather Thayer said. There was no responding twinkle in his eyes.

Rolling north from Sconnet after lunch, Adam told her that the old man wrote at least a letter a week, often a letter a day to various public officials, from the governor to the President. He had been doing it for forty years. ''He believes a citizen's voice should be heard,'' Adam said.

''Where does he get all those big ideas?'' Honor asked.

''From his hero, Walter Lippmann.''

''I didn't really like him,'' Honor confessed. ''He sort of turns nasty on you, without warnin'.''

''An old family habit. Want to quit now, when we can get it annulled quietly? I'll swear I was impotent the night before last, and we never even consummated it.''

''Stop now,'' Honor said. ''I don't think that's one bit funny.''

"Read the Sconnet *Sampler* to me," Adam said. "It will restore our sense of humor."

The Sconnet *Sampler* was the local paper. Honor read the report of a town meeting at which tempers grew ragged over whether the police force should buy a second patrol car. Even more intense was the argument over an ordinance to ban the wearing of two-piece bathing suits on Main Street. "Some of the summer people," declared one citizen, "don't wear enough clothes to pad a crutch."

The letters-to-the-editor column was full of arguments pro and con about the extraordinary statement the state's senator, Margaret Chase Smith, had made in the U. S. Senate exactly one week ago. She had recruited a half dozen other Republicans and lashed out at the nation's chief anti-Communist, Senator Joseph McCarthy of Wisconsin, denouncing his smear tactics and the atmosphere of fear and repression he was creating in the nation. Some letter writers accused Senator Smith of being a pinko dupe, other called her a great American.

"That's Sconnet," Adam said. "We give equal time to two-piece bathing suits and international conspiracies."

They entered Canada and took the ferry to Nova Scotia. It was dark by the time they reached the town of Casey. But they found their rooming house with no difficulty. It was run by a friendly couple named Winston. They were both blond Anglo-Saxon types with almost identical faces. He had been in the Canadian Army during the war and called Adam "Leftenant." In ten minutes, Honor was unpacking their bags on the huge double bed and Adam was calling a waterfront restaurant recommended by their hosts.

Toward ten o'clock they returned, stuffed with fresh lobster, the tremors of Sconnet forgotten. Adam had insisted on Honor splitting a full bottle of wine with him, even though she protested that she did not like alcohol. That line, he told her, was all right for a West Point drag, but it was unthinkable for an officer or his wife. Life on an Army post was a series of parties and those who could not hold their liquor were considered oddities, a fatal label.

"Why fatal?" she asked as he filled her wineglass.

"Oddities don't get made generals."

"You really want to be one, don't you?"

"Why not? Where else can a know-it-all get the power to make everyone agree with him?"

The wine made her amorous. She did a strip while Adam lay on the bed, watching, applauding, threatening to give a street whistle through his fingers. Then he imitated her while she lay on the bed naked. Suddenly they were both naked, making wild love to an unconditional unexpected climax, a letting go, a giving, richer, sweeter than anything she had ever imagined. Adam seemed equally amazed. He lay beside her, one hand between her thighs, the other on her breast, murmuring: "Aphrodite. Or is it Demeter, queen of the underworld? Or Helen? The marriage of Diogenes and Helen. Except he didn't believe in marriage, old Diog."

"Shush," Honor said.

"Good advice," Adam said. "I will try to imitate the brevity of my forebears."

"Adam," Honor said after a long glowing silence. "You asleep?"

"Not quite," he said.

"You know I told you my daddy got sick and died after he went in the Army durin' the war. It wasn't the truth. Like you and your momma and the roomers, it's—it's more complicated. He and my mother had the most awful fight about him goin' in the Army in the first place. They screamed and cursed and yelled at each other. She swore she wasn't goin' to live in some hellhole of a Georgia or Alabama backwoods town. He told her he didn't want her anyway, he was sick of her. Well, when the word came in 1944 that Daddy was dead, the story they told us was he got killed tryin' to take a gun away from a drunken soldier. But it turned out they were both in a brothel."

"A what?" Adam said sleepily.

"A whorehouse. It like to almost killed Momma. She didn't speak to me or anyone for weeks. It's why she sent me North to school, and kept me there no matter how many courses I flunked."

"Poor guy," Adam said.

"Is that what you really think?" she whispered. "I don't know what to think. I've tried to forgive him, understand him. But it still hurts me to think about it. He was such—a dignified man."

"With parents the best thing is to forgive and forget," Adam said.

"If she'd gone with him, it wouldn't have happened," Honor said.

"If there hadn't been a war, he wouldn't have gone. If the coin I flipped to choose between Annapolis and West Point had come up tails, I'd be a sailor. History is mostly accidents, honey. People, politics, kings, presidents, generals out of control."

"Adam. Don't ever do that to me. No matter what else you do, don't do that."

Adam laughed. "There's only one thing I'm going to do to you, over and over. I did it to you tonight and I'll do it to you tomorrow morning and I'll do it to you tomorrow night."

He kept his word.

They made sunrise love.

They made moonrise love.

They made salty love, fresh from a plunge in the freezing cove below the cliff face.

They made perfumed love, silken and nylon love.

They made outdoor love, in a field of goldenrod, beneath a sun that whirled and burned behind Honor's closed eyes.

They made harsh love and quick love and slow love. They made playful love and mocking love and serious love.

The days slipped by in a dream infinitely more total, more absolute for Honor than June week. She began to laugh, almost, at the romance of June week. It was playacting, childish stuff, compared to this giving and taking, this spring-becoming-summer in this magical northern land, where the noon sun was hot but the nights remained deliciously cool. They feasted on salmon and crab, scrod and flounder, she who had stubbornly refused to like fish. She drank wine and whiskey, she who had vowed never to touch a drop of the stuff that had caused her father's death. They went sightseeing and she grew tearful at the story of Evangeline, told by a guide in the village of Grand Pré. She who had flunked an English test on the damn poem in senior year in high school and almost didn't graduate.

On the way back from Grand Pré they saw a stable and a half dozen riding horses in a field. Honor insisted on stopping. The owner cheerfully assured her that the horses were for hire and there were a dozen miles of trails through the woods. Honor was stunned when Adam declined to join her in reserving a horse for the following morning.

"I don't know how to ride, and I'm not interested in learning," he said as they drove back to their boardinghouse. "Only the old Army stiffs, the MacArthur imitators, like Captain Rod Coulter, go in for it."

"I think you should learn. I think it goes with bein' an officer and a gentleman."

"I don't," Adam said.

The next morning, Honor arose and said she was going to ride—alone if necessary.

"Great," Adam said. "I've been wanting to dig into these."

He pulled a half dozen books out of his suitcase. They were mostly military histories of World War II by generals with names Honor only dimly recognized—Mark Clark, Robert Eichelberger. "I brought this for you," he said. He handed her a thick book. It was the collected stories of William Faulkner.

The books marked the moment when the honeymoon glow began to diminish. It did not disappear—far from it. At night, Honor was still able to restore it with her lips, her breasts, her welcoming thighs. But they no longer spent the whole day together. She went off for her morning ride, while Adam sprawled on a chaise on the porch overlooking the cove, a book propped on his chest. Honor usually got back from her ride about eleven and tried to read Faulkner's collected stories. She did not like them. Everyone in them was disappointed or crazy or defeated. They made the South look like such an awful place to live. The last straw was "A Rose for Emily," about a weird old woman who killed her lover. With a gasp of disgust Honor threw the book off the porch onto the sunny lawn. "I don't know any southern people like that," she said. "That man's a liar or a fool."

"He just won the Nobel Prize," Adam said.

He went down on the lawn and retrieved the book. "Don't ever do that again," he said. "You broke the spine." He showed her where the back had cracked and the pages had gotten loose.

"I don't give a damn," Honor said. "It isn't worth readin'."

That night she apologized for the ruined book and tried to make it up to him by being extra loving. The next morning she did not go horseback riding. She said she wanted to go sailing. Adam was not enthusiastic. "Won't your horse miss you?" he said.

"Adam. Don't be nasty."

Why couldn't he see that she wanted to do something that got him away from those damn books? Each day he was spending more and more time with them. She persisted in her desire for a sail. The Winstons kept a catboat for their guests, anchored just off the beach in the cove. Adam said he had forgotten how to sail. Honor reminded him that he had taken her sailing on the Hudson not three months ago. He said he meant sailing on the ocean. It was dangerous and she was a poor swimmer. But she persisted, pointing out that other guests, including a married couple in their sixties, had used the boat without any trouble. Around noon Adam relented. A heat wave had rolled up from the United States, making the cool water irresistible.

Before they left, Adam asked Mr. Winston what time the sun went down. He called the local weather service and got the exact minute. On the water, Adam kept looking at his watch. Suddenly he said it was time to head back to their cove. But the wind proved erratic, rising to languid puffs at best and then dying away entirely. By the time they reached the cove the sun was almost down. It lay on the horizon, a huge bleeding eye. The land, the houses, were all dark red and bronze.

"Look," Adam said. "Look at those flowers." She looked up and saw a line of goldenrod along the top of the cliff waving in the bloodred sun. For some reason the mixture of colors troubled her.

"Beautiful," she said.

But she didn't think they were beautiful. Neither, she suspected, did Adam. He stared up at them glumly as if they had disappointed him. He even seemed to lose track of where he was. He forgot to pull up the centerboard and the boat plowed into the hard ocean bottom. Honor, sitting in the thwarts, went flying into the bow, banging her head rather hard on a beam. Adam was terribly contrite.

He fussed over her as if she had fractured her skull. "I'm all right," she said. "It wasn't half as bad as fallin' off a horse."

"Are you sure you're okay?" Adam asked again as they labored up the wooden stairs on the cliff face to the house.

"Yes," she said.

At the house, Mr. Winston met them with a troubled look on his face. Honor wondered if he had seen the accident and was worried about her or about possible damage to his sailboat. "Say, Leftenant," he said. "I just got a flash over the radio. The Reds seem to be trying to start a war."

"Where?" Adam said.

"Korea. The North Koreans have invaded the South."

Adam's reaction amazed Honor. He laughed exultantly. "Son of a bitch," he said. "Grandpa was right for once in his life. Here we go."

Honor burst into tears. She wept partly because she was afraid Adam might get killed. But mostly because he did not say a word about their ruined honeymoon. She thought it meant he was glad to get away from her.

BOOK
TWO

BOOK
TWO

I

"Hey, anyone here from Woo Poo Five Oh?" Peter MacArthur Burke bellowed in his command voice.

From inside the connected row of paint-peeling wooden shacks that constituted junior officers' quarters at Fort Ripley, Kansas, came another command voice. "Nobody from the lousy 1st Regiment."

"I'll take the leavings. I'm desperate," Pete boomed.

Joanna sat in their 1947 Ford, which seemed in danger of vibrating into several dozen pieces. Dazed by the incredible heat, she barely managed to translate the Academy lingo. Woo Poo was West Point. Five Oh was the class of 1950. There were two regiments in the cadet corps, each of which claimed it was superior in all things.

Joanna's ears were still ringing from Pete's insistence on practicing his command voice all the way from Cincinnati. She had been his coach, reading him reminders on breathing and pronunciation from a booklet he had all but memorized at West Point. Its pages were thumbed brown and every other word was underlined. Joanna had never dreamed that giving orders such as "forward march" had to be taught—in fact were taught at the U. S. Military Academy. The booklet made her realize it was not as simple as it seemed to order several hundred men around a drill field. A man who did not know how to do it could burn out his voice in fifteen minutes, and end up screeching like a crow.

Appreciating this minor revelation and having Peter MacArthur

Burke bellow FOH-WAHD MAHCH, POAT HAHMS, PLA-TOON AH-TEHNS-HUNN in her ear for an hour at a time were two distinctly different matters. But it was not easy to stop Pete Burke once he picked up momentum. She had discovered that on their honeymoon. From the moment he heard the news about the war in Korea, Pete had become a man obsessed. On the beach, at lunch and dinner, he could talk about nothing else. What Captain Coulter had heard from his father the colonel about the South Korean Army. What the papers said about the tanks and artillery of the North Koreans, where their officers had trained, why they were walloping the South Koreans. He had rushed to the tiny library of the New Jersey shore town where they were staying and talked the librarians into letting him take out all six of their books on Korea, plus a volume of the *Encyclopaedia Britannica*. Joanna had tried to share his sudden fascination with the terrain, the history of this remote nation. But she had never had much interest in international politics, and her enthusiasm for industrial and agricultural statistics was nil.

"Do the Koreans have any novelists, poets?" she had asked, on the third or fourth night of the cram course.

"What?" Pete said, looking up from the encyclopedia. "I dunno."

Joanna stopped thinking about her ruined honeymoon and stared in disbelief at Fort Ripley's accommodations. A line from Karl Shapiro drifted through her mind: *Row houses and row lives*. A door opened. Out sauntered a dark-haired young man in a green Army shirt and baggy green pants. He had a narrow face with a long, sensitive nose and a dimple in the center of his smallish chin. "Hey, Lover," Pete yelled. They shook hands and exchanged punches to the shoulders and arms that would have crippled Joanna for life.

"When'd you get here?"

"Yesterday."

"What's the com like?"

"Eats shavetails for breakfast, preferably fried."

"Anybody else here?"

"Holliday, Callow, Flynn, Edison, Hardin. More due."

"Hey, we're going to have a good time. Come meet the wife."

He led his classmate over to the car. "Jo, this is Lover—I mean

Wilbur MacKenzie. We roomed together in plebe year. Isn't this a break?"

"Call me Lover," MacKenzie said. "My wife won't mind. If this big lug has any objections, don't worry. I can handle him with both hands behind my back. Special training in psychological warfare."

Lover tapped the side of his head. Joanna forced a smile. Comedy was hard to enjoy when the temperature was 96.

"He got the nickname from his rendition of 'Lover, Come Back to Me' in the showers," Pete said. "Come on, beanhead, help me get this stuff out of the car. I'm in eight. Where are you?"

"Thirteen."

"Good show. Let's get a party going tonight. Got to do something to cheer up the girls."

"What about cheering me up?" Lover said. "I'm married to a woman who tells me this isn't really hot compared to Fort Skillens, Arkansas, or Fort Brainard, Texas. Or the Canal Zone. Or Mindanao. I never should have fallen for an Army brat. I just wasn't thinking. I wonder if the Adjutant General can get it annulled."

"I thought her father was the Adjutant General," Pete said.

"He is," Lover said. "What do you think my next assignment will be if I send her back?"

"Airborne," Pete said. "But they won't issue you a parachute."

With Lover continuing to list the faults of his wife, the two second lieutenants lugged from the back seat and trunk of the Ford the blankets, sheets, dishes and pots Joanna had received as wedding and shower gifts. Joanna got out of the car and blinked into the glare. Between the barracks-like apartments a few feeble tufts of grayish grass struggled to survive the merciless sun. Up a baked back road lay Fort Ripley's central parade ground. Beyond it, as far as the horizon, lay a world flat enough to intimidate Christopher Columbus in his prime.

Joanna told herself she was glad to be here. It was where she belonged. She had come very close to a nasty argument with Pete to get here. He had wanted to leave her in Cincinnati with her parents. She had been appalled by his insensitivity. Why didn't he see that she felt displaced, superseded since Korea had exploded like an artillery shell in the middle of their honeymoon? She had been prepared to yield him to the Army after the honeymoon. But she had seen those first sixty days as hers, a time in which she would root their personal lives. Above all, the last two weeks, which they had planned to spend in Hawaii.

She had struggled to accept the disappointment as Korea shoved aside the novels and poetry she had hoped to persuade Pete to read and discuss. She tried to remember what he had whispered to her on their wedding night. *I love you, Joanna. I really meant what I said on that altar. For better or for worse, till death do us part.* She had been touched, almost exalted by that devotion. It was some consolation for what had preceded it.

It had obviously been the first time for both of them. Although she told herself to relax, to open herself, give herself, she had been so tense that he had had a terrible time entering her. Joanna had thought, perhaps hoped, she would be assaulted, overwhelmed. Instead, he had been afraid to hurt her and for the first few minutes prodded, pressed, prodded with practically no force. When he finally entered, all she knew at first was pain from the parted hymen. He began stroking at such a cautious pace that she still found it hard to escape some inner reluctance, a gap between her idea of the gift of herself and the giving. In some of the books she had read about married love (all written by priests or nuns), sex had been compared to the mystical ecstasy of the poems of Crashaw. She had hoped to become an "undaunted daughter of desires," part eagle and part dove. But she had not soared or swooped or whirled. There was only pleasure; not to be dismissed, of course; some of the surges of excitement that flowed from his strokes, from his lips on her neck, her breasts, were too undeniable, too rich. But it was still, on balance, a disappointment.

It remained a disappointment until Pete added the "extra added attraction"—lovemaking in the morning, when he came back from his daily swim and five-mile run along the beach. She found ardor came more quickly, deliciously, when she was half asleep, when it was half dream that his male thing was in her body, creating such overpowering sensations. She could close her eyes and imagine herself one of those Greek heroines, Leda or Eurydice, visited by a wandering god. She could open her eyes and see nothing but the fair freckled skin of his tremendous shoulders, the close-up landscape of his muscles as he scooped her into the hard hollow of his couching body. This was closer to love as she had imagined it—a sweet obliteration. But she remained grounded; no soars or swoops or whirls emerged from the surrendered self.

"Ready for the ceremony?" Lover MacKenzie said, his elbow cocked on the roof of the car.

"What?" Joanna said. She had lost touch with the present—the two lieutenants lugging the Burkes' household goods into Quarters 8.

"I'm carrying you across the threshold. Pete isn't up to it," Lover said.

"Get out of the way, spaghetti-legs," Pete said. Before Joanna could say a word, he picked her up and strode into Quarters 8 as if she weighed thirty instead of a hundred and thirty pounds. "Here it is," he said, setting her down in the empty living room. "I warned you it was going to be god-awful."

The living room was not much wider—and it was a good deal shorter—than the upstairs hall of her Cincinnati home. There was a tiny bedroom behind it and an even tinier kitchen beside that. A corner of the bedroom had been invaded to create a minuscule bathroom, with a shower stall instead of a tub. No one had painted the walls since they had been daubed an ugly brown early in World War II.

"It'll look better when we get some furniture in it," Pete said.

"I'm still glad I came."

"I am too, Jo. You don't know how glad. I was just afraid it would be so lousy you'd get discouraged. I mean—you're not used to this sort of life."

"I'll get used to it," she said.

He kissed her. "You're fantastic."

His extravagance troubled her. She disliked false compliments. She was not fantastic. So far, neither one of them was fantastic.

Following directions from Lover MacKenzie, they drove twenty miles toward the horizon and found themselves on the main street of Archer, Kansas, population 12,000. On the outskirts, towering grain elevators dominated the landscape. There was only one furniture store, Atkinson's. The owner was a fat, balding man wearing a Hawaiian shirt, which reminded Joanna of her lost honeymoon. He sat behind the counter, fanning himself with a newspaper while they wandered among his wares. It was all Grand Rapids stuff but there was no point in buying anything decent. Pete let Joanna make the decisions. She tried to be parsimonious. Still, a double bed and night table, a box spring and mattress, a couch, coffee table and two chairs came to a shocking $442.50.

Pete took out his checkbook. Mr. Atkinson shook his head. "Cash only for soldiers," he said.

"Wait a minute," Pete said. "I'm a lieutenant, a West Point graduate." He held up his ring. "I don't write rubber checks."

"Don't care if you're a general," Mr. Atkinson said. "Cash only for soldiers. We learned the hard way during the war. Nobody around here wanted Ripley reopened anyway. Won't do anything for us but bring in whores from Kansas City."

"It's bringing you four hundred and forty-two bucks right now," Pete said. "There'll be a lot of other guys looking for furniture."

"I got a sixteen-year-old daughter. Worried more about her than money. It's cash or no sale."

He threw the newspaper on the counter. The headline read: HEAVY FIGHTING IN KOREA. AMERICAN RETREAT CONTINUES. They trudged down the street to the local bank. "I'd rather sleep on the floor than pay him a cent," Joanna said. "I wish you'd go back there and wipe up the store with him."

"I don't think you'd really like sleeping on the floor," Pete said. "And if I wipe up the store with him I'll get court-martialed."

At the bank, a gray-haired vice-president was at least polite. They could not cash the check unless the Burkes opened an account, and they could not cash it today unless another bank—their home bank—would guarantee their credit. Joanna called her father, who quickly arranged for his bank to issue the guarantee. A half hour later, Pete counted out $442.50 to Mr. Atkinson, who promised to have everything delivered before sundown.

They bought groceries at a small local supermarket, Pete again letting her make the decisions. They drove back to Ripley through waves of heat that made the highway seem to shimmy and dip ahead of them. "How can you march, do anything when it's this hot?" Joanna said.

"It's about the same temperature in Korea," Pete said.

"I can't believe this is happening," Joanna said.

"I bet it's hotter in Fort Bragg," Pete said. "I can practically hear Supe bitching. He can't take the heat."

Adam had called them at their hotel in New Jersey a few days after the war began. He had told Pete he was switching to the airborne and urged him to do the same thing. Adam said that paratroopers were the logical response to the rampaging North Koreans. Pete stuck with the infantry. At first Joanna thought he was trying to delay going to Korea for her sake. She soon learned that Pete disagreed with Adam. Paratroopers were not going to stop the North Koreans. Only infantry would do that. "Adam's an angle player," Pete said. "He thinks he can outsmart the odds. Engineers were the best bet for peacetime, airborne when some shooting starts."

"What odds?"

"On making general."

She was struck by the harsh realism of Pete's mind, the matter-of-fact way he judged his best friend. Would he judge her the same way? she wondered. It was somewhat unnerving to recall that West Point slang for roommate was "wife."

By the time the telegram from the Defense Department arrived, canceling the sixty-day graduation leave and their honeymoon, and ordering Pete to report to Fort Ripley, he, not Adam, had been proven a prophet. No paratroopers were rushed to Korea to stop the Communists. Only infantry. Pete was as shocked as the rest of the country by the way the North Koreans mauled and routed them. He was convinced that the Communist tanks were being operated by Russians, and probably their artillery as well. No one was willing to admit that the little yellow men had a modern army and knew what to do with it.

They got back to Ripley as Mr. Atkinson's delivery truck was coming in the gate. Pete led the driver to their quarters and helped him unload the furniture. Lover MacKenzie appeared at the window to inform them that a class of '50 BYOB party would square off in his apartment at 2000 hours. Pete had to explain to Joanna that this meant 8 P.M. She began cooking sirloin steak and home-fried potatoes on the two-burner stove. Stupefied from the heat in the tiny kitchen, she bent down to check the steak. Flame burst from the broiler, scorching her hand and almost catching her in the face. She screamed for help and people rushed from other apartments. Pete raced from the lawn, where he had been working on the Ford. Before he got there, a large blond girl bawled: "Get a fire extinguisher," and the next thing Joanna knew, Lover MacKenzie was covering her flaming stove and steak with sticky foam.

The blonde, who turned out to be Martha MacKenzie, Lover's wife, explained that all the stoves were coated with years-old grease left by the previous owners. "I was lucky enough to notice mine before I cooked anything," Martha said.

"Oh, in Cincinnati Joanna probably had a maid that took care of things like that," said another voice. Joanna quickly connected it to a familiar face in the rear ranks of her rescuers—Ruth Parrott Hardin, still playing the character she had launched at West Point.

Pete thanked everyone for responding to the emergency and shook hands with several second lieutenants, said hello to their wives and ushered them out the door before asking Joanna if she was all right.

"My hand hurts." She held up her right hand. The back of it looked like underdone steak. Pete rubbed it with butter, wrapped it in a handkerchief and drove her to the base hospital. There was no doctor on duty. A sympathetic corpsman coated the hand with some soothing unguent, bandaged it and gave her some codeine pills for the pain.

They ate at a restaurant out on the highway. Fort Ripley's officers' club was not yet functioning. Joanna felt miserable. The heat, her throbbing hand, her failure as a housewife, made her want to put her head down on the table and weep. With obvious regret, Pete suggested that they skip the MacKenzies' party. Joanna insisted she felt well enough to go. She took a codeine pill and changed to a light green voile dress that she chose for its minimal weight. At Quarters 13, she found everyone was wearing sports shirts and Bermuda shorts. A few wives were even wearing short shorts.

Before she could retreat into a corner, Lover MacKenzie saw her bandaged hand and held it aloft. "Hey," he yelled. "The first casualty of old Five Oh. I think she deserves a Purple Heart, don't you guys?"

"And you want a Silver Star for putting the fire out?" someone said.

"Listen, if I hadn't braved those flames we'd all be sleeping in our cars tonight," Lover said. "I think we ought to organize a committee to warn incoming wives."

"Don't have to worry about Lover gettin' written up for anything he does in Korea," drawled a husky handsome Southerner named Holliday. "He'll take care of that himself."

"Sounds like he wants to take care of the wives too. You better watch him, Martha," Sam Hardin said. "He gets carried away by that nickname."

"Don't worry," Martha MacKenzie said out of the corner of her mouth. "One wrong move and the shavetail'll be in combat before he gets anywhere near Korea."

"See what I mean?" Lover said. "I must have been out of my mind to marry an infantryman's daughter."

Unbothered by Lover's humor, which Joanna thought was somewhat dubious, Martha took her arm. "Come on, honey, you've got a right to the only decent chair in the place."

In a moment Joanna was seated in an easy chair against the wall while her first Army party swirled around her. Across the room she heard Ruth Hardin playing the insider. "One thing you've got to remember. Never get too friendly with the wives of higher ranks. It can really hurt your husband's career. In the Army, everything goes by rank."

"Pete says your father's a general," Joanna said to Martha MacKenzie.

"I hope you don't hold it against me, like Ruth over there," Martha said. "She's got everyone thinking I'll send secret reports on their cooking and cleaning back to Washington."

"Was your father a West Pointer?"

Martha shook her head. "He did it the hard way. Started in World War I as a lieutenant."

"I thought almost all the officers in the Army were West Pointers. Pete says they're only about ten percent of the officer corps."

"But about eighty percent of the generals," Martha said.

The men stood by the door, most of them looking very young. A second lieutenant's bars did not automatically create maturity. Their crew cuts contributed to the boyish aura. But their conversation was not boyish.

"If they couldn't hold at Chonan and Chochiwon, I don't know how they can hold Taejon."

"I think they'll pull back to Yongdong."

"They've airlifted 3.5 bazookas to the 24th."

"Standard tactics. Frontal attack and outflank every time. If we had the manpower to hold the flanks we'd be slaughtering them."

Pete stood in the midst of his fellow second lieutenants, nodding, commenting. Joanna wanted to join him, ask questions, participate. She had involuntarily taken at least half of Pete's cram course on Korea. She had read everything written about the war in the newspapers and news magazines. But none of the other wives made the slightest attempt to join the men's conversation. They talked about their weddings and where they had gone for their honeymoons. Martha MacKenzie described the fun she and Lover had had motorbiking and sailing in Bermuda. Martha made it sound like they had spent half their honeymoon laughing, in spite of Korea. Joanna found herself wishing she and Pete had laughed a little more. She suspected it was not just Korea that explained it. She never should have let Pete choose Paradise Beach, New Jersey, for the first two weeks of their honeymoon. She had begun downgrading it—and New Jersey—within a day of their arrival. The perpetual humidity, the cheap cottages, hardly compared to the cool northern nights, the sprawling Victorian mansions on upper Michigan's Little Traverse Bay, where she had spent her girlhood summers. New Jersey's hot dogs were sadly inferior to a Cincinnati "coney," a frankfurter topped with chili and shredded cheese. New Jersey did not even seem to know that mocha-chip ice cream, secret of a happy Cincinnati childhood, existed.

Ruth Hardin strolled over to Joanna's side of the room. "Have you heard from George and Amy?'' she asked. ''We got a card from Paris.''

Joanna shook her head ruefully. ''I wish we could have afforded a trip like that,'' she said.

''I envy them George's assignment to Germany,'' Martha said. ''No worries about Korea.''

Ruth gave them both skeptical looks. She was sure Joanna was just as rich as Amy Rosser. Ruth seemed to think civilians were divided into rich and poor the way the Army was divided into officers and enlisted men. But she was more disturbed by Martha's remarks.

''Lucky?'' Ruth said. ''With all the connections Amy has? She's made damn sure George'll stay far away from Korea. I'm surprised your father didn't do the same thing for Lover.''

''What do you mean?'' Martha said.

''The Adjutant General can send a second lieutenant anywhere he pleases. Like a nice safe desk job in Washington.''

''Lover wouldn't consider such a thing. Neither would my father,'' Martha said.

''I know a lot of people who would,'' Ruth said.

''I don't,'' Martha said.

Ruth stood there, scowling, scuffing the carpet with her toe like a ten-year-old, incapable of extricating herself from the social blunder she had just committed.

''Ever live at Fort Wool?'' she asked.

''No,'' Martha said.

Ruth went doggedly down the complete list of her family's stops in their amazingly peripatetic Army life, which took them from Fort Wool to the Aberdeen Proving Ground. Whenever Ruth found a post they had in common, Martha invariably had liked it and Ruth had hated it. Martha's answers were curt but Ruth did not seem to notice her tone. Joanna found herself comparing Ruth to a big doll she had once owned. Ruth had the same pasty skin, the same stiff features squeezed on the front of her small face, the same emotionless eyes. Joanna's scorched hand throbbed dully and the codeine made her feel woozy, further disassociating her from the party. The different conversations became more and more entangled.

"You liked the Presidio? My sister and I had colds all the time we were there."

"MacArthur wants four divsons. Forty percent of our ground forces, for Chrissake."

"His mother was so *furious* at our wedding because her sister didn't send us a present."

"What happens if our guys run out of Korean real estate before we get there? Do we go amphibious?"

"I sure hope they open the commissary soon. Food prices are going out of sight. There's a lot of scare buying."

"What do you do when they attack using civilians for cover? Has there been any SOP on that?"

"Wouldn't you know, I got my period on the third day. The third day. I'm so damn irregular."

How could anyone worry about food prices, periods, when the men they loved stood a few feet away from them, talking about the war? Joanna wanted to be with them, sharing their calm courage, their knowledge of violence and possible death. Wasn't that where an Army wife belonged?

"I hate this," Joanna said to Martha MacKenzie when Ruth Hardin drifted away. "The men at one end of the room, the women at the other."

"A lot of Army parties go that way when there isn't any music to make them dance with you," Martha said. "Face it, honey, you're in a man's world."

"We don't have to accept the status quo. Will you join me?"

"No," Martha said, stopping Joanna as she started to get up. She looked down the room at the crew-cutted second lieutenants. "Let them alone. Let them talk war. It makes them feel better. They're worried. And with good reason. They were supposed to spend a year with troops and a year studying infantry tactics. Now they're going to teach them two years' worth of know-how in thirty days."

"Pete doesn't seem worried."

"None of them do. West Point trained them not to seem worried. But they're still worried."

The certainty in Martha's voice made Joanna wonder if Lover confided more of his personal feelings than Pete. The suspicion touched Joanna at her most sensitive point, almost forcing her to disagree, even though Martha was a general's daughter.

"Oh," she said. "I think you're feeling too sorry for them." She got up and strolled over to the second lieutenants. Pete was in the middle of telling them about his experience during the previous summer, when he went on training maneuvers with infantry and armored units at Fort Benning. "An infantry-armor team will do more than close air support to hold down casualties and build momentum in an attack. Tanks give infantry confidence. They're the interference—"

"What about the North Koreans' tanks?" Joanna said. "The newspapers say they're better than ours."

"Don't believe everything the newspapers say. Did they get your wedding announcement right?" Lover MacKenzie said.

"No. They spelled my grandparents' name wrong. S-i-e-g-e-l instead of S-i-g-c-l."

"Wasn't there a Union general by that name in the Civil War?" Sam Hardin asked.

"He was my mother's grandfather."

"You're real old Army. You make Martha look like a plebe," Lover said.

"Hope they got your picture right," said Sam Hardin. "You sure were one beautiful bride."

"Hey, is it true that Rosser tried to buy the number-one wedding slot to keep his heiress happy?" Lover asked.

"That's a dirty rumor. I wouldn't repeat that," Pete said.

Someone asked Joanna where she had spent her honeymoon. They began riding Pete about his devotion to New Jersey, which they insisted was the armpit of the nation. "We can get away with this now," Lover explained. "He can't strike a fellow officer. That wasn't true of a fellow cadet."

The war, its tactics, its future course, vanished in the compliments and good-natured kidding. Joanna saw with dismay that they would not, perhaps could not, talk to her about it.

The next afternoon, Joanna chose another dress from her trousseau, a blue silk shantung with a lapelled jacket. Pete donned a crisply creased khaki summer uniform, and they drove to the rambling wooden quarters of Fort Ripley's commander, Major General Harmon Strong. An enlisted man answered the polished brass knocker on the front door and admitted them to a shining center hall, where a framed Norman Rockwell print of a Fourth of July parade was the chief decoration. The orderly explained that neither the general nor Mrs. Strong was at home. Classmates who had already paid this traditional courtesy call had forewarned them to expect this reply. With several hundred second lieutenants arriving at Ripley in a single week, the general had decided it was impossible to greet all of them personally. Pete and Joanna left their cards on a silver tray beneath the Norman Rockwell print. Joanna peered into the spacious formal living room and the comfortable study on the opposite side of the hall and compared them with their three tiny sweltering rooms on Shavetail Row.

"Why do we live in a slum while he lives in splendor?" she said as they went down the front steps. "There doesn't seem to be that much distance between general and second lieutenant."

"R-H-I-P," Pete said. When she looked baffled, he translated: "Rank hath its privileges."

"But you're both officers."

"We're at the bottom, he's at the top," Pete said. "And believe me, honey, there is a distance. About twenty-five years' worth of distance."

"We're not living much better than enlisted men."

"Yes, we are," Pete said. "You want to see where they live?"

They drove west, across the base, for a full ten minutes. Joanna was amazed by the size of the place. It looked big enough to hold the entire city of Cincinnati. Presently they were surrounded by hundreds of shabby two-story barracks. Paint peeled from their walls, tar paper curled from their roofs. Grass was several feet high in the yards. Dozens of men in green fatigues were at work cutting the grass. At least half of them were Negroes.

"About two hundred men live in each of those crummy things," Pete said as they drove slowly down the street. Suddenly, he slammed on the brakes and yelled: "Hey, Sergeant. Sergeant Cartwright."

A squat scowling man in a uniform as crisply pressed as Pete's turned to peer into the car. "Yes, sir?" he said, and then smiled, revealing a shiny gold tooth on the right side of his mouth. "Is it Lieutenant Burke?" he said, saluting.

"Right. Ex-cadet," Pete said, returning the salute. He got out of the car and shook hands. "I was hoping they'd transfer some of you old-guard Benning types out here."

The sergeant chewed on his lower lip for a moment. "I can't rightly say any of us hoped that way, Lieutenant. But now that we're here, we'll do the job."

"Meet my wife," Pete said. He introduced the sergeant. "He was my instructor at Benning last summer. Sergeant Cartwright knows more about infantry tactics than anyone else in the Army," he said.

"I wish that was true. Nice to meet you, ma'am."

The sergeant glowered at the grass-cutting recruits. "We goin' to have our hands full here, Lieutenant. This place is fallin' apart. Toilets don't work in half the barracks. Can't open half the windows. Then there's the niggers. President says we got to make soldiers out of'm. I kinda think he's followin' the old infantry motto. 'Do somethin', even if it's wrong.'"

"I know what you mean, Sergeant. But it's an order. We've got to do our best to live with it."

Pete shook hands with Sergeant Cartwright again and got back in the car. "Why did you let him get away with that?" Joanna asked as they drove away.

"With what?" Pete said.

"That remark about the Negroes," she said.

"What was I supposed to say?"

"You should have told him to change his attitude. They're American citizens, human beings just like him, or you or me."

"Honey, the sergeant's from Alabama. He doesn't think that way. He'd just say 'Yes, sir,' and tell every sergeant in the Army I was a nigger-loving nut."

"You agree with him, don't you?"

"Not completely. But I sympathize with his problem. I don't think they're going to make very good soldiers. If you check their record in the last two wars, you might agree with me."

"Really, Pete. I'm amazed—almost ashamed. How can you say such a thing—as an officer—as a Catholic?"

"Honey, a green second lieutenant is in no position to lecture Sergeant Cartwright. He's been in the Army twenty years. He fought in damn near every major battle in the European theater. As for being a Catholic, I don't see what that has to do with it."

"Are you saying segregation is *right?* The National Catholic Conference on Interracial Justice has condemned it. The President—"

"I know what the President said. I'm just saying I agree with Sergeant Cartwright. It isn't going to be easy to work these people into the Army. It's a team, the Army. On a team you need people who respect each other, trust each other."

They were back at Shavetail Row. Joanna flung herself out of the car and stalked into their quarters. He was so *impenetrable*. She could not change his mind about anything. He was always right.

In revenge, she asked him to clean the stove. He did it cheerfully, oblivious to her anger and disappointment, cussing the sooty mess good-naturedly and emerging from the kitchen with a face and hands almost as black as one of the Negro recruits. "You look like you should be segregated," she said. He only laughed and took a shower. He did not even notice—or at least say anything—when she bitchily ignored her clean stove and served cold ham and potato salad for dinner. He even complimented her on the menu, remarking that it was too hot to eat anything else. Joanna sat there, picking at her food, feeling totally, hopelessly, excluded from his inner self, the only self that mattered to her.

"Gentlemen, we are going to master this fucker if it takes all night. Lover, it's your turn. Hardin, turn out the lights."

Pete did not realize how his voice carried through the thin walls of Shavetail Row. Joanna lay in bed a few feet away. In the humid darkness she could see the scene in her living room as vividly as if the bedroom wall did not exist. Twelve second lieutenants from West Point's class of 1950 crowded around her coffee table, on which crouched, like a huge obscene insect, a Browning Automatic Rifle. Every infantry platoon had two of these evil-looking things, and second lieutenants had to know how to take them apart and put them back together again—in the dark.

Joanna still trembled slightly at the memory of the shock when Pete appeared soaked with sweat and smeared with dust from his usual field exercise, and set the long gleaming gun on its stubby metal legs on top of her coffee table. "What in God's name is that?" she had said.

"That is the most beautiful weapon in the U.S. Army," Pete said.

"What's it doing here?"

"A lot of guys—Lover MacKenzie for one—didn't have the month I spent last summer, training with the infantry. Lover was Signal Corps, Hardin artillery. Korea's turning everybody into infantrymen. I want to make sure everyone knows how to repair this gun. It could save their lives. I asked Sergeant Cartwright to come around after supper and give us a talk on it."

At seven-thirty Sergeant Cartwright appeared. He was soon joined by the dozen members of the class of '50. Joanna distributed beer and pretzels and retreated to the kitchen to wash the dishes. The sergeant asked her to close the door and began his lecture.

"Gentlemen," he said, "you are lookin' at a weapon that can save your asses nine times out'n ten, if you treat her right. But she is a cunt, a beautiful temperamental cunt. You got to know how to handle her. Otherwise she will fuck you instead of the enemy."

Joanna heard every word. At first she was shocked. Was this how her husband and those other smiling, polite members of the class of '50 talked when their wives were not around? The sergeant continued, with an obscenity every third word. Gradually Joanna found herself listening with fascination. It was a special language, the way he manoeuvered *fuck* and *cunt* and *hump* and *prick* and *pussy* through the lecture. Finally she became ashamed of herself and ran the water in the sink to drown him out.

When she finished the dishes, she opened the door and asked if anyone wanted some more beer. The sergeant was saying: "Now consider this gizmo the clit. You gotta know where that is in the dark, just like—"

Pete jumped up, blushing—actually blushing. "Why don't you

leave us lugs to our own devices and maybe go visit Martha or one of your other friends?" he said.

She found Martha reading the *Ladies' Home Journal*. "Got room for a refugee from a sergeant's lecture about a machine gun?" she said.

"I thought it was a BAR," Martha said.

"It looks like a machine gun," Joanna said. "I never heard anyone talk that way before in my life."

"What way?"

"Every other word was—*fuck* and *ass* and *goose*—"

She was amazed to discover she could even say them. Martha laughed. "Most sergeants talk that way. So do most officers."

"Including your father?"

"Sure. But never in front of me or my mother. I remember one time I said *son of a bitch*. He damned near knocked my teeth out. He wanted me to be a lady."

"You mean they talk one way to each other and another way to us? All of them, officers and sergeants?"

"All men, as far as I know," Martha said.

"I think that's—that's infuriating," Joanna said.

"Why? It makes them feel better. That's what we're here to do, isn't it?"

"Do you really mean that?" Joanna said.

"In a way."

"I take it more seriously," Joanna said. "I want to share all of Pete's life. To be as close to him as possible. It's how I was taught to see marraige. Catholic marriage."

Martha whistled softly. "You're too deep for me, kiddo."

"Do you have a religion?"

"Sure. I go to church."

"What one?"

Martha shrugged. "Protestant is about all I can tell you. The Army chaplains are either Protestant, Catholic or Jewish."

"Don't Protestants try to make a connection between faith and marriage?"

Martha looked baffled. "They're just glad to have you show up on Sunday. I don't know about this sharing idea, Jo. The Army divides things up. There's a man's world and a woman's world. They think it's better that way."

"Who's they?" Joanna said. Whenever there was a discussion of Army policy, "they" regularly appeared.

"The guys who wrote the rule book a couple of hundred years ago. If you start bucking the system, Jo, the Army will drive you nuts. It's better to go with the flow."

Joanna stubbornly shook her head. Martha changed the subject to college. She had gone to Skidmore and majored in sociology. She asked Joanna if she had ever read *Middletown,* the classic study of a medium-sized American city. Joanna had never even heard of it. Martha recommended it. "It'll help you understand the Army," she said. "In peacetime it's not much different from Middletown. A war changes things, though."

For a moment Martha looked like she was going to weep. "Wow," she said. "I don't know what's wrong with me tonight. I guess it's the news from Korea. It keeps getting worse and worse. Let's numb the brain with some bridge."

Martha recruited Sandy Holliday, a Southerner with an accent twice as thick as Honor Prescott's, and Claire Flynn, a pert Bostonian. They played desultory bridge for the next two hours. Everyone finally agreed that it was time to go to bed, even if the BAR students showed no sign of joining them. "Might as well get used to sleepin' alone," Sandy Holliday said with a sigh.

Joanna returned to Quarters 8 and found Sergeant Cartwright had departed. The Browning Automatic Rifle was in two dozen pieces on the coffee table, and Pete was putting it back together. He told her to go to bed. They were all going to learn to disassemble and assemble the gun in the dark, and it was going to take a while.

"Like maybe two days and two nights," Lover MacKenzie said.

"One way or another, we're going to do it," Pete said.

Joanna went to bed and listened to their soldier's language through the wall. She imagined herself getting up, strolling out to join them, lolling on the couch while they grappled with their metal nemesis, asking casually: "Hey, guys, do you think you'll get that son-of-a-bitching cunt fucked into shape before dawn?" But she did not move. Eventually, the male voices dwindled and she slept.

• • •

Joanna awoke the next morning—and other mornings—to the war. The radio orated in the kitchen. "THE NEWS FROM KOREA CONTINUES TO BE BAD. UNDER HEAVY ATTACK, UNITS OF THE 25TH DIVISION GAVE GROUND EAST OF SANGJU." Through the thin walls from nearby apartments she could hear other stations. "HEAVY CASUALTIES AGAIN REPORTED IN THE 1ST CAVALRY DIVISION FIGHTING NEAR YONGDONG. THIS VITAL ROAD CENTER WAS ABANDONED LAST—"

"ONE REPORTER CLAIMS MEN OF THE 29TH INFANTRY REGIMENT WERE SENT INTO THE FRONT LINES NEAR CHINJU TOTALLY UNTRAINED. THEIR RIFLES WERE—"

Pete was taking a shower after his usual five-mile morning run. Joanna struggled into her bathrobe and stumbled out to the kitchen to start breakfast. She was not a morning person. It took her at least an hour to wake up. Pete was brisk smiling energy ten seconds after he stepped out of bed. He soon appeared in his olive-drab field uniform with its numerous straps and belts. He downed his usual big breakfast, orange juice, corn flakes, two eggs and a quarter of a pound of ham, while Joanna sleepily sipped coffee. It was just as well that her conversational ability was at a minimum because Pete spent the meal switching from station to station trying to get the latest news from Korea.

Pete kissed her goodbye and Joanna sat there for another half hour, listening to the radios. By nine o'clock she was awake and ready to start her day. She took out one of her college poems and started rewriting it. Each day she chose the style of a different poet—Muriel Rukeyser, Lawrence Durrell, Karl Shapiro, Dylan Thomas. She was trying to break the hold that T. S. Eliot and Thomas Merton had fastened on her imagination. It was exhausting work in the heat—but she thought she was making progress.

At their stopover in Cincinnati, Joanna had bought a dozen books by contemporary poets. She devoted most of her afternoons to reading them. She did not consciously avoid the company of her fellow wives. She was usually agreeable when Martha MacKenzie asked her to be a fourth at bridge or join her for a shopping expedition to the PX or commissary. Once a week she and Martha drove to Archer to buy some decent fruit and vegetables and a good cut of meat. The commissary's choice in these departments was unbelievably bad. Occasionally, Ruth Hardin went with them. She kept trying to get friendly with Martha, in spite of repeated rebuffs. When Ruth saw Joanna succeeding where she had failed, she attached herself as Joanna's friend. Either way, Ruth was a disaster. All she did was gripe about the commissary, the PX, the heat, the boredom of Fort Ripley compared to Schofield Barracks, which was where she and Sam would be if it were not for "this lousy war."

Unlike Ruth and other wives, Joanna did not feel bored. She was even secretly pleased that it was too hot to do any serious cooking. It left her more time for poetry. She was surprised—and a little intimidated—to hear Ruth tell Martha she looked forward to the day when she could entertain "in decent style." Other wives made similar remarks and exchanged complicated recipes for hors d'oeuvres and soups and main courses.

"Do people entertain a lot in the Army?" Joanna asked Martha.

"It can get pretty competitive," Martha said. "Some wives go all out. They're the ones who'll be pushing their husbands into the fully qualified promotion zone and kicking them out of bed if they don't make it. I told Lover that I wasn't going to play the game that way. My mother took it easy and Dad's done okay."

"What's the fully qualified promotion zone?"

Martha explained that since 1947 promotion was no longer by seniority alone, as it had been in the pre-World War II Army. Now there were two groups in each rank, from captain through lieutenant colonel, one called "fully qualified," the other "best qualified."

Not for the last time, Joanna found the Army's choice of language amusing and puzzling. "What if you're just qualified?" she asked.

"You're a civilian," Martha said.

"I don't think Pete will worry about who gets promoted first."

"That's because he'll be one of them," Martha said. "Everyone's got him spotted for a couple of stars."

"A general?" The idea was inconceivable to Joanna.

"He's a leader, Jo. Those are the guys they make generals."

That night at supper, Joanna told Pete what Martha had said. He laughed. "I wish she could get her father to put that in my file."

"Your file?"

"In Washington. Everybody's got a file. Everything you do right—or wrong—goes into it."

"I'm not sure I like that idea."

"How else can they decide who gets promoted?"

"Do you want to be a general?"

"Who doesn't? Right now I'm more worried about being a good second lieutenant."

A few days later, Pete returned from a day in the field and told Joanna to make sure her best dress was clean. Tomorrow, General Strong was giving a reception at the Officers' Club to welcome all the officers and wives who had left calling cards at his residence. Joanna chose the blue silk shantung she had worn to the general's quarters on their duty visit. But she found it hard to work up much enthusiasm for the reception. They were swallowed in a mob of several hundred couples. Most of the men were second lieutenants with ROTC commissions. The weather remained mercilessly hot. By 5 P.M. the club had been baking in the sun all day and was a giant oven.

Pete and Joanna went down the receiving line behind the MacKenzies. An aide, a captain with a loop of gold braid on his shoulder, smoothly forwarded each name to the general and his wife. What a bore, Joanna thought, shaking four hundred hands, flashing a polite smile in four hundred faces. "If this is what a general has to do," she murmured to Pete, "I hope you never become one."

"It's important," Pete said in a rather surly way. "For junior officers. For their morale."

General Strong was a short, balding, cerebral-looking man. Sweat gleamed on his forehead and his smile was becoming somewhat artificial by the time the Burkes and MacKenzies reached him. When he saw Martha, his expression changed to genuine delight. "Muggsy!" he said, and gave her a kiss. He shook Lover's hand with special cordiality and said something about having him and Martha over for cocktails. Then the general turned to his wife and said: "Look who's here."

Mrs. Strong was leaning on a cane. She had once been a handsome woman, but now the left side of her face had a sad droop.

Her hair was white. She looked ten years older than General Strong. But she was equally delighted to see Martha. "How's your mother?" she said. "Tell her how much I miss her."

"I will. How are you?"

"I'm getting better every day. I want to start riding but my commander-in-chief here won't let me."

"We'll see you later," the general said, anxious to keep the receiving line moving.

At the bar Pete and Lover got tall, deliciously cool tom collinses for themselves and their parched wives and they joined the milling throng in the ballroom of the Officers' Club. "General Strong was Dad's chief of staff during the war," Martha explained.

"How do you like her Army nickname—Muggsy?" Lover asked. "She didn't tell me that one until after the wedding."

"Dad pinned it on me when I was two years old."

"What's wrong with Mrs. Strong?" Joanna said.

"She's had a couple of strokes—the first one right after their oldest boy was killed in Italy in 1945."

When the reception line ended, the Strongs walked over to them. Mrs. Strong leaned heavily on her cane and dragged her left foot slightly.

"I've been scolding him for using that dreadful old nickname," Mrs. Strong said to Martha.

"When I saw you I was suddenly back in Fort Bliss in 1935," General Strong said.

"Happy days," Martha said.

"Sir," Lover said. "I understand you married a general's daughter too. Do you have any advice for me?"

The general's eyes twinkled. "Just remember to salute the first thing each morning. That keeps them happy until about noon."

"Don't listen to him," Mrs. Strong said. She turned to Martha and Joanna. "We're gradually getting this place organized. The Women's Club will finally meet next Wednesday."

"We'll be there," Martha said.

The general turned to Pete. "Is this the Burke who stopped the Navy fullback about eight times in a row last November?" he asked.

"I had a lot of help, General," Pete said.

"We can use that kind of defense out in Korea," General Strong said.

"We'll give it all we've got, General."

"How's the training going?"

"Couldn't be better, sir. We've got some great officers and sergeants."

General Strong nodded and smiled at Martha. "The Adjutant General promised me the best." He put his arm around Mrs. Strong. "I'm taking this lady home for a nap."

The general and his wife departed, she still leaning heavily on her cane, dragging her left leg. Odd, Joanna thought. He fought in the war and she's the wounded one.

Martha was also looking at Mrs. Strong. "Now I know why they've been slow about starting the Women's Club. He's afraid she won't be able to handle it."

"What's the Women's Club?" Joanna asked.

"It's something to keep you girls busy. So you won't start playing around," Lover said.

"It's where Army wives get a chance to make a contribution," Pete said.

"It's about midway between those two ideas," Martha said.

The Fort Ripley Women's Club met in the ballroom of the Officers' Club on the following Wednesday afternoon. It was still murderously hot. Mrs. Strong made a brief welcoming speech, urging everyone to participate in the club. It would help them become part of "the Army family," she said. Then she announced that a slate of officers would be elected. She introduced each nominee. They were all wives of colonels and lieutenant colonels. The second lieutenants' wives studied them and silently pronounced them dowdy. Their clothes were out of style and so were their hairdos.

Since there was no opposition slate, the officers were elected unanimously. The new president, a brunette built along the lines of a Wagnerian soprano, called for volunteers to staff a startling number of committees. There was a thrift shop committee, a Boy Scout and a Girl Scout committee, a bridge club committee, a drama club committee, an entertainment committee, a welcoming committee, a hospital committee, a day care center committee, and a committee to maintain liaison with the Enlisted Wives' Club.

Response was tepid among the second lieutenants' wives. They did not feel part of Fort Ripley. They had been there only a few weeks and their husbands would soon leave for Korea, making them civilians again.

"Aren't you going to work on any committees?" Martha asked.

"How much time will they take?" Joanna asked.

Martha shrugged as if that were irrelevant. She volunteered for the thrift shop, bridge club and welcoming committees. Ruth Hardin volunteered for the same ones. Among the few second lieutenants' wives who volunteered, almost all were married to West Pointers. Intimidated, Joanna put her name on the list for the drama club, hoping they would never get into production.

Joanna found it hard to explain to Martha or anyone else why she was so chary about her time. She was not at all sure she had any real talent as a poet. No matter how good she was, Joanna suspected that Martha would find it hard to accept poetry as an excuse for failing to respond to Mrs. Strong's call to duty. But Joanna never expected Pete to have a similar attitude. She was even somewhat surprised when he asked her how the Women's Club meeting had gone.

"Fine," she said.

"What committees did you join?"

"The drama club."

He looked dismayed. "That's all?"

She explained that she was reluctant to spare more time from her poetry. She had shown him several samples of her recent efforts and he had said they were "great." Now it became evident that his praise had been perfunctory. He shook his head, a frown on his formidable forehead.

"Jo—you've got to realize—"

"IN KOREA, AMERICAN TROOPS DUG IN ALONG THE NAKTONG RIVER, THEIR LAST NATURAL DEFENSE LINE—"

Someone had turned on the six o'clock news in a nearby apartment.

Pete stood there, listening to the somber voice retailing more bad news. His frown vanished. "It's not worth arguing about. Not now," he said.

Later that night, as they made love, two lines from Lawrence Durrell leaped into Joanna's mind. *The woman walks in the dark like a lantern swung. A white spark blown between points of pain.* Perhaps that was better than mystic swooping and soaring. Closer to the reality of an Army wife. But still poetry.

Two nights later, with the Kansas summer still blasting heat through the walls, Joanna was trying to decide between veal chops and liver and bacon for supper when Martha MacKenzie knocked and strolled in through the open door. Everyone kept their doors open in the hope, usually vain, of catching a breeze.

"Excitement," Martha said. "Look who's moving in next door."

A short, stocky Negro was unloading a blue Chevrolet, with the help of his wife.

"Dad told me we'd have a lot of them out here," Martha said. "They don't want to send them to Benning or any other southern post if they can avoid it."

"Shouldn't we do something to make them feel welcome?" Joanna said.

"What?" Martha said.

"I'm going to say hello."

"Don't you think you should talk it over with Pete first?"

"I don't have to talk this sort of thing over with him."

Joanna strolled out to the car. "Hi," she said. "I'm Joanna Burke. Welcome to Fort Ripley."

They both thanked her and shook hands. Their name was Elson, Shirley and Roger. Shirley was thick-lipped and heavily built. She wore her shiny black hair almost shoulder length with a bang down her forehead. Joanna warned them about the deficiencies of the commissary and advised them to shop in Archer.

"How about the Officers' Club?" Roger asked. "Are they serving dinner?"

"Yes," Joanna said. "We haven't eaten there. Pete gets home so late. We've only been there to a reception the general gave for new junior officers.''

"I don't think we ought to try the club just yet, Rog," Shirley said. "How about the restaurants outside? Are they segregated?"

"I don't think so," Joanna said. "But you don't have to go out. Why don't you take potluck with me and Pete tonight?"

They thanked her and said they had to go into Archer to shop anyway. Joanna invited them for a drink after supper. They accepted and she strolled back to Quarters 8. Martha MacKenzie and a clump of other wives were waiting at her back door. Among them was Ruth Hardin. They peered into the kitchen at her as if she were something in a zoo. "Did they say more are comin'?" asked blond Sandy Holliday in her heavy southern accent.

"I didn't ask them."

"Did he say anythin' about usin' the Officers' Club?"

"He said they might have dinner there."

"Just let him try it," Ruth Hardin said. "Old Harmon Strong will have him pitched out on his ear."

"I don't see how he can do that," Joanna said.

"It's an Officers' *Club*," Ruth said. "Just like a private club. I looked it up in *The Officer's Guide*. It quotes paragraph 2 of AR 210-60, passed April 3, 1947, which states that members of an officers' club have a right to make their own rules. I'll bet you a hundred dollars one of the rules will be no niggers."

"AR what?" Joanna said.

"Army regulations," Ruth said.

"I don't know what the general will do. Or what the regulations say," Joanna said. "I know what we should do. I've invited them over for drinks tonight. Would any of you like to join us?"

There was silence at the door. "Let me give you some advice," Ruth said. "The Army doesn't like troublemakers."

"Ruth," Martha MacKenzie said, "excuse me for talking like a sergeant, but you're full of horseshit. Lover and I'll be around, Joanna. What time?"

"Eight-thirty, nine."

Pete appeared at 7 P.M., dirty and sweat-soaked as usual. The second lieutenants had been on a field exercise, working with heavy weapons, mortars and machine guns, out on Ripley's firing ranges, miles from Shavetail Row. At Pete's suggestion, they had marched out and back, to get in condition for Korea. He showered and she served the liver and bacon she had decided on for supper. It was one of Pete's favorite meals and he attacked it enthusiastically, meanwhile telling her how much everyone was learning about infantry tactics. "I think we'll be able to do some good over there."

"Maybe we can do some good here, before you go."

She told him about the Elsons, her invitation, her nasty exchange with Ruth Hardin. Pete stopped enjoying his liver and bacon. "Holy Christ, Joanna," he said.

"What do you mean?"

"Why didn't you wait, talk it over with me?"

"What was there to talk about? Do you seriously think I *shouldn't* have welcomed them, invited them over tonight?"

"I seriously think it would have been a hell of a lot better if I did it. If I had a chance to go around and talk to a couple of key guys in this setup, guys like Lover who can soft-soap people, calm them down. In a day or two, maybe I could have arranged something. Instead, we've got a big split in the group, we've made enemies of the Hardins and their friends, and I've got to go around looking like my wife tells me what to do."

"Is that so terrible?"

"Yes," he snarled, bringing his fist down on the table with a crash that sent his coffee cup hurtling to the floor. "Joanna, in two weeks I'm gonna be in Korea, telling guys to go up hills and risk getting shot. They're not gonna do it for Lieutenant Casper Milquetoast!"

Joanna was devastated. The rage on his face said *I hate you*. Or *I could hate you*, which was almost as bad.

"But that's not the main point," Pete said, getting a broom out of the kitchen closet to sweep up the pieces of the cup. "The main point is to keep the Army united on this desegregation thing. You can't move too fast. You can't pull stunts on people."

"Do you think Lieutenant Elson should be admitted to the Officers' Club?"

"I don't know," he said. "That's up to the board of governors of the club. It's up to General Strong, really."

"You don't think it's a moral issue?"

"It's a command issue. The general will make the decision on the basis of the effect it will have on his command. If it's going to cause a big upheaval, tremendous dissension, I can see why he might say no. I hear there's going to be thirty or forty black officers here in the next couple of weeks. They could form their own club."

"That's disgusting," Joanna said. "It's immoral and disgusting."

He dumped the broken cup into the kitchen wastebasket, came back to the table and sat down. "Okay," he said. "That's your opinion. But if the general decides to go that way, keep it to yourself. What time is it?"

"Eight o'clock."

"That's good. I've got time to go down and talk to the Hardins."

He left his liver and bacon unfinished and charged out of the house to the Hardins' quarters at the front end of Shavetail Row. Joanna sat looking disconsolately at his empty place for fifteen minutes. Finally she picked up the cold food and threw it in the garbage. She stacked the dishes in the sink and showered and changed to a polka-dotted organdy dress. At 8:25 Pete appeared, looking more relaxed, if not exactly pleased with life. "The Hardins are coming," he said. "I talked it over with them. Smoothed Ruth down. I convinced Sam that the Academy had to set a sort of example in a situation like this. I'm sure Ruth is giving him hell right now for saying yes. Which means he'll probably hate my guts. You have really cut a lovely swath of destruction."

"I'm sorry," Joanna said tearfully. "I thought I was doing the right thing."

"Jo," Pete said. "If it were anyplace else, some suburb outside Washington or New York, it would have been the right thing. But not here. Not in the Army. Try to remember that there's a right way, a wrong way, and an Army way of doing things. Please."

"I'll try," she said.

The MacKenzies arrived promptly at 8:30. The Hardins showed up at 8:45. At nine o'clock there was still no sign of the Elsons. They finally appeared at 9:30. Joanna introduced them, and they apologized for being so late. "We've had quite a time getting our supper," Roger Elson said. "We tried the Officers' Club, but no dice. I wasn't a member. We tried two restaurants out on the highway. Full."

"All the empty tables were reserved," Shirley Elson said.

"Oh, that's so terrible," Joanna said.

"I'm kind of used to it," Roger Elson said. "I come from Hackensack, New Jersey. Everything is segregated there. Theaters, restaurants, swimming pools."

"I come from Westchester County across the river," Shirley said. "I remember one night Roger took me out to dinner. We tried twelve restaurants. They were all full."

"Where did you get your commission?" Pete said.

"ROTC, Cornell," Roger replied.

"Do you think you'll have any problems leading white troops?"

"No. But I think white troops may have problems following my orders. Excuse me, but after a night like this I can't help but think the average white American's head is so screwed up about Negroes, you wonder if there is any point in trying to unscrew it."

"Don't let it rattle you so much," Pete said. "You're not the only people who've had to deal with prejudice. I can tell you a few stories I heard from my Irish grandfather."

"It's not the same thing, man, believe me," Elson said.

Pete's brow knitted slightly, a sign of annoyance. Joanna could understand both men's reactions. It was hot and the Elsons were tired, depressed and angry. Pete had no enthusiasm for this party. Joanna anxiously shoved beer at everyone and turned up the electric fan. The MacKenzies began talking about the news from Korea, which continued to be terrible. Earlier that day Martha had spoken to her father on the telephone. He told her a story which had not yet gotten into the papers. Two days ago, on August 1, the Americans in Korea had withdrawn behind the Naktong River, the last natural barrier between them and the sea. As the rear guard, units of the 1st Cavalry Division, crossed the only bridge left standing, thousands of South Korean refugees tried to follow them. Three times the Americans had driven them back and warned them that the bridge was going to be blown up. Three times the refugees had surged after them. Night was falling, the North Koreans were getting closer. With the bridge still crowded with Koreans, General Hobart Gay, commander of the 1st Cavalry, ordered it blown up.

Pete shook his head. "That makes me glad I'm not a general," he said.

"Let me ask you something," Roger Elson said. "Would he have blown up that bridge if those refugees were white?"

"I don't know," Pete said. "I'd have to think about that one."

"Would you blow it, any one of you? If you were in his shoes?"

"Sure, I'd blow it," Sam Hardin said. "An order is an order."

"I don't believe you," Elson said. "I don't believe that General Hobart Gay would have blown it. If those people were white, if this stinking mess was happening in Germany or Austria, he would have put his guys back on the other side of the river and fought it out until the last refugee got across. You know why? Because a flap would have come out of Washington and blown him away for killing white people. But it's okay to slaughter a couple of hundred yellow people."

"What the hell are you talking about?" Lover MacKenzie said. "The Koreans themselves blew half a dozen bridges across the Han River a couple of weeks ago with three or four thousand people on them, including troops."

"We're talking about military necessity versus civilian hysteria," Pete said. "If the North Koreans get across the Naktong River, it's goodbye to the whole ball game."

"That wouldn't be such a bad thing in my opinion. I think we'd be better off getting out of there right now. Let 'em have the damned country."

"Lieutenant," Pete said, "I don't think much of your attitude."

"Oh, you don't?" Elson said. "What is this anyway? Some West Point secret society looking over the nigger officer material? So you can figure out ways to run him out of the Army? Well, let me tell you something, *Lieutenant*. Here's one nigger that isn't going to run. I've got friends in Washington who will put your ass—all three of your asses—in slings."

"We're all West Pointers, class of '50," Pete said. "That's about the only grain of truth in what you've just said. I was trying to give you a little advice, but I guess you don't need it."

"I don't need anything from any of you," Elson said. "I made it out of Hackensack on my own and I'm gonna make it through this Army on my own and be on my way as soon as my three lousy years are paid off."

"Hey, wait a minute," Sam Hardin said. He was smiling. Joanna was amazed. Pete looked like he was about to dismember Roger Elson. "Wait a minute. Let's get a couple of things straight. This young lady"—he gestured to Joanna—"invited you over for a drink because she thought it was the right thing to do. We're here because we agreed with her. No other reason. Let's not let the heat and stupidity of a few civilian restaurant owners spoil a good beginning."

"Let me second that motion," Martha MacKenzie said.

Pete still looked like he was liable to explode. But Roger Elson's rage perceptibly cooled. He looked at his wife. "The man's making sense, Roger," Shirley Elson said.

"I'm afraid I am a little uptight," Roger Elson said.

"Who isn't?" Lover MacKenzie said. "They're shooting real bullets out there in Korea. They didn't tell me anything about that in West Point. They promised me a year in the Signal Corps—learning how to answer some general's telephone."

Everyone except Ruth Hardin started smiling. Joanna got more beer out of the refrigerator. Pete revealed that he was from Hamilton, which was only about thirty miles from Hackensack, New Jersey. Sam Hardin told some funny stories about growing up on a Texas ranch where half the cowboys were black. Lover did an imitation of his father-in-law, the Adjutant General. By the time the Elsons went back to their quarters, the evening was a success.

"There's more to Sam than meets the eye," Joanna said after the Hardins and the MacKenzies left.

Pete nodded. "I can't figure out why he married Ruth. That makes me worry about his judgment."

Joanna was tempted to tell him what she had heard from Amy

Rosser at the Hotel Thayer. But she decided to say nothing. She owed Sam that much for rescuing her good deed from disaster.

During the next week, Joanna found it harder and harder to struggle out of bed on Pete's early schedule. She blamed it on the heat. Pete was very understanding. He said he would be glad to cook his own breakfast. Although she noticed this generosity did not include doing the dishes, she was grateful for the privilege of drowsing in the relative coolness of the morning, while the war news from Pete's radio and other radios murmured through the bedroom walls.

Each day Pete sat down on the bed in his battle dress to kiss her goodbye. One morning he was especially tender. "Wish you had time for an extra added attraction, soldier," she whispered.

He nodded, obviously thinking the same thing. But his smile was wan. "Only ten more days," he said. "Let's make the most of them."

She clung to him and almost wept. In the next apartment, occupied by an ROTC lieutenant and his pudgy wife, both from Massachusetts, a radio muttered: "North Korean forces crossed the Naktong River in battalion strength last night. Heavy fighting was reported—"

They kissed again and Pete departed for another field exercise. About fifteen minutes later, Joanna got up, washed her face and began combing her hair. Swirling up from deep inside her body came the most appalling nausea. The familiar face in the bathroom mirror dissolved. She clutched the sink and retched into it. Nothing came up but some filmy saliva-edged mucus.

Joanna stumbled back to bed and lay there in the August heat, trying to recall what she had eaten the previous night. Nothing that was likely to have gone bad. In a recent letter, her mother had warned her not to buy any desserts with custard in them and she had dutifully avoided them. She wondered if this was the onset of some fatal disease, perhaps leukemia. The thought was vaguely appealing. God was an ironist. While everyone shuddered at the thought of these heroic young men dying on the battlefield, He sent His messenger, death, to claim the innocent bride, to remind them all that He was the Ruler of the World, and His will must be humbly accepted. Years later, they would all remember Joanna, the earnest sad idealist, who tried to leave something behind her by befriending the first Negro officer and his wife to report to Fort Ripley.

"Joanna? Jo?" Martha MacKenzie called at the door. "Feel like going to the Women's Club bridge today? We're playing for an eighth of a cent a point. You could clean up. Win as much as twenty cents if you concentrate."

Joanna struggled into her bathrobe and reeled to the door. "I'd love to—but I'm feeling god-awful," she said.

Martha joined her in the living room. Joanna described her symptoms. "Oh-oh," Martha said. "When was your last period?"

"I—I haven't had one yet," Joanna said. "A book I read said that might happen—"

"I bet it did. You're pregnant, honey. My big sister had the same thing—morning sickness. For nine lousy months. I'm praying I'll be luckier when we decide to go for one."

Joanna simply could not believe it. With Pete being flung into a war after they had been promised no war, after their honeymoon had been disrupted and their plans for a year in beautiful Hawaii had been canceled, she had assumed that God, who was benevolent as well as ironic, a God of love, after all, would see to it that pregnancy did not occur. It was His decision, wasn't it, whether or not one of Pete's sperm swam uphill within her to meet one of her eggs and became a baby?

When we decided to go for one. That meant Martha was practicing birth control. According to the Catholic Church, that was a sin against nature, a moral blot, whether or not a person was a Catholic. Yet Martha did not seem in the least blotted. It apparently had no impact on her conscience whatsoever. "You don't—don't want a baby now?"

Martha frowned and dropped her offhand style. "I want one. But Lover says no. He wants to wait until he gets back from Korea in one piece."

"He will. They all will," Joanna said.

"No, they won't, Jo," Martha said. "They know it. We know it.

Don't kid yourself about that kind of thing. It's better to be—sort of braced for it.''

The Army brat, the general's daughter, was talking now. For a moment Joanna felt panicky, as if Pete were already dead. She remembered the prayers she had said for her brother's safety, prayers which had been answered by that government telegram in 1944. The memory seemed to coalesce with her nausea to declare that she had no control over any part of her life, not even her own body. She fought the panic, telling herself to accept the nausea, to accept God's will, even if she did not understand it.

At Martha's urging, Joanna got dressed and Martha drove her to the base hospital. Joanna wondered why Martha brought along several magazines. She found out why at the hospital, her first encounter with the Army's medical routine. (Her scorched hand had healed without a return visit.) The clinic section was jammed with enlisted men, wives, an occasional mother with a child, sitting on rows of wooden folding chairs. Joanna gave her name to the poker-faced nurse in charge of record keeping and sat down beside Martha. "I thought officers' wives would have a separate clinic," she said.

Martha smiled wryly. "They don't," she said, and handed her a copy of *Cosmopolitan*.

The nausea, which recurred in waves, made it difficult for Joanna to concentrate on the short stories in *Cosmopolitan*. They were better than Joanna expected them to be, one in particular by a writer named Kurt Vonnegut. Three hours later, having read every word in *Cosmopolitan* and the *Ladies' Home Journal*, she was finally summoned to a narrow room where a snub-nosed doctor named Walton Trueblood, who did not look more than twenty-five years old, nodded impatiently as she told her story, then ordered her to undress and lie down on a paper-covered examining table. He went into the next room and examined someone else. At one point his voice rose and Joanna distinctly heard the word *gonorrhea*. Dr. Trueblood returned and curtly ordered her to put her feet in stirrups that he hoisted to eye level from beneath the table. He put on rubber gloves and examined her vagina, whistling some silly tune like an auto mechanic. He squeezed her breasts, then told her to give him a urine sample. She stepped into a small toilet beside the examining room and supplied him with one. He told her to go back to the waiting room.

An hour later, she was resummoned to Dr. Trueblood's presence. "You're pregnant," he said. He glowered at her file. "What the hell's the matter with you? Don't you know your husband's on his way to Korea?"

"Of course I know it," she said.

"Then why aren't you practicing birth control?"

"I'm a Catholic."

"I don't care what you are. Does it make any sense to have a kid who may not have a father before he, she or it is born? A West Pointer, too. Doesn't say much for his judgment."

Dr. Trueblood was a captain. Joanna wondered if she had the right to object to this abuse, even if he outranked her husband. "Is there anything I can take for morning sickness?" she asked.

"Sure, but none of them work. Might be better to let you put up with it. If you heave hard enough, you may abort."

"How can you say such a thing?"

"Because I'm a scientist," he snapped. "And you, my dear girl, are an idiot. Here."

He scribbled a prescription on a pad. "Give this to the pharmacist."

Outside, Martha MacKenzie was still waiting for her. "Just in time," she said. "I'm down to my last short story."

Unfortunately, it took another half hour to get the anti-nausea pills from the pharmacy. "The guy who said 'Hurry up and wait' was the Army's motto must have been a doctor," Martha said as they drove back to Shavetail Row.

Joanna wanted to tell Martha about Dr. Trueblood's diatribe on birth control but she was afraid it might make Martha uncomfortable, or worse, argumentative. In her college daydreams, Joanna had imagined herself serenely rebutting non-Catholic arguments against birth control with irrefutable Thomistic logic. Between the heat of August and her morning sickness, all she wanted to do now was go to bed and cry.

Bed was where Pete found her when he came back from the field. She had stopped crying several hours earlier. But every time she stood up, the nausea returned. As Dr. Trueblood had predicted, the pills were worthless. She spent the last hour in an imaginary dialogue with Dr. Trueblood, in which she gave him clever, scathing replies. But in the end she only felt more disconsolate. Why did she always think of the perfect answer too late?

Then Pete was in the doorway, a frown of concern on his forehead. "Honey, what's wrong?"

"I'm pregnant."

He smiled. *Smiled*. He whooped. "Joanna, that's fantastic," he said.

He didn't know, he could not even imagine her nausea. How could he? But she still felt hurt, angry, at his total lack of sympathy.

"I suppose it is," she said. "But I've been so sick all day I don't feel like celebrating."

"But that won't last, will it?"

"Martha MacKenzie had a sister who felt this way for nine months."

"Maybe you just have to get used to it," he said, sitting on the bed and taking her hand.

"Oh, that's beautiful," she said. "That's easy to say. But wait'll you hear what I went through at the hospital."

She told him about Dr. Trueblood. "I think you should do something about it," she said. "Can't you charge him with unprofessional conduct or something? He has no right to insult me that way. And you. He said you had no judgment."

"Jesus Christ." Pete strode up and down the room, smacking his fist into his palm. "I'll talk to Quincy about it tomorrow."

The next day was Saturday. Pete made an appointment to see his immediate commander, Major Charles Quincy, at his quarters. He returned an hour later. Joanna's morning sickness was still horrendous, but she had gotten up and dressed, wearily telling herself that she could not spend nine months in bed. She was in no mood for the news Pete brought her.

"Quincy thinks we ought to forget it."

"Why?"

"He says it's Dr. Trueblood's prerogative, as a senior officer, to give me—and you—advice."

"In such an insulting way?"

"Are you sure it was as bad as you made it sound, Jo?"

"Of course I'm sure. Are you implying that I made it up?"

"No. But you're naturally more sensitive about it. He might not have thought he was insulting you. He was just trying to give us advice, as he saw it. Non-Catholics don't see anything wrong with birth control, Jo."

"He called me an idiot! If that isn't an insult—"

"Maybe you said something that upset him."

"I did nothing of the sort!"

By now she had no difficulty imagining the conversation between Pete and Major Quincy. Emotional woman. Supersensitive. Devout Catholic. In effect, they had concluded she was an idiot.

"Look," Pete said. "I can file a complaint with General Strong. He might order an inquiry. It could take weeks. Meanwhile, everyone else around here will be in Korea. I'd feel pretty bad about that. I'd feel like some kind of coward, Jo. This punk isn't worth the trouble. He's not a regular. Just some jerk they've drafted out of medical school."

None of these points made any impression on Joanna. All she heard was her husband's reluctance, amounting to a refusal, to defend her. "Well, I won't go back to him, no matter how sick I get. Maybe I'll lose the baby and make him a prophet. Then maybe you'll do something."

"Jo. I'm only a second lieutenant. I'm in no position to make waves. The Army's fighting a war out there in Korea. General Strong's going crazy trying to find trained instructors when half his best people get pulled out of here every week as replacements. He hasn't got time to worry about what a wise-guy doctor says about birth control."

He was right. But she was so hot, so sick, so miserable. She started to cry. He swept her into his arms. "I'm sorry you're feeling lousy," he said. "But I'm glad you're pregnant. I know that sounds crummy to you. But it's the truth, Jo. It's pretty rough out there in

Korea. It'll make me feel better, if I get in trouble, knowing I've left something behind."

"What are you talking about?"

"Major Quincy showed me his *Army Times*. The newspaper. Joe Shaefer got killed last week. Fifty's first casualty."

"I—did I meet him?" she said dazedly. It was too confusing, this abrupt journey from birth to death. Her morning sickness, her anger at Dr. Trueblood became doubly trivial.

"He was in my company in plebe year," Pete said. "I think I introduced him to you once, in Boodler's. He was from Ohio."

She had a vague memory of a lanky cadet with a blond crew cut who had joked with her about being in awe of people from Cincinnati. He was a farm boy from some tiny town outside Columbus.

"How did he get out there so soon?"

"He wasn't married. He was touring Japan on his leave, and had orders for the 24th Division. So he cut the leave short and reported."

"Oh God. I'm sorry to be bothering you with my—my stupid worries."

"They're not stupid, Jo. If I were a civilian, I'd loosen a few of Doc Trueblood's teeth. Or if there wasn't a war—I'd try to run him out of the Army no matter what it cost me. But I can't afford to miss this show in Korea—"

I can't afford to miss this show. The words came as naturally to his lips as the previous ones about anger and revenge, about his sympathy for her morning sickness. He could not wait to travel six thousand miles to risk getting maimed or killed in a country most Americans barely knew existed two months ago. Leaving her to cope with nausea and loneliness. *I can't afford to miss this show.* For the first time Joanna wondered if she could stand being married to a professional soldier.

II

Paris, bathed in early-summer sun, the Tuileries and the Bois all glowing green and sultry shadow, the air thick with warmth, rich with birdsong, Paris seemed to guarantee Amy Rosser everything a honeymoon needed to achieve romance. George made sure she kept her promise to compensate him for the denials of the previous summer. By day they prowled the shops, enjoyed the restaurants, and toured the Louvre and Versailles, where Amy as a *cum laude* art major lectured on styles and schools, techniques and trends. George amiably confessed to knowing nothing about art but he managed to ask intelligent questions. He got his turn to be the lecturer on a tour of World War I battlefields. They hired a car and drove out to the embankments on the Marne River where the 38th Regiment of the 3rd Division had broken the back of the great German offensive in the spring of 1918. They spent a whole day in the Argonne, where George's father had fought as a private. Lieutenant Rosser did a remarkable job of making the rather dull landscapes come alive with the drama and chaos of battle.

Back in Paris, Amy fell in love with the fall season's fashions, which were in all the shops. The Spanish or "gaucho" look was the rage—she had worn an American version of it to the graduation hop—and Amy bought a half dozen dresses with flounces and off-the-shoulder bodices, all in velvet or velveteen, the year's favorite fabric. She liked the way the dark colors complemented her skin and hair.

George was appalled at the cost of the dresses, over $1,500. Amy told him they were an investment in his career. George's reaction to this remark upset her. He said he was not at all certain he wanted to make the Army his career. He owed the government only four years of service for his West Point education. Thereafter, he was free to resign and he intended to consider the option seriously. He thought he might be able to make a lot more money as a civilian. Amy reminded him that they did not need a lot of money. At her graduation from Vassar, Mother had finally revealed the amount of the trust fund she had long promised to set up for her—$500,000. This would give them an income of at least $25,000 a year—a nice supplement to his Army salary. George said he was not sure that he liked the idea of being supported by his wife. She told him he was being middle-class and they had dropped the subject.

It had been replaced by an even more unpleasant topic: Korea. On Sunday morning, June 23, the day before they were to leave Paris for Rome, George had come running into their room at the Hotel Crillon to shout the news to her while she was taking a bath. They had been scheduled to have lunch with Major General Christian Carver, one of the old Army friends to whom Amy's uncle, Paul Stapleton, had written letters of introduction. Carver was on the staff of NATO. The general's aide soon telephoned to tell them that the lunch was canceled. The President had put U.S. forces on alert around the world. Everyone thought Korea might be a diversion to mask a major assault on Western Europe.

George had become impossible for the next few days. He had cabled his whereabouts to the Pentagon, as if he were a military genius without whom the war could not be won. He had wanted to cancel their reservations in Rome. Amy had had to practically throw a tantrum to insist on her right to have a honeymoon, no matter what was happening on some silly Asian peninsula six thousand miles away.

Rome was magnificent, as always. But George had been barely polite as Amy marched him through St. Peter's and the Catacombs and the Pantheon and the Forum, disgorging more of the art history she had learned at Vassar. He often interrupted her to ask nearby tourists if they had any late news about Korea. While they taxied to their next site, he strained his brain trying to read the headlines on Italian newspapers. At St. Paul's Beyond the Walls, he had deserted her in the middle of a commentary on the historic altarpiece to ask an American with a portable radio if he could get the Armed Forces station that broadcast from Germany.

By the time the newlyweds left Rome for Florence, President

Truman had committed U.S. ground troops and they had been promptly, amazingly routed. A new term, "bug-out," entered the Army's vocabulary. George had been dazed with disbelief. He had written a letter to John Stapleton in Japan, asking him what was happening. George had asked Amy if she wanted to write a few lines as a P.S. and she had scribbled: *Having fun getting thoroughly conquered in all those places you conquered under General Ike*. As she wrote, she noticed that George had told Johnny he was going to try to get transferred from Germany to Japan and was hoping to land in his armored battalion. *Grease your CO to keep a slot open or better yet ask for me, if he hasn't got too many green second lieutenants already*, George had written.

Amy had circled those words and written in the margin: *If you do, I'll never forgive you*. She had sealed the letter and mailed it when they went out the next morning to survey Florence. Then she went to work on George. As they strolled along the sullen dribbling summer version of the river Arno toward the Pitti Palace, she asked him how long he thought the war in Korea would last.

"I'm afraid it won't last long enough for me to get into it," he said. "The Far East Command guys like cousin Johnny are going to get combat experience while I'm over here touring museums. You can't get anywhere without combat experience in your file. If I'm going to stay in the Army—"

"George, it seems to me you ought to talk this over with some of Uncle Paul's friends. A second lieutenant needs advice."

"You've got a point," George said.

Mark Stratton, the first general who had time to see them, once Korea became a war unto itself, was living in an awesome turreted castle outside Vienna. George was eager to meet him. He had been one of Patton's toughest tankers. Amy was dismayed by both Stratton and his wife. The general was an ugly crew-cutted little blockhouse of a man with a snout of a nose over a wide mouth and bulldog chin. Everything he said came out in a roar. His wife, a small, frazzled-looking woman with watery eyes, said she hated living in a castle and seldom left the apartment on the top floor, where they met for drinks.

Worse, General Stratton gave George advice Amy did not want him to hear. "YOU'RE GODDAMN RIGHT I THINK YOU SHOULD GET OUT THERE. THE WHOLE IDEA OF THE U.S. ARMY CAN BE SUMMED UP IN ONE ORDER: RIDE TO THE SOUND OF THE GUNS. THEY COURT-MARTIALED FITZ-JOHN PORTER FOR NOT OBEYING IT AT SECOND MANASSAS AND THEY WERE RIGHT. IF I WERE LINCOLN I WOULD HAVE SHOT THE BASTARD." He went on to list a half dozen other generals who should have been shot in World Wars I and II for similar failures. Stratton was about to get another star and head home to the Pentagon, "where they can put a lock on my mouth," he said. He would see what could be done to get George transferred to the 303rd Armored Brigade—John Stapleton's outfit, which was already in Korea.

Amy would have left Stratton and his castle in a very bad mood—except for the stories the general told about her cousin and her uncle. He described how Johnny had captured half a German regiment and shot up an entire town in Sicily, with nothing, neither infantry nor artillery, to support his tank. He told how Paul Stapleton had saved the American beachhead in North Africa by fighting a battalion of Vichy French tanks to a standstill, although they outnumbered his tanks three to one. Amy could not help feeling that the afterglow of this praise had cast at least a shine on George.

"How did he get to be a general?" Amy asked, riding back to their hotel. "He's so crude."

"Most tank generals are pretty crude," George said. "George Patton's their model."

"When you get to be one," Amy said, "I expect you to improve on the model. I think a man can be tough without being crude."

"Sure," George said. "Sure." He stared indifferently at a baroque fountain in a square near the Hofburg Palace. "I hope to hell he remembers me when he gets to the Pentagon."

For a moment Amy almost panicked. He was out of control, everything was out of control—her honeymoon, her promised three years in Germany with hot and cold running servants and a domiciled husband. He would go to Korea and come back full of battle wildness like John Stapleton, or worse, tanker crudity like General Stratton, or worst, a cripple like her cousin Mark Stapleton, John's brother, who had lost an arm and a leg in a tank on Okinawa.

At the hotel, when George tried to make love to her, Amy refused him for the first time. She told him she could not stand the thought of him going to Korea. George tried to calm her down. Assuming that she was only worried about him coming back alive, he held her hand and told her combat was not that dangerous. Most people survived. He even had the statistics for World War II. Officer casualties were only 7.01 percent, and it got safer as you advanced in rank. For every second lieutenant that got killed, there were 38 dead enlisted men; for every captain, 80 enlisted men; for every major, 365; for every lieutenant colonel, 503; for every colonel, 2,206; and for every general, 6,796 enlisted corpses.

These calmly recited numbers revealed the analytic side of George Rosser's mind. It took Amy by surprise. It did not seem to jibe with the hot-blooded cadet who had pursued her to Paris, or the sweating, snarling wielder of a lacrosse stick. The revelation was unexpected but it made Amy feel better. She told herself George was a realist, like her. They had similar temperaments. Wasn't that the principal reason she had married him?

Amy remained unreconciled to George's going to Korea. But she did not argue with him about it for the rest of their week in Vienna. Instead she tried to make their nightly sessions in the bridal suite so enjoyable, George would find it unthinkable to ask for a reassignment. But George seemed to accept her extra efforts as nothing more than a compliment to his masculinity. He went right on buttonholing tourists, tuning in radios, searching for newspapers to get the latest word on the war. Amy began to fear everything depended on the advice George got from the next general they were to meet, thanks to Uncle Paul's letters of introduction.

Creighton Trask was deputy commander of an armored division headquartered in Regensburg. He invited them to cocktails at the magnificent hunting lodge in which he was living, six miles from town. Mrs. Trask was a crisp, charming woman who had graduated from Bryn Mawr. She and Amy got along beautifully. General Trask was a cooler, younger man than General Stratton. Trask advised

George to think twice about rushing to Korea. For an armor man, it was not much of a war. Europe was where the big tank battles were going to take place, where, waiting for the battle, big maneuvers were regularly scheduled. A man could learn more about armor tactics in Europe, even without a war, than he could ever learn in Korea. General Trask was convinced that Korea would not last very long. It might be over before George got out there, and then he would be rattling around Japan in search of a decent assignment.

The first part of this advice seemed to be confirmed by a letter from John Stapleton that awaited them when they reached Nuremberg on August 31.

Dear Cousins:

I guess you qualify for that title now, George. It would be great to see you out here. We need all the help we can get. But don't expect to fight from the turret of a tank. We hain't got no mo, as they say down South. We had nothing but T-24's. It was Army doctrine that only light tanks were fightable in the Far East. Too bad they didn't tell the Koreans. They're using T-34's, the best heavy tanks developed in WW II by either side. We went into the Naktong Bulge to support the 25th Division with our rolling egg-shells. In the first day's fighting, we lost 17 tanks out of 20. The next day we lost the other three. So yours truly is now an infantry lieutenant. It gives me new respect for the dogfaces. So far my platoon is the only one in the regiment that hasn't bugged out. It's no tribute to my leadership—just dumb luck. They sing the Bug-Out Boogie to me every night. With or without tanks, it's a real war, the only one around. I wouldn't pass it up if I were you, George. If Amy is as thoroughly conquered as she sounds, she won't miss you for a month or two. I always thought a thorough conquering was what she needed.

Yours,

Johnny

• • •

"What's that about you being conquered?" George said.

"By you, darling," Amy said. "It's what I told him in the note I added to your letter."

George simply nodded. He did not go in for linguistic subtleties, thank God, Amy thought. When she scribbled that note to John, she had not anticipated such a direct reply.

In Nuremberg, they discovered that George was assigned to a supply battalion which was headquartered in Mautbrunnen, a small town about twenty miles north of the old imperial city. Mautbrunnen nestled in a valley beside a branch of the Pegnitz River, with a medieval castle on a forested height above it. Unlike Nuremberg, which had been devastated by Allied air raids, Mautbrunnen had been untouched by the war. In its central square was an old German army barracks, called a casern, in which the battalion's enlisted men lived. Lieutenants and captains lived nearby in another casern, divided into three-room apartments.

Amy was dismayed by the dingy apartment and its quartermaster furniture. George was even more disappointed by his assignment to a supply battalion. He had come to Europe to learn about tanks, not to play nursemaid to trucks.

"This settles it," George said, pacing around their tiny living room. "I'm putting in for Korea. I wish I was there with Johnny right now."

"Calm down, darling," Amy said. "Read his letter again. He has no tanks. Do you really want to become an infantry officer? That's strictly for cretins like Pete Burke. Remember what General Trask said, about learning more right here."

"He thinks like a staff type. I agree with old Stratton. He's gut Army."

There it was again, that wild wayward streak that linked George to the mysterious loyalties of the male world, and threatened to leave her as husbandless as Mother, without even the right to complain about it. Amy told herself she preferred the analytic lecturer on combat casualty statistics, the realist. She was sure this romantic wildness was not natural to George. It was an aberration he had contracted from the duty-honor-country preachers at West Point. Not that Amy was opposed to ideals; she just did not think you should go out of your way to let them mess up your life.

Struggling for calm, Amy put on two of her Paris purchases, a pale blue haltered dress with a button-on cape and a matching cloche. George donned his tropical worsted khaki shade No. 1 summer uniform and they paid their required courtesy call on George's battalion commander, Lieutenant Colonel Willard Eberle, and his wife, Florence.

The Eberles lived in a picturesque Bavarian house just off the Mautbrunnen town square. They were both tall, which made Amy feel even smaller than her five feet nothing and more insecure. Florence Eberle had glossy dark brown hair that fell over her ears in a 1930's ripple remarkably like the style Amy's mother wore. Lieutenant Colonel Eberle was balding with large ears and a face that seemed rather small for his head. He looked more like an accountant than a soldier. But he talked in a gruff, direct way. So did his wife. Amy had never met a woman as direct as Florence Eberle.

While an orderly poured cocktails—manhattans, Amy's least favorite drink—Florence Eberle questioned Amy about everything but the size of her trust fund and the date of her last period. She seemed unimpressed by all Amy's answers until she learned that she rode.

"Good," Mrs. Eberle said. "So far, you're the only junior officer's wife who does. They're the biggest bunch of duds I've ever seen. I'm bored silly riding each day with Serena Casey—that's the exec's wife. Does Lieutenant Rosser ride?"

"No," Amy said. "George is a tennis player. He was on the West Point team."

"Willard, did you hear that?" Florence said. "Lieutenant Rosser was on the West Point team."

Lieutenant Colonel Eberle was telling George something about his experiences in World War II. He did not like the way he was interrupted.

"What West Point team?" he asked.

"Tennis," Florence Eberle said.

Lieutenant Colonel Eberle frowned. "I don't know whether we'll get a chance to profit from his prowess. He seems inclined to join his classmates in Korea.''

"That's ridiculous," Florence said. "You're the only Academy junior officer we've got. I told Willard to *demand* a West Pointer from G-1 to give the battalion some tone. We've got nothing but Rotcees and ninety-day wonders too lazy to go back to civilian life. I swear, I think Willard's lost most of his hair since he took command of this mess.''

"If I were you, I'd at least stay long enough to get on OER. That's sixty days minimum," Lieutenant Colonel Eberle said.

"Absolutely," Florence Eberle said.

Amy felt slightly breathless. They were talking a language she did not understand. Who was G-1? What was a Rotcee? An OER? All she knew was, she liked it. She liked private languages, especially ones that belonged to men. Florence Eberle had appropriated this one with consummate carelessness. Amy vowed to match her.

Lieutenant Colonel Eberle was telling George he did not think the Korean war would last very long. The Americans were rapidly building up supplies and reserves in their Pusan beachhead. The North Korean People's Army was having more and more trouble getting supplies down the peninsula from the North under American air attack. "Supply sounds dull, but it's the key to waging success-ful modern war—especially armored warfare," Lieutenant Colonel Eberle said. "Believe me, you won't be wasting your time in this battalion. Supply isn't as boring as it sounds, especially in an armored division.''

Amy blinked. Lieutenant Colonel Eberle had more or less said the same thing twice. She was soon to discover it was a habit.

"I certainly appreciate the advice, sir," George said.

"They're going on maneuvers next spring and we're going to win the best-in-division prize," Florence Eberle said.

While Lieutenant Rosser was mulling this advice, Florence breezi-ly continued, there was no reason why she and Amy could not do some riding together. Amy felt panicky. She had not mounted a horse since her junior year at boarding school. She tried to put off the inevitable by pleading a lack of a riding outfit. Mrs. Eberle said there was a well-equipped shop in Mautbrunnen. She could buy everything she needed and get it fitted in an afternoon.

"I'll look forward to seeing you here at the house at oh-eight-hundred hours tomorrow morning," Mrs. Eberle said.

Back in their apartment, Amy had George translate the portions of the conversation she had missed. G-1 was the officer in charge of personnel at division headquarters. Rotcees were ROTC lieutenants, ninety-day wonders were officers who had graduated from OCS during World War II. An OER was an Officer Evaluation Report, better known as an efficiency report. Senior officers were required to make these reports on junior officers every six months, or whenever an officer changed his assignment. Amy asked George to get her a copy of the form, known as WD 67-1. It was four pages long. In years to come she would often say every Army wife should study it, perhaps even memorize it. She learned more about the Army in the half hour it took her to read it than she had learned in the previous two years of dating and dancing at West Point.

On page one there was a section, "Estimated Desirability in Various Capacities," in which the officer filling out the report was supposed to assume he was a commander in a war. He rated the officer on whether he could:

a. Represent your viewpoint and make decisions at a higher headquarters.
b. Be responsible in an emergency calling for initiative, coolness, forceful leadership.
c. Work out an assignment requiring great attention to detail and routine.
d. Represent you where tact and ability to get along with people are needed.

The rating officer answered these questions on a scale of 1 to 5: 1 meant "don't want him," 3 meant "happy to have him." 5 meant "fight to get him."

Even more interesting was the job-proficiency section, in which the rating officer had his choice of marking "yes" or "no" beside statements such as: "becomes dogmatic about his authority," "fol-

133

lows closely directions of higher echelons," and "never makes excuses for his mistakes." The final page rated personal qualifications in the same way: "worries a great deal," "has admiration of officers and men alike," "a quiet unassuming officer." Amy saw at a glance that even some of the apparently innocuous descriptions could have a fatal effect on a man's career. Having met two generals in the last few weeks, and noticed the decisive way they stated their opinions, it was clear that worriers did not make generals. "Never makes excuses for his mistakes" implied that there were a lot of mistakes to make excuses for. Again, the victim was damned with faint praise. The same thing was true for the quiet unassuming officer.

As far as Amy was concerned, the report settled the argument about Korea. She told George she thought he would be out of his mind to pass up the opportunity to stand out in a crowd of dum-dum supply officers and go out there to compete with hundreds of other second lieutenants and first lieutenants already in combat. How could he get noticed, except by some sort of Medal of Honor heroics that would probably leave him crippled or dead? George muttered uneasily about the importance of combat experience, but he did not really have an answer.

The next morning, Amy arrived for her ride with Florence Eberle at exactly 0800 hours. Florence granted her an approximation of a smile. "Serena Casey's always fifteen minutes late. Drove me nuts. I grew up on punctuality in the old Army."

Amy contrived to look sweetly puzzled. "What do you mean, the old Army?"

By now, Florence was behind the wheel of a dark green Opel Kapitan, a prewar German sedan which the battalion mechanics had restored and polished to an almost unreal perfection. "The old Army, God bless it, was—well, the old Army," Florence said. "I was born into it, at Fort Baxter, Arizona, in 1908. My father was a captain, commanding a cavalry company. It was still Indian territory. Bands of drunken Apaches would get off the reservations and raise occasional hell. We had Irish sergeants who'd fought with Crook and Custer out on the plains. Daddy was West Point class of 1895. Almost every officer was an Academy man. You knew, if a man was an officer, he was a gentleman. That just isn't true anymore. But we're going to do our damnedest to get back to it."

Florence Eberle proceeded to condemn the post-World War II Army in her most unsparing style. The influx of civilians with democratic ideas had wreaked havoc on the distinction between officers and enlisted men, the heart of the old Army. When she arrived in Europe to join Willard after the war, there were officers and enlisted men eating from the same kitchens! Associating in public! Sitting at the same tables! Unthinkable. The Army had soon put a stop to those practices. But it still had a long way to go toward changing the attitudes of the "civilian transplants," as Florence called them, in the officer corps. They did not know how to give *orders*. They were apologetic about their privileges. Ridiculous, Florence snorted. What they had to do was restore West Point's style to the Army, from bottom to top. That was why she hoped Amy would persuade George to forget Korea. The 310th Supply Battalion's junior officers badly needed a West Pointer on which to model themselves.

As they strolled to the riding stables on the outskirts of the Erlengstegen Forest, north of Nuremberg, Florence casually added that George would not regret it. If all went well with the battalion, Willard was slated to become a full colonel and move up to G-1 at Division. A West Point classmate, Arthur Drinkwater, had the job at the moment.

Colonel Drinkwater, Florence Eberle continued as she thrust her left foot in the stirrup and slung the other long leg over the saddle of her horse, was a tennis addict. He played the game every morning and every evening if he had the time. His wife was almost as addicted. Several times they had invited the Eberles to Regensburg to play with them. But Willard was a mediocre player and Florence was terrible. Perhaps some intensive lessons from Lieutenant Rosser could improve their game enough to enable them to lose respectably.

"There's nothing wrong with that," Florence said as the German stablekeeper rushed out with a stool, enabling Amy to get her foot in the stirrup and mount Blitzen, the formidable horse he had selected for her. "The important thing in the Army is not to make a fool of yourself in public, ever."

Amy found these words of warning agonizingly apropos on that first morning's ride. Florence Eberle enjoyed a brisk pace and the path through the forest was full of hollows and abrupt turns. Low-hanging tree limbs along the border on both sides were another menace. What would Mrs. Lieutenant Colonel Eberle think if she looked back to find Mrs. Lieutenant Rosser flat on her back in the dirt? Several times Amy almost dropped the reins and clung to Blitzen's neck. The horse, with typical equine perversity, sensed her uncertainty and did all sorts of stunts, dancing sideways, bounding down into hollows with unexpected dashes, then abruptly slowing on the upgrade and almost sending her out of the saddle headfirst. But Amy managed to remember enough horsemanship to survive.

That evening, sitting somewhat gingerly at their quartermaster-issued dining-room table, Amy told her husband what she had learned on her morning ride. "George, if you walk out on the Eberles, I hate to think what your first OER will be. Your first one. If the man who makes out that report likes you, he'll give you the benefit of the doubt on every question. If he doesn't, you're a gone goose, no matter how well you've done your job."

"Eberle won't make out my OER," George said. "My captain will."

"But Eberle makes out *his* report, and the captain isn't going to downgrade someone who's pleasing the battalion commander."

George chewed on a chunk of lamb chop, obviously somewhat amazed by how much his demure society wife was learning about the Army.

"Florence says everyone in the Army's got to have a patron, if they hope to get anywhere."

"I'll take General Stratton," George said.

"He forgot who you were ten minutes after you walked out of that castle," Amy said. "A person remembers you when you do something for them. Something that makes them look good."

George stopped talking about Korea. On the morning he reported for duty in H Company of the 310th, Supply Battalion Lieutenant Colonel Eberle summoned him and his captain to headquarters and outlined step one in his game plan. Lieutenant Rosser was to take his platoon and drill it into a model for the rest of the battalion. George had been one of the commanders in Beast Barracks at West Point, in charge of turning new plebes into cadets. He soon discovered that draftees in a supply battalion did not respond to drill with the same alacrity or enthusiasm as appointees to the U. S. Military Academy. The men began calling him Lieutenant Von Rosser behind his back. George broke the revolt by transferring several of the worst offenders to the infantry. He divided the platoon into squads and forced them to compete with each other for weekend passes.

Slowly, with the help of a veteran sergeant that Lieutenant Colonel Eberle transferred from his headquarters company, the 2nd Platoon of H Company started to look like soldiers. Their shoes shone, their guns and equipment gleamed. Meanwhile, the captain began climbing all over the ROTC lieutenant in command of the company's 1st Platoon. He soon had his men drilling into the twilight too.

On September 15, Lieutenant Colonel Eberle held a battalion review in a small sports stadium just outside Mautbrunnen. H Company marched with a precision that made the rest of the battalion look like sleepwalkers. Amy, sitting on the reviewing stand beside Florence Eberle, felt the kind of thrill she had experienced at West Point as George and his men swept past, responding to the order "Eyes RAHHeet!" with a simultaneous snap of 175 heads to salute the commander and the colors.

The next morning, at officers' call, the daily meeting of the battalion's company commanders, Lieutenant Colonel Eberle told his captains that they had one month to bring their companies up to the standard set by H Company or they would be relieved. Amy followed this continuing drama from two points of view. George frequently came home cursing over the latest relapse of one of his men who had gotten drunk and been arrested by the MP's in Nuremberg or shacked up with some German girl and was listed as AWOL. George tended to overdramatize these setbacks. From her almost daily rides with Florence Eberle, Amy knew that things were going very well. The Eberles were delighted with George's spit-and-polish campaign—and his tennis lessons.

Every day at 4 P.M. and on Saturdays at noon the Eberles played doubles with George and Amy. George preceded the match with some coaching on the backhand, forehand, lob or smash and gave a brief critique of their performances—including Amy's—afterward. Florence Eberle improved rapidly, but the lieutenant colonel persisted in lunging for the ball instead of getting set and stroking it. Florence bought a full-length mirror and made Willard rehearse his strokes before it every night for an hour. His form improved dramatically although he still hit the ball out five times out of ten.

Finally, not without some trepidation, George pronounced them ready to confront the Drinkwaters in Regensburg. The Eberles drove down there on the weekend after the battalion review and came back beaming. They had lost both days' matches by respectable scores. The Drinkwaters had invited Brigadier General Trask, the division's deputy commander, to dinner and everyone had gotten along beautifully. Willard had described his campaign to win the best-in-division for the supply battalion and General Trask had been so impressed he asked for a detailed report on it.

By this time Amy was spending most of her days and a fair number of her evenings with Florence Eberle. She acted as her social secretary, writing invitations for her dinner parties and helping her plan menus. Florence averaged three dinner parties a week. She devoured the *Stars and Stripes* and the *Army Times* to see who was being transferred or promoted, and above all, who was coming to Nuremberg or its vicinity. She had a file with at least a thousand cards in it, each a dossier that included the names of a man's wife and children, where the Eberles had met him or his wife, their likes and dislikes, interests and background.

George and Amy were regular guests at the Eberles' dinner parties. They enjoyed showing off the battalion's resident West Pointer and his Philadelphia Main Line bride. After each party, there was a half-hour "critique" in which Amy and George were advised on how to improve their performance at the next dinner. Certain guests were more important than others. Usually they were West Pointers. Local German officials were strictly window dressing and could be ignored with impunity. Commanders of nearby supply battalions and their wives had the highest priority. A friendly neighbor shared spare parts and hard-to-obtain equipment and was understanding if one of your men had an accident or got into a brawl with one of his soldiers.

While Florence and Willard lectured, Amy found herself making a private critique of their dinners. The food was unrelentingly bland, nothing but the tired vegetables and third-rate meat sold by the commissary. Florence's silver, which she had probably inherited from her mother, was ornate nineteenth-century stuff. It looked ridiculous with her plain white PX china. The ecru lace tablecloth, also no doubt inherited from her Army parents, was another mismatch. If the dinners succeeded—and Amy wondered if any of them really deserved that level of acclaim—it was because Willard made sure the orderly poured the drinks with a heavy hand.

Amy yearned to do some entertaining on her own. But it was practically impossible in the two-room apartment the Army had issued them. George's captain invited all the company's lieutenants and their wives to a beer blast a week or so after they arrived. Amy agreed with Florence's estimate of the women as duds. They talked about their trips around Germany, obvious sightseeing like a boatride up the Rhine. Amy said she could not wait to visit Bamberg, whose Romanesque cathedral was one of the most famous in Europe. They looked blank.

Amy was also less than enchanted with the class of '50 parties that George rushed to attend in Nuremberg. There were about a dozen members of the class in and around the city. Their wives were not as relentlessly middle-class as the 310th Supply Battalion wives, but they seemed disoriented by Germany. They complained about the poor food available at the commissaries and the shoddy goods at the PX. The men talked about Korea, nothing but Korea. Everyone had letters from friends out there, telling what it was like.

At first the stories were all grim. The defensive war in the Pusan perimeter was bitter and bloody. A half dozen class of '50 graduates were killed, making Amy wonder if George had recited his statistics in Vienna merely to calm her down. Toward the end of September, however, the letters from Korea became exuberant. Douglas MacArthur had landed two divisions at Inchon, far to the north of the attacking People's Army. They slashed across the waist of the peninsula to recapture the South Korean capital of Seoul, trapping the Communists in a deadly vise. The People's Army collapsed and the war was transformed from a desperate defense to a victory-piled-on-victory offensive.

The Police Action, as President Truman called it, seemed over. George signified his abandonment of dreams of combat glory by buying a new German car, designed by the renowned Dr. Porsche. It was an odd little humpbacked thing called a Volkswagen. George said it was the best-built car in the world for its price. He insisted on paying for it with his own money—what was left of it after the honeymoon.

Then came another letter from John Stapleton.

Dear George:

As Gene Autry used to sing, I'm back in the saddle again. I hope you're singing a similar song, with a more enjoyable double entendre. I'm talking about the turret of a tank, a beautiful shiny new M-26 with a 90-millimeter cannon and a couple of machine guns. Not enough armor to take a direct hit from a T-34, but still a nice machine. Anyway, now there aren't any more T-34's. They're all rusting in ditches and gulches along the Pusan Perimeter while us old cowhands are rolling north, shooting up the poor Commies almost at will. I saw General Stratton in Seoul the other day. He says he met you in Europe and tried to get you transferred out here but your battalion CO screamed you were "essential to the success of his mission." What the hell are you doing over there in Germany, George? I bet the bastard's mission was hunting ducks and he enjoyed having an Academy type as his gun bearer. I'm not sure I'm going to like the Army without a war. Not until I make general, anyway.

Give Amy a kiss for me. Tell her I haven't seen many Korean girls worth conquering.

Best,

John

The letter made George grumpy for a week. Complaints about his recalcitrant platoon, about spending four years near the top of his

140

class at West Point and ending up as a drillmaster, filled their evenings. Amy offered him neither sympathy nor soothing advice. She was in a rotten mood herself. She blamed it on the apartment, its three claustrophobically tiny rooms, its cheap quartermaster furniture. When George came moaning in the door for the fifth consecutive night, Amy told him to grow up. He answered her in kind and they had their first fight. A night and day of icy silence followed. When George came home the following evening, Amy apologized for being so bitchy. George kissed her eagerly and said it was his fault. Amy said maybe neither was to blame.

"I think it's this rinky-dink squirrel cage," she said, gesturing contemptuously at their quarters. "I hate it. Florence thinks we should move so I can do some decent entertaining. She's appalled at the level of the social life in the battalion."

Amy had put the idea in Florence Eberle's head earlier in the day and obtained her approval. Later she had visited the office of the leading lawyer of Mautbrunnen, who had steered her to a widowed cousin with a four-room cottage for rent in the hills above the town. Amy had taken one look and put down a hundred-dollar deposit— one month's rent. She did not anticipate any problems with George. But he turned out to be dubious. He said he was uncomfortable enough, playing Eberle's tin soldier. The other officers in the battalion were barely civil to him. He was worried about making enemies who would knife him later. A move to a cottage that cost half a second lieutenant's monthly salary would only make everyone more hostile.

Amy told him he was being ridiculous. "Florence says there's only one way to do things in the Army. Put your best foot forward and keep it there. Eventually, even the second-rate people have to admit your quality."

"Florence is living in 1935. The Army's never going back to that little in-group setup, where everybody knew everybody else. It's going to stay big and get more and more impersonal. Guys can do things to you in the Pentagon or in Army headquarters that you'll never even know about."

"I don't agree with you," Amy said. "There'll always be enough of the best people, the old Army people like the Eberles, around to take care of each other. That's where we belong, by instinct, by—by inheritance.''

George lit a cigarette. "Maybe," he said.

For a moment Amy wondered if George, behind his West Point façade, was still the middle-class son of a California hardware store owner. She had assumed that West Point had made him an officer and a gentleman in every sense, above all in the assumption that he was superior to the mediocre majority. Was George wearing the aura of another West Pointer? Was it possible for some extraordinary men to cast a glow on those they chose to like? She suddenly remembered thinking that very thing while General Stratton was praising John Stapleton.

No, Amy told herself, no. She had chosen a safer, more dependable man than that wild tanker. George was still a soldier, still a man who could give orders, make men obey him. If he doubted himself, because of his background, she would give him confidence, she would sustain him. His success would be her success.

They drove out in their Volkswagen to look at the cottage she had found. As Amy expected, George found it irresistible. It was so close to Mautbrunnen, yet it had a view down the river valley past the town almost to Nuremberg. A huge stone fireplace dominated the living room. "Think of the fun we could have smooching in front of that," Amy said. The bedroom had a big double bed with a handcarved headboard full of Hansel and Gretel figures. George's opposition collapsed. They moved in the next day.

By now it was well into November. That night there was frost on the ground. George built a fire from the ample amount of wood left them by Frau Kinder, the cottage owner, and they lay in front of the blaze drinking dark beer from multicolored Bavarian steins. "Wait'll you see what I do with this place," Amy said. "We're going to get back every cent we spend on it. In terms of your career. There's no need to be afraid of being a little bit better, George. That's what a leader is, isn't he? And a leader's wife—"

"Maybe you're right," George said. "Right now the leader would like to do something to his wife that has nothing whatsoever to do with his career."

In the dancing firelight, Amy made love with honeymoon enthusiasm. She told herself she was teaching George another valuable lesson. Make me happy and I'll make you happy.

The first party Amy gave was a beer and bratwurst affair for H Company's officers and their wives. It was an unqualified success. The wives went into paroxysms of admiration over the cottage's handmade Bavarian furniture, including a genuine cuckoo clock. The men could not get enough of the bratwurst and sauerkraut. Frau Kinder had given Amy the recipe.

A few days later George was telling her that his colleagues in H Company were much more friendly and relaxed. One party had defused the envy generated by the Eberles' invitations. Amy followed up this triumph with a party for the Nuremberg contingent of the class of '50. She served *Regensburger*, a fat, heavily spiced pork sausage, and *Rauchbier*, smoked beer from Bamberg, which had a strong taste and a high alcohol content. Again, Frau Kinder had suggested the menu and it was a tremendous success. Several of the lieutenants had to be poured burping into their cars. The wives, some of whom had been rather condescending about George's assignment to a supply battalion, were stunned by the cottage. They tried to find out where Amy had learned so much about German food. She smiled, accepted their compliments, and told them nothing.

Amy immediately began planning her next party. She again turned for help to her landlady, Frau Kinder, who lived alone in a small apartment in Mautbrunnen. Her town house in Nuremberg had been destroyed, along with the rest of the city's historic center, by American air raids. She had a livid scar on her cheek from a bomb fragment. By now, Amy had learned that she was the widow of a colonel who had been killed on the Russian front. She had also lost a son, a captain, in Tunisia. When Amy expressed her sympathy, Frau Kinder had shaken her head. "They did their duty," she said. Frau Kinder introduced her to Frau Kress, the wife of a German major who had lost both legs above the knees when his tank hit a mine in Italy. Frau Kress sold Amy a set of deep green Meissen china that had been in her family for six generations. Major Kress, wasted and waxen in his wheelchair, watched the transaction with mournful eyes. Amy paid four hundred dollars in cash. The dollars were worth ten times that much on the black market.

Amy had already hired Lena, who before the war had been Frau Kinder's brawny maid of all work, to keep the cottage scrubbed to a state of cleanliness attainable only in Germany. For her next party she hired Hilda, Frau Kinder's rotund former cook. Amy wrote out invitations to Lieutenant Colonel and Mrs. Willard Eberle, Major and Mrs. Francis Casey, and Captain and Mrs. Thomas Walton. He was the commander of H Company.

They all arrived precisely at seven-thirty. Amy found it hard to get used to the way Army people arrived on time. There was no such thing as being fashionably late. Everyone admired the living room, with the fire leaping in the grate, Mozart playing softly on Amy's hi-fi.

"It's a find, a real find," Florence Eberle said.

"But how can you afford it?" Serena Casey said. "It must cost a fortune."

"Hardly. It's a bargain, thanks to the power of the dollar," Amy said.

"How much?" Florence said, in her usual blunt style.

"A hundred a month," Amy said.

"There aren't many second lieutenants who can afford that, my dear," Serena Casey said.

"Or captains either," dark-haired Grace Walton said, smiling somewhat nervously.

They could have been sisters. Both were chunky women. Serena, a redhead with a pugnacious chin and a wide, rather mean mouth, was smarter and far more sure of herself than Grace. Amy concentrated on Grace, not even looking at Serena, as she explained how unhappy she had been in the casern. "I guess I'm just not used to apartment living. Florence thought it would be nice if somebody at George's rank had room to do some entertaining."

"That's right," Florence said. "In the old Army, a second lieutenant had quarters about this size. He was expected to live like a gentleman."

"Gee," Grace said. "I kind of like the casern. But I'm used to apartment living. I grew up in the Bronx."

Florence gave her a look that consigned her to nonperson status.

There were no people from the Bronx in the officer corps of the old Army.

Serena remained hostile. She had done little riding with Florence Eberle since Amy Rosser arrived. When Hilda emerged from the kitchen with a plate of tiny frankfurters for hors d'oeuvres, Serena said she was surprised to see Amy had hired a German servant. She did not like the Germans. They were overcharging the Americans for everything. Serena found fault with the Army policy of hiring German civilians to work in the PX and commissary. They were rude and unhelpful.

"I admire the woman who owns this house," Amy said. She told them Frau Kinder's comment on the death of her husband and son.

"I wish to God we had more of that spirit in our Army," Florence said. "We would have had a lot less bugging out in Korea."

Amy smiled tensely. She had not expected her dinner party to start with a running battle. But so far she was winning it. Serena Casey scowled at her from beneath her bangs, which came down almost to her eyebrows.

The men were already talking about Korea. Lieutenant Colonel Eberle said he had gotten a letter from a West Point classmate who was commanding an infantry battalion in the 1st Cavalry Division. The North Korean Army was finished but the American commanders on the ground with the troops were worried about another army. At Unsan, on November 1, a company of the 1st Cavalry had been mauled by Chinese Communist troops. Florence Eberle said there was only one solution to that problem: the atomic bomb. Her husband agreed.

"But I don't think we'll have to go nuclear, Flo. I doubt if we'll have to drop the big one. No one's seen a Chinese soldier since that brush with them at Unsan. Not a trace of a Chink," Willard said, repeating himself in his oracular way. "Intelligence thinks Unsan was just a bluff. But it'll take more than a bluff to stop Doug MacArthur. He announced the final phase of the offensive yesterday. The troops'll be home by Christmas. What Doug MacArthur announces, Doug MacArthur does."

How does Florence stand him? Amy wondered. She said it was

time for dinner and led them into the dining room. She took a last, satisfied look at the candles glowing on her silver and her Meissen china and stepped into the kitchen for a final conference with Hilda. When she returned to the dining room, the women were seated and Willard Eberle helped her into her chair.

"Reminds me of the dinner I had with that countess in the Loire in 1944," Willard said. "Remember me writing you about it Flo? Same kind of china."

"Yes," Florence said.

"Amy doesn't have a title, I don't think," George said with a forced laugh.

Something had gone wrong and Amy did not know what it was. Hilda served the first course, a Nuremberg favorite called *Ochsenmaulsalat*, a spicy cold meat salad, touched with oil and vinegar. Florence Eberle took one bite and said: "Willard, I'd be careful of this. You know what onions do to you."

"Much too sharp for me too," Serena Casey said. "Frankly, I'll take good old American cooking anytime."

"I think it's interesting to enjoy the food of the country, like the wine," Amy said.

"My father tried that in China in 1915," Florence Eberle said. "Ate nothing but Chinese food. He was stationed in Szechuan Province, the spiciest cooking in China. He wound up with an ulcer."

The meal slid rapidly downhill. No one said a word about the wine, Monzinger, one of Germany's best. The main course, a Munich specialty known as *Kalbshaxe mit Knödel*, veal shanks with dumplings, was eaten without cavil but only Grace Walton praised it. Lieutenant Colonel Eberle seemed to enjoy the dessert, *Nürnberger Lebkuchen*, Nuremberg gingerbread, served with whipped cream.

The conversation limped. Major Casey, who shared his wife's thick neck and aggressive chin, talked of his boyhood in Iowa, where his father owned one of the state's largest dairy farms. His father wanted him to retire from the Army and take over the farm. Serena hated Iowa and wanted him to stay in the service. Florence said she hoped he would take Serena's advice. Serena began discussing the whereabouts of officers and wives who had been transferred from the battalion over the past year—a conversation which totally excluded Amy and George. Amy could not believe Florence was really interested in what these nonentities thought of Fort Hood, Texas, and which of their wives had recently given birth. But she listened with apparent fascination. She even tolerated a report on Grace Walton's transferred friends.

Immediately after coffee, the Eberles announced they were leaving. The others echoed them. Amy sat there, numb with dismay, while they trooped across the living room into the bedroom to get their coats. The men emerged and stood by the door, talking with George. The ladies were using the bathroom. Amy drifted uncertainly toward the door of the bedroom. Inside she heard Serena Casey say: "Who does she think she is? A second lieutenant's wife entertaining with that kind of silver and china."

"She's new to the Army," Florence said, halfheartedly defending her protégée. "She'll have to learn the hard way, I'm afraid."

Amy fled back to the men. She listened to Willard telling his juniors Korea would be a nice assignment once they got it thoroughly pacified. The ladies emerged from the bedroom and everyone thanked Amy for a wonderful dinner and vanished into the night. The door slammed and Amy almost wept. She paced the living room, muttering: "God! *God!*"

George asked her what was wrong. "Didn't you notice anything? During dinner?" she snapped.

"No," George said.

She told him what she had overheard Serena Casey and Florence saying in the bedroom. George sighed and put his arm around her. "Ame," he said. "I know you're only trying to do your best for me. But Serena Casey's got a point. You're rushing things. I'm a second lieutenant. The Army works by rank. You can't make the CO and his wife look bad."

She walked away from him, to stare into the fire, imagining how Johnny Stapleton would have handled Willard's remark about her china. Johnny would have made a joke out of it. *Didn't you know Amy was a countess? Her father's the Duke of Bala-Cynwyd. Everybody calls him Duke for short.* Or he would have stopped her from buying it. She would have listened to his advice, because it would have been given in language she understood. *That's too much good taste for the U. S. Army to handle, coz.*

They went to bed as soon as the cook departed. Amy shrugged away from George's tentative touch. She stared sleeplessly into the darkness for a long time, thinking about how she could be living in Japan, a far more interesting country, waiting to give Johnny a hero's reception in Tokyo for Christmas. Instead of listening to George grouse about the latest AWOL Negro private or the stupidities of some bonehead corporal from Tennessee, she could be hearing real war stories, how Johnny's cannon and machine guns had mowed down hundreds of those stupid little yellow men.

What would George do, what would everyone do if she just *left*, if he came back here from Mautbrunnen tomorrow night and found her gone, nothing but a note saying sorry it hasn't worked. Then a cable to Johnny. General Stratton or her Uncle Paul would find a way to get it to him.

IN TOKYO WAITING TO BE CONQUERED.

AMY

Dreams, dreams. She finally drifted into a shallow sleep. There the dreams were bad. Johnny was in a tank, smiling from the turret, the way the conquering Germans had ridden through Paris in the newsreels in 1941. She was standing in the road, waving to him. There were dozens of other tanks behind him. He did not seem to see her in the road. Instead of stopping, his tank gained speed. The huge cannon swung menacingly back and forth. *Stop*, she cried. But it was too late, the monster was rolling over her and he was still in the turret smilling.

"Amy. Christ. Wake up. Wait'll you hear this."

It was George. He was turning on the radio beside their bed. The radio in the kitchen was already blaring. An announcer on the Armed Forces Network was reporting in excited tones the latest news from Korea. Massive Chinese armies had attacked the Americans. The 2nd and 25th divisions were in danger of being overwhelmed along the Chongchon River. "It could be the signal for a Communist

148

attack worldwide. I'm getting down to Battalion. I'm sure we're going on general alert.''

"Isn't Johnny with the 2nd Division?" Amy asked.

"Yeah," George said.

For the next four days, everyone in the American Army in Germany listened numbly to their radios and read disbelievingly in their newspapers about the new war in Korea. China, with its millions, had attacked without warning and the Eighth Army was reeling back in disarray. On December 1, when Frau Kinder came to collect her rent, she shook her head and said: "I hope you will have no more bad news. But it is very hard to make war against such people. I remember my husband's disgust with the Russians. You killed them and killed them and there were always more of them. Asiatics are all alike."

Each night after supper George got out a map of Korea and studied the battle that was raging along the Chongchon River. He said that the 2nd Division and the 25th Division were being torn apart by Communist columns striking across the river deep into their rear, cutting off their lines of supply. Each day, Amy sat by the radio listening to the confusing repetitive reports. American planes were massacring the Chinese. The Americans were retreating. The Chinese had broken contact and were retreating to Manchuria.

George went to a briefing in Nuremberg, supposedly to get the latest inside information, direct from the Pentagon. The briefing officer, a colonel in Army Intelligence, talked for forty minutes, using maps to show the audience where Communist armies were massed, from the North Sea to the Balkans, apparently ready to strike at any moment. During the question period, George had asked: "Sir, do you have any idea what they might do, aside from what they can do?"

"Young man," the colonel had said. "I don't have a clue. Neither does anyone else."

Shopping in the commissary, Amy met Serena Casey. She was almost frantic about the Russians. Lieutenant Colonel Eberle was sending Florence to Paris. The rest of the wives were staying here, within fifty miles of six Russian armored divisions. Had Amy read what the Russians had done to the German women when they took Berlin?

With this kind of hysteria ringing in her ears, Amy drove home to the cottage on the hill. There she found a letter slipped under the door. It was from Florence Eberle. It began by thanking her for the delicious dinner the other night. She was off to Paris for a few days' shopping. She had wanted to take Amy with her but Willard thought it might have a bad effect on morale. However, if Amy decided to join her, she would be at the George V.

Still in the club, Amy thought. But did she want to be in the club? In this supposedly all-powerful, all-victorious Army that let ignorant Chinese walk all over them? An Army with intelligence officers who did not have a clue?

That night, Amy had a different kind of dream. It was snowing and she was walking across a battlefield where an army had suffered a terrible defeat. She was wearing nothing but her nightgown and a blanket which she clutched around her shoulders. Past wrecked tanks and trucks and jeeps she trudged, with dead men lying everywhere. There was not a sound, not even the sigh of the wind. It was terrifying.

The next morning, Frau Kinder appeared with her sad scarred face, her gray hair in the usual efficient bun. "May I ask you a favor?" she said. "This is the sixth anniversary of my husband's death. We spent our honeymoon in this cottage. Would you let me spend an hour here with my memories?"

Amy was glad to escape the cottage. She drove to Mautbrunnen, wondering if she had somehow picked up some echo of death and disaster that belonged to the cottage, to all of Germany. Surely that was the wreckage of a defeated German army that she had passed in the night. In Mautbrunnen, she drove around aimlessly. She passed the barracks and nearby headquarters of George's company. He was coming out the door of the gray stone building with the saddest expression on his face. She stopped and beeped her horn at him. He walked toward her, head bowed, like a man at a funeral.

She knew. She knew before he spoke. "Ame," he said. "I was just talking on the phone to a guy from the class of '49 in Nuremberg. He just got word from the Pentagon that Johnny's dead. He was supporting an infantry company on the Chongchon. The

Chinese started to cut them off and the infantry bugged out. Johnny stayed to hold the road and cover their retreat. He finally ran out of ammunition and they got him with a satchel charge.''

What was a satchel charge? She didn't know, she didn't care. All their special languages became hateful to her. The special ways they said things to avoid saying the brutal truth, that they killed people and people killed them. She realized she had been shaking her head back and forth, saying no, no, from the moment George began talking. Tears streamed down her face.

"There were two tanks with him. They bugged out too. I wish I'd been there. Maybe I could have helped.''

Yes, why weren't you? Amy thought. Maybe you would have died instead of him. But she knew that was stupid. They would both be dead. Maybe that would be easier, all the same. She did not think she could ever let this man touch her again. Poor George. She was like those tyrant kings and queens who executed the messenger who brought the bad news. With a gasp of anguish, she slammed the Volkswagen into first gear and drove wildly back to the cottage, passing Army trucks on hills and curves, daring death to take her too. The road was a blur. Only luck kept her alive. At the cottage, she blundered into the living room to find Frau Kinder putting on her coat.

Amy stared into her proud ruined face and thought: *I am like you now. A widow too.* But a widow who was forbidden to mourn, who could only grieve in secret. Frau Kinder noticed her tears but was too polite to ask what was the matter. She probably thought it was a lovers' quarrel between the lieutenant and his bride.

Where would she go to mourn? Amy wondered as Frau Kinder departed. What were her memories, her shrine? The front seat of her Chrysler coupe? The rank rooms of New York's side-street hotels? The whispered words on the Stapleton farm: *Would you like a little education, cousin Amy?* That reckless smile, the feel of him, the sense of his animal power.

Amy saw how she had lied to herself, how she had concealed her secret hope that somewhere, in Hawaii or Texas or Japan or Paris, she and John would meet again and love again, freely, wildly behind the façade of her marriage. No, more than a façade, a refuge to which she could again retreat to escape him when fear of him outran desire. Secretly hoping that this would not happen the next time. Secretly dreaming that by then the Army would have somehow tamed or refined him or inspired him with a wish to meet her, not merely to fuck her. To meet her as his beloved, proud and confident and trusting. Oh.

Now she knew what army she had passed in the cold silent darkness of her dream. She looked out the window. Snow was falling. Six thousand miles away, it was also falling on the shallow icy river with the meaningless name Chongchon. On its banks stood an American tank, its sides blackened by flame and explosion. Around the tank lay the bodies of dozens of Chinese in their padded uniforms. Behind the tank, she was soon to learn, lay a trail of other tanks and trucks and jeeps containing thousands of dead Americans. An American army had met bloody defeat in North Korea. There were many mourners like her, groping the wreckage for broken hopes.

III

"On Christmas Day?" Joanna said. "A telegram on Christmas Day?"

Her father looked like he was going to collapse. He was remembering another telegram from Washington, six years ago.

"Open it," her mother said.

They were in the living room, dominated by the eight-foot Christmas tree, decorated with old-fashioned ornaments the Sigel family had brought from Germany a hundred years ago. Joanna ripped open the yellow envelope with the malicious rectangular eye and unfolded the telegram. Nausea surged in her bulging stomach. The world had become as misshapen as she was.

THE SECRETARY OF THE ARMY HAS ASKED ME TO EXPRESS HIS
DEEP REGRET THAT YOUR HUSBAND, FIRST LIEUTENANT PETER

M. BURKE, HAS BEEN WOUNDED IN KOREA ON DEC. 20, 1950, AS A RESULT OF HOSTILE ACTION. A CONFIRMING LETTER FOLLOWS.

WILLIAM E. HANNEGEN
MAJ. GEN., U. S. ARMY
ACTING, THE ADJUTANT
GENERAL

Joanna passed it to her mother, who read it aloud to her father.

"Thank God," he whispered. "He's only wounded. I don't think I could have stood it if—"

"Why don't they tell you how badly he's wounded?" Joanna said.

"They may not know," her mother said with her usual common sense.

"Maybe I should cable Adam Thayer. I had a letter from his wife only yesterday."

Honor's letter had been full of offhand chatter about how interesting Japan was, how much fun she and Adam were having in Koke-Do, a resort town near Kyoto. The letter had seemed unreal. It was hard to believe it came from the same part of the world that had meant nothing but anguish to Joanna for the past five months. Adam had gotten into the airborne, but the Army had decided paratroopers were too valuable to use as infantry, so they were holding them in reserve in Japan. Just wait, Joanna had thought. Just wait until he goes into combat. Then you won't be so offhand.

She had reproached herself for such a mean-spirited reaction. Just because Honor had not lamented the war did not mean she was free from worry. An Army wife kept her fears to herself and smiled in public.

The phone rang. Joanna realized she had been sitting beside it for several minutes, thinking these dismal thoughts. She picked it up and a long-distance operator said she had a call for Mrs. Peter Burke from Tokyo. In a moment Adam Thayer's voice crackled faintly across eight thousand miles. "Joanna? I'd say Merry Christmas but it's not very merry out here. I'm calling about Pete. He's been wounded."

"I know. I just got the telegram from the Pentagon."

"Those idiots sent you a telegram on Christmas Day? When we take over that place, I'm going to have a special firing squad set up to execute dodo bureaucrats. I just saw Pete. He's in Gorgas Hospital in Yokoshima, about forty miles from here. He's in pretty bad shape. But they say he'll make it. I told the big lug he can't die on us. He's got the DSC, which means he's a guaranteed general."

"Where is he wounded?"

"Mostly in the chest. He got hit about six times charging a Chinese machine gun that was blocking No Name Pass, the escape route for the whole 2nd Division. The general and a flock of colonels were watching down on the road. Big Peter couldn't have had a better audience. He took out the gun with a grenade and bayoneted six or seven Chinks who were trying to protect it. A whole Chink company decided they were fighting Superman and took off. It opened the pass for a good third of the division. Unfortunately, the Chinks came back and closed it an hour later. They've wiped out half the 2nd Division. It's unbelievable, MacArthur's stupidity—"

"What should I do, Adam? Should I come out there? Or will they send him back here?"

"They're not going to move him. I think it would help if you came out. He started giving a farewell message to you. He's that low. He acts like he lost the goddamn battle instead of MacArthur, sitting on his fanny back here in Tokyo babbling about home by Christmas while the Chinese moved a whole army around his flanks."

"Where could I live?"

"You can't get quarters on an Army base. But you can live on the economy for practically nothing. The exchange rate—the black-market one, not the legal one—is incredibly in our favor. How pregnant are you?

"Six months."

"Didn't waste any time, did you? Does the Pope give out medals? I'd say you rate at least a Bronze Star."

"Can you meet me at the airport? I'll cable you—"

"I'm afraid not. We're stationed about nine hundred miles south of here, at the other end of the country. But I'll find somebody to take care of you, if I have to go all the way to Doug himself."

Unreal but this was reality. Unreal. The words kept repeating themselves in Joanna's mind as she flew west, in spite of her father's frowns, her mother's protestations. America had become unreal in the last five months. America went about its business, oblivious to the war in Korea. Twenty million people watched Ezzard Charles defeat Joe Louis on television. The down-to-the-wire pennant race between the Dodgers and the Phillies created a national frenzy, and there was almost as much excitement when Purdue's football team defeated Notre Dame and Army lost to Navy, ending two famous winning streaks. Everyone was buying TV sets. People discussed Faye Emerson's cleavage, Milton Berle's latest antics, far more often than they mentioned the war. Car sales boomed and so did Las Vegas, Nevada. *Life* magazine ran a picture of the 400 repulsive people, the 63,000 silver dollars, $300,000 in chips and tokens, the dozens of packs of playing cards required to operate a casino for a single night.

America's indifference intensified the feverish interest with which Joanna followed the war. To an amazing degree it erased all the negativities, the doubts and hesitation, she had felt about being an Army wife. The pregnancy, the sense of carrying Pete's child also helped. But the war was the major catalyst. She clipped articles about it and pasted them into a scrapbook which Pete and his son (she was sure the baby was a boy) would read in future years. She underlined and circled references to the 9th Regiment of the 2nd Division, to which Pete had been assigned. Above all, she waited for his letters. The first one arrived the day after Labor Day.

Dearest Joanna:

We had some trouble last night. I lost my first sergeant and about twenty men in my platoon. The men are pretty shaky. This is some country. It's as hot as Kansas and the smell that comes out of the rice paddies is unbelievable. They put night soil into them. I hope you're feeling better. Regards to your folks.

Love,
Pete

Joanna was enormously disappointed. She had made him promise to write her every day, imagining the letters would give her a sense of being with him, of knowing and feeling the fury and savagery of battle, the fatigue of marching and countermarching. Succeeding letters were equally brief and vague. They followed a formula. Comments on the weather, references to "trouble" or "quite a brawl" or "a rough time" in the previous days or nights. A hope that she was feeling better. Regards to her folks. Only once did he add a comment that was even slightly personal. "I'm in luck. Lover MacKenzie's commanding a platoon on my right and Sam Hardin's on my left. Sam's really great. A born fighter."

The letters baffled her. Could this man be experiencing the same war the correspondents wrote about, ambushes by treacherous Communists disguised as civilians, human-wave assaults by an enemy to whom life was cheap, panicky American troops who bugged out and left their officers behind to die? She dutifully pasted each of Pete's letters into the scrapbook, but they were dead spots, vacuums of non-information in her history of America's so-called Police Action in Korea.

In her daily letters, Joanna sent Pete news of West Point classmates, which she gleaned from corresponding with Honor Thayer, Amy Rosser, Martha MacKenzie, and from reading the class of '50's newsletter in *Assembly*, West Point's alumni magazine. Occasionally she hinted that she wished his letters told her more about what was happening to him. A week later she got a reply that told her more than she wanted to hear.

> Dearest Joanna:
>
> I've got some terrible news to tell you. Lover MacKenzie was killed last night. I think I mentioned that he was commanding a platoon in the next company. They got overrun in the dark. We counterattacked at dawn and drove the enemy back. We found Lover and a half dozen other men dead. Be sure to write Martha a letter. Tell her how sorry I am.
>
> Love,
> Pete

She had just received a cheerful letter from Martha, full of jokes about the "future cadet." Martha was staying with her family at Fort McNair in Washington, D.C. Impulsively, Joanna had telephoned instead of writing. A mistake. Martha had just received the telegram from the Pentagon. Trying to be a general's daughter, she thanked Joanna and said something about knowing the risks. Then she broke down and sobbed: "Oh Jesus, Jo, I wish I'd done it your way, had a baby, something to hold, something to remember him by, besides a couple of snapshots."

It had made Joanna feel acutely guilty because she wished she was not pregnant. At least five times a day she wished it, sometimes in anger, sometimes in disgust. Her nausea had subsided to the first half hour of each morning. But the daily retching left her feeling exhausted and depressed for several hours. She disliked everything about her pregnancy, from the doctors who poked and peered into her vagina and lectured her about holding down her weight to the way it made her an object of her mother's solicitude, a kind of grown child.

The pregnancy—or was it simply being married?—seemed to alter the shape of her mind as well as her body. For the first time she found herself resisting her mother's opinions and decisions—with unpleasant consequences. They began by arguing over whether Joanna's morning sickness was mostly imagination, a bad habit which she could overcome with a little willpower. Mother had never been sick a day with her pregnancies. Then came the shock (to Mother) of discovering that Joanna had bought her own maternity clothes with no prior consultation. The final really violent disagreement had come when Joanna announced she was going to Japan. Her father and sister Beth dutifully agreed with Mother, as usual. But Joanna resisted them all. In her mind, Pete's courage became a sort of metaphor from which she borrowed strength.

On the day she bought her plane ticket, Joanna had driven to her father's showroom and asked him how much he would give her for their 1947 Ford. "How about fifteen hundred?" he said.

"That's four times what it's worth. I don't want charity—"

"Look. I want you to get out there to see Pete. I haven't said anything at home. I decided a long time ago it was better to have peace than argue with your mother. She never quits.''

It was a stunning glimpse into her parents' marriage. For the first time Joanna saw weakness on her father's handsome face. She understood what it had cost this mailman's son from Cincinnati's West Side to marry his strong-willed German heiress. Had she been subconsciously looking for a different man, for strength, when she chose Pete?

From California, a Pan American Strato Clipper flew Joanna west to Hawaii, nine exhausting hours. They landed at dusk and she got little more than a murky glimpse of Diamond Head, Waikiki, and the other pleasures and panoramas she would have been enjoying if war had not exploded in Korea. The next day, after a restless sleep in a motel near the airport, she flew west again to Wake Island, Guam, and Manila. Again she saw little beyond the airport perimeters. She was too tired to do any sightseeing and the airline did not encourage it, apparently working on the assumption that all passengers were morons in danger of missing their planes. From Manila, the following day, it was another nine brutal hours to Tokyo.

Between meals and snacks and dozing, Joanna read the most talked about novel of the year, Ernest Hemingway's *Across the River and into the Trees*. She found it a hateful, appalling book. The central character, Colonel Cantwell, with his totally amoral attitude toward the world, his utter indifference to whom he killed and why, outraged her. This was not a portrait of the professional American soldier, imbued with the ideals of West Point. Cantwell was an aberration, a nihilistic monster.

Joanna finally abandoned Hemingway for her scrapbook. Page after page, she reread the agonizing story of the last six months in Korea, studded with Pete's brief, frustrating letters. Not even his promotion to first lieutenant early in November, his appointment as executive officer of the company, his promotion to company commander when his captain collapsed with pneumonia in North Korea, evoked any emotion. They were reported in the same flat monosyllabic style, with the same closing line: "Hope you're feeling better. Regards to your folks."

In her outrage against Hemingway, Joanna vowed that as Pete recovered from his wounds (and he would recover, she had perfect faith, she whispered to God) she would persuade him to tell her everything that had happened to him. Perhaps, if he told her enough, it might make a book. Her literary ability and his heroism would create a monument. The wish was intensified by her growing confidence as a poet. By imitating a dozen different poetic styles, she had begun to forge one of her own. But she had not yet written anything worth publishing. Her poems lacked intensity, hard, felt images from experience. Perhaps by sharing Pete's life, his heroism and suffering, she would find them.

Joanna's ears began to ache. They were losing altitude. The pilot told them to fasten their seat belts, they would be landing at Tokyo's Haneda Airport in fifteen minutes. Soon she was looking down on the charcoal-gray and dark green landscape of Japan, the gateway to the strange Oriental world that had almost killed her husband. Joanna felt anxiety prowl her flesh. What if Pete was some kind of basket case? What if Adam had not had the courage to tell her the truth?

No, if there was one thing Adam did consistently, even dangerously, it was tell the truth. Joanna found herself hoping he would be there at the arrival gate, in spite of what he had said about being stationed nine hundred miles away. She felt in need of a friendly face.

Adam had cabled her that she would be met by a familiar name, if not a face. He had discovered Ruth Parrott Hardin's mother working as a volunteer at Gorgas Hospital. Ruth's father had been promoted from sergeant to captain and was stationed at a nearby replacement center. But there was no sign of Mrs. Parrott at the arrival gate. Husbands greeted a dozen other wives on the flight and rushed off to the baggage-retrieval area, leaving Joanna standing alone, feeling grotesque and betrayed. Two military policemen strolled past, big mean-looking men wearing white helmets and billy clubs dangling from their belts. She asked them for help. Their policemen's glares vanished. They seemed delighted by the opportunity to help an Army wife in distress. One MP went to get her baggage while the other escorted Joanna to their airport office, where a fat red-faced sergeant named Kennedy telephoned Gorgas Hospital. Mrs. Parrott was nowhere to be found. Sergeant Kennedy, who had a sleeveful of hash marks, denoting twenty-two years in the Army, meditated. "Can't leave this young woman wanderin' around this airport and can't drive her clear to Yokoshima," he said. "Gettin' dark outside already. How'd you like to spend the night at a Japanese inn?"

Joanna said that any place with a bed would suit her. The sergeant explained that Japanese inns did not have any beds, which sometimes disconcerted Americans. Joanna assured him that she could sleep on a bare floor if necessary.

In twenty minutes she was in a jeep with a canvas top, driven by a Negro MP. She shivered as the damp penetrating cold of Japan in January seeped into the vehicle. Soon they were rolling through a densely populated district on Tokyo's outskirts. The houses were little more than shanties, many of them open to the street. In a surprising number of them, Japanese girls wearing American dresses slouched invitingly.

"Is this what I think it is?" she asked.

"You mean a red-light district, ma'am?"

"Yes."

"They got thirteen of them just like this one. Lot of people gettin' rich over here, ma'am."

The Japanese inn was on a quiet road about a mile beyond the red-light district. Joanna was met in the lobby by the smiling proprietor in a business suit and a young girl in a kimono. They bowed and helped her put on a pair of soft slippers and led her down corridors of polished wood to her room. She was charmed by its elegant simplicity. The sliding door was decorated with a gold leaf and watercolor landscape. The floor was covered with clean matting. In a small alcove hung a pictorial scroll behind a vase of flowers. The bathroom was a less pleasant discovery. The toilet was a hole in the floor. Joanna needed to use it. By the time she finished, she was sure she had ruptured something. The baby's weight added additional strain to muscles unaccustomed to squatting.

In the bedroom the maid offered her a thickly padded kimono. Another maid appeared with tea and delicious cakes of various sizes. She asked Joanna when she wished to have her bath and eat dinner. To her hostesses' evident dismay Joanna said she was so tired she preferred to go to bed immediately. They spread a heavy quilt on the floor, put a pillow stuffed with some sort of grain on it and bid her a polite good-night. Joanna lay down on the quilt, curled up on her side and fell asleep almost instantly.

Several hours later, she was awakened by a chaos of shouts, screams and crashes. Most of the voices were American. They came toward her down the corridor. A hand flung open the sliding door and four soldiers and three Japanese girls in cheap rayon dresses peered at her.

"Aw hell, this one's taken," said the tallest of the soldiers.

"Maybe she'd like to join the fun," said the soldier next to him. His arm curled around one of the Japanese girls and his hand cupped her breast.

The proprietor of the inn came running down the hall in his bare feet, his shirt outside his trousers. He threw himself in front of the door. "Gentlemen, you must leave immediately. This lady is wife of an officer in your Army."

"Well, big deal, Tojo," said the tall soldier. He punched the innkeeper in the face and sent him hurtling into Joanna's room. He lay on his back, groaning.

Another half dozen soldiers appeared in the hall with more Japanese girls. "Listen, we ain't got all day. The MP's are gonna be lookin' for that truck," one of them yelled. "Let's get our pussy and split."

They surged down the hall and threw other guests out of their rooms. All were Japanese men and they got beaten up when they resisted. The innkeeper herded them into Joanna's room and spoke to them in Japanese. They bowed and smiled painfully at Joanna while she clutched her kimono about her. "Military police coming soon," the innkeeper explained in English. "I have special telephone to them."

For the next ten minutes drunken shouts and whoops resounded through the inn. Then came the crash of heavy boots in the hallway. Sergeant Kennedy and a dozen of his brawny assistants glared at Joanna and the frightened Japanese. "Where are they?" he growled.

The innkeeper pointed down the hall. Soon more chaos erupted; shouts, curses, cries of pain. Several of the invaders were dragged past Joanna's door semi-conscious. The girls, some of them still pulling on their dresses, were herded down the hall after them. The sergeant came to the door to apologize. "Them boys are goin' back to Korea tomorrow. They're bringin'm over here for five days' rest and recreation. Causin' us all kinds of trouble."

Joanna slept fitfully for the rest of the night. She was still dozing the next morning when a hand rapped urgently on her door. Joanna opened it and confronted a beefy woman with a small pursed mouth and button nose. She wore an old black cloth coat, frayed at the sleeves, and ugly black shoes. She looked like a prison matron. "Mrs. Burke? I'm Betty Parrott," she said.

"Oh yes. I guess there was some mix-up."

"No mix-up. I told that wise guy second lieutenant friend of yours it was a long ride from Yokoshima to that airport and I was drivin' a car that might break down and he should tell you to be prepared to cope with bein' on your own for the night. I also told him it was ridiculous to have you comin' out here six months pregnant to see a man you can do nothin' for. Becomin' one more headache for the Army in Japan. As if we don't have enough. I told my daughter Ruth to stay home until she's guaranteed official quarters on a base. I told her West Pointers and their wives don't have any special privileges in the Army. You better get that through your head, fast."

Joanna nodded numbly at this diatribe until the implication of the remark about Pete penetrated her sleep-fogged brain. "You mean Pete is so badly hurt that—that—"

"He's not a vegetable if that's what you mean," Mrs. Parrott said. "But he might as well be one. He's in a funk. Never talks to anyone. Seems to think he's responsible for losin' the war. Maybe he's just shocked to learn West Pointers can get shot like anyone else."

Joanna had never met anyone like Betty Parrott. She emanated hostility and a warped authority. Briskly barking orders, she had Joanna flinging on her clothes, hurling toilet articles into her suitcase, agreeing to skip breakfast so they could get on the road without delay. As they drove through Tokyo, Joanna tried to make polite conversation by asking about Ruth. This only triggered another diatribe. Ruth was in San Francisco, alone and miserable, living in a furnished room. "I told her she was nuts to marry an Army man and especially nuts to go for that yo-yo from Texas, with no connections. What's his father? A ranch hand, for God's sake. If you want proof he's got no brains, I just heard he's gonna extend his tour in Korea. Spend another six months tryin' to get killed."

Joanna dropped Ruth as a topic. By now, they were rolling down Tokyo's main shopping street, the Ginza. Joanna was amazed by the flourishing department stores and the huge office buildings, with exotic Shinto shrines on their roofs. She remarked that not as much of the city had been destroyed by American air raids as she had been led to believe.

"Personally I wish the whole damn country had been flattened and kept that way for a hundred years," Mrs. Parrott said. "My brother was killed on Bataan. In the Death March."

That topic too seemed exhausted. Joanna waited for several minutes, hoping Mrs. Parrott would propose another subject. She did not say a word. "I heard your husband's been promoted," Joanna said.

Mrs. Parrott snorted. "He made captain during the war. Then came the big RIF. They broke him back to sergeant. That's what he was when we were at West Point. Now they've promoted him to captain again."

"What's a RIF?" Joanna asked.

"Reduction In Force. You don't have to worry about it. West Pointers don't get riffed. Not back to sergeant, anyway. After the war there were too many officers. So they gave everyone the choice of getting out or going back to their old ranks, if they wanted to hang on to their pensions. Now the Army's in hot water in Korea and they need officers again. So presto, they're handing out commissions. When this thing finishes they'll pull the same crap."

Most of the traffic on the road was Army vehicles. Mrs. Parrott seemed to feel she had the authority to pass them at will. She blasted her horn and roared around them on the narrow two-lane highway. Meanwhile she denounced the generals running the Army as a pack of frauds and fools. The biggest of them was "Dugout Doug," as she called MacArthur, the hero who had deserted his troops on

Bataan. "If it wasn't costing so many men, I'd be cheering the mess he's making of Korea," she said.

Between fear of sudden death beneath a truck's wheels and bafflement at Mrs. Parrott's attitude, Joanna felt dazed by the time they reached the Gorgas Army Hospital outside the city of Yokoshima, about forty miles south of Tokyo. Her escort led her briskly into the big rectangular building. An elevator took them to the third floor, where they entered a ward that seemed a half-mile long.

Everything was white and very still. "All critical cases at this end," Mrs. Parrott said. They walked past beds where men lay motionless. Many had tubes up their nostrils or attached to their arms. Bottles of plasma or clear liquid dripped above them. Smashed arms, legs, were rigged on pulleys. Bandages covered half, sometimes a whole face. About halfway down the ward, things changed. Several men were sitting up, propped by pillows. A balding man who looked as old as Joanna's father was reading a magazine. In the next bed she saw Pete.

His left arm was in a cast. There was a small bandage on the right side of his throat and a huge swath of white gauze on his chest. He was unbelievably gaunt. All surplus flesh had vanished from his face. Worst of all was his expression. It was unutterably sad.

"Jo," he said, "Jo."

She started to put her arms around him. Mrs. Parrott caught her coat. "Don't lean on him," she said. "He's got a very serious thoracic wound. They had to take out a rib and a section of his left lung."

Joanna picked up Pete's right hand, which was limp and cold. She pressed it to her face and started to cry. "Now that isn't going to do him any good," Mrs. Parrott said.

"Betty," said the balding man in the next bed. "Why don't you just draw the curtains around Captain Burke's bed and get the hell out of here?"

He had one of those craggy, classically American faces, a cross between Gary Cooper and Randolph Scott, without their stoic caution. His smile was rakish and uncomplicated. Before his hairline receded, he must have been a handsome daredevil. He reminded Joanna of someone. Who? She did not have time to think about it.

Betty Parrott drew the curtains around the bed and sulkily told Joanna she would be downstairs in the volunteers' lounge.

In semi-privacy, Joanna managed to kiss Pete without leaning on him. His lips seemed cold, inert, like his hand. "Did I hear you being called captain?" she said.

"Yeah," he said. "They promoted me again. Tomorrow, Mac himself is coming down to decorate me. Adam went to the Dai Ichi Building—that's Supreme Headquarters—in Tokyo and reminded one of the Five Oh guys on staff there that MacArthur was my middle name. He bucked it to the PIO flacks and they decided it was great publicity for the general when he needs it most."

His voice was soft, empty. She was baffled, frightened by this different man confronting her. "Are you—in pain?"

"No."

"It seems to me you ought to be more excited. Happy. I mean—I am. I'm so proud of you."

He shook his head. "Don't say that, Jo. You shouldn't be proud of me. Nobody should. I don't deserve a medal. I wish I could refuse it."

"Why do you feel that way? Adam told me what you did. Saved half of the division. You—"

He just stared at her. Her voice trailed away.

"I lost my company, Jo. My whole company. My first command. I lost them. They're all dead. I should be too."

"But was it your fault? It must have happened to other companies. I read the papers. I kept a scrapbook. The Chinese took you by surprise. The whole Army."

"But it was my *command*, Jo. My responsibility. I made a promise to those guys. If they stood and fought, they'd get help if they were wounded. I'd get them out, no matter what. I'd never leave one of them behind. They believed me. Now they're all dead."

For Joanna it was simultaneously frightening and exalting. He was telling her this, sharing his pain with her, pain he could reveal to no one else. "Darling, darling," she said, pressing his hand to her lips again. "It wasn't your fault."

She started to tell him what Adam had said about MacArthur

being an idiot. Pete shook his head. He became violently angry. "That's the wrong attitude," he said. "I told Supe that when he came up here. There's only one way to act if you're a professional soldier. Shut your mouth. Dig in, build up, and wait for a chance to even the score."

Joanna found herself recoiling from these grim words. She preferred the other husband, the one who had reached out to her for sympathy, forgiveness. Could the two men be inhabiting the same body?

The next day, Joanna got her first glimpse of Army panoply and the frenzy that a visit from a famous general can inspire. She had spent the night in a minimally furnished room in a barracks-like nurses' quarters on the grounds of a nearby Army base. A short pop-eyed first lieutenant knocked on her door at 8 A.M. and handed her several sheets of paper. One was a schedule for General MacArthur's visit. Every moment was carefully blocked out.

1130 HOURS	GENERAL MACARTHUR ARRIVES
1135 HOURS	RECEPTION IN CENTRAL LOBBY
1140 HOURS	REMARKS TO PRESS AND STAFF
1145 HOURS	TOUR OF EM WARD #11
1200 HOURS	TOUR OF OFFICERS' WARD #14
1215 HOURS	AWARDING OF DSC TO CAPTAIN BURKE
1230 HOURS	DEPARTURE

A second sheet, from the major in charge of information at the hospital, instructed her to be at Captain Burke's bedside no later than 1130 hours. This meant she could not see the general arrive, or join in the reception in the lobby. Joanna was irked. They apparently considered women idiots who could not get anywhere on time. She decided to be disobedient.

Precisely at 1130 hours a helicopter clattered to rest on the hospital lawn. General and Mrs. MacArthur, both smiling, emanating an assurance Joanna doubted she could ever attain, entered the lobby, followed by at least a dozen officers and press aides. The hospital staff was drawn up in ranks, nurses and doctors on one side, enlisted corpsmen on the opposite side of the big lobby. Everyone was wearing crisp, freshly pressed uniforms. At the back of the lobby, in gray volunteer uniforms, stood several ranks of Army wives. Betty Parrott was in the first row. Joanna stood behind the doctors. She heard one of them say: "This is ridiculous. We should be upstairs operating. I heard they had a thousand casualties yesterday."

General MacArthur shook hands with the spare gray-haired commander of the hospital, a brigadier general, introduced Mrs. MacArthur and his aides and then walked to the microphone. He said he was here not to inspect but to congratulate everyone for the superb job they had been doing, under terrible pressure. He wished he could meet and thank each of them personally. Then, in a more somber voice, he said that the Eighth Army had been attacked without warning by a vicious and powerful adversary but he hoped, before long, to make the Chinese Communists regret it.

The commander of the hospital now motioned Betty Parrott from the ranks of the volunteers to introduce her to MacArthur. "She's going to join us for your tour of the wards, General," he said. "She's one of our most faithful volunteers and a MacArthur supporter from way back. Her brother was on Bataan."

Smiling greedily, Mrs. Parrott shook hands with the man she had been condemning to Joanna yesterday. She all but bowed to Mrs. MacArthur. The general and his entourage departed for the enlisted men's ward. The first lieutenant who had delivered the day's schedule to Joanna rushed up to her. "Mrs. Burke," he said, "you were told to be upstairs with your husband at eleven-thirty hours. The general will be there in less than thirty minutes."

"It'll only take me two minutes to get upstairs in the elevator," Joanna said.

"That's not the point," the lieutenant said. "You should do what you're told. You're not entitled to ignore orders just because your husband's getting a medal. We hand out a couple of dozen medals a month around here."

Joanna was hurt, baffled, angry. She was only beginning to discover that competition and its unlovely concomitants, envy and hostility, were as endemic within the American Army as they were outside it.

On the third floor, Pete was sitting almost upright in bed, propped by two extra pillows. He was wearing clean pajamas and a dark blue robe. He told her that a barber had given him a shave and haircut. They had moved the men and beds on either side of him to make room for the award ceremony. Pete looked glum, as if he were still thinking about refusing the medal.

General MacArthur and his party appeared precisely on schedule. He stopped and spoke briefly to a half dozen other wounded men as they moved down the ward. At Pete's bed things were much more ceremonial. The entourage flowed around the hero. Flashbulbs popped as General and Mrs. MacArthur shook hands with Pete and Joanna and congratulated them. The general asked Pete what rank his father had had in the World War I Rainbow Division.

"Sergeant, sir."

The general nodded, smiling. "The Rainbow will always be my first love," he said. "I learned about war with those men. I remember the night my father's dearest friend, General Summerall, came into my command post in the Argonne and told me that he wanted the Côte de Châtillon the following day or a report of five thousand casualties. I told them the Rainbow would take that hill or he could report every man in it as a casualty. And my name would be at the head of the list. We took it. I gave out a dozen of these medals afterward. Most of them were posthumous."

Joanna wondered if it was possible to love a division. Wasn't the general really in love with his own glory? Or was it a kind of melancholy gratitude to the men who had died at his command? She shivered, gazing at MacArthur's lined, resolute face, and compared him with modest, smiling General Harmon Strong at Fort Ripley. It was hard to imagine MacArthur taking his wife home for a nap. Or Mrs. MacArthur, as erect and determined-looking as the general, ever needing one.

Far more than Eisenhower or Patton or any other World War II leader, MacArthur had been the prototype of a general to Joanna. Face to face, she was somewhat disappointed to discover he looked old. The backs of his hands were covered with liver spots. His one or two remaining hairs lay limp and lonely on his bald head. He had a decidedly visible old man's paunch.

An aide handed General MacArthur the citation and the medal. He read the citation in his most sonorous tone. It described the action in detail, adding generous words of praise, such as "in complete disregard of his own safety" and "demonstrated the highest standards of leadership and personal courage." The general pinned the medal to Pete's robe. It was a bronze cross with an eagle in the center. Below the eagle was a scroll with the inscription: "For Valor."

It was 1225 hours. The general shook hands again. Mrs. MacArthur asked Joanna where she was living. "I don't know," Joanna said. "I just arrived."

The general turned to Mrs. Parrott. "I want this young woman to have the best accommodations available. Officially, we are not encouraging wives to come out here. But the Army is always ready to make exceptions."

Mrs. Parrott agreed heartily, eating still more of her words of yesterday. She assured the general that she would personally supervise getting Mrs. Burke settled. The MacArthurs departed. Within five minutes, the clatter of their ascending helicopter passed over the hospital. Joanna smiled at Pete. All her irritation at the Army's rigid ways and officious people had vanished. Now she knew only one emotion: pride.

The next day Pete announced that he wanted to get out of bed. The doctors allowed him to put his feet over the side. The following day he stood up and walked a few steps on Joanna's arm. Soon he was striding the ward, taking physical therapy in the hospital's gym. The balding man in the next bed, who had gotten rid of Betty Parrott on the first day, gave Joanna all the credit. "Before you got here, he spent most of his time brooding about his lost company. I told him I lost a whole regiment on Bataan. But he wouldn't listen to me or anybody else."

Pete introduced Joanna to Colonel Arnold Coulter. He was the father of Rodwell Coulter, the West Point tactical officer who had verified Pete's refusal of the Cadillac convertible. Joanna was vaguely disappointed to learn that Pete had shared with others his anguish about losing his company. But the smiles he gave her each time she visited, the eagerness with which he asked her about the baby's signs of life, enabled her to brush aside this wayward emotion. As Pete convalesced, she hoped that he would tell her more—everything—about his five months under fire in Korea, sharing the pain, the sadness, as men around him died and others suffered terrible wounds. She wanted to know, to understand what sustained him, what he thought and felt from day to day. Although she said nothing to him about a book, she still secretly hoped she would write one out of his memories. If anything, the medal ceremony had sharpened this wish.

Pete refused to talk about it.

"What was it like, fighting on the defensive around Pusan?" she would ask.

"Hot," he would say. "Hot and messy."

"Were the casualties as heavy as they said they were?"

"Yeah."

She tried to get him to describe the battle with the Chinese on the Chongchon, and the chaotic retreat. "Cold. Cold and messy. The details aren't worth remembering, Jo," was his answer.

"As far as I'm concerned, everything that happened to you is worth remembering."

He took her hand. They were sitting in the pavilion at the end of the ward. "I wish that was true, Jo."

Gradually, Joanna became aware of the silences that engulfed them. They did not seem to trouble Pete in the least. She could not abide them. She struggled to fill them by talking about her growing interest in Japan and things Japanese. Adam Thayer was largely responsible for her enthusiasm.

Adam had called several times in the first few weeks to get the latest word on Pete. After Joanna told him the recovery was on schedule, and exchanged an equally brief inquiry-and-answer about Honor, they talked about the Japanese. Adam thought they were a fascinating people. He called them the Yankees of the Orient. To understand them, he insisted that she had to study Buddhism, above all, Zen Buddhism. He shipped Joanna books on both subjects as well as translations of Japanese poetry rooted in the Zen tradition.

For Joanna, Buddhism was an emotional and intellectual shock. For the first time she discovered the narrowness of her Catholic education. No one in sixteen years of Catholic schools had so much as hinted at the existence of this tremendous spiritual enterprise, begun when Gautama Siddartha became Buddha (the Enlightened One) beneath a giant fig tree at Gaya, India, five centuries before the birth of Jesus Christ.

Here was a faith, with its own scriptures, its own savior, which still permeated half the world. One had to take it seriously on this score alone. Even more startling was the discovery that it preached a way of life that called for humility, self-denial and compassion. Most amazing was the assertion of classical Buddhism that Enlightenment could not be summed up in words. To someone whose head had been stuffed with Catholic philosophical formulas, it was almost a revelation in itself to read:

> For whatsoever is affirmed is not true
> And whatsoever is denied is not true

To Adam, already a savage skeptic of all creeds, this was manna. To Joanna, it was unsettling doubt. She saw why Adam liked Zen Buddhism, which was a Japanese adaptation of this central insight. It reflected the stoic, martial nature of the Japanese people and their long struggle to wrest a living from their narrow rocky islands and the sea around them. Zen insisted that satori or enlightenment came, not from meditation in a jungle hut or cave, in the style of Indian Buddhists, but from forcing the mind to abandon its penchant for abstraction, while living an everyday life surrounded by ordinary things and tasks. Zen mocked the mind's ability by asking impossible questions, such as: "What is the sound of one hand clapping?" The Zen poet P'ang-yun wrote:

> How wondrously supernatural
> And how miraculous this!
> I draw water, and I carry wood!

For a thoughtful Army wife in Japan in the winter of 1951, Zen's flirtation with absurdity had a special appeal. The war churned on in Korea. Casualty lists lengthened with enough names of '50 classmates on them to elicit groans of distress from Pete at least once a week. Among them was Sam Hardin, who was sent to an Army

171

hospital at Okawa Machi, about a hundred miles away. Joanna asked Betty Parrott if she was going to see her son-in-law. "Too far," Betty said. "It's only a leg wound. I talked to him on the phone. I asked him if he was through trying to be a hero. He hung up on me."

Joanna went up on the train to visit Sam. He was in terrible shape. His right leg had been smashed by a shell. The doctors were still talking about amputation, but he refused to consider it. Pain contorted his face as he told her: "Maybe I'll die. But that's okay. Dying's easy. That's about the only thing I've learned so far. Staying alive—keeping your head together—that's a lot harder."

"I'll say some prayers for you," Joanna said.

"Say some for the leg. I'm okay but the leg needs help," he said, with a flicker of his cadet grin.

"All right. For the leg."

"How's my wonderful mother-in-law?"

"She's—fine."

"No, she isn't. She's a miserable bitch." He fought the pain for a moment. "See what I mean about dying? It makes everything easy. Like telling the truth."

"You're not going to die," Joanna said. It was an automatic response.

"Probably not. My old man used to say I was too dumb to get killed. Started breaking horses when I was eleven. The wilder, the better. Surprised the hell out of him—and myself—by getting into West Point. I'm still pretty dumb but I'm starting to ask some questions. Like what the hell are we doing over there in Korea? It doesn't make any sense, Jo. What do you think?"

The question surprised her. It was not something Pete would ever have asked her. "I don't know," she said. She told him how disgusted she had become with the indifference to the war at home.

"I guess we're on our own," Sam said. He looked past her for a moment, his face transfixed by pain and sadness. For the first time Joanna realized the intimate connection between a soldier's morale and his feelings about his country.

"Is Ruth coming out to Japan?"

Sam shook his head. "Her mother still says no self-respecting officer's wife should set foot on foreign soil until she's guaranteed a house on a U. S. Army base.''

"I—I don't like Mrs. Parrott very much," Joanna said.

"Who does? Not even her husband can stand her. He gets boiled every night. One of the reasons I married Ruth. Let me take you away from all this. Makes you feel like a big shot, to say that to someone. I never had much of a chance to be a big shot on the Four Star Ranch. Ah—''

He turned his head away. She was sure it was not the pain in his leg that made him do it. "You don't want my personal story.''

"I'm here to listen," Joanna said, remembering somewhat guiltily her ready acceptance of the other reason Sam had supposedly married Ruth, their secret sexual liaison at West Point. The reason she had just heard made the other story seem shabby and cruel. How naïve they all were, even when they thought they were being sophisticated.

They chatted about the war, American politics, sports—Sam had been on the boxing team at West Point—for another half hour. When Joanna told him it was time for her train, Sam held her hand and tears came into his eyes as he tried to tell her how grateful he was for the visit. She suspected that not many people had been kind to Sam Hardin growing up.

Back in Yokoshima, she told Pete Sam's question about the war. Pete nodded, not in the least surprised. "It's a real problem, motivating troops over there," he said. "I dropped all the stuff about God and country. I could see it wasn't working, after one kid said to me, 'I'm ready to die for my country but not for this hellhole.' I just told them we were here and the enemy was over there and it was up to us to do the job, to fight or get killed.''

"That's pure Zen," Joanna said.

"What?" Pete said.

"Japanese Buddhism," Joanna said. "I told you Adam sent me some books on it. Maybe they ought to start teaching it at West Point.''

"They don't teach any religion at West Point," Pete said.

"Zen isn't really a religion. It's more a philosophy.''

Joanna gave Pete a book by the Zen master D. T. Suzuki. He gave it back to her a few days later, saying he enjoyed the part about the Zen approach to fencing, which taught that defense and attack should be almost simultaneous. But it only applied to hand-to-hand combat. In vain, Joanna tried to explain that attack represented life, the external world, and defense one's response to life. The Zen master was trying to tell us to eliminate the two abstractions, self and life.

"The next time I see Supe I'm going to break him in half for turning you into a philosopher."

"You don't believe women should think?"

"Nothing like that. For showing me up." He put his arm around her. "Jo, I'm just a big dumb mick who loves you."

They were alone on one of the hospital's pavilions. Outside rain drizzled from the gray February sky. In the distance, the flat-topped houses of Yokoshima huddled beneath humps of hills. Joanna started to cry.

Joanna did not even attempt to share with Pete her enthusiasm for Japanese poetry. She devoured it, that winter of 1951, that winter of war. Much of it was written by women, which pleased her. Even poems written by men had a feminine quality to them, they were so brief and delicate.

> To what shall I compare
> This world?
> To the white wake behind
> A ship that has rowed away
> At dawn!

> Loneliness does not
> Originate in any one
> Particular thing:
> Evening in autumn over
> The black pines of the mountain.

She read these in her Japanese house, wrapped in a Japanese winter kimono, while her housekeeper, Mrs. Togo, polished the already gleaming woodwork or cooked in the tiny kitchen. She had

174

not become a Japanese house dweller voluntarily. After General MacArthur's decree, Joanna had thought that she would be installed in substantial quarters on the American Army base near Yokoshima. Formerly the headquarters of one of the occupation divisions, it was now a processing center for replacements en route to Korea. But Joanna swiftly learned that even Douglas MacArthur could not defeat Army regulations. Betty Parrott informed her that it was "against regs" for a wife to live on a base to which her husband was not assigned. Joanna had rushed to Pete in search of arguments and was told Mrs. P. was right. An appeal to General MacArthur might change things, but that was not Pete's style. He did not want to give anyone the impression that he thought his medal made him privileged in any way. So Joanna found herself living in a Japanese house in the hills above Yokoshima, with a marvelous view of Tokyo Bay and Fujiyama.

At first, Joanna found the house intriguing. It was so simple and bare. The small garden beyond the sliding panel walls, with its two dwarf trees and three humps of rock surrounded by gray gravel, emanated a serenity that suited her mood. She moved in on a sunlit day in mid-January, and the place seemed like an exotic gleaming dollhouse. Mrs. Togo greeted her with smiles and bows. She knew exactly four words of English, *hello*, *goodbye*, *eat*, *bath*, but even this did not seem a drawback. The next day winter returned. The sliding doors, both the *shoji*, the paper panels, and the *amado*, the wooden panels, were closed. The house became a dark cocoon. Drafts rose through the floor, although Mrs. Togo energetically laid straw mats everywhere. The damp ugly cold filled the house. The only heat emanated from the hibachi full of smoldering charcoal, which warmed nothing beyond a range of two feet.

The total lack of furniture, except for ankle-high tables and miniature dressers, soon became a problem. Joanna's back, which ached periodically from the weight she was carrying up front, began to torment her. Reading by the feeble light on the *andon*, the rectangular paper-covered floor lamp, left her eyes throbbing. There was no such thing as a comfortable sleeping position on the heavy quilt, the *futon*.

Yet she stubbornly refused to abandon the house, or fill it with

American lamps and furniture, as most other wives living on the economy in Japan had done. The house was part of a test which life, fate, God, she wasn't sure how to designate the controlling power, was giving her. A test of her spirit, in a way that she had never imagined in her college daydreams.

Mrs. Togo, the widow of a naval officer killed in the battle of the Coral Sea, was delighted by Joanna's interest in things Japanese. Each day in the late afternoon, they walked across the garden to the small house in the corner and practiced Cha-No-Yu, the Japanese tea ceremony. This above all Adam had enjoined Joanna to learn. He said it would make the meaning of Zen, of her Japanese house, come alive for her.

Mrs. Togo borrowed stone lanterns from her father's garden to illuminate the *Roji,* or dewy path to the teahouse. Each lamp had been designed by a tea master of a previous century. She offered Joanna a list of possible names for the tearoom, among them *Tokyo-do* (East-Seeking Hall), *Mokurai-an* (Silent Thunder Hut) and *Myogi-an* (Wondrous Joy Hut). Joanna chose *Fushin-an*—Doubting Hut.

Mrs. Togo showed her how to arrange the utensils in the *Mizuya,* the tea kitchen, and for a flower arrangement recommended *Nage-iri* (Thrown-in Flower), a single flower in a vase. They painstakingly rehearsed the thirty-seven steps in the order of the tea ceremony, from bringing in separately the water jar, tea bowl, tea spoon and caddy and hot-water ladle, to the precise folding of the napkin, to the final withdrawal of each utensil and the farewell bow to one's guests from the threshold.

Watching Mrs. Togo perform each movement in the prescribed way, designed to demonstrate its inevitability and the inevitability of all things, Joanna soon despaired of achieving Japanese perfection. But she did see and admire the inner purpose of the ceremony, the same inner purpose that guided all Japanese art, to achieve beauty with economy, to simplify and ultimately to toughen the spirit.

On the wall of her tearoom Joanna hung the verses of the tea master, Sen No Rikyu. They emphasized the importance of a pure heart and an untrammeled mind in the performance of Cha-No-Yu. They coincided in spirit and tone with the Zen koans Adam sent her. Over the centuries, Zen masters had composed thousands of these cryptic sayings, ranging from single phrases to elegant four- and eight-line poems that toyed with meanings in a deliciously ambiguous way. Adam sent Joanna one about an amorous woman who denied her love. She riposted with one about a "fearsome and solitary" monk who enjoyed his monkishness.

This passionate pursuit of Zen further isolated Joanna from the Army wives she encountered on her visits to the hospital. They had little in common anyway. All were in their late thirties or early forties, wives of majors, lieutenant colonels and colonels, the only officers with enough seniority to get housing on a base. They were nice enough, often inquiring about her health, offering to shop for her at the commissary or the PX. But they had no interest in Japan beyond a tourist willingness to see recommended sights such as the Imperial Palace in Tokyo.

Childbirth was now only a few weeks away. Joanna was the lone maternity case at Gorgas Hospital. The doctors regarded her with irritation or boredom, depending on their temperaments. She never saw the same doctor twice, and the examination was always perfunctory. Except for her persistent morning sickness, she had no alarming symptoms to report. Blood pressure, urine samples, all remained normal—which made her utterly uninteresting compared to the medical dilemmas that machine-gun bullets or shell fragments caused in the human body.

Joanna could not decide whether she should be casual or angry about this neglect. Or whether to call it neglect. She was healthy and strong, her mother's daughter. There was no reason to think she would have a difficult birth. Her mother had "enjoyed"—that was the word she used—having her three children. But she was not her mother's daughter in so many other ways; she could not help but wonder if her reaction to this experience would also be different. She thought of the Zen saying: *Satori (enlightenment) is to be sought in the midst of Samsara (birth and death).* Before long, she would have a chance to test that murky directive.

"Excuse, please. Can spare a dime to part-time Samurai?"

"Adam!" Joanna flung her arms around him and kissed him on the cheek.

He was looking marvelous, tanned and lean, his jump boots gleaming, his paratrooper's jacket adding bulk to his thin torso. His red beret, tilted at a cocky angle, gave his stark face a vaguely Japanese cast.

"How did you find me? How did you get here?"

"Answer to question one: Called hospital. Talk to Captain Pete. He say stop, bring you down. Second lieutenant always obey captain. Answer to question two: Fly to Tokyo on Army plane. Leave wife behind. Too bad you pregnant nine months."

"Stop," Joanna said. "You are crazy. How's Honor?"

"Turning into moose. Gets more yellow, eyes slant all the time."

Moose was the standard GI name for Japanese girlfriends. It was derived from Japanese *moussa*, meaning sweetheart. But it had long since acquired a derogatory overtone among Americans.

"I wish you'd brought her," Joanna said, only half meaning it.

"Don't let wives of Samurai on U. S. Army planes. Honorable spouse lies miserable in our hut at Koke-Do, reciting poem of old woman in Tales of Ise, who loved warmhearted Captain Narihira:

> Shall I have to sleep
> All alone tonight
> On my narrow mat
> Unable to meet again
> The man for whom I long?"

"Captain Narihira struck me as a bit of an idiot," Joanna said.

A Japanese nobleman who flourished around A.D. 800, Narihira spent most of his time falling in and out of love with women from sixteen to a hundred and sixteen, and writing tormented poems about it.

"Typical attitude of Western woman who resents warmhearted man who loves all women indiscriminately. Japanese woman more philosophical, thank Buddha."

Joanna escorted Adam through the house. He praised her refusal to succumb to Western luxuries such as a bed. Honor was threatening to leave him unless he scrounged at least an American mattress somewhere. The garden made him envious. His house did not have

178

one. He wanted to know if Joanna had learned the tea ceremony from Mrs. Togo and immediately asked for a demonstration, even though *Ikkyaku Isshu*, One Guest and One Host, was a special case. While Mrs. Togo beamed, Joanna put on a kimono, bowed and led Adam along the *Roji* to the Doubting Hut, a name he instantly approved. Studying the verses on the wall, he pronounced them entirely satisfactory, except for one, in which the poet claimed to have reached such a state of enlightenment that in her heart there was "no stir of attraction or disgust."

"Even Zen can be carried too far," Adam said.

As prescribed in *Ikkyaku Isshu*, Joanna allowed Adam to arrange the single flower in the vase, and pour the water that gave it life, while she brought the tea things from the *Mizuya*, then added the final drops that brought the water to the very brim of the vase.

After the ceremony, which was conducted in the traditional complete silence, they relaxed, sipped more tea and discussed Zen. Adam was more interested in the self-mastery Zen offered than he was in kensho, self-insight, or satori, enlightenment. He enjoyed the cruel and bizarre answers that Zen masters gave to their pupils in order to shock them into understanding that there is no understanding. One slammed a gate and broke a pupil's leg to make his point, another hurled a learner into a freezing river, a third invited a prize student to his house for supper, then served him cow dung.

"Now I understand why the Japanese make good soldiers. We ought to make Zen part of the Army's basic training. Maybe teach it to a few generals, too."

"Does everything have to come back to—or down to—the Army?" Joanna said. For the first time she realized how much she had liked the idea that she was Adam's spiritual comrade in their joint exploration of Zen. It hurt her to find him coolly, callously going his own way, transferring all meanings to the same reality that dominated Pete's mind—the Army.

"Yes. That's our satori," Adam said. He smiled at her for a moment, rather bleakly. "I'm discovering there are several kinds of enlightenment. The Zen version might have helped me get through the Academy with a little less angst. I came close to quitting that

179

scholastic version of Alcatraz about six times. Then there's the enlightenment of discovering the real Army after enduring unreal West Point.''

He began telling her about his Airborne Regimental Combat Team. He did not make the paratroopers sound like the elite of the Army. The 158th RCT was, he said, largely composed of semi-rejects from the two airborne divisions in the States. When they had been ordered to form the 158th, they had seized the opportunity to dump their lemons in somebody else's lap. Adam's battalion commander was a West Pointer whom he called ''Two-Gun Tim.'' He swaggered around with a pair of revolvers on his hips, à la George Patton, and specialized in abusing second lieutenants, both on duty and in the Officers' Club, where he got drunk almost every night. Two-Gun Tim had taken a particular dislike to Adam when he found out he had transferred from the engineers. That meant he was a hive at the Academy and Two-Gun hated hives. If the 158th went into combat, Adam and the two thousand men in the battalion would have to obey life-or-death orders from this obnoxious drunk.

''How did he get promoted to lieutenant colonel?'' Joanna asked.

Adam smiled in the same bleak way. ''Making sense out of the Army promotion system is comparable to studying metaphysics. I believe it was one of your Catholic heroes, Chesterton, who defined that as searching a pitch-dark room for a black hat that isn't there.''

Suddenly Adam abandoned his habitual irony and sarcasm. Gray light spilled from his New England eyes, illuminating his somber face. ''I can see already, if I'm going to stay in this Army, I'll have to go it alone. Have you read the Samurai's creed?''

Joanna shook her head.

''It's the most important thing I've read in my life.''

''Recite it for me.''

He turned his head slightly away from her, toward the scrolls on the wall of the Doubting Hut. She sensed he was speaking not only to her but to some spiritual presence which he wanted her to recognize and worship with him.

''I have no parents; I make heaven and earth my parents.

''I have no magic power; I make inward strength my magic.

''I have no armor; I make righteousness my armor.

"I have no body; I make fortitude my body.

"I have no design; I make opportunity my design.

"I have no friends; I make immovable mind my friend.

"I have neither life nor death; I make the Eternal my life and death."

"Adam," Joanna said. "That is so beautiful."

They sat in silence, sharing the moment, incapable of knowing its inner meaning, its future power.

Adam looked at his watch. "Holy Bushido, it's almost twelve o'clock. Gotta get down to the hospital and knock rings with the hero. It isn't often mere lieutenants are allowed to socialize with the high command."

At the hospital, Captain Burke greeted them with an impatient scowl. "What happened?" he asked. "Did he parachute into the wrong city?"

With trembling hands, Adam lit a cigarette and became a sneering Frenchman. "How dares he talk that way to an officer of the Legion?" he intoned through his nose. "To tell you z'truth, *mon capitaine*, I was trying to seduce your wife, but I could not get my arms around her."

"That's mean," Joanna said.

"It's either twins or an All-American defensive tackle, with his shoulder pads on."

Pete grinned. Joanna told them they were both heartless. They ignored her and began discussing the war. In Korea, the Eighth Army, under a new commander, Matthew Ridgway, had gone over to the offensive and was smashing the Chinese back toward the 38th parallel. Casualties were heavy on both sides. Pete was disgusted. He agreed with General MacArthur, who called it an accordion war. It violated everything they had been taught at West Point about winning wars with maximum speed by applying maximum force. Adam said it was a new kind of war, limited, by tacit agreement on both sides. America was not used to fighting such a war. You had to go back to the eighteenth century to find one.

"Professional soldiers ought to be able to understand limited wars," Adam said. "They don't need a crusade, a war-to-end-wars propaganda barrage, to motivate them. The trouble is, MacArthur and a lot of other generals have fought their wars with citizen soldiers and absorbed the crusader philosophy."

"But we've got to use citizen soldiers, draftees. There aren't enough professional soldiers to go around," Pete said.

The hospital loudspeaker system interrupted them with a familiar call. "ALL ON-DUTY PERSONNEL PLEASE REPORT TO RECEPTION AREA IMMEDIATELY." Another shipment of wounded had arrived from Korea.

Suddenly Joanna felt as if a war had begun inside her body. An invisible enemy seemed to be shoving a bayonet through her pelvis. She gasped.

Pete grabbed her hand. "Is it—?"

"I—I think so," Joanna said.

They looked around. There was not a doctor or a nurse in sight. "Do you have a room reserved?" Pete asked.

Joanna shook her head. "They said it wouldn't come for another two weeks."

"Where do you go to see the doctor?" Adam asked.

"An outpatient clinic. On the first floor, in the back."

"Take her there. I'll find a doctor," Adam said.

He raced down the ward. Pete, his arm clutching Joanna against him, as if he thought she might collapse any moment, rushed her to the elevator and along the first-floor corridor to the white-walled clinic with its stainless steel sterilizing units and glass cabinets full of menacing instruments. It was empty. Pete helped her onto the examining table just as she got her next contraction. She clung to him and heard him gasp: "Christ, this is worse than combat."

"This is just the opening skirmish—Captain," Joanna said.

Adam came in with a young nurse, a lieutenant. "The doctors are up to their eyeballs," he said. "They claim there's nothing to worry about for the next couple of hours, anyway."

"Is there a room available?" Pete asked.

The nurse shook her head. "We were going to put her in one of the senior officers' private rooms. But they're all full. The Chinese broke through the 2nd Division's front and tore apart a lot of command posts. We're loaded with colonels and brigadiers."

"I'm all right here," Joanna said.

"Are you timing your contractions, honey?" the nurse asked. She had one of those impersonal Grade B movie faces, acceptably good-looking but indistinguishable from a thousand similar faces.

"I'd say about ten minutes apart, for the first two."

"They'll probably stay that way for an hour or two. You better get out of those clothes and let me prep you. In the meantime, you two gentlemen could find a corpsman and tell him we need a bed in here. She can't spend the night on this table."

Pete and Adam went in search of the bed. Joanna undressed and put on a hospital gown. The nurse shaved her pubic hair and took her pulse. She asked which of her worried escorts was her husband. "The red-haired one," Joanna said.

"I'll take either one," the nurse said. She opened the door and discovered Pete and Adam had found a bed. They wheeled it in and the nurse helped Joanna into it. She patted her arm. "Everything's going to be fine as far as I can see. When the contractions get down to every five minutes, send the lieutenant up for a doctor."

"Which one?" Joanna asked.

"Whoever's free," the nurse said. "You're gonna have to get them between operations. They'll be going all night, from the way things look."

The contractions stayed at every ten minutes for several hours. Daylight faded from the examining room. Pete and Adam sat beside her, Pete holding her hand. Adam described how he and Honor had won first prize at a masquerade party at the Officers' Club in Koke-Do. She went as a Geisha, he as a Samurai. He tried to explain to Pete the similarity between Zen satori and the indoctrination of incoming cadets at West Point. "Remember the time when you suddenly knew you were going to hack it, no matter what they did to you? When ten minutes before you were thinking of turning in the costume? That's satori, enlightenment."

Pete looked dubious but he was too worried about Joanna to argue with Adam. Every few minutes he squeezed her hand and asked her how she felt. She would say fine and then change her mind when a contraction hit.

About eight o'clock the bag of waters broke and the contractions began coming every five minutes. Adam raced upstairs to find a doctor. He came back looking worried. "They're all either operating or sleeping," he said. "I've got another nurse, a major this time, who said she'd be down to take a look."

The pain was beginning to disorient Joanna. She clung to Pete and whimpered every time it started. She was drenched in sweat, although the room was chilly. "I don't think I've seen that palace of pearls yet," she said to Adam.

"You'll see better than that," Adam said. "You'll see the boat sailing before the wind."

"What the hell are you two talking about?" Pete growled.

"Zen koans," Adam said. "They take your mind off what's happening to you." He took Joanna's hand. "Repeat after me:

> *Our body is the Bodhi tree*
> *And our mind a mirror bright*
> *Carefully we wipe them hour by hour*
> *And let no dust alight.*"

Pete grabbed Adam by the shoulder and spun him around. "Supe," he said, "if we're going to say any prayers, it's going to be to Jesus Christ, not Buddha."

"That wasn't a prayer."

Pete stepped between Adam and Joanna and took her hand. "Do you want to pray, honey?"

"No," she said. "Not yet."

For the first time she had a glimmer of what Zen tried to do: not merely toughen the soul but render it independent of the ambiguous God that Christians worshipped. She suddenly wanted that kind of strength, wanted it fiercely. But it was beyond her. Each time the pain began, her will collapsed and she fled helplessly to the only God she knew, crying why, why, begging please, please end it.

The nurse finally arrived. Joanna told her the water had broken. "Getting close," the nurse muttered. "Sorry I can't get excited, honey. I've been in the operating room for the last eight hours. I'll give you some Demerol. That'll ease the pain."

Joanna saw she had a syringe in her hand. Before she could object—and she wasn't sure she wanted to object—the needle was in her arm. Things became more and more disconnected. She would doze and then cry out as a really bad contraction began. When she awoke it was black night outside. The windowpanes were like a mirror. She saw Pete, gazing down at her, anguish on his face. She heard Adam shouting at someone over the telephone. "I don't care how many dying men you've got upstairs. We may have a dying woman, a dying baby down here."

"Is the baby dead?" she asked Pete. She didn't care about herself any longer. She would be glad to die. But she did not want the baby to die.

"No, no," Pete said. "Supe's just trying to scare them. We still haven't gotten a goddamn doctor down here."

A young doctor, whose white, exhausted face was vaguely familiar, appeared in the examining room. He too was drenched in sweat. A surgical mask dangled from his neck. He took her pulse, timed her contractions and snarled at Pete: "Pull up her gown."

"What?"

"Pull up her gown. How the hell am I going to examine her?"

Pete obeyed the order. The doctor made the usual examination. "Hell," he said, "the cervix is barely dilated. She won't be ready for hours."

"But she's in labor, Doctor, terrific labor," Pete said.

"Nobody ever died of labor pains. I'll give her some Demerol."

"She's already had some."

"A little more won't hurt."

He took a syringe from a cabinet on the wall, filled it from a bottle in the cabinet and gave Joanna another injection. "Can't you stay with her, Doctor?" she heard Pete ask.

"My friend, I've got ten men upstairs with internal bleeding that has to be stopped sometime in the next hour or they're going to be dead. I've got two intestinal resections and a stomach resection ahead of them."

"Sure, Doctor, sure," Pete said. "We'll sweat this out. If we just knew who to call. When it's time."

"There isn't anyone available. They've got allergists operating up there, for Christ's sake. We're swamped. The next time you guys fight a war, remember to draft twice as many doctors as you did for this one."

Joanna drifted down into confused darkness, across which pain streaked like flashes of black lightning. Once she stood under a Bodhi tree with two Zen masters in saffron robes and wide-brimmed, down-slanting straw hats that covered their faces. She recited the poem Adam had given her.

> Our body is the Bodhi tree
> And our mind a mirror bright
> Carefully we wipe them hour by hour
> And let no dust alight.

The smaller of the two masters raised his head. She saw it was Adam. The larger one raised his head. She saw it was Pete. "You still haven't got it right," Adam said. "You don't belong here."

"I do," Joanna said, violently angry. "I do. I'll prove I belong with you."

Suddenly she was awake. It was no longer black night outside. The windows were dirty gray, the color of the February sky. An older doctor, looking extremely angry, was standing beside her, roaring: "Where is this woman's file? You mean to tell me no one has even looked at this woman's file?"

The older doctor kept on shouting as he examined Joanna. His voice rose crazily through the sheet over the lower half of her body. "Here it is, General," said a nurse, thrusting the file at him. He placed it on Joanna's stomach and paged rapidly through it, then uttered another roar. "Look at that. Look at that pelvic measurement! You mean to tell me not one idiot on this staff bothered to look at that measurement? This woman can't have a child by vaginal delivery. Prepare her for a Caesarian."

"We don't have an operating room available. Or a surgeon," the nurse said.

"We'll do it right here," the general growled. "I'll operate. Get six corpsmen in here and scrub this place down immediately."

Joanna liked that decision. She would rather have her baby here than upstairs, in the wards and operating rooms that reeked of battle death. The corpsmen moved her into the next room, full of files and a desk, while they scrubbed down the examining room. The contractions were still coming every two minutes and she found it difficult to follow Pete's explanation, but she gathered Adam had gone to the quarters of the hospital's commanding general at 4 A.M. and shouted him out of bed to examine his only maternity case.

Nurses shooed Pete away and began preparing her for the operation. Why hadn't some doctor she had seen told her about the measurements? They probably thought the word *Caesarian* would scare her. Was there something about her that suggested instability? Weakness? Her habitual self-criticism and everything else vanished as more needles sank into her arm, her back. Numbness seeped through her body and it was black night again, dreamless this time.

When she awoke it was day, bright sunlight pouring through the window of a narrow room. Pete sat on one side of the bed, Adam on the other side. She drowsily thought that if she could have them both for husbands, she would be perfectly happy. She would live with Adam until his mockery and extremism unnerved her and recuperate for a year with Pete's stability and sincerity. Then she remembered the labor, the dreams, the general. "Is the baby all right?" she asked.

"A six-pound eight-ounce plebe, class of '73," Adam said. "I just taught him the manual of arms. He responded beautifully."

"He's fine. Are you?" Pete asked.

"I think so," she said.

"I'd say she rates a Combat Infantryman's Badge, at least," Adam said.

"The hell with that. The Medal of Honor," Pete said. "You've got more guts than the whole class of '50 combined. What do you want to name him?"

"Tom. After my brother."

"Okay with me."

"Son of a gun," Adam said. "I was sure it would be Adam."

"Listen. That kid's going to have enough trouble with you for a godfather. A goddamn Buddhist."

"A Congregationalist Buddhist."

"I love you," Joanna said to both of them, and slipped into more blank black sleep.

IV

SOMEONE was hissing in her ear and Honor Prescott Thayer did not like it. He or she was interrupting a lovely dream. She was riding across a glowing green meadow, the horse taking delightful bounds in the high grass. The meadow swept ahead of her over rolling hills, uninterrupted beauty, America, not stupid Japan, where every other foot was smelly rice paddies or some other kind of farm and the rest rocky ridges and ravines. Honor awoke to find Mrs. Kasunabe, their Japanese housekeeper, leaning over her.

"Breakfass, Mssss Taya," said Mrs. Kasunabe.

"*All right,*" Honor said, and sat up. She ran her tongue around the inside of her mouth. Furry. She was hung over again. It wasn't even a real party at the Officers' Club this time. Just everyday—or night—routine drinking and dancing. It wasn't her fault. Someone was always getting Honor another drink. They loved to get drinks for Honor. They liked to dance with Honor, the majors and the colonels. She was their pet wife. Sexy Honor. She did not really like it, but she did not know what to do about it.

Adam did not seem to mind. But the other officers' wives minded. Honor found that upsetting. One of the trials of her adolescence had been the bitchy way other girls had treated her, because boys liked her looks. She had tried to talk to Adam about it, but he had dismissed it with a cocky "Ignore them." He did not seem to realize that if you ignored them you had no friends.

Through the open door Honor could see Adam on the sunny porch of their house, a book on his lap. Another damn book about Japan, Honor thought. That was all he read these days. You'd think the Japs had won the war, the way Adam talked about them, their Samurai this and their Zen that and their—

She hoped he was not reading the book he showed her last month. The love book, he called it. He had bought it in a bookstore in

188

Kyoto. A public bookstore. It had pictures of women doing the most ungodly things to themselves and letting men do the most ungodly things to them. Adam had shown them to her and talked about how great it was that the Japanese had no guilt about sex and then suggested, actually suggested, that they try some of those things. She had told him—

It had been a nasty fight. He had called her inhibited. Honor Prescott *inhibited?* If he knew how close she had come to being uninhibited before she met him. She had told him that if making love to a woman in the respectable honorable way that had been good enough for generations of American men did not satisfy him, there was something wrong with him. If he noticed the attention she got on the dance floor, it should be obvious that there wasn't an officer in the 158th Regimental Combat Team who wouldn't jump at the chance. Not that she intended to give it to any of them but—

That was the last Honor had heard of the love book.

Struggling to her feet, Honor felt a familiar ache in her bones and glowered down at the *futon*, the Japanese quilt on which she had been sleeping. Adam had finally promised her a mattress to replace it. She glared at the stylized paintings of kimonoed ladies bowing to resplendent Samurai on the walls of their tiny sitting room—bedroom. It did not make any sense, living like the Japanese. Only two or three other couples in the 158th RCT were doing it. Joanna had tried it and abandoned it when Pete came out of the hospital. She had imported a bed, chairs and other American amenities. They had visited the Burkes two months ago for Thomas Adam's christening. Adam had been the godfather and Honor had acted as proxy godmother for Joanna's sister.

Thinking about Thomas Adam, the cutest little red-headed baby she had ever seen, put Honor in a better mood. She brushed her hair and washed the sleep from her face in their Western-style bathroom, for which she thanked God every morning. Joanna's house lacked one, as did the Japanese inns at which Adam was so fond of staying on weekends. Honor Prescott Thayer was simply not born to squat. No wonder Japanese women were so humble. Putting on her blue-and-white kimono, Honor strolled out on the porch, overlooking the town and its valley. Adam, wearing a blue kimono with fire-breathing red dragons on it, was discussing *mushimono*, Japanese steamed food, with Mrs. Kasunabe. Honor's coddled eggs were on her plate. Before Adam sat fermented bean soup and some sort of omelet, with little fish around it. He was always trying new Japanese recipes. Honor hated their food even more than she hated almost everything else about the Japanese. Mrs. Kasunabe bowed, hissed something about enjoying "breakfass" and withdrew.

Honor grabbed the book out of Adam's hands, sat down on his lap and kissed him. "How's my paratrooper this mornin'?"

"Okay. How's the paratrooper's wife?"

"She'll be perfectly happy if you get her a mattress to sleep on."

"I told you. The sergeant's working on it. If there's one on Kyushu, he'll find it."

"You and your sergeants. Haven't they gotten us into enough trouble?"

"They run the Army, sweetheart. The generals only think they run it."

"That's not what the junior officers' wives think."

"You know what I think of the junior officers' wives."

Honor dropped it. She did not want to start the argument again. A month ago, George Buckley, the master sergeant in Adam's company, had punched the captain, the company's commander, in the jaw. Sergeant Buckley was immediately arrested and held for court-martial. Adam had been drawn into the case by his platoon sergeant, Fred Hammer. At the court-martial, Adam testified for the master sergeant. Adam said he believed Buckley's version of the quarrel—that the captain had called the sergeant an obscene and insulting name. He was the only officer who testified for him. Buckley was acquitted, to the indignation of most officers and their wives. For several weeks, Honor had been cut dead by some of the wives at the Officers' Club and at the PX and commissary.

The night of the court-martial decision, Adam had invited Hammer and Master Sergeant Buckley, a huge, drawling Georgian, to the house for dinner. Honor had liked Buckley, a modest man who said little. But she had disliked Fred Hammer. He had brought his moose, his Japanese girlfriend, who spoke almost no English. He had made cruel jokes about her stupidity all night while the poor girl smiled politely and laughed when she thought her sergeant was being funny. Her father was the mayor of Koke-Do and Honor gathered he and Hammer were in a kind of partnership, changing American money on the black market.

Adam's irascible battalion commander, Lieutenant Colonel Timothy Blackwell, who had disapproved of his testifying in the court-martial, had given Adam a reprimand for the dinner invitation. He was told that the Army did not encourage socializing between officers and enlisted men. Adam had respectfully (which, knowing Adam, meant the exact opposite) disagreed with this policy, citing the 1946 report by General James Doolittle on the reorganization of the Army, which recommended such fraternization. Lieutenant Colonel Blackwell informed Adam that the Doolittle report had never become U. S. Army policy.

Sergeant Hammer had not been invited again. But Adam was still fond of him. He liked Hammer's old Army style. He had been in almost twenty years and knew all the tricks. He persuaded Adam to let him exchange their dollars for yen on the black market at 400 to 1, enabling them to go tripping off to Kyoto and stay at Japanese inns and buy a beat-up old 1936 Buick. He helped Adam weed the deadheads and crybabies out of his platoon and dump them on less fortunate lieutenants.

Honor had barely given a thought to Hammer lately. The unpleasant episode into which he had drawn Adam was rapidly becoming ancient history. She told herself she was enjoying their tour in the 158th Regimental Combat Team, in spite of Japan and the Japanese. Her original fear, that Adam would use the war to get away from her, had proved groundless. Instead, the war had added excitement, adventure, to their marriage. As she sat down to breakfast, she waved cheerfully to blond Sally Hoban, standing on the porch of an identical house, about fifty yards away. Sally's father was a congressman from Florida. Angled from Sally's house, facing the Thayers' house, was another porch, on which Lieutenant Archibald Baker and his skinny wife, Patty, were breakfasting. Her mother was a Randolph, which meant something in Virginia. Patty did not wave. She and Archie were having *problems*. Everywhere they went, they crept into corners for intense conversations.

These junior officers' quarters were all built in groups of three around an inner court. At this moment, all the lieutenants were on their porches having breakfast. Honor rather liked the idea. She liked almost everything about the Army, so far. The tiffs with the other wives were not the Army's fault. By and large, she liked most of the wives, and when they were not waxing jealous or getting embroiled in arguments on their husbands' behalf, they liked her. At least, she tried hard to get them to like her, to make it clear, woman to woman, that she had no pretensions because of her looks. Some of them were getting the message pretty well.

It was a beautiful June day. Fat puffy clouds drifted lazily in the blue sky. She was going to *enjoy* herself today. Lunch at the Officers' Club, a swim in the pool, maybe canasta with Captain Clark's wife, Rita. Clark had replaced the captain who got slugged and he had been very cool to Adam at first. But Honor shared Rita's passion for canasta and Rita was from North Carolina. Between canasta and talking one southern girl to another, Honor had done a lot to change Captain Clark's mind about Adam. Things were now cordial enough to issue a dinner invitation. The Clarks were coming tomorrow night. Which meant she had some shopping to do. No matter what Adam said, she was not going to serve them Japanese food.

"Koke-Do, you're okeydoke," Honor said to the postcard landscape, repeating a remark Adam had made when they arrived eight months ago. The hillsides around them were full of dwarf trees and picturesque waterfalls. The town of Koke-Do nestled at the foot of the valley, along the sea. They could not believe their luck, pulling this resort, once reserved for vacationing officers of the Japanese imperial staff. One more proof that it paid to go airborne.

"Do you think we'll stay here for the summer?" Honor said, cracking one of her coddled eggs.

"Good chance," Adam said. "Last we heard, the Chinese were advancing to the rear at a rapid rate."

The 158th Airborne Regimental Combat Team was in ready reserve for the Eighth Army in Korea. The main airborne divisions were still in the United States, standing by to meet Communist threats elsewhere in the world. The 158th was a composite of men from these divisions—a lot of them screw-ups and bad apples, according to Adam. But he had a tendency to see the worst in people, a habit which she reminded herself to change. Another Airborne RCT, the 187th, commanded by one of the young hotshots of World War II, Brigadier General William C. Westmoreland, was stationed about a hundred miles away. A third RCT, composed of infantrymen, was being put together in northern Japan. Pete Burke had just been appointed aide to the general commanding it. A regimental combat team was bigger than an ordinary regiment; it had its own artillery, tanks and other supporting elements.

The war continued to be a bitter struggle between a revived Eighth Army and their Chinese Communist adversary. Adam said it was like two gladiators fighting in a closet. Every movement inflicted injury. But the advantage now seemed to be with the Americans, thanks to their massed artillery and air power. The Eighth Army had apparently survived the greatest shock of the postwar era—even greater than the defeat inflicted by the Chinese at the Chongchon River—the dismissal of General Douglas MacArthur. The 158th Airborne's officer corps had been badly split by it—most of them siding with MacArthur. Adam had sided with President Truman, making more enemies with his gift for quick comebacks whenever an argument developed. Honor had warned him and finally pleaded with him to hold his tongue.

During the week, Honor saw little of Adam between breakfast and dinner. Brigadier General Addison Foreman, the commander of the 158th, was determined to keep his men battle-ready. He had them out almost every day on twenty-mile route marches through the countryside or on the firing range at a nearby Army reservation. A lot of other wives complained about boredom, but Honor did not mind the long lonely days. "What did they expect?" she sometimes asked Rita Clark, as she dealt another hand of canasta. Rita said she thought it helped to be southern. People from the South had an aptitude for Army life. Honor liked that. She wanted to feel part of the Army. It made her feel closer to Adam.

Scarcely a week went by without a practice jump. Some of the wives got unstrung when their husbands jumped, but Honor had stopped worrying when Adam told her it was a lot safer than horseback riding. She had never missed a chance to watch a jump at Fort Bragg. It was so spectacular, the way the small black bodies dribbled from the bellies of the planes and blossomed into those magical chutes. Honor liked everything about the airborne, from the gleaming Corcoran boots to the brash red berets. Above all, she liked the idea that the airborne were the best, the elite. That was where she and Adam belonged.

"What's on the schedule today, another hike?" Honor asked.

"Twenty-four miles," Adam said. "Have the water boiling."

"You're queer for that tub," Honor said.

"I'm queer for you, when you come out of it."

Adam liked the game they played with their Japanese bath. So did she, up to a point. She would sit on the porch and watch the companies come down the hillside from their march, many of them on the double, chanting, "ONE TWO THREE FOUR WHAT THE HELL ARE WE FOR: AIRBORNE!" Twenty minutes later, Adam would arrive in his jeep, covered with grime and dust. She would have a mint julep waiting for him. He would down it in one gulp and undress, flinging the dirty clothes in the laundry basket for Mrs. Kasunabe to worry about. She undressed too and they put on terrycloth robes and entered the bathing room, two steps down from the living room, with a wooden lattice over the cement floor. In the center was the tub, a huge egg-shaped contraption, part metal stove and part wooden vat divided into one large and two small compartments. She would have the tub already full and heated to parboiling.

With water from one of the small compartments, she would play the Japanese wife, soaping Adam's long, much too skinny body, talking about how she wanted to get him back to some Army base in the States and feed him corn pone and pork chops and grits all day until she fattened him up. Then Adam would soap her, playing little games with his fingers until she slapped his hand away. Sometimes Adam would get so excited it would be standing straight up and she would be embarrassed. It was not very pretty to look at. Then he would tell her to give him the "cure" and she would douse him—and it—with ice-cold water from the washbasin and they would plunge into the hot tub. They would float around in there and Adam's hands would be traveling all over her again under the water.

She liked it, but she did not like it, because he said he was treating her like a Japanese wife and she was afraid he was going to ask her to do some of those ungodly things in the love book. He hadn't so far—they made love in the regular way. But he wanted her as soon as they came out of the tub—before supper. That made her feel strange. It was hard to come back to earth and start cooking on the little two-burner stove. She tried to explain this to Adam but he would not listen to her. He wanted her when he wanted her, he said. That put her in a bitchy mood and she retaliated by decreeing that every other night was more than enough for any man.

The telephone rang in their bedroom. Mrs. Kasunabe was rolling up the *futons* to stuff them behind one of the sliding doors. Adam stepped past her to pick up the phone. Honor saw his back stiffen. "Yes, *sir*. Yes, *sir*. I'll be there in five minutes," he said.

He slammed down the phone and whirled to speak to her from the shadowed room. "We're going in. Pack my stuff. I'll be back here in less than an hour."

"In where?" Honor said.

"Where the hell do you think?" Adam said, flinging off his kimono. "The Chinese have launched an offensive. They're tearing the South Korean Army apart."

"You just said they were retreatin'."

"That's how good generals launch offensives. They make you overconfident, let you overextend, then wham."

Adam was tugging on his boots, jamming his trousers into them, frantically buttoning his shirt. His hands were shaking. Was he afraid? Honor refused to believe it. She refused to believe any of it. "You said we'd be here all summer."

"You'll be here," he said. "Just check my gear. I'm pretty sure it's all ready."

She sat numbly on the porch before their unfinished breakfast and watched the jeeps from all the officers' houses in the valley tearing down the dirt side roads, leaving funnels of dust behind them. They met on the main road and streamed up the macadam to the airfield and the surrounding quonset barracks. Honor found Adam's field glasses and focused them. She could see men running out to the fat-bellied planes.

Behind her she heard someone sobbing. Fran Slattery stood in the doorway. She had walked right into the house, into my house, Honor thought, wishing the Japanese Army had put locks on the doors of their vacation houses. Fran and Joe Slattery had the house on the right. They were both from Connecticut. He was a World War II veteran who had been recalled from the active reserve. Fran was at least thirty and looked forty, one of those sloppy sloping women who always seem to be on the verge of coming apart, a hem drooping here, a slip showing there. Now she was coming apart emotionally.

"Honor?" she said. "I just wanna see—I mean, from our side you can't see much. It's awful, isn't it? It's gonna be worse than the Bulge, Joe says."

"Don't be silly," Honor said. "The 158th will tear them apart. They're the best outfit in the Army."

"No matter how good you are, you can't fight off odds of a thousand to one," Fran said. "That's how the Chinese fight. Oh Jesus, I keep thinkin' Joe's taken enough chances. He was in the Bulge, at Bastogne. Normandy."

"Maybe it's a drill," Honor said.

"No," Fran Slattery said. "It's the real thing."

"They're startin' the engines of the planes," Honor said, using the field glasses to avoid looking at Fran. The propellers were turning. It was like a war movie. Exciting.

"Marge?" she heard Fran Slattery call. "I'm out here with Honor."

Marge Thomas joined them, cigarette dangling from her lower lip. She and Fran were best friends. Marge's husband, Oscar, was an ex-sergeant who had decided to move up to lieutenant when Korea gave him the opportunity. If Honor had to choose one word to describe Marge, it was *used*. She had a bizarre head of curly brown hair and a wide meaty face, dominated by a thick-lipped scornful mouth. She had been an Army wife for fifteen years and knew all the scores. Several times, when she had had too much to drink, she had called Oscar Thomas names that Honor never heard before in her life. Marge's raspy voice easily penetrated their thin Japanese walls. Honor could not believe such a woman was an officer's wife.

Adam had told her it was a big Army, too big to be officered exclusively by West Pointers. They had to take the officers where thay could find them and Oscar Thomas was a first-class fighting man.

"Oh, Marge, isn't it awful?" Fran Slattery said.

"Bad," Marge said. "About as bad as you can get. Give him a good kiss—or something better if you have time—when he comes back for his gear. It may be the last one."

"Really now," Honor said. "You're bein' ridiculous."

"Oh. We got a lady general here. You think just 'cause they jump outta those planes and yell 'airborne' that bullets can't put holes in them? I thought that way once. My first husband, Charlie, was the biggest, roughest son of a bitch I've ever seen. The first day in North Africa a sniper plugs him in the head. So much for old Charlie's muscles."

She drew deeply on her cigarette. "Bullets go through West Pointers too, honey."

She hates me, Honor thought, hates me for what I am, a person of taste and refinement, and I hate her, she is trash. She ignored Marge Thomas and admired herself for the way she held the glasses with perfectly steady hands and watched the propellers whirling faster and faster while the roar of the laboring motors flowed down the valley to engulf them. The sound seemed to unhinge Fran Slattery's already slipping self-control and she began sobbing. Marge Thomas said Fran needed a stiff drink and led her away to administer it.

Honor checked Adam's field pack and added an extra dozen antimalaria pills, although she didn't have the foggiest idea if Korea was malarious, or whatever they called it. Everything else was there, and his .45 pistol was hanging in the closet. She took the gun out of the holster and hefted it. It was an incredibly black and menacing thing. Its cold metal made her shiver. Let those other cows weep, this was what being an Army wife was all about.

She sat on the porch sipping coffee and watched the trucks lugging gear out to the planes, the work crews piling it on the elevators that raised it into the bellies of the big Globemasters. About ten-thirty, the jeeps began returning from headquarters. Once more they left dramatic funnels of dirt behind them as they mounted to the houses on the hillsides. Adam was driving his jeep. Oscar Thomas sat beside him. Joe Slattery sat in the back. They all looked grim.

"It's bad," Adam said, in an unintentional echo of Marge Thomas. "Half the Eighth Army's left flank is gone. Two South Korean divisions have just disappeared. We've got to plug the hole before the Chinese get in our rear."

"You'll do it," she said, and put her arms around him. He was rigid. She felt his heart pounding against her cheek. His hand brushed mechanically at her back. "Yeah," he said.

"Airborne," she said. "Why are you so—nervous?"

"First time. Everyone's nervous the first time." He kissed her briefly, harshly. His lips were as dry and stiff as a piece of Brillo. He grabbed his pack and headed for the door. "Oh, listen, Fred Hammer's not back from Kyoto. I left him a note about getting that mattress you want. He might have time to do something about it."

Adam was gone before she could thank him, reassure him, tell him how touched she was, *ennoble* the moment somehow. Going into battle, the last thing he thought of was a mattress. Ugh. It was hard to believe her paternal grandfather, that proud old man whose portrait glared down at her from the living-room wall during her childhood, discussed mattresses before he rode off to join General Lee at Bull Run.

Honor went out on the porch and stood there, waiting for Adam's farewell wave. Five minutes, ten minutes, there was still no jeep. Then she realized he was sitting in it, waiting for the others, who were saying goodbye to their wives like men, not frightened boys. Her husband, her West Pointer, was afraid. Afraid to the point of panic on the eve of his first battle.

Finally the jeep appeared. Adam sat beside Oscar Thomas, who was driving. Adam looked like a boy, a teen-ager at best, in contrast to Oscar's slabby bulk. Joe Slattery hunched in the back, hanging on to both sides of the jeep as they bounced down the side road. From all the other roads, the jeeps appeared again, racing to their rendezvous at the airport.

A few minutes after the last jeeps disappeared into the byroads among the quonset huts, the companies came out in long swift columns. As they reached the concrete edge of the airport they broke into a run and went on the double to their planes. Down the distance, Honor could hear their cheers. The propellers began turning, the motors roaring again as they trotted up the boarding ladders, then the doors closed and the planes began wheeling toward the runways. For the next hour the valley trembled with the thunder of their take-offs. They rendezvoused overhead in prescribed formations before vanishing into the blue northwest sky.

They were gone. It was hard to believe. The same spring sunshine glowed on the green hills, the frothing waterfalls, the dwarf trees. Honor's life, which had seemed so interesting and exciting when she awoke this morning, was suddenly a blank. There would be no dance at the Officers' Club tomorrow night. There would be no more moonlight picnics in the hills. There would be no more trips to Kyoto or other shrine towns, unless the wives went in a group, a dreary idea. For the first time Honor realized how essential Adam was to her Army life, even if he was with her only a few hours a day.

She took the jitney bus to the Officers' Club. The place was like a giant funeral parlor. Wives sat around the pool like zombies, staring into space. Some, like her friend Rita Clark, were getting smashed. Honor ate a chicken-salad sandwich and went to the PX to get some shampoo. "Need any liquor, Mrs. Thayer?" asked the tall, somewhat effeminate sergeant who ran the place. "It's going fast. Everybody wants to drown their sorrows, I guess." Honor said no, thank you. She did not intend to do any drinking while Adam was gone.

She got back to the house about six and noticed a jeep parked beside the Baker house. Odd. It was from headquarters. Could Archie Baker have gotten killed already? He was dumb enough not to duck, Honor thought. Marge Thomas had her phonograph on, loud as usual. It sounded like Harry James or Sammy Kaye playing some thirties song. Marge's door was open. Fran Slattery reeled out as Honor crossed their little courtyard, with its single dwarf tree in its square of gray gravel. She was slobbering drunk. "Hey, come on, Honor," she yelled. "Have drink. It's only way—"

"No, thank you."

"Better'n what a lot of other people are doin'," Fran said.

"What do you mean?"

"See that jeep next door? That's Captain Whosis from headquarters. Been up there all afternoon with Mrs. Baker. FFV. I'm beginnin' to think that doesn't mean First Families of Virginia."

"That's not funny."

Fran nodded drunkenly. "Know it isn't. Marge says happens sometimes. When outfit ships out. Collapse of moral—morale—you name it."

"Don't look so shocked, Honor honey," Marge Thomas said from her doorway, drink in hand. "Only a few officers are doing it so far. You should go down to Prefab Heaven, the enlisted men's village. Everyone's drunk and fucking everything that walks. Ask Fran. She saw it too."

Fran Slattery crossed herself, wide-eyed. "Honest, Honor."

"Too many combat veterans in this outfit. Too many Army widows, like me, with horny memories," Marge Thomas said. "What the hell. Why not let them have their fun? The headquarters boys are going tomorrow."

"That is a digustin' attitude for an officer's wife to—"

A jeep pulled up outside. A man emerged from the twilight carrying a large object over his shoulder. "Mrs. Thayer? Honor?"

"Yes?" Honor said, turning.

"Fred Hammer. I got your mattress."

She remembered how much she disliked the way Sergeant Hammer called her Honor when he met her on the street in Koke-Do a few days after they had had him to dinner.

"Well, for Chrissake. Old Freddie," Marge Thomas said. "Haven't seen much of you since you shacked up with Miss Black Market of 1951."

Hammer resembled Marge Thomas in a vague way. He had the same kind of wide thick-lipped face and heavy-boned frame. In the twilight he looked vaguely menacing, a figure from the lower depths of life. He smiled at Marge Thomas. "Us dogfaces aren't supposed to fraternize with the officers, Marge."

"Bullshit," Marge said. "You're welcome here anytime. I keep telling Oscar that dropping his stripes was the biggest mistake he ever made. I bet you and that black-market moose are making ten times what we're making."

"Maybe five times," Hammer said. "Where do you want this, Honor?"

"Oh, just put it—by the door to the porch. Where did you get it?"

"General Foreman ordered it. Got here a day too late. He's not going to be able to use it where he'll be sleeping tonight."

"Christ, are they in the lines already?" Marge Thomas said.

"Hell yes," Hammer said. "They got casualties already. At least five killed in Able Company of the 3rd Battalion."

"Jesus," Fran Slattery said. "That's Joe. Oh God—"

She ran back into Marge Thomas's house. "Join us for a drink, Fred, once you get rid of that load," Marge said.

As Hammer lugged the mattress toward the door to the house, Marge leered at Honor and added, "Can't imagine what use you've got for that now, honey."

Honor glared at her and followed Hammer into the house. He dumped the mattress and departed. Honor contemplated the padded mass and groaned. Adam was right. It did look god-awful in the tiny Japanese room. She would keep it until he came back and then get rid of it. Smuggle it up to General Foreman's palatial hunting lodge on the mountaintop in time for him to celebrate his return to Mrs. Foreman. Although it was hard to imagine that bony, totally controlled politeness machine being sexy.

Honor sat on the porch and picked at some sukiyaki Mrs. Kasunabe had left on the stove for supper, then decided to wash her hair and take a bath. Soak her troubles away. She lit the fire and soon had steam rising from the big vat. She stripped off her clothes and soaped herself, casually admiring her legs, which everyone agreed were as good as Betty Grable's.

She shampooed her hair and plunged into the steaming vat. Ohhh, dissolving, worries, fears, wishes, everything dissolving. Through the thin walls came the croak of a male laugh. Then Marge Thomas started playing her phonograph again, another big band in the mediocre middle range, with a greasy male vocalist singing "Amapola," one of Honor's least favorite songs. She put her hands over her ears, and drowned out the music, so that only the beat reached her. She bucked her belly to it in the steaming water, creating delicious sensations in her thighs.

Footsteps on the gravel outside, then thumping in the house. Suddenly Fran Slattery's long wan face was in the door, her eyes bulging with shock and fright. "Honor. If you saw what she's doin' to him—what he's doin' to her. I wouldn't. I'm a good Catholic. I'd—lock the door. Put somethin' in front of it."

She was gone. What in God's name was she talking about? Honor sprang from the tub, toweled herself dry and put on her blue kimono. She went out on the balcony. Down on the road she saw jeep headlights, figures walking near them, shouts, bursts of drunken laughter. "Fuck'm all!" someone yelled. From one of the nearby houses came a woman's cry: "Don't. Don't. Help me, someone."

Honor whirled to gaze at the door to the courtyard. How did you lock a sliding door? What was the point in putting something in front of it? Then she heard the wooden frame hiss open. A man's bulky body filled the doorway to the porch. It was too dark to see his face.

"The boys are kinda wild tonight. A lot of them know they may be dead tomorrow or the next day," Fred Hammer said.

"Are you here—to protect me?" Honor said, one hand clutching the kimono at her breasts. The breeze crept under it and opened it from the waist down. She clutched at the lower cloth with her other hand.

He laughed nastily. "I sure as hell don't want to hurt you. I just thought maybe we could exchange favors, before I go airborne tomorrow. I think about you a lot, Honor. When I'm stickin' it into the moose, I close my eyes and think it's you. I was doin' the same thing next door, with old Marge, when she passed out. She never could hold her booze, old Marge."

"Get out of here or I'll start screamin'."

"Honor. You shouldn't talk that way to me. You know what might happen? I might let your husband get killed. I might even kill him."

"What are you talkin' about?"

"Second lieutenants die pretty fast in a war, Honor. Nobody bothers to notice whether the bullet gets them from the back or the front. Nobody wants to know. On the other hand, if you're nice to me, really nice, I can almost guarantee to bring him back alive."

"I will count to three. If you're not out of here—"

"Combat's wild, Honor. The craziest most confusing goddamn experience you've ever imagined. Bullets, noise, fear. The first time, trying to command men, you think you've got to be a hero. I'll let him be one. He'll end up dead, like all the heroes."

With one sweep of his arm he ripped her kimono off and flung it across the porch. He must have eyes like a cat, Honor thought. A cat or some other animal that saw in the dark.

The night wind chilled her flesh. She felt it against her breasts, her arms, her buttocks. He stepped onto the porch and she saw in the paler darkness that he was naked. "Let's look at it this way," he said. "I've never had high-class pussy like yours and you've never had low-class cock like mine." His hand covered her pubic hair and she felt his palm rotate into it. "Ohhh, that is really smooth," he said. "I thought about doin' that every time I saw you strollin' around in those goddamn short shorts."

The porch railing cut into her back. The palm of his other hand was rotating against her left breast. She smelled his breath, thick with whiskey, as his tongue slid along her neck. He stepped back and seized both her hands and wrapped them around his swollen penis. "Feel that," he said. "Old Marge worked me up to that. You wouldn't want me to waste that, would you?"

He whirled her into the bedroom with a flick of his arm. Will God permit this? Honor wondered. Will I permit it? How could she stop him? He could kill her with those arms, those hands, if she tried to fight him he could kill Adam. What had happened to the Army she loved, the Army of the day, of light, the Army of order and command, polish and pride? It had vanished into this darkness, become an Army of chaos, evil, fear, of women crying in the night. A woman could not stop a creature like Hammer, she could only permit him in this Japanese darkness that permitted so much so far from home. Mother, did you ever—

Oh. His mouth was warm and wet between her legs, then she was face down on the mattress and he had entered her from behind in one swift sure thrust. She felt almost nothing at first, beyond the shock, the knowledge of him within her. Everything down there was soft and yielding from the bath.

It would be like the bath, she thought, she would let the darkness become the bath and dissolve into it, he would be nothing but water, heat. Then his hands found her breasts and he stroked her once, twice. She felt the hard harsh authority of his flesh. There was a swirl of excitement that blurred and then blended into a shudder of rage and revulsion. "How's that?" Sergeant Hammer whispered. "The lieutenant ever give you anything like that?" Another stroke and he lifted her to her knees, still in her, and the strokes went deeper. She began to weep, tears of rage and shame and fear while the callused hands ground her breasts and the dwarf trees bowed beneath the darkness on the hills above them and the waterfalls trickled and flares fell over the murky hell of Korea where Adam the shavetail crouched. For him with fear and loathing and love, I will let this Army animal, Honor prayed, now that it was clear that God was permitting it.

Then he was out of her and she was lying face down on the mattress again. "That was really great, Honor," Sergeant Hammer said. "Don't worry about gettin' knocked up. I had a boot on it. And don't worry about the shavetail. Old Fred is gonna take good care of him."

With that goodbye, he vanished into the darkness, his natural element.

Honor spent the night in a weird half-sleep, talking to the distant living and the more distant dead. She vowed to her mother that she had not encouraged Hammer; never, by a word or glance. A lot of wives wore short shorts around Koke-Do. She asked her father why he had let it happen. She had thought that wherever he was, he watched over her, somehow. Now she wondered if he wanted her to become a whore, if he preferred that kind of female to respectable women like her mother.

Honor reacted to the morning with dread. Morning meant she had to try to resume her daylight self. She would have to become Honor Prescott Thayer again. It was impossible. She could not live a lie.

She would never be the same, nothing would ever be the same again.

That first day, she did not go out at all. She ate nothing. She told Mrs. Kasunabe to go home at noon. A few minutes later, a hung over Fran Slattery knocked at the door and wanted to know if she was all right. "I'm fine," Honor said through the closed door. Fran asked her if she wanted to join her for a bloody mary at the club. "No, I've got a headache," Honor said. Fran departed and enormous panic surged through Honor's body. Was she ever going to be able to face anyone again? She found a half-empty bottle of scotch in the kitchen and drank some of it. She felt better and slept the rest of the day. She woke up around 1 A.M. and spent the rest of the night weeping silently.

The next day Mrs. Kasunabe said they were out of eggs and milk. Honor had to go out. She wore sunglasses to conceal her red-rimmed eyes. As she stood at the commissary check-out counter. Marge Thomas came in the door. She looked at her in that confronting way. "Hi," she said. "Headache better?"

"Yes, thank you," Honor said.

Again panic stormed through her body. They were talking about her. Marge Thomas knew. She had told Fran Slattery, who had the biggest mouth in the regiment. Honor went back and bought a bottle of scotch. She did not go out for the next two days. She drank the scotch and slept about half the day and half the night. She wept without warning now, day and night.

Fran Slattery knocked on her door again around noon on the third day. She wanted to know if Honor was okay. Honor opened the door wearing her sunglasses and said she was fine. "I'm just worried about Adam, that's all." Fran agreed it was a worry. But what could they do except hope God answered their prayers? Fran urged her to come down to the Officers' Club and play some canasta. Honor said she did not feel up to it.

That afternoon, the messenger of death arrived. He was the Protestant chaplain, a short low-slung man with a square red face that always seemed to be saying excuse me. His jeep stopped at Honor's house. She saw him coming from the porch. She held her breath, telling herself: *If it's what I think, I'll die.* The chaplain knocked on Fran Slattery's door. No answer. She was playing canasta at the club. He knocked on Honor's door. She told him where to find Fran.

"Is Lieutenant Slattery—?"

"Yes. He was killed by a mortar shell the day before yesterday."

That night, Honor was awake but dry-eyed. Fran Slattery wept for her. Her sobbing seemed to shake the house, the earth. The next day she left. Honor did not say goodbye to her. She heard Marge Thomas trying to console her. *The minute they die, we wives are gone,* Honor thought. *We don't exist anymore.*

The picturesque flowering landscape, the expressionless Japanese, the bare house, all seemed to mock her. She started to hate Adam for abandoning her in this never-never land. Two days later, another messenger of death arrived, the Catholic chaplain this time. He stopped at Patty Baker's house, and she too was soon gone. That afternoon Honor drank more scotch and ignored Marge Thomas when she knocked and asked if she was all right. Marge came back with an MP who shoved open the door and blundered into the house. Honor became hysterical and wept and screamed that it was none of the Army's business whether she went out of the house to their goddamned Officers' Club or their goddamned lousy PX or rotten commissary. It was the way her father had sworn at her mother. She had never talked that way before. She was appalled. That was when she knew she had to tell somebody.

Joanna? She was the one real friend Honor had in the Army. But Honor shrank from telling her. She would be sympathetic. But she would somehow imply that Honor should not have let it happen. Honor did not like the way Joanna tended to see herself as superior, to lecture accordingly.

Her mother? If she were closer, if Honor was sure she would not lose her head, she might tell her. But she had seen her lose her head twice, when her father joined the Army in World War II and when he was killed. No, Mother was liable to write her congressman, call the President.

A chaplain? They were supposed to understand such things. But they were so absorbed in their double roles as morale builders for the men in the lines and messengers of death here at the base she could not imagine them taking her seriously. She could even imagine them saying it was too trivial, too accidental, for them to worry about now, when men were dying every day in front of their eyes.

Honor finally decided there was no one to tell except Adam. He would have to decide what to do. She would tell him eventually; why not now, when there was still a chance to punish Hammer? There were other sergeants who could replace Hammer. All the sergeants liked Adam for defending Master Sergeant Buckley. They might even shoot the son of a bitch Hammer for what he had done to Lieutenant Thayer's wife. That was what she really wanted. She hated the idea of testifying at a trial—a court-martial, telling a group of officers, people she would later have to talk to and dance with, what Hammer had done to her.

Honor wrote to Adam that night. Her tears kept smudging the words. She mailed the letter the next morning, after another round of doubt about Adam's reaction to it. A dismal week passed. Two mails arrived from the front without an answer from Adam. Would he call? There was some kind of communication center at headquarters, where they got messages direct from the field.

The chaplains came and went with their messages of death. Still no word from Adam. Finally, as balmy June ebbed into a sweltering July, and the Chinese, pounded bloody by American planes and artillery, abandoned their offensive, Adam replied.

Dear H:

I've just been through 48 hours of heavy fighting and I'm not entirely convinced I'm still alive. I read your letter and wished for a moment I wasn't. Sergeant Hammer was killed yesterday trying to drag a wounded man to safety when our counterattack stalled. I just recommended him for the Silver Star. What to do? You can't court-martial a dead man. I don't know what's to be gained now for you or for me if we told the story. It's so ugly. The best thing, it seems to me, is to bury it with Hammer.

Love,

Adam

207

• • •

It's so ugly. Those were the only words Honor saw, the ones that fulfilled her dread. Adam felt she was defiled. He would never love her again as they had loved in the sparkling midnights and cool dawns of Nova Scotia or the ferocious heat of Fort Bragg in July or even here, before supper on their Japanese quilts, with that love book threatening her peace of mind. He would never love her again in that deep way she had won from him, almost, she sensed, against his will. Never again.

V

OUTSIDE the house, August sunshine beat down, almost as hot in Japan as it had been in Kansas. Mrs. Togo sat in the garden singing a nasal Japanese song to six-month-old Thomas Adam Burke in his cradle. On an end table beside the bright green wing chair in which Joanna was sitting lay the latest issue of the service newspaper, the *Stars and Stripes*, with a huge headline: MASSACRE IN DEATH VALLEY. The war had become a stalemate, with random explosions of combat as the two armies jockeyed for control of strategic valleys or hills. Joanna had lost interest in it. The two soldiers she cared about most, Pete and Adam, were no longer in Korea.

Be happy, Joanna told herself. Why aren't you? Everything is going beautifully. Your husband is an aide to an influential general. You have a beautiful baby, and almost no work to do for him, thanks to Mrs. Togo. You should be happy. You even have time to write poetry, and you think—hope—it's pretty good. Different, anyway, no longer imitations of anyone.

She heard a jeep engine straining up the hill to their door. In a moment Pete opened the gate and Honor came up the path, smiling. She was wearing a white cotton dress with a red belt and red-trimmed pockets and sleeves. The sun sparkled on her spectacular red hair. She was wearing it quite short, with a mass of tight curls on top. Was that why she looked older? Behind her strolled Adam in his paratrooper's uniform, with silver first lieutenant's bars on his shoulders. He was so thin he looked boyish. Honor, who had gained weight, looked ten years older.

As Honor drew close and Joanna opened her arms to kiss her, she noticed that her eyes did not match her smile. They were clouded, averted, and had grayish circles under them. *Something has happened*, whispered a voice in her mind as they embraced and exclaimed the usual phrases.

Adam did not kiss her. He bowed, Japanese style, and said: "Greetings, honorable madam. Your dust-covered guests have arrived, dreaming of the pleasure of tea in your far-famed Doubting Hut."

"Oh," Joanna said. "I've—I've given that up. You'll have to settle for gin."

"What—is—gin?" Adam asked, wrinkling his brow and smiling like an ultra-polite Japanese.

"I wish you really didn't know," Honor said. "I wish neither one of us knew."

"Have you ever seen anything this thin?" Pete asked, spinning Adam around to examine him. "I had trouble finding him at the railroad station. He was standing sideways. No wonder the Chinks couldn't hit him."

"I lost the weight doing an exercise you've never tried, dumdum," Adam said. "It's called thinking."

"Let's sit in the living room," Joanna said. "It's the coolest place we'll find."

They walked toward the house. With its sliding doors open on two sides, it looked like a stage set. The oversized Western furniture, in the bizarre colors Japanese manufacturers favored, added to its unreality. It was a silent commentary on Joanna's flustered confession to Adam that she had virtually abandoned her Japanese life style and the study of Zen Buddhism since Pete came home from the hospital. At her urging he had tried the Japanese way for a week. He had eaten sukiyaki and sampled sushi and let Joanna serve him tea in the Doubting Hut. Then, in the mildest but firmest imaginable way, he had told her that he preferred the steaks and chops and ham and eggs from the commissary, even if they weren't very fresh. He wanted a bed, because his wounded chest ached badly after a night on the *futon*. He wanted chairs, a couch, a table, because he did not like sitting on the floor. As for Japanese tea, he would take American coffee anytime.

In the house, Adam regarded the green wing chairs, the overstuffed vermilion couch with disdain. "You've still got this stuff cluttering up your beautiful house?" he said. He had denounced the furniture when he and Honor came up from Koke-Do for Tom's christening.

"It's more comfortable," Joanna said.

Behind her surrender was a reason she could not explain to Adam. A week before Pete left the hospital, she had extracted a concession from him that made bargaining impossible. She had told him that she wanted to avoid another pregnancy for at least six months. Her mother was partly responsible for this idea. Along with a silver porringer and the announcement that she was creating a trust fund to pay Thomas Adam Burke's way through college, Mother had written Joanna a brisk letter urging her to practice rhythm. She said she had practiced it throughout her marriage with complete success. Joanna was predisposed to take this advice. The memory of her twelve hours of labor pains and nine months of morning sickness was still fresh. Pete was agreeable until Joanna constructed a chart of her erratic menstrual cycle with the help of a doctor at the hospital. They found that she had only four or five safe days a month.

In the house, Honor insisted on an immediate inspection of Thomas Adam. Mrs. Togo brought him in from the garden. Honor bounced him on her lap and talked nonsense to him. "The blob," as Pete called him, gurgled agreeably in return. Joanna felt uneasy. She rarely played with the baby. Pete picked him up far more often. Did the memory of those labor pains make her antagonistic to the child? No, Joanna told herself. It was Mrs. Togo's fault. She monopolized him. Even now, she hovered at Honor's elbow and soon recaptured her charge.

Pete collected drink orders. Honor asked for iced tea. Adam and Joanna agreed on tom collinses. Adam talked about the wild hail-and-farewell party the 158th RCT had given for them and a half dozen other couples who were leaving for the States. "Too wild," Honor said. "I don't like to see you get drunk. I don't like to see anyone get drunk. There's too much drinkin' in the Army, there really is."

"I agree," Joanna said, puzzled by Honor's sudden puritanism. There was definitely something wrong. Honor was not the relaxed, self-confident girl she had known at West Point. Or the wife in love with the Army and with her husband who had visited them for Thomas Adam's christening. She spoke with a strained unreal vehemence. She was twitchy, tense. Her mouth, when she was not smiling, had a tiny droop of unhappiness in each corner.

Joanna did not probe to find out what was wrong. She was still too polite, too separate. She did not see herself as belonging to anyone except Pete, even though he continued to resist the kind of intimacy she wanted. Besides, she was more interested in another topic. Adam had telephoned from Koke-Do to tell them that the Thayers were homeward bound and would be passing through Tokyo at the end of the week. He had refused to say a word about his new assignment until they were face to face, except to describe it as "unbelievable."

"What's this fabulous new assignment?" Joanna asked as Pete distributed the drinks.

Adam accepted his ice-filled glass from Pete and leaned back in the wing chair. "Harvard," he said.

"Haavahd?" Pete mocked. "Since when have they joined the Army?"

"The Army's joining them. It's the wave of the future, big shot. I corresponded with Uncle Abe from my foxhole. He tells me the Army's decided to load up with M.A.'s and even Ph.D.'s. I asked him for Harvard and he got it for me."

"Good God. I thought I was through with school," Pete said.

"Who's Uncle Abe?" Joanna said.

"George Lincoln, head of the Academy's social sciences department," Adam said.

"Harvard," Joanna said. "That's wonderful, Adam."

Did she sound tepid? She hoped not. She hoped her smile was wide and sincere. She was happy for him. But she could not avoid or deny the wish that she could go with him. Not because she preferred him to Pete. But because she infinitely preferred Harvard to Japan or West Point or Germany or even Hawaii.

"I'm not so sure I'm goin' to like it," Honor said. "We're goin' to be poor as the proverbial church mice among all those New York and Boston swells."

"I told you, that idea's out of date. It's a national school now. You may even find a few Southerners with enough brains to get in. There's got to be at least one or two."

"What will you study?" Joanna asked, inwardly flinching at Adam's abrasive tone.

"International affairs," Adam said. "I've already got a title for my thesis. 'Limited War versus Limited Men.'"

"Marvelous," Joanna murmured.

Adam suddenly dropped his air of blithe self-congratulation. "I really twisted old George's arm for the deal," he said. "I needed it. We both needed it. It'll do us good to get away from the Army for a year or two."

He looked at Honor in a strange, somehow mournful way. Again Joanna scented trouble. Pete was simply baffled. "What's wrong, Supe?"

"This goddamn war," Adam said, clutching his drink with both hands. "It doesn't make any sense. When you see half the men in your company getting killed or wounded to capture a hill. When you get to the top and there's another hill just beyond it. It's just too damn idiotic. A half dozen times, I lied. I said we couldn't advance. I doubled my casualty reports. I knew my leader, old Two-Gun Tim, got so rattled under fire he wouldn't remember what I said— assuming he was sober in the first place."

Pete was appalled. "Supe," he said. "That can't be tolerated. What about the companies on your flanks? Did they advance and get creamed because you weren't there to protect them?"

Adam shook his head. "I stalled the whole damn advance."

"That's even worse."

Joanna was confused. Pete was angry. He was denouncing Adam for a moral failure. Even more confusing, Joanna could see that Adam felt guilty about it. What he had just told Pete was a kind of confession, but Pete was not prepared to give him absolution.

"It's not an Army over there anymore. It's a collection of strangers," Adam said. He called the rotation system, whereby enlisted men were replaced after a year and officers after six months in combat, the worst idea the Army had ever perpetrated on itself. "It's destroyed the basic idea of an Army, regimental pride, company loyalty. All the GI's care about is survival. All the officers care about is CYA."

"That means cover your ass," Honor said. Joanna was dismayed to see that she did not seem to take Adam's outrage seriously. She lit a cigarette and told Adam he was boring everyone. Adam ignored her. His eyes—very angry eyes—were on Pete.

"Two-Gun Tim—and a lot of other battalion commanders—made captains sign a statement that their bunkers could take a direct hit from an enemy shell. That way, if anyone got killed, it was the captain's fault."

Pete shook his head. "It's just a way of making sure the captain's doing his job. The colonel's not an engineer. He can't tell if the bunker's been built according to specifications just by looking at it."

"I talked my captain into refusing to sign the statement," Adam said. "Two-Gun caught him with a Korean girl in the bunker and brought charges against him. I went to see the crumb and told him I was going to prefer charges against him for a party he threw when we were in a rest area. It was a goddamn orgy, naked Korean whores dancing on the tables. Two-Gun dropped the charges."

"And you made an enemy for life," Honor said.

It was obvious from Honor's remark that Adam had never tried to explain the Samurai's lonely creed to her. Joanna felt even more confused. She was simultaneously sad about Honor's marriage and angry about her own, angry at Pete for never telling her any of these hard truths about the Army. Why was he so determined to keep her naïve?

"Supe," Pete said, "I don't think the girls want to hear this sort of thing."

"Why not?" Adam said. "It's their Army too. They're in it with us."

"No, they're not," Pete said. His vehemence seemed out of

proportion to the disagreement. Was he still angry at Adam for disobeying orders in combat? "What happens over there is—is between us. We've got to live with it. But they don't. They shouldn't. We're trained to do it. We took an oath to do it."

"Burke's version of the Army. A private horror show," Adam mocked.

"It's not private. I agree with you, rotation stinks, the whole war stinks. But that's the way the civilians want us to fight it. We may not like it, but they're the ones who call the shots."

"I don't agree," Adam said. "I think the civilians need to be told what shots to call. Otherwise there won't be anyone around to do the shooting."

"What the hell are you talking about? Four months in combat turned you into an appeaser? I think we're doing pretty well in Korea. We're showing the Communists aggression doesn't pay."

"I wonder if they think so. Even with a ten-to-one kill ratio in our favor. I suspect they think they're still ahead."

Listening to these closest of friends, West Point roommates, Joanna heard a fundamental disagreement about the U.S. Army's purpose, and the part that an officer should play within the Army. Pete's reaction to Korea was typically Irish-American—traditional, conservative, but hardly timid. He responded wholeheartedly to the idea of the Army as the defender of freedom throughout the world. Adam with his New England roots saw himself as the inheritor of the right to question and even to shape this mission. Pete was upset by Adam's hostile skepticism, which, being Adam, he pushed to an extreme. Adam was equally distu___d by Pete's acceptance of the system.

"Are you going to stay in an Army that's ordered to commit gradual suicide?" he said.

"I told you when we were yearlings, I was in it for the distance. I thought you felt the same way."

"I'm having second thoughts," Adam said. "Maybe Honor is, too."

"I'm not," Honor said. "I don't want to be the reason you quit. You love it, Adam, no matter what you say about it."

Joanna sensed two conflicts, neither of which she understood. The more immediate one was between Adam and Pete. She saw that Pete meant more to Adam as a kind of symbol, the personification of a moral style, than Adam wanted to admit. Between Adam and Honor there had always been an intellectual gap. Now something else had been added, a darker, more ominous shadow. Joanna could only hope it would pass.

They managed to submerge conflicts and shadows in more drinks followed by a steak dinner which Mrs. Togo cooked. Honor revealed that the Thayers had decided to have a baby, and she might already be pregnant. Pete talked about his admiration for Arnold Coulter, the colonel he had met in the hospital. When he was promoted to brigadier general and given command of a new Regimental Combat Team, he had made Pete his aide. Joanna remarked that she was writing poetry again and Adam insisted on seeing some samples. He pronounced them "good to excellent." They talked about absent friends. Sam Hardin's leg had healed and Pete had persuaded him to volunteer to command a company in the new Regimental Combat Team. Adam wondered if he was unable to face going home to Ruth.

Martha MacKenzie, Lover's widow, had married his West Point roommate, Victor Kinsolving. Amy and George Rosser were deep in Army politics. George's boss, Lieutenant Colonel Willard Eberle, had been promoted to G-1, personnel chief of the 4th Armored Division, and Amy seemed to be giving George most of the credit for it. They were eagerly awaiting a suitable reward. "Amy won't be satisfied with anything less than the NATO command," Adam said.

The evening ended abruptly when Pete looked at his watch. "Holy smoke," he said. "The last train to Tokyo leaves in five minutes."

They were all—except Honor—a little drunk. Adam kissed Joanna boldly on the mouth. "Get rid of this junk, I adjure you," he said, gesturing toward the furniture. "Or you'll never see the boat sailing before the wind."

"Come on, Samurai Sam," Pete said, dragging him down the path to the gate.

"I hope you're right—about being pregnant," Joanna said to Honor.

"I hope so too," Honor said.

They were gone. While Mrs. Togo cleaned up in the kitchen, Joanna wandered down the dewy path to the Doubting Hut and switched on the light. In the glow of the small bulb the place looked abandoned. A spider had woven a web around her teapot. She thought about Adam at Harvard, criticizing the Army. She told herself she admired, yes, even loved, Pete's way, his courage and stubborn devotion to duty. Was he aware of the implied comparison between him and Adam in her mind? She suddenly wanted to show him—and Adam, in some remote unadmitted way—that she did not regret her June week choice. But it was not a safe night, according to her rhythm chart.

She heard the jeep return. Retracing the dewy path, she reached the house as Pete entered it from the other side. He sighed and said: "They made it."

Mrs. Togo departed with a bow and a weary smile. Joanna nursed Thomas Adam while Pete took a bath. She decided to skip a bath and put on a nightgown. She lay on the bed and watched Pete emerge from the bathing room, a towel around his waist, and go to the bureau to get clean pajamas. Her eyes focused on the ugly scar of his chest wound, which ran from his left nipple around his body to his backbone. She sprang out of bed and threw her arms around him. She was trying to say she loved him, to tell him she wished she could say it more explicitly. But Pete did not respond with affection. He froze; a strange, almost angry expression appeared on his face. She touched the scar with her fingers. "They hurt you so much," she said.

"Jesus Christ," he said, shoving her away. "Are you turning into some kind of weirdo?"

She fled sobbing into the living room. After slamming several bureau drawers, Pete followed her to apologize. "It's this rhythm thing," he said. "Wanting you and not being able to have you."

She clung to him and begged him for a few more months. "I'm not as brave as you want me to be, I know it," she said.

He denied it, without enthusiasm. They went to bed. She read rejection in the way he turned his back to her. Indifference in the way he so quickly fell asleep. If he had given her a little more time, she might have been ready to risk an unsafe day, in spite of Mother's advice. Why wasn't he more patient with her? Why did he insist on inflicting so many of his attitudes, his likes and dislikes, on their marriage? She brooded about his refusal to tell her the truth about the war. It typified their relationship.

A mild hangover and lost sleep combined to make Joanna feel wretched the next day. She decided to skip her four-hour stint as a gray lady. The hospital had more volunteers than they needed now, anyway. Casualties had dropped steeply since the war became a stalemate and the Army had opened a half dozen other hospitals in Japan. Joanna spent the morning in the garden, reading Zen koans. It was the first time she had read any since Pete was discharged from the hospital.

After lunch, she decided to clean the Doubting Hut. She was in the middle of this sweaty task when she heard the tinny tinkle of the telephone. Mrs. Togo answered it and informed her it was "Coptin Brrk." She found Pete's last name impossible to pronounce.

"Hope you're in the mood for another big dinner," Pete said. "General Coulter's wife has finally arrived. He's invited a couple of old friends of theirs. Two generals."

Joanna did her best to get in the mood. She told herself she should enjoy these command-performance dinner parties to which they were regularly summoned since Pete became an aide. The guests were usually interesting and important. Arnold Coulter seemed to know dozens of generals and diplomats. They seldom did more than make boring small talk with her. But the wife of a newly promoted captain was hardly on their level. When Pete arrived in his jeep with the general's star on it, she was ready, smiling, in her best black dinner dress.

As Pete changed into a fresh uniform, he briefed her on the generals she was about to meet. "One's a three-star named Mark Stratton. He and Coulter got out of the Academy together, class of '22. He was a big tank general in Europe. Flatten'm Stratton, they called him. He's got his aide with him, a major named Ingalls. He's class of '43. From Massachusetts. Saw some tank action in Europe. And Major General Christopher and his wife. He was a big deal in the capture of the Philippines. His wife is from Idaho."

In spite of her prior exhortations to herself, Joanna felt irritated. "Why don't you let me find these things out for myself?" she said. "I'm not five years old." It was not the first time she had been irked by Pete's insistence on briefing her so elaborately before a dinner party. She saw it as a lack of confidence in her. The name he had called her last night—weirdo—reinforced this suspicion. She only half listened to Pete's explanation.

"Joanna. It just helps—it smooths the converstation. General Stratton thinks he's pretty damn famous. If you ask him what he did in World War II, his nose will be out of joint for the night. So would Christopher's, for that matter. He thinks he captured the Philippines single-handed."

"General Coulter isn't such a prima donna."

"He's different."

She was struggling to like General Coulter, even though the more time she spent with him, the more certain she was that he could have sat for Hemingway's portrait of Colonel Cantwell in *Across the River and into the Trees*. Hunting was Coulter's favorite sport. He had killed everything from lions in Africa to grizzlies in Alaska. He loved war and could describe in amazing detail how it felt to lead a bayonet charge or watch a BAR mow down a company of attacking enemy. But his career had a most un-Hemingway-like curve in it. He had been captured on Bataan and imprisoned by the Japanese for four years. They had treated him abominably, starving and torturing him. But they had been unable to break his spirit. It had been an ultimate test of his manhood and he had passed it. He even seemed to admire the Japanese for their remorselessly thorough brutality.

"What's Mrs. Coulter like?"

"I have no idea. She can't be too bad, with a son like Rod Coulter."

Joanna still did not completely share Pete's admiration for Captain Coulter, who was now a company commander in the 2nd Division in Korea. He had flown to Japan for the party celebrating his father's star and seemed even more stiff and formal than he had been at West Point. Everything Rodwell Coulter said had a slightly unnatural resonance. "After due consideration," he told Joanna, "Edna and I concluded that it would be better if she stayed in the States. My mother emphatically concurred.'' It took Joanna several days to realize that he reminded her of Douglas MacArthur. There was the same aura of solemnity, the same sense of interior drama, the feeling that Captain Coulter was not merely talking to you, he was performing for you, playing the part of the totally dedicated soldier. He was so different from his father, Joanna found herself looking forward to meeting his mother.

Soon the Coulter house was visible on its hilltop, although they had to travel another half mile of winding road to reach it. The house had belonged to a Japanese admiral in the days when nearby Yokosuka had been headquarters for the Imperial Navy. It was decorated in a weird mixture of Western and Oriental styles, one room full of overstuffed clumsy furniture worse than anything Grand Rapids ever committed; the next room bare and graceful, with a *kamidana*, or god shelf, bearing a miniature Shinto temple guarded by two porcelain lions. Behind a sliding panel was a small room containing an elaborately carved, gold-lacquered Buddhist shrine. Against opposite walls were a stuffed tortoise and a stuffed crane, symbols of longevity. The garden, three times the size of Joanna's pocket version, was pure Japanese, with an oval pool in the center of it, and rugged hills, symbols of eternity, beside a teahouse at the far end.

Most generals' wives Joanna had met thus far had been different in appearance but similar in manner. They had been variations on the Mrs. MacArthur model, charming, friendly, but very self-controlled and understated in makeup and dress. Blanche Coulter immediately announced herself as different. She was wearing an off-the-shoulder black chiffon dress, with a Spanish flounce to the skirt. She wore her rather frayed black hair in an equally pronounced way, combed to the right side of her face. She had large, thyroid eyes and a small mobile mouth. It was a flapper's face, now lined and excessively made-up, emanating a feverish, somewhat artificial intensity.

''You're the girl who had the baby in the middle of a battle,'' she cried when General Coulter introduced Joanna. ''Arnold told me about it.''

''Not quite, Blanche,'' the general said. ''She was in the hospital. The hospital was sort of reluctant to admit it, that's all.''

"There are only two places to have an Army baby," Blanche Coulter announced. "Washington, D.C., and West Point."

"I'll remember that," Joanna said.

"What the hell's this?" bellowed General Stratton. "The Army's having babies now?" He was an ugly, stocky man with a flat head, a snout of a nose and a square jaw.

"What are you going to do about it?" Blanche Coulter said. "Court-martial us? Run us over with one of your silly tanks?"

General Stratton and his aide, Major Newton Ingalls, were introduced. Ingalls was built along his boss's bulky lines, but was much better-looking and had a far more agreeable manner. Stratton insisted that he only wanted to straighten out one thing: who had the babies, the Army or the "camp followers"? If the Army had them, they were government property and maybe Congress could eliminate the draft.

"I think you know more about camp followers than I do," Blanche Coulter said. "I heard you had one in your tank all the way across Europe."

"In my tent," General Stratton said. "There isn't enough room to do anything in a goddamn tank."

"Now I know why I chose the infantry, sir," Pete said.

The general began declaiming on the uselessness of infantry unless they were supported by tanks. Lanky, jut-jawed General Wayne Christopher joined the argument. He was an infantryman and so was General Coulter. General Stratton began taking punishment from front, flank and rear. Mrs. Coulter extracted Joanna from the argument and joined Mrs. Christopher, who was a smooth, smiling Mrs. MacArthur-model wife. They both wanted to hear more about her adventure giving birth. Joanna was flattered by the attention, but thought it was best to play it down. "I'm sure there would have been no problem, if the fortunes of war hadn't overwhelmed everybody."

"That's the wrong attitude," Mrs. Coulter said. "The Army has put you through a most ungodly ordeal. Has you husband made it up to you?"

"I—I don't understand," Joanna said.

"Made it up. Whenever something like that happened to me, I

insisted that Arnold make it up. I'd say you deserve a trip to Hong Kong, at least."

Joanna glanced at Mrs. Christopher, trying to see what she thought of this idea. She looked politely but blankly amused. Did she agree? Behind their smiling façades were all generals' wives as imperious as Blanche Coulter?

"Being in the Army is a fate which should not befall any woman," Blanche Coulter continued. "She has a right to be recompensed. Regularly." She glared across the room at the generals and their aides, who were now in a sober conversation about the use of tanks and infantry in Korea. "They get combat pay and medals. What do we get?"

An orderly appeared carrying another round of drinks. Joanna accepted a second scotch and soda with some misgivings. She had begun drinking hard liquor at parties since Pete became the general's aide. Beer seemed too gauche and Coca-Cola or ginger ale too juvenile. Several times she had come home with her head spinning. Blanche Coulter took a hefty swallow of her drink and asked Joanna what she was doing for servants. Joanna told her about Mrs. Togo.

"I came out here on only one condition. I would not have to let one of *them* in the house." She began telling Joanna what she had gone through in Manila in 1942 when the Japanese captured the Philippines. There had been repeated threats of rape and mutilation. At one point they had told her that her husband had been executed. For Blanche Coulter, the Japanese became monsters and she had no intention of letting the peaceful smiling civilians of the Occupation change her opinion. She had come to Japan for only one reason, she said. "I have a premonition, amounting to a certainty, that Roddy will be wounded and I intend to be here to nurse him. I have no great faith in Army medicine, as I am sure you will understand," she said to Joanna.

Beneath the heavy makeup and the flamboyant style, Joanna began to see a suffering woman, someone who had experienced a dimension of Army wifehood that stirred in Joanna a profound, dangerous sympathy. She began telling Blanche Coulter about her ambition to write a book with Pete about his experiences as a company commander in Korea.

"Why, I think that's a wonderful idea, don't you, Wayne?" Blanche Coulter said to General Christopher as he turned away from the masculine circle to take another drink from an orderly.

"What?" he said.

"Mrs. Burke's going to write a book with her husband about our disaster in Korea. Don't you think it could be fascinating—especially if they wrote the whole truth—what Arnold told me in his letters? The utter cowardice of the troops and the incompetence of half of the officers."

"I don't think junior officers should write books," General Christopher said.

"Who's writing a book?" General Stratton said.

"Captain Burke, apparently," General Christopher said. He had a long lean face, a good match to his lanky body. Joanna had thought he was rather mild-mannered when he smiled and said hello. Now she suddenly saw another side of his personality. The smiling mouth was gone.

"A half dozen reporters have been trying to get me to write a book," General Stratton said. "I told'm to get lost. I'm no horn blower. Only horn blowers write books."

He was drunk. So, Joanna suspected, was General Christopher. But it affected him in a different way. "Are you going to include your difficulties at the hospital?" he asked her. "To make sure the Army comes out looking completely rotten?"

"What's wrong with that?" Blanche Coulter said.

"No," Joanna said. "I was only thinking of helping Pete write about his combat experiences."

"And what do you think this will accomplish? Are you trying to make him a general before he's thirty?"

"Sir," Pete said. "It's something we've discussed—but I told Joanna I had no interest in it. I tried to explain to her that it wasn't practical."

"Have you kept a diary, like so many other ambitious junior officers?" General Christopher asked.

"No, sir," Pete said. "I'm not the diary type."

An orderly summoned everyone to the dining room, furnished in massive Spanish colonial mahogany which the Japanese admiral had apparently looted from the Phillippines. Joanna hoped the book would be forgotten in the transition. But General Christopher was relentless.

"I found out one of my battalion commanders was keeping a diary on Luzon," he said. "I relieved him immediately. Diary keepers are all assassins, in my opinion, assassins of their commanders' reputations."

"Captain Burke said he *didn't* keep a diary, Wayne," General Coulter said.

"I agree with Wayne," General Stratton said. "Never thought about it before, but I agree with Wayne."

"I don't," Blanche Coulter said. "I think you're just a bunch of glory hogs and don't want anyone else to get any credit for doing anything but dying. I'd like to see a captain write a book, describing generals—and colonels for that matter—as they really are."

"Calm down, Blanche," Arnold Coulter said.

"I am perfectly calm, General Coulter," Blanche said.

"Sir," Pete said to Coulter, looking more and more desperate. "I assure you that I have never even thought of keeping a diary. And I have no intention of writing a book."

"I know you don't, Pete," General Coulter said. "You've got Arnie Coulter to vouch for the fact that you're the kind of soldier everyone in this business has got to respect. Old Arnie was lying down there on a jeep in No Name Pass last December, watching those Chinks walk that machine gun closer and closer to his morphine-filled torso, when you went up that hill and took out that gun and the whole company of slant-eyes supporting it."

By now, Joanna was wishing she could slide under the table, like an embarrassed child, and disappear. Major Ingalls seemed to be the only one who had any sympathy for her. "My wife wanted me to write something about my company commander experience in Europe," he said. "It's probably the most intense human contact a man has in the Army. He feels responsible for all those lives."

"The Pentagon might have let you get away with that," Arnold Coulter said. "But they won't let anyone tell the world how unprepared we were to fight in Korea."

"We were not unprepared," Wayne Christopher snapped. "If

223

we'd had a week—two weeks—to get even one division up to combat strength in men and equipment—"

"Crap," General Stratton growled. "You and Doug were sitting out here playing emperor instead of running an Army. Proves what I've always said. Army should stay out of government bullshit. Let the politicians screw it up on their own."

"How much time did you have to get the 10th Armored ready to fight before you went into Africa?" Christopher said. "Twelve months. You didn't have a President who declares war one day and tells you to fight it the next. Why blame the Army for Truman's idiocy?"

"I'm not blaming the Army. I'm blaming MacArthur," Stratton snarled. "Maybe if somebody told the truth, people would stop thinking he's Jesus Christ and Alexander the Great combined."

"Hear hear," Blanche Coulter said. "Another reason for Captain Burke to write his book. I could tell some stories about the Great Ham that would add considerable spice to it."

"Maybe we ought to change the subject," General Coulter said. "Will Army have a winning football season next year? What do you think, Pete?"

While Joanna sat dazedly, Pete examined Army's prospects, position by position. The orderlies began serving the dinner. Mrs. Christopher asked Blanche Coulter if she planned to do much shopping while she was in Japan. "I don't expect to leave this house," Mrs. Coulter said. Mrs. Christopher demurred. "It's fun," she said. "There are some marvelous buys in the small towns around Tokyo. Pottery, lacquerware. Even the Ginza is fun now. There are lots of things in the stores. *Ginbura*, the Japanese call it, Shopping the Ginza."

Somewhat nervously, Mrs. Christopher discussed the ethics of buying yen on the black market. General Christopher let her do it, as long as she did not tell him about it. She usually had one of their orderlies handle the transaction. With the official price 15 to a dollar and the black market price 360, it seemed almost insane not to deal. "It makes shopping so much more fun," she said. "Buying things with make-believe money."

"Are you breast-feeding the baby?" Blanche Coulter asked, all but leaving Mrs. Christopher in the middle of a sentence.

224

"Yes," Joanna said.

"In my day, it was formula. If you think that was easy to prepare on Mindanao, with 110-degree heat and a million crawling, flying insects and maids who barely knew the meaning of soap and water—"

The wine, a Château Haut something or other introduced by General Coulter with great fanfare, flowed freely. The orderlies served steak and baked potatoes. The generals, their rivalries apparently soothed by Pete's briefing on West Point's football team, began discussing the integration of blacks and whites in the Army. Arnold Coulter thought it was a good thing, long overdue. Wayne Christopher, with that bluntness which Joanna had begun to realize was a trait among generals, disagreed. Integration might work in combat, he said. But here in Japan it was already turning into a nightmare for the Army. He described some of the riots they had recently had in Tokyo's red-light districts when blacks and whites began patronizing the same bars and brothels.

Joanna recalled the disorder she had encountered on her first night in Japan. "Why doesn't the Army just shut down all those places?" she asked. "We're running the country, aren't we?"

The generals looked uncomfortable. "It's a question of morale, Mrs. Burke," General Christopher said. "Soldiers expect that kind of entertainment. You've got to give it to them, if you expect men to fight."

"You mean American soldiers won't fight unless—"

She saw desperation contorting Pete's face again. This was another unsuitable topic of conversation.

"Let's put it this way, Joanna," Arnold Coulter said. "When you ask a dogface to squat in a rifle pit up to his knees in rainwater in January and take on a couple of thousand screaming Chinese, you can't expect him to act like a Boy Scout when he's on leave."

"War does terrible things to the moral sense, Mrs. Burke. It's so cruel, so random," Major Ingalls said.

"I think it's social class," Wayne Christopher said. "Enlisted men haven't changed that much, even with the draft."

"Roddie doesn't agree. He says it's a new Army," Blanche

Coulter said. "He says an officer has to lead by example. I think that's ridiculous, don't you?"

"A true believer," General Coulter said with his quick rakish smile, which seemed to mock the idea—but not quite.

The party broke up rather quickly after coffee. General Stratton said he had a conference at 0800 tomorrow with the "paratrooper," General Matthew Ridgway, the new supreme commander in the Far East. General Christopher apparently had a long day every day trying to keep order in Japan. As he shook hands with Pete, Joanna was dismayed to hear Christopher say: "I hope you won't write that book, Captain." Pete swallowed hard and assured him that it would remain unwritten.

Joanna and Pete were left alone with the Coulters. "Don't let Wayne Christopher upset you, Pete," General Coulter said. "He was my executive officer in the Philippines, before the war. A born martinet. He was First Captain of his class."

"I understand, sir," Pete said.

"Well, I think Pete and Joanna should write the book," Blanche Coulter said. "If I had any literary talent I would have written one about your adventures."

Joanna tried to explain that she had never intended to blacken the Army. General Coulter smiled and nodded. "You just didn't realize how touchy certain generals are about their reputations."

"Certain generals?" Blanche Coulter said. "I've never known one who wasn't."

"Joanna," Pete said. "You've got a customer expecting a midnight snack. No one can give it to him but you."

"I want to see that young fellow as soon as possible," Blanche Coulter said. "Will you bring him up here?"

Joanna said she would be delighted, any day. Mrs. Coulter said she would call and make a date.

"What a fascinating woman," Joanna said as they started the five-mile downhill drive from the Coulter home.

Pete just grunted.

"It's sort of shocking, to think the Army actually believes that you have to supply enlisted men with prostitutes. It's really—immoral."

226

Pete said nothing.

"Don't you think so?"

"I wouldn't know. I'm not a general."

"You don't have to be a general to see what's wrong with it. The policy is immoral."

"What the hell am I supposed to do about it?"

"Nothing. I'm just shocked—that's all."

He drove down the mountain at an alarming speed. Several times Joanna clutched the side of the jeep to keep from lurching into the road on a curve. Gradually, she realized he was angry. At the house, Mrs. Togo was doing a flower arrangement. The baby was "fast ashreep," she said. Pete said good night and she bowed her way out the door. He took off his tie and flung it over the green wing chair. Joanna went into the bedroom and took Thomas Adam from his crib. He rubbed his eyes and puckered grouchily. Like father, like son, she thought.

Back in the living room Pete was pacing up and down. Joanna began to nurse Thomas Adam. Pete got out some scotch and poured himself a hefty belt. Finally he said: "How could you do that, Joanna?"

"Do what?"

"Bring that up? The book."

"It just came naturally. I thought Mrs. Coulter would be interested."

"Interested. Couldn't you see at a glance that she's got a screw loose? Maybe a couple of them? Don't you have any judgment?"

"No. I guess not. I guess I'm just a weirdo."

He slammed his glass down on an end table and paced again. "I said I was sorry about that. Are you going to throw it in my face every time we have an argument?"

She burped Thomas Adam, changed him and put him back in his crib. He would sleep until Mrs. Togo arrived at 6:30 A.M. The world's most cooperative baby. She returned to face his glaring father.

"You don't seem to realize what you just did. Got me a reprimand from a two-star general. Got me marked down in his book as a guy who keeps diaries, a glory hound."

"I doubt if he'll remember it. He was pretty drunk."

"If he doesn't, his wife will."

"I still don't see why you can't write it. Is the Army afraid of the truth? Isn't it a free country?" For a moment she was so angry she started to cry. She managed to suppress the tears but the words exploded between them. "You still don't understand why I wanted to write it, do you? It makes me wonder what you think marriage is all about. When I try to get close to you, to find out what you feel about war, combat, being wounded, you shove me away and tell me I'm a weirdo. Put me off with one-sentence answers. What was it like around Pusan? Hot and messy. Is that the kind of answer to give to someone who's trying to love you, to share your life?"

She saw he was truly, genuinely astonished. He had never gotten even a glimmer of how she felt. But his surprise blended with his anger, his memory of the humiliation she had just inflicted on him at the Coulters' quarters. "You know why I don't tell you? Because I don't want you to know about it. It's too goddamn horrible for you to know about. For anybody to know about but the guys who go through it."

"I don't believe that," she said.

"All right," he said. "I'll tell you how Lover MacKenzie died. They swamped him with one of their human-wave assaults. He surrendered, he and a half dozen other guys who were cut off around his command post. The Communists tied them up with barbed wire, our own barbed wire, throat to toe, with their hands behind their backs. The next day we counterattacked, and knocked them off the goddamn hill. Just before they ran, they shot the enlisted men in the head. They poured gasoline on Lover. They must have gotten it from one of our tanks. They poured gasoline on him and set him on fire. That's what we found at the top of the hill."

Joanna shook her head. She was numb. Pete took it to mean she still disagreed with him.

"Not enough? You want to know how I lost my company? Really lost my company? That first night on the Chongchon, we did better than any other company in the regiment. G and H on our flanks were wiped out in their holes. We held our ground. But we had a lot of dead and wounded. I got the wounded back to an aid station. The

228

next night was the same story, only worse. The Chinks hit us from three sides. I lost all my sergeants and corporals.

"Then they told us to pull out. A couple of tanks took up a blocking position on the road. We got into trucks and the aid-station people loaded the wounded into the convoy right behind us. I had maybe eighty men left. We went about ten miles and stopped. We sat there for hours. We could hear firing up ahead. It was getting dark. Suddenly some of the aid guys come running down the column screaming the Chinese have us surrounded and it's every man for himself.

"It was total panic. Everybody jumped out of the trucks, jeeps, and ran into the hills. They didn't know where they were going. They just ran. I managed to catch one guy by tackling him. We spent the rest of the night wandering around, trying to find some others. By morning I'd collected six. We headed back to the column, but most of it had moved during the night. The aid-station trucks, with all our wounded, were sitting there, isolated.

"As we started down the hill toward the trucks, we heard aircraft coming in low. Air Force Phantoms. They had orders to destroy all abandoned vehicles. Before we could move, they dropped three cans of napalm on the trucks. We could hear the wounded screaming, burning alive inside them."

He was shaking, weeping. "My men, Jo, my men."

She groped her way across the room to him, half blinded by tears. "That's enough, enough," she whispered. "I understand now, I really do. I'm sorry I made you tell me."

"I want you—I need you here, Jo. You and the kid. If you weren't here, I'm not sure I could go back over there. I need to know you're here, waiting for me."

How could she resist wounds of such dimensions? She accepted the role of healer, restorer. Not seeing then that it inflicted on her a passivity, an obedience that she would gradually find intolerable. She led him into the bedroom and began to unbutton his shirt.

"It's not a safe day," he said.

"The hell with it."

"Are you sure?"

"You heard me. The hell with it."

"Jo."

He was kissing her, undressing her, lifting her onto the bed. But as he caressed her breasts, as his fingers found her clitoris, her bold words began to transmute into something strange and dangerous. They became part of what was happening in her body, an inability to open herself without fear, to give herself beyond doubt. Pete had opened himself to her, half in anger, true, but also in anguish, above all, in honesty. She could not achieve a similar honesty. The fear of another pregnancy, of another nine months of retching misery, another night of agonizing labor, stood between her and that perfection. This changed the meaning of *the hell with it*. The words skittered and scattered and finally dissolved in the gush of his coming, a tremendous surge of semen that she accepted in her body and fled in her mind. When it was over, when he cradled her against him in that strong commanding way, the words returned with their new meaning.

The hell with being a Catholic.

The hell with not being able to love in freedom. Without fear.

In bed, Pete turned his broad back to her and seemed to go to sleep almost immediately. Joanna lay there, trying to get a grip on what was happening to her. She groped backward for the Zen self that she had tried so hard to fabricate before Thomas Adam's birth. That Joanna seemed to have vanished, to have never been more than a creature of wish, dream, incapable of confronting the reality of this formidable soldier husband. Yet that woman, who had tried to find a new stance, another way of facing reality, was not forgotten. Perhaps she was also not as insubstantial as she seemed. Perhaps she still existed, like a negative print of a photograph, waiting for an event that would restore the flesh, the color of reality.

The next afternoon, Blanche Coulter appeared in Joanna's doorway, apparently oblivious to her declaration that she would never leave her hilltop house. A 1951 Chrysler, driven by an orderly, purred in the street. Blanche was wearing another high-style outfit, a violet suit with large dramatic buttons and a coat with spectacular lapels. She said that she had come "to see this famous baby." She bounced Thomas Adam on her lap for two minutes, pronounced him a darling and gave him back to Mrs. Togo. "I'm on my way down to the Officers' Club to see an old friend," Blanche said to Joanna. "Why don't you come along?"

Joanna recognized an order when she heard one. At the Officers' Club, to Joanna's dismay the old friend turned out to be Betty Parrott. Betty's father, it seemed, had been master sergeant of General Coulter's company when he had been a captain in the Philippines. Joanna sat there, a polite smile on her face, while they reminisced about prewar Manila days. It sounded like a lovely life. Even the sergeants' wives had had servants. Everyone spent their summers at Baguio, a resort in the mountains. In the 1930s, General MacArthur added his aristocratic presence. While the old Army girls talked, they drank. Betty Parrott had three rye and ginger ales and Blanche Coulter had two bloody marys. Joanna sipped a tom collins. Betty Parrott's good humor declined with each swallow of her third drink. She began denouncing her son-in-law, Sam Hardin, for letting Pete persuade him to become a company commander in General Coulter's Regimental Combat Team, Task Force Delta.

"I warned him that he was going to get his a-s-s blown off this time for sure. I told him Arnie Coulter specializes in taking chances and everybody who goes into action with him winds up a casualty sooner or later. But he'd rather listen to your hero husband."

"I thought Delta was staying here, in reserve," Joanna said.

"They'll be in Korea before the end of the month. Ridgway's going over to the offensive."

"Are you sure?" Blanche Coulter said. "Arnold promised me three months, minimum."

Betty Parrott only reiterated her prediction. With her usual disregard for eating her words, she asked Blanche if she could get Captain Harold Parrott into Task Force Delta. He was tired of shuffling papers at the replacement center. This time he wanted to hold his rank and he needed some combat time to do it. Blanche said she would talk to Arnold about it—and about a few other things. "He promised me three months," she said, frowning ominously.

Driving back to the house, Blanche Coulter told Joanna not to take offense at Betty Parrott's manners. "Old Army people like her are common. But they're loyal. They know the Army."

"She hates it—the Army," Joanna said.

"Of course she does. Any sensible woman hates the Army. My mother told me I'd hate it. So I had an advantage. I joined up with my eyes open."

"Was your mother an Army wife?"

"Dear God, no. You've heard of the Rodwells in Chicago?"

"I'm afraid not."

"Mother was a Rodwell. My father was a Palmer. Surely you've heard of them. I was the youngest of three girls. I was determined to marry someone different. So I went on a world cruise and met Arnold in Hawaii. We got engaged and married the same week."

They were inching along one of the crowded back streets of Yokoshima. Japanese women hurried past in brilliant kimonos. The sliding doors of all the houses were open to the street. Various merchants—shoemakers, fishmongers—were at work, often with their wives toiling beside them. Bright paper lanterns and flags dangled from roofs and wires. Several women with babies strapped to their backs sat on the steps of a Shinto temple.

"Horrible people," Blanche Coulter said through clenched teeth. "These horrible people ruined everything for us. Arnold would be a four-star general today. We'd done everything right. We knew everybody—Marshall, Somervell. Arnold was the same rank as Eisenhower, Bradley, the whole bunch from the class of 1915. Then these people captured him. Arnold sat out the war while all the stars fell on Ike and his pals."

She shoved another cigarette into her white pearl holder and with no warning, changed the topic. "I felt so sorry for you last night. Wayne Christopher is a boor. You're like me, you take things to heart. It doesn't work in the Army, my dear. The Army doesn't believe in heartbreak. It doesn't exist for them. If it did, they wouldn't be soldiers."

They were at Joanna's house. Blanche Coulter was smiling in her intense forced way. "Goodbye, my dear. Let's do this again soon."

So Blanche Coulter had been one of those wives who had been determined to make her husband a general, to do everything that her money, her beauty, could contribute to this goal. What made her failure doubly painful was Arnold Coulter's ability. As Pete explained it to Joanna, Coulter had a record as a troop leader and expert on the Far East second to no one in the Army. He had been one of the organizers of the Philippine Constabulary, which had fought heroically on Bataan. But the fortunes of war had flung him into limbo for the crucial years of his career and now he was in another kind of limbo, far behind his contemporaries. "He wouldn't have even made brigadier if it wasn't for Korea," Pete said.

"It seems so unfair," Joanna said.

"The general says an Army career is like getting married. It's for better or worse, and you've got to expect some of the worse."

Joanna was not sure she liked the comparison. But she accepted it without contradiction. "I hope we don't turn out like them," she said. "She's so bitter."

"That's her fault," Pete said. "She's got the wrong attitude."

What's the right attitude? The question teetered on Joanna's lips. But she said nothing. She was afraid it would sound dumb—or hostile.

Perhaps even then she sensed that she shared Blanche Coulter's inability to accept the decrees that history, events, inflicted on a human life. For the first time, thanks to Blanche Coulter, history had become personal to Joanna. She realized that she was part of its often brutal process, that history happened to people. Somehow, her brother's death in World War II had never seemed historical. It was a minor elegy in the swelling national triumph. Did history's hulking presence only become apparent in defeat? In 1951, the vast majority of Americans did not know the taste, the feeling of defeat. Only Army people, those who had been in the lost battles, knew it.

Perhaps that was why she did not share Pete's disgust when he came home a few days later to report that Captain Harold Parrott had just become the deputy adjutant of Task Force Delta. "The old man'll do anything to keep Blanche happy," he said.

"What's wrong with him?"

"He's a drunk. He keeps a bottle in his desk. But the general's probably right. We won't have time to worry about him once the shooting starts."

"What shooting?"

"They're sending us over to Ten Corps. To spearhead a new offensive."

"I wish you didn't look so happy about it."

He got the message. "I'm not happy about leaving you and Tom. But—"

She told herself she was learning. She was not really hurt.

A few days later, Joanna was giving Thomas Adam his five o'clock feeding when a jeep stopped in front of the house. She assumed it was Pete. It was, with General Coulter beside him. Blushing, Joanna hastily buttoned her blouse. "Sorry," Coulter said, flashing that reckless, charming grin, which looked too young for his weathered face. "I just dropped in to say goodbye. And ask you to keep Blanche company. She's pretty upset about me going into combat again. With Roddie out there already."

"Of course," Joanna said.

"Don't wait for her to call you. Go up there once or twice a week. With the little guy."

"I'll be glad to, General."

The Task Force left for Korea the following morning. Joanna got the usual cryptic letters from Pete. She learned more about what they were doing from *The Stars and Stripes*. Delta joined the Eighth Army's massive tank-and-artillery-backed offensive that pushed the Chinese steadily north, inflicting huge losses. The Chinese Army began showing signs of disintegration. Companies and regiments surrendered en masse when they were cut off by fast-moving tank columns. Suddenly the Communists agreed to talk truce. The offensive ground to a stop. Pete, echoing General Coulter, was appalled. Another month and they would have destroyed the Chinese Army, perhaps ended the war, he said. But the politicians in Washington had to make good on their repeated protestations that they wanted peace.

Meanwhile, Joanna tried to keep her promise about seeing Blanche Coulter. She took a taxi up to her house twice in the first week. Each time, she was dismayed to discover that Betty Parrott was already there, eagerly pouring drinks for herself and Mrs. Coulter from the general's private supply. Blanche was delighted to see little Tom, for about five minutes. Then she went back to discussing the war. As usual, Betty Parrott had inside information, no doubt from her husband. Delta had fought well but casualties had been heavy. No matter what some fire-eaters said, maybe the truce was not such a bad idea.

"What about the 2nd Division. Casualties heavy there too?"

"Very," Betty said.

Blanche Coulter began to weep. "What happens to Arnold doesn't matter anymore," she said. "But if Roddie dies—"

She talked in a violent hysterical way about her son's future. He was certain to become the youngest general in the Army, the first man in his West Point class to wear stars. The Army owed it to her. People, very important people, had promised her.

"Why in God's name is he commanding a rifle company?" Betty Parrott said. "Why isn't he back on staff?"

"Because he's his father's son," Blanche said. "In spite of all I've tried to teach him, he still worships that maniac." She laughed bitterly. "You know, MacArthur wanted to take Arnold with him. When the Great Ham went on the lam from Corregidor. Arnold said he'd rather stay with his men. And then he said: 'I think you should stay too, General, no matter what our commander-in-chief says.' That's one reason Arnold never got a star, after he finally got out of the goddamn Jap prison. World's leading expert on the Far East. He sits four years in Washington writing memorandums because MacArthur doesn't even want to hear his name, much less see him."

History, Joanna thought. The Army was infested by its own history, as well as the nation's history. History that broke hearts. She shuddered and for the first time felt truly afraid of the future. She could see why history tormented the wives more than the husbands. The men at least had the consolation of duty done, courage proven. That solace seemed denied to the wives.

The course of the war accentuated everyone's sense of helplessness. The Communists used the truce talks to spout propaganda while their Army dug deep into the Korean hills along the 38th parallel. In several places they held menacing high ground from which they could launch a devastating offensive when they chose. The American Army decided it could not tolerate this advantage and savage seesaw fighting erupted for his high ground, which reporters soon nicknamed Heartbreak Ridge. Task Force Delta was not involved, for which Joanna thanked God. But the 2nd Division bore the brunt of it and each visit to Blanche Coulter became a process of waiting for the hysteria, the crying jag, to burst out, letting it run its course, then putting her to bed.

Joanna began to dread the visits. She preferred to work at the hospital, writing letters for or reading to the wounded. Then came that gray day in early November, a time when the Japanese landscape begins to acquire its funereal winter look. Betty Parrott stopped outside the house in her snorting old Plymouth. Joanna instantly sensed something was wrong. Betty never encouraged her visits to Blanche Coulter. She considered her a rival. Joanna came out of the house to find Betty standing beside the car. "He's KIA," she said.

"Who?" Joanna said, almost collapsing, thinking it was Pete.

"The hero, Captain Rodwell Coulter, West Point '45. I want you up there. I can't face this one alone."

It began to rain on the way up to the house. By the time they got there it was pouring. They stumbled in the door and found Blanche Coulter sitting in the small room that contained the Buddhist shrine, staring at the impassive face of the Enlightened One. She knew. General Coulter had called her during the night.

"Maybe they're right," she said, without turning around. "The Japanese. The Orientals. It's all fate. All written in the stars ten thousand years ago."

"Sit down in here," Betty Parrott said, leading her into the living room. "Let me get you a drink."

Blanche continued to talk in an empty monotone to Joanna while Betty bustled in the kitchen. "Arnold said he died like a soldier, his face to the enemy. On Heartbreak Ridge. He said there wasn't a round of ammunition left in any of their guns."

"We know they're soldiers. Why do they have to prove it?" Joanna said.

"They have to prove it to each other," Blanche said. "They're really boys, you know. Bang you're dead. They don't believe it until it happens."

Betty put a dark brown glass into Blanche's hand. "I really— don't think you should drink that," Joanna said.

"Why not?" She downed the drink in one long swallow. "You must understand one thing. I can't endure lectures. I taught that to Arnold a long time ago. But I could never teach him the other lesson. That we need—comforting. They don't know how to comfort us. All they can do is tell us to be hard like them. I shall try my best."

She handed the empty glass to Betty Parrott. With a sneer at Joanna, Betty went out to the kitchen to refill it. She refilled it a half dozen times before Joanna left, using her baby as an excuse. By that time Blanche Coulter barely knew where she was. She smiled politely at Joanna and thanked her for dropping by.

Gray November slipped sullenly into December. Joanna went up to see Blanche Coulter less and less. Betty Parrott was now bringing her some kind of pills from the hospital. Blanche drifted dazedly around the house in long lacy black negligees, which Joanna found embarrassing, they were so blatantly sexy. Blanche gave Betty money for the pills—Joanna never knew how much and talked almost exclusively to her about prewar days in the Philippines.

Joanna wrote a frantic letter to Pete, full of accusations against Betty Parrott, and tore it up. What was to be gained from plunging him into the middle of a quarrel which both he and General Coulter could easily dismiss as female jealousy? She could not stop Blanche Coulter's disintegration any more than she could stop the war, which rumbled on while the truce negotiators talked and talked at Kaesong. Pete's letters were nothing but groans of frustration and boredom. The wounded trickled into the hospital as usual; some lived, some died.

On Christmas Day, Joanna could not avoid a visit. She arrived to find Blanche in the bedroom talking on the telephone to General Coulter, telling him she was fine. "In some ways I feel closer to Roddie now than I did before. I know he'll never change, never grow away from me now," she said. "And guess who just walked in? Joanna Burke. Is Captain Burke there?"

Joanna and Pete said conventional things. Merry Christmas.

Thomas Adam had gained another five pounds. The front was quiet. Blanche Coulter smiled dazedly. Joanna hung up and Blanche lurched to her feet and led her into the living room, where she had set up a Christmas tree. She gave Joanna a present. "Something to remember me by," she said.

Joanna broke the gold cord and opened the white box. The gift was one of those black lace negligees that had become Blanche's favorite costume.

"Mrs. Coulter," Joanna said. "There's a psychiatrist at the hospital. Maybe if you talked to him instead of relying on—on—"

"On Betty? I don't rely on her. I use her. I will use her as long as it suits me."

There was more pride and more despair here than Joanna had ever encountered before. She retreated into silence, allowed Blanche to pour her an eggnog, and left as Betty Parrott came leering in the door. Later that day, just after she signed the register and went on duty at the hospital, Joanna encountered Betty, also wearing the gray volunteer's uniform. They were in an empty second-floor corridor.

"I'm—I'm terribly worried about Mrs. Coulter."

"The Duchess? Nah. I've seen her go through this act before. In the Philippines, when Dugout Doug dumped her. They had a big affair, you know. Back in the States—"

Joanna shook her head angrily. She did not want to hear any more of the bitter truths of the old Army. But Betty Parrott was unsilenceable.

"You wouldn't feel so sorry for her if you knew her way back when," she said. "If you knew how she shit on me and my mother and father in the Philippines and every other enlisted man and their families wherever she's been stationed. She used to make my mother wash her personal laundry because she didn't like Filipinos handling it. They weren't white. Old Arnie let her get away with it. He let her get away with everything. She was so goddamn rich."

Joanna could only recoil from this hatred oozing up from the Army's lower depths, contained behind smiles and submissions and salutes. Was this at the heart of the Army, this barely controlled rage, this cruelty? How could she keep this evil out of her own life, her son's life, retain, somehow, the ability to love Pete, love everyone?

238

That night it snowed. But the morning was clear. Mount Fuji's white cone was visible in the west. Joanna decided to make one more try to help Blanche Coulter. She told herself that if she got there early enough to spend a few hours with her alone, it could make a difference. Betty Parrott was like the spirit of evil, a malevolent force sucking Blanche back into the dangerous past of ruined hopes and lost happiness.

It was only a few minutes past 8 A.M. when Joanna arrived at the house. "Blanche?" she called. "Mrs. Coulter?"

The front door swung open to her touch. She moved cautiously through the Japanese room, with its lion-guarded Shinto temple and symbolic tortoise and crane. "Blanche?" she called. The smaller shrine room was empty. The golden Buddha sat alone, staring enigmatically. The bedroom was also empty. The bed was still made. "Blanche?" Joanna called, more nervously now.

The winter wind sighed around the roof. Its chill touched Joanna's cheek. The sliding door to the garden was open. She stepped into the world of gray gravel and jutting stone. Perhaps Blanche was in the tearoom at the far end. Joanna began to walk along the *Roji*, the dewy path, wondering if she could get Blanche interested in the tea service. Then she saw her.

The general's wife was face down in the icy pool in the center of the Japanese garden, her black negligee floating around her like the petals of a drowned flower.

VI

"I DON'T want to go skiing. I find the class of '50 singularly boring."

"Okay. Okay. Do you mind if I go?"

"Yes, I do. I don't enjoy rattling around this apartment by myself. I feel like a ghost from the twelfth century every time I look out the window."

First Lieutenant George Rosser shook his head and pondered the snow falling on the medieval shops and houses of Donaulingen, one of the oldest of the picturesque cities on Germany's Romantic Road. Amy knew what he was thinking: *You're the art major, the expert on old paintings and old buildings. Here I've given you the living museum to end them all and you're still miserable. What the hell is the matter with you?*

Donaulingen was only a hop and a skip in their Volkswagen to Augsburg, headquarters of the U. S. Army's European Logistics Command (EURLOG). There, in an office on Philippine-Wepser-Strasse, behind a desk as empty as his mind, sat George's new boss, Major General Carl Lightfoot. Not far away, in her town house opposite the historic Palasthotel Drei Mohren, sat his wife, Margaret, Amy's nemesis.

Amy knew what George was trying to do, suggesting that they join a class of '50 ski trip to the Bavarian Alps that he had helped organize. It would put some distance between her and Mrs. General Lightfoot for a few days. It was thoughtful-selfish, like so many things George did. He loved to ski and was good at it. Amy did not like to ski, perhaps because she was not very good at it.

Was it the snow? Amy wondered, glancing uneasily at the thick white flakes drifting silently down through the twilight. Was she going to be spooked by snow for the rest of her life? She ordered herself to get a grip on her nerves. She was being ridiculous. It had nothing to do with the snow. It had nothing to do with memories, mourning. She was living in the present, dealing with reality. She was not the sort of person who spent her life bemoaning lost dreams, fantasies that were impossible in the first place. The reality was: the class of '50, European division, were a boring lot. Their wives were worse. The thought of spending a long weekend with them in a ski lodge made her retch.

She had every reason to be in a rotten mood. Another dismal six months confronted her, 180 days of trying to keep Margaret Lightfoot happy. An impossibilty. Of watching George trying to keep her happy, an even larger impossibility. Under her breath, more than once since June, Amy had cursed Florence Eberle.

From Florence's point of view, everything had gone according to plan. More tennis with Willard's West Point classmate Colonel Drinkwater had led nicely to Willard's promotion to full colonel and his succession as G-1 of the 4th Armored Division. The promotion had been guaranteed by the 310th Supply Battalion winning the best-in-division prize on maneuvers in May. It was the first time a supply battalion had ever won. Not a few of the white points had come from the West Point smartness with which the battalion marched in the post-maneuvers review in Nuremberg.

With Willard Eberle in charge of personnel, George waited impatiently for his reward—as did Amy. When it came, it seemed at first to be more glorious than anything they had dared to imagine. Not merely promotion to first lieutenant, but appointment as aide to one of the best-known fighting generals in the Army, Carl Lightfoot. Florence Eberle had called Amy from Regensburg to assure her that she would love Margaret Lightfoot, she was old Army, born at West Point, where her father had been a professor. One of the Lightfoots' many friends at the Pentagon had called the commander of the 4th Armored and asked the general to give the Lightfoots the best social aide they could find. The general had bucked the job to Willard, who suggested George.

Then came reality. Carl Lightfoot was not going to take command of one of the armored or infantry divisions in Europe. He was going to EURLOG, a strange assignment for a fighting general. Amy and George told each other it was probably temporary. They were right—but not in the way they wanted to be right. They both sensed something was awry, from the moment they met the Lightfoots and their military aide, Captain Kenneth Bourne, at the Stuttgart airport. General Lightfoot was a hulk of a man, with permanent five o'clock shadow on his hollow cheeks and jutting ridge of chin. A Texan, he walked and talked like a rancher. His wife was also large, and as padded with flesh as the general was lean. She was dowdy but formidable, with a wide flat face and an aggressive chin.

"I hated this country the last time we were here," Margaret Lightfoot said.

"No, you didn't, sweet. You had a real good time," General Lightfoot said.

"We were in Cologne. A decent city. They're all Communists here, from what I've been told."

"That's Worms," the general said. "Lot of Communists in Worms. It won't be so bad, you'll see. We'll have the grandchildren over. Lot of good sightseein' round here."

"Yes, sir," George said, and started talking about the castles and walled towns on the Romantic Road.

"Romantic Road," Margaret Lightfoot said. "I've never heard such an asinine name in my life."

They debarked at the town house and went up the steps. Margaret Lightfoot frowned at the Palasthotel Drei Mohren across the street. "What's that old pile?" she asked.

George began telling her it was a very famous hotel, where Czars and Kaisers and other celebrities, including Mozart and Goethe, had stayed.

"It'll probably be noisy and keep me awake all night," she said.

Inside, Mrs. Lightfoot strode around the town house, which was furnished in stark 1920s Bauhaus style. "This is ridiculous," she said. "I feel like I'm living in a gymnasium. I want the whole thing redecorated."

"The whole thing?" George said before he could stop himself.

"The whole damn thing," Mrs. Lightfoot snarled. "Are you in charge of EURLOG's petty cash?"

"No, ma'am," George said.

"We'll take care of it," General Lightfoot said. "You just caught Lieutenant Rosser by surprise. I'm sure he and his wife are ready and willin' to help you."

"I'm ready to start right now," Amy said. "I love decorating houses."

"Well, I don't. So I'll let you do all the work," Margaret Lightfoot said.

"I think we're all worn out from the trip," General Lightfoot said. "We'll see you folks in a day or two. Leave your phone number with Captain Bourne here."

The next day George had a drink with Captain Bourne at the Officers' Club. He was an ROTC graduate who had won a Silver Star in Korea. He told George why Carl Lightfoot was in EURLOG.

True to his reputation as a fighting general, he had launched a series of aggressive probing actions when he took command of the 38th Division in Korea, early in May of 1951. Fierce fights for nameless hills had erupted, causing heavy casualties—at a time when Washington did not want any casualties. Reporters started calling him "General Heavyfoot" and "Callous Carl." He had been relieved of his command and transferred to EURLOG with orders to keep his mouth shut for a year and then retire. The general was pretty philosophic about it, but Mrs. Lightfoot was furious and determined to exact all the revenge in her power.

After a week of dealing with Margaret Lightfoot, Amy could scarcely conceal her dismay. She found it hard to believe that anyone could be angry about her husband being forced to retire as a major general. Especially a husband like Carl Lightfoot, who seemed (to Amy) lucky to have risen that high. His only topics of conversation were hunting and fishing. Amy was amazed when George disagreed with her. Voicing an outrage that he had apparently caught like an infection from Captain Bourne, he said Lightfoot was a great soldier and what the Army had done to him was a damnable disgrace. Lightfoot had been Patton's favorite brigadier in World War II, famous for the way his brigade advanced as fast as or faster than the tanks. In Korea, he had simply obeyed orders to secure his front against a possible Chinese offensive. When the press started howling, the Pentagon had thrown him to the editorial wolves.

Amy, exhausted from drives to Munich and Frankfurt to find antique furniture and wallpaper for the great town-house redecoration, was unimpressed. "I still say he's a simpleton and you ought to call Willard Eberle and demand a new assignment."

"I couldn't do that to the old man," George said. "He'd know why. Besides, he's going to take me and Bourne hunting in the Vosges Mountains next month. Where he and Patton used to go."

"And leave me to play whist with Maudlin Margaret?"

Whist was Mrs. Lightfoot's favorite game. She and the general apparently played it by the hour.

"Isn't she going to do any entertaining?"

"How can she when her house looks like the inside of a puzzle factory?"

243

Amy saw to it that George did not go hunting. She told Margaret Lightfoot about the expedition and she refused to part with George, who, after all, was her aide too. Geroge spent the week supervising a team of German painters who were gilding the ceiling of the town house. With Amy's help, Mrs. Lightfoot was restoring it to its eighteenth-century splendor.

Missing the hunt in the Vosges put George in an extremely bad mood, but he still refused to ask for a transfer. Instead, he gave Carl Lightfoot something to do. At EURLOG the general's responsibilities were zero. He told his two aides that he hated to be useless. Did they have any suggestions about how he could make a contribution in his last year in the Army? George suggested investigating the large amount of equipment that was being stolen from Army supply depots. He told of the frequent shortages of spare parts and fuel that he had encountered while serving in the 310th Supply Battalion. General Lightfoot liked the idea. He had George draft a memorandum, suggesting a series of spot checks for which he would need a staff of twenty men. Under orders to keep Lightfoot happy, lest he tell what had really happened in Korea, EURLOG gave him what he wanted. Within a month the "Lightfoot Brigade" had found enough evidence to suggest a major scandal lurked inside the EURLOG command, with officers as well as enlisted men involved in selling U.S. equipment to Germans on both sides of the Iron Curtain.

George began having a good time but Amy continued to be miserable. Mrs. Lightfoot finally got her house decorated to suit her late in October and gave a dinner for a half dozen colonels and the commanding general of EURLOG. Amy expected the main topic of conversation to be Korea and had George brief her on all aspects of the stalemated war. Instead, Mrs. Lightfoot turned the dinner into a right-wing political forum. She said there was a Communist conspiracy in the Pentagon and that explained the "no win" war in Korea, the sabotaging of patriot generals like her husband. To Amy's amazement several people at the table agreed with Mrs. Lightfoot.

Although Amy had planned the dinner down to the choice of brandy and port (consumed by the generals and colonels in astonishing quantities), she was scarcely noticed at the table. Mrs. Lightfoot, wrapped in her rage and gloom, was too busy orating on Commu-

244

nism to give her any credit. When they got home to Donaulingen, Amy swore and threw things around their apartment. "I am not going to do another thing for that bitch," she screamed. "I want to go home."

George was dismayed. He told her that he was making a reputation for himself in the logistics field. Hadn't Willard Eberle told them supply was a place where a smart soldier could go places in the modern Army? George was beginning to agree with him. The Army was woefully lacking in management techniques. Every little supply depot and motor pool was a law unto itself. It was time to bring some order out of the chaos and he was beginning to think he was the man to do it.

That was when George began suggesting ways to get Amy away from Margaret Lightfoot, if only for a weekend. The ski trip was the latest idea. Amy knew he was trying, rather desperately, to keep her happy. This seemed to make her all the more determined to foil him. Why? Why was she refusing to be happy? she asked herself. Was Margaret Lightfoot really that much worse than Florence Eberle? Wasn't she merely another valuable lesson in the ways—and in her case the woes—of an Army wife? Would Florence Eberle let a screw-loose cow like Margaret Lightfoot make her so miserable?

Amy stared out at the falling snow. George was saying: "You know, half the time I get the feeling you don't like me very much anymore."

"That's silly," Amy said, feeling a whiff of panic.

"Or you're taking something out on me. Something that sure as hell isn't my fault. I can't figure out what's happening to us."

She had not been very romantic lately. Worse than lately. For a good six months. Make that nine. At first, she had tried to manage her grief over John Stapleton's death by letting George have her whenever he wanted her. Which was often. But it did not work. The grief, she now saw, was still there. So she started to blame him for the failure to consume it with his hungry lips, erase it with his eager hands. When that failed, she had tried loneliness, avoiding love. She told herself she would conquer grief as the strong and the tough conquer their disappointments, with a defiant "so what." But that was not working either.

"It's this job," she cried. "It's such an utter total zero. A waste of a year."

It was a lie, a misrepresentation and a rather inept one. George did not let her get away with it. "The hell you say. Lightfoot's giving me credit all over EURLOG for Operation Spot Check. We're going to launch another one, Operation Tightwad, studying unit finances, housekeeping costs."

"It's a zero for me, then. Don't I count?"

"Ame, is the old girl that bad? I don't get it. She was a pain in the tail when she was decorating the house but—"

But I won't do anything. I won't entertain. I won't go out. I sit home and stare at the falling snow. Is that what he's going to say? Maybe I'll tell him why.

The telephone rang. George answered it. "Hello. Mrs. Lightfoot? Sure. Amy's right here."

George handed her the telephone. "Mrs. Rosser?" Margaret Lightfoot said in her imperious way. "Where can I find a baby nurse?"

"I—I don't know."

"Oh—you don't have any children, do you? I keep forgetting. Would you look into it tomorrow, first thing? My grandchildren are arriving for Christmas and we don't want to be tied down to their schedule."

"I'll take care of it, Mrs. Lightfoot. I'm sure we can find one."

Christmas 1951 was coming. It was less than two weeks away. And she was launching her own home-by-Christmas offensive. Bitter, bitter, the tricks memory played on you, she thought. Christmas and falling snow and a smashed tank. Men were still dying in Korea. George had stopped complaining about his lost combat experience. She had won that battle. But she had suffered a shuddering defeat in another, more secret war. Maybe there was a lesson to be learned from it, a lesson her mother never learned from her endless arguments with her father. Stop trying to impose your feeble female will on men and events. Accept the best and the worst with an indifferent smile. Gallantry, that would be her goal from now on.

Amy acquiesced to the ski trip. She got her German cleaning woman to find a baby nurse for the Lightfoots' grandson. The following day she and George drove across Germany, picking up a caravan of '50 classmates at Karlsruhe, Würzburg, Stuttgart. They passed through the shrine town of Oberammergau, and along the Alpine Highway to Garmisch in the Bavarian Alps. The scenery was spectacular, the weather perfect, and Amy's gloom gradually diminished. She found the class of '50's husbands and wives had no inkling of the truth about General Lightfoot and she felt no compulsion to tell them about it. Instead, she talked briskly of the waves George was making with his investigations at EURLOG.

On Saturday, in bright sunshine belying December, they lunched on the terrace of the Gasthof Reindl, with the majestic Zugspitze, Germany's highest mountain, and a half dozen other peaks looming around them. The men were all determined to ski "Zug." Most of the wives said they would be satisfied with the four-mile walk to Grainau, with its superb views. As they strolled along the snowy road, one wife, a cherubic-faced blonde named Martha Kinsolving, fell in step with Amy.

"I met a friend of yours when my first husband was training in Kansas," she said. "Joanna Burke."

"Oh yes. I owe her a letter. I owe about a dozen letters. Mrs. Lightfoot keeps me running from dawn to dusk."

"I had a letter from Joanna about a month ago. She and the baby are fine but she's sick of Japan. I'm afraid she's going to be there for a while. Pete's become an adviser to one of the South Korean divisions."

Amy's brain clicked into gear. "You're—you were—Martha MacKenzie. Joanna mentioned you." *Her father's a general*, Joanna had written as if this was a matter of no consequence. "Your first husband was—was—"

"Killed in Korea."

"My God. That must have been terrible."

"It was rough for a couple of months. But you get over it."

How? Amy wanted to ask. But she only nodded and said: "I lost a cousin. A very dear cousin. John Stapleton. He was with the 2nd Division."

"Class of '49? I met him. He dated a friend of mine who went to Ladycliff. Broke her heart, I'm sorry to say."

"He had—had that reputation," Amy said. Each word was an immense weight that she lifted from the center of her body. She fought an impulse to weep.

"Oh wow! Look! What's that? I think it's the Eibsee," voices chorused.

They had rounded a curve in the road and the other wives were gazing in awe at the glittering lake with the tremendous rock wall of the Zugspitze rising above it.

"I was lucky," Martha said, continuing their private conversation. "I found someone else I could love. Vic's a wonderful guy. Being born in the Army helped a little too, I guess. You know other people who've gone through it. You know what to expect—and what's expected of you."

"Yes," Amy said. She barely heard the last two or three sentences about the Army. She was riveted by the previous sentence. *I found someone else I could love.* "Yes," she said again. She watched the word float out of her mouth and drift into the blue sky. If it echoed around George on the slope of the Zugspitze, what would he say? *Bullshit?*

That night, with wintry stars glinting outside the window, Amy nestled close to George in their double bed and whispered: "I hope you didn't give everything to that mountain."

"Just about," George said drowsily. They had consumed flagons of dark beer at dinner. But he decided not to pass up the opportunity. Not many offers had come his way lately.

Maybe that was why it was wrong. He didn't linger over anything. He just wanted to get it over with so he could get to sleep and be ready for a full day's skiing tomorrow. Amy felt nothing. She kept hearing Martha MacKenzie Kinsolving say: *I was lucky. I found someone else I could love.* Afterward, she decided she felt worse than nothing. She felt violated. *Fucked.*

No, wait. Amy spent most of the night staring into the darkness trying to find an alternative to that feeling. The next day she looked and acted like a zombie. Martha Kinsolving invited her to join several other wives in a cable-car ascension of the Wank, the second-highest peak in the Bavarian Alps. She realized she could not endure it. She could not endure Martha and her resignation. She could not endure the sight of so much snow. She could barely tolerate looking out the hotel window at the snowbanked roads and white fields. Snow recalled the dream, the defeated army, the wrecked tank. She told Martha she was getting her period and felt rotten.

George and Amy drove back to Donaulingen late that afternoon, arriving at their apartment around midnight. George was in a cheerful mood. As usual, he had not the slightest perception of her feelings. He ignored the way she answered him in monosyllables as he discussed the assignments of other members of the class. Some of '50's best men were talking about resigning as soon as they fulfilled their required four-year stint. A few disliked the postwar Army with its reliance on OER's. They thought it was too impersonal. Others were disillusioned by rotten commanders—martinet lieutenant colonels, incompetent majors, hostile captains.

Amy listened and did not care. She knew George was testing her opposition to early retirement. She wanted to care but she did not care. By the time she stumbled into bed in Donaulingen, she was ready to weep at the vacuum inside her.

The next morning, at eight, the telephone rang. George, already awake and cooking his breakfast, answered it. A moment later the phone was being thrust into Amy's hand. "It's Mrs. Lightfoot."

"Mrs. Rosser? I hope it's not too early. I've been up since five, playing with my guest. Do come down and see him sometime this morning. Maybe you can take his sister out for a stroll around Augsburg."

George drove her to the Lightfoot door and went on to EURLOG, headquartered in a building around the corner. In the living room of the town house, on an eighteenth-century sofa upholstered in green baize silk which Amy had ransacked Munich to find, sat Mrs. Lightfoot, tickling a small boy who was propped against the cushioned back. Not since she arrived had Amy seen Mrs. Lightfoot in such a good humor.

"Mrs. Rosser," she said, "let me introduce you to Carl Logan Lightfoot the third. Isn't he the best-looking baby you've ever seen?"

Carl Logan Lightfoot III. Amy gazed into his round baby face and suddenly she knew what she had to do to regain her grip on herself, on her feelings, on life. That night, after supper, she sat down on the sofa beside George and put her arms around him. "Hey," he said, "this is an unexpected pleasure."

She kissed him. "George," she said. "I think it's time we had a baby."

She did not tell him the rest of it. That the baby would be a boy and he would be named John Stapleton Rosser. It was better not to tell George everything.

BOOK
THREE

I

Krrackumph. The sunrise gun boomed across the precise lawns and litterless streets, the rectangular parade grounds and row houses and barracks of Fort Stanton, New York. In Quarters 275, a tan attached wooden house identical to three others in its group, and to six other groups on the street, a red-headed five-year-old was already awake, squirming beside his mother on the living-room couch while she read *Charlotte's Web* to him. In the past year Joanna had assembled a small library of the best in children's literature. Unfortunately, Thomas Adam Burke, now usually called Tom, did not agree with his mother's literary taste. He thought books about talking spiders and pigs were dumb and declared that he would rather have "a story" from *A Picture History of the Tank,* a book his father had given him for Christmas.

"It's time to stop anyway," Joanna said. "I've got to get breakfast."

Suddenly the opening lines of a poem caromed through her mind.

> *From an altitude beyond delight*
> *The blind parachutist prepares to plunge*
> *Into the heart of the city*

Joanna got up and scribbled the words on a pad on the government-issued maple desk in the corner of the living room. She stared at them for a moment. Where had they come from? Did it have something to do with Adam Thayer being a paratrooper? Superfluous question. It did not matter where poems came from. The important thing was to get them written. She added two more lines.

> *For centuries he flew into the sun*
> *Until impossible brightness taught its lesson*

"Can we have pancakes for breakfast?" Tom asked as he pulled the tank book from beneath an end table.

"No. Pancakes are for Sunday. They take too long to make."

She went out to their narrow kitchen and began cooking bacon and eggs. The greasy odor of the frying bacon swirled around her as she scrambled the eggs. She struggled to control her nausea. When the eggs were firm she poured cornflakes into bowls, orange juice into glasses. "Breakfast," she called.

Pete arrived first, his khaki shirt pressed to razory creases on the sleeves, his red hair shining, his skin glowing from his shower. He exuded health and good humor. "How are you feeling?" he said, giving her a kiss.

"All right," she said. It was what he wanted to hear. There were only so many complaints about morning sickness a man could stand.

"Tom?" she called.

"Snap into it, Mr. Ducrot," Pete said, using a West Point name for plebes. Tom came rocketing into the kitchen. "Sorry, sir!" he said, his eyes smiling. Pete and Joanna had taken him along to West Point last fall when Pete gave a lecture to the first-classmen on his combat experience in Korea. Tom had loved the place. He sat on his father's shoulders and watched the Corps pass in review, scampered up three flights to Daddy's old room in North Barracks, spent hours in the military museum admiring guns and uniforms.

A cockroach dashed across the counter by the sink. Pete killed it with his hand. "Jo," he said. "You've got to keep this place cleaner or those critters will eat us alive."

"Everybody has them," she said.

"We wouldn't have as many of them if you did the dishes after every meal."

Two and a half years in Japan with Mrs. Togo doing all her housework had spoiled her, Joanna thought. It was a shock to return to servantless America and discover how much time it took to cook meals, clean house and keep track of a small but very active boy.

"What's on your schedule today?" Pete asked as he ate his cornflakes.

"A Women's Club bridge," Joanna said. "I'd like to skip it."

"You skipped last week's, Jo."

She heard the reproach in his voice. His assumption that she would participate in the Women's Club had been another shock to Joanna when they returned from Japan. Living off the economy in Yokoshima, with the nearest base a replacement center, she had felt no compunction to join its Women's Club and Pete had not insisted on it. But living on a Stateside base changed the rules for a lot of things. Major Burke had bought a copy of a book called *The Army Wife* and given it to Joanna for Christmas. He said it would save arguments. The book enjoyed semi-official status as a compendium of good advice on everything from moving to entertaining to decorating a house. When the Women's Club came up, Pete pointed to the pertinent passage. *It is every wife's duty not only to join but to take an active interest in the Women's Club.* Major Burke made it clear that he expected Mrs. Burke to do her duty and then some. It was not enough to join the weekly bridge club. Almost every wife did that. He wanted Joanna to be active on at least two other committees.

"We're having the Floyds and the McQuades to dinner tonight."

"I know. But the club's important, Jo. You know why. I explained it to you. Besides, I think it's good for you to get out of the house and meet other wives. You've got to learn to get along with all kinds in the Army."

Ever since they had returned from Japan in 1954, Pete had reiterated how anxious he was for them both to be outgoing, sociable. He did not want anyone to think that his rapid rise to major, thanks to his combat record in Korea, had given him or his wife a swelled head.

"All right, I'll go," Joanna said.

"Atta girl," Pete said.

On brave old Army team, Joanna thought. If only she were a team, life would be a lot simpler. There were times when she wondered if her husband—and the Army—thought she was three or four people. They apparently expected her to be an enthusiastic committeewoman, a dedicated wife and mother and a gracious hostess. The hostess side was the third shock she had received when they returned from Japan. When they arrived at Stanton, invitations poured in from old friends and new acquaintances. Pete expected her to return all of them in what he called a "reasonable" time—and to entertain better than the veteran hostesses with whom she was competing. He "critiqued" her first half dozen meals, from the hors d'oeuvres to the dessert and found them wanting in various ways.

Pete went off to his training battalion to spend the day planning marches and field exercises to turn draftees into soldiers. Joanna did the breakfast dishes and went into the bedroom, where Mr. Ducrot was supposed to be dressing himself for school. She found him shining a brown shoe with a brush from the kit his father had given him for his birthday. The kit had been an idea ahead of its time. Whenever Tom used it, Joanna had to spend ten minutes cleaning him up. Today was no exception. The hand holding the shoe was covered with brown polish. There was a smear on his right cheek. "Tom," she said. "Those shoes were all right."

"Daddy said they should be four point oh," he said, using the Army phrase for a perfect inspection.

"Three point eight is good enough," Joanna said.

She hustled him into the bathroom and scrubbed the hand and cheek, then back into the bedroom for a rapid insertion into his shoes and snowsuit. One minute later, the bus arrived at the door to take him to kindergarten at the post school. Her next-door neighbor, Beatrice Lamm, stood on her steps watching her two sons, one of them Tom's age, the other three or four years older, board the bus. "Feel like a cup of coffee, Jo?" Beatrice said.

"I—"

Joanna's mind was a blank. She could never think of an excuse to avoid Beatrice Lamm. She was nice enough, in her salty Montana way, but she could talk all morning. Pete had told Joanna to accept these neighborly invitations unless she had a good excuse. Beatrice's husband, Major Theodore Lamm, was an OCS graduate who was eight or nine years older than Pete. He had something of a chip on his shoulder about the Army's supposed favoritism toward West Pointers, which made it doubly important for Joanna to be friendly with Beatrice.

It was ten o'clock before Joanna got back to her quarters, after listening to Beatrice Lamm denounce the commander of Fort Stanton, Major General Lucius Atwater, for ordering the MP's to arrest any child found wandering on or near the parade ground. Her youngest, Teddy, Jr., had been picked up yesterday and taken to the post jail. She had had to go down and claim him. Joanna winced at the thought of what Pete would say if this ever happened to Tom. He had spent an hour explaining to both of them that the base commander held every officer responsible for the conduct of his children.

> "I DON'T KNOW BUT I'VE BEEN TOLD
> HONEY, HONEY
> RUSSIAN GIRLS ARE MIGHTY COLD
> HONEY OH BABY MINE"

Three or four hundred male voices chanted this marching song as they passed the head of the street on the way to a firing range or an obstacle course. Joanna had liked this training-base routine at first. Lately the voices had become intrusive. There was no place, not even in your bathroom, where you could escape the Army.

Joanna sat down at the desk and read the opening lines of her poem. It could be a good one. She had not written—or, to be exact, finished—a poem for a long time.

During her last year in Japan, while Pete was back in Korea, she had written almost a poem a week. She had sent a batch of them to Adam at Harvard. He had submitted several to *The Atlantic Monthly* and the poetry editor had liked one enough to publish it. Seeing the poem in print had been the most exciting moment of her life. But no one in her personal circle except Adam had liked it. The poem was about an aristocratic woman who faced a life without hope and chose death. Joanna's mother thought it was "atheistic," and Pete, reading it in a command post in Korea, thought the resemblance to Blanche Coulter was too strong. He hoped General Coulter did not read *The Atlantic*.

Joanna wrote two more lines of the new poem about the parachutist.

> *Now the era of questioning is over*
> *The machine is in its final fatal dive*

The telephone rang. "Mrs. Burke? This is Sally England. How are you? Would you be willing to head up a committee to welcome the next lecturer in our anti-Communism series?"

"I—I suppose so."

"Could you come over to my quarters tomorrow afternoon to discuss it?"

"I'm on duty at the Thrift Shop."

"Oh, yes. How about the following afternoon?"

"I'm giving a book report to the Reading Club."

"Then let's make it lunch at the Officers' Club tomorrow."

"Fine."

Joanna hung up grinding her teeth. Sally England was a colonel's wife, president of the Women's Club. The series of lectures on anti-Communism was a brainchild of Mrs. General Atwater. Each lecture was more boring than the previous one, but every member of the Women's Club made sure she was there. There was no need for a committee to welcome each speaker. But the Army—including its wives—could not do anything without forming a committee to discuss it.

Joanna looked at the kitchen clock. It was 11 A.M. She had to clean the living room and dress for the Women's Club bridge. She would spend the rest of the afternoon shopping at the commissary, then cooking dinner. She went back into the living room and stared forlornly at her poem. A disconnected line, a piece of what had been an organism, emerged. She scribbled it down.

> *An Army of one with loneliness his guidon.*

Joanna whizzed around the living room waving a dust rag, vacuumed the rug, and drove to the post school to pick up Tom. She left him at the day-care center run by Women's Club volunteers and drove to the big stucco Officers' Club for the luncheon and bridge.

Escaping Beatrice Lamm with a wave, she paid fifty cents for a scotch and soda that contained a lot more liquor than she wanted to drink, and chatted with two captains' wives, whom she had gotten to know at the Thrift Shop. They discussed the odd winter weather, which thus far had left Fort Stanton free of its usual six or eight feet of snow, and warned her about an outbreak of measles that seemed to be sweeping the base. As everyone sat down to lunch, the head of the bridge committee, the wife of a colonel whose name Joanna could never remember, seized her arm. "Mrs. Burke," she said. "We sat you at a table with three captains' wives. I hope you don't mind. They're really more your age."

Joanna was tempted to tell her that she thought this preoccupation with rank was silly. But she also knew by now that rank was inescapable from the top of the Army to the bottom. It determined where and how a family lived, it influenced the treatment a man and his wife and children received everywhere on a base in subtle, often invisible ways. Simultaneously Joanna was annoyed by this small hint that a lot of people thought Pete's promotion to major was premature.

Unfortunately, the captains' wives were as rank-conscious as everyone else. They expected Mrs. Major to be the best bridge player and more or less dominate the conversation. Joanna was not a very good bridge player and today she was terrible. Lines from the poem kept drifting into her mind. She decided to change the menu for the dinner. She had been going to make chicken divan. Something less complicated would give her an hour this afternoon to work on the poem. Between menus and the image of her blind parachutist plummeting down on her symbolic city, she lost all track of the game. She bid four hearts after her partner had bid three spades and was trounced. Twice she forgot which suit was trump. She kept smiling and saying she was glad they were only playing for a tenth of a cent a point. She and her partner lost a dollar in the final accounting and Joanna insisted on paying it.

Feeling like an idiot, she picked up Tom at the day-care center and drove to the commissary. There she discovered a mob of shoppers. It was payday. When was she going to remember not to shop on payday? But there was only so much room in her tiny refrigerator and she had spent yesterday afternoon at the dispensary, getting her monthly pregnancy checkup. To her surprise, she saw the same doctor she had seen on her previous visit and he remembered her.

Joanna did not get out of the commissary check-out line until three-thirty. Tom was complaining that his head hurt. Was he getting the measles? She drove home sorely tempted to violate the base speed limit of 20 m.p.h., fiercely enforced by General Atwater. Pete had tried to explain that the general was strict about such matters because statistics on everything—accidents, crime, illness—went down to Washington and if the figures for the base were above the norm it made the general look bad. There were always companies of marching men on a training base. If a single car plowed into one, a dozen men could be killed. Pete was quick to defend the Army way of doing everything. "I still think Atwater's a grouch," Joanna had said.

The next day Tom had asked Pete why General Atwater was a grouch. This had produced another lecture from Pete, with citations from *The Army Wife* about the danger of criticizing the Army or the commanding officer when the children were around. He pictured Tom grandly informing the son of General Atwater's aide, with whom he went to kindergarten, that his daddy thought the general was a grouch.

"AROUND HER NECK, SHE WORE A YELLOW RIBBON
SHE WORE IT IN THE SPRINGTIME
AND IN THE MONTH OF MAY"

A company was marching back to their barracks. Joanna got stuck behind them. Some thoughtful sergeants kept the men out of the center of the road. Thoughtless sergeants never bothered. They seemed to be in the majority.

At home, Joanna took Tom's temperature and found it was normal. He zoomed out to play with Teddy Lamm, Jr. Joanna sat down at the desk and gazed wistfully at her poem. Two more lines meandered into her head. But they did not connect to anything. She was losing it. The thing was becoming a muddle. It was four o'clock and her dinner guests were arriving at six. She rushed into the kitchen and went to work on her hors d'oeuvres, Swedish meatballs. They were a chore. Pete thought the hors d'oeuvres were very important in a meal. Putting your best foot forward, he called it. She had never dreamt that this big man's man would take such an interest in her housekeeping and cooking, nor that such things could have an influence on his career. But she had tried—she was trying now—to respond to the pep talk he gave her about an officer and his wife being a "team." She had agreed that sit-down dinners were a far more impressive way of entertaining even if they were more work. She had spent hours practice-cooking elegant but inexpensive main courses, such as chicken curry, beef bourguignon.

Setting the table, Joanna was dismayed to see that her silver candlesticks, a wedding present from her sister, had tarnished. She gave them a few quick rubs and rushed back into the kitchen to prepare the main course. It was roast beef, a definite budget breaker. And the time she had hoped to rescue, thanks to its simplicity, had been lost on the commissary check-out line and the 20-m.p.h. drive home.

> "THE OLD GRAY MARE SHE AIN'T WHAT SHE USED TO BE
> AIN'T WHAT SHE USED TO BE
> AIN'T WHAT SHE USED TO BE"

Another company went chanting past the head of the street. Joanna took a shower so the bathroom would be free for Pete. By five-thirty, she was back in the kitchen wearing a long dark red skirt and a white nylon blouse, washing lettuce for the salad. Pete came in, kissed her and asked her how she was feeling. "Fine," she said. He wanted to know how the bridge club lunch went. "Fine," she said. Satisfied that all was well, the major retired to shower and dress for dinner. Fifteen minutes later he returned to the kitchen in full uniform and said: "Jesus, Joanna, didn't you dust in there?"

"Yes. But in kind of a hurry."

"There's dust an inch thick on one end table."

"Dust it yourself if you're that worried about it," she said, trying to sound good-humored.

Major Burke dusted the end table.

Majors Floyd and McQuade arrived with their wives promptly at six. The men had Pete's job—executive officer—in other training battalions in the regiment. Their wives, both trim, smiling, brown-haired, greeted Joanna while their eyes roved the house. It was an unofficial inspection tour with Joanna hoping, in spite of herself, for at least a 3.8. "I love those curtains," Marcia McQuade said, gazing at the crossed white organdy tiebacks Joanna had chosen for the front windows. "But they're going to get dirty. We get a lot of soot blown this way from Syracuse and Rochester."

"So I've noticed," Joanna said.

"I said the hell with it and put up drapes—brown drapes," Sue Floyd said.

"You just don't have the old-get-up-and-go like these young folks," Bob Floyd said.

Pete smiled, ignoring the reference to his rapid promotion. "Joanna's quite a hausfrau," he said.

The rest of the party went reasonably well, with only a few remarks from the wives about Joanna being the Army equivalent of Cinderella, enjoying quarters infinitely superior to what they had had to endure at her age. The men discussed the difference between combat in World War II and Korea—a put-down of sorts for Pete, no doubt.

The guests left early, saying nice things about the Swedish meatballs and politely avoiding the roast beef, which Joanna's erratic oven had overcooked. Pete helped her do the dishes. In the living room, Joanna sat down at the desk and stared at the poem. She was very tired and no lines came.

"Jo," Pete said, "how much did that roast beef cost?"

"Ten dollars."

"I thought we agreed we'd stay away from expensive main dishes like that."

"We did but—"

Since they came back to the States, finances had been the subject of numerous family conferences. A major's pay of $3,300 a year did not go far in the America of 1956. They ended each month dipping into the savings they had accumulated while Pete was in Korea drawing combat pay and she had lived for next to nothing in Japan. They could buy clothing and food at the PX and commissary at well below civilian prices. But the meat was not much better than the frozen stuff the Army had purveyed in Japan and the PX's taste in women's clothing was atrocious. Joanna could not resist shopping off the post for a good dress, an occasional choice cut of meat.

"I went for something simple—that would practically cook itself," Joanna said.

"It cooked itself a lot too long. I don't think there was an inch of rare or even medium meat on it. I was sort of embarrassed to carve it."

"The oven's temperature control doesn't work. I called that sergeant down in maintenance about it twice this week."

"I'll give him a buzz tomorrow. Let's eat cheap for the next couple of days. Meat loaf, hot dogs."

Joanna nodded.

"Remember that slogan I gave you. Economize and organize. If you'd follow that weekly schedule in *The Army Wife* you'd have time to cook dishes that don't cost an arm and a leg."

Joanna nodded. The schedule called for washing on Monday, ironing on Tuesday, intensive cleaning of different parts of the house on other days, mending and removing spots from clothes, polishing silver, defrosting the refrigerator, checking supplies, and marketing on Saturday morning in time to "enjoy the weekend with your husband." It made no mention of mornings and afternoons of Women's Club volunteering, weekly bridge, sit-down dinners or visits to the dispensary.

"Otherwise it was a nice dinner," Pete said. "Let's go to bed. You can put them in your hostess file tomorrow morning."

He thought she was sitting at the desk doing one last chore for Major Peter MacArthur Burke—adding the Floyds and McQuades to the file he had urged her to keep. Again it made perfect sense. You met so many people in this big Army it was impossible to remember their nicknames, children's names.

Something in the expression on her face must have made him

realize she was not working on her hostess file. "Wasn't that what you were doing?"

"No—I—I was fooling around with a poem. But it's all right, it's—it's—"

She almost said "dead." Was she going crazy?

But she did not finish the sentence. She turned her back on the dismembered lines of her poem and went to bed with her husband.

"WHO ARE THE ENEMIES OF CHRIST IN AMERICA TODAY? ATHEISTS? NO. THERE AREN'T MANY ATHEISTS IN AMERICA. BUT THERE ARE A LOT OF SECULARISTS, PEOPLE WHO TELL THEMSELVES AND OTHERS THAT RELIGION DOESN'T MATTER, WHO ARRANGE THEIR LIVES AND WHO TRY TO ARRANGE OUR COUNTRY AS IF GOD DIDN'T EXIST. OUR GODLESS PUBLIC SCHOOLS—"

Joanna sighed. Since she came back to the United States, she had found the sermons at Sunday Mass extremely boring. Perhaps it was a problem of the Army chaplain corps. Perhaps it was the times. So many chaplains seemed obsessed with the dangers of Communism and secularism. Perhaps becoming a chaplain made priests think they were talking to the church militant, for whom they had to serve as combination cheerleaders and early-warning systems.

Beside her, Tom started to squirm. He looked up at his mother and silently mouthed *I'm hungry*. Pete stared at the pulpit, apparently fascinated, although Joanna suspected that he was really working out plans for tomorrow's training exercise. Several times recently she had made a passing remark about a sermon and he had revealed by the vagueness of his answer that he had tuned out Chaplain Martin early.

Blanche Coulter's suicide had restored a spiritually shaken Joanna to the Catholic Church. General Coulter had resigned his command, and when Pete returned to Japan, Joanna had taken shelter in his calm, steady faith. For a month she had ignored safe days and loved him with a strange passive ardor. She let him lift her by slow degrees from a sadness that seemed at times too overwhelming to bear. They had gone to Mass and communion every day in the

Gorgas Hospital chapel. This burst of devotion was really a retreat, an evasion of the meaning Blanche's suicide threatened to inflict on Joanna's soul. Only in the subterranean world of her poetry did alternate meanings lurk, expressing themselves in oblique images.

Passivity became her prevailing pattern. When Pete took Arnold Coulter's advice and volunteered to become an adviser to the South Korean Army, Joanna stoically accepted another year of living in Japan, on an Army base north of Tokyo. Pete came back from the front every two months for five days of love. In the fall of 1952 she became pregnant again. The morning sickness recurred but she did not let it discourage her. Then came the first miscarriage, an ugly gush of blood and tissue between her legs in the bed at dawn.

Pete's Korean division was fighting off a massive Chinese assault. KMAG (Korean Military Assistance Group) ignored the hospital's request for an emergency leave. She had to endure the loss alone. Other KMAG wives were helpful. But she had wanted Pete there to hold her, to mourn the little death with her. When he finally arrived a month later, there was nothing left but vague sadness, which Pete thought he could dispel with a cheerful "Let's try again."

He did not cheer her when he announced that he had extended his tour for another six months. She accepted his explanation, that the South Korean Army needed men with his advisory experience. They, not the Americans, were the main targets of the Chinese attacks. He did not seem to notice that the tepidity with which she accepted this decision extended to their lovemaking. Not that it made much difference to her ovaries. She became pregnant again. This time the nausea was very difficult to bear. She resented or resisted the idea that no matter how she felt in her heart and head, nature went about its generative business in the basement.

After three months of retching, she had another miscarriage, a gory mess that required an ambulance, blood transfusions. A week later the war in Korea ended. Soon Pete was back, talking about trying again. This time she retreated to rhythm for three months, until they returned to the States. Even on safe days, she found the dread of another miscarriage seriously interfering with her response to him. Her old reluctance to become pregnant had produced a mental negation. This was physical. She literally shrank from his rush of semen and from him. Pete did not seem to notice. Or if he did, he said nothing.

Chaplain Martin finished his sermon and resumed the Mass. Soon the bells for the offertory rang. Joanna bowed her head and read the prayers in her missal. She joined the priest in asking God to accept "this spotless host, which I, your unworthy servant, offer to You, my living and true God, to atone for my numberless sins, offenses, and negligences." Lately Joanna had begun to read these and other prayers with a growing skepticism. She was not conscious of even a few sins, offenses, and negligences, much less numberless ones. Perhaps that was proof of dangerous spiritual complacency. But she did not feel complacent. If anything, she felt discouraged. There was little in the prayers of the Mass and absolutely nothing in Chaplain Martin's sermons that dealt with such a feeling.

As the Mass continued, Joanna found herself compiling a rueful list of derelictions. She could not seem to manage all the tasks of the Army wife. In the past month she had skipped another Women's Club bridge, she found the New Year's Eve party at the Officers' Club an exhausting bore, she owed at least four dinner invitations, she was still a less than perfect housekeeper, she had lost track of Tom twice in the past week and let him wander off their street. Were these sins, offenses, and negligences?

While his wife floundered, Major Burke performed all his duties, social and official, with smiling, striding, ever more confident ease. During his year as a senior instructor at TIS, The Infantry School, at Fort Benning, Georgia, he had qualified as a paratrooper and a ranger. In the past ten months at Fort Stanton he had organized battalion football, basketball and baseball teams that had won post championships. His superiors exhausted their adjectives, praising him in the Officer Efficiency Reports.

On the altar, the bells of consecration rang. As Chaplain Martin raised the white host, Joanna read the words of Christ at the Last Supper. *All of you take and eat of this, for this is my body.* Next, the gold chalice was lifted heavenward and Joanna read: *This is the chalice of my blood of the new and eternal covenant: the mystery of*

266

faith: which shall be shed for you and for many unto the forgiveness of sins.

Unworthy, she thought. Perhaps she was unworthy, as the prayer in the offertory intimated. She told herself to compare her petty discontents to Christ's awesome sacrifice. She focused on the words *the mystery of faith.* It was impossible for her to understand why she was being sent these pregnancies and miscarriages. She ordered herself to thank God for having an understanding husband, a healthy son.

Her knees began to ache on the hard kneeler. No foam-rubber pads for Army chapels. She shifted her position and felt it, the wetness, between her thighs. Simultaneously, a jagged pain, like an internalized bolt of lightning, ran down her pelvis. No, she whispered to God. No. Not again. Weirdly, she thought of Lover MacKenzie as the North Koreans poured gasoline on him. There was no sense, no purpose to it. She did not want to think that all life was like a battlefield, rife with random death.

"Pete," she whispered. "I'm bleeding."

She sat back and there it was, spots of dark blood on the wooden kneeler. Her pants were already soaked. It was bad and it was going to get worse. Tom stared, pop-eyed.

Pete whirled. One of his battalion's captains, a beetle-browed Italian-American named Jack Conti, was sitting behind them. "Jack," Pete said, handing him his car keys. "Get my car. We've got to get Joanna to the hospital." Jack's bubbly blond wife, Eleanor, asked if she should come. "Take care of Tom," Pete said.

Jack Conti raced down the aisle. Pete picked up Joanna and strode after him, past dozens of staring eyes, wondering faces. Within thirty seconds of reaching the street, Captain Conti had his car, a 1950 Ford, even more decrepit than their 1951 Chevrolet, at the curb. "I couldn't get your car started," he said.

Pete thrust Joanna into the back seat and threw himself into the front seat. "Floor it," he said. Jack sent the old car roaring for the hospital, ignoring the 20-m.p.h. post speed limit. As they turned a corner, tires screeched, the car lurched, and Conti gasped: "Christ, that was the general."

With the violent lurch, Joanna felt more jagged pain and a gush of blood. She was ruining her best dress, her green A-line. Disgusting, she thought. The whole thing was disgusting. Bleeding all over herself, in the back of somebody else's car, possibly dying. Why? They screeched to a halt in front of the hospital. Pete and Jack Conti had a terrible time getting her out of the car. She was unbelievably weak. Pete finally got her in his arms and charged up the steps into the hospital.

There was no doctor on duty, only a short, balding corpsman.

"My wife's having a miscarriage," Major Burke snapped. "Call one of the doctors."

The idiot started to dial the telephone on his desk. "Get us a bed first," Pete snapped.

The corpsman rushed them into the first room on the corridor. At least it isn't a ward, Joanna thought. She did not want any more eyes on her. Semi-strangers like Jack Conti were bad enough. They had been to a potluck supper at the Contis'. She owed them an invitation. Pete deposited her on the bed, got her winter coat off and held her hand. Out in the hall she heard someone talking in a very loud, angry voice. It was General Atwater. "I don't give a goddamn," he roared. "The speed limit on this base is twenty miles an hour and I want you to obey it, Captain."

"Yes, General. Yes, sir," Jack Conti said.

Pete rushed into the hall. She heard him explaining to the general that it was his responsibility. His wife was having a miscarriage. The general was not impressed. "I want a report, including a signed statement from the doctor, on my desk tomorrow morning," he snarled.

Joanna felt another gush of blood. I could die, she thought, maybe I'm dying now. Would that satisfy the foul-tempered bastard? What idiocy. She remembered how she had felt giving birth to Tom in Japan. Resigned, even proud to die, a heroic mother. But not this way, not when there was nothing left but a mangled blob of flesh that her body, God, had for some reason rejected.

"Sir, Major," the corpsman said as Pete returned. "I got the duty doctor on the phone. He wants to know if it's serious."

Pete lifted Joanna off the bed. "Look at that," Pete said, nodding at an oval of dark red blood.

"Why the hell don't we have decent doctors?" Jack Conti said. The corpsman scuttled out, convinced. "It's going to drive me out of the Army."

"They're all draftees," Pete said. "Serving under duress. They could be making a lot of money outside."

It took twenty minutes for the doctor to arrive. In the meantime, the corpsman, alarmed at the amount of blood Joanna was losing, started giving her plasma. The doctor, whose name was Kingsley, looked and acted like a carbon copy of the young snot who had lectured Joanna on birth control at Fort Ripley, Kansas. "This better be a real emergency," he said. "This is the third weekend in a row I've been dragged in here for problems that could have easily waited until sick call on Monday."

"I think it's an emergency, Doctor," Pete said. "We're hoping against hope we can save the baby. We lost the last three."

"So I see," Dr. Kingsley said. He was reading Joanna's file. "Three miscarriages in the last thirty months. Did you ever hear of a modern idea called contraception, Major?"

"We're Catholics," Pete said.

It was his turn, Joanna thought. His turn to get the lecture. She had gotten it with the last two miscarriages.

"So am I," Dr. Kingsley said. "But that doesn't mean I agree with the Vatican's asinine attitude toward contraception."

Pete swallowed, perhaps trying to control his temper, perhaps intimidated. Joanna could not tell. "My wife and I don't think that way, Doctor."

"I advise you to start," Kingsley said, "if you want Joanna around for a few more years."

"Is she—in danger now?"

"She would be," Dr. Kingsley said, taking her pulse, "if she didn't have the blood in that bottle running into her arm."

"Can you stop the bleeding?"

"Major," Dr. Kingsley said, "all we can do is prevent the worst effects of nature's destructive tendencies."

Pain knifed through Joanna's pelvis. "Oh God," she said. "I'm getting more cramps."

"You're obviously going to abort. Why don't you step outside, Major."

A blond nurse appeared, wearing slacks and a green jacket. She had been summoned from her quarters too, and was looking grumpy about it. Her name was Sweeney. Joanna had seen her on previous visits to the hospital. Sweeney and the corpsman got her on a rolling table and took her down to one of the operating rooms. In about twenty minutes the fetus aborted but the placenta remained in her uterus and the bleeding continued. Dr. Kingsley had to give her an injection of the hormone oxytocin to expel this last fragment of her pregnancy. The bleeding soon stopped. Within an hour, she was back in her room. Pete sat beside her looking disconsolate. She felt weary and defeated.

"Why?" she said. "Can you tell me why?"

Pete shook his head.

Nurse Sweeney gave her a sleeping pill. The next morning, she opened her eyes to find Dr. Kingsley standing beside the bed. "Aw, nuts," he said. "Snow White opened her eyes before I got a chance to kiss her."

She was tempted to tell him he was not Prince Charming. He had dark brown tightly curled hair and a snub nose. His mouth had ironic downturned corners. Like Adam Thayer's.

Dr. Kingsley sat down on her bed. "Three strikes in your game isn't necessarily out," he said. "Theoretically, you can go on getting pregnant until about the age of forty-five, if you get to the hospital in time to get your blood transfusions when you abort."

"It may not happen the next time. One doctor told me—"

"Mrs. Burke. Joanna. Face up to the fact that you've got a problem. I think it has something to do with a fairly rare hormonal deficiency. A guy I worked for at Harvard Medical School has done a study of multiple miscarriages. I think you ought to go up there and see him before you let that big Irishman near you again."

"Are you really a Catholic?"

"Sure I'm a Catholic. Fordham University, 1950. I'm a Catholic who thinks for himself."

Joanna wondered if you could stay a Catholic and disagree with something as fundamental as birth control. But she did not have to agree with Dr. Kingsley's moral theology to take his advice about going to Boston. Nothing in her Catholic education forbade her to listen to modern science. On the contrary, she had been taught that there was no conflict between science and reasoned faith. Pete felt the same way. If there was a problem, science and religion together would find a way to cope.

Dr. Kingsley arranged an appointment with his man in Boston. Pete telephoned Adam, now in his third year of graduate school at Harvard, to make a hotel reservation. Honor insisted that Joanna stay with them.

Adam met her at the Trailways Bus depot in foggy, rainy Boston. He was in full uniform down to his jump boots. "Still wearing it?" she said.

"Sure," Adam said. "It still drives them crazy. They want to believe the Army is like those lugs in *From Here to Eternity.*"

In his occasional letters addressed to "Dear Captain and Moose" while the Burkes were in Japan, Adam had portrayed himself as a man embattled, defending himself against the condescension that Harvard deans and dons instinctively displayed toward West Point. In defiance, he had vowed to wear his uniform everywhere and get the highest marks in every course.

"How's Honor?" Joanna asked as they crawled through downtown Boston's heavy traffic.

"Ask her," Adam said.

"What's wrong?"

"What do you think?"

"I don't know."

"I don't know either."

"Yes, you do."

"Ask her. Maybe you can help."

In the Thayer apartment on the third floor of a narrow Victorian house in Cambridge, Honor greeted her with southern warmth. "Jo, I'm so *glad* to see you," she said, kissing her exuberantly.

Even with her red hair unbrushed and wearing a cheap house-dress, Honor was still beautiful. Her figure was showing signs of spread, no doubt the result of two children in quick succession. Three-year-old Elizabeth, called Pookie, clung to her mother's skirts and refused to look at the visitor, even though she was assured that she was face to face with her godmother. One-year-old Matthew Ridgway Thayer, named for Adam's favorite general, was equally unimpressed.

The apartment was a mess. Children's toys mingled with books piled on end tables and coffee tables. The couch had a deep sag in its center, which suggested its innards were resting on the floor. Joanna soon discovered that there were only two bedrooms, and thought she was destined for the couch. "Listen," she said to Honor after Adam departed for the library, "I really feel I'm crowding you. I can afford a hotel. There's nothing to spend money on in upstate New York."

"Adam won't mind the couch," Honor said. "He sleeps on it half the time anyway. He hardly ever gets back from the library until after midnight. Once I get to sleep, I don't like to get wakened. I have to take another pill and I'm like an old woman with the blind staggers all the next day."

That night, without even a try at cleaning up the living room, Honor had a dinner party. Joanna asked her who the guests would be. "Some Harvard brains Adam wants you to meet," she said.

Joanna instantly recognized the name of the first guest to arrive. Carleton Haines was the poetry editor at *The Atlantic Monthly*, the man who had accepted her poem. He was tall and stooped, with a pale blond mustache and shaggy pale blond hair above a face that seemed to be all profile. His wife, Annette, was his physical opposite, a chunky vigorous woman with stiff black hair, cut in a pageboy. She was getting her Ph.D. in international affairs, like Adam. With them came a *New York Times* reporter, curly-haired, boyish-looking Don Marble, who was attending Harvard on a Nieman fellowship.

"Well," Carleton Haines said in a voice that carried a trace of a southern accent, "it's nice to meet a contributor to *Antithesis*."

Joanna looked blank. "Didn't this Prussian clod tell you?" Annette Haines said, glaring at Adam.

"I like surprises," Adam said, opening a big straw-covered bottle of Chianti.

"The Atlantic Monthly was too commercial for me," Haines said. Don Marble guffawed at this declaration. Haines remained unruffled. "I am now the editor, publisher and proofreader of a new magazine, *Antithesis.* I've selected another of the poems you sent Adam for the first issue. The one about the toy soldier."

"Congratulations," Don Marble said. "I wrote a piece on Korea for it and he turned it down. Said it was too establishment in tone. I only suggested they should have court-martialed MacArthur."

"How about a reading?" Annette Haines said.

"I happen to have a copy of the masterpiece right here," Adam said.

"It's not a masterpiece. Just a good poem," Carleton Haines said.

"Thank you," Joanna said.

Adam handed her the poem. Joanna scanned the almost forgotten words.

"I wrote this in Japan during the war. I called it 'Microcosm,'" she said in an uncertain voice.

"Read it," Adam said.

> *"On the rug's flowery battlefield*
> *The toy soldier dies*
> *In the enemy mind. It is all a dream*
> *He drank when he was six. The metal gun*
> *The tongue fired, the argument*
> *Has become the world's.*
> *In the cold mud the word becomes*
> *The bullet and sticks and stones*
> *The perilous accidents of Babel.*
> *He dreams suddenly of impossible futures*
> *Probable pasts. A warm bed.*
> *A cold nun in a crowded classroom.*
> *If only they knew the world, he thinks,*
> *I might believe. But it is all so childish.*
> *As mournfully*
> *The corpsman stoops to take his number."*

"Bravo." "That's a poem." "Great," said her little audience.

Joanna blushed and sat down. She had read it too fast, without any of the feeling it deserved. They were being kind.

"Any work in progress?" Carleton Haines asked.

"I haven't written anything—since I came back to the States. Almost eighteen months," Joanna said.

"You've been too busy having miscarriages," Adam said, handing her a glass of wine. "You see before you an interesting subspecies of the genus femina Americana. Roman Catholicus. Her body is in the twentieth century and so is about half her mind. The other half is in the twelfth."

"That poem sounds like she's doing some thinking of her own," Annette Haines said.

Adam shook his head. "Poetry has nothing to do with thought. The good stuff springs direct from the unconscious."

"That's where eighty percent of your arguments come from. But you presume to call them thinking," Annette Haines said.

With that abusive start, the conversation whirled away in directions and at a pace Joanna had never experienced. Communist parties in Italy, China, Algeria, Chile, were discussed, debated, praised or dismissed, names of foreign poets, Neruda, Arrabal, Mayakovsky, were flung into the vortex to prove or disprove a point. It was totally different from the talk that was standard among wives at Army parties—children's antics, moving woes, shopping tips. It pained Joanna to realize how she had accepted the Army life style, in which the men talked assignments, exchanged war stories, while the wives talked their own brand of shop. She recalled her feeble attempts to oppose this tradition at Fort Ripley. How pathetic, how naïve, those gestures seemed now. After five years in the Army, she had begun to accept so many habits as necessities. It was the war, she thought. Once you got even a glimpse of war, you retreated, in effect, you said to them, do it your way, do everything your way.

Suddenly, Annette Haines was asking Joanna a question. "Do you find much evidence of McCarthyism in the officer corps? Adam claims it's nil, especially since the senator attacked the Army last year. An incomprehensible blunder."

Joanna shook her head. "As far as I can see, the Army's not interested in politics, unless it involves their budget."

Returning from Japan in the fall of 1953, Joanna and Pete had been amazed by the furor over Joe McCarthy. They had been even more startled to discover that their relatives on both sides were passionate advocates of the man. He obviously aroused a certain tribal instinct in many Catholics. Joanna's sister Beth and her husband were ardent McCarthyites. Pete's father practically worshipped the senator from Wisconsin.

"Some officers' wives echo him now and then," Joanna said. "Our general's wife at Fort Stanton is batty on the subject." She talked sarcastically about the almost total boredom created by the lecturers on anti-Communism imported by Mrs. Atwater. Everyone except Annette chuckled approvingly. Annette was disappointed. She had obviously hoped to hear stories of wild-eyed majors and colonels plotting anti-Communist coups.

Adam beamed at Joanna. She felt enormously pleased that she had helped him prove the Army was not a collection of right-wing dunderheads.

"I am a prophet without honor around here," Adam said. "Everything I say is suspect, because I wear a uniform."

"Oh, bosh. Stop trying for the martyr's robes," Annette Haines said.

Honor emerged from the kitchen with a macaroni-and-cheese casserole and they adjourned to the table in the dining area, Adam lugging the Chianti. The wine and the conversation continued to flow. By now it was clear that Annette was a Marxist, with utter contempt for the capitalist system. Carleton Haines, on the other hand, claimed that he had no political opinions. Poetry was his only passion.

The talk swerved to the Korean War. "I predict Adam's thesis on limited war will get him demoted to private," Annette said.

"Why?" Joanna asked.

"Annette wants to believe the Army thinks the way it marches," Adam said. "In step. I keep telling her it's changed. Korea has shaken a lot of people's assumptions. Do you think Ridgway could

275

have gotten away with telling Eisenhower and Dulles to get lost when they wanted him to save the French in Vietnam last year?''

"Everyone at Benning thought we were going in," Joanna said. "Pete even started studying Vietnamese.''

"We can't make the same dumb mistake twice," Adam said.

"Korea was dumb?" Joanna said. "The whole thing?"

"Do you think they're going to let him get away with saying that?" Annette asked. "Doesn't that mean a lot of generals were dumb?"

"The State Department was a lot dumber," Adam said.

Joanna found herself remembering the talk Pete had given at West Point on his combat experiences in Korea. He described the horrendous casualties, the frequent heroism, the occasional cowardice of his men. A cadet in the audience asked him if he thought it was worth it. Pete had responded with a speech within the speech, about his admiration for the Korean people. He discussed the year he had spent with them as an adviser. He had found them as brave, as ready, perhaps more ready to die for freedom than the Americans. Yes, Pete said. The American deaths were worth it. Even his own death would have been worth it, to defend these people.

Now she heard Adam telling his Harvard friends that all that blood and courage was a mistake, a geopolitical blunder. America was brave but stupid. The Koreans were not worth the cost. She found it hard to accept this as wisdom. It ridiculed too many memories—Pete weeping for his lost company, Sam Hardin in agony from his shattered leg. Joanna suspected Adam would find it hard to sell his ideas to a lot of fellow officers.

"Adam," Honor said. "When I listen to you go on this way, I get to thinkin' you're too smart for your own good."

"That's something you'll never have to worry about," Adam said.

The Haineses and Marble eventually went home and Adam announced he was off to the library. He had wangled a key, which enabled him to work nights at a table in a corner of the stacks. He was driving himself to finish his courses and write his Ph.D. thesis in three years. Joanna went to bed with Honor, remembering somewhat wistfully the nights they had chatted at the Hotel Thayer

276

in 1949 and 1950. But this time Honor took a pill—and was soon asleep. Joanna lay awake thinking about the evening, the clash and thrust of opposing ideas and opinions. Could she ever be anything more than a spectator like Honor? Perhaps not. Perhaps . . .

The next morning Adam drove her through more rain and mist to Massachusetts General Hospital for her appointment with Dr. Stephen Ricemayer. He was a handsome man with friendly blue eyes and an unlined face made somewhat incongruous by a shock of white hair. After five years of Army doctors, it was refreshing to talk to a medical man who seemed to take a personal interest in her. They chatted about Cincinnati, where he had several ex-students practicing medicine. He asked numerous questions about her eating habits, her health, her religion, her attitude toward having children, and about the circumstances of each miscarriage. He made a careful pelvic examination, then took blood and urine samples and told her to return the following day.

Back at the Thayer apartment, Joanna spent the day getting to know her godchild. Pookie gradually abandoned her suspicions of the intruder and solemnly displayed all her toys, one by one. She saved until last her most precious possessions, an Army helmet and a rifle. "She's Daddy's girl," Honor said. "She's goin' to be so disappointed when she finds out she can't go airborne."

Honor kept complaining about being groggy. "When I drink wine and take one of these doggone pills, I don't wake up till noon," she said.

"You didn't have any sleeping problems in our old roommate days at the Hotel Thayer," Joanna said. "What's wrong? Doesn't Harvard agree with you? Adam's doing the studying. You don't have to worry about entertaining majors and colonels with wives who give your living room a barracks inspection—"

Honor did not think any of this was even mildly amusing. She seemed to be fighting back tears. "There's a reason I don't sleep well, Jo," she said. For a moment she seemed to glare at Pookie, standing there in her green overalls and white shirt, her olive-drab helmet cocked on her small head, the toy rifle on her shoulder. "But you don't want to hear my troubles. You've got enough of your own."

"If it would help you to talk—"

Honor told Pookie to play in her bedroom and sat down on the couch with Joanna, the sagging center cushion between them. "The first night after Adam went into combat in Korea—a sergeant—the sergeant of his company—raped me," she said. "It's never been the same between me and Adam, since."

Weeping, one hand clutching the front of her blouse as if she were still trying to defend herself against the memory, Honor poured out the story, which included her conviction that it had affected the way Adam felt about her sexually.

Joanna was appalled. But she found it hard to focus on the reality of the rape and its effect on the Thayers' sex life. Retreating from the central image, she concentrated on trying to reassure Honor about Adam. She told her it was not fair to draw such a conclusion now. Adam was under a terrific strain, trying to complete in three years a program that took most men five years. "Wait till you get on a base and start living a regular Army life. You'll be so busy you won't have time to brood. Adam will come down from the intellectual stratosphere. It'll be like—like the honeymoon."

No, too extravagant. She could see Honor was tempted to ask her if life with Pete at Fort Stanton was like their honeymoon. "We're not goin' to a base. We're goin' to Washington. He's goin' to work in the Pentagon."

Joanna rattled on for ten minutes about how interesting Washington, D.C., would be. Honor kept nodding but she was not really listening. Joanna realized that she herself did not believe a word that was coming out of her mouth. She sat there, battled at her inability to comfort Honor, fighting a dim, panicky suspicion that life was incomprehensible. Things simply happened without any plan, guidance, meaning. Did this mean that her devotion to her Catholic God, in whose name she had had three miscarriages, for whom she had become Joanna-the-good-girl, dutiful wife of Major Peter MacArthur Burke, was as wasted as Pete's heroism in Korea?

The next day Adam again drove her through the seemingly perpetual rain to Massachusetts General Hospital. Dr. Ricemayer sat her down beside his desk, piled with medical journals, and told her the results of his tests and examinations. "You have precisely the problem Dr. Kingsley diagnosed. A rather rare deficiency of certain hormones that make it almost impossible—extremely unlikely—that you will carry another baby to term. In fact, you were very lucky to do it once."

"How did I get that way?" Joanna asked.

"We like to think of nature as efficient. She—or it, if you prefer—is actually rather slipshod. A certain percentage of babies are born without feet, hands, adequate brains. In your case you were born without these hormones."

"Can't they be supplied—in pills or injections?"

"I'm afraid not. They haven't been reproduced synthetically."

"What can I do? I told you I was a Catholic."

"If you go ahead and risk another pregnancy, I would advise total bed rest from about the second month."

"Total bed rest? I'd need a servant. I have a five-year-old son. A husband who expects—"

"I know. And I couldn't guarantee that it would work in the first place. That's why I recommend tubal ligation for most women with your problem. It's a very simple operation. You'd be in and out of the hospital in a day."

"The Catholic Church forbids that too," Joanna said.

"I know. I sympathize with Catholic women. I really do."

"I'll have to think it over, Doctor."

"All right. Call me later today at this number—" He handed her a card. "I can arrange to have it done tomorrow."

Honor looked expectantly at Joanna as she came into the apartment. "Good news, I hope?" she asked.

Joanna shook her head and told her what Dr. Ricemayer wanted to do. "I think you should get it done," Honor said. "I'm half tempted myself. Two's all I can handle and that diaphragm gets to be an awful pain. Half the time I get it in because I think Adam's goin' to and I want to be romantic and say yes with no fussin' and then he doesn't and I feel hurt and mad—"

"It's against my religion. The Church says—"

She tried to explain to Honor but it did not sound very convincing. Honor shook her head. "I wouldn't presume to tell you what to think, religiously, Jo," she said. "But—"

You don't sound like you believe it. Was that what Honor was tempted to say?

"I'll have to talk it over with Pete," Joanna said.

"Don't!" Honor said. "Don't tell him. Tellin' Adam about the rape was the worst thing I ever did, Jo. Believe me."

"I couldn't not tell him."

"What do *you* want to do?"

The question startled her. She had always thought of herself as Honor's superior and she was, intellectually. Was Honor more in touch with her natural self, her instincts as a woman? Joanna suddenly knew undeniably, unforgettably, that she wanted the operation. She wanted to escape her dread of another pregnancy. She wanted to be able to love Pete freely without fear.

"I want to do it," she said. "But I've got to talk to Pete about it."

That night after supper she telephoned him at Fort Stanton, reversing the charges. "Hello," she said. "How's everybody?"

"Great. Just got Mr. Ducrot squared away."

"What are you eating?"

"Let's see. Tonight we had hamburger and french fries. Last night we had french fries and hamburger. What's the word from the Harvard doc?"

"Dr. Ricemayer says he doesn't think I should get pregnant again. If I do I'll have to spend eight months in bed. I've got that hormone problem, as Dr. Kingsley suspected."

"Jesus, Jo."

"Dr. Ricemayer thinks I should have my Fallopian tubes tied. So I won't conceive again."

"What does the Church say about that?"

"They say it's wrong. A sin. But Pete—I think—I really think I should do it."

She meant it. Even now, hours after her talk with Honor, she meant it. She began to wonder if her religious thinking had been subtly but irremediably altered by her encounter with Buddhism in Japan. Wasn't Catholicism, all of Christianity, just one among many faiths?

280

Pete Burke did not think so. "Joanna," he said. "How can you say that? If you're doing it for me I'd rather— It means we could never have another kid."

"I know. I wanted—as many as you wanted—"

A lie. Or a half-truth, by putting it in the past tense. She had wanted as many as God sent her, in the dreaming naïveté of her engagement days. Now? She thought of the last eighteen months. Not a single poem.

She stopped, overwhelmed by guilt. She could see Pete in his T-shirt and khaki pants, sitting on the couch, his huge shoulders hunched, disappointment staining his wide freckled face. If ever a man was born to have a big family, it was Pete Burke.

"They can perform the operation up here. Dr. Ricemayer says it will only take a day in the hospital."

"Wait a second, Jo. This is too big a decision—is Supe sitting there telling you to go ahead with it?"

"I haven't said a word to him about it."

"I don't want you to do it, Jo. In fact, I absolutely forbid you to do it. I want you to come back here and consult a couple of other doctors. I didn't like that guy Kingsley's attitude in the first place."

"They'll just tell us to practice rhythm. You know how much you hated it, what it did to us, in Japan. We snapped and snarled at each other every day."

"I don't remember any such thing. I'll practice rhythm if that's what we've got to do. I'm ready to take the rough with the smooth, Jo. That's life. I couldn't respect you or myself if I let you dodge responsibility this way."

She suddenly remembered another part of the speech Pete had given at West Point last year. The final question from the audience had come from a cadet who asked him if he had been afraid in combat. Pete said every soldier was afraid. But most men got used to it. Looking over the cadets' heads at Joanna in the back row, he compared a soldier's fear to the anxiety of a woman who had a rough time having children but went on trying to have them. No, Joanna had thought, the comparison mixed too many things, birth and death, biology and psychology. She remembered it now with a sinking heart. She saw that he considered the whole thing part of orders he had received from God, to be obeyed as implicitly as a command from a general or a colonel.

> *Take that hill, Burke.*
> *Yes, sir.*
> *Marry that woman for better or for worse, Burke.*
> *Yes, sir.*
> *Keep her pregnant even if it kills her.*
> *Yes, sir.*

It was the Corps. Duty-honor-country applied not only to the battlefield, to the training camp, it applied everywhere. How could she, Joanna-the-good-girl, find herself hating such moral purity? Hating it and admiring it at the same time.

Driving her to the bus depot the next morning, Adam said: "I gather the news from Dr. Ricemayer was not good?"

"Correct," Joanna said.

"And Big Peter won't let you do anything about it."

"It's none of your business, Adam."

She stared straight ahead into the streaming windshield. In March in Boston rain was apparently a permanent part of the atmosphere.

"Yes, it is. I still love you. Even though I'll probably never touch you for the rest of our lives. I care about what happens to you. To him too, for that matter."

"What is going to happen to me, prophet?" she said, her voice suddenly thick with tears.

They were in heavy traffic, edging past the Public Garden. Boston, where so much American history and literature began, sat stolidly in the downpour, looking dull, nondescript. Ahead of her and off to the right she could see narrow twisting streets, a mélange of shops and office buildings. Boston looked old, tired, corrupt. It was just a slightly larger version of Pete's home town, Hamilton, its government a coterie of Irish politicians. She thought of Robert Lowell's description of the Public Garden by night, the moon like chalk on the water, desolation, ruin everywhere, ending in that devastating two-word sentence: *Everything's aground.* That was how she felt.

"Little by little, you're going to change," Adam said. "You're going to stand up to him, be your own person. I lived with Pete for three years, I know what he's like. He does everything by the book. His trick is, to do it better than the book. I bet he's got you running from morning to midnight, giving sit-down dinner parties twice a week, working on every Women's Club committee in sight. The Army superwife. Pete wouldn't be satisfied with anything else. Am I right?"

Joanna shook her head. But she was not signifying her usual disagreement with Adam's extremist opinions. It was simple incomprehension, that words spoken by one human being to another human being could have such devastating impact. Fragments vibrated in her brain like the shockwaves of an explosion.

> Better than the book.
> Army superwife.
> I know what he's like.

The dazed blast victim went through the motions of dissent. "It's not quite that bad. Some of it is necessary, Adam. The Army has—traditions."

"Most of them asinine," Adam said. "The Army is a dinosaur with its nose in the twentieth century and the rest of its head and body in the nineteenth."

For the next five hours Joanna was an inert passenger, sitting beside a streaming bus window, gazing mournfully out at the soggy landscape of western Massachusetts and northern New York. Harvard Square, Boston, literary and historic, receded. She thought about her early frustrated wish to share Pete's Army experience. They were sharing it now, they were partners, a team; but it was not the kind of sharing she wanted, not a sharing between equals. It was the sharing of the leader and the led. A sharing on the leader's terms. *On, brave old Army team.*

In Syracuse, Pete was waiting for her at the bus depot in his dark green raincoat. He was alone. He told her that Tom was having such a good time playing with Teddy Lamm it seemed a shame to inflict a two-hour ride on him.

"Colonel Carswell's wife called to invite us to dinner on the twentieth," Pete said as they walked to the car. "I accepted. That's going to be a tough invitation to return."

Colonel Carswell was Pete's regimental commander. His wife had a private income and liked to entertain lavishly.

"I didn't tell her why you were in Boston. I don't think you ought to tell anyone, Jo."

"Why not?"

"It's a hard thing for anyone who's not a Catholic to understand. I'm afraid they might think—well—that it reflects on my judgment."

"You mean they're liable to put it in your OER?" she said. "Refuses to let his wife have her tubes tied."

"Of course not. It's more subtle than that. But we're both being judged all the time, Jo."

He did not try to talk to her again until they were out of Syracuse's downtown traffic. His voice was mournful. "I talked to my uncle the Monsignor on the phone. He says tubal ligation is absolutely forbidden. It's worse than abortion, in his opinion. He says—every time we made love, it would be an—an abortion because the seed wouldn't have a chance for life."

That's idiotic, she thought. How can you abort what hasn't been born yet? But she did not want to argue with him about the theology of abortion and sterilization. Already she was envisioning a moment when she would sit down with him and have a frank talk about their whole life together, about what she owed him as a wife and what he owed her as a husband, about her lost poems and his career. She wanted to tell him how much she was prepared to love him, if he freed her from the fear of another pregnancy and gave her more time to be herself, a poet, a dreamer.

Pete talked ruthlessly, carelessly through this wish. "We'll go to Syracuse or Rochester and see a specialist. Work out a chart that will give us more time together, maybe."

Five instead of four times a month? she thought.

"We'll work it out, Jo. It may be rough on us for a while, but you're worth it to me. You'd be worth it to me if they told me I could never touch you again."

Baloney, bushwah, bullshit, she thought. That was not Pete Burke the husband talking. It was Major Burke the leader, inspiring her to follow him into the valley of the shadow. Through the rain that seemed to be falling on all of America, she saw the barbed-wire-topped outer fence of Fort Stanton. Behind it stood the barracks, row on row, the square and rectangled areas between them, the huge parade ground with its reviewing stand, where General Atwater surveyed the troops each Saturday. There was the wide squat Officers' Club where she played mediocre bridge with the other officers' wives on Wednesday afternoons and danced with their husbands on Saturday night and talked about the weather and measles and lost luggage and smashed furniture from the last move. She saw all of them, the officers in their uniforms and their wives in their inexpensive but tasteful dresses trying to live like ladies and gentlemen in a country that did not pay them as much each month as the average ditchdigger earned in a week, she saw their earnest smiles and probing eyes and their hands raised to admonish her. They were all on Pete's side. They liked this world where there was not a speck of garbage in any gutter, not a sign of litter on any lawn. Utterly different from the dirty twisting streets and haphazard mixture of buildings in corrupt Boston or other American cities. Order, purity, honor, courage, comradeship, they shouted at Joanna. All here, made visible, possible, by authority of the commanding general and the traditions of the service.

As Pete turned in the gate and received the white-helmeted policeman's salute, Joanna suddenly found it difficult to breathe. Within her body began to beat the wings of some blind trapped thing, bird or spiritual creature of the blood, perhaps her own heart, adrift in the suddenly empty space that her vacated flesh had become. Breath and then no breath as the wings beat and she struggled to still them. How? Wishes were as feeble as her own draining arms, as her gasping mouth. She tried to pray but her throat was filled with nothing but feathery violence.

She was sure she was dying. She was having her first anxiety attack.

II

"Two thousand dollars!" Adam snarled. "We owe your mother two thousand goddamn dollars? Why didn't you tell me?"

"I *tried*," Honor said. "I tried a dozen times. But you wouldn't listen. You wouldn't listen or think about anything but that damn thesis."

"I would have thought about two thousand dollars," Adam said in the same snarling voice. "Especially if you told me we were going into debt to your idiot mother."

"Honey, I wish you wouldn't talk about her that way. She *is* my mother and she's been real generous to us."

"And now you tell me I've got to put up with her every weekend or she'll garnishee my salary? Such as it is?"

"Don't be silly," Honor said. "It's just bein' family. We're livin' in the same state. She'd like to see her grandchildren. I just mentioned it would make things easier about the money, that's all. She could see for herself how far a captain's salary goes."

"Nuts to that. I'll be goddamned if I want pity from a pinhead."

"Adam, you're bein' awful rude. She *is* my mother. I don't say she's the most marvelous person in the world. But she is my mother and she was always very good to me. I'm her only child and I think she's got a right to see her grandchildren. Even if she didn't loan us the money to finish your goddamn thesis and get your Ph.D. so you can prance around actin' like the smartest captain in the whole damn Army."

"Maybe I am the smartest captain in the whole damn Army. That's not saying much."

"It doesn't give you the right to insult my momma!"

"Oh Christ, don't start crying again."

Honor saw Adam, saw her husband through a film of tears. It was not the first time she had seen him that way in recent months.

Joanna's prophecy, that Adam would relax and regain his old cheerful self once the ordeal of the Ph.D. was over, only made Honor wince, when she remembered it. Instead, Adam kept changing in the same direction he had begun changing in Cambridge. He didn't even look the same. He had always been thin. Now there was a gaunt, skeletonic quality about him. He smoked constantly, two or three packs a day. His eyes were gray hollows, circled by darker gray patches. Seldom did Honor see the reckless smile, the flash of witty mockery, that had charmed her. His mouth, at least when he talked to her, seemed perpetually poised between bitterness and anger.

Part of the reason was her fault, Honor knew, or half knew, when she could think about it clearly. She had tried to talk to Joanna about it but there were some things that you could not say even to a close friend. She simply could not or would not—her body would not respond to Adam when he came back from Korea. Part of that was Adam's fault. She had started to tell him the whole story of the rape, every detail. He had stopped her in his curt way and told her he did not want to hear it, he had told her to forget it. He did not seem to understand how much she needed to tell it, to put it outside her body, her mind.

Honor had hoped that a return to Virginia, to her home state, and escape at last from Cambridge, would restore her old self, and with it their honeymoon love. She had not had a dream about the rape for almost a year. But in Virginia she had met a new antagonist: the Pentagon. Harvard had been bad enough, the incredible demands the professors made on a man, as if he were nothing but a machine to read books and write papers. The Pentagon was worse. Everyone was expected to work a twelve-hour day and take home a full briefcase. It was worse than Cambridge, where Adam often went for whole days without talking to her. Now he had two excuses, the

Pentagon and the books he had to read to keep up with the field of international affairs.

At the Pentagon, Adam was assigned to something called the Coordinating Group, which was supposed to do the thinking for the chief of staff. Adam was the only captain in the group. The rest were majors and colonels. They were supposed to be the best brains in the Army. But Honor did not think much of the way they operated. They were out to challenge the military policy of President Eisenhower and his administration, which was starving the Army. General Ridgway, Adam's hero, had resigned in protest against the Eisenhower budget slashes shortly before Adam arrived at the Pentagon. Someone in the Coordinating Group had told Adam to steal Ridgway's resignation statement from the files—it had been classified top secret—and leak it to Don Marble, *The New York Times* reporter Adam had met at Harvard. The story had caused a big flap. Honor had warned Adam that stunts like that could wreck his career. "I'll worry about that some other time," he told her.

Honor had talked the whole thing over with Ruth Hardin, whom she had met while shopping in the Fort Meyer commissary. Sam had just been promoted to major. He was at the Pentagon in "ops" (operations, where the combat types worked, Ruth explained). She seemed to think there was something wrong with being a combat type, even though it had paid off for Sam with an early promotion. Inevitably, Ruth knew all about the Pentagon. She told Honor that the Coordinating Group was a waste of time. They weren't going to change the Army. If they kept on making waves, "Engine Charlie" Wilson, the Secretary of Defense, was going to chop their heads off.

They compared notes on mutual friends. Honor told Ruth that Pete and Joanna Burke would soon leave Fort Stanton for the Military Academy, where Pete would be a tactical officer. Joanna had just had another miscarriage. Ruth said she always knew Catholics were dumb, but Joanna deserved a special prize. Honor was tempted to defend Joanna by telling Ruth about the visit to Boston, the tubal ligation Joanna almost got, but she decided it was something that should stay private. Ruth reported on the Rossers, who were in Ankara, where George was in JUSMMAT. Honor had to ask what that meant. "Joint U. S. Mission Military Aid for Turkey," Ruth said. She used acronyms and special Army names for everything.

"After three years at Harvard, I don't rightly feel like I'm in the Army," Honor said.

"I wish I could say that," Ruth said. She was still trying hard to be a character.

When Honor told Adam what Ruth had said about the Coordinating Group, he had gone berserk. He had screamed at her in front of the children, called her a buttonhead and ordered her to keep her mouth shut about what he was doing at the Pentagon. They had not spoken for two days. They still wouldn't be speaking if he hadn't apologized.

A few days later, she had tried again, urging him to call his guru, George Lincoln at West Point, and ask for a transfer to the faculty there. She would love to spend two or three years at the Academy. Joanna and Pete would be there; it would be a sentimental reunion. Adam warned her, in the same snarling voice with the same snarling mouth that confronted her now, not to tell him how to manage his career. "I'm in the goddamn Army to do something, be something that matters. I don't want to spend my life yakking to a lot of beanheads."

The knowledge of his wife's disapproval seemed to infuriate Adam. He had gone out of his way to pick fights with Honor, to find fault with her cooking, to criticize the way she let Pookie and Matt watch television so much.

Adam shoved his chair back from the dining-room table, where the argument about her mother visiting them, which had now become the argument about the money her mother had loaned them, had started. "I'll take out a bank loan on Monday," he said. "I'll pay back every goddamn cent of that two thousand dollars at one crack."

"Adam, you're crazy," Honor said. "We can't do it. We can barely meet the payments on this house and keep the Volkswagen runnin'."

"Then I'll get a second job."

"Doin' what?"

"I don't know. Maybe driving a taxi. I know another captain

who's doing it. There's a major two offices away from me who's selling used cars. I incline to the taxi. Who knows? I may pick up some interesting leads for Army Intelligence."

"Don't be ridiculous. You're workin' too hard already."

"Then maybe you should give up your horseback riding. How much does that cost a month?"

"Forty dollars. It's the only fun I have. Besides—"

She did not have the courage to tell him that her mother was paying for this pleasure already. The admission would only bring on more snarling. Why didn't he understand, appreciate, how much horseback riding meant to her physically as well as emotionally? All the magazine articles she read urged women to take more exercise. She had dieted desperately for their last six months in Cambridge to get down to her pre-maternity weight. Even though nobody in Cambridge gave a damn. Not once in the three years they had spent there had she received a compliment or even a comment about her looks, which were twenty times superior to those of every faculty or graduate student wife she had met, even with the extra fifteen pounds she had gained. Only when she was about to say goodbye to Harvard did Honor realize how much she missed the Army's sociability, the Saturday-night dances at the Officers' Club, the compliments implied and occasionally spoken, the attention that a pretty woman got from real men, instead of being ignored by those ivy-covered doubledomes whose only thrill was discussing Karl Marx or that other German Adam was always quoting, Clausewitz.

Virginia would be different, Honor had told herself. It was different all right, it was worse than Cambridge. It was not the Virginia Honor knew in Charlesville, only thirty miles from the North Carolina border. That Virginia was the real South. In their development house in Annandale, she might as well have been living in some suburb of New York. Almost all the neighbors were Yankees, government bureaucrats whose wives talked nothing but politics all day. Most of the time Honor ate lunch and dinner alone with the kids. At night she tried to make conversation with a husband who was too tired to talk when he finally got home. According to the class newsletter in *Assembly,* the West Point alumni magazine, there were several dozen '50 graduates in the Washington area. But Adam did not seem interested in getting together with them. Honor found it especially depressing to be back in her home state and lonely. It seemed a personal insult.

The telephone rang. "Is this Honor?" a woman's voice asked. "This is Ruth Hardin. How are you?"

"Just fine. It's so good to hear from you. What's up?"

"I've been delegated to round up Five Oh types for an Army–Navy game TV party. Want to come?"

"Sounds lovely. Just tell us where and when."

Honor took down the information. Adam stood watching her, his hands on his hips. "I don't want to go," he said.

"Well, I do," Honor said, "It's the first invitation we've gotten, for God's sake, and we've been here five months."

"You go, take your horse," he said.

Honor grabbed the first thing her hand could reach—a book from a shelf near the telephone—and threw it at him. She grabbed two more and threw them. One hit Adam's upraised arm and crashed into the dishes on the table. The others flew past his head and thudded against the dining-room wall.

"You are not goin' to talk to me that way! Ever again! If you do, I'll walk out of here and I won't come back!"

Adam picked up the books that had hit the dining room wall. "You broke the spines. Remember I told you on our honeymoon? And look at this—"

He lifted the third book off the table. They had had pot roast for dinner and it had landed in the gravy. Its open pages were smeared with cold brown goo.

"I'll do it to every damn book in the house. Maybe then you'll talk to me when you come home."

"I talk to you," he said, wiping the gravy off the book with his napkin.

"What's for dinner? Turn down the TV? Keep those kids quiet? I don't call that talkin'."

"It's the best I can do," Adam said.

"You don't love me anymore, do you? You think I'm—I'm unclean or something. Is that it?"

"No," he said, still trying to wipe the gravy off the pages of the book.

"What is it then? Don't you realize you never even touch me unless I ask for it? I have to *remind* you that it's been ten days or two weeks. What is it? I don't look any different, I don't act any different."

"I'm tired all the time, that's all. I told you what's going on at the Group. They've got me rewriting everything."

"Damn the Group. I wish I never heard the word."

"Then what the hell are we going to talk about? It's all I think about sixteen hours a day. It would never occur to you to do anything with a book but throw it—"

She searched his tired face for love. She saw, or thought she saw, a man with a withered heart, a man who had lived too long, too narrowly, in his mind. "Adam," she said, "let's get out of here. Let's ask for reassignment anywhere. Germany, Korea. Some place where you can calm down and start livin' like a normal human bein' again."

He shook his head. "You'd have more trouble sleeping on an Army base. You'd see Sergeant Hammer every time a set of stripes went by your window."

"That's not true, Adam. I'd feel safer, actually, on a base, where there's MP's, a real police force. When you stay halfway to dawn at that damn Pentagon, I'm terrified by every little noise, alone here. A woman got raped two blocks away, last week. I told you about it."

He shook his head again. "I couldn't quit the zoo now. The game is just getting good. We've got the lions up on their stools. Will they stay there? Will they decide to have us for supper? I've got to find out."

The zoo was the Pentagon. The lions were the generals. Honor did not understand the rest of it. She only knew it sounded like trouble.

That night Adam made love to her in a cold efficient way. None of the old jokes, teasing. It was swift, silent, too swift for her to catch up to him once she realized his pace. She had been tempted to refuse him but she was afraid of what he might do, what else he might say. It ended disastrously, with her lost, trapped in a vise of involuntary refusal, not much different from the early Harvard days.

Afterward, she lay there trying to decide what she felt. It was not the feeling of sadness, loss, that she remembered from Cambridge. Then, the failure had been her fault; at least, it had been within her. Adam had been considerate, tenderly forgiving when she had wept and said she was sorry, and vowed her poor response had nothing to do with him. Only later, when he had been absorbed by the Harvard rat race, had the coldness, the distance, started to come from his side of the bed. She had tolerated it because there was an ending, a departure date on the calendar. Now there was no date, no calendar. His nastiness, his indifference, was becoming a way of life. She was not going to tolerate it. Honor Prescott was not the sort of woman a man could treat that way. She thought of her best Charlesville boyfriend, Bobby Southworth, a lawyer now, of a half dozen other men she could have married by lifting an eyebrow. By God, she was going to show Adam Thayer that Honor Prescott was not just any old wife he could kick around.

Except that she did not want to show him. She only wanted to belong to him, to hold him and be held by him. She lay there weeping confused bitter tears.

Two weeks later, they drove past the massive walls of the Pentagon, crossed the Potomac and went forty miles into Maryland to the development house of Ruth and Sam Hardin. Sam greeted them in old slacks and a sport shirt. Everyone was wearing similar clothes, except Charlie McAdoo, who showed up in his blue uniform. He was among the hundred or so members of the class of 1950 who had gone Air Force. They were one of the last West Point classes to have this option, before the Air Force opened its own Academy in Colorado. Charlie claimed he had been on duty in the Pentagon War Room that morning, but he got a razzing anyway from the rest of the group, who were all Army. A lanky drawling Alabamian, Charlie responded in true rebel style, telling "the creepers and crawlers" to go to hell.

"I wish you'd all worn your uniforms," Honor said. "Then maybe I'd feel like an Army wife for a few hours. Down here I swear I think sometimes I'm married to a civilian."

"Not a very well paid one either," Ruth Hardin said.

Everyone looked so cheerful, even Ruth and Sam Hardin, Honor was swept by dismay, remembering her quarrel with Adam. Sam Hardin displayed his eighteen-month-old son, who had his father's pugnacious jaw. Sam said he had him enrolled in the West Point class of 1975. "Over my dead body," Ruth said, barely pretending to smile. But no one paid much attention to her. The party got under way. Everyone had brought their own drinks, mostly beer. Adam drew hoots when he produced a bottle of Chianti. The razzing doubled when he declared wine was the drink of the aristocrats, beer of the slobs.

The football game was the highlight of the afternoon. They watched it on the Hardins' television, growing more and more excited as Army, rated as the underdogs, rallied to win. The era of ever-triumphant Army football, as '50 had known it in their cadet days, was over, and it made this victory so much the sweeter. Afterward, they cooked hamburgers on two oblong griddles Ruth Hardin put over the burners on her kitchen stove. The men exchanged Pentagon gossip. Most of them were action officers on various staffs. They were given assignments—actions—which they were expected to complete with maximum speed. There were tales of generals and colonels who thought maximum meant miraculous. Others told of frantic efforts to soothe congressmen with drafted sons or nephews who claimed their sergeants were mean to them. There were horror stories about colonels and lieutenant colonels who had gotten on some general's shit list and sat in basement offices with nothing to do. Everything Honor heard only further convinced her that the Pentagon was a plague spot in which Adam was staying out of sheer perversity.

Sam Hardin surprised Adam by telling him he had read his Ph.D. thesis on limited war. Before General Ridgway departed, he had circulated copies of it among his staff, and the general for whom Sam worked had given him one.

"I can see why Ridgway thought it was important," Sam said. "It gives the Army a purpose it hasn't had lately."

Adam acknowledged the compliment with a nod. Another classmate new to the Pentagon wanted to know what Hardin was talking about. Since when had the Army lacked a purpose?

"Since they tested the H-bomb," Sam said. "And decided the Air Force could deliver more bang for the buck."

"Maybe beating Navy today will be the first step in the Army's renaissance," Adam said. "After three straight losses in the battle of the budget, we're about to counterattack."

Everyone knew Adam was with the Coordinating Group, which gave him an inside track to top policy. They wanted to know what he meant.

"We've gotten our chief of staff to agree to fight for a new Army, one that doesn't just sit on its tail in Germany and Korea and train draftees over here and watch them disappear in two years, while the Air Force gets all the money and publicity."

"What do you mean, fight?" Sam Hardin asked.

"Just that. Get the papers, TV, Congress on our side. Raise hell."

This was pretty exciting news. Adam was suddenly the star of the party. Honor wondered why he was talking so recklessly. She soon learned that the Coordinating Group was sending colonels and majors all over the country, recruiting key officers at the Army's schools and posts, lining them up to back the effort.

"Isn't all this goin' to overheat Engine Charlie a little?" Sam Hardin said. "Not to mention the general in the White House?"

"Maybe a public hotfoot is what they need," Adam said. "Maybe they'd take us seriously if they knew just how angry the officer corps is about the way the Army is being treated. In fact, I've been telling the Group that we ought to get together a petition signed by every lieutenant and captain in the Washington area, to show Ike just how deep the anger goes. How many of you guys would be willing to sign it?"

Everyone looked at someone else, disbelief, uneasiness on each face. "Supe," Hardin said, "they've got a word for that sort of thing: mutiny."

"Baloney," Adam said. "They couldn't court-martial all of us. The Army'd never recover."

"The hell they couldn't," Sam Hardin said. "The Army's got a real strong instinct about junior officers tryin' to take over."

"But the generals are with us. They've promised to go down the line."

"Did they put it in writing?" Sam asked. Several heads nodded in silent agreement. They were all wearing civilian clothes, but it was obvious that Sam was the only major in the group. The Army feeling for rank ran deep.

"Are we all men of honor or aren't we?" Adam said. "Are we going to sit around and let these blue-suited Air Force creeps walk away with forty-six percent of the budget when all they can do to win a war is drop a nuclear bomb? Do we care about the country, the Army, or don't we?"

There was an embarrassed silence. Sam Hardin forced a smile and looked at Honor, who had been sitting with the rest of the wives eating her hamburger and drinking beer from a bottle. "Supe," Sam said, "I think you're out of our depth. Maybe not your depth, but ours. We haven't spent three years at Harvard thinking about this. Most of us have been training draftees in Texas or driving tanks around Germany."

"I don't know how you can get so intense about Pentagon politics, Supe," Charlie McAdoo said. "When you got a wife like Honor to lure you home from that five-sided squirrel cage every night."

Everyone seized on the remark to evade Adam's proposal. "Yeah, let the colonels worry about it, Supe. If they get chopped down they've got pensions to console'm," drawled another Southerner.

"Anyway, you've been blabbing with an Air Force spy right here in front of you," someone else said.

"We know they know what we're doing," Adam said.

"Just in case, I switched on my tape recorder," Charlie McAdoo said. "It's disguised as my belt buckle."

"What do you think of it all, Charlie?" Sam Hardin asked.

"Hell, I'm not paid to think," Charlie said. "I just like to fly."

"Spoken like a true Air Force intellectual," Adam said.

Everyone got uncomfortable. Adam did not seem to know they had stopped being serious. "I've got some Elvis Presley records," Ruth Hardin said. "Shall we roll up the rug and try a few rotations?"

They rolled up the rug but no one wanted to dance to Elvis. They still preferred the big band music of their cadet years. Ruth put on Benny Goodman's "Juke Box Saturday Night." Honor looked over at Adam. He shook his head. Sam Hardin started dancing with one of the other wives. Honor felt the music running through her whole body. She strolled over to Charlie McAdoo, who had come without a wife.

"Want to try a few spins, fly-boy?" she said.

They swung into the smoothest snappiest lindy Honor had done since the one she danced with Adam after the Army–Notre Dame game in New York in 1949. Whirling left, whirling right, Honor realized that she had not danced at a single party in their three years at Harvard. Nothing but stupid endless discussions. Charlie boogied away from her. Honor matched him step for step. Once Adam could dance this way. Now he was over there on the sidelines, looking sour.

Honor gave Charlie the pelvic ripple that had helped her and Bobby Southworth win the lindy prize at Charlesville Central High School two years running. "Hey," she said. "How come we two southern stompers didn't do more of this at West Point?"

"Fate," Charlie said. "Cruel fate. I think it was also against regulations."

"I hate regulations," Honor said.

She was in the mood to ignore a lot of regulations. She hoped Adam was noticing that there were still some men around who could see Honor as something more than a cook, diaper changer and commissary shopper.

"We oughta do this more often," she said. "Who knows what it could lead to?"

"The way Adam's lookin' at me, it could lead to murder," Charlie said.

"I thought you fly-boy types liked to take chances."

Someone put on "Hot Canary" by Harry James, then "I Don't Care If the Sun Don't Shine" by Tommy Dorsey. They kept on dancing. Charlie wanted to know where she got her stamina. Horseback riding, she told him. Four hours a week. How about him? Charlie said the planes flew themselves, which meant he had a lot of stamina left over for other things. Was it going to waste? Honor asked, all the while moving her nicely dieted hips, letting her eyes suggest the kind of games she used to talk about playing when she was in a hell-raising-father's-daughter frame of mind back in Virginia, one of the reasons her mother shipped her North to Norwood, where her virginity was well and expensively guarded.

Adam did not know anything about that year in Honor's past, the last year of World War II, the year when she thought she might be Scarlett, not Melanie after all. She had let Bobby Southworth and one or two others come so close to having it. Going North had saved her, somehow. Cooled her blood or something. Maybe that was why she had married a Maine man. She wanted to mix some cooling fluid with her hot southern blood. But she didn't want ice water. That's what she was beginning to think she'd gotten. Ice water or iced vinegar.

Honor started sugar-footing, taking two quick steps on the break, pivoting to her left, shifting her weight to her right foot and raising her right hip—oooh. She reversed it and swung the left hip into action. Charlie McAdoo responded with a Texas Tommy, reaching around to catch her right wrist and spin her out, backhanded. Then tuck-in turns, one after another, whirling her to him, then spinning her out in the opposite direction, her skirt up around her hips, Charlie simultaneously spinning. *Yesssss!*

"Triple lindy," she yelled, and they started doing three steps to the beat. Fantastic! Dancing was sexy, no doubt about it, almost like doing the real thing standing up. And *fun*. My God, when was the last time Honor had some fun?

Adam stepped between them as Charlie spun her into another break. "Gotta get home," he said. "I'm working on a big paper."

"The party's just gettin' good!" Honor said. "If you got to be a poop along with bein' a mutineer, just go along. Charlie'll get me home eventually."

"Come on," Adam said, grabbing Honor's arm.

"Keep your hands off me," Honor said. "If you're not interested in touchin' me in private I'm not goin' to let you paw me in public."

The words just flew out. Sam Hardin definitely heard them. His head jerked round. So did Ruth, standing on the sidelines. She almost smiled. Everyone else kept dancing. Except Charlie McAdoo. "Hey, we're only trying to have a good time. I don't want to start a war here," he said.

Adam just looked at Honor, stony-faced. "I'll wait for you in the car," he said.

They did not speak until they crossed the 14th Street Bridge into Virginia. "I'm sorry I said that," Honor said.

"Are you sorry about the rest of it?" Adam said.

"What?"

"Dancing with McAdoo. After I tell everyone that the Air Force is screwing the Army, that they're the enemy, you start dancing with the only Air Force guy in the crowd."

"I don't know what you're talkin' about. It was just a pleasure to dance with somebody who enjoyed himself a little. With a real man. Not a worn-out paper-shufflin' intriguer like you're turnin' into."

"I proved I was a man in Korea."

"Huh. I remember the day you went into combat. You like to shook your buttons off, you were so scared."

Again, the words just flew out on her hot-tempered breath. Their effect on Adam was scary. His face seemed to turn to stone. He drove in silence for a good ten miles. Then he began to talk in a low flat voice.

"This is a warning. I know exactly what you're doing. You're trying to get me out of the Pentagon so you can go to some training base or West Point where you can dance at the Officers' Club every Saturday night and have all ranks slavering over you the way they did in Koke-Do. You're trying to run my life in the same humiliating way your mother ran your father's life until he found the guts to tell her to get lost. Keep it up and I'll tell you to do the same thing, no matter what a divorce does to my career."

All Honor heard was the hate, the rage in this diatribe. It made no sense to her. "Adam, I never wanted to humiliate you," she said. "I love you. Honest. It was the beer. Those words—I mean—I was mad at you. But I still love you."

"Sure," Adam said.

She had shown him. Now he was showing her. Fighting tears in the darkened car, Honor realized a kind of war had been declared.

III

Happy New Year, hon. It's another girl. Just as pretty as the first one.''

Amy Rosser glared at George—and coincidentally at God. She had been so certain that the first child was going to be a boy. Instead, three-year-old Georgianna Rosser was walking around at this very moment in their apartment on Gazi Osman Pasha Hill above Ankara, while she risked her life in this third-rate Turkish hospital to have another baby, who *had* to be a boy.

"What do you want to name her?" George asked.

"I don't care," Amy said. She had named the first one Georgianna, as if she was trying to remind God of what she had intended. Defiantly remind Him. George, without a clue to what she was thinking and feeling, as usual, was immensely flattered by it. She had told herself that it might be better to have the boy as the second baby. There would be less possibility of hurt feelings when he was named John Stapleton Rosser. Now she was confronted by another girl. She absolutely refused to name it. Let George do it.

"Hon," George said, taking her hand. "I don't care whether it's a boy or girl. I kind of like presiding over my own little harem."

As usual, George's sense of humor was pathetic. *"I* wanted a boy," she said.

George grinned. "I'm ready to try again, anytime."

Fuck you, Amy thought. Maybe she and the baby would both die before they got out of this horrendous hospital. Maybe that was the perfect solution. It was all so stupid. They should never have come to this idiotic country in the first place. They would not have come if George had listened to her instead of to that bonehead Pete Burke when they met at their fifth reunion. Pete convinced him that everyone ought to have some experience as a military adviser. Just because that Irish-American cluck had been promoted to major before George even made captain. What could you expect, if someone was dumb enough to stay in Korea, risking his life until the last shot was fired? The Army had to reward that kind of foolhardiness, or go out of business.

Florence Eberle, with whom Amy corresponded faithfully, advised her not to worry about who was ahead of whom on the promotion track for the time being. Eventually everyone who was going to stay in the race for general more or less caught up at the lieutenant colonel level, and then the jockeying for the rail positions began. But George worried anyway, so here they were in Turkey on New Year's Day 1956, with George gone for weeks at a time teaching these moronic Orientals how to handle American tanks, leaving her and his female namesake wandering forlornly through Ankara's third rate bazaars breathing the ubiquitous smog.

What made it even more frustrating was the near certainty that George could have picked off a graduate-school assignment with a simple request for one. They had come home from Germany and spent a boring year at Fort Knox, Kentucky, where George took his required advanced course at the armor school. Amy had heard about Adam Thayer's rising fame and spent the last six months at Knox urging George to apply for graduate school with all possible speed. Adam's doctoral thesis on limited war had been circulated through the highest levels of the Pentagon and Adam had landed a choice assignment on the Army staff. The graduate-schooled officer was the wave of the future, and Amy, following another Florence Eberle dictum—imitate success—had even selected the ideal subject for George to study—industrial management. He had ignored her and applied for Turkey.

If all this was not enough grist for gloom, they were out of Washington at a time when her father, of all people, might be able to help them. Eisenhower's election had put the Republicans back in power after two decades in the political wilderness. Judgeships, ambassadorial posts, government commissions by the dozen offered, at last, a cornucopia of political appointments. Her father, on the advice of his cousin, Paul Stapleton, had become an assiduous giver to the Grand Old Party, and had loaned his distinguished family name to fund-raising appeals on behalf of Ike and other candidates. Teddy Kemble was rewarded by a title and a desk in the upper reaches of the Central Intelligence Agency. It was really rather boring work, he told her in his self-deprecating way. But he was enjoying Washington. All sorts of old school friends were in town, including his ex-Yale roommate, who was an undersecretary of defense. Subsequent letters revealed little but Teddy's talent for traveling around the world purportedly to confer with intelligence agencies in other countries, leaving Mother in Washington, complaining and gaining weight.

Now, a year later, all these frustrations and disappointments coalesced around this final disappointment, another baby girl. Final because Amy had no intention of going through another nine months of discomfort and disfigurement. God, or whoever was running the world, would have to get along without a John Stapleton Rosser. The mere echo of that name in her mind aroused a deeper, blacker anger. She lay there staring at the ceiling while George experimented with names. Agnes after his mother? Grace after her mother?

"Why not Grace? Your mother would like it."

"I don't care," Amy said.

"How about Florence? We could ask the Eberles to be the godparents."

"I don't *care*," Amy said.

Pain throbbed beneath her double-thick sanitary napkin. They had performed an episiotomy to ease the delivery. It was a relatively minor procedure, but the idea of being cut down there by a surgeon's knife repelled, offended Amy. Dr. Cubuk, the tubby Turkish doctor who had delivered the baby, appeared in the doorway. "How is our little peasant?" he said in his vaguely English accent. Although he had studied medicine in London, Cubuk had served in Korea with the Turkish brigade and liked Americans. During the delivery, he had started calling her a peasant because she did not make a sound, no matter how much the contractions hurt. "Are you ready to commence the spring planting this afternoon?" Dr. Cubuk continued.

"She's feeling a little disappointed, Doctor," George said. "She was hoping for a boy."

"You see, I told her she was turning into a Turk. That is typical of a peasant woman's attitude. Girl children are despised. But I didn't expect to see such primitive opinions in the mentality of a graduate of Vassar College."

Dr. Cubuk worked for the U.S. Army, which rented a floor of the Turkish Army's main military hospital. The diet kitchen was run by a Turkish woman, who fried everything, even vegetables, and "improved" their taste with generous dollops of olive oil. She spoke very little English and no one could persuade her to cut down on the olive oil. The Americans called her Scheherazade because she had a thousand and one dishes and they all tasted the same. Was it the thought of eating this slop or was it being called a peasant by this idiot Turk, who had discussed Hemingway's "Farewell to Limbs" with her during the delivery, that made Amy want to weep?

She thought of the kitchen of her apartment on Gazi Osman Pasha Hill with the perpetual collection of pots of boiling water on the stove, a necessity in Ankara because the city's water was polluted. She thought of the miserable commissary in the basement of the JUSMMAT building, where you could buy little besides butter, flour, coffee, sugar, canned milk and, for some reason, sauerkraut. She thought of the boring New Year's Eve party which she had been attending last night when the labor pains began. She thought about the whole miserable unkempt city of Ankara, sitting in its bowl of smog below the bleak treeless hills. She remembered a remark George had made when they argued about going to Turkey— "Ankara's the same latitude as Philadelphia." She started to cry.

"It's okay, hon, it's okay. She's a beautiful baby," George said for the tenth or eleventh time, as the tears streamed down. He was not used to seeing her cry. She had stopped crying by the time he came home that day in Germany when he told her John Stapleton was dead.

She finally agreed to call the baby Grace, after her mother. The hell with Florence and Willard Eberle. What had they done for her, anyway? They would ask George's dum-dum ex-roommate, Sam Hardin and his moronic wife Ruth, to be the godparents. Sam was working in the Pentagon, the seat of Army power, where George Rosser would be if he had taken his wife's advice.

As soon as George left, the tears began again. Dr. Cubuk came in and asked her if she wanted to nurse the baby. She shook her head, still weeping. Scheherazade arrived with a tray of fried meat and vegetables splattered with olive oil. Amy pushed it away and continued to weep.

She wept most of the day and most of the night. Finally, around dawn on the second day of the year 1956, she stopped and lay in her bed, wondering what was happening to her. Was she losing her mind? No, Amy decided. Nor did it have much to do with John Stapleton either. A sensible realistic woman did not weep for someone dead four years. No, her problem was Ankara, and George. He was having a wonderful time playing war with his Turks in their tanks while she went slowly crazy here in this plague spot of the Middle East. Except for a week's leave in Beirut, and another week sailing the Greek islands, they hadn't even done any traveling. It was all war games, endless discussions at parties about what great tank country Turkey was, the marvelous Anatolian Plateau, so flat, barren, perfect for an armor genius. George Patton would have loved it.

The trouble was, George Rosser was not an armor genius. Every time she thought she had cured him of his romantic infatuation with being a tank battle hero, he relapsed. Lying there in her bed on the third floor of the Turkish military hospital, eating Scheherazade's vile food, going through the motions of trying to breast-feed the baby to please Dr. Cubuk, making small talk with George when he visited, Amy began to formulate a plan to avoid a repetition of this disastrous assignment.

Step one was her inability to breast-feed little Grace. Dr. Cubuk was baffled. Her breasts were small "but not insignificant." Amy did not bother to tell him that she took the baby off her breast the moment he left the room. She hated breast-feeding. It hurt, and there was something basically annoying about having this gurgling creature tugging at her anatomy. By the time she was ready to leave the hospital, Dr. Cubuk had given up and Grace was on formula.

At home, on Gazi Osman Pasha Hill, George had organized a party, with the help of their next-door neighbor, Helen Palladino, and the other captains' wives in the building. They had taken up a collection to buy Grace a silver spoon. Helen, who lived down the hall, was JUSMMAT's reigning beauty. She had a willowy body and a face that might have served as a model for a Pompeian wall painting, long-nosed, with high, aristocratic cheekbones. She would have made Amy uneasy and undoubtedly broken a few hearts in the mission, but she was a clown, always twisting her mouth, popping her eyes and talking too fast in a Brooklyn accent.

Helen presented the spoon. "We want this kid to remember Turkey. When she gets old enough, you can tell her she was born with a silver spoon in her mouth and what's more, it was sterilized."

It was the perpetual lament of all the wives, the danger of hepatitis and intestinal diseases. Not only did all water have to be boiled; all fruit had to be peeled; all vegetables had to be cooked in a chlorine solution. The kitchen walls were damp with steam, the apartments reeked all day.

Next came the ritual of showing Georgianna her little sister. Everyone cooed. Georgianna did not seem especially enthusiastic. She only cried and said she wanted to hold the baby some more when Amy decreed it was time to go to bed. Georgianna was a whiny child. Amy already suspected she would not like her much more than her own mother had liked her. Not that Amy had whined. That had been Mother's specialty.

They sat around exchanging the latest Rank Hath Its Privileges stories. In the tight little world of the mission, with only about a thousand officers and enlisted men and their dependents, the foibles of the higher ranks were a constant topic. Generals, colonels and lieutenant colonels lived on the upper reaches of Gazi Osman Pasha Hill where the smog was thinner. In school, in the Boy Scouts, their children bossed around the children of the lower ranks. Among themselves, the uppers were just as rank-conscious. Helen Palladino told the best story of the night. "General Bloop"—she inflated her cheeks to suggest a certain brigadier—"and Honey Chile"—she gave a perfect imitation of the mincing walk of the general's Georgia-born wife—"moved into that apartment reserved for lieutenant colonels while their house was being painted. They got one of the two apartments in the building that don't have washer-dryers. This meant Honey Chile would have to share the washer-dryer in the basement with the wife of the junior lieutenant colonel who got stuck with the other apartment. Guess how Honey Chile solved it?"

Helen repeated the mincing walk and Mrs. General's wide insincere smile. "You can use it on Saaaty night because we'll be goin' out then. I'll take the rest of the week. I like to do my washin' a little at a time."

Amy never told any of these stories. The transients, the ones who did not plan to stay in the Army, the lightweights, like Helen Palladino, whose husband was an ROTC graduate, were the ones who retailed them by the gross. When Amy heard one, she only smiled and said something innocuous, such as "Oh dear."

The talk shifted to other vexations of life in Ankara—the endless stream of peddlers who came to the door selling fruit, vegetables, pottery, wood and water, the beggars who specialized in pestering Americans, the servants who remained impervious to English and to cleanliness. "We got charming news yesterday," Helen said. "Flavia is going to have to get rabies shots."

"Oh no!" Amy said. "One of those damn cats?"

Helen nodded glumly. Ankara swarmed with stray cats, who were very wild. They fed on garbage, which often made them rabid. They frequently bit and scratched children and the Army's doctors insisted on the painful weeks-long series of rabies shots when this happened. The Palladinos' daughter, Flavia, was Georgianna's age.

"I'm glad I didn't know it when I was in the hospital," Amy said. "I would have been out of my mind with worry. When it comes to watching Georgianna, Sophia is a complete idiot."

Sophia, their Turkish maid, happened to be standing about a foot away, clearing some dirty glasses from an end table. She smiled and nodded eagerly when she heard her name. It was one of the few words she understood.

As soon as the last guest departed, and Sophia put Grace to bed in a bassinet beside Georgianna, Amy went to work on George. "I'm

306

very worried about the baby," she said. "I can't nurse her. We'll have to rely on formula. I dread what could happen with this contaminated water."

"We boil it," George said.

"I know. But I'm not sure if we boil it enough for an infant. Georgie has had diarrhea for a month, you know. I've had to put diapers on her again. It's made her very weak and susceptible to infection, in my opinion. Now this thing with the cat is the last straw. Sophia can't or won't watch Georgie when she goes out. I can't go out if I've got to double-boil the formula water and mix the stuff myself. It'll take half the day."

"What's the answer?" George said.

Amy sensed from his tone that he already knew it. She frequently forgot that George was not stupid. There was just something dull about him, something in his manner, which was too unassuming. But now was not the time to deal with such minor matters. She had a plan and she was not going to change it.

"I could go home early," she said.

"Aw, Amy."

She knew what he was thinking. Six months of celibacy. It was what he deserved, Amy told herself, for wishing this ordeal on her. If anything, his reaction reassured her that she was doing the right thing. No sign of resentment, anger, the sort of thing that led solitary husbands to play around. Turkey was the perfect place to leave him. It was practically impossible to date a Turkish woman. Anyway, Amy told herself, six months wasn't that long. Since she had just given birth, it would be six weeks before George could make love to her, even if she stayed. She wouldn't be very enthusiastic if she was still trying to cope with life in this pesthole. Instead, when she greeted him in Washington, D.C., they might be ready for a second honeymoon.

She was going to Washington to make sure George's next assignment was graduate school, preferably in the capital, at Georgetown or George Washington University. Left to him, it was liable to be Germany (those damn tanks again) or something as insane as Korea. Graduate school would be nailed down with Florence Eberle's help. Willard had weathered Command and General Staff School and was now working for the deputy chief of staff for personnel. Everything would be arranged without argument long before George taught his last Turk how to steer a Sherman tank for JUSMMAT.

George groaned about how grisly life would be in a BOQ (Bachelor Officers' Quarters) and how much he would miss her and Georgianna. But he could not deny that Turkey was risky for a new baby on formula. And Sophia *was* an idiot.

Within a week, Amy was packing. They made up a white lie about her mother being ill to explain her departure. She left, trailing clouds of sacrificial-glory—going home, with two small children, to nurse an ailing parent. She told George she was going to live with her parents, who had rented a house in northwest Washington, D.C. Amy actually had no intention of doing such a foolish thing. Her mother would spoil Georgianna silly in two weeks.

George almost cried when he said goodbye to them at the airport. Georgianna, Daddy's girl, wept until she got hysterical. Amy had to slap her face when they got on the plane and warn her that she would not get a speck of dessert if she didn't shut up. She finally subsided into sullen brooding, another bad habit which Amy reminded herself to change. For the time being she had her hands full feeding Grace and savoring the skill with which she had executed this strategic withdrawal.

In Washington, D.C., everything went according to plan. Mother and Father met her at the airport and were given a week to gurgle over their granddaughters while Amy house-hunted. She finally bought a medium-priced three-bedroom colonial in Alexandria, in a development that did not look too Levittowny. Each house was on a half-acre plot. Most of the neighbors were majors or government bureaucrats. George would be a major in a year or two if all went well.

The children were extracted from their grandparents' grasp. When her mother begged her to let Georgianna stay for another week, Amy took considerable pleasure in saying no. *You never spent that much time with me*, Amy thought. *Now we're even for all those hours I spent sitting outside the music room while you trilled your brains out.*

It took a month for her furniture to arrive from Turkey. Meanwhile, she retrieved her silver and china, which she had stored in Philadelphia. Over lunch at the Fort Halleck Officers' Club, she reestablished her friendship with Florence Eberle, who spent the first half hour deploring the Army's new green uniforms. Florence said they were nothing but a stupid attempt to make the Army look modern and thus compete with the Air Force, which was getting almost half the defense budget these days. Willard was trying everything to get out of personnel and into the missile program, which was where the power curve was moving. But for the first time, Florence seemed unsure of herself. It was hard to tell what was happening to the Army, she said, and damned Eisenhower throughout her third martini as a traitor to the Corps and possibly to the country.

Amy also called Honor Thayer and invited her to lunch at the Fort Halleck Officers' Club. Honor accepted with alacrity, and after her second martini talked rather loosely about Adam's job at the Pentagon. She seemed bitter about the amount of work they were making him do and the "riskiness" of it all. Honor was as beautiful as ever and as dumb, Amy concluded. She also concluded that she wanted to learn more about this Coordinating Group for whom Adam toiled.

As soon as her house was organized, and she found a black girl to take care of the children, Amy invited Honor and Adam to dinner with her mother and father. Adam was surprisingly gaunt and hollow-eyed. He did look like he was working too hard. Teddy Kemble was scarcely privy to the inner workings of the Eisenhower administration, but he knew enough to support their party line on most things. When the conversation got around to Army affairs, Teddy naturally echoed Engine Charlie Wilson's "more bang for the buck" philosophy, which was based on Secretary of State John Foster Dulles' massive-retaliation doctrine.

Adam proceeded to demolish him. "What are we going to do, Mr. Kemble, if the Communists capture Guatemala? Or Cuba? Drop an H-bomb on them? That vaporizes the whole country. Is anyone else going to be very enthusiastic about asking help from the United States if that's our answer to everything?"

United States military policy, Adam said, was in the grip of Air

Force generals who had formed an unholy alliance with the Navy to outvote the Army on everything. "Before they're through," Adam said, "I predict they're going to try to eliminate the Army completely."

Ridiculous, her father sputtered. The Army had too many friends in the Administration, even without the President. He himself was an Army man. Teddy nattered about his hero cousin, Paul Stapleton who was close to a number of influential senators. One of Teddy's oldest friends was an undersecretary of defense. He was an Army man too. Adam raised an eyebrow. "Would you be interested in telling us what's going on inside Wilson's office? It would be awfully helpful to get some word of any advance moves, along the lines I just described."

Teddy Kemble refused to take Adam seriously. But he said he would see what could be done. Amy had to listen to the latter part of the conversation with one ear because Honor insisted on talking about children. She wanted to know if Amy was going to try for a boy. Amy's mother vapidly said she hoped so. Amy dismissed the idea with a shake of her head.

"What a shame George couldn't be here," Adam said as they departed. "When *is* he getting back?"

"In a month or two, I hope," Amy said. Honor had already asked that question earlier in the evening. Amy had given the same answer, although the truth was four months, and described at length her reasons for coming home with the baby. While she made Ankara sound like an overcrowded leprosarium, she wondered why Adam leaned on the *is*. Did he know something? How could he?

The next day, Adam was on the telephone asking if her father had contacted his old friend the undersecretary. His boss at the Pentagon was very interested in opening a line of communication. Amy felt excitement stir her blood. She phoned her father and lashed him into action. He said he was afraid of making a fool of himself. He talked about the unpleasant things that might happen if the Defense Department thought the CIA was trying to play some dirty tricks against it. Amy pulled out a few stops in her emotional repertoire. She asked him if he cared about the country. She asked him if he cared about her. Rather than answer no to both questions, Teddy took his friend the undersecretary to lunch at the Cosmos Club.

Wonder of wonders, it developed that the undersecretary was not very happy about the way the Air Force generals and the Secretary of Defense were talking about the Army. There really were memorandums being written, suggesting that the Army be reduced to 100,000 men. Her father, his voice a little shaky with excitement, reported this to Amy on the telephone two nights later. Keeping her voice perfectly calm, Amy called Adam at the Pentagon the next day. "I've got some interesting news," she said. Before she could say another word, he told her that he would call her back on another phone.

Ten minutes later, her doorbell rang. There stood Captain Thayer in his paratrooper's uniform, his Korean battle star gleaming dully on his ribbons. "If it's really interesting," he said, "it can't be said over a telephone in the zoo. You never know what's being tapped. We're reasonably certain all the Coordinating Group's phones are."

"You're joking."

"Amy dear," Adam said, strolling past her into the hall, "do you know why the late Secretary of Defense James Forrestal jumped out that window in 1949? Because he found out, among other things, that his phone was being tapped by his own admirals."

Amy was wearing old slacks and a blouse. Her hair needed washing. Adam caught her glancing in the hall mirror with evident dismay and said: "It's all right. I like my ladies rumpled now and then. It makes them human. Which is a way I've never quite thought of you."

"Human?"

"Your determination to be perfect in all things visible and audible daunted me. Otherwise I might have tried to compete with George for that trust fund."

"Dear old Adam," she said. "As charming as ever. Can I get you some coffee?"

"I live on the stuff. Black."

They were alone in the house. The maid had Grace and Georgianna out for the morning. Amy led him into the sun-filled kitchen and apologized for serving him instant coffee. He said he'd forgotten there was any other kind.

"What's the news?" he said.

She told him.

"Beautiful," he said. "Just as we suspected."

"I can't believe it," Amy said. "The Army's only got nine hundred thousand men now. What would happen to everybody?"

"We'd be riffed," Adam said. "The biggest rif ever."

"What happens now?"

"We need documentation. Copies of some of those memorandums. Tell your father to ask the undersecretary to get them. I'll pick them up here."

My God, was she glad she had gotten out of Ankara. To have missed something like this! "What will happen then?"

"At the right moment, I hope, we unleash a publicity barrage that blows them out of the sky and sea. That's what I'm recommending. But I'm only a captain. The chief of staff is a very nervous man. And a politician besides. His secretary, the brigadier, is another one."

"They must be insane. Wilson and the Air Force, I mean. What can they be thinking?"

"Governments don't think. They react to pressure. The Air Force has already got forty-six percent of the military budget and they're cocky enough to try for another twenty. The Navy's reasonably contented with the twenty-nine percent they've got, so they're pitching in with the fly-boys. Leaving the Army with about five percent. Enough to post a couple of regiments here and there to guard the radioactive ruins after the bomber jocks drop the big ones."

"It's serious, isn't it?"

"Very."

"You look like it's—wearing you down."

"A little."

She thought of George in Ankara, teaching Turks the difference between left and right. Would his face ever wear the haunted weariness she saw on this man's face?

"I'll tell my father. I'm sure he'll pass it along."

"Fine. When we communicate, I think it might be a good idea to use code names. How about Priscilla and Miles?"

He still remembered the half-joking argument about their ancestors they had had at West Point. Amy found that curiously flattering.

"Priscilla and Miles it is."

They stood up and moved simultaneously toward the kitchen door. They met in front of it. "And poor George won't be home for another four months. What's wrong?" Adam said.

"I told you—"

"I've got a friend in personnel. He looked him up. No request for a transfer. Every evidence of completing his tour without demur or complaint. Like a good soldier."

"I just hated the place—"

"You know," Adam said, "I always thought Miles got all he wanted from Priscilla after she married John."

Amy started to say no. But the word locked somewhere deep in her throat.

"I've got an hour," Adam said, stepping back, making sure she was free to choose. "I told them you lived out in Annandale, near me. I don't trust anyone, not even the boys in the Group."

Amy reached out her hand. He met it halfway. Had she intended to shove him away? Or was she trying to show him that she too wanted something, perhaps consolation, perhaps a union that would be part of the tempo that their intrigue stirred in her blood? She wanted to feel that tempo beat in everything, she wanted to see if it could do miraculous things to an act that had hitherto been merely pleasurable.

Don't think of betrayal, forget Honor's woebegone face at the Fort Halleck Officers' Club, temporarily erase George, baking in his tank on the Anatolian Plateau—

She stopped in the doorway of the master bedroom, staring at the four-poster from their cottage in Mautbrunnen. George had insisted on buying it as a memento. She had not been enthusiastic about any mementos from that cottage, but she had been unable to think of a way to stop him. On the bureau was a picture of her and George outside the chapel at West Point.

Adam stood behind her, his hands cupped over her breasts. "Don't stop now," he said. "Don't think. Except about wanting, letting go."

"No—down here," Amy gasped, and led him along the short hall to the still undecorated guest room. It had a new bed, there was nothing on the wall but a mirror. A motel, Amy thought, it could be a motel room. Adam could be a stranger she was meeting elsewhere, a necessary price she had to pay to become part of this larger thing, the intrigue, the struggle for billions of dollars, for control of the Army.

"Undress me," he said as he fumbled with the buttons of her blouse. "I hate passive women."

"We shouldn't," she said. "What if they find out?"

She took off his tie and unbuttoned his shirt.

"That's what makes it special. The danger," Adam said.

He had her blouse off. He unhooked her bra, unzipped her slacks and pulled them down, taking her underpants with them. She stepped away from the clothes while he kicked off his shoes and took off his pants. They were naked. He drew her to him, his hands finding all the right places. My God, it was special. Her heart was pounding. Something else beat in syncopation in her temple.

But where was it going to lead? Did it make any more sense than her affair with Johnny Stapleton? Once and for all, banish that ghost, maybe that was what she was doing, laying the ghost. But this was not Johnny, this skeletal cerebral man who was whispering: "Slow down, slow down, we've got an hour."

What if the maid came home early? What could she say? How could she explain, even to three-and-a-half-year-old Georgianna, what Mommy was doing in the guest room with Captain Thayer? Adam's car was in the driveway. What if her neighbor had seen the trim young paratroop officer arrive? Would she notice that he left an hour later? A major's wife, Denise Harkness, lived at the end of the block. Her husband was studying at the Army Industrial War College. Who knows whom she might know? Class of '50 graduates at the college? Officers from Fort Knox? The Army was too big, too confusing to keep track of individuals.

But it was happening, irreversibly happening. They were on the bed. He was placing her hands around his erect penis. So different from George, so much more methodical, cool, yes, even cold, he was in perfect control, the smile in his eyes was a kind of distant laughter. Did he know what she was thinking, how scared she was? For a moment she teetered between dislike, anger and letting go.

Then she remembered. "My diaphragm. I haven't—"

"Don't worry. I've got the insurance." He opened his hand and showed her the condom crumpled in his palm.

"You came prepared."

"Hopeful," he said. "Call it hopeful."

He knelt beside the bed, spread her legs and thrust his tongue deep into her. Johnny had done that once. She had declined to return the favor. Was it one of the tests she had failed with him? "A sensual—intellectual," she gasped.

He said nothing. He mounted, entering swiftly, surely, awakening guilty memories of George's more modest husbandly satisfaction. Was it simple wish, physical desire, that had brought her to this bed? It was somehow comforting to think of it that way, more easily forgiven. The old married lady just got horny, that's all.

But Adam did not tolerate such simplicities. "Close your eyes," he said, "Imagine we're doing it in the War Room at the Pentagon. Have you been there yet? I'll take you someday. It's the damnedest place you've ever seen. Push a button and voices, lights, come at you from Panama, Japan, Korea, Vietnam, Iran, Germany, England, Greenland."

Stroking while he whispered these insane outrageous words. Was he making fun of her? Was it all a joke? Fuck the little society bitch? Did he mean it? Could she move, live inside this darkness? She always kept her eyes open with George. Sometimes she turned her head away because he made strange faces when he approached climax—as if he had somehow just stubbed his toe. But this?

"What do you see, what are you feeling, Priscilla?" he whispered, stroking slowly now.

Nothing? She could not admit nothing. "Nice," she whispered. It was nice if the maid did not come home early, if the major's wife was cleaning out her closets and hadn't looked out the window lately.

"Not good enough. I want a thousand flares, a flight of F-100's, a free-fall drop from twenty thousand feet opening five hundred feet from the ground as the Army's favorite weapons system, in constant use since George met Martha, prepares—to—fire—"

Not very loving, she thought, as she felt ever so faintly the pulsing begin within the condom's sheath. Not very loving or romantic. George often whispered "I love you" as he came. But she was not looking for love or romance here. She was looking for excitement, right? Excitement and something else that had no word to describe it, that smiled or leered somewhere in this darkness.

She thrust her belly against him, holding her breath, fiercely seeking the answer in his bony maleness, clasping the wish to her searching breasts. Yes, yes, she willed, fiercely insisting on a new kind of coming.

She waited for him to lie beside her, hold her. But he vanished from her darkness. She opened her eyes to find him lying on his side, smiling at her. He put his hand on her pubic hair, a gesture of possession that she almost resented. "That was great," he said.

"I'm flattered," she said. "Especially coming from you. Married to a beauty queen."

"Too much of a good thing makes for complacency. She just lies there, assuming the mere vision creates ecstasy."

"What happens now?"

"We trust each other a little more. We—share a little more. For a while."

He began to tell her about the Coordinating Group, what they were doing. Compiling an arsenal of facts and arguments for the great confrontation. Recruiting allies in the press. He told her about his friendship with *The New York Times* reporter Don Marble. How they were using Marble to probe upward into the *Times*'s hierarchy, feeding him their position papers for secret circulation, promising him an exclusive, if the *Times* in turn promised to go down the line with the Army in the battle that was going to erupt. Recruiting other allies in the House and Senate.

They lay there, on the guiltless guest-room bed, both still naked, while Amy listened, learned. Part of her education, part of her life, she thought, life that was suddenly suffused with the wildness she had tasted in Johnny Stapleton's arms and something larger, much more exciting than wildness. She found herself liking the nakedness, the thrust of his cool eyes up her thighs through the dark tangle of hair he had caressed to her pleasing belly and breasts.

"What's in it for you, for Adam?" Amy asked.

He smiled crookedly, briefly, an acknowledgment that he appreciated the question. "If it works, the colonels will be generals within the year. Adam'll be a major. We'll all be on our way."

"If it doesn't work?"

He smiled again. This time she did not like it. She glimpsed a recklessness she did not approve. "We'll have had some fun," he said.

So they began their dangerous game. The fucking, which is how Amy soon thought of it, became more intense, but it never dominated the scenario. More and more she began to suspect that Adam was only mildly interested in it. This hurt her on one level. On another level it freed her from a fear of entrapment.

Then Adam began to visit her when there were no memorandums, no messages to collect; at night, parking on the next block, walking to the house, going immediately to the guest room, where the shades were drawn, lights dimmed against casting shadows. Amy sensed a need deeper than sex, a need to talk about what was happening to the government, to the Army, what might happen if they failed. Adam taught her to see the Army as a kind of country within the country, not a unified organized modern nation, but a survival from another era, a collection of independent duchies, with generals as barons, carving out territories, fiercely resisting anyone's attempt to rule them. Another time he spoke of it as a dinosaur, a beast of awesome power, with a very small brain. He saw himself and the Coordinating Group as Dr. Frankenstein, trying to put a modern brain in the monster's head. They were the hope of the Army. It was the first time the Army had marshaled the best thinkers and used them as a force, instead of abandoning them to wander forlornly through their careers, making brilliant recommendations which everyone ignored.

Most of the time Amy simply listened. Sometimes she made cautionary comments about the confrontation psychology the Coordinating Group was pursuing. "Wouldn't it be better to approach Eisenhower privately?" she said. "I can't believe he'll go along with a plan to dismantle the Army, if he's approached as a West Pointer by fellow West Pointers."

"It's been tried," Adam said. "We're convinced he's senile. He burned himself out in Europe. That's only a smiling shell of General Ike over there in the White House."

She sensed, at times, a certain hysteria in the whole thing, perhaps a product of the Pentagon's claustrophobic atmosphere, perhaps a shock reaction to the very real possibility that the Republicans, mesmerized by the power of America's atomic weapons, were preparing to destroy the Army. In mid-April, the undersecretary told her father that Secretary of Defense Wilson and Admiral Radford, Chairman of the Joint Chiefs of Staff, had decided to make the proposal in the budget for the coming year, which would be released early in the summer.

Adam made a growling sound in his throat when he heard this news. "Now we have no choice. There's been some talk in the Group about holding back, just making threats but keeping the whole dirty business inside the zoo."

He fucked her with unusual enthusiasm that night. Little bites, pinches of delight. He let her get on top, a position she found very exciting. They were like creatures from some primitive culture where women as well as men were warriors. More and more she traveled with him in her mind, to the Pentagon, saw the generals and the colonels behind their desks, hefted the pieces of lethal paper they were shuffling.

"Will we keep this up after John Alden gets home, Priscilla?" Adam asked her.

"I don't know," she said. "I don't know if it would be—possible. Or wise."

Already, George's letters were a problem. They were so full of endearments, of kisses for her and for the children, of laments about the dreariness of life in Ankara without them.

"If I left the Army, would you divorce George and marry me?"

"What would you do if you left?"

"There's a future for civilians in the Defense Department. Maybe more than there is for Army officers."

"You'd have to become a politician. Or a bureaucrat. You wouldn't be any good at either of them."

He laughed briefly. "You're probably right. But I hope we'll always be—special."

"A sentimental streak. I can't believe it," she mocked. He looked hurt. For the first time she saw him as vulnerable. She regretted the words. "Let's not decide anything yet. Let's enjoy what we have," she said.

The Coordinating Group moved inexorably toward the confrontation. Problems—such as *The New York Times*'s insistence that their regular Pentagon reporter write the story, which caused Adam's friend, Don Marble, to quit the paper in a rage, symptoms of cold feet among several three- and four-star members of the general staff—only proved to be delays. At 3 A.M. on May 17, Amy's telephone rang. "This is Miles. Can I come over?" Adam said.

"Of course," she said.

"Have a drink ready. A strong one."

He arrived looking more exhausted than she had ever seen him. His eyes were glazed with fatigue, his skin had the brownish withered quality of an old newspaper. She handed him a double scotch and soda and he gulped it down. He had been working, he said, for forty-eight consecutive hours. Cold feet were rampant on the general staff. They had demanded revisions of various memorandums which attacked the Air Force directly. They had canceled a series of magazine articles which Adam had written, proving the Air Force's ineffectiveness in Korea. *The New York Times*'s Pentagon reporter was difficult and imperious. He did not trust Adam and Adam did not trust him. He made endless demands for verification of almost every line in the Army's papers.

"Marble knew me from Harvard. He knew I had a brain," Adam lamented. "This guy sees me as just another captain. In the Pentagon that's synonymous with pencil sharpener."

Nevertheless, the assault was launched. The *Times* was going to break the story on May 19. They began holding their collective breaths. That morning, Sunday, the doorbell rang at nine o'clock. Amy almost stopped breathing. The maid was still feeding baby

Grace her second bottle of the day and Georgianna was in the living room watching television. Was Adam crazy enough—?

Amy opened the door to discover a delivery boy with a dozen fresh roses. The card was signed: "The Coordinating Group." Amy suddenly wondered if Adam talked about her to the colonels. Would she go through the rest of her life in the Army known as a great lay? She didn't trust him. It occurred to her that she did not trust any man.

"Who sent you the flowers, Mommy?" Georgianna asked.

"Grandma," Amy said.

In the box with the flowers was a copy of the front section of the *Times*. There it was, the bombshell, on page one. MILITARY FORCES SPLIT ON ARMS POLICIES. A rather tame headline. The story went on to describe "profound conflicts" within the Defense Department. At the head of the list was the question whether "the big bombs" would deter Communism. The more Amy read, the more disappointed she became. It was all written in the *Times*'s worst gray-lady style, full of jargon which the reporter had taken verbatim from official documents. "Will nuclear weapons be stalemated by parity between the United States and Russia?" he asked. Another paragraph, subtitled "Issues in Interservice Discordance," argued against "excessive reliance on one form of military power." Amy could see legions of readers going to sleep. Worse, the reporter revealed that he had obtained staff papers from the Air Force attacking the Army's arguments with equally obfuscating jargon.

The next day's story was even more disappointing. Abandoning the Army entirely, the reporter devoted columns to an Air Force attack on the Army's Nike missile, which the Air Force claimed was incapable of shooting down planes or enemy rockets. That night, about ten o'clock, Amy got a call from Adam. "As Napoleon said on the way home from Moscow—can I stop for a drink?"

"Sure," she said. He sounded odd.

He arrived with a smile on his face. "I didn't expect to see you looking so happy," she said.

"Why shouldn't I be? I'm drunk. I'm trying to stay drunk. It isn't easy on a captain's salary."

"It's that bad?" she said as she poured the scotch.

"It's worse than bad. It's all over. The Coordinating Group is finished. The colonel in command got orders for Alaska. A half dozen other guys are on their way to Korea, Germany, Afghanistan, you name it."

"And Captain Thayer?"

"He's getting coffee for a colonel named Eberle. They've confiscated all our files."

"I hope my name isn't in them."

Adam smiled briefly. Very briefly. "You were ready enough to share the glory, Priscilla. Why not share the shame?"

"Because—"

She hesitated for a split second before saying it. When it was spoken, it left no doubt about the future.

"—it wouldn't be fair to George."

Adam did not like it. She saw that he had come here looking for a partner to share his pain. For a moment Amy felt guilty. But she did not have any sympathy for him. Sympathy was not her strong suit. Anyway, he had used up his right to it by insisting on the other thing, the fucking.

"You don't have to worry," he said. "This guy Eberle from personnel is a dodo. He's been put in charge of our dispersion. He thinks all I did was sharpen pencils, like the other captains in the zoo. I've managed to sneak out the juiciest stuff, including the memos Daddy got us, right under his nose."

He began to denounce the chief of staff, General Maxwell Taylor, and his secretary, Brigadier General William Westmoreland, as cowards and double-crossers. They had promised to back the Coordinating Group and they had now collaborated to destroy them.

Amy refused to follow him. "Maybe the whole thing wasn't realistic in the first place, Adam," she said.

"Oh. Then why did you go along for the ride? Was it just for the fucking?"

"I'm glad you think of it that way too," she said. "It'll be easier to stop."

"Will it?" Adam said. "I want you—maybe I need you now more than ever. Jesus, Amy, don't you *care?* If not about me, then about the Army, the country?"

No one had ever asked her that before. George assumed that she cared about him, the children, a woman's caring. But Adam was not asking for this; he was willing to forgo it if she had the other thing, the man's caring, the kind that created those smiles of suppressed affection between father and son, that sent Pete Burke up a machine-gun-swept hill in Korea, that made Johnny hold the road in his doomed tank while the yellow men swarmed around him with their satchel charges. Amy flinched from the cost of this caring, the pain. "Why did it go so wrong?" she said.

"Because everybody lost his nerve. And *The New York Times*, with their goddamn theories of objective journalism, decided they had to tell all sides of the story simultaneously. And—"

He gulped his scotch.

"Aw, hell, let's forget it. Let's get drunk and make believe we're doing it on Engine Charlie Wilson's desk with the Joint Chiefs standing around saluting. Then we'll go back to playing the game."

It wouldn't be fair to George. Why did those words suddenly seem so depressing? Was she, had she been pursuing another secret dream, personified by this reckless drunk now grinning so desperately at her? A dream of wildness beyond anything she could expect George to achieve. Why not get drunk this once, get drunk with Adam and see what she found in the darkness?

She poured another double scotch for Adam and a triple for herself. "Here's to the Group," she said.

After the second drink, things became blurred. Later, she had a vague memory of Adam standing naked on the guest-room bed, pretending his erection was a Browning Automatic Rifle, meanwhile reciting an old poem, written by a West Pointer in the thirties. It described soldiers fighting and dying meaningless deaths for Caesar, Genghis Khan, Napoleon. But the born warrior remains undaunted.

> *"I see these things, still am I slave*
> *When banners flaunt and bugles blow*
> *Content to fill a soldier's grave*
> *For reasons I shall never know."*

She remembered reeling toward him, also naked, deciding that she was going to do something heretofore unthinkable to express her affection for the Army's favorite weapons system. Whether she did, what else they did in their drunken despair, Amy refused to remember, easy enough because it was all lost in alcoholic darkness, half memory. All she really remembered was waking up the next morning and staring into Georgianna's eyes. The child was standing beside the bed in her pajamas. "Mommy," she said, "I'm hungry."

Amy sat up, violently frightened. Was Adam in the bed? No, he was gone. At least the bed was empty. "Where are your pajamas, Mommy?" Georgianna asked.

"I forgot them."

She snatched up her clothes from the floor and fled down the hall to the master bedroom, where she dressed with the frantic haste of a schoolgirl. It was 9 A.M. Her head was splitting down the middle. The maid would be here any moment. Was Adam lying unconscious somewhere in the house? A frantic search. Nothing. Amy gulped coffee and sat down at the kitchen table, numb. The maid arrived bearing *The Washington Post*. There, splashed across the front page, was the story of a meeting of the Joint Chiefs of Staff, convened by Engine Charlie Wilson, the Secretary of Defense, at which the Secretary denounced their public quarreling. At the White House, President Eisenhower was saying the same thing. The Secretary said the President was "a little unhappy." It took only a minor talent for reading between the lines to perceive that Ike was furious.

Never again, Amy thought. She would never let Adam Thayer in this house again. The son of a bitch was insane. How could she let him seduce her that way? Not merely physically, but spiritually. Seduce her toward his mad reckless uncaring. The crucial thing about Amy Kemble Rosser was, she did *care*. About herself, about her children. About her husband. She could not wait to tell Adam that.

She never got a chance. Instead, the same florist's delivery boy arrived with a dozen yellow roses, and a note: *What a way to say goodbye.*

Two weeks drifted past, ending the unmerry month of May. George's letters became more ardent. He would be home by the Fourth of July. Like a creature conjured by a god and now dismissed, Priscilla sank slowly back into Amy's day-to-day stream of mothering, shopping, writing to George. Occasionally, alone in the morning, she would find herself waiting tensely for the telephone to ring. She tried to understand what she had liked about it, besides the excitement. Ultimately she decided it was the camaraderie, the way Adam had treated her like a partner, like a man. They would, she thought mournfully, have made a marvelous team. But it could never be. Realistic, you are realistic, Amy told herself fiercely. You can't change what's happened, you can't even do much about what's going to happen.

Then came a delayed explosion, *The New York Times* published the story of the plan to reduce the Army to 100,000 men. The reporter referred confidently to documents leaked by an officer on the Army staff, including memorandums from the Secretary of Defense. That very morning, the telephone rang. Amy answered it breathlessly, determined to say no to another visit. But it was not Adam. "Darling," Florence Eberle said, "I haven't seen you for two months. Let's have lunch."

At noon they were sitting down in the dining room of the Fort Halleck Officers' Club, its wide windows looking out on miles of rolling Virginia hunt country. "Did you read the papers this morning?"

"Yes," Amy said.

"Willard called me. He said he's never seen or heard of such a flap. Engine Charlie's raving about demoting generals, court-martialing the Joint Chiefs. He wants to know who leaked those memorandums from his files. Naturally they suspect someone who's had a connection to this Coordinating Group."

Amy nodded noncommittally. The Group had been mentioned in *The New York Times* series.

"Willard's been in charge of cleaning them out," Florence continued. "He kept one of them to handle the paper work, a Captain Thayer, one of those thinky types they produce in the social sciences department at West Point. Do you know him?"

"Oh yes," Amy said, and explained in jolly tones her friendship with Honor and Adam.

Florence ordered another martini and insisted on Amy joining her. "Now comes this flap. Suddenly Air Force Intelligence produces a report on Captain Thayer. He seems to have been more involved in the Coordinating Group's planning than you'd expect, for a captain. I always said those social science doubledomes were a bunch of Bolsheviks. No respect for rank, tradition, chain of command . . .''

Florence sipped her martini. Suddenly Amy did not like the way Mrs. Colonel Eberle was looking at her. ''This intelligence report has some rather strange data in it, Willard says. About you, of all people. About visits that Captain Thayer paid to you at all hours of the day and night.''

''He—he is an old friend,'' Amy said.

''Old Army friends—of the opposite sex—don't call on wives whose husbands are overseas at eleven and twelve o'clock at night. Once at three in the morning.''

''It had nothing to do with—what you think,'' Amy said.

''I hope not. A bad reputation—of that sort—is the worst thing that can happen to an Army wife—''

''We were—trying to help the Army.''

''God knows it needs all the help it can get. How?''

''My father has a friend—an old school chum—he's one of the top civilians in the Pentagon. He offered to leak certain things like the plan to cut the Army back to a hundred thousand men. My father passed them to me. Adam came—to pick them up for the Coordinating Group.''

''How fascinating. I'm afraid, now, this friend of your father's has become a liability. The President is extremely angry about this latest leak. I told you what Engine Charlie is saying. Who is he?''

What would Adam say? Amy thought. *Stuff it, Florence. We don't rat on our friends.* But Florence knew things about the Army Adam would never learn. She proceeded to tell Amy a few of them.

''We didn't ask your father's friend to stick his neck out. At the moment, the Army—that is, the chief of staff—needs very badly to make a gesture of peace to the White House and the Secretary. Otherwise, God knows what they'll do.''

Translation: What they'll do to the boys wearing the stars, the ones sitting on top of the show. The generals are ready to do anything to protect the twenty-five or thirty years they have invested in those stars. Amy could understand it. That is, Amy the realist could understand it. Amy, Adam's comrade-in-arms, detested it. *Stuff it, Florence,* whispered Adam's voice in her head.

Then she heard her own voice, realistic but unnervingly elegiac: *I wouldn't be fair to George.* Comrade Adam had said goodbye. The yellow roses had long since wilted and been consigned to the garbage can. She told Florence the undersecretary's name.

"Ah," Florence said. "Now about Captain Thayer. Do you think he could be responsible for the latest leak? The reporter mentioned documents. Willard was sure he had confiscated every scrap of the Coordinating Group's files. This leak is making him look very foolish."

Amy drained her second martini. The gin seemed to turn her blood to sludge. She found it an effort to speak. But she had to say it. She had to prove to Florence that Adam meant nothing to her, he was a courier, nothing more.

"I wouldn't be surprised," she said. "He's a very strange one. Amazingly reckless, defiant, for an Academy graduate. I remember him saying something to me about smuggling out files."

"Amy," Florence said, with a smile that somehow looked cannibalistic. "You can't imagine how helpful this will be. Excuse me while I make a phone call."

Florence ordered a third martini for both of them and strode off to the lobby. Amy sat at the table, looking around her at the majors and colonels, an occasional general, feeding their faces. Among them were several tables of wives, no doubt chatting about children, parties, assignments. Amy suddenly found herself resenting their ordinary lives. Were they ever called on to make the sacrifice she had just made? No. So it followed, as the night the day, that they did not deserve life's larger rewards. There was only one way that she could tolerate the shame and loss she was feeling. By winning the prize at the end of the game, the prize that went to the best—

What? Betrayers, slayers, flayers, emasculators, she didn't know what to call them.

No. Players. That was all she would admit. They were all playing the game. She was just starting but she was learning fast. She was going to be very good at it.

Florence returned, beaming. She raised her brimming glass of gin and ice. "Willard says there'll be an Army Intelligence team at Captain Thayer's house with a search warrant in an hour."

Amy smiled. Not, she hoped, wanly. "I trust I can claim a modest reward."

"Name it. Willard will be in a position to deliver."

"It's time George got an advanced degree. I was thinking of industrial management. He could go to George Washington University, then move over to the Pentagon the next year."

"Consider it done," Florence said. She drained her drink and beckoned a waiter. "Time to eat."

Behind the menu, Florence added one more line. "That Air Force Intelligence report. Willard said he was going to shred it."

It was the best way, the only way, Amy told herself. She would let George think he won the graduate-school assignment on his own, that it was a testimony to his prowess at teaching Turks how to steer tanks.

"I'll have the chef's salad with Russian dressing," Amy said.

IV

A NORTH wind moaned across miles of prairie, driving snow against Joanna Burke's bedroom window. She was back in Kansas; a Kansas no longer blazing in the summer sun; instead, a world of sempiternal snow and sleet. *Fitting*, whispered a voice in her head, *fitting*. She frequently recalled Robert Frost's poem about how the world would end, not with fire, but with ice. These days, ice seemed to be forming everywhere in her life, on her bedroom windows, in her flesh, on her marriage.

They were at Fort Leavenworth, home of the Army's Command and General Staff School, one of the primary "Stations of the Cross," as Adam Thayer called them, on the road to becoming a general. It was a grueling mental ordeal, especially for Major Peter M. Burke, who was far from a born student. He was competing against some six hundred mostly older officers, majors and lieutenant colonels who had risen at the normal pace to these field grades. Only a few men from '50, such as George Rosser, who had finished near the top of the class, were with him.

It was a compliment to Major Burke's exemplary record that he was here at all. Of the 7,000 Regular Army majors currently in the service, only half had qualified for CGSC. The 7,000 other majors with reserve commissions were automatically eliminated. But at the top of the Army there were only 500 generals, and the separation of those who would reach the stars and those who would fall short began here.

Leavenworth was where an officer not only was taught how a division, an army, a corps—a group of armies—worked; he was expected to demonstrate that he could command these huge organisms. Week after week, he toiled over plans and problems as if he were in charge of operations (G-3) for the 20th Infantry Division or supply (G-4) for the Thirtieth Army. In the six-hour-a-day classroom routine he had to war-game the Thirtieth Army across China or set up a base of operations for the 12th Armored Division in Rumania. He spent 231 class hours studying the infantry division, 111 hours on the armored division, 164 hours on airborne operations and other types of unconventional warfare, 270 hours on armies and corps. Supplementing this classroom grind was a minimum of four hours of nightly homework. For Pete Burke, this stretched to six and frequently eight hours. At the end of the term loomed nine four-hour examinations, each a knuckle-buster.

While Major Burke tried to cope with this trial by intellectual fire, his wife, who should have been running his house, controlling his rambunctious eight-year-old son and entertaining the numerous officers whose opinion of him might influence his career, was flat on her back in her bed twenty-four hours a day, reading and writing poetry. Worse, she did not show much remorse for her dereliction. She even seemed to be taking a perverse pleasure in it.

Joanna had actually welcomed the pregnancy; by the time it came, she was ready to use it as a weapon in the covert war she was waging with her husband. Okay, hero, she was saying, here's your chance to be really heroic. Following Dr. Ricemayer's advice, the moment she discovered she had conceived she retreated to her bed and announced that sex, social entertaining, even keeping house were banned for the next eight months.

After she returned from Boston to Fort Stanton, Joanna had tried to maintain the role of Army superwife, with the help of tranquilizers. An Army doctor carelessly gave her Thorazine, one of the strongest of these new drugs, and she had drifted through her days in a near stupor. Poetry was impossible; she even stopped reading. A letter from Carleton Haines, looking for more poems, nerved her to throw the pills down the toilet and fight the anxiety in a more direct way. She used Pete's refusal to free her from the fear of another pregnancy to free herself from the role of superwife. She blamed her anxiety on their sexual dilemma. She swore that she was only getting four hours' sleep a night. This made a midday nap essential. Once this was conceded, she blamed her miscarriage at Stanton on the exhausting pace Pete had set for her. She withdrew from the Women's Club and abandoned sit-down dinners. She resigned from the team.

In the summer of 1956, they moved to West Point. On this most sociable of Army posts, Pete had looked forward to entertaining former professors and numerous classmates who were working as instructors in one of the academic departments or, like him, as officers in the tactical department. Pete was disappointed and skeptical about Joanna's excuses. But he too put on a mask of complaisance. His career, he tried to tell himself, was not as important as his wife's health and God's command to increase and multiply. But he soon noticed that Joanna did not use her withdrawal from the superwife sweepstakes to rest and relax. On the contrary, he frequently found her at the typewriter when he came home for lunch and she was at it again when he came home for supper. Around her on the floor would be ten different drafts of a poem.

Carleton Haines was publishing her in almost every issue of *Antithesis*. He sent samples of her work to friends on other little magazines, and they shared his enthusiasm for her cool tough imagery. But there was very little enthusiasm for her poetry at home. Instead there was a growing swarm of comments about the length of their "owed" list. Major Burke was not assuaged when she wiped the list clean with a hectic open-house Christmas-season buffet. That was not the way an Army career officer, who had been medaled and marked as a comer, should entertain.

There were nights when Joanna awoke tormented by guilt, racked by new, more subtle anxiety. She found it hard to accept this devious self, who warred by subterfuge, this saboteur of the love she had so confidently proclaimed as her ideal. Enthusiasm slowly drained from their sex life even during the months they were not practicing rhythm. She tried to get Pete to read her poetry, to understand and perhaps love the secret self that was emerging there, a woman who looked at life with wide cold eyes and transmuted what she saw into bold images. She wanted him at least to be proud of that Joanna. He curtly refused even to try. He had begun to perceive the game she was playing, the way she had blind-sided him. They drifted through dinners of sultry silences, breakfasts when he talked exclusively to Tom. She heard the edge of sarcasm in his voice when he asked her if she thought she could handle an extra guest for dinner—one of the class of '57 cadets whom he thought was especially promising. Little by little, Joanna sensed her resistance crumbling. She began blocking on poem after poem. She would have inevitably surrendered if she had not received an unexpected reinforcement: Adam.

He had arrived at the Academy as a refugee from the Pentagon wars, trailing clouds of massive disillusion. The Army, he proclaimed, was finished. It was only a matter of time before the Air Force and the Navy picked all the flesh off the corpse of the old dinosaur, who had chosen to commit suicide rather than go down fighting. He hurled maledictions on the heads of everyone from the chief of staff to the President.

For Pete it was just one more example of Adam's tendency to go to extremes about everything. But Joanna saw the spiritual dimension of Adam's disillusion. He had experienced an enormous disappointment in the meaning, the purpose of the Army and she had to know why. During a picnic on the shore of Lake Poplopen, near the cadet summer training camp, he told her the story of the Coordinating Group and their massacre. She had been appalled. She wanted to know what had happened to each of the colonels and she was given the details of trivial assignments, supervising the ROTC in Florida, baby-sitting Nike missiles in the Chicago suburbs. Most of these bitter, bewildered men were resigning from the Army. The Group's leader had already handed in his papers, after being investigated three times in a single year.

What made the disaster particularly upsetting to Adam was the Coordinating Group's enthusiasm for his Ph.D. thesis on limited war. As he explained it to Joanna, the thesis was not the crude criticism of Korea as the wrong limited war in the wrong place that Annette Haines had led her to believe at Honor's dinner party that evening in Cambridge. The heart of Adam's thesis was a phrase he had coined—"coercive war." This was a contest in which victory went to the side that lasted longest—that "coerced" the other side into quitting by inflicting unacceptable casualties. Americans, with their emphasis on the value of each individual, were simply not prepared to fight such a war against an Asian enemy for whom life was cheap. If the Coordinating Group had won its battle, Adam's insight would have become part of the Army's doctrine. The National War College, the Command and General Staff School, would have begun devising counterstrategies, to avoid or avert coercive wars. Now the idea was likely to become one more of the thousands of other suggestions for changing the Army's rigid ways that moldered in Pentagon files.

"Are you going to let all this destroy your faith, Adam?" Joanna had asked.

"I like that way of putting it," Adam said, looking past her at Pete and Honor and the three children, who were rowing toward them in a borrowed boat. "For the first time I see the value of associating with true believers."

Adam accepted her challenge. He stopped denouncing the Army. Events—or the non-occurrence of the event he was predicting—helped. The Army was not devoured, although it still had no realistic, overall mission in the American defense posture. Muddling through became the policy of the second Eisenhower administration.

While Adam "vegetated"—his term—in the West Point social sciences department, teaching a course on revolutions, he made Joanna, her poetry and her childbearing problems, his hobby. He praised the poetry extravagantly, to Pete's obvious discomfiture.

Simultaneously, he mocked the West Point Women's Club and the whole idea of Women's Clubs around the Army world. He called them a last vestige of involuntary servitude, and insisted that half the chores that Women's Club volunteers performed, such as manning day-care centers, should be paid for by the Army. He also scorned the Army's passion for social entertaining, which reached a climax of sorts at the end of the fifties. The Army, Adam said, had a peculiar genius for turning what should be a pleasure into a duty, a necessity. To Honor's dismay, Adam forbade her to entertain anyone, anytime, no matter how many invitations they owed.

While he was disrupting one aspect of the Burkes' marriage, Adam sought to restore sanity to their sex life. The new progesterone pill, he informed Joanna, was the answer to her Roman prayers. He had friends at Harvard dig out articles by Catholic theologians calling it a morally permissible form of birth control. The same friends put Joanna in touch with John Rock, the Massachusetts Catholic doctor who was one of the first physicians to test the pill. Rock assured her it was safe, and moral. Pete conferred with his uncle, Monsignor Clancy, and with the West Point chaplain, both of whom disagreed. It was an ironic commentary on Pete's commitment to Catholicism that he refused to seize this opportunity to remove Joanna's prime excuse for refusing to be an Army superwife. Perhaps by that time he knew that she was prepared to resist his summons to duty, teamwork, under any circumstances. Perhaps it had become a point of pride with him, a resentful determination to win at least one battle in his war with his deviously rebellious wife—even if it was a Pyrrhic victory.

The argument boiled over when Pete's spiritual commander-in-chief, Pope Pius XII, condemned the pill as direct sterilization and forbade Catholics to use it. As far as Pete was concerned, this was decisive. But Adam said the Pope was like a staff officer who had never been in combat. He gave unrealistic orders. Adam reiterated this opinion when he and Honor dropped in for a farewell drink the night the Burkes left West Point for Fort Leavenworth.

"I begin to think your friend Pius may have destroyed the Catholic Church with that order," Adam said. "It's the first time in history that the Church has ever taken a position that women instinctively oppose. For two thousand years the Church has been pro-woman. Fighting for marital stability, against sexual excess."

"I admit, on the surface, the Pope's decision is hard to understand," Pete said. "I'm worried about Joanna. But we've got faith." He glanced uneasily at Joanna, as if he were afraid she might contradict him. "Faith gets you through a lot of things in life that you don't understand."

"As someone said, faith is great but it's doubt that gets you an education," Adam said.

"I've told you a hundred times, that's the wrong attitude," Pete said. "You don't understand every order you get in a battle. Only wise guys like you think they should hold up a whole advance because their casualties might get too high—and maybe include them."

Adam flushed. Once more Joanna sensed Pete's moral power over him. "I don't think the comparison is apt," Adam said.

"I don't think a lot of things you say are apt either," Pete said. "But you're a friend, so I put up with you. I don't tell you how to run your life."

Pete was warning Adam, not very obliquely, that he did not appreciate his interference in the Burkes' marriage. Joanna hastily changed the subject to Leavenworth, the Command and General Staff School.

"Amy and George Rosser will be there," she said. "I just had a letter from her. George's been promoted to major."

"You've got my sympathy," Honor said. "You'll get dragged to a dinner you'll never be able to match. Some damn Austrian wine and a saddle of beef with spices direct from Bavaria."

"Watch out for Amy," Adam said. "She'd determined to make George a general."

"Since when is that news?" Joanna said.

"It can lead to the theory that George's chances will be improved by killing off the competition."

A growl of anger in Adam's voice as he said these last words made Joanna wonder if he was talking about a personal experience. But Honor only waved a deprecatory hand and said: "Adam, honestly, you exaggerate everything."

Within a month of their arrival in Leavenworth, Joanna became pregnant and retreated to her bed. Pete stoically accepted her declaration of inertia. "We can handle it," he said. He turned to the Women's Club, to the Army wives' sense of solidarity, for help. The response was heartening, in one sense. The president of the Women's Club organized a revolving committee who cleaned the Burke quarters, did the Burke shopping, cooked the Burke lunches and dinners and took charge of Tom when he came home from school. Major Burke was thus able to solve such problems as maneuvering an army group across China with a minimum of distraction.

For Joanna, Pete's solution was far from satisfying. She had to face up to the malice that was part of her original decision to take to her bed. She also had to take her punishment for it in the daily doses of gratitude she had to display to the volunteer wives, and in listening to them describe the perquisites and pleasures of Fort Leavenworth, which she was missing. In the fall, almost everyone had taken riding lessons. A number of wives were playing golf and tennis. The Officers' Club had the best food in the Army. Amy Rosser was one of the queens of the post, entertaining in marvelous style, each dinner featuring some recipe she had acquired in Germany or Turkey. Other wives were ransacking cookbooks to match her.

Most of Joanna's volunteer housekeepers were good-natured and sympathetic. But Amy was another matter. Before her first visit was over, she knew all about Joanna's miscarriages and obviously regarded her as somewhat simpleminded. Amy also wanted to know when and if Pete was going to graduate school. She was shocked when Joanna said he had no interest in it. George had gotten his Master's in industrial management at George Washington University, and Amy was urging him to try for a Ph.D.

On her next visit, Amy wanted to know if Joanna thought Tom was hyperactive. Had she talked to the post doctors about putting him on drugs? Joanna could only gasp. Tom was a supercharged, totally physical boy, crazy about all sports; incontestably his father's son. Each morning he ran five miles beside Pete and did dozens of push-ups, chin-ups, jumping jacks. After school he zoomed around the post with a gang his own age, occasionally getting into mild trouble with an officious MP for running across some colonel's or general's sacrosanct lawn. But in the evening, after watching one or two shows on television, each of which he was required to negotiate with his mother, he devoured children's history books. Joanna was tempted to tell Amy that her son was not hyperactive, but she would worry about Amy's daughter Georgianna if she were her mother. The child was just too icky pretty, posing and simpering like a teen-ager, always just so in what looked like a party dress.

On Amy's next visit, she concentrated on finding out all about Joanna's poetry. She said she had heard a lot about it from Adam Thayer, when their tours overlapped in Washington, D.C. Joanna got out her published poems, which now numbered some two dozen. Carleton Haines's little magazine, *Antithesis*, was still her best market. But she had published other poems in the *Kenyon Review*, *Transaction*, *Far Point*—all magazines that had prestige in the world of poetry. Amy read the poems without comment and asked Joanna how much she was paid for each one.

"Nothing, usually," Joanna said.

Joanna was sure this admission would further confirm her simpleminded status. Instead, in an unexpected burst of enthusiasm, Amy asked if she could publish some of the poems in a Women's Club newspaper that the wives were starting. Flattered, Joanna told her to take her pick.

A week later, Pete came home for supper, stomping in a heavy-footed way that Joanna had learned to associate with irritation. She heard him slamming doors and muttering under his breath. She heard Tom, watching cartoons on TV, ask: "What's the matter, Dad?" Then Pete was in the bedroom, a piece of paper clutched in his hand.

"Joanna," he said. "I don't want to—I mean, I know you're supposed to have peace and quiet. But—"

"What's the matter?"

"These poems. In this excuse for a newspaper. Especially that one." He thrust the paper at her, jabbing it with his thick index finger.

CLAM
Pry me open
With the tip of your bayonet

> *Soldier*
> *Probe my pink contrary flesh*
> *With your tongue*
> *Taste my silence.*

"What the hell are you trying to do? Make me look like a goddamn pervert? A laughingstock in front of the whole damned post?"

Joanna smiled. "You're not the soldier in the poem. It's a dramatic monologue between a woman and a soldier. Any soldier."

"Bullshit!" Pete roared. "Your name is on it. Joanna Burke. Any sensible person is going to assume—".

Suddenly Joanna felt a need, a wish, to talk honestly with him—something she had not done for a long time. "Maybe it is you. Maybe it is me," she said. "Maybe I'm trying to say something to you about loving me in a way, in a place, you haven't reached."

Pete was aghast. "Joanna, I never thought—I mean—I've got too much respect for you—

"Jesus," he roared, regaining his anger. "How can you talk about something like that in public? Have you gone out of your goddamn mind? You're going to see the psychiatrist tomorrow. I'll carry you to the hospital if necessary."

She realized that he thought the poem referred to sexual technique, cunnilingus. "Pete, it's not sexual. There may be a sexual overtone. But the thrust, the meaning of the poem is spiritual. Taste my silence, the woman says. The part of a woman that a man so often ignores."

He either totally refused or totally failed to understand her. "Joanna, I have had all of the intellectual poetic bullshit from you I can take. I have allowed you—for the sake of your health—for the sake of the baby we've been trying to have—to sit home and write this goddamn stuff instead of doing what everyone else's wife is doing—making a contribution to the Army, to their husbands' careers. But when you start humiliating me in public, that's it. From now on, if you insist on writing poetry, I want to see it before you publish it."

336

"Go to hell!"

It was out in the open now, four years of suppressed anger and resentment. Major Burke loomed over her bed, fists clenched, veins bulging in his massive neck. "Don't talk to me that way, Joanna."

"I'll talk to you any way I please. You *let* me sit home and write this goddam stuff? My poetry? You *let* me? Who the hell do you think you are, Major? Who do you think you're talking to? Some private who's going to wet his pants when you start screaming at him? I'm not your servant. You don't *let* me do anything. I'm a college graduate. An intelligent woman. I've gone on trying to supply you with children at the risk of my life. But you're not satisfied with that. You want the rest of it too, the sit-down dinners, the whirlwind commiteewoman, out there kissing Mrs. General's fanny, just in case you're not smart enough to get to be a general on your own."

He took it. He didn't flinch. He just took it head down, glowering. Was it stupidity? she wondered. Or some other kind of impenetrability? She let her rage run completely, cruelly wild. "Now you're going to tell me how to think and feel. To write only poetry you approve. Go to hell! When and if I have this baby I'm going on the pill and I don't care what you or Uncle Monsignor or the Pope say about it. Once we settle that, maybe we can do something about your oafish indifference to all the things I appreciate. Most of the time it's a chore to make conversation with you about anything that doesn't have some connection to the Army, your marvelous career."

Was that incomprehension she saw on his face? Or pain? He did not give her a chance to find out. He turned his back on her and walked slowly out of the room. She was left alone with the wreckage of her marriage. Five minutes passed. Joanna felt the child stir in her womb. She lay there, dazed, not quite sure whether she was surviving the explosion.

Tom appeared in the doorway, looking frightened. "Mommy," he said. "What's the matter?"

"Nothing," she said.

"Daddy's in the kitchen. He told me to go away. Why did you yell at him?"

She didn't answer him. What could she say?

337

"Did he punch you? Teddy Lamm says his father punched his mother once. Last year. She took out his gun and said she'd shoot him if he ever touched her again."

"No, he didn't punch me."

"Are you going to get a divorce? Teddy says his mother's always talking about it."

Joanna was too astonished to say anything at first. "No, we're not going to get a divorce."

"That's good. Because if you did, we'd have to leave the Army. That's what Teddy says, anyway. I'd hate that. I really like the Army."

Joanna felt a different antagonism, half fear, half dislike, stir deep in her mind. But she blocked it. Now was not the time to face it. She had too much to face already. "I'm glad you like the Army," she said. "I like it too."

"Then why were you fighting with Dad? Teddy Lamm's folks fight about whether his dad should stay in the Army or not. His mother says they should get out."

"Married people fight about lots of things. Daddy didn't like one of my poems. He thought it made him look silly."

"Did it?"

"No. Of course not. I wouldn't do such a thing."

"Can I see it?"

"No. You—you wouldn't understand it."

Was that skepticism she saw on that freckled eight-year-old face, his father's face, without the grimness inflicted by Korea, a glimpse of Cadet Burke's innocent pride and optimism? Oh God, she was making a mess of everything, marriage, motherhood, her soul's salvation. She was turning her back on all of them. Or had they just turned their collective backs on her? Symbolized by the silent back of Major Peter MacArthur Burke, USA? Panic, the beating wings of the anxiety condor, throbbed in her throat. But she clung to her anger, remembering Adam's prophecy. *Someday you're going to stand up to him.*

"Come over here," she said.

Tom gingerly approached the bed.

She sat up and kissed him. "It's nothing for you to worry about," she said. "Most married people have fights. But they make up after a while. It's not so different from boys who are friends. You have fights and make up, don't you?"

"It depends on whether you win or lose," he said. "I had a fight with Charlie Packer last week. I flattened him. We haven't made up yet."

"Go watch TV until Daddy calls you for dinner."

It depends on whether you win or lose. A half hour later, Tom reappeared, carrying her dinner tray. Usually, Pete brought it. She ate it, alone. She spent the night reading *The Ugly American*, an indictment of American bureaucrats in Southeast Asia. It was an upsetting book, a thinly fictionalized account of the way American officials failed to adapt themselves to the people they were supposed to be helping. When she finished it, she was startled to note it was after midnight. Her door was still open. Light streamed in from the living room. Usually Pete came in around 11:30, asked her if she needed anything and kissed her good night. He had taken to sleeping on the living-room couch, because he regularly studied past midnight and did not want to wake her up when he went to bed.

Joanna got up, went to the bathroom, closed the bedroom door and dozed off. She awoke in the dark with the phone clanging in her ear. The luminous clock on the night table told her it was 2:05. The phone rang three times. She finally picked it up. Simultaneously Pete picked it up in the living room.

"Pop? Is it you?" Pete said.

"Hope I didn't wake ya, Pete."

"No sweat, Pop. I won't be in bed for another two hours."

"Jesus. Workin' ya hard."

"They're separating the men from the boys out here, Pop."

"Pete, I gotta call ya, when the ol' lady, y'know—"

"I know, Pop."

Arthur Burke was drunk. He had developed a bad habit of calling Pete late at night. His life had become a nightmare to him. His older son, Arthur, a detective, had been killed in a shoot-out while Pete was at Fort Benning, in 1954. A shift in his city's political power structure had forced Arthur, Sr., into retirement. He was a lonely disappointed man, mourning his dead son, desperately reaching out to the living one. He apparently did little but drink and feel sorry for himself.

"Pete, I can't handle it. I keep thinkin' Artie, y'know? M'fault, Pete. No fuckin' good. Never was. But wan' ya to have things, y'know? A decent glove. Mem' the catcher's mitt I bought ya? How Artie got sore cause his glove—"

He started to weep. "Jesus, Pete. I still got the old gun. Gonna use it. It's best way. Ol' police special. Bes' way, Pete, don' think? Y'soldier. Y'know what it means. Bes' thing to do when y'licked, right?"

"No. You can't do it, Pop. For Mom's sake. For little Tom's sake. You haven't seen much of him but he thinks a lot of you, Pop. I've told him about you. The things you did when you were a patrolman. Shootin' it out with those three boogies in front of O'Donnell's grocery."

"Really? Y'tell'm that one?"

"Sure. And I don't wanna tell him that you took the easy way out, Pop."

"But when y'finished, Pete. When's no use. When Artie—"

"He wasn't your fault, Pop. It's just something that happened. It hurts like hell but it's the way things happen. Now go to bed, Pop. I've got a lot more work to do tonight."

"Okay. Thanks, Pete. Give'm hell now. Thanks—"

The line went dead. Joanna carefully hung up the extension. She lay there in the darkness. She heard Pete go down the hall to the bathroom, urinate, then run water in the sink. A snort. He was bathing his face to stay awake. His footsteps thudded back to the dining-room table, where books and charts and maps were a foot thick. For a full hour Joanna lay awake and the white line of work, of weariness, still gleamed beneath her door. He was still there, hunched over the books, struggling to absorb doctrine and procedure, the Army way to do things, when and if he became a major general or lieutenant general, trying to produce a plan using "agreed solutions" for an operation like the invasion of Rumania. Had she lost interest in what he was studying because the problems seemed so distant from reality, both practically and chronologically? It would be at least fifteen years before Pete even became eligible for promotion to general. And there did not seem to be much likelihood of American armies invading Rumania or maneuvering across China in the near future. Slowly, as the line of light beneath her door persisted, Joanna realized she had also lost interest in how many hours he was working each day and night. Her unspoken anger had been like a pair of blinders that enabled her to see only what she chose to see.

Finally, at 4:30 A.M., the light beneath the door went out. Once more she heard the masculine bathroom sounds, then the thudding footsteps, the crunch of the heavy body on their sagging couch. She dozed off and awoke to another familiar sound: "Four five six seven eight nine—" Tom and his father were doing push-ups in the living room. They had already completed their daily five-mile jog. Ten minutes later, Pete came to the bedroom door. His face was an impassive mask. But she saw the hollows of weariness beneath his eyes.

"Do you need anything?" he asked.

"No," she said.

Again, before she could say another word, the broad back confronted her. So that was the name of the game. She would show him two could play it. She would be just as hard, just as unforgiving.

Her volunteer for the day was Jane Skelton, wife of a lieutenant colonel from the class of '48. She was a placid, hefty blonde, an extremely good-natured person, but a tremendous gossip. She knew everything that was happening on the post, and seemed to feel it her duty to pass it along to Joanna. Gossip was obviously Jane's favorite entertainment and she assumed Joanna was equally interested. Positioning herself in the bedroom doorway, a dustcloth in her hand, a blue apron draped around her ample figure, Jane began her morning's monologue.

"Well, we just had our first breakdown," she said. "And it's only January."

"Breakdown?" Joanna said.

"Sure," Jane said. "They average three or four a class. Haven't had a suicide for a couple of years. In the twenties they had so many they had to close the school for a while."

"Where did you hear that?" Joanna asked.

"Sue Lynch. Her father taught here before World War II."

"Who—who broke down?"

"Lamm. He got drunk last night and beat hell out of Beatrice."

"That's terrible."

"Sue says most of them don't crack that way. They just stop coming to class, and get quietly transferred. I'm going to start slowing Brad down. How many hours does Pete study each night?"

"A lot," Joanna said.

"Brad too. I don't know anybody that doesn't. Except George Rosser. Amy claims he goes to bed before midnight without fail. But I don't believe a word that bitch says."

Joanna chose not to denigrate Amy, although she was remembering what Adam had said about her killing off the competition. Had Amy published her poems hoping they would embarrass Pete?

"All is not as serene there as it seems to be, from what I hear," Jane said.

"Oh?"

"Pat Folley was with them in Turkey. JUSMMAT. George spent two years over there. But Amy left after eighteen months. According to what Pat tells me, George had something going with a girl named Helen Palladino. That was why Amy went home. She was driven from the field, one might say."

"Really," Joanna said.

"Those military assistance assignments are murder on marriages," Jane said.

"So I hear," Joanna said.

She could not imagine Amy letting another woman drive her from any field, whether the contest was dinner parties or sex.

"I understand Mrs. Perfect was over at the hospital the other day with a terrific case of migraine."

"Oh."

"You know what that's a sign of."

"No."

"Sexual dissatisfaction. I read an article on it in the *Ladies' Home Journal*."

Jane disgorged more Army gossip. Another reduction in force was on its way, a fifty-thousand-man cutback. A lot of people were being sent to Laos, although no one was talking about it very much. There was a nasty little war heating up in the jungles over there and in South Vietnam. Jane's husband, Brad, was a paratrooper and they seemed to be the prime candidates for Laos. You had to parachute into the damn country. Jane was hoping they'd skip Brad. "I was a wreck all the time he was in Korea. That's where I gained all this weight. When I worry, I eat."

After serving Joanna an egg-salad sandwich for lunch, Jane departed, leaving the patient to brood away the afternoon. When Pete came home, he did not bother to say hello. Once more, Tom brought her dinner. Once more, Joanna slept poorly and awoke to find the slit of light beneath her door at 2 A.M. Once more it remained there, like an accusatory leer, until 4 A.M. For a week, the pattern repeated itself; Saturday and Sunday brought no significant change. Pete spent most of both days at the library. They spoke, when they spoke at all, in brief, toneless sentences.

"You want anything?"

"No."

"Who's coming today?"

"Amy Rosser."

"We're out of sugar."

"I'll put it on the list."

At the end of the week there was another 2 A.M. telephone call from Pete's father. This time Joanna did not listen on the extension. But she guessed from the haunted grimness on Pete's face the next morning that the same anguish, the same sick threat had been discussed.

"You want anything?"

"No."

It was becoming the sign and countersign. Their code for continued war. Another week, a third week, a fourth passed. Blizzards piled on blizzards, in true Midwest style. The ice seemed to coat the house. Then came another phone call. Joanna yearned to pick up the receiver. There was a cry of pain in the living room. "Ah, Jesus!" She stumbled to the door and blinked across the living room to the dining area, where her husband sat in his sea of books. "Ah, Mom. I prayed so hard for him. I know you did too. He wasn't a bad man,

Mom, he just didn't think about it until it was too late. It was the system, the lousy rotten system. I'll get a plane tomorrow, Mom. Now try to calm down. Call the Monsignor.''

"What happened?" she asked.

"The old man," Pete said, rubbing his fist into his streaming eyes. "He finally did it. He drove the car into the Passaic River. Made it look like an accident."

"Maybe—it was. He was drinking so much."

"Go to bed. What the hell do you care?"

"I do—"

"Okay, you do. Go to bed."

"Pete—I'm so worried about you—"

"Go to bed."

She crept back into her dim room, her cave. The next day, Saturday, Pete flew home for the funeral. Joanna lay in bed, his anguished words, *the system, the lousy rotten system,* burning in her mind. She remembered going to his brother's funeral, what Pete had told her then about the greasy politics of his home town, where corruption was taken for granted. It was why he had chosen an Army career, he said. He wanted a job where a man did not have to sell out to get ahead. She had been touched by his moral determination, then. Now she trembled at the growing fear that it might destroy him, with her help.

Pete returned from the funeral late on Monday, barely spoke to Joanna, and stayed up all night, finally falling asleep at the table, his head on his arms. In the morning, Tom came into Joanna's bedroom and asked if he should wake up his father. A few nights later, after staring at the usual crack of light beneath her door for two hours, Joanna got up and went into the living room. Pete was not asleep. He was just sitting there, staring dully ahead of him. He looked dazed, ravaged, like some of the wounded from Korea that she had seen in the hospital at Yokoshima.

"Pete," she said, "please go to bed."

"I can't do it," he said. "I'm just not good enough."

"I don't believe that," she said. "If you graduated from West Point—"

He did not seem to hear her. He seemed to be talking to himself.

"Why the hell did you marry me, if you knew I was such a dumb cluck?"

"You're not a dumb cluck. And I loved you. I still love you."

Was that true? Did she have to surrender her anger to say it? Become submissive, humble Joanna again?

"I'm going to wrap this up. Ask for a reassignment. You can have a divorce if you want it. I'll stick it out for twenty. Give you half my salary—more if I can afford it—"

She saw, she heard, catastrophic defeat on his face, in his voice. He had been pushed beyond his strength. Command and General Staff School alone was enough to do this to a man who already had inferiority feelings about his ability as a student. To ask him to bear the burden his wife, his father, had inflicted on him was too much. He could not say, perhaps did not even know, what was happening. He was not an introspective man.

She reached out for him, half blinded by tears. She had to touch some part of him even if she could not offer him her swollen body. She seized his hands. They were shockingly cold and inert. "Pete," she said. "I'm sorry. I wasn't really angry at you. It was at the Church, for what we've been put through. And at the Army, for teaching you that you—and your wife—ought to do everything better than the book. It isn't your fault—or mine. Korea mixed everything up for us. By the time we started living on a real Army base you were a major but I wasn't ready to be a major's wife."

"So what?" he said.

"I'm asking you to forgive me—just as I'm ready to forgive you. Maybe forget is a better word. I want to forget the last few years and love you the way we did for those five-day leaves in Japan. When you were with KMAG. Do you remember them the way I do?"

"Yeah," he said, his head down, refusing to look at her; perhaps from weariness, perhaps wariness.

"We can have more days like those—if you let me act—live— according to my conscience."

"What about my conscience?"

"Can't you live with—love someone even if you think he or she is doing the wrong thing? Look at your father. You loved him, didn't you?"

"I didn't have any control over him," he said. "I'm responsible for you. I'm the head of this family. But you can't command—lead—someone without respect. I never got it from you. Because you think I'm stupid."

"You're not stupid. I've lived with you for almost nine years. I know you're not stupid. We have different minds, different interests—"

She felt like a surgeon trying to staunch wounds in the middle of a battle—wounds that the surgeon had inflicted.

"You said you can barely talk to me."

"Pete, that was anger. War. Can you understand that? You hit me, hurt me about the poetry. I hit you back, hurt you. Wives and husbands are very good at that, hitting and hurting."

"None of the guys've said a word to me about the poetry. I guess they think it's women's stuff. None of their business."

She swallowed that humiliation without comment. Penance, she thought.

"But I can't hack this, Jo. With or without you." He shoved at the books and papers on the table, as if he wished he could push them over the edge of the world. "I'm just not a student. I wouldn't have made it through the Academy without Supe to pound stuff into my head."

"I don't believe that. On the contrary. I think that anyone unfortunate enough to room with Adam Thayer would inevitably end up thinking he was stupid. Adam treats everyone that way."

A lie, or at least an exaggeration. But she was desperate.

"You think so?" asked the weary, beaten pupil confronting her.

"I know it. He managed to give me an inferiority complex, just talking to him on the dance floor."

Liar, liar, chanted a voice in her head. Was it her secret poet's voice? "Have you flunked anything?"

"No. But I'm way down in the lower third of the class. Where I was at the Academy. I wanted to show them I could do a lot better, out here. At the Academy, football took so many hours each week."

"There's nothing wrong with the lower third of the class. Especially out here. Martha Kinsolving told me in her last letter that when her father was here he got 95.6 in map reading and finished forty-seventh in the course. With that kind of competition, the

Army's got to be more interested in seeing whether you can get through here. Stand the pressure."

"Maybe," he said.

"I think you need a coach," she said. "Take it from an old student, after a certain point it's better to go to bed. Come to bed with me now. And promise me you'll sleep tomorrow until you wake up. I'll keep the house quiet. I'll rest on the couch."

"Okay," he said.

He did not even bother to put on his pajamas. He let her lead him into the bedroom and strip off his shirt and pants. He fell into the bed in his underwear. She put her arms around him. He smelled sweaty, musty, as if he had just crawled out of a foxhole. Maleness. It had been so long since she had breathed it, she found herself trembling. What was it? Desire, the wish for him to hold her, take her? She put her arms around him and kissed him. "I'll always love you," she said. "Remember that. No matter what I say or do, I'll always love you."

Another lie? whispered that subterranean voice in her head. Another bandage on the wound, applied by the guilty surgeon? No, Joanna vowed. It was the truth. Staring into a darkness that was also an image of the future, she clung to the vow, to the love that she had almost destroyed, as one of her few remaining certitudes.

The next morning she got up at nine-thirty and made her somewhat wobbly way to the living-room couch. From it she could see the dining table, still covered with Pete's books and papers. She decided to straighten them up. Pete looked like he might sleep for a week. Tom was playing at a friend's house. There would be no housekeeping help today, Saturday. Once more she risked getting to her feet and began stacking the books on some shelves Pete had mounted on the dining-area wall. After resting a moment, she tackled the papers. As she reached out to pull a sheaf of them into a pile, her fingers touched something large and unyielding beneath them. She knew what it was. Slowly, she lifted the disordered mass and stared down at the gun. It lay on its side, the long flat chamber flush to the table, the round blue-black barrel pointing at her. *Oh, my God*, she thought. *Oh, my God.*

She sat down slowly in a dining-room chair. Was it possible?

Could he? She did not know. She did not want to know. After about five minutes, she picked up the gun and put it on the shelf in the hall closet. She felt a need to wash her hands. Lady Macbeth? She murdered her husband's rival, not her husband. Stop, she ordered herself. She had not murdered anyone. It was the Army's fault, with its superhuman demands on its best men. The goddamn Army, as Adam so frequently called it. She remembered Honor's complaints about the brutal hours at the Pentagon. The Army took advantage of loyalty, dedication, to push men beyond their endurance, in pursuit of an unattainable perfection.

But the gun had been there. It had been lying beneath the papers, inches from his hand last night. Would he have used it if she had not come out to talk to him? Would he have yielded to his dead father's voice, pulling him down into the darkness with his brother, with Lover MacKenzie and the hundreds of others he had seen die in Korea? For the first time since Korea she feared for him. It was a new, unnerving fear, a mixture of sympathy and responsibility, a recognition of her part in his life, the power of her words to wound him in ways almost as deadly as enemy bullets.

Once she went to the closet and reached up on the shelf to touch the gun. It was real. It had been there.

Tom came home at 5 P.M. full of enthusiasm for the movie he had seen at the post theater, *The Bridge on the River Kwai*. He described the explosions that destroyed the bridge as "terrific." He wanted to know if the Japanese had treated American prisoners as rottenly as they had treated the British. She said yes.

"Boy, I'd like to plug a few of them when I grow up," Tom said. He looked baffled when she told him that the Japanese were now our friends and allies. She asked him if he remembered Mrs. Togo. He shook his head. She was only a dim memory. "She sends you a birthday card every year. She loved you," Joanna said. She told him how Mrs. Togo had wept and kissed him when they said goodbye to her. He looked vaguely disgusted.

"Where's Dad?"

"Still sleeping. You'll have to be very quiet tonight."

"Charlie Skelton said I could stay over at his house. He's got a terrific collection of toy soldiers."

348

"What did his mother say?"

"She said it was fine with her."

Joanna called Jane Skelton just to make sure. She was agreeable. "What's one more?" she said. Nothing fazed Jane. She and Brad had four children. After a quick supper from the pot of stew brought over by Jane the day before, Tom departed for the Skeltons', who lived only a few doors away. Joanna put the dishes in the sink and returned to the couch. She was barely settled when she heard the thump of bare feet in the short hall.

Pete swayed in the doorway. "Jo," he said. "The gun. I just remembered it."

He stared at the clean table.

"I put it away," she said. "On the closet shelf. I hope it isn't loaded."

He said nothing. He went into the closet and she heard the click of metal. He came out and sat down on the couch. "It was loaded," he said.

"Pete," she said, hearing her own voice as a half groan, half cry.

"I wasn't going to use it. I know some guys have out here. I couldn't do that to you, to Tom. But I had to face it. I had to walk right up to it and face it."

He did not look at her. He seemed to be speaking to someone or something directly in front of him. His voice sounded sullen, or perhaps just drugged with sleep.

"You'll never do it again. Promise me," Joanna said.

"I hope not," he said.

He left her with that non-assurance and stumbled back to bed. She spent the night dozing on the couch. Late the next afternoon, Pete emerged from the bedroom again. He looked resurrected. Some of his normal color had returned to his face. The gray hollows under his eyes had vanished. Without a word, he picked Joanna off the couch and carried her back to the bedroom. "Okay, coach," he said. "That was good advice. Now what?"

"Go out and run five miles," she said. "Come home and watch television. Don't start studying until tomorrow night."

The scholastic athlete obeyed his coach. He also promised to stop studying at midnight, no matter how much he still thought there was to be done. The gun on the table receded into memory. Joanna never tried to talk to Pete about it again. But more than once it appeared in her dreams. Other guns appeared in her poetry, when she began to write it again. In one poem called "Browning's Automatic Rifle," she chose most of the language from an official Army manual describing its operation, blending it with the language of the typical instructor. Carleton Haines called the poem an ironic tour de force and promised to publish it in an early issue of *Antithesis*. She did not show the poem to Pete. He knew she was writing poetry but made no demand to see it. Had they established a wary truce? Or was it a genuine peace?

Winter drizzled into spring, into Easter, into blooming, bountiful May. The volunteer housekeepers came and went. As exams loomed, the scholastic athlete informed his coach that he was going to study until 1 A.M. The doctors at the base hospital, indifferent to such exigencies, decreed that the baby was ready to deliver. The decision to perform another Caesarian had long since been made. Pete drove her to the hospital and obeyed a final order from the coach—to go home and study. She did not feel deserted. Her doctor, the nurses, could not have been more considerate. The Army seemed determined to improve on its previous obstetrical performance. Joanna drifted into the anesthetic darkness wondering if it would be a boy or a girl. She did not really care. She was thinking more of the future than the present, her future with Pete.

She awoke to organ music playing on someone's radio or television. Pete was standing by the bed with Tom. Spring sunlight streamed into the room. "Girl or boy?" she whispered.

"A girl. You've evened the odds," Pete said.

"I wanted a boy," Tom groused. "You can't punch a girl. She'll cry."

"Have you punched any girls lately?" she said.

"No. But I'd like to punch Georgianna Rosser. She got me into a lot of trouble. She called the MP's and told them I was throwing mudballs."

"At what?"

"At her."

"I socked him with a hundred demerits," Pete said. "No dessert for a week."

"Did he hit her?"

"Right between the eyes," Pete said. "I think it was her mother who called the MP's."

They decided to name the new arrival Cecilia after Joanna's mother. "We'll call her Cissie, for a while," Joanna said. "Cecilia's too much of a mouthful for a little girl."

Tom liked the nickname. "It's the truth," he said. "She'll be a sissy, like most girls."

"You may be in for a surprise," Joanna said. "Did you know I was the best third baseman in the neighborhood when I was your age?"

"You're kidding me," Tom said, truly amazed.

The next day Joanna wrote to Dr. Rock and asked him to send her a supply of the birth control pills and instructions for taking them. They were not yet licensed by the government, so they were not available at the hospital. When Pete visited her after supper, she asked him to mail the letter. He looked at the name and address and knew what was in the envelope. "Are you sure you want to do it, Jo?" he asked.

"Darling, don't look so sad. It's for both of us. We'll both be so much happier. I promise you."

She did not realize what a dangerous thing she was doing, promising a man happiness. She only saw that Pete's acquiescence conceded her changed status, her new power, in their marriage. Pete was admitting his need for her, not merely sexual, but emotional and spiritual, his need for her love. She saw how uneasy this made him. He preferred the other relationship, the one he understood best, the leader and the led. Joanna sensed the fragility of the balance they had struck. She told herself it would work. She would make it work.

Unspoken, as they faced each other there in the sunny hospital room—she in her green-and-white kimono, a souvenir of Japan, he in his khakis—was her role in their Army marriage, member of the husband-wife team. They talked of other things. Joanna tried to calm Pete's moral uneasiness by telling him that next year's Vatican

Council summoned by the new Pope, John XXIII, might alter the Church's stand on the pill. Pete said he could not understand how something could be moral under one Pope and immoral under another one.

Pete talked about the state of the Army and the world, as it looked in that spring of 1960. The southern states of America were in turmoil. The Reverend Martin Luther King and his followers were leading protest marches and sit-ins against discrimination and segregation. Pete hoped his next assignment took them far away from that social and political whirlpool. Nobody wanted to command troops with reporters swarming around them. "One wrong order, even one wrong statement, and your career is kaput," Pete said.

"I had a letter from Honor," Joanna said. "Adam's volunteering for Laos. He's going down to Fort Bragg to train at the Special Warfare School."

Pete shook his head disapprovingly. "Those counterinsurgency guys are like the paratroopers, only worse. Trying to be an army unto themselves. I'll stick with the big Army. I wouldn't be surprised if we all get a lot more involved with Indochina. I just had a letter from General Coulter. He says that whole region is starting to cook. He's been out to Vietnam twice this year."

Arnold Coulter had retired from the Army and was now with the CIA. But Pete still considered him his patron, eminently worth consulting on his career. For Joanna the mention of his name evoked Blanche Coulter, a memory she preferred to forget.

"Honor says they'll probably go out to Hawaii after Bragg. That's where most wives are staying while their husbands are in Laos."

"We might wind up there too," Pete said. "Coulter thinks I ought to try for a slot in the 44th Division—battalion exec or a G-3 staff deal. I can start studying Vietnamese again in my spare time. Not many guys have had my experience—advising the Koreans for eighteen months."

Hawaii. Her lost Hawaiian honeymoon rose to mock Joanna. What would it be like to go there now, no longer the dreamy bride, but the would-be loving wife? "Yes," she said automatically, not really grasping the direction in which Pete's mind was moving. For the moment all her anxieties were personal. She had no inkling that she and her husband were both in the inexorable embrace of history.

The class of 1960 graduated from the Command and General Staff School while she was in the hospital. She heard the band playing for the graduation review, imagined the solemn speech by the guest speaker, the deputy chief of staff, and was privately glad she was missing it. She was sure it was the same sort of government double-talk she had heard at West Point ten years ago.

A nurse brought in the baby and Joanna breast-fed her. She was a little blond beauty, only six pounds but perfectly formed, with the most delicate sheen to her skin Joanna had ever seen. She glowed when the nurse told her Cissie was Leavenworth's prettiest baby of that year.

As Cissie finished dining and gave a burp and a contented sigh, the graduate arrived, a broad smile on his face. Joanna had not seen him looking so happy in a long time. "I can't believe it," he said. "I finished in the top thirty percent."

"Fantastic," Joanna whooped. She grabbed his tie and pulled him down on the bed for a kiss.

"Hey," he said, tightening his tie. "Are you trying to get me out of uniform?"

"Eventually," she said, in a mock sultry voice.

Pete's smile was a little tentative. Did he really want a sexy wife? she wondered.

"Rosser finished number one. Got the George Marshall prize. Made me pretty proud of old '50."

Joanna made a face. "Amy will be insufferable. Give me some good news."

"I've gotten our next assignment."

He took a sheaf of papers from inside his coat and threw it on the bed. REQUEST FOR ORDERS, it began, and with the usual Army jargon, it ordered Major Burke to report for duty at Schofield Barracks, Oahu Island, Hawaii, on July 1, 1960.

"We're going to catch up to that honeymoon," Pete said.

She was touched by those words. But she did not let them weaken her resolve. Nor was she surprised by the Hawaiian assignment.

353

What Pete had said a few days earlier about Arnold Coulter's advice made the announcement something of an anticlimax. She was glad he had forewarned her. She was ready with a suggestion that would never have come from Joanna the dreamy bride.

"Let's make it a real honeymoon," she said. "Let's live off the base—in a beach house."

"What?" Pete said. "Schofield's one of the most beautiful posts in the Army. You'll love it."

Joanna shook her head. "Pete, I want to have my own schedule, my own life. If we live at Schofield, we'll go right back to what drove me crazy at Fort Stanton. No time for myself."

He started to shake his head angrily. She had to stop him before he stated plainly what she was doing—demanding both halves of the loaf, sexual freedom and social freedom.

"You don't need an Army superwife, Pete. You can make it on your own. You've proved that out here."

He was still shaking his head, his eyes averted now. Had she reached him? Had she penetrated the muscular armor and spoken to the uncertain son of an Irish cop who lived within it? "It's the truth, Pete," she said. "You don't need that kind of wife. But you do need a woman who loves you, who cares about you. Every man does. I want to be that woman. Give me a chance to love you, Pete, on my terms, in my own way."

He paced up and down the room, his eyes still averted. Cissie gave another contented gurgle in Joanna's arms. "Jo, you know I love you. I want you to love me. I just can't understand why you won't—work with me," Pete said.

"Darling, I will. I'm willing to do a reasonable amount of entertaining. We can have dinner parties at a beach house. It'll just be different from Schofield's style, more informal, relaxed. I can still do some things for the Women's Club. I just won't be at their beck and call."

Still he paced, refusing to look at her, at the child, proof of their love, in her arms. She tried once more to penetrate the muscular armor. "Are you afraid to be a little different? Do you have to do everything by the book?"

He stopped and stared out the window at the sun-baked parade ground. "Okay," he said. "Okay. Maybe I have been pushing too hard. Maybe I can afford to coast a little." He turned to face her and the baby, his arms folded across his broad chest. Where had she read that this was a defensive gesture? "Maybe it will do us both good to relax for a year."

"Pete, it'll be great, I promise you."

"I hope so."

The smile was forced but the wish was sincere. Wasn't that the most she could expect from a man who put duty ahead of happiness? I'll change that, she thought. I'll change everything about us, she vowed, foolishly believing in her new power and in the magic of Hawaii.

V

No question about it, Amy Rosser told herself as she dressed with her usual care, she loved Fort McConnell. It was in the Georgia countryside about midway between Atlanta and Savannah, which meant marvelous Atlantic Ocean beaches were within an hour's drive. As headquarters for IV Corps, it was a small post, with only 4,000 men, most of them communications specialists. This meant a higher type of enlisted man and fewer discipline problems. The roomy red brick houses around the central parade ground, where the commanding general and the post colonels lived, were over a hundred years old. Radiating off the parade ground were a half dozen other streets with smaller but equally comfortable houses for lieutenant colonels and majors. All the quarters were in excellent condition. The IV Corps commander, Major General Henry Hamburger, knew how to extract an ample housekeeping budget from the Pentagon. The general was also a fanatic about neatness, order. Every blade of grass on every lawn at Fort McConnell was cut, every hedge trimmed to precisely the same height. Amy liked that too.

In her letters to Joanna Burke and other friends, Amy described

George's assignment as SGS—secretary of the general's staff—to Major General Hamburger as a dream job, exactly what a man who had graduated first in his class at the Command and General Staff School might expect. Amy never mentioned her role in that achievement, although she was inclined to give herself at least half the credit. She had hired one of the post carpenters to build a study for George in the basement of their quarters at Leavenworth. Every night George had descended to this virtually soundproof isolation chamber and stayed there for five or six hours. Saturdays and Sundays, which the less ambitious types took off, Amy slowly promoted from half to three quarters to full working days. George had grown somewhat irascible toward the end of the ordeal. But he had to admit when he graduated first in the class that it had been worth it.

Willard and Florence Eberle were living in one of the colonels' houses on the McConnell parade ground. Willard was G-1 to Henry Hamburger, who was an old friend. Major General Hamburger had been a lieutenant in the cavalry under Florence's father, Edgerton Hackworth, and toiled for him later in pre-World War II Washington. Hamburger liked to tell stories about old Edgerton, the toughest, meanest colonel in the U. S. Army. Hamburger himself did not play the tough guy. He claimed to be an idea man, a "creative" general. Among his more recent ideas was a project to revive the cavalry, complete with bugle calls. He had George researching all the contested areas in the world where a horse would be more useful than a tank. So far, the only place George had found was Andorra.

In her more realistic moments, Amy admitted to herself that General Hamburger was an idiot and IV Corps was a paper operation, consisting of a half dozen skeleton brigades and divisions scattered through the lower South and Texas. She and George had been sucked into Hamburger's orbit by the Eberles. As the general's personnel man, Willard had picked up a few brownie points by getting Henry an SGS who was ceritfied as one of the brightest young officers in the Army. George had grave doubts about letting Willard run his career. But Amy told herself—and George—that a year or two with Henry Hamburger wouldn't hurt. One of Patton's followers—in effect his publicity man—Henry had gotten to know dozens of correspondents and politicians during World War II. He had gone back to the Pentagon after the war and without leaving the five-sided nightmare for so much as a day, had risen smoothly to his present two stars. Henry Hamburger was the supreme Pentagon politician, and if Willard thought he was worth studying under, Amy averred, George Rosser should find it equally profitable.

The general's wife, Millicent Hamburger, was also worth studying. From the Charleston aristocracy, she had powerful political connections of her own in Washington. Her style was a nice combination of democratic good humor and upper-class taste. Florence Eberle hung on Millicent's every word the way Florence expected Amy to hang on hers. Amy suspected she could easily displace Florence in Milly Hamburger's affections. But she kept her place in the pecking order. She had learned a few things in the last ten years. Besides, Willard Eberle was slated to become a brigadier and secretary of the general staff at the Pentagon next year, if all went well (that is, if General Hamburger gave him a maximum OER). Amy had already decided to aim George at that Pentagon SGS job like a veritable guided missile.

Amy drew the nylon stockings up her tanned legs. She had been playing tennis three times a week with Florence and Milly and a revolving fourth partner, usually some colonel's wife, selected by Florence with a nice eye for who deserved the honor. Amy was dressing to meet Milly and Florence at the Officers' Club to inspect the ballroom decorations for the St. Patrick's Day party. Practically the entire Women's Club had been working on them for two days. Florence was president of the Women's Club and Amy was her executive officer. She spent hours on the telephone each week making sure all the committees were functioning smoothly.

As she put on her slip and adjusted it in front of the mirror, Amy felt a flutter of nerves. She and Florence had taken a calculated risk and decided not to consult Milly about the decorations. She had a maddening inability to make up her mind about anything until the last minute. If Mrs. General was in a bad mood, she might decide to dislike everything. If so, they would be up all night, and volunteers for future decorating committees would be as hard to find as Henry's extinct cavalrymen.

A moment after the flutter of nerves came a throb of pain in the back of Amy's head. No, she thought, straightening the skirt of her tweed suit, not a migraine, now. The headaches had begun in Washington, D.C., the year after George came back from Ankara. It had been a difficult year. Although George claimed to like his graduate course in industrial management, he had been surly most of the time. She had not been especially charming either. She had found Adam Thayer much harder to forget than she had anticipated. After one especially bad fight, George had moved into the guest room. Amy let him get away with it for over two months. She realized now she was trying to expiate Adam. Curiously, the migraines seemed to stir affection in George. He returned to her bed and they had been reasonably contented for the past eighteen months.

A howl of pain downstairs made Amy twitch. The howl grew louder as it ascended the stairs. Five-year-old Grace burst into the room, weeping. "Look what Georgie did to me," she bawled, clutching her cheek.

Amy yanked her hand away and saw two deep scratches down the small rounded cheek. "Georgianna!" she shouted. "Come up here."

A slow silent ascent ensued. Eight-year-old Georgianna eventually appeared in the doorway. She looked too much like George, the same bland imprecise features; not unhandsome but nothing that defined the character, that suggested a lineage, like Adam Thayer's face.

Why in God's name was she thinking about that maniac now? He was on his way to Laos to get himself killed. Part of the reason, Amy suspected, was a broken or at least badly chipped heart.

"Why did you scratch your sister?"

"Because she was trying to turn the channel on the TV. I wanted to watch the afternoon movie. She likes those stupid cartoons."

"There's nothing wrong with cartoons. Come over here."

Georgianna walked slowly over to her mother. Amy slapped her in the face, hard. Georgianna raised her hand to her cheek, and pulled it away, as if she regarded it as a gesture of weakness to admit that the blow had hurt.

"Now we're even," Amy said, putting on her gold earrings.

"What do you mean even?" Georgianna cried. "I didn't hit you."

"Say one more word and you'll get another whack," Amy said. "Grace, go in and wash those scratches. They could get infected."

"Yes, Mother," Grace said. Amy, checking her earrings in the mirror, saw Grace stick out her tongue at Georgianna, who made a threatening fist. Georgie was exasperating. She had a good mind, but she refused to study. She had almost gotten left back at the post school this term. Lately, Amy simply reported her depredations and derelictions and let George deal with her. Along with being lazy, she was precocious. Amy had caught her reading her father's copy of *Playboy* last week. She had told George to keep that disgusting magazine out of the house.

On her way out, Amy ordered Georgie to put TV dinners in the oven if she wasn't home by six. She was hoping that if all went well at the inspection, Millicent Hamburger might invite her and Florence for cocktails.

Amy drove to the Officers' Club in her new Volkswagen. In the ballroom, Helen Palladino, a familiar face from Ankara days, was teetering on a stepladder, wrapping the last of the green crepe paper around a chandelier. The Palladinos had reported for duty at Fort McConnell less than a week ago. Jerry, Helen's husband, was still a captain. He was bitter about missing a second promotion round from his age group. It practically guaranteed that he would have to resign. Apparently it had something to do with a poor OER that he had gotten in Turkey.

Other wives were rushing around putting the last of the favors on the tables. Amy paused to examine the huge papier-mâché statue of St. Patrick that Nancy Edmiston, the shapely blond wife of Captain Walter Edmiston, General Hamburger's aide, had created. The saint was wearing combat boots and had a big IV Corps patch on his chasuble. Nancy was miffed because Amy had virtually usurped her role as Milly Hamburger's companion. Amy made a point of praising the work of art. She had decided to kill Nancy with kindness. Florence Eberle waved to Amy and told her to watch the club's front door and escort Millicent up the stairs to the ballroom the instant she appeared.

Amy went down just in time to find Millicent venturing into the lobby in her wide-eyed fluttery way. One of the general's orderlies was holding the glass door. Upstairs, everyone stopped and practically came to attention when Millicent walked in. She smiled sweetly and said hello to each wife on the committee, Florence handling the introductions. Amy noted that they had lined up by rank. She liked that.

"I feel so guilty, letting you poor things do all the work," Millicent said in her modified South Carolina accent. "But it looks wonderful. I obviously wasn't needed."

"Now's the time we need you, Milly," Florence said. "When we're on the brink of judgment day, we need someone with judgment."

"Don't tease me, Florence," Millicent said. She strolled into the center of the room and oohed over the statue of St. Patrick. Mrs. General gazed up at the ceiling, with its green streamers, at the green crepe paper on the chandelier and green napkins and green (sprayed) roses on the tables, and said: "Too much green."

"But it's St. Patrick's Day," Florence gasped.

"Blue is just as Irish as green," Millicent said. "My great-grandfather Denis Hooper O'Brian was one of the founders of the Hibernian Society in Charleston, you know. He didn't have a speck of green in his coat of arms. Blue. I think half the streamers should be blue."

"We'll get right to work," Florence said.

Millicent O'Brian Hamburger departed. Two hours later, while officer husbands and children sat in their quarters with rumbling stomachs and souring tempers, the wives had replaced the last green streamer with a blue one. Florence looked everything over, and decided there was still too much green. Off came the crepe paper on the chandelier, to be redraped in blue, another hour's work. Florence sent everyone but Helen Palladino and Amy home at seven o'clock. It was after nine by the time they finished. Helen kept muttering nasty remarks about Florence, Millicent and the Army. Amy said nothing. She was not enjoying herself, but it was part of the job.

Florence finally pronounced the ballroom finished and Helen

asked in a very surly way if she could be "liberated." A lot of the good humor she had displayed in Turkey seemed to have vanished. Some people don't know how to tolerate disappointment, Amy mused. After Helen left, Florence turned on all the lights and surveyed the ballroom. "We shouldn't have sprayed those damn roses green," she said. This had been Amy's idea and had been greeted with enthusiasm when it was suggested. "I'll come over tomorrow morning and spray them blue," she said. Florence said that would be lovely.

They stopped in the lounge of the Officers' Club to have a martini. There was no need to hurry home. Major General Hamburger had a reputation for working his staff late. The lights in the headquarters building frequently burned until midnight. George had begun grousing about it a month ago. Willard Eberle at G-1 was particularly harassed. Hamburger was always pecking away at senior officers in his command, transferring or replacing them for trivial reasons, or harassing them with petty criticisms that prompted them to ask for reassignment. Willard and his staff were drowning in the paper work these reshufflings generated. Florence called Henry a fusspot and a birdbrain, but Amy could detect a certain affection for him, nonetheless. Even when he was commanding a mostly paper outfit like IV Corps, he kept busy, generaling. That was what the Army was all about, the exercise of command.

They discussed the other wives in the Women's Club. As usual, there were a few workers and a lot more drones who showed up at meetings and volunteered for committees only because it was expected of them. The new generation of junior officers' wives seemed particularly delinquent to Florence. Amy agreed.

Florence cited Helen Palladino's negative attitude. "How well do you know her?" she asked.

"She lived down the hall from us in the same apartment building—in Ankara."

"I'd watch her if I were you."

"What do you mean?"

"Nothing in particular. I'd just watch her. I gather she misbehaved quite a lot in Turkey. More than she admits to anyone."

"Oh? With whom?"

"That's not in her husband's file. But they used words like *promiscuous.*"

Amy was shocked. Helen had seemed so innocent, wacky but essentially innocent, when they said goodbye in Ankara. But she had stayed there another eighteen months. A wife could do a lot of deteriorating in Ankara in eighteen months.

At home in Quarters 76, Amy found George on the couch watching "Gunsmoke" with his arm around Georgianna. "I hope she's done her homework," Amy said.

"She has. I went over it," George said.

Amy dined on tuna-fish salad and went upstairs and got out the dress she was wearing to the dance the following night. She wanted to make sure the pleats were all ironed to exactly the same width. It was an emerald green, with a nice drape that disguised her overlarge fanny, strapless, in the current style, which Amy disliked. She had no cleavage worth looking down. Helen Palladino did. Was that the answer to her promiscuity in Turkey?

George wandered into the bedroom. "Hamburger is not to be believed," he said. "He fired the PIO officer today because he couldn't get a story about him in the Washington papers. He thinks this Fourth Force is the greatest idea to hit the Army since the Sam Browne belt."

The Fourth Force was General Hamburger's variation of an idea recently initiated in one of the airborne divisions, Operation Overdrive, which called on everyone to work longer hours and produce better statistics for Washington. Hamburger's Fourth Force was supposedly his addition to the big three factors in a good Army— Command, Discipline and Morale. General Hamburger called his Fourth Force Spiritual Commitment. He had kept the Public Information Officers busy writing speeches and finding public occasions for him to orate about this brainstorm. Amy had accompanied George and the Hamburgers to several of these affairs. After chewing on rubber chicken and gritty peas, they had to listen to Henry tell why IV Corps might be important after all. It did not have enough troops to fight a decent battle, but it had produced an idea that he believed could revolutionize America's fighting men—maybe even the whole country. "Yes, the Fourth Force may make IV Corps more famous than all the battles it never won," Henry would say, and then he would be off, denouncing the social and religious laxity of the time, which was grist for the Communist propaganda mill. It was all true, Amy often thought, but why did he have to make it so boring?

"I got a letter from my brother Bill today," George said. "They just passed out the bonuses for 1961. He got thirty thousand dollars. That gives him eighty thousand for the year. Incredible, isn't it?"

Amy found herself wishing brother Bill would electrocute himself with one of his amazing new circuit breakers, or whatever it was his electronics company produced. Bill was making more money than any son of a hardware-store owner ever dreamed was possible. George's other brother, Harry, was working for Texas Instruments, another of these growth companies, and doing almost as well. The inevitable comparison made George restless about the Army as a career. The slump which everyone expected once the economy resumed a peacetime status showed no signs of occurring. People with investment know-how were making fortunes. But Amy's trust fund was administered by the fuddy-duddies the bank had put in charge of it when her father fell on his face in the Depression. Now, with a go-go market that was made to order for his incurable optimism, Teddy Kemble was in a wheelchair, crippled by a stroke. Life was unfair. Amy knew that long before John F. Kennedy said it.

Amy made no comment on brother Bill's bonus. George read her silence correctly. She was not going to get into another argument about changing careers. She put away her dress and they got ready for bed. As she bathed, she found herself vaguely wishing that George would make love to her. Instead, he started an argument about her slapping Georgianna. He did not believe in hitting kids, especially girls. Amy replied sharply that she believed the punishment should fit the crime. He told her she favored Grace. By the time they stopped bickering the grandfather clock in the hall was bonging midnight, and Amy was in no mood for love.

The next night at the St. Patrick's dance, everything went beautifully for the first two hours. Millicent Hamburger adored the decorations, especially the blue roses on every table. The general, his brush mustache twitching, congratulated the wives who had decorated the ballroom and said St. Patrick was a good example of a man who understood the Fourth Force. Maybe Americans should imitate him and drive out a few of the snakes that were infesting the country. George danced his required round with Mrs. Hamburger, and General Hamburger essayed a rumba with Amy, warning her in advance that old cavalrymen were terrible dancers. "I never think of you as old," Amy said, which inspired the general to suggest they stay on the dance floor for a waltz that followed the rumba.

Out of the corner of her eye, she saw George drift past, dancing with a girl in a green dress that was at least five years out of style. She was rather tall and had long gleaming black hair. It took Amy a moment to realize it was Helen Palladino. On the way back to the table, she obeyed Florence's injunction to watch Helen. She and George stood talking after the music stopped. He kept his left arm around her waist. They had been dancing rather close during the waltz. But no closer than Amy and General Hamburger, who was what Army wives called a "hugger." In Ankara, Helen Palladino could tell you the dance-floor proclivities of every officer in JUSMMAT; she had the terminology down—"squeezers," "huggers," "sticks," "stompers"—the complete gamut. Helen had made it sound funny, then.

Amy told herself she was being ridiculous, letting Florence upset her. She tried to listen to General Hamburger, who was telling her that the guerrilla war in Vietnam was heating up. If his Fourth Force idea took hold, there was a good chance that he might get out there, as deputy commander of MAAG—the Military Assistance Advisory Group. Would she mind if he took George with him? "Of course not," Amy said.

"Didn't think you would," Hamburger said. "Florence's told me about you. Army all the way."

Amy turned to discover George and Helen Palladino still on the dance floor, almost the last couple there. George finally woke up and started back to the table. As they parted, he gave Helen's hand a squeeze. He regained his seat beside Florence Eberle, and Amy heard him telling her that he had not seen Helen since Turkey. No trace of guilt on his smooth affable face but . . .

When the band returned from its break, George danced with

Florence. Willard Eberle descended on Amy. She spent the next five minutes fox-trotting into the medals and decorations on his chest—the fruit salad, as Florence called it—while Willard talked about the troubles he was having with black officers and sergeants who could not get housing off the base. Willard thought the answer was reassignment. The Army could not be expected to change the minds of the civilian population. But the blacks seemed to think the Army or the federal government should use everything short of nuclear weapons to force people to rent them houses. A hell of a mess.

Terrible, Amy murmured once or twice, and shifted her cheek to prevent a wound from one of Willard's battle stars.

Next Amy danced with General Hamburger's guest, a reporter from the Associated Press named Arthur Conkling, who was an admirer of the general from World War II days. Conkling was at Fort McConnell to learn all about the Fourth Force program. He was a short flabby-faced man who had had too much to drink, and he stepped all over Amy's feet as he told her stories of his combat reporter days.

Suddenly Amy stiffened in Arthur Conkling's arms. George was dancing with Helen Palladino again, this time with both arms around her waist, as they revolved to a dreamy fox-trot version of "Wouldn't It Be Loverly." He was smiling at her in a way that sent needles of pain dancing through Amy's forehead. Once more they repeated the routine of intense conversation after the music stopped.

At home, after General Hamburger had treated them to a superfluous nightcap in the cocktail lounge, a half dozen possible questions crowded Amy's tongue. How many times did you dance with Helen Palladino? Why were you holding Helen Palladino so close? Do you think you can get away with something like that right in front of me? All of them sounded semi-hysterical and remained unspoken. The next morning, after George left for headquarters, Amy went through his dresser drawers and the drawers of the secretary, where they kept the bills. Nothing. She descended to the cellar and went through his luggage. Nothing in the small pieces. His trunk was under her trunk. She dragged and tugged and pulled hers off with a crash that echoed through the house. By now she was grimy with sweat and dust. The big brown trunk with his initials on it was unlocked. It had a tray on top for smaller articles. She lifted it out. There, in the bottom corner, was a small cache of letters.

Upstairs, without bothering to wash her hands, she read them. The first one began:

Dearest George:

After you said goodbye, I cried for two hours. I played Sinatra's "Night and Day" at least twenty times. Jerry is still up on the border. I hope he stays there another week; I need time to pull myself together. But I know you're right. It was a beautiful thing and it's better to remember it that way. A precious memory. We both have responsibilities to other people. I'll try to measure up to them. I'm not sure if I can. We're so right for each other. Does it make sense to deny something like that? I'll try to believe it does.

Love,
Helen

The letter was addressed to a box number in Washington, D.C. George obviously had decided the situation was so intense it had to be decompressed by mail. Succeeding letters told of Helen's demoralization, her loneliness and feelings of guilt and failure as she tried to replace George, first with her husband, who was in the field with the Turkish Army for weeks at a time, then with "someone else." Behind her jokes Helen was a hopeless romantic. There were, of course, no copies of George's letters to her, but as far as Amy could see from Helen's comments on them, he mixed realism with nostalgic passion in a calculated attempt to calm her down.

What to do? Amy wondered as she returned the letters to the trunk, shoved it back in place and piled the smaller luggage on top of it. She decided to do nothing for the time being. She felt no special sense of outrage. Discovering the letters made her feel, if anything, calmer, more in control. She even found herself thinking about George in a new, curiously sexy way. Suddenly George was a challenge. Before this discovery, Amy thought, studying her trim body in the bathroom mirror after showering away the grime and sweat of the cellar, before this George had been—what?

There. That was all. Just there.

That night, George did not escape Henry Hamburger's clutches until ten o'clock. The children were in bed. Amy had made a pot of *choucroute*, and kept it hot for him. She sat at the table with him and asked him for the latest gossip from headquarters. Nothing much, George said. Henry was getting more and more interested in Vietnam. Something was cooking on that front, somewhere. He had ordered George to subscribe to *The New York Times* and several other papers. The general's aide, Walter Edmiston, would henceforth brief him daily on what they were saying about Southeast Asia.

George looked at the eleven o'clock news and trudged upstairs to bed. Amy put on one of her frilliest nightgowns, a pale pink with a lace bodice, and hinted broadly to George that she would welcome some sexual activity. He stumbled into bed apparently without noticing it, leaving her awake, gloomily wondering. This performance was repeated the following night, when George again came home at ten muttering about Henry Hamburger and his "goddamn Fourth Force bullshit." He had spent the day—and night—editing a booklet for the troops. The next night he managed an earlier escape and was home for family dinner. Amy served *coq au vin*, which Georgianna refused to eat. In a fury, Amy ordered her away from the table. George was disgruntled at her harshness and they barely spoke to each other for the rest of the night.

The next day was Saturday. George went off to headquarters—not unusual—to catch up on his paper work. He said he would eat lunch at the Officers' Club. Georgianna and Grace departed for a Saturday play group that the Women's Club had organized. Amy decided to cook a spinach quiche and invite George home for lunch. Who knows what might happen afterward if they added wine to the menu, she thought, remembering afternoons in Paris.

About eleven-thirty, she telephoned headquarters. Hamburger's aide, Walter Edmiston, answered the phone. Sorry, he said, but George wasn't here. He hadn't seen him. Amy telephoned Helen Palladino's quarters. A baby-sitter answered the telephone. Captain Palladino was in Washington, D.C. Mrs. Palladino was out.

A trip to Washington was ridiculously simple for a general's SGS to arrange. There were innumerable errands on which a captain could be sent. He would go eagerly, grateful for this crumb of attention from headquarters. Never knowing what the SGS and his wife had in mind. Or in bed. Yes, that was where George and Helen were, at this very moment. In some motel, a safe twenty or thirty miles away. Amy sat down at the kitchen table and breathed the eggy, crusty smell of her spinach quiche. She was being defeated. She had accepted Helen as a challenge and she was being defeated.

Her head began to ache. She opened the wine and began eating the quiche. She ate half of it and drank half the wine before she stopped, appalled. She was reacting like her mother. This was how Mother had added forty pounds to her figure. Amy rammed the cork back in the bottle and put the rest of the quiche in the refrigerator.

All afternoon Amy wandered through her house, touching pieces of furniture, the Louis Quinze couches and chairs they had bought in Paris, the oriental rug from Turkey. She remembered the gossip about marital woes that had drifted across bridge tables at Fort Leavenworth. The thought that she and George might become one of these tidbits appalled her. But she still felt no outrage. Only an enormous disappointment. Why didn't he give her a chance? She was ready to remind him that she was very good in bed. But he would not give her a chance.

George came home about five, avoiding her eyes, muttering out of the corner of his mouth about the paper work Henry created. He looked guilty. Amy decided to let him stew in that useful juice for the time being. Face to face, she felt less defeated and disappointed. Perhaps it was the silent admission of the strength of the word *wife* in George's oblique eyes.

But defeat and disappointment remained her nightly experience in the bedroom. Even on the one night when George suggested they make love. Amy tried to feign a terrific excitement, a breathless pleasure. But George did not respond. She may have increased his guilt, but she did not emerge with any other indication of victory. When she suggested a Saturday drive to the beach—one of their favorites was only about fifty miles away—George said April was too early for such expeditions, and besides, he was still far behind Henry in the paper-work marathon.

Once more, on Saturday, Amy called headquarters. This time she got a warrant officer who said Major Rosser was not in his office. At the Palladinos' quarters, Helen's husband, Jerry, answered the phone. He said Helen was visiting an old college friend who lived in Spartanburg, South Carolina. Amy said her call was not important. Just some Women's Club business.

On Monday, around noon, Amy got a call from Florence Eberle. She suggested lunch at a restaurant in Emery, the nearest town to Fort McConnell. There were no decent restaurants in Emery, and it was odd for Florence to lunch off the base. She usually felt uncomfortable surrounded by civilians.

On the road, Florence told Amy that big things seemed to be brewing in Washington. Milly Hamburger had a cousin who was a power on the House Armed Services Committee; he had had a lot to do with making Henry a general. According to the congressman, President Kennedy had decided to up the ante in Vietnam. He was sending a four-star general, Paul Harkins, to take charge of a new Military Assistance Command, which was a much more potent setup than the Military Assitance Advisory Group that had been sending advisers into the field with South Vietnam's excuse for an Army. There were lots more slots in a command and Harkins, like Henry Hamburger, was an old Patton man, which meant there was a very good chance that he might ask for Henry as his deputy.

"All of this, Amy dear," Florence said as they ordered at the restaurant, which was attached to a Howard Johnson's motel, "may explain to some extent the reason I am about to give you some rather unpleasant news—and some advice to go with it."

"Oh?" said Amy, clutching her martini on the rocks.

"Your husband is fooling around with Helen Palladino. He took her here—to this motel—last Saturday. Only ten miles from the base. You'd almost think he *wanted* to get caught."

Florence practically chugalugged her martini. For some reason this statement of adulterous fact seemed to disturb her. Amy, groping for a stance, a way to deal with what she had just heard without groveling, sensed a vulnerability Florence had never previously displayed.

"Are you sure?" she said.

"Of course I'm sure. That cutesy little sneak, Nancy Edmiston, saw him. God knows what she was doing here in the first place. She says she was just having lunch. Anyway, she told Milly, who pinned her ears back and got on the phone to me. So the situation is contained, for the moment. Now it's up to you."

Amy writhed. Should she confess everything, admit her defeat, her humiliation? No, humility was preferable to humiliation. "What should I do?"

"You only have two choices, my dear. Break him. Or leave him. I went through the same thing with Willard in 1946. We were married in 1935, you were married in 1950. Your problem confirms my suspicion that it's an eleven-year, not a seven-year itch that causes the trouble. Rank is part of it too, I think. They imagine that a field-grade rank entitles them to certain freedoms. You have to disabuse them of that notion. It isn't a pleasant task, I assure you."

Florence ordered another martini. Amy joined her. "I wish—I honestly do—wish that I didn't have to say any of this. Most of the time I try not to think about what I went through with Willard. He had this French mistress when I arrived in Europe in 1946. A little something he picked up when they liberated Paris . . ."

Florence glowered into her martini. "I reminded him that I was Edgerton Hackworth's daughter. I'd been taught to shoot a gun at the age of eight. I don't recommend it as a solution—or really think it will be necessary with someone like George. There's a crude streak in Willard. His father was a sergeant who won a DSC in World War I. Yours is a different situation. I think you can appeal to George's more rational fears. The Army tends to lose interest in divorced officers. The ambitious ones only need to be reminded of this in the right way."

Break him. Or leave him. Amy stared at Florence Eberle's horsy face, the wide mouth with the corners pulled back as if an invisible bit was in place. No, she thought. I will not become Florence. I will become something else. Just what, she was unsure. She was not discounting or dismissing Florence's advice. But she did not want to be married to a Willard Eberle, a crude fuzzy automaton. She still wanted to win her woman's—wife's—victory against Helen Palladino. She still wanted to conquer this suddenly sexy soldier, Major George Armstrong Rosser.

Lunch arrived, two chef's salads, covered with bottled French dressing, oozy orange stuff that made Amy's stomach curl. Florence dug in with her usual indifference to food. "We can do the obvious things, of course. Transfer Captain Palladino out of here to Vietnam or Germany or Iceland. That might be the best place. No, I take that back, it's a hardship tour. That would leave Helen around unattached."

A hardship tour was a one-year overseas assignment, sans wife and family.

"Maybe England would be better. Or Lebanon. I hardly need add that if you can solve this thing, George will go to Vietnam with Henry. Willard has found him invaluable in getting the right kind of decisions out of Henry. They're still a very good team, Willard and George."

"From what I hear," Amy said, "it wouldn't take much to make Captain Palladino resign. Maybe that's the simplest way to handle it."

"A court-martial?" Florence said. "Those things can be sticky. You get a few idealists on the board, with pie-in-the-sky ideas about justice. Or a few meddlers who want to get to the bottom of the whole thing—"

"I don't mean a court-martial. Just another bad OER," Amy said. "He's already gotten one from Turkey."

"He'd resign now, if he had any brains," Florence said. "One bad OER is all anyone needs to ruin him. Everybody who knows anything is giving everyone else a max."

"Who's his commanding officer?"

"I'll find out. He's in the Public Information section. One or two tough assignments might be enough. I'll put Willard to work on it."

Interesting, Amy noted, how she had to do the thinking. The problem had Florence rattled. Amy was tempted to ask for more details of her pitched battle with Willard in Paris. But she was wary about trying to cross the gulf between major and full colonel. She still needed Florence more than Florence needed her.

Was Willard Eberle taking George out to lunch today? Were they talking it over man to man? *That little Italian cunt isn't worth it, George. Stick with me, kid, and when we get to Saigon we'll have enough Vietnamese pussy to last us a lifetime. We'll go home and be faithful to those bitches we married for another year at least.*

She could talk that way to George. *I can do anything that little Italian cunt can do, better. Just give me a chance, you dumb shit. I'll fuck you till your eyes pop.*

Meanwhile, Amy listened to Florence discuss the problem of the Founder's Day Dinner, the annual bash of the local West Point Society. It was touchy because you couldn't ask wives of non-graduates to work on the decorations, which considerably reduced the woman-power. Florence thought it might be best to execute a strategic withdrawal and let the wife of some other staff colonel, maybe Jane Skelton, whose husband was Hamburger's G-3, cope with Milly's inability to make up her mind about anything until the last minute.

"A good idea," Amy said.

Break him. Or leave him. She was not going to leave him. But what if George wanted to leave her? Panic crawled up Amy's flesh. Never. George recognized a good thing when he saw it. She had her faults but she was a good thing.

That night, George did not come home until eleven. Amy was panicky again. How did she know if he was working for Henry Hamburger or working on Helen Palladino? Luckily, Helen phoned. She said she was returning Amy's Saturday call. She sounded tense. Amy said she had wanted to ask Helen if she was interested in becoming a Cub Scout den mother. The Women's Club was having trouble finding volunteers, because the job often involved Saturday meetings. "I know everybody likes to keep their Saturdays private," Amy said.

Helen said she would think about it.

When George came home, Amy was reasonably calm. She waited

for him in the bedroom, propped against the carved headboard of their Bavarian bed, arms folded. "George," she said when he came into the room. "I know all about Helen and you."

"I figured you did," he said. "I went down to the cellar to get her letters out of my trunk and give them to her. I noticed everything'd been moved."

"You son of a bitch," she hissed. "And you still went to that motel with her?"

"Yeah. You want to know why? Because I love her."

Amy almost cowered against the headboard. It was love, that cruel mysterious word, said in a way that he had never said it to her. It had a timbre, a depth, she had never heard in his voice. Perhaps he had said it more gently, more wistfully to her in their honeymoon years. But she wanted the other thing, the gutty hungry sound of it. She never desired him more than she did right now, as he stood there, cocky, defiant, his legs spread. But the desire blended with a searing sense of loss.

"It's that simple?" she said. "She's that much better than I am in bed?"

Fuck. She's a better fuck? Why couldn't she say it?

"You know it's not that simple. It was an accident. I realized how many things I disliked about you. How much I put up with. But we were—married. I love our two kids. I tried to forget it when I came home."

"Stop, you're breaking my heart," Amy said.

"It's the truth," George snarled.

Amy liked the way anger looked on his face. It made him formidable. She suddenly remembered the day she had watched him play lacrosse at West Point. The battering he had given and taken with those dangerous sticks.

"Then I went for a walk with Georgie one day. She said to me, 'Mommy's funny. Sometimes she sleeps without her clothes on. And she forgets to wake up in the morning in her own bed. She's in the guest room.'

" 'Alone?' I said.

" 'Oh yes,' Georgie said. 'The man who used to come at night is gone away by then.' "

"You bastard," Amy said. "You knew it all this time and you never asked me about it?"

"I was waiting for you to tell me about it. Show at least a shred of remorse. But you don't work that way. It's got to be all your way or nothing. Perform, George, when Amy cracks the whip. Who was it?" he said, standing over her.

Amy shook her head. "I don't want to talk about it. I did it to—to help you. Believe it or not."

He slapped her in the face, banging her head against the headboard. It hurt. But it also excited her enormously.

"Bullshit," George said. "Bullshit." He raised his hand to hit her again.

"It was one of the colonels in the Coordinating Group," she said. "Adam Thayer introduced me to him."

"That figures," George said, dropping his arm. "A colonel. Prestige, power. That's all you care about. You don't give a shit what kind of a job I've got to do as long as it looks good out front and you can play princess around the post. You don't care what I've got to put up with from that asshole Hamburger. You don't care about me or the kids for that matter. Sometimes I think you're a goddamn monster."

He sat down on the end of the bed, facing away from her. Through the daze of pain and humiliation, Amy saw that movement, that choice of position, as a hopeful sign.

"What are you going to do about it?" she said.

"I don't know. I've been thinking about resigning. Asking you for a divorce. Helen's marriage is falling apart. Jerry blames his bad OER in Turkey on her. He doesn't know about us. She got a bad reputation over there after I left and this colonel made a pass at her. When she told him off in public, he creamed Jerry."

"You'll be miserable," Amy said.

"I told you I love her," George said.

"George, face it. You're a soldier. You'll be miserable as a civilian married to that Frank Sinatra fan. She has no class, George. She'll lead you straight to some humdrum suburb and get you elected president of the PTA. I'll help make you a general, George. I know how to do it. You know why I slept with the colonel—besides being lonely and missing you? For us, George. To find out what he knew. The Coordinating Group was at the white-hot center of the Pentagon that year. If they'd pulled it off, they would have owned the Army. We would have gone with them. But they blew it. That was a lesson too—watching them self-destruct. A lesson in how the real Army works. George, I've already taken you inside the power curve. You're on your way to the top, if you don't lose your head or your nerve. I know Henry Hamburger is a jerk and Willard Eberle is no prize either. So what? Are you going to grow up and realize some jerks get to be generals? Or are you going to spend the rest of your life feeling sorry for yourself because the Army doesn't work the way they told you it did at West Point? Face it, George, that true blue Corps and the Corps stuff is strictly for adolescents."

George shook his head. He was only buying 50 percent of it. He was still yearning for the never-never land of idealism. Or was it for the sometime-sometime land of Helen's boobs?

"I didn't love the colonel. I've never seen or heard from him since you came back. He's probably out of the Army by now. But you know something, George? He was a good fuck."

George spun and glared at her, astonishment mingling with outrage.

"In some ways, some very essential ways, I don't think we've ever understood each other," Amy said. "You've insisted on seeing me as some sort of Lady of the Lake, so fragile or so polite or whatever that I'd really rather do it with my eyes closed and the lights off. That's not me, George. I'm more inclined to do it with you out in the middle of the parade ground some dark night. Or in the back seat of a car. I like excitement, George. If I've been a bitch, maybe it's because you haven't excited me. You haven't let yourself go. You haven't treated me like a soldier's woman."

Anger and pain now mingled with desire on his face. Yes, desire, she had him, he was facing her now, one leg up on the bed, leaning toward her. Amy savored the supremely dangerous game she was playing. She could easily lose. If she was wrong, if that inner core of toughness, that harsh masculine lust she was challenging, did not exist inside George, he would flee back to Helen's sentimental consolations.

Break him. Or leave him. No, Amy thought, this was much better. This was her alternative. She rode the inrush of desire, of sudden wild wish that her own words produced in her. "George," she said. "I know I'm a bitch in a lot of ways. But I still want to be your wife. In every way."

"Ame. Ame." He was kissing her. But not in a tough or angry way. He was cradling her in his arms in his usual tender style. "You don't have to talk that way to me. I still love you. I guess I felt—you didn't love me very much. Now that I see how much our marriage means to you, I mean—to make you say, pretend things so totally foreign—opposite to your background, your upbringing. I've never had any desire to treat you that way—"

Was she winning or losing? Amy wondered dazedly as he undressed her. Didn't he *hear* what she had said to him about excitement? Her fear—or was it her intuition?—was correct, there was no tough lusty soldier inside George, he was his Methodist mother's son all the way. With women he only heard what the spirit of sweet sententious love (with a modest flavoring of self-interest, like a slice of lemon in a heavily sugared iced tea) allowed him to hear. Amy still wanted the spirit of lust, of comrade-in-arms-manship, of daring mockery of rules and respectability. She wanted combat thrusts, not sentimental strokes. She wanted sybaritic extravagance, not ladylike satisfaction. She wanted outrageous proposals, not murmurs of renewed affection. She would even welcome slaps, if that was the price she had to pay for the other things. At the very least, she wanted snarls, grunts, guttural growls of pleasure. But it ended with the usual husbandly sigh of release, relief, contentment.

"I can't believe I hit you," George said. "I'm sorry. It was inside me, eating away, for such a long time."

"It's all right. I deserved it," Amy said.

"I think I understand—about the colonel."

"I understand—about Helen."

She was winning, breaking him in her own way, she thought with a shiver of regret. All right, she would be satisfied with that. Winning was better than losing to a sentimental Italian from Brooklyn.

She would have to find her excitement elsewhere. In her imagination, in the Army and its power, its panoply, its prestige. She told

376

George what Florence had told her about General Hamburger's hopes of going to Vietnam. "If you're on the winning team out there it will be a lot more important than Korea in your file. Milly Hamburger's congressman cousin says the Kennedys are frantic about the Southeast Asia situation. They can't afford another fiasco like the Bay of Pigs."

George agreed. "But I can't see why anyone in his right mind would want Henry around."

"You don't appreciate Henry because you're too close to him," Amy said. "He's very good with the press. It's a skill you ought to cultivate. You've either got to be very good at something or have some clout somewhere to move ahead in the Army."

"Or be full of shit," George said.

She tolerated his cynicism. She had him back in her bed, in her marriage. Tomorrow she would call Florence Eberle and reverse the engines on Captain Palladino. Instead of running him out of the Army with a bad OER, it would be better to promote him to major as soon as possible, and transfer him to someplace innocuous, like Alaska. It would probably be easier for Willard Eberle to handle than the other routine.

As for the Rossers, that reunited husband-wife team, it was on to Saigon—and victory.

VI

LET EVERY NATION KNOW, WHETHER IT WISHES US WELL OR ILL, THAT WE SHALL PAY ANY PRICE, BEAR ANY BURDEN, MEET ANY HARDSHIP, SUPPORT ANY FRIEND, OPPOSE ANY FOE TO ASSURE THE SURVIVAL AND THE SUCCESS OF LIBERTY.

THESE words from President John F. Kennedy's inaugural speech, hand-lettered by the wife of a lieutenant colonel on the staff of the 44th Division, hung on the wall above the dining-room table at which Joanna Burke sat, struggling to finish another recalcitrant poem. Through the screens came the warm rush of the Pacific trade wind.

Joanna had gotten both her wishes. She was taking the pill, which meant she was theoretically free to love her husband every day of the month. She was living in a house on Mo Ka Lei Beach on Windward Oahu, a full hour's drive from Schofield Barracks with its formal white buildings and stiff old Army atmosphere. There were a dozen other officers' families on the half-mile-long beach. Unlike Schofield, where a wife had to wear stockings and carry gloves every time she went out of her quarters, Joanna's uniform of the day was the long colorful Hawaiian tent dress, the muumuu, and single-strap thongs called go-aheads. The Burkes' cottage was surrounded by flowering trees and blossoms. In the summer they could climb up on the garage roof and pick bananas for breakfast. The nearest house was a hundred yards away. Could there be a better place for two people trying to restore a shaken marriage?

The first night, summer heat all but vibrated in the trade wind. "Let's go for a swim," Joanna said. In the dark water, she began to kiss Pete. She pulled down her bathing suit and moved her breasts against his chest. "Let's do it on the beach," she said. "Like the natives."

He let her swim ahead of him to the shore. On the sand she began to shimmy out of her bathing suit. "Wait a minute," he said. "How do we know who walks along here at night?" He led her into the house, where they discovered the baby had awakened and was crying. Tom was also awake. He said the wind kept scaring him. By the time they settled the two children in their beds again, and retired to their bedroom, her ardor had vanished. They made love, but it was in a dutiful, alarmingly passionless way.

That was the beginning of Joanna's rueful discovery that she was not going to catch up to her lost Hawaiian honeymoon. What made it heartbreaking was the way they both tried to make Mo Ka Lei work. Pete bought some used scuba equipment, including a spear gun, from the previous tenant of their cottage. He soon became an expert spear fisherman, often catching a supper of juicy moi (mullet) or opakapaka (pink snapper), which Joanna learned to cook on the brick grill in their yard. Pete explored the brilliant undersea world of the reef off their beach. Joanna and Tom often went with him, using snorkels to watch him move with marvelous grace beneath the turquoise water. Pete taught Tom to bodysurf, and tried once more to teach Joanna. He had made the effort on their honeymoon at the Jersey shore. But she was again unable to master the split-second timing the surfer needed to catch the wave at the right moment. Nevertheless, a visitor watching the sunburned major and his tanned smiling wife and laughing nine-year-old son emerging from a swim would have reckoned them to be a model of familial happiness, a married Robinson Crusoe, a veritable apotheosis of natural man, reveling in the pleasures of paradise.

The observing stranger would only be one more proof that the interior of every marriage is a closed world. If nothing existed beyond Mo Ka Lei, if the major and his wife had been true inhabitants of the timeless world of Hawaii's native innocence, they might have been happy. But every weekday, the major got into the rusting 1954 Chevrolet that sat under the carport and drove up the unpaved dirt road between fields of pineapple and sugarcane to the main highway that took him to Schofield Barracks. There he sat in a white-walled office and worked on field training plans for Brigadier General Newton Ingalls, the 44th Division's deputy commander. Major Burke ate lunch at Schofield's splendid officers' club, with its crisp white tablecloths and smiling waiters. He dined with other majors and perhaps a lieutenant colonel or two, all of whom were living at Schofield Barracks. Returning to work, he walked past their pristine quarters with their carefully tended lawns and thought of his ramshackle bungalow with its weedy garden on Mo Ka Lei. Being a perfectionist, he often worked late on his plans and memorandums, which meant that he got back to Mo Ka Lei long after dark. Twice his decrepit car broke down and he did not get home until after midnight. He often spent half his weekend working on the car to make sure it would get him to work on time. He found it harder and harder to be cheerful with his relaxed smiling wife, who showed him the poems she had finished in the previous week and babbled to him about how free, how happy she felt on Mo Ka Lei.

Joanna saw the decline begin, within a week of their arrival, when they made the required duty call on the division's chief of staff, a formidable bald-headed colonel named Tumulty, and his wife. The Tumultys had just returned from the Philippines, where they had bought several pieces of teakwood furniture, including a complete dining-room set, which blended perfectly with the tropical architecture of their Schofield quarters. Mrs. Tumulty, a petite pretty blonde, asked Joanna how she liked her quarters. Joanna began explaining that they had decided to live off the base, on Mo Ka Lei beach. Mrs. Tumulty was frankly amazed. Joanna realized that Pete and Colonel Tumulty had stopped talking about Fort Leavenworth and were listening to her increasingly strained explanation.

"I just felt Joanna needed a rest," Pete said, taking over the conversation. "She had a baby at Leavenworth—after a few miscarriages. It was a terrific strain for both of us. She had to stay in bed for almost eight months."

Mrs. Tumulty became all sympathy. She agreed that Mo Ka Lei was a wonderful idea. Colonel Tumulty seconded the motion. "You must come down and visit us," Joanna said. "The cottage is a wreck but the beach is lovely."

Pete's mouth tightened, his eyes hardened. Joanna knew she had made a mistake. She soon discovered it was a double mistake. "Must be an hour away," Colonel Tumulty said.

"We don't expect you to come down, sir, unless you're in the mood some weekend," Pete said.

Joanna realized Colonel Tumulty thought she expected them to go all the way to Mo Ka Lei to return this duty call.

Not even an unexpectedly pleasant duty call with Pete's boss, Brigadier General Ingalls, rescued them. At work Pete had reminded Ingalls of their previous meeting in Japan, when he was Lieutenant General Mark Stratton's aide. Ingalls still had his burly, bulky tanker's build and the quizzical friendly eyes Joanna remembered. His wife was a tall thin brunette, with a lively delicate face. "Margo," Ingalls said as he shook Joanna's hand, "this is the girl I told you about—the one who wanted to close all the red-light districts in Japan."

"Bravo for you," said Mrs. Ingalls.

"The Army's Carry Nation," Ingalls said.

"I learned my lesson that night," Joanna said. "I buried my hatchet."

"Still writing poetry?" Ingalls asked.

"Yes," Joanna said. "How—do you know about that?"

"I read that sample you published in the Women's Club newspaper when you and Pete were at Fort Leavenworth," he said. "I was on the faculty out there last year."

Joanna found herself smiling inwardly. If Amy Rosser had intended to embarrass her, the dirty trick had boomeranged beautifully.

The general began asking her opinion of various modern poets. He was an avid reader of poetry, of all kinds. He said his taste ranged from Kipling to Kenneth Koch.

"It's all her fault," Ingalls said, gesturing to Mrs. Ingalls. "She got me hooked on it at an early age."

"What does Major Burke think of your poetry?" Mrs. Ingalls asked.

"He tolerates it," Joanna said, smiling at Pete.

"I don't understand one line out of three," Pete said.

"That's not a bad average for modern poetry," General Ingalls said. "Reading it is like talking to a woman, Pete. Lugs like us only get about a third of what they're trying to tell us. Fortunately they don't expect much more."

"We live in hope that you'll *listen*, once in a while," Mrs. Ingalls said.

"Just keep promising, that's my formula. It's worked so far," Ingalls said, giving his wife an impudent smile.

"Humph," Mrs. Ingalls said, and asked Joanna if she liked her quarters. Pete recited the Leavenworth-difficult-birth explanation. Mrs. Ingalls was properly sympathetic. "I'm sure you'll get a lot more poetry written down there," she said. "We'll just get along without you at the Women's Club."

"Oh, I want to do something," Joanna said. "I'm not trying to go AWOL."

"Of course not," Mrs. Ingalls said. Joanna was sure by now that she understood everything.

"What a pleasant surprise they are," Joanna said as they drove past Kaena Point toward Mo Ka Lei beach. "It's nice to know somebody that intelligent gets promoted to general."

"He didn't make general because he likes poetry," Pete said

"I didn't say that."

"Too bad we can't capitalize on it."

"What do you mean?"

"He'd probably return our duty call—if he didn't have to drive an hour into the boondocks to do it. He'll probably invite us to dinner. We might invite him back—if we had a decent place to entertain him."

"Pete, is it that important? I'm so happy at Mo Ka Lei. Tom loves it too. Doesn't that mean anything?"

"Sure. It means you've gotten your way. You've won this round. But I've got some rights in this deal too. The next round—or the one after it—belongs to me. Fair enough?"

"I suppose so," she said, feeling more and more disheartened.

From that beginning they progressed (or declined) inevitably to dinner invitations from other majors and lieutenant colonels on the division staff. They drank cocktails in inner courtyards, beside splashing fountains, they ate in formal dining rooms, with tranquillity, order oozing from the foot-thick walls. Everyone wanted to know why they were living on Mo Ka Lei and Joanna began to dread Pete's stolid explanation, and the flood of female sympathy it inevitably released. Guilt gnawed at her nerves. She returned invitations by urging everyone to visit them as soon as possible for a Saturday or Sunday swim, and bring their friends. For several weekends she felt like she was running a beach club. By Monday she was exhausted. Everyone seemed to have a good time—except Major Burke. Their haphazard cottage with its woven mat rugs and bamboo furniture—they had stored their Stateside furniture in an Army warehouse in Seattle—could not possibly match the gentility and formality of Schofield Barracks.

Politeness and proximity required them to socialize with the other Army families on Mo Ka Lei. They were all captains or lieutenants, for whom no housing was available at Schofield Barracks or at other Hawaiian posts. Major Burke was not a snob about his rank. He patiently served his liquor to the captains and lieutenants and conversed with them about their problems with sergeants and AWOL's, and other mundane matters which seldom concerned an officer on the division staff. Joanna talked babies and clothes and cooking with the young wives and listened to Pete with her other ear while guilt gnawed deeper into her nerves. She could almost hear Major Burke critiquing the party, critiquing Mo Ka Lei, critiquing his wife. She could almost hear him explaining that majors, ambitious majors, concentrated on socializing with their own rank or the rank just above them. They did not waste their nights and their liquor talking to captains, half of whom would quit the Army for one reason or another before they ever got to the next promotion zone.

One night a captain named Ben Shaughnessy, from the class of 1956, asked Pete why he had chosen to live on Mo Ka Lei. Joanna braced herself for the standard explanation. But Pete either had grown tired of repeating it or did not feel it was necessary to dissemble to the lower ranks. "It was Joanna's idea. She wanted to go native," he said. Fortunately, Ben and his busty wife, Lyle, drank very hard. They were both too sloshed to hear the resentment clang in Major Burke's voice. But his wife heard it.

Inevitably, Pete's negative feelings crept into their bedroom, the place where almost all disguises fail and so many compromises collapse. Joanna soon stopped advertising her new sexual availability. Without invitations, Pete ignored her for two weeks at a time. When she wondered aloud about it, he put Sunday night on his schedule as their time for sex. Joanna wrote a poem called "Fuck Night," in which a wife told her husband what she thought of his attempt to systematize their love life. *Are you keeping records on me, like the ones you keep on the car?* the wife in the poem asked. *Can I look forward to a lube job at 6,000 miles?* She did not send the poem to Carleton Haines or anyone else. It went into the bottom drawer of her desk. It soon had company, as the secret self that spoke in her poetry became more and more disturbed. She tried to avoid blaming Pete—or herself. Floundering, desperate, she looked for help elsewhere.

For several successive weekends, the public self, Joanna the wife and mother, found a babysitter for Cissie, urged Pete and Tom into their Chevrolet and toured the island, hoping Hawaii's beauty would work its reputed magic on them. They drove to Hauula and toiled up the one-mile trail to watch the Sacred Falls plunge eighty-seven feet into the gorge, while above them the Koolau palis loomed against the blue sky, sheer walls of green and brown stone, a primordial mass carved by eons of water erosion on the soft lava rock. They sought out Waimea Valley and its famous falls, and picnicked on the shimmering sand dunes of Waimea Bay. They absorbed the breathtaking vistas of Pali Pass as it descended to Windward Oahu. They gazed from Kolekole Pass on the white perfection of Schofield Barracks. Pete explained to Tom that this was what the Japanese pilots saw as they roared down the pass on December 7, 1941.

"Gee, Schofield looks beautiful," Tom said. "Why don't we live there?"

"Your mother wanted to go native," Pete said.

In September, when Tom went to school, they discovered that behind its postcard beauty Hawaii had some alarming social problems. Tom got off the yellow bus at their back door and announced that he had no desire to return. "They hate me," he said. "I'm the only haole in the class. And they're dumb, Mom. Half of them can't even speak English."

Joanna knew that most of the children at the country school came from families of the Japanese and Filipinos who worked in the fields behind Mo Ka Lei. She had no idea of the savage antagonism they entertained for all whites. Pete was far more disturbed, not only by the race prejudice but by the low scholastic level of the school. Most of the children in the fourth grade could not read, Tom said. Later that night, after Tom had gone to bed, Pete paced up and down the living room, asking Joanna how she could defend Mo Ka Lei now. Tom could be going to the post school at Schofield. Associating with other Army children, instead of fighting for his life and learning nothing, down here on the beach.

"All right," Joanna cried. "I'll live at Schofield. I was wrong. I admit it. Ask for quarters."

"It'll take a year," he said. "When you turn down quarters, you go to the bottom of the list."

They lived for the next four months with that admission echoing

384

in their living room and bedroom. A thousand hours of sighing trade winds could not blow it away. Joanna began to distrust, to suspect the experience at the Command and General Staff School, which she thought had renewed their marriage. She had forced Pete to admit his need for her but it had not lessened—it had possibly deepened—their antagonism. More and more she saw their relationship, not as a contest between her and the Army for Pete's affection, but as a contest between her and the Army, period. He *was* the Army, striding from the car each night to stare gloomily around their house, rating it at 0.4 instead of 4.0, picking up toys and wet bathing suits that Joanna had allowed to accumulate during the day, telling Tom to put on a clean shirt for dinner, to get his hair cut to a regulation length.

Pete spent more and more time at Schofield. He took Tom up there almost every weekend for a review. He started having dinner at the Officers' Club one or two nights a week, then working until ten or eleven. Coming home, he would pad through the dark house in his stocking feet while Joanna lay awake, listening, wondering if darkness made the casual disorder, the cheap beach furniture more tolerable to his Army eyes.

Joanna began to dread her own visits to Schofield. By day the tropic sun seemed to explode off the white buildings, the immaculate lawns, the quiet walks and streets, insisting on purity, nobility, all the abstractions she both admired and feared. By night the softer electric lights played romantically on the shadowy old buildings, mocking her naïve theory that romance was synonymous with white sand and the murmuring ocean. The inevitable New Year's Eve party at the Officers' Club had been a kind of climax. She spent the evening straining so hard to be charming, witty, she could not get to sleep for hours after they returned to Mo Ka Lei. She wandered through the house in the trade wind, fighting an impulse to weep.

Not even John F. Kennedy's inaugural speech rescued them. They had heard it together on a rebroadcast on the night of January 20. Pete had been tremendously excited. "At last we've got a President who knows something about leadership," he said. "If he means it, we'll chase those guys out of Cuba and Vietnam in a year."

Joanna tried to use the soaring rhetoric to prove to Pete that she was still an Army wife. As they went to bed, she put her arms around him and kissed him. "I'm proud I've got the kind of man the President was talking about," she said.

Pete responded with some of the ardor she remembered from other days. But the net effect was still far from the emotional splendor she had once imagined she would find in Hawaii.

"I'm not making you very happy, am I?" she said.

"Yes, you are. I'm not complaining, am I?"

"No. But you're not—not as loving. I mean—I don't feel you love me as much as you did ten years ago. That makes me sad. To think—after ten years—we've lost instead of gained—on the love front."

"Maybe it's the pill."

"You mean you still—"

"No. It's your business. Your soul. But it changed things. I don't admire you as much as I did. I mean—I know it's a good thing and it's made you a lot happier and that makes me happier. But I don't admire you the way I did when you—took the risk."

"You're telling me I should endanger my life? I should—"

"I'm not telling you to do anything. I'm just telling what I feel. You asked me and I'm telling you. I still love you. But that other thing—that made me sort of—feel close to you. It isn't there and I miss it."

She saw, in fear and trembling, how his mind worked. A soldier's mind. What did she expect? He had that love of danger, that willingness, almost eagerness, to confront death. She remembered the gun on the table at Fort Leavenworth. *I had to look at it, touch it,* he had told her. Her courage, or what he thought was her courage, had been an arousing, exciting thing to him. Was that all? Or was it the feeling that he was mingling life and death within his arms, was that what he missed?

No, too sick, don't accuse him of such a thing, Joanna warned herself, fighting desperately for her love.

"Is it only the pill? Or is it living here, at Mo Ka Lei? Would it change things if we lived at Schofield?"

"I don't know. We'd have to try it."

Pressed against him in the bed, Joanna sensed him again as an armored man, a compound of muscle and metal that she could never penetrate. Which made his penetration of her meaningless, even gross. No, she told herself. Stop that kind of thinking. Where were those thoughts coming from? "I still love you," she said. "I love what you stand for. Why can't you love me as I am? I'm willing to let you go—anywhere you want to go—Vietnam, Laos. I'll follow you there if they let me. If they don't let me, I won't sit home and curse you, like some wives do. I don't try to run your career like Amy Rosser runs George's."

"I do love you," he said. The sighing trade wind swept the perfunctory words out of his mouth and sent them spinning across miles of empty ocean. Joanna wept.

A month later, Major Adam Thayer called from Fort Bragg. Honor had kept Joanna in touch with Adam's progress in the Special Forces. The commander of the training school at Fort Bragg had made him an instructor in counterinsurgency warfare as soon as he finished the basic course. But Adam was determined, to Honor's distress, to get into the mounting guerrilla war in Laos and South Vietnam.

"How are things in paradise?" Adam asked.

"All right, if I could just stop my lord and master from wishing he was living at Schofield Barracks."

"How did you ever lure the Old Regular away from the base? That's the crucial point your letters have never revealed."

"I threatened to deprive him of access to my body. That didn't work of course, but when I suggested I might tell the general's wife what I really thought of the Women's Club, he capitulated."

"Atta girl. Old four-point-oh Burke may have met his match in you."

For a moment she hated both of them for being so heartless.

"Listen, just because I'm finally promoted doesn't mean I can afford small talk at long-distance rates. I'm calling to put you to work. You are hereby ordered to find us a house, preferably on Mo Ka Lei Beach. The Thayers will be flying toward you in two weeks' time. Either produce or stand by to double up in your bungalow."

"That's marvelous! How long do you expect to stay?"

"I expect to stay about a week. Honor a year at least."

"A week?"

"Yeah. Long enough to pack my parachute and make sure the Air Force knows how to read a map of Laos."

"Oh, Adam."

"Jesus, you sound like Honor. I want a stiff upper lip and a nice teary kiss. If that's a contradiction in terms, the hell with it."

"I'll look for the house. Give my love to Honor."

Joanna called the real estate agent who had rented them their cottage. He had a house available at the opposite end of the beach, next door to Ben and Lyle Shaughnessy. It was a good half mile from the Burke cottage. But it was the same beach. Joanna put a deposit on it. She cabled Adam and Honor the news and told Pete when he arrived home from Schofield that night.

He shook his head and grunted skeptically at the prospect of Adam parachuting into Laos. "They can't use firepower, I guess they're trying brainpower."

"What do you mean?"

"We've been more or less sticking to the Geneva agreements, which limit the number of men we can put into Laos. The North Vietnamese are sending in whole regiments. It isn't the healthiest assignment in the world. These Special Forces drops are covert. If they get it we can't even complain about it."

The Special Forces were being air-dropped into Laos to work with the hill tribes along the Vietnamese-Laotian border. The tribesmen—traditional antagonists of the Vietnamese—were very primitive people but good fighters, Pete explained. The North Vietnamese put a high priority on trying to stop the United States in this attempt to organize a guerrilla army on their flank.

"It's getting worse out there, isn't it?" Joanna said. "In South Vietnam too."

At the New Year's Eve dance, the men had talked about nothing but Vietnam.

Pete nodded. "I'm going to start listening to my language tapes again."

She put her arms around him. "I don't think I can take another war," she said.

"Go on," Pete said. "You'll be glad to get rid of me."

She shook her head, angrily denying the half-truth. She wondered if he was really saying he would be glad to get rid of her. He saw how hurt she was and covered the comment with a laugh. "I'm only kidding," he said.

Two weeks later, the Burkes met Adam and Honor, eight-year-old Pookie and six-year-old Matthew at the Army terminal in Honolulu. They looked somewhat the worse for wear after their ten-hour flight. Pete draped leis around their necks and Joanna snapped some pictures with a camera her mother had given them for Christmas. Pookie was still a skeletonically thin female version of Adam. Matt was a handsome chubby redhead, obviously the beneficiary of Honor's genes. Adam was in his Special Forces uniform, which included the tight paratrooper's jacket and jump boots and the green beret that President Kennedy had authorized them to wear. Honor and Joanna exchanged kisses and Pete mashed Adam's hand and said: "You look like you're going to a St. Patrick's Day costume ball."

"Watch it, big boy," Adam said. "Men have been disemboweled for cracks like that."

"Oh, I'm scared silly," Pete said in a high-pitched voice, intimating that the rest of the Army was not impressed by the Green Berets' much publicized training in hand-to-hand combat.

They piled the bags in the Chevrolet's mildewed trunk and whisked the Thayers out to Mo Ka Lei. Tom and a Japanese friend from his class in school were waiting on the porch of the Thayer bungalow. Cissie, now almost one, was at home with a baby-sitter. Tom urged Pookie and Matthew into bathing suits and the younger generation raced off to explore the area. Adam stood on the porch, telling Pete with calculated malice how lucky he was to be living here instead of stuffy Schofield. Honor was not so impressed with the house, which shared the flimsy construction of the Burke cottage. "There's no glass in the windows?" she said. "How do you keep out prowlers?"

"We haven't had a single one down here," Joanna said. "I know they're common on other beaches. I think they know who lives here. Lotta malihinis wit boom-boom."

"That's Hawaiian pidgin for strangers with guns," Pete said.

Lyle and Ben Shaughnessy strolled over, Ben with a cocktail shaker full of bloody marys under his arm. They sat on the porch and Honor and Lyle got neighborly, in spite of the six- or seven-year difference in their ages and the distance between genteel Virginia and small-town Arkansas. Lyle was Ben's high school sweetheart. Joanna was sure he was going to regret marrying her. She was too loud, too satisfied with her smug high school cheerleader personality to make it as an officer's wife.

The men talked about Vietnam, Laos, the growing war. According to Adam, the North Vietnamese were sending thousands of armed infiltrators into South Vietnam. Kennedy had to make a decision, fast, or there would be no government to support over there.

"I think the whole thing's crazy," Honor said. "Droppin' a man into the jungle, where there isn't a single *white* man to help him, expectin' him to teach a bunch of savages how to fight a war when they're barely beyond usin' bows and arrows—"

"That's what makes it interesting," Adam said. "Maybe we can teach them how to fight the guerrilla way. Instead of teaching them how to fight the Battle of the Bulge, or the Argonne, which is what the brass is feeding the Laotian and South Vietnamese regulars."

"You can't win a war without an organized army," Pete said.

"You can lose a guerrilla war with one. The French proved that already."

That was the way the conversation went for the next week. Adam barely noticed Joanna. He spent all their time together arguing with Pete about the relationship between the Special Forces and the Regular Army, and their relative merits in the struggle to save South Vietnam and Laos from the Communists. As Adam saw it, giving the South Vietnamese and other Asians outside the Communist orbit the right training to resist guerrilla warfare was crucial. Guerrilla tactics were simply the first stage of a coercive war—which the Communists had learned to fight in Korea. If the Army could train the Asians to stop the Communists at the guerrilla level, there would be no need for large numbers of American troops, no danger of America being sucked into another coercive struggle.

Adam wanted Pete to join the Green Berets. He said they needed more West Pointers, men with his kind of medals and battle experience, to win the big Army's respect. Pete refused to even consider it. But Pete was not averse to telling General Ingalls about the presence of his ex-roommate in Hawaii. Ingalls invited Adam to a private lunch at the Schofield Officers' Club, at which he lectured the division staff on the situation in Indochina as the Special Forces saw it. In spite of his maverick tendencies Adam was a star and it did not hurt Pete to associate with him.

After Adam left for Laos, Joanna realized he had never even asked to see any of her recent poems. She knew that it was ridiculous to balance her small personal life and talent against Adam's absorption in a struggle for the lives and allegiance of millions of people. But it left her feeling vaguely depressed, almost abandoned, on Mo Ka Lei. Adam was as entangled with the Army as Pete. In his own proud, more oblique way, he was equally ambitious. She remembered asking him in Japan: *The Army, does everything have to come back to the Army? Yes*, he had said, *that's our satori*.

Joanna found it more and more difficult to finish a poem. She would begin with a decisive image, a dramatic first stanza, and falter at the halfway mark. Something seemed to be crippling her will or her imagination. Sometimes she found herself blaming Honor. She spent the weeks after Adam left predicting his doom, weeping on Joanna's shoulder about the bad dreams she was having. For a while, Joanna selfishly welcomed these laments (while she tried to sympathize) because they gave Pete a chance to see another wife's reaction to Army life. But Honor soon began to get on her nerves. She did not like Mo Ka Lei. After a visit to Schofield, she asked Joanna why in God's name she had turned down quarters on such a beautiful base to live in beachcomber squalor? She was unimpressed by Joanna's repeated reassurance that Mo Ka Lei was safe. Honor collected newspaper stories of assaults on tourists and residents by mixed-bloods, the juvenile delinquents of Hawaii.

On the day Pookie and Matt started school, Honor's dislike not merely of Mo Ka Lei but of Hawaii reached a climax of sorts. That afternoon she arrived on Joanna's porch in a blue-and-white muu-muu, practically hysterical. "Pookie says they laughed at her and punched her in the school bus because she's *white*. They call her by that damned name—what is it?"

"Haole," Joanna said. "I know it's not very nice. But they're just children. And they are the majority."

"I don't care what they are," Honor said. "I'm not goin' to have my daughter treated like a nigra. Look. Look at that lump over her eye."

She pointed to Pookie, who stood a few feet away, staring at them. She seemed indifferent to her bruise, but Joanna felt compelled to be sympathetic. "Oh, that's terrible," she said. "How did it happen, sweetie?"

"They pushed me when I was getting off the bus. I hit my head on the door. Tom says he knows who did it. He'll beat him up tomorrow."

"No, he won't," Joanna said. "The best thing to do is try to be friends with them. They're too many to fight."

"They probably carry knives, like their older brothers," Honor said. "Honestly, Joanna, I know you don't agree with me, but I think they're worse than American nigras, they really are. They're worse than the Japanese in Japan too. At least they were polite."

"They're Americans," Joanna said. "I guess they tend to be uppity."

"Uppity!" Honor found Joanna's liberalism trying. "Last night some of them broke into a house near Kahaluu and stabbed a lieutenant near to death and beat up his wife. I can't sleep a whole hour at night, with the wind tearin' through the house, flappin' the curtains. Every noise I hear makes me think it's one of them. I swear I'm turnin' into a nervous wreck."

Joanna found herself wishing Honor away, elsewhere, anyplace but on the beach at Mo Ka Lei. Over the next few weeks, she visited Joanna less and less. She spent most of her time at the other end of the half-mile-long beach with her hard-drinking next-door neighbor, Lyle Shaughnessy. Why was she letting Honor drift into such company? Joanna asked herself, more than once. She had no answer beyond the uneasy suspicion that when she looked into Honor's unhappy face, she was seeing a mirror image of her own marriage.

Two months later, as the hot muggy Kona weather turned the trade wind languid and made writing a poem an enormous effort, Joanna received a letter from her mother. The Welshes were coming to Hawaii for a second honeymoon and also to look the islands over as a possible retirement haven. It was a shock to realize that her father was sixty-five and her mother sixty-seven. Joanna had kept in regular touch with them, writing dutiful letters at least once a month. Her mother wrote more often. Her letters frequently irritated Joanna; several paragraphs were invariably devoted to her sister Beth and her ever-growing family. They now had four children. Still more kind words were lavished on Beth's husband, Bob, who was now executive vice-president of American Dynamics. His salary was $60,000 a year. He and Beth had bought an eight-room house in Indian Hill, only a few blocks from the Welshes. With a little help from his father-in-law, Bob had just gotten into the exclusive Camargo Country Club. Sister Beth was imitating Mother's example and rapidly becoming a mover and shaker in the Junior League. Mother's letters were also crowded with the names of high school friends who had married doctors or lawyers or Procter and Gamble executives and were now living in the posh Montgomery or Hyde Park sections of Cincinnati. The young marrieds were all traveling to Europe as their parents had before them and vacationing each summer in family compounds in Michigan or Maine.

Time and *Newsweek* regularly amplified Mother's reports of prosperity in Cincinnati with buoyant statistics about America's incredibly productive economy. Every college graduate in sight seemed to be getting rich—except Army officers. The boom was the main reason why a startling number of junior officers, including a lot of West Pointers, were resigning their commissions. Only a few nights ago, Ben Shaughnessy had had a long talk with Pete about whether to quit or stay. Lyle wanted him to get out. Along with calling the officer corps a collection of stuffed shirts, she kept telling him he could make five times as much money outside.

Mother and Father arrived early in June. Pete and Joanna were at the airport to greet them and watch while the Hawaiian tourist board's entertainers twanged their ukuleles and dropped pink leis around their necks. Joanna kissed her mother dutifully and her father fervently; still unable to break the old habit. They were both looking remarkably youthful, except for an abundance of gray hair. Mother had teased hers and added a touch of blue. She was wearing a light green suit with a stylish stole neck. Joanna said she looked more like a New York socialite than a sedate Midwest matron. Her mother laughed and said everybody her age in Cincinnati had "gone glamorous." She blamed it on Jackie Kennedy.

They were staying at the Royal Hawaiian Hotel in a room with a perfect view of Diamond Head and Waikiki. Her mother said she could not wait to see Joanna's house and their "private beach" at Mo Ka Lei. "It's not exactly private," Pete said dryly, eyeing Joanna. In her letters she had said the beach was "practically private." Mother had a habit of improving on everything her children did. In conversation with her bridge club she probably had Pete promoted to brigadier general by now.

They had dinner with the Welshes at the Royal Hawaiian. Joanna's father was inordinately interested in how Pete liked the Army these days. He wanted to know why he had not volunteered for the Green Berets. Tom Welsh seemed to think this intimated a decline in Pete's enthusiasm for the military. It was an inadvertent testimony to the publicity the Green Berets had received since they attracted President Kennedy's interest. Pete tried to explain the Army's rather cool attitude toward the Special Forces.

"It takes so long to get promoted in the Army," her mother said. "How long have you been a major now?"

"Six years. I'm still fairly young for a major," Pete said.

"It's a life sentence, the Army," Joanna said. She hastily forced a smile, trying to lessen the negative implication of the remark.

Her father chose the wine for dinner. "The Rothschild sounds good. We're celebrating," he said.

The sommelier clanked off to get the bottle, which probably cost more than Pete made in a week. With warnings about their humble abode, Joanna invited Mother and Father to dinner the following night. Her father rented a car and drove down in time to see the sunset. Her mother gazed at their flimsy cottage, with its screened but glassless windows, eyed the paint peeling from the sides under the relentless assault of the ocean's dampness, and said it looked like "fun." Joanna gritted her teeth, almost wishing she were not so diplomatic. Inside, a certain order had been imposed on the living room and bedrooms and porch. Joanna's cost cutting and lack of enthusiasm for decorating were still all too visible in the flowered drapes and curtains, the woven mat rugs. Again Mother was diplomatic. "It must be wonderful to decorate for yourself this way, according to the custom of the country."

The dinner was pleasant enough, even though the wine was only Almadén. Pete had caught the fish off the beach that morning. The grandparents doted on Tom and Cissie. During cocktails, her mother insisted on holding Cissie on her lap. It gave Joanna a glimpse of her mother's intense maternal feelings. She simply did not have them to the same degree.

After dinner, Pete wanted to know if he could be helpful in the Welshes' search for a retirement home. He had talked to some old Hawaiian hands at Schofield Barracks. They recommended Maui, one of the outer islands, as an ideal place. Her parents were surprisingly evasive. They said they were already leaning toward Arizona. They just thought they should check out Hawaii.

"I guess the real reason we came out here, Pete, was to talk to you," her father said.

"Yes," her mother said, in her emphatic way that eliminated the "I guess" from her father's diplomacy.

"I'm going to sell the dealership. It's worth about a million dollars. Five times what we paid for it."

"Good news," Pete said.

"Right. But I don't need the money, Pete. It's been a very profitable business for a long time now. Even in the Depression Cadillacs sold pretty well. I'd like to keep it in the family."

"How?" Pete said, although he certainly saw what was coming.

"I'm ready to give it to you for a nominal sum. Say two hundred thousand. You could borrow that from any bank in Cincinnati, and pay it off in five years. The business would be yours free and clear. When Joanna's mother and I pass on, we'd take into account the estimated value in our wills, leaving Joanna's sister Beth enough cash and stock to make sure she doesn't feel cheated.''

"That's tremendously generous of you, sir, and I really appreciate it," Pete said. "But I don't know a thing about the car business.''

"You could learn it in six months. I did. You've got all the things you need to make it big. A great war record. A good personality."

"What do you think, Joanna?" her mother said.

Joanna was not thinking. She sat there, too dazed even to feel. Did her parents have any idea what they were doing to her? They were offering her escape from budgeting every nickel and dime, from abrasive generals and rumors of war, from Women's Club committees and trivial conversations about moves, children and commissary prices, escape from a nomad's life of new assignments every year or two, escape to the safe comfortable world of Cincinnati, where she would always be Joanna *Welsh* Burke, surrounded by girlhood friends and relatives, mistress of a ten- or twelve-room house in Indian Hill or Hyde Park with at least a cleaning woman and possibly a cook, escape to stability, permanence for her children.

"I—I don't know," she said. "It's Pete's decision."

Did Pete hear something less than dedication in those pale words? He did not meet her eyes as they flickered in his direction. He put his big hands on the table, as if he needed to hold it down, as if the table, the whole house, was about to rocket off into outer space.

"Mr. Welsh, I can't express—I don't have Joanna's gift for words—I can't tell you how much I appreciate your thoughtfulness. I know I haven't been able to give Joanna everything you'd like to see her have."

"That's not true. The offer has nothing to do with that—even if it was true," her father said, glancing uneasily toward her mother. "I've put a lot of my life into the business, Pete. I'd like to see it stay in the family. I'd feel—like part of me was still in it. I'd like to think maybe young Tom might run it someday, after you."

"I understand. I wish I could accept it. I know it may sound crazy to you. But I feel I owe something to the country for my West Point education. And I think—this may sound even crazier—I think the country needs me right now. I've got some skills, some experience, the country—the Army—could use."

Not since Pete spoke to the cadets at West Point about his combat experience in Korea had Joanna seen him so nervous. He tried to lessen the obvious disappointment on her father's face and the even more obvious disapproval on her mother's face. "I'm afraid the Communists are on the offensive. They're giving us a rough time around the world."

He gestured to the framed words from John F. Kennedy's inaugural speech on the wall above them. "I take pretty seriously what the President said about being ready to meet hardships—pay a price—to defend freedom. I don't think I'm a one-man Army—but I am one of the guys he needs to make it work."

"You're sure, Pete?"

"I'm sure, Mr. Welsh. And thanks again."

"Once we sell it, it's gone beyond recall," her mother said.

"I know that. Maybe—if you'd suggested this last year, Mrs. Welsh, when I was breaking my head at the Command and General Staff School, I might have been tempted. The Army seemed to be going nowhere and so did I. Now the President—well—he seems to have gotten the country moving. The country and the Army. He's asked everyone to stand up and be counted."

"I think Mr. Kennedy is vastly overrated," her mother said. "I see nothing but more blunders like the Bay of Pigs."

"You're talking to one of the original Ohio Republicans, Pete," her father said, nodding toward her mother. "I understand what you mean. You're a born soldier."

Pete nodded. "Thanks, sir," he said.

In years to come, Joanna hoped she would remember this moment the right way. Not with self-pitying regret, but with pride. She *was* proud of this big earnest man who sat opposite her at the dining-room table in their cheap Hawaiian bungalow. Outside in the carport was a rusting six-year-old Chevrolet. He had about $3,000 in a Honolulu savings bank. These were his tangible rewards for ten years of service to his country. He had a wife who had turned out to be anything but the girl of his romantic dreams. Who would blame him for seizing this chance to inherit a million-dollar business, to say goodbye to duty-honor-country in the great American tradition of looking out for Number One?

Joanna suspected the whole trip, the proposition, had been her mother's idea. By the end of the evening she was sure of it. Defeated in the frontal assault, Mother resorted to a series of attacks from the flanks. One disquisition virtually gave them a room-by-room estimate of the cost of her sister Beth's new house. This maneuver was succeeded by an annotated report on a half dozen equally prosperous couples who were Joanna's contemporaries, told in a somewhat bewildered style to underscore the amazing amounts of money people were making. It was a replay of her letters, aimed at Pete. He simply smiled and said it was great to hear that the country was so prosperous. Maybe they could afford to let the Army expand a little, and buy some of the new weapons they were developing, like rocket-firing helicopters, modern tanks.

At last her parents departed for the Royal Hawaiian after enlisting Joanna as their tour guide for the next five days on Oahu. Pete helped her do the dishes. They barely spoke, beyond exchanging comments on how healthy the old folks looked.

As he folded the dish towel on the sink, and she mopped the counter, Pete said: "Are you sorry?"

"About what?"

"That I said no."

She continued mopping. "I've never been prouder of you in my life. Including the medal in Japan."

He turned her around to study her face. By now he had learned to suspect what she said. He knew words came too easily to her.

"Do you really mean that?"

"Yes," she said, facing him, facing more years of cheap furniture and dirty sinks and probable wars. "Every word."

She prayed—a prayer without her old confident faith—that she was telling the truth.

"Jo," he said. "Jo." He drew her to him in a deep tender kiss.

How strange life was, Joanna thought. Love renewed here, beside the sink, her cheek caressed by hands smelling of dishwater. Renewed by something as totally unexpected, as unromantic, as the visit of a strong-willed mother and a retiring father. His arm around her waist, Pete led her through the living room into the bedroom. As he began to undress her there flared in her mind with incandescent amazement not only her pride in him but her gratitude for his refusal. She did not want to live in Cincinnati as Mother's creature, her husband equally captured by cringing gratitude. She had lost her taste for Cinci chili, coneys with cheese, mocha-chip ice cream. She had no desire to compete with sister Beth and a dozen other social climbers for leadership in the Junior League. She did not care if she never shopped again at Pogue's or Gidding-Jenny. Life with Major Peter M. Burke was far from perfect but it was hers, it did not belong to anyone else. Her mother had just tried to steal her life from her. Joanna rejoiced in this man's strength, which had enabled him to block the attempt, to refuse the temptation.

That night their love transcended barriers. For a little while they lived in the world of commitment and found it more exalting, more meaningful than pleasure or affection. Soon their hands, their lips spoke these almost lost realities and the combination burst upon them like a breaking wave, sweeping Joanna down into a lovemaking more passionate, up into a giving more absolute than she had ever achieved before. It was a fusion of their different idealisms into one unforgettable thing, a marvelous compound of flesh and spirit.

It was more than Hawaii, although it happened in that seemingly carefree place. It transcended romance, poetic or sentimental, it soared beyond the rigidities of self and systems. It was love, the absolute thing-in-itself, which she could never deny again, without risking the loss of her soul. As he came in her she met him with a trembling elation, her first genuine orgasm in a long time. *Something good has happened*, she thought. *Something wonderful.*

She lived for two weeks in the afterglow. Nothing bothered her, not even Mother's complaints about Hawaii's smog and her father's disappointment at the puny waves that broke on Waikiki. Pete changed too. He gave her squeezes and offhand kisses—something he had stopped doing when they started to come apart at Fort Stanton, six years ago. He still worked long hours at Schofield but when he got to Mo Ka Lei, he relaxed. He began to talk about how beautiful it was, how much he enjoyed it.

At the beginning of the third week, Pete returned from Schofield looking unusually weary. Or was it sad? "What's wrong, soldier?" Joanna called from the kitchen window as he walked from the car toward the back door.

He stopped there in the shadow, blinking at the sunset on the ocean. He held up one hand to cut the glare. It made him look like he was warding off a blow.

"Kennedy's doubling the number of advisers in Vietnam. I'm on the list. We leave for Saigon next Sunday."

Joanna remembered the elation with which he had left her for Korea. This time, he really seemed sorry to go. Progress of sorts?

"I'll see what I can do about getting you out there with me," he said.

VII

When they begin the Beguine... The old song wandered past, competing with the trade wind and the crash of the surf. Honor Thayer sat on the porch of her house on the beach at Mo Ka Lei reading a radio message that had just arrived from Saigon. *Still hanging on here with my noble savages. Almost all our friends have been good boys and gone home like the diplomats say they should. The other guys are still around, of course, shooting anything that moves. So lately my warriors have been keeping very very still. Kiss the kids for me.*

It was insane. Adam was up in the mountains along the border between Laos and Vietnam, living with a tribe of primitive people called the Meo, trying to get them to fight the Communists. Several hundred American advisers had also gone into Laos to help the Royal Laotian Army fight the local Communists, the Pathet Lao, who were getting help from the North Vietnamese Communists. But the Royal Laotian Army turned out to be the biggest bunch of

400

cowards that ever put on uniforms. They ran away in every battle, leaving Adam and a dozen other Special Forces officers stranded in the mountains. Then the diplomats negotiated a truce that was supposed to neutralize Laos. The North Vietnamese Communists and the Americans were both supposed to withdraw their troops. But only the American advisers went home. The Special Forces stayed and so did the North Vietnamese Communists. They went right on fighting a secret war.

All she ever heard from Adam were these radio messages that he sent to Saigon once a month. Saigon sent them to CINCPAC (Commander-in-Chief, Pacific) here in Hawaii, and they sent a lieutenant down to give them to Honor in an envelope marked "eyes only." She was supposed to burn them as soon as she read them. Before the Americans got kicked out of Laos, Adam had written her letters about what a wonderful time he was having with the Meo. They were like the American Indians, he said, proud, noble, unspoiled, brave. Tell Joanna, he said, that they had restored his faith in human nature.

Tell Joanna. That had made Honor feel strange. She wasn't really jealous of Joanna. But it hurt her, that Adam presumed his wife didn't understand what was bothering him. He had been miserably low after the rout of the Coordinating Group. He had lost all his idealism about the Army. Honor had been just as upset. It was like watching Ashley wither and die before her eyes.

It was she who had nagged him into seeking refuge at West Point, after the Army Intelligence people had descended on their house in Annandale and all but tore it apart to find the papers Adam had smuggled out of the Pentagon. She had put up with his neglect, his drinking, once they got to West Point. He rarely touched her, sexually. Sometimes she got so angry she was tempted to play around. There were lots of good-looking bachelor officers at West Point, serving tours as instructors. But Adam was so low, so down, it would have been cruel to do such a thing. In her heart she signed a truce with him. She had never wanted a war, anyway. Except . . .

What the hell day was it? She walked somewhat unsteadily into the kitchen and peered at the calendar. December 12, 1962. She glared sullenly at the perpetual Hawaiian sunshine. It was easy to forget what day, month, year it was on this goddamn island. December 12 meant Adam had been gone almost fourteen months.

Honor freshened her drink and went back out on the porch to resume her thinking about truce and war. She had almost started a new war with Adam about that name on the pad on his desk. It had come through because he pressed so hard when he wrote the note with a ballpoint pen. *Dear Priscilla*. Who, Honor had asked, was Dear Priscilla? A Pentagon secretary, Adam said. Who did she work for? Honor demanded. Priscilla works for SGS, the secretary of the general staff, Adam had said. The next day Honor had called SGS and asked for Priscilla. No such animal at SGS, they told her. Adam had looked her straight in the eye and told her Priscilla had gotten fired. She was involved in helping him steal documents and leak them to the newspapers and she had gotten fired. Honor had finally believed him when the Army Intelligence people ransacked the house and Adam had said very bitterly: "Priscilla must have talked." Honor believed him, except . . .

Adam had stopped making love to her—or practically stopped— before the Coordinating Group collapsed. He was so exhausted, from the hours he was working, Honor did not think much about it at the time. Only after Dear Priscilla did she start to wonder. Which made her think, sometimes, when they got to West Point and Adam still ignored her, that she wouldn't declare a truce.

Then came the Special Forces, John F. Kennedy, and suddenly Adam was his old self. Full of energy, writing articles for Army magazines, arguing that the Green Berets were the answer to the problem of guerrilla warfare. Off they had whirled to Fort Bragg. She had loved Bragg, loved the Special Forces people. They were all *men*. They were like the airborne, elite, but smarter, tougher, Adam said. Then he was gone, parachuting into Laos, leaving her on this godforsaken island with Joanna. Then Pete had left for Vietnam and Joanna started taking courses at the University of Hawaii. Honor hardly ever saw her.

The last day with Adam, on the way to the airport, he had looked at her in that not-quite-nice smiling way and told her the old Army saying that a wife had one of three things in Hawaii, a baby, an affair or a nervous breakdown. That was when she sensed that he actually wanted her to fool around with someone else. That was when she thought of Priscilla again and wondered if she was an officer's wife, someone who might even be waiting for Adam in Laos. There were a lot of officers' wives living in Southeast Asia now, in Saigon, Vientiane, Bangkok. Joanna said she expected to get a call from Pete almost any day, telling her to start packing. How did she know Adam was telling the truth, with these radio messages from the jungle? He could be down in Vientiane, the capital of Laos, every weekend, living it up with Priscilla.

Maybe it was not that bad. Maybe Adam had said that stuff about an affair because he was feeling guilty. Maybe he wanted her to fool around so he could confess to her and she could confess to him and they'd be even. Adam had a conscience, she knew that much. It bothered him to be rotten to her. When he got drunk, he'd admit it. He'd call himself a bastard and tell her to leave him.

"Honor? Hon?" called a voice from the left side of the house. Soon a face and body emerged to go with the voice. Lyle Shaughnessy had fluffy blond hair, a little girl's mouth, dimpled cheeks and a curvaceous figure, concealed, at the moment, by the standard costume of the Army wife on Mo Ka Lei, a muumuu. Lyle's husband, Ben, was serving as an adviser in Vietnam under Pete Burke. Before he left, all the Shaughnessys did was fight.

"There you are," Lyle said. "Pam Todhunter 'n' me are goin' for a swim at De Russey. Want to come?"

"No. It's my turn to sit with the older kids when they come home from school."

"Oh, bother. Why can't they mind themselves?"

"Tommy Burke's a menace. He leads Pookie astray. She can't swim worth a damn and he tempts her to go out a mile with him."

"Seems to me the great brain Joanna ought to just wham hell out of him. But I suppose that ain't in her theory of raisin' the perfect kid."

"I guess not."

Joanna and Lyle had disliked each other on sight. Lyle wanted to have a good time. Joanna almost didn't know how to have a good time anymore. She was too busy organizing things, worrying over

Vietnam, Laos, Korea, getting her Master's degree in English literature at the University of Hawaii. She scared Honor, she was so intense. She said she could not write any more poems, she "blocked" (she called it) everytime she started one, because she felt so guilty about the way she had treated Pete. Honor tried to calm her down, to tell her that Pete was wrong too, expecting her to give sit-down dinners twice a week while she was going through God knows how many miscarriages. But she would not listen. She was like Adam. She did not know how to relax and enjoy herself. She always had to be doing something to improve herself like writing poetry or reading a book. Joanna had gotten together all the Army people on the beach to hire a day nurse, a fat, good-natured Japanese mamma-san, for the pre-school kids, which gave everyone a lot more free time to take hula lessons, shop, relax at the Army beach at Fort De Russey, and gave Joanna time to take courses at the university.

"You hear from Adam?" Lyle asked.

"Just the usual radio message. It's so crazy, leavin' him in Laos and sendin' everyone else home."

Lyle just shrugged. Her interest in national strategy was zero. "I heard from Ben. He's goin' to get a medal, he says. I can't believe it. That bubblehead gettin' a medal?"

Lyle was always cutting her husband down. It may have been a habit she started in fun, but now it was half serious. It was one of several reasons why Joanna did not like Lyle. Honor did not approve of it either, but she was inclined to think it was just a younger-generation thing, trying to be smart. Honor liked Lyle because she was young. Not that Honor Prescott Thayer was old at thirty-five. But she didn't feel young anymore. Life didn't just jump out of her the way it did out of Lyle. Those ten years, from twenty-five to thirty-five, what a difference they made.

Honor knew that Lyle considered her and Joanna ancient. They had been through the Korean War, for God's sake. Lyle was only fourteen years old when that fuss started. Joanna didn't approve of Honor spending too much time with Lyle. But she was her next-door neighbor and Joanna, aside from being a half mile down the beach, was gone most of the week at the university. It was either hang around with Lyle and her friend Pam Todhunter or sit brooding about Adam. Some choice.

Pamela Todhunter was another person Joanna did not like. Pam and Lyle had similar chunky bodies and pug-nosed faces, but Pam was dark and California sophisticated, while Lyle was Arkansas natural. Pam's husband, Jeremy, was a psychiatrist at Schofield Barracks, one of the Army's drafted doctors. They lived on the beach to get out of the "goddamned Army atmosphere." They both despised the Army and everybody in it. Pam Todhunter's two favorite topics were how much money her husband would make as a psychiatrist in Beverly Hills when he got out of the Army and the weird hang-ups that Army people had, if the stories her husband heard from the wives at Schofield Barracks were any sample.

After one night with her, Joanna had been so outraged she had written a letter to the commanding officer at Schofield Barracks, accusing Dr. Todhunter of violating his code of ethics as a doctor and an officer. But Pam's tales were only a little worse than the usual gossip that floated around Army posts from wives who worked at the hospital as volunteers. As far as Honor knew, the commanding officer at Schofield did nothing about it. Pam Todhunter was still yakking.

"Hey, listen," Lyle said. "Pam's having a farewell party tonight for some of the 44th Division types. They've got a raft of'm goin' to Nam. You know that lieutenant colonel who beats up on his wife all the time? They'll be there. And that major who can't get it up? Ought to be fun, standin' around watchin' them, them never knowin' how much we know."

"No, Joanna's stayin' late at the university tonight. I promised to cook dinner for the kids."

"Joanna, Joanna. Jesus, Honor. That girl doesn't do nothin' but take advantage of you."

"She's a good friend. I told you, we got married the same day at—"

"Oh, sure. But that doesn't mean you should let her walk all over you. Tell you what. When she does show up, and you unload the brats, come walk up the beach. It's goin' to be real informal. Nothin' but muumuus and go-aheads."

"I'll see. Thanks for thinkin' of me, Lyle."

"Just tryin' to put some life in the party. When you get goin', Honor, you're the one who can do it. Ain't no one can do the hula the way you do it, except maybe one of the purebloods."

Honor had won first prize in their hula class. She had written Adam about it; he had never even mentioned it in any of his messages. Maybe the parachute containing that letter had drifted off course. Honor finished her rum Coke and went into the kitchen to mix another one. She returned to the porch and picked up a copy of *Redbook* magazine. Maybe read a short story. They had good stories in *Redbook*. She flipped toward the back and stopped as her eyes were caught by the title of an article: WHEN A WIFE IS SECOND-BEST. She flung the magazine across the porch and started to cry.

Almost exactly twelve hours later, Honor's eyes were dry. She was not very dry but her eyes were dry. She had a rum Coke, a real one mixed by Dr. Jeremy Todhunter, not the kind she mixed for herself, barely flavoring the Coke, a real rum Coke waiting for her. Meanwhile she was swaying in the middle of the Todhunters' living room while a thousand steel guitars seemed to pour from Dr. Todhunter's stereo and beside her Lyle Shaughnessy was trying to hula too but doing a god-awful job of it, she just couldn't dance, and besides, she was pretty drunk. Honor was not drunk, she had barely arrived at the party after Joanna had told her she shouldn't go and she had finally told Joanna off. Yes, off. Told her Honor had a right to a little fun in life and if her husband wasn't going to supply it, if he thought it was more important to play hide and seek with some weird natives in Laos, that was his business, but it wasn't any of Joanna's business to tell Honor what to do when the problem was *nothing* to do.

That's it, Jo, don't you see? Honor asked in the private part of her mind while the hula happened in the rest of her and the steel guitars crashed, loud enough to be heard in Tahiti. *Aloha Oe, Aloha Oe!* Officers, most of them around Lyle's age, young ones, stood around clapping and yelling. None of the senior officers had accepted the Todhunters' invitation, the way it looked. Everybody here was young and mostly bachelors.

One big brute, a captain about Pete Burke's size, put his arm around her waist. She slapped it away. "The hula's a solo dance, a dance to the gods," she said. Joanna had told her that. Joanna was into Hawaiian folklore.

"Hey, I got an idea," Pam Todhunter yelled. "They're having a dance tonight at the Schofield Officers' Club. Let's crash it and get Honor to do the hula on one of the tables. Show the stiffs how the natives dance!"

It was definitely not a good idea. Schofield Barracks was *old* old Army. You wouldn't dream of walking into the Officers' Club without at least tailored Bermuda shorts and preferably a best dress, chiffon, silk, linen. But Honor was as disgusted with the goddamn Army as she was with Joanna and Adam. They wouldn't let her live at Schofield. But they couldn't stop her from living it up at Schofield. What the hell. She knew Pam Todhunter just wanted to thumb her nose at the Army and that was all right with Honor. What did Adam, her husband, care? Only thing he cared about was the strategic blah-blah of the logistic something-or-other.

Into cars they piled for the wild ride down the coast highway and up into the mountains to Schofield. The big captain was sitting next to Honor and he had his hands all over her. He was resigning from the goddamn Army as soon as he finished his tour in Vietnam. Played football at the Academy. Kept talking about how the Army'd cost him $100,000 of pro football salary. Honor kept slapping his hands away. "C'mon, I'm 'n old married lady," she said.

"Don't stop the young married ladies, why should it stop you?" he grunted. Lyle Shaughnessy was jammed into the corner on the other side of the car with some lieutenant all over her. As they passed a streetlight, Honor caught a glimpse of his arm a mile up her muumuu.

Suddenly Honor saw Adam smiling at her in that not-nice way, asking her which it would be—the affair, the baby or the breakdown? Where was he now? Maybe sitting in some hooch with one of those silly cigars he'd started smoking stuck in a corner of his mouth and a couple of those little Laotian honeys consoling him.

Tough guy. Can't make your mind up whether you're Rhett or Ashley. Maybe I'll show you some Scarlett.

They were at Schofield. Ignoring the speed limits, roaring past the whitewashed barracks and company headquarters to the Officers' Club. Everybody out. Inside the band was playing "Night and Day." They could hear the music, but sanity or cowardice or something took over and the captain and the lieutenant said maybe they just ought to sit in the cocktail lounge and let the brass glare their disapproval on the way out. Crashing the party might make the commanding general a little more excited than they wanted him to get.

Pam Todhunter called them a couple of sunshine soldiers and said at least they ought to have Honor do a hula on one of the tables, and they all got around in a circle after the big captain planted her on the table and howled what they thought sounded like Hawaiian music, and Honor started to hula. But the dance was breaking up and officers in dress blues and their wives in evening gowns came into the lounge for a nightcap. Some of them looked familiar and Honor felt horrible and got down. She wanted to be them, walking back to their quarters on this marvelous old post, husbands and wives, arm in arm, dedicated to each other, to the Army, to the country. Why was she married to a man who sneered at what he called the Big Army and said the Pentagon was a collection of fatheads and the country was a screwed-up mess that didn't know where it was going or what it was doing in places like Laos and Vietnam?

More rum Cokes, she didn't know how many later, Honor found the big captain helping her to her feet. The lights were going out in the lounge, the waiters and bartenders were all gone except one. It was hard to tell who was drunker, she or the captain or Lyle Shaughnessy. They seemed to have picked up one or two other junior officers, equally drunk. Only Dr. Todhunter and Pam weren't drunk. They just watched everyone with little superior smiles. They reminded Honor of Adam—the Adam she did not like.

The big captain insisted on Honor doing one more hula and away they went, roaring "Aloha Oe!" In the car Honor fell asleep or passed out or something. When she woke up the big football hero captain had his hand inside her muumuu and inside her bra playing with her left nipple. "Hey," she said, "hey, cut out." But she didn't sound very serious. Wasn't very serious. She was too drunk. She was having a *time*. Father's daughter, what the hell. Momma always was a pain in the ass. Singin' hymns to Jesus. Momma's girls just don't belong in the Army. Not when you got a bastard of a husband who wants you to fool around and maybe is fooling around this very second with those Laotian girls. She saw pictures of them on TV welcoming some UN committee. Beauties, every one of them, smiling as they handed bouquets of peace flowers to the diplomats. What did they give the soldiers? Easy to guess.

They were taking off her muumuu, heaping leis over her head, was it her idea? Do a *real* hula. Dr. Todhunter turned up his stereo and the music poured out on the beach. But Honor couldn't stand straight, couldn't keep her feet in one place, couldn't move anything right. Boof. Sit down on the sand, hell with it.

Skinny dip, someone yelled, and lurched past her to splash into the water. The big captain or someone was pulling off her bra, grabbing at her pants. She rolled away from him and half ran, half fell two or three steps into the water and the cold blasted her in the face; it seemed as cold as Nova Scotia, the cove of her honeymoon, silken love, moonlight love, morning love. Oh, Adam, Adam, why?

Whaaaat? The big captain was after her again, his hands on her pants, pulling them down, off, to her knees, she grabbing for them, trying to stand in the shallow water, and he laughing, lunging against her, crashing splashing down on top of her, her head under, drowning, Jesus. She thrashed, slashed at him with her nails. He gurgled and rolled away. On her feet again, pulling up her sodden pants. Lyle Shaughnessy was on the beach on her hands and knees in a splash of light from the Todhunters' door letting two officers do things to her, giggling, shaking her shiny blond head like a horse, while Pam and Jeremy Todhunter stood on the porch watching the Army animals with superior smiles on their self-satisfied California faces.

"Hey, you fuckin'—" It was the big captain, stumbling toward her, clutching his private things with one hand, his face with his other hand. "You fuckin' bitch, you kneed me in the balls—"

"No," Honor said, backing away from him. "No. Please."

It was Koke-Do again.

The whole thing is so ugly.

What am I, unclean?

Adam, why, why?

Honor started to run down the beach toward her house. She only got about ten steps when the captain landed on top of her and they went crashing, smashing this time into sand, not water, sand that sent pain searing across her right cheek. He flung her on her back, straddled her. "Whatsa matter, you one of them teasers, like to get a guy's rocks but no fucking? I'm gonna be in Vietnam the day after tomorrow and the way I figure it, the goddamn Army owes me one and you're gonna give it to me."

Honor started to scream the kind of scream she had wanted to scream at Koke-Do instead of hiding in silence in that Japanese house for so many days. A scream that flung everything inside her, hope love Melanie Ashley God Army Adam America into the black star-spangled Pacific sky. A scream that annihilated Harvard the Pentagon West Point Pookie Matthew, Joanna Burke and Nova Scotia and Fort Bragg and Laos and Vietnam and Korea and Charlesville Virginia and horses and happiness Adam sneering and Adam smiling and Adam snarling and Adam lying, a scream that was like a flame thrower destroying all the good things and the bad things. An atomic scream that reduced to particles Waikiki and Mount Kaala, Hanauma Bay and Diamond Head, picture-postcard Hawaii with its Oriental faces peering hatred from its beaches and mountains. A scream that said nothing and everything. A scream that was not merely coming from Honor, it was Honor.

He tried to stop it, the big captain, but she bit his hand and kept screaming. There were people around her, pulling him away, and she kept screaming. Dr. Todhunter was kneeling beside her and she kept screaming. He shoved something in her arm and she kept screaming. If she stopped screaming Honor would stop. That was what she was starting to believe. Honor was her scream and her scream was Honor. She kept screaming into the darkness that seemed to fall on her like a toppling palm tree.

When Honor woke up she was in bed in her own house. She was wearing a nightgown. Pookie appeared at the door of the bedroom, looking scared. The big eyes, the narrow intense face, were so much

Adam, Honor started to cry. "Are you all right, Momma? Your cheek—" Pookie said.

Honor realized her cheek was aching. So was her arm. She pointed to the hand mirror on her dresser. Pookie gave it to her. Little Matt took Pookie's place in the doorway. Honor gazed in horror at her reflection. The right cheek was scraped raw. Around the lacerated flesh was a blue-and-purple bruise. She fell back on the pillow and began to weep even more violently.

"I'll get Aunt Joanna. She'll know what to do," Pookie said, and ran out of the room.

"No," Honor cried. "Come back."

But the screen door slammed. Pookie was gone. "Go after your sister. Tell her to come back," Honor told Matt. He ran obediently after her. But neither came back. Pookie was not about to take any orders from her drunken slut of a mother. Maybe the child saw them carrying her back last night. Maybe she had heard her screaming on the beach.

Screaming.

Suddenly she wanted to scream again. Not drunkenly, in protest against what was happening to her. But for pity, kindness, forgiveness. For Adam. Maybe not a scream but a cry, a whimper, a plea. For Adam.

Slam of a door. There stood Dr. Todhunter, without his little smile. "Honor," he said. "I thought I ought to stop in and see if you're feeling all right."

She shook her head, while the tears flowed. "I want my husband," she said. "I want my husband back."

"He's in Laos."

"I want him back. I need him back."

"Sure you do. All the wives feel the same way." He avoided her eyes and scratched the back of his ear for a moment. "That was a bad scene last night. I should have stopped it."

"I just want my husband," Honor said.

She kept crying while Dr. Todhunter tried to talk to her and finally wrote out a prescription for some pills that would calm her down. Slam went the screen door and Joanna was in the doorway in a yellow-and-white-striped muumuu. Honor only wept violently.

"I want Adam, Jo. Call CINPAC and make them bring him home."

"What happened? What's wrong with her?" Joanna asked Dr. Todhunter.

"The party got a little rough last night. She's upset," Dr. Todhunter said.

"Some party," Joanna said. "I just got a call from a friend of mine whose husband's on the division staff at Schofield. She says everybody from the general down is talking about the way you people acted at the Officers' Club. I told you to stay away from these people, Honor—"

"Jo, please, don't talk to me that way," Honor said.

Pookie was standing in the doorway, those big gray eyes, Adam's eyes, seeing everything. "I just want Adam. Ask Adam to come home," Honor said.

Dr. Todhunter inclined his head, urging Joanna out of the bedroom. While Pookie stood there watching her weep, Honor could hear Todhunter talking to Joanna about last night.

"Episode—

"Potentially serious—

"Husband's tour—"

Joanna came back and sat down on the bed and put her arms around Honor. It made her feel a little better, but she still kept crying.

"Darling, if they brought Adam home now—it could hurt his career. I know that sounds cruel. But—"

"I don't care. I want him home. I can't stand thinkin' about him out there. I want him home or I'll start screamin' again."

"Screaming?"

"Screamin'. If you don't believe me, I'll—"

"No, don't." Joanna kept hugging her. Honor let the scream dwindle inside her.

"Are they really talkin' about me at Schofield?"

"Yes. But you know how the Army is. It'll all be forgotten with the next rumor from Saigon or something."

"Don't lie, Joanna. I'll never be able to go near that post again. I'll be too ashamed. Oh, Jesus, I gotta get off this island. I hated it from the minute I saw it. All these damned Japs and Chinese and mixed-bloods.''

"It's a beautiful place if you'll only try to understand it. And not judge its faults too harshly.''

Typical Joanna. Honor started to scream again. In the doorway, Pookie put her hands over her ears and burst into tears. Little Matthew stared incredulously and then ran away. Honor kept screaming and then sobbing and then screaming.

"I want my husband. Don't tell me I can't have my husband.''

SCREAM.

"I want Adam. I want my husband, call him, Joanna please.''

Sobbing.

SCREAM.

She didn't know how long it lasted. Eventually Dr. Todhunter came again and injected something in her arm and the blackness fell on her again, not like a palm tree this time but like part of the ceiling.

Everything got very confusing after that. Sometimes Joanna was there, but they were not in the bedroom or even in the house. There was no sound of the surf and when Honor asked for Pookie, Joanna would just say she was all right. When Honor wanted to know if they were still talking about her at Schofield, Joanna said no, it was all forgotten, in a way that made Honor cry because she was so obviously lying. Then a doctor would show up and talk to her about her mother and father and what had happened to her as a teen-ager with men making passes at her and she answered him with words that fell out of her mouth like stones on the floor, words that didn't mean anything to her anymore, but he wrote them down on a sheet of paper because they seemed important to him. Then she stopped answering him because she began to think maybe the doctor was working for the general, the commander of Schofield, and they were going to punish her for what she had done, corrupting the morals of the Army or something, and she would cry in Joanna's arms and ask her when Adam was coming.

"Tomorrow," Joanna said.

She didn't believe her, of course. They were only trying to stop another screaming attack.

"Hello," said the Green Beret in the doorway, so thin he looked exactly like a paratrooper in Korea that Pete Burke had made jokes about ten years ago. Adam. In the doorway of her room, smiling at her. Not angry, not even that mean mood that made his mouth like a scar across his face. None of that sort of thing. Just Adam, smiling, taking her in his arms, holding her for a long, long time.

"Oh, Adam," she whispered. "I want to go home with you. Home to Bragg or West Point or any place but here. With you."

"We're going," he said.

Behind them in the doorway stood Joanna, misty-eyed.

"And I'm going to Saigon," she said. "I just heard from Pete."

"They need all the help they can get out there," Adam said.

BOOK
FOUR

I

"CONGRATULATIONS, Mrs. Burke."

"Congratulations."

"Mrs. Burke, would you and the colonel and the children pose for one more picture with General Harkins?"

Outside, Saigon sweltered beneath the tropic sun. In the air-conditioned press room of the five-story headquarters of MACV (Military Assistance Command, Vietnam) on Pasteur Street it was deliciously cool. The day, Joanna's second in Saigon, was delicious in every way. Major Peter MacArthur Burke had just become a lieutenant colonel. As twelve-year-old Tom Burke watched admiringly and his three-year-old sister squirmed impatiently in his lap, Joanna had helped austere General Harkins, COMMUSMACV himself, pin the silver oak leaves on Pete's broad shoulders. Then Army photographers took pictures and PIO officers handed out press releases about the victory that the Vietnamese 25th Division had won in Quang Ngai Province with Lieutenant Colonel Burke's advice. The Viet Cong had left 226 dead on the battlefield. There were about a dozen reporters at the ceremony. Tieless, in rumpled slacks and sports shirts, they contrasted almost defiantly with the freshly pressed khakis of the MACV officers. The newsmen's questions surprised Joanna. They were so skeptical.

"Is the two hundred twenty-six body count an estimate or an eye-witness statistic?"

"Eyewitness," Pete said.

"American or Vietnamese?"

"American. I counted every one personally."

A grisly image which Joanna hastily shoved from her mind. It did not fit into an otherwise delicious day.

"Do you feel this will turn the war around in Quang Ngai Province?"

"No. But it's a good beginning. The 25th is a new division. They fought very well for green troops."

"You would still consider the province contested? Far from secure?"

"Of course."

"But this victory has changed the entire atmosphere in the province," General Harkins said. "I was up there yesterday to inspect the 25th Division. The main roads are comparatively safe for the first time in a year and the people are bringing in intelligence."

"That's right, sir," Pete said, suddenly rather nervous. "And of course, the strategic hamlets have proven themselves. I think we've shown the people they're safe, now."

"Exactly," General Harkins said.

Joanna had an uneasy sensation that Pete's words were not spontaneous. Unconcealed skepticism twisted the reporters' mouths. They picked up their press releases and departed. General Harkins looked annoyed. He shook hands with Pete and Joanna in a rather perfunctory way and also departed, leaving his staff to host the small party that followed. Joanna was pleased to see balding Bradley Skelton, whose wife, Jane, had been one of her most entertaining volunteer housekeepers at Fort Leavenworth. Brad was now a full colonel. An even pleasanter surprise was smiling Major George Rosser, who kissed her and asked for her telephone number. He said Amy wanted to invite them to dinner as soon as possible.

George introduced his boss, Major General Henry Hamburger, a somewhat pompous little potbellied man with a brush mustache, who heaped extravagant praise on Pete's performance as an adviser. Blushing, Pete said that there were a dozen officers advising other ARVN (Army of the Republic of Vietnam) divisions who deserved at least as much credit. General Hamburger shook his head. "This is no time for modesty," he said. "We need to shout our victories from the housetops. You should have told those yellow journalists the province was secure. Security is a relative term, Colonel. We can stretch it a little, for the sake of the mission."

"I understand, sir."

"The war is going well?" Joanna said.

"We've taken the momentum away from them," General Hamburger said. "It's only a question of time and training now."

Standing there in the reception room of MACV's headquarters on her second day in Saigon, surrounded by these confident men in their crisp khakis, with rows of battle ribbons and decorations on their chests, Joanna gratefully accepted their optimism. Why shouldn't she? It was what she wanted to hear. Although her husband had been in Vietnam for almost a year, it was not a real war to her, any more than it was to most Americans. Pete's letters left her with the impression that the Vietnamese were doing all the fighting. Nothing she heard that day at MACV altered this idea. She went back to her apartment in a celebratory mood, ready, even willing, to tolerate Saigon's atrocious heat and humidity, the ancient plumbing, the strange insects that crawled everywhere. She was in Vietnam to prove to herself and to her husband that her renewed commitment to him and to the Army was no accident. Joanna wanted to be among those Americans who were ready to bear any burden, meet any hardship, support any friend in the name of liberty.

The following day, Joanna thought this commitment would be deepened by a ceremony at the Gia Long Palace on Saigon's main boulevard, Tu Do Street. As they inched through the traffic, Pete translated the Vietnamese names for her. "Gia Long means independence. Tu Do means freedom. These people know what they're fighting for."

Joanna was puzzled by his defensive tone. It struck her as a minimum expectation, that the South Vietnamese knew why they were fighting. At that precise moment, however, she was more concerned with suffocating. With the windows closed, the cab was a sauna on wheels. She started to put down the window on her side.

Pete stopped her. "Always keep the windows closed," he said. "That way you never have to worry about a hand grenade landing in your lap."

In the vast main hall of Gia Long Palace, beneath a thirty-foot-high ceiling studded with whirling fans, some two dozen Vietnamese Army officers, white-suited civilian officials and journalists in their usual motley garb chatted and sipped champagne dispensed by circling waiters. A small stocky officer and a tiny strikingly beautiful woman detached themselves from the group and walked toward the Burkes. The woman was wearing a white silk ao-dai, the traditional Vietnamese costume, which consisted of a high-necked ankle-length tunic, slit to the waist, and loose silk trousers. In a moment Joanna was meeting Major General Dat Le Bu, with whom Pete had worked as an adviser in Quang Ngai Province, and his wife, Thui. The general pumped Pete's hand and said something jovial in Vietnamese, to which Pete replied. Thui stood on tiptoes to kiss Pete on both cheeks in the French style and turned to Joanna. "You have the bravest husband in Vietnam," she said. "Perhaps in the world."

"Thank you," Joanna said.

Another Vietnamese officer rushed up to them. "Excuse me, General—Colonel—the President is arriving," he said. "Will you follow me?"

Everyone put down their champagne glasses and proceeded to the far end of the hall, where several rows of chairs awaited them. Joanna and Thui were seated in the first row. Pete and the general stood in front of the audience. Ngo Dinh Diem, the President of the Republic of South Vietnam, entered through a nearby side door. Pete had explained to Joanna that Americans called him Diem (pronounced Zee-yem) although it was actually his first name. Vietnamese names were reversed. President Diem was a squat somber little man of about fifty who walked in an odd flat-footed way, his toes pointing out, like a penguin. With him came a slimmer, younger Vietnamese man and a still younger woman. Unlike Thui, who used almost no makeup and wore her hair in a simple black fall, caught by a silver clasp, this woman strove for effect. Her hair was an intricately piled coif, with delicate bangs on the forehead. Her makeup was excessive; cheeks rouged, lips crimson, amazingly long nails with shocking-pink polish. She had several rings on her fingers and a gold bracelet on each wrist. Her ao-dai was a dramatic purple.

"Who is she?"

"That is Madame Ngo, wife of the President's brother, Ngo Dinh Nhu, who is there beside her. He is the President's counselor and strong right arm," Thui said. "We women like to think Madame Ngo—most Americans call her Madame Nhu—is his strong left arm. She heads our Women's Solidarity League."

While TV cameras whirred, the President pinned the National Order, a medal for heroism, on Lieutenant Colonel Burke and General Dat. The President then let his brother take charge of the ceremony. Counselor Nhu made a speech in which he declared that the victory in Quang Ngai was proof that Vietnamese could work with Americans and retain their dignity by sharing a common bravery. He said this not once, but about a dozen times in various ways, with frequent references to abstractions such as equality and power, the state and the nation, the people, the masses, morality, responsibility, human rights. He closed with an attack on the atheism of the Communists that sounded like several sermons Joanna had heard at Mass in the mid-1950s.

The speech lasted forty-five minutes. Joanna hoped the ceremony was over. She had not yet adjusted to Saigon's humidity and felt exhausted, even though it was only about 11 A.M. But Madame Nhu now stepped to the microphone. She also spoke in English for the benefit of the TV cameras. She said that she too was proud of the victory in Quang Ngai. She agreed that Lieutenant Colonel Burke and General Dat deserved their medals. But there was another person in the room who deserved a medal too. "Madame Dat," she said. "Would you come here?"

Thui walked to the microphone. "You see here a valiant woman, who served beside her husband in spite of repeated Communist attempts to assassinate her and her children," Madame Nhu said. "She helped organize the Women's Solidarity League of Quang Ngai. She is in the great tradition of the women of Vietnam, the tradition of the Truong sisters, who drove out the Chinese invaders in an earlier century."

While Thui stood with humbly lowered eyes beside her, Madame

421

Nhu gave a thirty-minute speech on the importance of Vietnamese women in the struggle against Communism. She discussed the relationship between freedom and morality. One could not exist without the other, she declared. That was why she fought the Communists. The women of Vietnam believed in God and they would never accept an atheistic immoral tyranny. Joanna felt her brain glaze as more abstractions clogged the hot thick air.

Madame Nhu finally finished and the waiters returned with more champagne. Joanna joined Pete as President Diem told him how much he admired West Point. "Along with your military skills, you must try to impart your moral code to our Army," he said. "Duty, honor, country, they are great ideals."

"Have you visited the Military Academy, sir?" Pete asked.

"Only as a tourist, when I was a refugee from the Communists in the early fifties. I lived in a monastery in the Hudson River valley. I sometimes wish I were back there, with nothing to do but pray for my country."

Pete had told Joanna the President was a Catholic. He looked so Oriental it seemed natural to ask him if he had become a convert during his American visit. He shook his head. "My family has been Catholic for over two hundred years here in Vietnam." He smiled in a weary way. "That is, if I recall my history, longer than the United States has been a country. Yet some of your embassy officials tell me Catholicism is foreign to Vietnam and I have too many Catholics in my government. When I visited West Point I noticed that the Protestant chapel is much larger and more expensive than the Catholic chapel. Do Catholic cadets feel discrimination in this?"

"No, sir," Pete said. He was having trouble trying to follow the President's line of thought.

"Sometimes I think I will never understand America," President Diem said. "It is the Protestant mentality, with its indifference to history, tradition. Some of your embassy officials seem to think that the Marxist-Leninism of the Communists is more native to Vietnam than Catholicism. Why is that Russian creed not exposed in your newspapers as a foreign faith?"

Joanna found Diem's mixture of plaintive resignation and sarcasm somewhat unnerving. She was glad to let Pete answer him. "We have no control over our newspapers, Mr. President," he said.

"Ah yes. That is the great pity."

Counselor Nhu took the President by the arm and drew him and Pete into a conversation with General Dat. Madame Nhu and Thui Dat gravitated to Joanna. "I understand you have just arrived in Vietnam," Madame Nhu said.

"The day before yesterday."

"I hope you will not develop nervous symptoms like so many of your countrywomen."

"I'm sorry—I don't know what you mean."

"They hear a single terrorist bomb and they cry hysterically and take the first plane home. We are engaged in a struggle to the death here."

"I'll—try to be brave," Joanna said, starting to resent the superior tone in which she was being lectured.

Madame Nhu launched into a vehement monologue on American morals. Spiritual superiority was a necessity in the war with Communism and she was worried because Americans seemed to lack it. They sneered at her for banning lascivious dances such as the Twist. She was interrupted by her husband, who informed her that the President was leaving. Hands were shaken, polite phrases exchanged, and the leaders of South Vietnam departed. Most of the Vietnamese Army officers and officials stayed, drinking champagne and chatting with each other or the reporters.

General Dat said something to Pete in Vietnamese. It sounded sarcastic. Pete shook his head and made a helpless, palms-up gesture. Thui Dat explained to Joanna that Counselor Nhu had just told her husband that he was being transferred to Hue, capital of Thua Thien Province. She was pleased, because it was her birthplace. Her parents still lived there. "I hope you and Colonel Burke will come visit us," she said. "It is an interesting and historic city."

They parted with warm expressions of friendship. On the way home in the cab, Pete looked unhappy. Joanna asked him what was wrong. "Transferring Dat," he said. "It's a mistake. He was just getting to know his troops. Diem and Nhu have to learn to let the Army alone."

"It would also help if they gave shorter speeches," Joanna said.

"Listen, they've got enough people criticizing them. Don't you start."

"Do we have to like everything about them, just because they're against Communism?"

"They're in a lot of trouble. They need all the help they can get."

The words stirred an uneasy memory of Adam's ironic smile as he said the same thing in Hawaii.

A month later, Joanna watched a tan Army bus pull away from her apartment-house door. The bus's windows were covered with wire mesh to deflect hand grenades. In the front sat a military policeman wearing a flak jacket, an M-16 automatic rifle at his side. Near him sat a nurse. A familiar face was dimly visible, grinning from the rear window; her son, Tom. He was on his way to the American School at Tan Son Nhut Air Base, where armed guards would escort him and his fellow pupils into a classroom with more wire mesh on the windows and sandbags around the outer walls to protect them against heavier explosions. Tom, who, like most twelve-year-olds, considered himself indestructible, loved all aspects of these military precautions. Joanna found it harder and harder to look at that school bus without a quiver of apprehension.

By now Joanna knew that terrorism—or its threat—was an everyday reality for Americans in Vietnam. Time bombs had been planted in American jeeps. Grenades had been flung at Americans in taxicabs, and at the American Ambassador in his limousine. An American sergeant had been ambushed and killed on the outskirts of Saigon on Christmas Day. A civilian employee of the U. S. Embassy had been assassinated while vacationing at the seaside resort of Cap St. Jacques. Few if any American families enjoyed the lawns and gardens of their villas. It was too easy for a terrorist on a motorbike to flip a grenade over their walls.

All of which made Joanna grateful to be living in an apartment, even if it was at the intersection of Le Van Duyet and Phan Dinh Phung streets, one of the busiest corners in Saigon. Broad Le Van Duyet Street was constantly jammed with Saigon's usual mixture of

American cars, Renault taxis, motorbikes and motor scooters, bicycles and pedicabs.

Joanna slowly climbed the dark stairway to her fourth-floor apartment, inhaling the acrid mixture of French coffee and cigarettes left by its former inhabitants and the odors of American cooking contributed by its present tenants. On the first floor, a phonograph was playing "I Wanna Hold Your Hand"; on the second floor a woman's voice was caroling: "What a friend we have in Jesus." There were many different kinds of Americans living in Saigon, and a fair cross section of them was in this apartment building.

By the time Joanna reached the fourth floor, the mushy humidity of Saigon had her gasping like an old lady of seventy. In the kitchen of her apartment, Mrs. Truc her mamma-san, or amah, as they were called in Vietnam, was feeding three-year-old Cissie her breakfast. Mrs. Truc's face was as wrinkled and brown as the dried mud on Pete's combat boots when he returned from a trip to the Mekong Delta, south of Saigon. Only Cissie could make Mrs. Truc smile. Her husband had divorced her and married a Communist in 1945. He now lived and worked in North Vietnam and had another family by his second wife, who was related to prominent Communists.

"Mommy, I have to go," Cissie said in her high chair.

"Cau tieu, cau tieu," Joanna said to Mrs. Truc in her pidgin Vietnamese. Mrs. Truc seized Cissie and hustled her into the bathroom. When they returned, Mrs. Truc said that was the third time this morning. Joanna gave Cissie a teaspoonful of polymagma, the drug of choice for Saigon tummy. She took one herself for good measure. Americans in Vietnam depended on polymagma to save them from endless embarrassments.

Moisture oozed from the kitchen walls. Part of it was the Saigon humidity. More came from the big pot of water perpetually boiling on the stove. Any American who drank Saigon's water unboiled was inviting amoebic dysentery. Joanna washed down the polymagma with a glass of sterilized water which she poured from a gallon-sized vodka bottle, a favorite American storage vessel. She stood beneath the big-bladed ceiling fan, which the Americans called Casablancas, and tried to get a breath of semi-cool air.

A knock on the door. Karen Lindstrom stepped into the room like a vision of America. Her milky skin and shining blond hair, her sweet smiling mouth, proclaimed innocence, Eden. She had a blond three-year-old in her arms, completing the picture of an American Protestant madonna. Karen and her husband, Bruce, who were United Church of Christ missionaries, lived directly beneath the Burkes on the second floor. They were from Minnesota and were frankly bewildered by Vietnam.

"Jo," Karen said, "would you mind watching Donny while I go down to the city hall and try to get a permit to open our church?"

"Not at all. Cissie would love the company," Joanna said.

"Jesus is trying to tell us something, but I don't know what it is," Karen said, setting Donny down on the floor. "We've been here two whole months and we still can't get permission to give a service. The Embassy people say it's because we won't pay bribes."

Joanna nodded sympathetically. "Pete tells me it's a bad habit left over from the French colonial days. Most officials expect something under the table. He says it reminds him of New Jersey."

"We don't do that sort of thing in Minnesota," Karen said.

Privately, Joanna thought the Lindstroms (Bruce was also blond, tall and noble, a perfect Protestant Jesus) were rather ridiculous, trying to bring their simple-minded version of Christianity to a land where far older faiths had been flourishing for centuries. But the Lindstroms' undeniable goodness, their eagerness to help Saigon's numerous poor, made up for their deficiencies, which included a tendency to mention Jesus in every second sentence.

Joanna let Mrs. Truc take charge of Donny Lindstrom and confronted a pile of unanswered letters. Beside the mail were fifty pages of her unfinished thesis on William Carlos Williams, all that she needed to complete to get her Master's degree in English literature from the University of Hawaii. She decided the mail was more important.

From the top of the pile Joanna took a letter from Honor. Adam was back teaching at the Special Forces School at Fort Bragg. Honor loved the place. She was still on tranquilizers but otherwise she felt good. *No problems*, she wrote, underlining it. Joanna hoped she was right. From the last letter Adam had written to her and Pete, Joanna saw numerous problems, more military than marital. But she had begun to wonder if these two things were really divisible in Army marriages.

Adam's experience in Laos had only reinforced his ideas about how to fight the Communists in Indochina. He told a reporter at Fort Bragg that the Army should quintuple the Special Forces program and completely retrain the South Vietnamese Army as a counterinsurgency team. He mocked the American regular Army advisers now flooding into Vietnam, claiming they were only training the Vietnamese to repeat the blunders of the French. The Pentagon brass, who did not like the Special Forces in the first place, had been incensed, and Adam's commander had ordered him not to say another word to reporters without official permission. Adam was fuming over the reprimand and over the Army's refusal to make the Special Forces more than a "publicity operation," a military sideshow. Pete shook his head and reiterated his opinion that Adam had made a grave mistake, joining the Green Berets.

Joanna did not have the military expertise to evaluate Adam's proposal. But by now she knew enough to suspect that some of the Pentagon's wrath emanated from a resolve to silence any officer who dared to suggest that the war in Vietnam was not going well. Her first intimation of this unpleasant truth had been the ceremony at the Gia Long Palace. Far stronger hints of trouble emerged from a lunch at the Caravelle Hotel with Amy Rosser and her friend Florence Eberle, whose husband was G-1 at MACV. Amy dropped this fact into the invitation as if it guaranteed Joanna's acceptance. She had to make an effort to remember that G-1 was personnel and important on any staff. The man in charge of assignments.

The restaurant on top of the Caravelle was a glass-walled, glossily modern affair, with spectacular views of the sprawling city. From above, Saigon looked like a huge village; the green shade trees lining the boulevards and avenues created a rustic impression. Only when you remembered the traffic clogging the streets, the crowds swarming on the sidewalks beneath the greenery, did the real Saigon return.

"It's spectacular up here at night," Amy said. "You can see the flares and Willy Peters—the white phosphorus shells—being fired by troops on the outskirts of the city. When they spot a VC they open up with bright red tracer bullets from all directions.''

Joanna nodded. ''We can see the show from our apartment. My twelve-year-old would-be paratrooper stays up half the night watching for it.''

Amy asked about Honor. She had heard rumors of trouble in Hawaii. Joanna told her as little as possible. She called it a ''mild'' nervous breakdown. Amy tsk-tsked over the damage to Adam's career. Joanna had avoided talking to Adam about that during the few hours she had seen him in Hawaii. She had concentrated on telling him how sick Honor had been, how much she needed tender loving care.

''Sam Hardin just finished a tour out here as an adviser in the Delta,'' Amy said. ''He had the most beautiful Vietnamese mistress you've ever seen. There's an awful lot of that going on over here. These Vietnamese women are incredibly attractive, don't you think? I wouldn't let George Rosser over here for ten minutes by himself.''

Joanna nodded mechanically, thinking that was one worry Pete had never caused her.

''I see where Martha Kinsolving's father just retired. Do you keep in touch with her?''

''Yes.''

Amy nodded approvingly. ''A general's daughter knows *so* many people.''

The conversational direction changed when Florence Eberle arrived. A tall, hard-eyed, no-nonsense type, Mrs. Eberle plunged them into Saigon politics. She had just spent an hour with Madame Nhu, who was in a kind of permanent tantrum over the way American reporters were ''slandering'' President Diem and her husband, Counselor Nhu. Since the Army and the U. S. Embassy refused to silence them, she seemed to think it was the responsibility of the American wives to change their minds by ''constructive argument.''

''A waste of time,'' Amy said. ''Nothing is going to change those wise guys. They're all Communist sympathizers. We've just got to win the war and make them eat their words.''

428

"*All* of them are Communist sympathizers?" Joanna said.

"Amy doesn't mean the old hands, the people you'll meet at General Hamburger's parties," Florence Eberle said. "She means the young smart-aleck types from *The New York Times* and those kinds of newspapers. Left-wing, Jewish-controlled. So smart they think it's patriotic to sympathize with the Viet Cong."

Joanna was intrigued. She found herself wanting to meet someone with such an outrageous opinion. He sounded like he would make Adam seem tame.

"We need people young enough to talk to these smart alecks," Florence Eberle said. "And you're literary. Amy tells me you write poetry."

"Occasionally," Joanna said. She had not finished a poem since Pete left for Vietnam a year ago. Ironic, when she theoretically had had all the time she could possibly want, a war had erupted between the secret self who wrote the poems and the public Joanna, the Army wife who had renewed her commitment to her soldier husband in that kitchen on Mo Ka Lei. She knew—or half knew—she had fled to the University of Hawaii, to the study of other poets, as an escape, even when she told herself she was trying to free her blocked imagination.

"Is there any truth to what the reporters are saying?" Joanna asked. "In private, Pete sounds discouraged sometimes."

"He shouldn't talk that way even to you," Florence Eberle said. "Now that he's here in Saigon, he has to get on the team and stay on it. So do you. The President and his brother need our help. They—and we—are surrounded by enemies. Half their generals are scheming politicians—"

Before Florence Eberle finished, she had damned practically everyone in South Vietnam except Diem's family and the staff of MACV. Even the American advisers in the field were "irresponsible" about the way they talked to reporters. They also let the South Vietnamese colonels and generals "poison their minds" against the Ngos.

Above all, Florence Eberle praised Madame Nhu. She orated on her leadership, on the power of her Women's Solidarity Movement and her other creation, the Women's Paramilitary Corps. At the

429

National Day military parade in October, a thousand uniformed girls, armed with carbines and submachine guns, had marched "magnificently" past the reviewing stand.

"Will they be used in combat?" Joanna asked.

"Why not? The Viet Cong use women," Florence said.

Joanna began to suspect that Madame Nhu awakened something personal, an unspoken wish, in Florence Eberle, and perhaps in Amy too, from the fervent way Amy agreed with her. Madame Nhu was exercising public power, not manipulating it behind the scenes, as the Army forced politician wives like Amy and Florence to do.

That night, the Lindstroms gave a party to welcome Joanna and Pete to Saigon. The other dwellers in their vertical American village came to shake hands and drink the punch—one bowl spiked, the other unspiked—which the missionaries (who drank the unspiked) supplied in endless quantities. Pouring himself a large glass from the spiked bowl as Joanna approached it was a tall blond-haired reporter with a narrow acne-pitted face she remembered from Pete's promotion ceremony.

"How does it feel to be brainwashed?" he asked.

"I wouldn't know," Joanna said.

"I saw you getting the party line from Mrs. Eberle, Madame Nhu's keeper, at the Caravelle today. Didn't she tell you all the reporters in Saigon were Commie finks?"

"Only about ninety percent," Joanna said.

He grinned approvingly. "I bet I was near the head of the condemned list. Carl Springer, defamer of President Diem."

"I don't think you were even mentioned. But I'll be glad to see what I can do about getting you on the list. What time would you like the firing squad to call?"

"Hey, you're a live one. I didn't think the colonel would have a wife like you. I thought you'd be as straight-arrow as he is."

"He lets me handle the curves," Joanna said.

"I'm not putting Pete down," Springer said, raising his glass. "I'll drink to him. He's the best damn soldier I've seen in Vietnam. I spent two weeks in Quang Ngai with him. You know what that means?"

Joanna shook her head. "He never tells me the grisly details."

430

"They were the hairiest two weeks of my life. I drove the back roads with him at all hours of the night. He did that all the time to show the locals that the dark didn't belong to Victor Charlie. We stayed overnight in villages that had been creamed by the VC the previous night, where morale was zero. I flew with him on operations with the ARVN. The sight of Pete, a major, amazed the troops. No officer in the ARVN above the rank of captain ever goes into the field. The little guys were even more amazed when Pete spoke to them in their own language. That's something only about ten percent of our advisers can do.

"I sweated out a half dozen contacts with him in those two weeks. I've never seen anyone like him under fire. There's no fear in the man. He communicates it to the troops, somehow. I don't pretend to understand it. But I saw what those little guys did for him. He made them think they were as big as he is. Whenever the VC found out he was in command, they just got the hell out of there.

"When I got back to Saigon, it took me two days to stop shaking. That's what two weeks with him did to my nerves. He lived that way for nine months. It paid off. He made the 25th Division into a fighting outfit. He turned Quang Ngai from a VC recreation zone into a contested province. But what happens, after the division wins their first serious victory? Diem transfers General Dat to a meaningless staff job in Hue. According to the grapevine, the Penguin was actually displeased with the win because the division's casualties were too heavy. Diem is a total ignoramus about warfare. He thinks the score should always be a thousand to nothing in the ARVN's favor or someone's goofed. Some people say he's not quite that dumb, he just acts that way because he's afraid to let any general get too famous. He knows the people are looking for someone—anyone—to replace him and his two-faced brother and weirdo sister-in-law and their little circle of Holy Roman fanatics."

Springer told Joanna about an interview he had had with President Diem. It had lasted six and a half hours. The man had droned on about everything from the meteorology of Vietnam to the problem of eliminating the turnip bug. Such interviews were not unusual. A two-and-a-half-hour session with Diem was considered a quickie. As a result, papers were piled two feet high on his desk, waiting for his decision. The man had spent most of his life as a meditating monk, a scholar. He was the worst possible choice to lead a nation fighting for its life.

Carl Springer was about twenty-five years old. He wore his blond hair in a boyish cowlick down his forehead, and fussed at it continually as he talked. He made Joanna feel matronly. "Carl," she said, "I know how you feel. I felt the same way in the early days of Korea. You barely remember that war, I suppose. The Americans were routed at first. It was a nightmare. But we pulled ourselves together and—"

Springer shook his head angrily. "Pete tried to sell me that idea already. This isn't Korea. It's Vietnam."

He was so sure of himself, so proud of his negative case. "Do you think there's any hope?" she said.

"Not until we get rid of Diem."

"You seem so *pleased* by it all," Joanna said. "Why?"

"I'm not pleased," Springer said. "I'm mad. Mad as hell. It infuriates me to see men like Pete risking their lives for the wrong reason."

"But he thinks it's the right reason."

"No, he doesn't. He's seen enough in Quang Ngai to change his mind. Ask him. He knows the Communists are the Vietnamese patriots, and our guys are left-over French puppets."

Pete sauntered over as Springer delivered this final denunciation. "What's this guy doing?" he said. "Still handing out the Viet Cong's line?"

"He says the ARVN are all puppets."

"The French gave them a Maginot complex, that's true. But they're not political puppets."

"The Viet Cong may have a line. But so does MACV," said a voice on their left.

Pete introduced Joanna to Tony Emerson, a dark-haired Buddha-shaped State Department career officer. He was soon joined by his wife, Clara, who matched him in girth. Neither was a jolly fat person; at least, not that night. They were in an even worse mood about Vietnam than Carl Springer. When Pete denied that MACV had a party line, Emerson tapped impatiently on his glass and said:

"No, they've got a program. A brainwashing program. They give every politician who comes out here the treatment. They all go away calling Ngo Dinh Diem the Winston Churchill of Asia."

Wilson and Isabel Canty joined the fray. She was small and gaunt, with wispy hair that kept straying off her head. He was also short, with a dead-white, cadaverous face, full of hollows topped by deep-socketed, luminous eyes. Canty was with the Agency for International Development. They nodded agreement while Tony Emerson denounced the government of Ngo Dinh Diem. It was a dictatorship, he said, practically indistinguishable from the Communist dictatorship in the North. Wilson Canty talked disparagingly of Counselor Nhu, with whom he was working on a program to resettle tens of thousands of Vietnamese in fortified hamlets. "I don't trust him," he said. "You can't pin him down. Everything is always tomorrow, tomorrow, he has to talk to the President but the President is meditating or some goddamn thing."

Isabel Canty said she could not stand Madame Nhu. "If that woman gives me one more lecture, I'll start screaming," she said. She sneered at Madame Nhu's attempts to reform Saigon. "Why doesn't she or her husband do something about the terrorists? Isn't he head of the secret police?"

A nerve began twitching in Isabel Canty's cheek.

"That's one reason he isn't too popular," Pete said. "But he's doing a pretty good job. Terrorism is down about thirty percent in the last four months."

"One of my best friends had a grenade thrown into her villa's front yard last night," Isabel Canty said.

"North and South Vietnam could switch flags," Tony Emerson said, "and no one would know the difference."

"I don't agree," Pete said. "Diem isn't perfect, but we can win with him if we can get him to let the ARVN fight. I think he might have done that already if President Kennedy had approved our recommendation for forty thousand American troops to throw the Communists back on their heels for a couple of months."

"When are you people going to realize a military solution is not the answer?" Tony Emerson said.

433

The contempt in his voice made it clear that this had become a very serious discussion.

"We know it's not the whole solution, Tony," Pete said. "I spent half my time in Quang Ngai helping people to grow better rice, eradicate rats, raise pigs. But you've got to protect people when the other guys are ready to kill them if they side with us. All the political and economic solutions in the world won't do you any good if the VC can come into a village in the middle of the night and chop off the schoolteacher's head and disembowel his wife and children. They did that in a half dozen villages when I first went to Quang Ngai."

The civilians all stood there, shaking their heads. Pete was wasting his breath. They had their own solution to the dilemma of Vietnam. More democracy, more freedom. They all but hooted Pete out of the room when he said Vietnam was a primitive country and the average peasant wanted strong leadership, not democracy. He lost them completely when he tried to defend Madama Nhu, arguing that Saigon was a corrupt city that needed moral reform.

"You call banning the Twist moral reform?" Clara Emerson asked.

"From what I hear she's slept with every general in the Army. The ones who refuse her are ruined," Isabel Canty said.

"That's what I hear happened to your friend Dat," Carl Springer said.

"I don't believe those rumors," Pete said. "She's a devout Catholic. She's got four children."

The Lindstroms listened, wide-eyed and confused. The missionaries instinctively sided with Pete. They thoroughly agreed that Vietnam needed moral reform. The other civilians, sophisticates all, were unimpressed by Pete's earnestness. They saw it as thickheaded military stubbornness. Joanna suspected most of them even took his courage for granted. Only Carl Springer, who had driven the midnight roads and flown in the fragile helicopters with him, knew what the Army was asking its officers to do in Vietnam. But Carl was equally contemptuous of Pete's political opinions.

"Sink or swim with Ngo Dinh Diem," Carl said. "That's the Army's motto."

"He isn't perfect," Pete said. "But he's a patriot."

More hoots. Pete smiled gamely. He was only a junior lieutenant colonel and these were the civilians, the people who decided how the Army fought its wars. Besides, they were all Americans. They all agreed on the fundamental point—that Communism had to be stopped in Vietnam, somehow. He let them have the last word.

The following night, Arnold Coulter invited them to dinner in his villa on Tu Do Street, not far from Saigon's red brick cathedral. Coulter had been in Saigon for over a year, as part of the huge CIA mission. He and Pete had already met several times. Joanna had found herself wishing there was some way she could evade the invitation. She did not want to think about Blanche Coulter now. She dreaded the possibility of a conversation about her death. To her relief, the general simply greeted her as an old comrade, in his cordial but somehow impersonal manner. She was disconcerted to discover he was wearing a brown toupee. It did not make him look younger. The creases in his face had become crevasses. But he still had his ageless daredevil's smile, which flicked on and off in a semiautomatic way as he introduced Joanna to the other guests. They had a bewildering variety of Vietnamese names, only one of which she was able to remember. It belonged to a small gentle-eyed woman who looked at least twenty years younger than Coulter. "This is my wife, Dieu," he said.

Pete looked surprised. "We've decided to make it legal," Coulter said to him.

The cocktail conversation was a mixture of French, English and Vietnamese. Pete tried to keep Joanna in touch with the Vietnamese parts and she caught fragments of the French. The Vietnamese were all opposed to Diem and his brother and spent most of the dinner denouncing them. Coulter was trying to find out from them if there was another South Vietnamese politician around whom the country could coalesce. They could not seem to agree on one. The women were as involved in the discussion as the men. Dieu, sensing that Joanna was being left out of the conversation, began asking her about her children, where she lived in the United States. The other women dropped politics and asked her if it was true what they had heard about American women's sexual freedom. Had it increased with the pill? Joanna found herself defending the virtue of her countrywomen. She got the impression that no one believed a word she said. Behind their deferential manners, these people had already drawn some harsh conclusions about Americans.

It was Joanna's first Vietnamese dinner. Pete had muttered something rueful about Coulter's habit of eating the food of the country. But Pete had said nothing about *nuoc mam,* an incredibly pungent fermented sauce made of drippings from sun-ripened fish. The Vietnamese put gobs of it on their rice, and used it as a dip for almost everything else they ate. The main course was roast chicken, chopped into small pieces, bones and all. Another course, obviously a delicacy, was hard-boiled duck eggs with embryos inside their blackish yolks. Joanna ate it all, dreading the intestinal aftereffects. In some ways it was harder to watch Pete, the devotee of American food, gamely gulping it down, including the *nuoc mam.*

After the Vietnamese departed, Arnold Coulter led Dieu, Pete and Joanna into a small sitting room and served an excellent French brandy. "I think you convinced a few people tonight, Pete," he said.

"Would someone kindly tell me what he was saying?" Joanna said. Pete's halting Vietnamese had not seemed very impressive to her.

"He was telling them that the lower ranks in the Army like Diem. It would be very dangerous to change the government now. He was urging them to put pressure on Diem to let the Army fight harder, to take the offensive against the Communists."

So the CIA was using Pete too, trying to shore up the Diem government. Coulter explained the purpose of the dinner. It was useful to let these people complain about Diem. They let off steam and then realized there was no alternative to him. In a paradoxical way, it put pressure on the President to change his policy toward the Army and also to broaden his government. At least one of the people at the dinner was secretly working for Diem and would report the meeting.

Coulter smiled wearily. "Asian politics is loaded with intrigue, and just between you and me old Arnie's getting a bellyful of it here in Saigon."

He discussed American politics in a much less resigned tone. There was a group within the Kennedy State Department who thought that Diem should be eliminated one way or another. Their attitude was echoed by a substantial number of people working in the U. S. Embassy. The CIA and the Army were trying hard to prevent this idea from gaining momentum. Unfortunately, most of the Saigon press corps favored the State Department solution. "It's an insane idea," Coulter said. "As insane as it would have been to dump Syngman Rhee during the Korean War, although we knew he was an irascible old son of a bitch. We built him into a symbol of Korean patriotism. We've got to do the same thing with Diem. There just isn't anyone else around."

"He is a good man, narrow but good," Coulter's wife, Dieu, said. "And brave. Ho Chi Minh captured him during the war with the French and tried to persuade him to join the revolutionary government. Diem refused. They argued and then Diem said: 'I think I will go now,' and just walked out. Ho did not dare to touch him. My first husband was working for Ho at the time. Diem's courage won his admiration and when Diem returned to Vietnam in 1954, my husband changed his allegiance to him."

"And Ho promptly murdered him," Coulter said.

Arnold Coulter told how the Communists had killed Dieu's husband and her five-year-old son in a machine-gun attack on their car. Dieu herself had been badly wounded. Her husband had been chief of Quang Tri Province, which borders North Vietnam.

"Ho's convinced that Communism grows from the point of a gun," Coulter said. "We've got to show him that a gun shoots both ways. That's why we need guys like Pete around."

Joanna smiled, accepting the compliment. She was remembering what Carl Springer had said about Pete's readiness to take repeated risks. She simply could not accept his soldier's fatalism about exposing himself to danger. She could not stop thinking about it as luck, a quantitative idea. Sooner or later luck ran out. The law of averages demanded its murderous toll.

Pete did not feel that way. Speaking confidentially to Coulter, his Army father, he said he wished he were back in Quang Ngai getting shot at. He did not like his current assignment at MACV. He thought he had been brought to Saigon to help plan major operations against the Viet Cong. It was a logical conclusion for a graduate of the Command and General Staff School. Instead, he had been assigned to General Hamburger's section and spent most of his time shepherding reporters around the country. MACV apparently thought they could still get some mileage out of the man who had won the big victory at Quang Ngai. But the war was not going so well in most other provinces. Pete was told to try to prevent his newsmen from seeing "negative material." This was virtually impossible. Pete had no control over how well or badly the ARVN fought in a specific operation. Nor could he predict what the Viet Cong were going to do. He was in a constant sweat that had nothing to do with the Saigon humidity. Hamburger had made him feel that if a reporter wrote a negative story, it was Pete's fault.

"Hamburger's an idiot," Coulter said.

"The trouble is, he'll write my efficiency report," Pete said.

Coulter shrugged. "Everyone who counts knows Henry is a birdbrain," he said.

Pete looked unhappy. On the way back to their apartment, he sighed and said, "I'm afraid the general's getting out of touch with the Army. He doesn't appreciate what one bad OER can do."

"What can it do?"

Pete stared gloomily from the taxi's back seat at the floodlit presidential palace. "Ruin your career."

"Why?"

"They're all inflated. You don't give a guy anything less than the highest rating, unless you want to ruin him. I rated Ben Shaughnessy at Quang Ngai. He's not the worst captain in the Army but he's sure as hell not the best. He's a good guy in a fight but he's careless, maybe a little lazy, about doing the whole job. I gave him a three—in the middle—on desirability. They sent it back from MACV and asked me if I was trying to run him out of the Army. So I gave him a five."

"It's crazy," Joanna said. "How could the Army let something like that get so out of control?"

"I don't know. It's just human nature, I guess. The Army's so big, the people in personnel, the generals who sit on the promotion boards for the higher ranks, don't know anyone personally. They don't ask whether the guy who wrote the report is an idiot. If it's a bad report, you're finished. Especially a guy at my grade.''

Joanna was amazed to discover that all the signs of favor and approval Pete had received so far, his decorations, his early promotions, meant so little. If anything, he seemed to feel more defensive, more vulnerable.

A week later, she saw in cruel detail what this implied. Pete escorted a *Look* magazine reporter named Harlan Kane to his old province, Quang Ngai. They stayed two days. Pete returned to their apartment on the evening of the second day, looking extraordinarily glum.

"What's wrong?" Joanna asked.

"The VC ambushed a 25th Division patrol. They killed Ben Shaughnessy."

"Oh, Pete."

"He tried to rally the company. The bastards all ran away except one guy. He died beside Ben."

Joanna remembered Ben Shaughnessy talking to Pete on the porch at Mo Ka Lel about whether he should stay in the Army or get out. She was sure Pete had had a lot to do with his decision to stay. She threw her arms around her husband. "You must feel awful," she said.

"Yeah," he said. "That *Look* reporter, Harlan Kane, is coming over after dinner. I've got to work on him. Can you keep the kids out of the way?"

"I'll try," Joanna said.

Harlan Kane was a stocky pop-eyed young man wearing a black handlebar mustache that he probably hoped would make him look older. Pete shook his hand, thanked him for coming over and introduced him to Joanna. She left them as Pete poured hefty drinks and began explaining the situation in Quang Ngai. "If you see the big picture, Harlan, I don't think you'll overstate the importance of that ambush."

"Now wait a sec, Pete. They wiped out a whole damn company."

"I know—but two weeks ago the VC lost a whole company in—"

Three-year-old Cissie could not understand why Daddy was

unavailable for her evening's entertainment. Tom kept prying open the door to the living room so he could listen to the military details. Joanna furiously ordered him to do his homework. She realized half her anger was caused by the thought that her husband was required to explain away an American defeat to this brash young stranger. A defeat in which one of his friends had died. Why did duty-honor-country require the man whom Carl Springer called the best soldier in Vietnam to become a wheedler?

The next morning, Pete got a call from MACV before he left the apartment. He hung up and told Joanna to put on a good dress. They were going to the airport for a memorial service for Ben Shaughnessy. On the first floor, they met Carl Springer emerging from his apartment. He eyed Joanna's dark blue linen dress and asked: "Where are you going so gussied up at nine o'clock in the morning?"

"Out to the airport to see a friend of ours off for home," Pete said.

They saw Ben Shaughnessy off for home. A chaplain said a nondenominational prayer over the flag-draped coffin in a bare room next to the American morgue. The Burkes were the only mourners. Enlisted men carried the coffin outside, where an honor guard of Vietnamese rangers wearing red berets came to attention. An oily-looking Vietnamese staff officer read a statement, declaring that Ben's death was "of untold grief to his Vietnamese comrades-in-arms." The officer's flat, emotionless voice subtracted all meaning from the words. He took a medal from a maroon velvet pillow held by a soldier beside him and pinned it to the American flag. Joanna thought of Ben putting on a makeshift grass skirt at one of their parties on the beach at Mo Ka Lei and doing an absurd hula.

"I wish I could believe Lyle will shed some tears for him," Joanna said on the way back from the airport. She had told Pete about Lyle Shaughnessy's role in Honor's breakdown.

"Write her anyway," Pete said. "I'm going to write. It'll be something for her son to read when he gets older."

That night after supper, Carl Springer strode into their apartment in a surly mood. "I had lunch with Harlan Kane today," he said.

"He told me about the big black eye we got in Quang Ngai. Why didn't you tell me about it?"

"Carl, we're neighbors. But that doesn't mean I'm supposed to keep you informed of every skirmish in Vietnam."

"Skirmish, hell. The VC creamed half a regiment, Kane says. They killed Ben Shaughnessy."

"A company. They beat a company. A patrol, Carl."

"And killed Shaughnessy. Give it to me straight, Pete. Is Quang Ngai sliding right back into VC control? Jesus, Pete, this is my story. I spent two weeks with you up there, risking my ass. Why can't you level with me?"

"Carl, I am leveling with you. Calm down. Sit down. One dead captain, a company lost, doesn't mean the whole province is down the drain—"

Pete spent the next hour trying to convince Springer that the ambush was just a minor incident in the seesaw guerrilla war. Once more Joanna had to keep the children in their bedrooms in the rear of the apartment. She lay on the bed in her room reading a short history of Vietnam that she had found in the U. S. Information Agency library. The book gave her a modest grasp of the country's strange past. Its southern third had been ruled for centuries by the warlike Khmers of Cambodia and its central third by the Chams, who paid homage to the same Hindu gods. The northern third had been ruled by the Chinese. Then the French arrived in the eighteenth century and conquered—and incidentally united—the nation.

The front door slammed. Joanna threw aside the book and went into the living room. Pete was sitting in a wing chair with a drink in his hand, looking morose.

"I'm beginning to think you ought to ask for a reassignment," Joanna said.

Pete shook his head. "I've got to stick it out for a couple of more months, at least. If I made a move now, Hamburger would consider it a personal insult and write an OER that would keep me a lieutenant colonel for life."

He finished his drink and stared gloomily into the glass. "He may do it anyway if I run into a few more VC ambushes."

"I don't like the way we're fighting this war," Joanna said.

"I don't like it very much either," Pete said. "Unfortunately I don't have three or four stars on my shoulders, so I can't change it."

"What about duty-honor-country?" she said. "The idea that an officer tells the truth at all times?"

"I haven't told anyone a direct lie yet," Pete said. "I just avoid telling the whole truth."

Pete looked so miserable Joanna felt guilty about harassing him. "I'm sorry," she said. "I don't completely understand what's going on. You just seem so unhappy. I'm worried about you."

He smiled ruefully. "Thanks."

They spent the rest of the evening like most parents, Joanna helping Tom with his homework—for some reason, not one of the five schools he had attended so far had taught him how to spell— Pete reading to Cissie from *Winnie-the-Pooh*. The sight of the big soldier solemnly recounting the adventures of Christopher Robin and his friends to the blond-haired little girl in his lap was enough to make Joanna glad she had come to Vietnam.

Going to bed, Joanna felt amorous. She wanted to restore the sense of solidarity, union, she had threatened with her sharp questions. But Pete had Vietnam on his mind. He had decided to tell her the whole truth about the war, as he saw it. He spread a map of Indochina on their double bed. Somehow the sight of it there disturbed Joanna. But she did not object to it. She looked over his shoulder as he explained what was wrong with the grand strategy of the American defense of South Vietnam. "See how Laos runs along the western border? It gives the Communists a sanctuary to retreat into—and a road to supply their troops. We call it the Averell Harriman Highway. He negotiated a neutral Laos for us."

"But Adam said the Laotians wouldn't fight."

"I know. They make the Vietnamese look like tigers."

His finger continued down the map. "Along the Cambodian border, it's more of the same. A so-called neutral country loaded with rest areas, supply dumps for the VC."

"What's the answer?"

"Time. It's going to be a long, slow process. We're going to be out here ten years, with at least this many American troops in the country. We can win it, if Diem lets the ARVN fight. Man for man, they're just as brave as the VC, if they get the right kind of leadership. But it'll take ten years to develop a decent officer corps.''

"I don't like the idea of a ten-year war."

"I won't fight it alone. They'll rotate us in and out."

Joanna sat down on the bed beside him, thinking of Ben Shaughnessy's flag-covered coffin. "But is it worth winning? I mean—is it worth the deaths? You know what Adam said about Korea. Could it be true here?"

Pete glared at her the way he often glared at Adam after arguing with him for an hour. "Adam has delusions of grandeur. It isn't a lieutenant colonel's job to ask those kinds of questions. If the President, our commander-in-chief, tells us to fight out here, even to stand and die out here, that's what we're supposed to do. We're not supposed to ask whether it's worth it."

"I I guess not," Joanna said, retreating before his anger. "But why is there so much divisiveness? Why do reporters like Carl Springer say the people are against us?"

Pete got up, thrust his hands in his pockets and walked over to the window. He watched two or three flares rise into the sky on the outskirts of the city. "The educated people—like General Dat and Thui—most of them are with us. They realize the Communists want to destroy their religion, their freedom. But the peasants don't understand."

Two more flares rose and fell like dying souls. "That's the difference in this war," Pete said, watching the flares. "There isn't any battlefield. You've got to fight with civilians all around you. Most of them aren't on anyone's side. They just wish both sides would leave them alone. I feel sorry for them. Especially when we use napalm. I hated to go through a village after the planes hit it with napalm."

"Why are we doing that?"

"That's the way the ARVN—the South Vietnamese Army—likes to fight. Artillery, planes, helicopters. Everything but going after the

VC on the ground, where it really counts. We don't have any control over them, really. We give them the weapons and the advice. But most of the time they do it their way."

"That's crazy," Joanna said.

"It's not very bright," Pete said. "But we've got to let them make the decisions. Otherwise they really will just be our puppets. We've got to show them we're different from the French."

"Napalm," Joanna said. "You mean our planes—the ARVN's planes—whoever's flying them—drop napalm on villages with women and children—civilians—still there?"

"If it's a VC village and they stand and fight inside it." Pete was growing more and more morose. He folded up the map of South Vietnam. "It's an ugly goddamn war. Sometimes I think Adam and his Special Forces friends are right. We should never have given the ARVN tanks and artillery and planes. Just rifles and machine guns and mortars and the training to go into the jungle and get the other guys. But it's too late to take away the heavy stuff now. The ARVN depend on it. They'd panic without it."

Pete put the map of Vietnam in a bureau drawer. Joanna realized with dismay that she no longer felt amorous. She was profoundly disturbed by what she had just heard from her husband. This war was different. Suddenly she heard Carl Springer saying: *This isn't Korea. This is Vietnam.*

Two weeks later, the Burkes received a renewed invitation from General Dat and his wife to visit them in Hue. They flew up the following weekend in a Beaver, a small Army support plane that ferried personnel and reporters around Vietnam. General Dat's aide met them at the airport and drove them to a white stone villa within the walled citadel that comprised half of this beautiful city on the poetically named Perfume River. The general greeted them at the door with a cheerful "Hello. I am delighted to see you."

"And that is all the English he has learned," said his wife, Thui, who was looking even more beautiful than she had looked in Saigon. She was wearing an ao-dai with a pale blue tunic over white trousers. Her fall of dark hair shimmered in the sun.

The Dats had two children, almost exactly the same ages as Tom and Cissie. Their little girl, Sa, gravely welcomed Cissie to her nursery. Her amah, who looked like Mrs. Truc, took charge of both girls. The Dats' son, Le, had a spare bicycle waiting for Tom and they went racing off to explore Hue from a twelve-year-old point of view. The adults were free to enjoy themselves.

Thui, who had learned her English at a Catholic college in the Philippines, was Joanna's guide for a tour of Hue, the former capital of the Nguyen emperors who had ruled Vietnam with French backing in the nineteenth century. The Chinese culture of the North had triumphed in Hue. The imperial family and their enormous retinue had lived in the three-mile-square walled citadel. Joanna was awed by its spectacular palaces and pavilions, with their lacquered columns, doors painted with golden dragons, huge bronze urns flanking shallow stairs that led to gardens and pools. It was a magnificent imitation of the Forbidden City in Peking.

Joanna told Thui she was reading a history of Vietnam. Thui surprised her by looking downcast. "I fear it will not make you admire us," she said. "You Americans are so proud of your independence. We have been ruled by foreigners for almost two thousand years—Indians, Chinese, French. We are used to being a subject people."

The sadness shaded into bitterness with these last words. "Have you read the Italian Machiavelli? He wrote: 'Honor is impossible in a defeated country.' Your husband has no doubt come to tell my husband to side with the other generals in a coup to overthrow President Diem. I do not think he should do it. What do you think?"

Joanna was speechless. If this was the purpose of Pete's visit, he had not shared it with her. She was discovering the power of upperclass Vietnamese women, who often managed the money in their families and participated as equals in their husbands' politics. Thui talked frankly about Dat's career in the Army. He had risen to general largely through the influence of her family, which had long been friendly with President Diem's family. Both families were Catholics. Dat had converted from Buddhism when he married Thui. "Now I fear he is turning back to Buddhism. He is angry because the President has not given him a command. He sits in headquarters and shuffles papers. His family and the monks here in Hue tell him Diem favors the Catholics too much. They may be right but I think an officer should be loyal to the government that appoints him, don't you?''

Joanna agreed and added that she knew nothing about the purpose of Pete's visit. She had thought it was purely social. For a moment Thui looked disappointed. She obviously assumed Joanna was lying. They continued their tour of Hue, visiting the immense tombs of the emperors on the outskirts of the city and some of the numerous Buddhist pagodas, thronged with gray-robed monks and nuns and youthful novices. The sweetish smell of burning joss sticks filled the air. Aged scholars with wispy beards wandered past. The old men ignored the visitors, but Joanna noticed several of the younger monks glaring at them. Thui grew nervous and suggested they leave. The Buddhists were angry at the Catholics because of a dispute over the right to display the Buddhist flag. The government had banned it but recently allowed the Catholics to fly the Vatican flag while installing two bishops.

Joanna and Thui went home and drank tea from delicate blue porcelain cups in the small garden of the Dat villa. Thui showed Joanna her library, which included French and English novels and poetry. That night, Thui's father and mother, Mr. and Mrs. Nguyen Hong Binh, came to dinner. They were both smiling, sophisticated people who spoke fluent French but very little English. With Thui's help, they discussed American and Vietnamese politics. Mr. Nguyen had gone to Hue's Quoc Hoc High School with Ho Chi Minh in pre-World War I days.

The main course was bouillabaisse, not one of Joanna's favorite meals. But she ate it, discreetly avoiding the inevitable dishes of *nuoc mam*, which their hosts put on the rice and everything else. Mr. Nguyen declaimed on Hue as a city of peace and culture, indifferent to the power-hungry commissars of Hanoi and the greedy capitalists of Saigon.

Pete said he too admired the people of Hue. But there would be no freedom for their religion or culture if the Communists won the war. Mr. Nguyen said he did not think of it as a war. If the government was patient, and maintained its strength in the cities and heavily populated districts, the Communists would grow discouraged and their cadres would diminish. Eventually, the leaders would give up and join the government, or go back to Hanoi. Patience was the important thing. Americans were too impatient. They did not understand Vietnamese history, which was a long story of resistance, then accommodation to the government in power, if it lasted long enough. Mr. Nguyen knew many Communists. They were men of culture. They did not want to spend the rest of their lives in the jungle.

Pete kept shaking his head while Thui translated this lecture from French into English. He raised his wineglass and said he did not agree, but he was still prepared to drink to the people of Hue. Joanna could see that Mr. Nguyen was offended by this gesture, which amounted to dismissing his argument. But he smiled and drank to his daughter's uniformed guest. Joanna wondered if he had said the same thing to French officers ten years ago, with as little effect; if his ancestors had not advised Cham and Chinese military men and accepted their dismissals with the same polite futility. There was something elusive and sad about these older people that Joanna found disturbing. They were Asian poetry and Pete was hard American prose.

Their son-in-law had been captured by this prose. General Dat spoke vigorously but politely, saying he too disagreed with his father-in-law. They were facing a new situation, a more determined enemy. They could not follow the old ways and rely on so-called ancient wisdom.

On Sunday, Pete and Joanna attended Mass with General Dat and Thui at a village church east of the city. Joanna had expressed interest in seeing a village, and Thui had suggested this one, on the right bank of the Perfume River, where most of Hue's Catholics lived. The parish priest was a middle-aged man named Buu Dong; he was short and thin and rather nervous, but he had a radiant smile and great personal warmth. After Mass, he escorted them through the cluster of straw-thatched huts, each a single room divided by a bamboo curtain. "Poor people, poor people," he said in French, which Thui translated. Most were farmers who worked the rich soil in the area. Only a few owned their land. In his bare rectory, a four-room wooden house, Father Dong served coffee and pointed to a picture on the wall. It was Ho Chi Minh. "I tell my people to pray for him, because he is our friend, too," he said. Pete was dismayed. On the way back to Hue, Thui explained that there were numerous Viet Cong in the area and Father Buu was trying to live in peace with both sides. General Dat, freed from the constraint of being polite to his father-in-law, said in French that the priest was *un imbécile*.

"If you gave him more protection, I bet he'd take down that picture," Pete said.

"We have no soldiers with your courage," Thui said. "It is just like it was in Quang Ngai before you came. The night belongs to the VC. They can come and kill him anytime they wish. All we can do is pray for him."

For a moment Joanna found herself wishing that she shared Thui's fervent Catholicism. But all she could summon was a kind of nostalgia for the daily communicant of 1950. She had abandoned that ancient, intricate boring faith and replaced it with an American faith, in which the vague God of Washington and Jefferson presided over a world waiting, yearning, to share her country's freedom and prosperity. Like most Americans in 1963, the third year of John F. Kennedy's presidency, Joanna believed that this promise of freedom—and the readiness of soldiers like Pete to defend it—was the answer to Vietnam's chaos. But Joanna was beginning to wonder if this faith could create a nation out of a tangle of hostile peoples and religions in a land that had not experienced either unity or self-government for the past seventeen centuries. Again she remembered what Carl Springer had told her on her second night in Saigon. *This isn't Korea. It's Vietnam.*

That was sounding more and more ominous.

II

TOWELED and fresh from her bath, Amy Rosser slipped into the white silk trousers of the ao-dai with a small shiver of delight. She had bought a dozen of these Vietnamese ensembles. She loved the caress of the silk against her thighs, the idea that beneath the flowing, so very feminine tunic, she was wearing trousers. The combination somehow armed her for the battle of wills and emotions that Saigon had become. Amy paused for a moment, savoring the pleasure of it.

She still had it; her Vietnam high, she called it in moments of self-communion. She still had it, in spite of George's decline. Lately poor George was having trouble responding to her invitations. Saigon's enervating humidity, the growing pressure under which he was working at MACV, often left him less than passionate. At least, that was how Amy explained his torpor. It was *not*, she was certain, a yearning for Helen Palladino. They had definitely banished that threat during their first memorable months in Vietnam.

Everything had been so deliciously right, in those shining days. The Army's new helicopter tactics were winning the war. The Vietnamese upper class rushed to make friends with the new commanders at MACV. The advisers, some of them George's '50 classmates or friends from earlier classes, others younger captains, made marvelous dinner guests. It was like being able to invite a different soldier of fortune to your table every nght. They arrived in floppy Anzac hats, red berets, captured Viet Cong sun helmets, and talked casually about kill ratios and body counts, ambushes and air strikes, homemade "lance bombs," spike foot traps, exotic VC strongholds like the Iron Triangle. Occasionally, one of these dinner guests was killed only a few days or weeks after sitting at her table (or the table of some other MACV wife) and there was the painful but still somehow exhilarating (or exalting) necessity of writing a mournful letter to his wife.

These fighting soldiers were the most glamorous but by no means the most important part of the American "country team" in Vietnam. There were the civilians from the U. S. Embassy, the numerous members of the U.S. AID (Agency for International Development) mission and their wives, the people from the U. S. Information Service, Air Force officers from the Tan Son Nhut Air Base, polite bland young men from the CIA and their equally bland seniors, even the Special Forces commanders with their green berets, whose style so many young advisers tried to imitate, all these people had to be met and mastered socially, persuaded to understand the Army's central role in this business of rescuing Vietnam from Communism.

Beyond this challenge was the country itself, so strange, so spectacularly beautiful in places like Nha Trang, Hue, Cap St. Jacques, so weirdly dangerous and impenetrable in its jungles and wild highlands. More and more, Amy felt that Vietnam was no one's country, it belonged to those who could subdue it. Comprehending it was impossible, unnecessary. The Vietnamese were so polite, so elusive, so stubborn.

Early in 1963, these two contradictory feelings, the opportunity, perhaps the necessity of conquering Vietnam and the disillusionment with the Vietnamese themselves, began to emerge in the American community. People came back from weekends at Cap St. Jacques or the highland resort of Dalat raving about the breathtaking beaches, the mist-wrapped mountains. Then they would exchange the latest story about the Vietnamese who wouldn't. It didn't matter exactly what they wouldn't. That almost became irrelevant. Wouldn't take American advice, wouldn't respond to American persuasion; wouldn't was a national habit.

Around the same time, George began to echo the harassed stridency of his boss, Major General Henry Hamburger, director of

Strategic Plans and Policy at MACV. A more exact title would have been director of Strategic Publicity. Henry was having a harder and harder time getting the Saigon press corps to cooperate with him. That was when the Headway Reports Henry wrote for COMMUSMACV, General Paul Harkins, began to acquire unrealities that George muttered about when he and Amy were alone.

Amy studied herself in the shadowy bedroom mirror. Her breasts were white dark-tipped cones against the tan she had acquired at the pool of the Cercle Sportif, a prewar French country club. She liked the tan. She wanted to look as sensual as she felt about Vietnam. There was something deeply, darkly arousing about this place, sprawled on the tropic edge of Asia, lapped by the China Sea. Amy remembered a bachelor adviser telling her bemusedly about the direct guiltless sexuality of Vietnamese women. She found herself wanting George that way, in all the positions, letting him do everything to her and returning the favors. But something stopped her from suggesting it to him. And George, left to his own devices, was—alas—George. Amy found herself wishing for Adam. He would appreciate the blend of excitement and desire she was feeling.

But Adam—and imitations of Adam—were forbidden. She had made that promise to herself—and by implication to George—in response to Helen Palladino. Maybe Helen was the reason she hesitated to suggest Asiatic pleasures to George. She did not want him to start wondering if the woman who had told him she liked a good fuck was the real Amy Rosser. That might make him suspect there had been others besides that mythical Pentagon colonel in her bed. No, Amy reiterated, again banishing vagrant thoughts of Adam. She would have to let imagination, wishful daydreams, satisfy what life refused to supply.

For today, there was a full measure of intriguing tasks to anticipate. She was on her way to lunch at the villa of Madame Pham Do Khiem, wife of one of Saigon's most important generals. She and Florence Eberle wanted Madame Pham to join them in a visit to an orphanage which the Vietnamese-American Association had organized for children of soldiers killed by the Communists. When their mothers remarried, these children were often unwanted and sometimes abandoned. It was going to be a struggle to persuade Madame

Pham to go with them. For a lady to be seen dishing out soup at an orphanage was unthinkable in Vietnam. Amy and Florence had already lost this argument with two other Vietnamese generals' wives. They had offered to send their cooks. Millicent Hamburger had ordered Amy and Florence to press on. Eventually, one of these stupid women would realize the value of such a picture in American newspapers.

Tonight the Rossers were going to dinner at the Hamburgers'. Amy had helped Millicent plan the menu, a judicious combination of French and Vietnamese, which would not tax the digestion of the guests. Wilson Canty, one of the top people in AID, was going to be there, along with Peggy Hankinson, a reporter for *Life* magazine. She was pro-American, a positive thinker. They hoped to sell her a story on the strategic hamlets, the Diem regime's answer to the Communists' control of the countryside. The hamlet program, which involved resettling millions of peasants, had been viciously criticized by some reporters. Canty and Pete Burke had been escorting Hankinson around the hamlets. The Burkes would be there tonight, Joanna with her earnest do-gooder's smile, in which Amy no longer quite believed. If she knew what her husband was doing, her innocence was a remarkable performance. But Amy was inclined to think Pete was telling her as little as possible. That was what she would do if she had a moralist like Joanna for a wife.

The telephone rang. "Don't leave your house," Florence Eberle said. "The Buddhists are on the rampage again. Another monk just did the barbecue bit."

"Where?"

"In Hue. The Saigon mob was waiting for the signal. They're charging out of the Xa Loi pagoda in all directions. Have you got a gun in the house?"

"George's forty-five."

"I'd keep it handy."

"What about Madame Pham?"

"The hell with her. She'll probably say no, anyway. I'll call her."

Amy was irked. This was the fifth or sixth Buddhist monk who had incinerated himself in protest against the Diem regime. Each time, mobs of monks and their supporters had rioted through the streets of Saigon and other cities, burning cars and buses, fighting with the government's police, attacking Americans. Two weeks ago, Amy had been driving Georgianna and Grace home from the Cercle Sportif in the aged Citroën she had bought from the previous tenant of their villa. A Buddhist mob had swirled around them, pounding on the roof and fenders. They began rocking the car, preparatory to turning it over. Amy blew an S O S on the horn and Vietnamese riot police had fought their way to them, just in time. Georgianna claimed to be terrified by the experience and tried to use it as an excuse to avoid school. Amy had told her she was an officer's daughter and hustled her onto the school bus the following day. Personally Amy enjoyed the encounter. It made marvelous dinner-party conversation.

Taking off her ao-dai, Amy pulled on slacks and a blouse and went downstairs to roust her cook, Mrs. Loan, from her midday siesta to make her some lunch. On the way, she inspected the living room, supposedly cleaned that morning, and found dust beneath the lamps on the end tables flanking the couch. She summoned the maid, Mrs. Loan's sister, and once more lectured her on moving the lamps instead of dusting around them.

"And keep Comrade Ho in the kitchen," she said, pointing to a green lizard who was perched on one of her gold-trimmed lampshades. Comrade Ho was a necessity to keep the insect population down. But the sight of him still gave Amy the creeps.

Upstairs, Amy checked George's .45. He had taught her how to use it at the Military Police pistol range near Tan Son Nhut Air Base. The gun had a full clip. If any of those Buddhist fanatics came this way, she was ready for them. She went out in the yard and checked the barbed wire and broken glass on the villa's outer walls. It was all in place. They would have to come through the gate.

Alexandre Dumas Street was only two blocks long. It was utterly peaceful. Nothing but the hum of insects, the distant beeps of Saigon's traffic, could be heard. Tucking the .45 in the belt of her slacks, Amy strolled next door. In an identical eight-room villa lived Brooks Turner, the UPI correspondent. He was a total cynic but a tired one. He disliked the young snots who dominated the Saigon press corps and as a reflex rooted for the home team.

Brooks was recovering from last night's party. Amy and George had stopped in for a nightcap on the way home from a dinner at the Eberles'. The villa had been full of pretty Vietnamese girls doing the Twist. Brooks, who had just shed his third wife, an Australian who had taken a hate to Saigon, sat in his living room, clutching a bloody mary. He was an elongated gray-haired man with a mouthful of misshapen teeth that gave him a sharklike grin.

"What the hell are you doing with that cannon?" he said in his graveled drinker's voice.

She told him about the Buddhist suicide.

"Son of a bitch," he said. "They're playing for keeps."

"And you still think our beloved CIA is funding them to dump Diem?"

"Of course."

Turner reiterated his jaundiced view of the American government. One hand never let the other hand know what it was doing. Americans could not stop competing with each other. The State Department constantly tried to screw the Army and vice versa. The CIA, as the newest and nerviest kid on the block, played the game a little rougher than the rest of them. Amy liked Brooks's cynicism. It was a refreshing antidote to George's attempts to convince himself that the country team in Vietnam was involved in a noble cause. Amy had long since decided the cause was exceedingly dubious. Which made it all the more interesting to try and win the game anyway.

Brooks went off to get the details on the burnt Buddhist and Amy returned home. The afternoon passed peacefully on Alexandre Dumas Street. At three Mrs. Chiang, a small smiling Chinese, arrived to wash and set Amy's hair and do her nails. At four-thirty Miss Hua, a younger, more muscular Chinese, appeared and briskly covered all parts of Mrs. Rosser with fragrant oil, then vigorously rubbed and kneaded and slapped her. This weekly massage had come to mean almost as much to Amy as sex with George.

Major Rosser came home in a scowling, snappish mood. "You heard about the Buddhist?"

454

"Yes. Florence Eberle canceled our lunch because of it. She had me sitting here with your forty-five, expecting the worst."

"That's exactly what we might get," George said. "Christ Almighty, I told you this guy Hamburger was a jerk and we should let him go over here and play his games without us. We had the perfect excuse when he told you you couldn't make the dependent list. Instead, you offered to pay your own way."

"Don't be an idiot. Think of how many people you've met since we got here. Generals, diplomats, newspapermen. You're being noticed, George, and that's vital."

"Noticed as what? The yes man of a dimwit."

"What's the latest word from Washington?"

"As of this morning, one more burnt Buddhist and Diem was through."

"I can't understand it. Why doesn't the CIA, the chief of staff, somebody, get through to Kennedy and explain that these bald-headed blabbermouths are Communists?"

"Nobody can prove it. Besides, the Embassy people are behind them one hundred percent."

"Brooks Turner says the CIA is financing them."

"I wish he could prove that. Some people in the CIA have been playing a very strange game. Your story checks out pretty well."

Sitting around the pool at the Cercle Sportif, Amy had heard Joanna Burke mention going to dinner at General Coulter's villa. She told George, who learned Coulter was in the CIA. The Army Intelligence people at MACV soon acquired a dossier on Coulter, who seemed to be in Saigon on a special assignment. His persistent association with Vietnamese who opposed Diem was alarming, George said. Even stranger was Pete Burke's friendship with him.

"I don't think Pete is smart enough to work with the CIA."

"What does he have to do?" George said. "He can talk to advisers when he takes journalists into the field. He can pass the word that Diem has to go. Half of them are ready to agree with him. He lets them tell their ARVN counterparts after he gets back to Saigon."

"Maybe I could get Joanna to talk about it. Have her to lunch here someday. You could bug the room."

George shook his head, in a weary, halfhearted way that irritated and alarmed her. "He'd never tell her, why should he?" He trudged across the room to the bar and mixed himself a double martini. "You know what Diem told Harkins today? If the Embassy keeps pushing the Buddhists, he's going to start talking to Hanoi. How would that look on my record? Executive officer of the Office of Strategic Plans and Policy, the man who processed the papers that surrendered South Vietnam."

George's panic ignited a knot of nerves in Amy's forehead. Her skull throbbed. She mentally cursed Buddhists and Catholics. She had not had a migraine since she arrived in Vietnam. It was outrageous, the way the Army was being isolated by its supposed allies; it reinforced Florence Eberle's contention that you could not trust civilians.

Amy tried to reassure herself—and George. "As long as Diem stands firm, and the South Vietnamese Army stands behind him, what can a bunch of priests and a few thousand rioters do?"

"Ruin us in Washington. That's where the real battle is being fought. It's a public relations war. And we're losing it. Those civil rights jerks around Kennedy think the Buddhist monks are like the southern freedom riders. Defenders of a persecuted minority."

"No matter what happens, Hamburger will be all right. He and Milly know too many people. Stick with him and he'll stick with you."

"We don't have any choice," George said. "We're stuck with him."

That night, during dinner at the Hamburgers', Amy began to sympathize with George's panic. The latest burnt Buddhist dominated the conversation. The first one had torched himself in the street outside Joanna Burke's apartment and she had yet to get over it. She gave them all a replay, her poetic gifts making it so vivid they could practically smell the scorching flesh.

Isabel Canty, a wispy little woman with a pointed nose and dangly stringy hair, kept knocking the Diem government. Something must be terribly wrong with it, went her sappy reasoning, if men committed suicide to protest against it. *Life* magazine's Peggy Hankinson was in a rotten mood because she had spent the last two days plodding around strategic hamlets in the Mekong Delta and missed the Buddhist riot here in Saigon. Worst of all, Wilson Canty, their AID spokesman, said he was disappointed in what he had seen in the hamlets they visited. The people the government had resettled in them did not look happy. Very little of the equipment they had been promised—electric generators, medical supplies, weapons— seemed to be reaching the hamlets. All during Canty's remarks Pete Burke just sat there, sipping his wine, chomping down his duck and rice, impassive as a Buddha.

Major General Hamburger struggled to glorify the hamlets program. He recited COMMUSMACV Paul Harkins' favorite poem, some Kipling thing about the futility of hustling the East. Henry argued that the happiness of the peasants in the strategic hamlets was immaterial. The important thing was they were no longer vulnerable to Viet Cong attack. When Hankinson still looked dubious, Henry committed his reserves. He reminisced desperately about his days as Patton's deputy, when he had handed a neophyte Peggy Hankinson some juicy stories. It was an almost pathetic appeal to gratitude. If Amy had been sentimental, she would have been touched.

Hankinson, a tiny, alarmingly thin woman who smoked small black cigars and wore her curly black hair cropped boyishly close, looked confused and weary. She kept saying she did not understand Vietnam. No one talked frankly to her about anything. She wanted to believe her old friend Henry was being straight with her but—

After dinner, they went out on the terrace of the Hamburger villa for coffee. Amy invited Isabel Canty down to a corner of the terrace to look at some interesting flowers. "For God's sake, stop talking about the government as if you were a Viet Cong sympathizer," Amy said. "And don't say another word about that barbecued Buddhist. Don't you realize what's at stake here? A story in *Life* magazine. Eight million circulation."

Isabel almost burst into tears. "I'm sorry, my nerves are shot," she said. "I'm going home, with or without Wilson. I've been on Librium for six months but it isn't working anymore." Vietnam was hopeless, a madhouse, she raged. She hated everything about it.

The party wobbled to a close without Isabel Canty saying another word. But Peggy Hankinson's doubts about the strategic hamlets had deeper roots. "What happens if I do a story about how great they are and the day before it hits the newsstands the VC wipe one out? Colonel Burke here didn't seem to think much of their defenses."

"I can't believe Colonel Burke would say such a thing," General Hamburger said. "You must have misunderstood him."

"I told Miss Hankinson I was afraid they couldn't withstand a determined attack in battalion strength, sir," Pete Burke said.

"But the VC haven't made a battalion-strength attack anywhere in the Delta," Hamburger said.

"A lot of advisers think they're moving to that stage, General," Pete said.

"I don't. No one in MACV, at the level where responsibility for analyzing intelligence rests, thinks so."

"It's just my opinion, sir," Pete Burke said. "Miss Hankinson asked me for it."

"Colonel Burke's like a lot of soldiers who've been promoted because of outstanding combat records. They don't understand staff work, the accumulation of data to assure careful decisions," Henry Hamburger said. "I'll stake my professional reputation on it, Peg, those hamlets are secure."

Hankinson left, promising to discuss the whole situation with her editors and let Henry know about their decision. It was not an upbeat finish to the evening. The Cantys left next and suddenly it was an all-Army party. Henry Hamburger gave Milly some sort of private signal and she suggested that the ladies might want to powder their noses. She led Amy and Joanna upstairs to the master bedroom. Its wide windows overlooked the terrace. Amy dropped into a chair by one window and pretended to enjoy a breeze. Joanna went into the bathroom. Milly said something about too much wine and went down the hall to another bathroom. Amy was left alone to hear what was being said on the terrace below her.

"Goddamnit, Burke," Henry Hamburger snarled. "Are you or aren't you on this team?"

"I'm on it, General," Pete said, "as long as you want me on it."

"An Army officer who fools around with CIA spooks is very liable to ruin his career."

"I don't know what you're talking about, General."

"I'm talking about your friend Coulter. Don't you think we know you have dinner at his house regularly? And you tell the Vietnamese they ought to get rid of President Diem?"

"I don't say anything of the sort, sir," Pete said. "I just tell them that I think the ARVN could beat the VC, if the government would let them fight."

"It amounts to the same thing."

"Sir, I don't agree. I'm making those statements at General Coulter's request. He's an old friend of mine. I was his aide in Korea."

"He won't be able to help you when you need it, Burke. In five years, he won't have any friends left in the Army."

"Sir, I've never depended on General Coulter for anything but advice. As for my career, I've just tried to do my best in every assignment."

"You call what you just did your best? Telling that woman the hamlets aren't secure? Blowing a chance to get a story in *Life?*"

"I didn't volunteer the information, sir. She asked me."

"That's irrelevant."

"I don't think it is, sir. I'm perfectly willing to accept the policy of not telling the whole truth, sir. But I will not tell anyone a direct lie."

Silence.

"I don't believe you, Burke. You're unreal," Henry Hamburger said.

"I would like to ask my classmate, Major Rosser, if he thinks I should lie in support of our policy, sir."

The son of a bitch, Amy thought. He is tougher, smarter than I thought he was.

"I told you it was irrelevant, and that's even more irrelevant," Hamburger roared.

Joanna emerged from the bathroom. Amy gave her a warm smile and used the facilities. When she came out, Milly Hamburger was showing Joanna some ivory statues of Hindu gods that she had bought in Bangkok. Joanna was able to give her the theology and folklore about each one. Milly was dazzled and asked her to write it all down for her. Amy said Joanna was also an accomplished poet.

"Somewhere I've got a copy of the Army newspaper at Leavenworth, where we published a half dozen of her poems," Amy said. "I'll dig it out for you."

Milly said she would love to see it. Amy thought Joanna gave her a somewhat peculiar look, as if she suspected her motive was not entirely pure. Amy stilled her conscience by telling herself that Lieutenant Colonel Burke's motives were not very pure either.

When they returned to the terrace brandy was served. General Hamburger puffed furiously on a cigar. George looked like he had just swallowed strychnine. Pete Burke examined and reexamined his huge hands. The conversation limped around several topics. Joanna said she was reading some Vietnamese epic poem, and finding it rather dull. Milly Hamburger rhapsodized about her trip to Bangkok. Amy reported her attempt to silence Isabel Canty and the hysteria it had evoked.

"I wish we could get rid of that whole AID operation," Henry Hamburger said. "They aren't loyal. They have no concept of loyalty. If we had genuine top-to-bottom loyalty out here, we'd be winning this war right now."

He glowered ominously at Pete Burke as he said this.

Joanna said she wanted to get home to make sure her twelve-year-old was in bed and not watching fire fights on the outskirts of Saigon.

"Is he still hyperactive?" Amy asked. It was a bitchy question but she was furious at Pete for dragging George into his duty-honor-country act. Joanna denied Tom had ever been hyperactive. "Maybe that's the wrong word," Amy said, smiling, her voice full of false jollity. "I just remember the time he almost gave Georgianna a concussion when he hit her with that mudball at Fort Leavenworth. The MP's were always after him for something out there." Amy knew what General Hamburger thought of Army parents who did not control their children. He had given several lectures on the subject and issued numerous reprimands at Fort McConnell.

The Burkes departed. Instead of fulminating, Henry Hamburger slumped in his chair. "I don't understand that fellow," he said. "I just don't understand him. Is he sincere?"

Amy was amazed. Pete had intimidated the general. But only for a few minutes. Henry told Millicent about his exchange with Lieutenant Colonel Burke. "I think you should accuse him of insubordination," she said. "Go to Harkins and accuse him."

"No. That would open a can of worms," the general said. "You graduated with him, George. What do you think?"

"He was always—well—a sort of literalist, sir."

Amy could see anger on George's face. But it was clashing with his Methodist conscience. He knew Pete Burke was sincere and could not quite bring himself to deny it.

"I think he left literalism behind him a long time ago, George," Amy said. "Along with his sincerity."

That was all Hamburger needed. "We'll settle scores with him in due time. With him and the other prophets of doom. We're going to pull this thing out, children. Mark my words. We'll pull it out. This Buddhist confrontation is what we need to shock Diem and his brother into action. Just before I left headquarters tonight, I heard Paul Harkins saying it was the best thing that could possibly have happened."

Driving home in their Citroën, George got more and more angry at Pete Burke. "That was a hell of a thing to do. Putting me on the spot that way."

Amy said nothing. She was pleased to see him discovering that true blue types like Pete could be dangerous. At home, her pleasure evaporated. Georgianna and Grace had had another fight. Georgie had thrown Grace's favorite doll, an exquisite golden-robed Siamese dancer, into the villa's fishpond. The motive was revenge. Grace had brought home a note from the principal of the American School, informing Amy that she did not think Georgie merited promotion to the fifth grade. The principal said she had given the note to Grace because she did not trust Georgianna to deliver it. She had apparently failed to deliver two previous notes about her disruptive conduct in class and impudence to the teacher when corrected.

Amy was furious. "You won't go to a movie, you won't go to the Cercle Sportif, for the whole summer," she shouted.

"Go to hell," Georgie said.

Amy slapped her in the face. "Someday I'll make you sorry for that," Georgie said. For a moment Amy was almost afraid of her.

She considered taking a hairbrush to her. But George arrived in his pajamas and bathrobe and once more tried to play the peacemaker. Even he found it hard to dismiss the principal's letter. He said he was very disappointed, and Georgie burst into tears. "I hate that school. I hate this country," she said. "Why can't we go home?"

Amy took the Siamese doll downstairs to clean the muck off it. She left George trying to explain to his sobbing daughter how important it was for him to stay here and help General Hamburger beat the Viet Cong.

After consultation with the American School's principal, Amy decided to ship Georgie home to her grandparents for the summer, under orders to study five hours a day with a tutor. She looked so thin and sad at the airport Amy felt sorry for her. But her sympathy dwindled when Georgie refused to kiss her goodbye. George was upset and urged Amy to try to be more affectionate with the child. He was worried about her. Amy, relieved to be rid of her for two and a half months, promised him she would try. Privately, she resolved not to give an inch in what she considered a battle of wills.

The rest of the summer of 1963 was politics and more politics, all tumultuous. Saigon seethed in its monsoon-drenched steam bath. The Buddhists continued to march and riot. Worse, they returned to their suicide tactics. Amy was in the Central Market, helping Milly Hamburger shop for a present for a niece, when screams of horror and panic erupted. They turned to see a monk standing there, engulfed in flames. He had apparently soaked his robes in gasoline and walked to the market before striking the match. Milly Hamburger was very upset. She went to bed for a whole day. Amy found herself unbothered. She gave a dinner party for ten people that night.

The next day Amy and Florence Eberle had lunch with Madame Nhu. She was as wacky in her own way as her spooky male relatives. But she had guts. In 1960 Diem had almost surrendered to a coup led by a battalion of paratroopers. Madame Nhu had persuaded him to hold out until loyal troops rescued him. Madame Nhu's solution to the Buddhists was equally combative. She wanted President Diem to arrest every monk in Vietnam. They were all Communists, she said. She was not in the least bothered by their penchant for fiery suicides. She said she wished they would barbecue a monk every day. She would even supply the gasoline.

Amy passed the remark along to Brooks Turner, who wrote a story on it. He did not, of course, quote Amy as his source; a good thing, because reaction in Washington was very bad. Other reporters in Saigon asked Madame Nhu if she had really said it and she emphatically affirmed it. The reaction in Washington was even worse, according to George, who saw all the confidential communications from the Pentagon that flowed across Henry Hamburger's desk. Amy said nothing to George, but she was confused and disgusted by her chickenhearted countrymen. Instead of seeing Madame Nhu as a courageous woman, the leader of an embattled nation, they heaped abuse on her as a barbarian, while saying practically nothing about the atrocities the Viet Cong committed every day. Amy began to see the whole press corps, even apparent anti-Communists like Brooks Turner, as the enemy. They did not really care about anything but a good story, no matter how much damage it did.

Instead of galvanizing Diem and his brother, as Henry Hamburger predicted, the Buddhists seemed to immobilize them. The President became more and more recalcitrant about making even the slightest concession to the monks. Worse, Counselor Nhu became more and more openly hostile to Americans. He refused to believe MACV was not a party to the Buddhist agitation. Madame Nhu stopped seeing Florence Eberle, and the Vietnamese-American Association's activities expired. Luncheons with wives of Vietnamese generals at the Cercle Sportif or the Caravelle ceased. Henry Hamburger grew hollow-eyed. George fretted and feared the worst. For once, it began to look like he was going to be right.

With no warning, President Kennedy announced that the American Ambassador to South Vietnam, Frederick Nolting, was being replaced by Henry Cabot Lodge. An all-out backer of Diem, Nolting had gotten along well with Paul Harkins, the commander of MACV. Nolting had no pretensions to military expertise and never criticized MACV's approach to the war. But the Ambassador was the civilian commander of the country team and could in theory make many waves. From mid-August, the Cercle Sportif, the PX and the Officers' Club were abuzz with rumors about what Lodge might do. The insiders feared that he would junk the military strategy which MACV had been following and switch the whole show to a counter-insurgency operation. In this scenario, the Special Forces people, of whom President Kennedy was so fond, would take over the war. Every officer in Saigon would be wearing a green beret. The regulars would be sent home in disgrace.

"I can't believe they'd ever do it," Florence Eberle told Amy beside the pool at the Cercle Sportif. "But anything is possible with those crazy Irishmen in the White House. They're unstable, ready to question everything."

On another morning at the pool, Joanna Burke fed the rumor with a letter from Adam Thayer, who was an instructor at the Special Forces center at Fort Bragg. Adam said they were talking about quadrupling the size of the center, and opening others overseas, in Okinawa, the Philippines and Vietnam. "Adam told Pete to send him his head size. He'd see if they had a beret big enough."

"You mean you'd let him become a Green Beanie?" Amy said, using the term of contempt the regulars had invented for the Special Forces. "Very few of them are Academy graduates, from what I hear. It's just a way for a bunch of hustlers to push their careers."

Joanna shrugged. "Pete says some of them have done a lot over here already, working with the tribes in the hills. He'd probably qualify, without even having to take the course. He speaks Vietnamese. He's certainly got the combat background."

Amy considered this a direct dig at George. She vowed to repay it eventually. The possibility that it might be true took priority over revenge, for the time being. What to do? George was not the Green Beanie type. He was an organization man. That was what the Army had said it wanted, all during the fifties. How could they change signals so totally in 1963? She began to hate Jack Kennedy and his grinning entourage, an emotion which came easily to her Republican instincts. She had allowed herself to be diverted by Kennedy's panache; she had let the feeling that they were all part of a new generation mislead her.

The news of the change in Ambassadors galvanized President

Diem and his brother, at last. They declared martial law and launched a ferocious assault on the Buddhists in Saigon, Hue and other cities. Saigon was a chaos of mobs, troops, frantic journalists and frightened Americans. The Ngos had acted without any consultation with MACV. They used elite troops, personally loyal to them, and tried to blame the attack on the South Vietnamese Army. The reaction in Washington, George reported, was disastrous. Kennedy seemed close to giving up on Diem. The President practically said so on national TV.

The new Ambassador, the suave patrician New Englander Henry Cabot Lodge, tended to confirm this impression. It soon became clear that he considered Diem expendable. Amy and the other Army wives, talking to Embassy and AID wives at the Cercle Sportif, found out why. The civilians were defecting, and blaming the Army for the whole mess. One top AID man had actually accused MACV of lying. He said the war was being lost. Worse, Lodge seemed inclined to believe him. Another AID man went back to Washington and told Kennedy that the strategic hamlets program was a complete flop. He accused the Diem government of lying and said the Army was in collusion with them. Kennedy responded by announcing that the Secretary of Defense, Robert McNamara, and his chief military adviser, General Maxwell Taylor, were being sent to Vietnam to make an on-the-spot reassessment of the situation.

Even in Saigon's humidity, the news sent an anticipatory chill through MACV. The Secretary of Defense could sweep the whole Military Assistance Command out of Saigon at the stroke of a pen. Everyone thought the Special Forces people looked alarmingly smug. Virtual panic ensued when Joanna Burke told Amy that Adam Thayer, newly promoted to lieutenant colonel, was coming out on the same plane as the Secretary to assume unspecified duties at the Special Forces headquarters. For the Secretary even to associate, however remotely, with an officer who had openly criticized the Army's program in Vietnam was unthinkable. Adam suddenly assumed an importance out of all proportion to his rank.

These successive shocks demoralized Amy almost as much as George. She clung to Florence Eberle's somewhat desperate contention that General Maxwell Taylor would protect them, somehow. He had chosen Harkins as COMMUSMACV. He couldn't zap his own man without ruining himself. As for Robert McNamara, the Secretary of Defense, he was just a civilian. He'd been here before and they had run him around the country, showing him the good news and carefully concealing the nasty stuff, keeping the correspondents at arm's length. They could do it again. MACV was in charge of planning the Secretary's itinerary.

This task proceeded to consume most of George's waking hours. A dozen different itineraries were composed by the MACV staff under General Hamburger's direction and critiqued by everyone from Pete Burke to General Harkins. A foot-thick Headway Report was compiled on every conceivable aspect of the war. Friends in the Pentagon worked on the assistant secretary for public affairs to persuade him to make an optimistic statement on the situation as soon as possible after the Secretary's arrival. This, went the unfolding strategy, would lock the Secretary himself into a positive conclusion, even if he was troubled by minor negatives.

At last the diplomtic D day, September 25, arrived. General Harkins and his aides clustered on one side of the airport ramp, Ambassador Lodge and his entourage on the opposite side. As McNamara and Taylor approached, both groups surged forward and Amy watched unbelievingly as two State Department flunkies stepped in front of General Harkins and left him flailing there for a crucial ten seconds, while Ambassador Lodge strolled debonairly down the ramp to shake McNamara's hand. After the blocking force rushed a mass of photographers and reporters. Harkins could only cry haplessly: "Please, gentlemen, please let me through to see the Secretary."

Watching that show of force, Amy concluded war between the civilians and the military had been officially declared. She also concluded there was a very good chance that Generals Harkins and Hamburger and company might lose it. Which made her all the more determined to invite Adam Thayer to dinner to find out what was going on.

Adam soon appeared among the four dozen or so members of the Secretary's entourage. Presidents and cabinet members never went anywhere without a private army. "Adam," she called. "Colonel Thayer."

He turned, smiling. His green beret was cocked over his left eye.

His jump boots gleamed. He looked so alive, so confident. For a moment Amy wished George, the weary deskbound aide, did not exist. Here was a soldier with answers, a man who thought he could conquer Vietnam. She suddenly wanted him to take her the same way, with the same casual certitude. She was drunkenly, scarily alone with him in some hot dim Saigon room, letting his hands explore her moist flesh.

"Mrs. Rosser," he said. "What a pleasant surprise."

A hundred yards away, the reporters and soldiers and diplomats still swirled around Secretary McNamara and General Taylor. Amy struggled to reclaim her habitual self.

"I—I was hoping you could come to dinner tonight. Just you and the Burkes and George, of course, if he can get away."

"Sounds great," Adam said.

Amy offered him a ride into Saigon. He was staying at the Brink Hotel until Honor and the children arrived. "Oh, I'm so glad," Amy said as they edged into a stream of traffic that included a half dozen Army trucks and jeeps. "I was afraid you'd be up in the hills with the tribesmen."

"I'll be on staff here in Saigon, for a while at least," Adam said. "How are George and the girls?"

She told him about her problems with Georgianna, who had refused to come back to Saigon. She was going to spend a year with her grandparents in Bala-Cynwyd. Adam bragged lightly about his oldest, Pookie, who was apparently something of a genius. "Matt, unfortunately, has Honor's IQ," he said.

The dinner was a complete frustration. Adam ate her duck à l'orange and told them nothing. He said he wasn't even sure why they put him on the Secretary's plane; possibly it was because he had made a study of the Laotian economy, which was based mostly on opium, and McNamara wanted a briefing on it. That was the only thing they talked about when he was summoned to sit beside the Secretary for the first hour out of Hawaii.

It was such a blatant lie Amy was tempted to call him on it. But George was looking so hangdog, staring at Adam's and Pete Burke's silver lieutenant colonel's oak leaves, she let the conversation go and it drifted all over the place, from Vietnamese poetry to Joanna's heebie-jeebies over burning Buddhists. She had apparently seen another one, outside Saigon's cathedral a month ago. Pete Burke didn't seem in the least interested in whether there was going to be a tilt toward the Special Forces. No doubt because he would get the information from his old roommate on the sly, some other time. George drank too much and talked loosely about the gloom that was engulfing MACV.

"I really can't believe what Lodge did today," he said. "I really can't believe it."

"I wouldn't take it too seriously, George," Adam said. "As far as I can see, no one in Washington knows what the hell to do about this situation. If you guys have a plan, you've got just as much chance of selling it to the Secretary as Lodge has."

"The trouble is," Pete said, "we don't have a plan. Except more of the same old thing."

"Ah," said Adam, and added nothing more than a smile.

Much as Amy hated to admit it, Pete was right. The next four days witnessed MACV's desperate attempt to sell McNamara the status quo. Everything went well at first. The assistant secretary for public affairs issued a paean of optimism about the progress of the war within twenty-four hours of the Secretary's arrival. The Saigon press corps growled its contempt, as expected. But the Secretary, whirling in helicopters and planes from I Corps to II Corps to III Corps, plodding through hamlets and advisers' compounds and watching armored personnel carriers rumble across the rice paddies, did not have much time to think about it. Everywhere he saw hard-jawed young captains and majors who told him everything in their province was A-OK, the VC were on the run.

But Amy early spotted the fatal flaw in MACV's campaign. The Secretary was living at the U. S. Embassy, and Lodge had his ear for breakfast and dinner. McNamara turned down most of the carefully orchestrated nighttime social program Henry Hamburger had planned for him as too tiring, after his full day in the field. "You should have put him in Hamburger's villa, and moved Henry and Milly to the Palace Hotel," she told George, who only groaned and nodded gloomily.

At last, McNamara and General Taylor, who had been strangely silent and rather distant with his friends at MACV, went home. A few days later came a statement from the White House that puzzled reporters—and appalled the loyalists at MACV. The Kennedy communiqué expressed concern about the government's policy toward dissenters like the Buddhists, urged the Vietnamese to fight harder—and predicted most of the advisers would come home by 1965.

That night, at dinner with the Eberles and some other MACV colonels and their wives, the gloom was thicker than the Saigon humidity. Everyone knew—or thought or feared they knew—what it meant. MACV was going to be dismantled, piece by piece, and the war was going to be handed over to the Special Forces, who would try to transform the ARVN into Green Beanies. There was even a rumor that 1,000 advisers would be recalled by the end of the year. Withdrawing 1,000 officers was the equivalent of subtracting 50,000 men from MACV's operations. They sat there damning the Kennedys and Maxwell Taylor. If the regulars could not win this war, if they had to take lessons from a bunch of freaks who liked to live in the jungle and dine on snakes, they were on their way back to the nightmare of 1956, of massive budget cuts and unsettling basic questions about the whole purpose of the Army.

Amy went home demoralized. Suddenly she was back at the airport, looking at Adam for that scary surrendering instant. She tried to resist it. She tried to persuade George to console her. She put on her sheerest nightgown and lay on the bed, waiting for him to emerge from the shower. All he did was pour himself a nightcap and complain about the way Henry Hamburger was treating him. With contempt, even suspicion. Because of that question Pete Burke had asked the other night. A hell of a thing.

At 3 A.M., still sleepless, Amy lay there, listening to George snore. Anger mingled with images of Vietnam, with desire and conquest and power. Then Florence Eberle's frowning face. Amy lay on her side, half fetal, half odalisque, and let her fingers play at love. She was sixteen again, furtive, frightened by the pleasure which was her only friend in the gaggle of simpering teen-agers to which her parents had consigned her in the name of education. But now she was no longer that fearful child, she was a woman, and no one, including her husband, seemed to notice it. Waves of wish swelled in her belly, her throat.

It had to be done. In spite of Florence, God, husband, child. She went downstairs, padding through the bare rooms in her nightgown to the antique French telephone in the kitchen. She called the Brink Hotel. A sleepy operator put her through to Colonel Thayer's room. "Miles?" she whispered. "This is Priscilla. I can't stop thinking about you."

"Interesting. I'm halfway through a third cigar, doing the same thing."

"Where can I see you?"

"With or without George?"

"I'm serious."

"With or without Mrs. Eberle?"

"I—I was hoping you didn't know about that."

"I like solving puzzles. Especially ones that have blown up in my face."

"Does that mean you're not interested?"

"I'll always be interested in fucking you, Priscilla. Because you're very good at it. But I don't want to get fucked in the process. I like to be in charge."

"Give me a chance to prove I'm sorry."

"This requires some staff work. Where can I call you?"

"I'll be here all day."

It was close to noon when he called. "A taxi will pick you up in a half hour. He'll take you to an empty villa on Pham Van Dong Street. Go out the back door of the villa and across the garden to the gate in the rear wall. A taxi will be waiting there to take you to a junk on the river. Wear an ao-dai and one of those conical hats with a veil. With your tan, you should pass for Vietnamese."

Everything went according to plan. She already owned one of the broad-brimmed conical Vietnamese hats. She often wore it to the Cercle Sportif as a sun hat. She rode to the empty villa and walked swiftly through it to the second taxi, whose driver was Chinese, unusual in Saigon. He drove her to the waterfront and pointed to an ancient-looking junk tied to the wharf. It looked so decrepit and dirty, for a moment Amy recoiled. Then the multiple stenches of the waterfront engulfed her. The sun beat down with tropic ferocity. The air shimmered with heat. Around her swarmed Vietnamese fishermen, dock workers, children. Women crouched over pots full of steaming rice. She began to like the idea of Adam taking her in the junk's hot foul cabin, a few feet above the fetid river. It was part of Vietnam and she was here because she wanted to be part of it too, part of the conquest.

She walked up the gangplank and the cabin door opened. Inside she found herself in an air-conditioned room paneled in blond oak, as modern as any suite in the Caravelle Hotel. Adam sat at the table, which was set for lunch. Cold lobster, white wine. "How do you like this?" he said. "One of the CIA's little toys."

They started with martinis, then proceeded to the lobster, the wine. The martini must have been a double. Amy felt more and more relaxed, careless, as Adam filled her wineglass for the third time and teased her about betraying him to Florence Eberle in 1956. "I had a friend check George's record and saw the connection. Did you think you were ruining me? Did you care?"

"I—I was frightened," Amy said. "Florence can be very formidable."

"I'm sure she can. Anyway, it didn't matter. Old Miles was fighting the Army's battle. They couldn't throw him out on the street. For one thing, he knew too much. He didn't even get a bad OER out of it. Just a mild depression."

"Which has apparently lifted."

"Yeah. How about Priscilla? Still clinging to her old true blue warrior, Major Speak-for-Himself?"

"Yes."

"What's she doing here?"

"I'm—she's not sure." Amy felt uneasy. This was not what she had imagined. This sanitized air-conditioned interior was too American. Adam was misreading her as badly in his own way as George did.

"Maybe there's only one way to find out," Adam said. "Let's go downstairs."

He led her down a companionway to an equally cool compartment with twin beds in the center of it. Amy stood there, passive, subdued, while he undressed her. She lay down on the bed and watched him undress. It was the same lean, sinewy body. He seemed to like what he saw from his side. "Haven't gained an ounce, have you?" he said.

He slid his finger into her vagina and held it there, while the palm of his other hand descended on her right breast. "Priscilla, we could have done a lot together, if you'd only been willing to get rid of that John Alden character."

"Maybe you should have—spoken—a little louder—for yourself, Miles," she said, half liking, half fearing what he had begun.

"No. Your trouble is you want everything. You won't admit you can't get it."

"Are you sure—that isn't—your problem?" she said.

"Of course it is," he said, his finger moving inside her. "That's why we could have been so good together. We would have known exactly how and why to console each other."

"Where—did I go—wrong, Captain Standish?" she said. "Did I forget to do something for you? Like this?"

She sat up and took his penis in her mouth. He smiled down at her. "Living in the Orient has been good for you."

He stepped back, lifted her under her arms, flipped her down on her knees on the bed and entered her from behind. She saw them in a mirror on the opposite wall. The smile on his face was unchanged. Cold, uncaring. Amy did not like it. This was not the old comradely sex, the almost-love of Washington, D.C.

Cupping his hands over her breasts, he stroked her once, twice. "Did George send you?" he said.

"No."

"Florence?"

"No."

"But you still think, when this is over, I'm going to tell you everything."

"No. I—"

I came here to be part of Vietnam? Part of you, the conqueror? She could not say that. She could only let him continue his obscene

472

stroking in the air-conditioned bedroom. Icy now, the temperature was plunging every second.

"Here's the joke, Priscilla. I've got nothing to tell. I don't know any more than you do. Any more than Kennedy does. No one knows what's going to happen out here. I told you that the other night. But you wouldn't believe me."

"You—wouldn't—believe me."

Each word a stroke. Each stroke a subtraction. He was reducing comradeship to pleasure in this icy American bedroom. Reducing pleasure to obscenity. Reducing obscenity to hatred.

"I've got nothing to sell," he said. "You've got nothing to buy. There's nothing between us but this. How much you like the way I fuck you. And vice versa."

No. Comrades we were once, why not again? cried wish.

Betrayed, sighed memory.

Tears started from Amy's eyes. They felt as hot and thick on her cheeks as blood. "You bastard," she said. "To think—I almost loved you."

"I feel the same—indefinite regret."

"Then why this why—?"

Was it the tears? Did they make his regret keener than he wanted it to be? He suddenly seized a fistful of her hair and pushed her head down until she was crumpled on the bed. A moment later he came, a throbbing rush of semen without joy or affection. An ultimate reduction.

Amy lay face down on the bed for a long time. She felt nothing. She was airless, weightless in the cold unreal room. She was nowhere, neither in America nor in Asia. She was no one.

Cigar smoke drifted around her. She raised her head and looked at him. He was sitting on the other bed, still naked, smoking. He took a deep drag.

"I'm sorry," he said.

"I deserved it," she said.

"There really isn't anything to tell."

"I told you I didn't come here for that," she said.

A clever lie, or the truth at last?

"It will have to stop, when Honor gets here."

"I know. What time is it?"

"Three o'clock."

"We have until six. Turn off that goddamn air conditioner. This is Vietnam."

He understood. They lay there on separate beds, waiting for the temperature to rise. Adam opened two portholes. The river's noise and some of its odors drifted into the cabin. In a half hour, there was a sheen of sweat on her arms. Her palms were moist. She lay down beside him on his bed and filled his mouth with her tongue.

They began.

Again.

III

"ADAM, you always ruin everything!

"That's what I said, Lord, I fairly screamed it at him when he told me he wanted to go to Vietnam.

"They'd invited him to teach, *teach*, mind you, at the Command and General Staff School, you well know that's the most beautiful post in the Army outside West Point. I could hardly wait to live there. The schools are great and poor little Matt was *not* doin' well in first grade at Bragg. The school was integrated, of course. I don't believe there is such a thing as a good integrated school. Pookie just burns up the books everywhere, but Matt needs a *good* school and now we're in this place where they got to study with guns all around them. My God, how can they expect to teach anything when a child isn't sure he's safe? Colonel Ellsworth, Adam's boss at Bragg, urged him to take the CGSS assignment, he said it wasn't often they invited people to teach there without even graduatin' from the place, General Westmoreland was one of the few. It just shows how hipped the Army is all of a sudden on this counterinsurgency thing, I mean Adam had his pick of slots, he could've gone back to the Academy or stayed at Bragg or gone to the Pentagon. You know that entry on the efficiency report where it says, 'Fight to get him'? That's the way it was for him all of a sudden. Lord, it's changed from the way it was before the Kennedys arrived. Then most everybody was fightin' *not* to get him. His name was mud after that Pentagon flap in '56.

"But noooo, Adam's got to go to Vietnam. He says he doesn't want to be a teacher, them who can't do teach and he wants to *do*. He wants to *apply* the theory. Even if he gets killed doin' it. So here we are, right in the middle of a revolution, practically. Wonderin' if *we're* goin' to get killed. But he hasn't touched me, Jo. He hasn't so much as touched me and we've been here a week. Don't you think that's strange?"

Librium. It was God's gift to Army wives, Honor thought. She could spill all that out here with Joanna and smile.

She just did not let it bother her. Adam was just Adam and she was learning to live with him, like the psychiatrist at Fort Bragg advised her to. That psychiatrist was totally different from Dr. Todhunter. He was an older man, someone she trusted. She told him about the rape in Japan, every detail, for the first time she told someone everything she remembered. It made her feel so much better, so much more ready to adjust to Adam with the help of lovely, government-issued Librium.

"They're all under—so much pressure. Things are getting really frantic," Joanna said.

Joanna had not changed. Still the same naïve romantic. Ready to forgive and forget no matter what a man does. A year or two with Adam would make her grow up. Maybe I ought to rent him out, Honor thought.

"He's havin' an affair. A wife can tell. He's done it before," Honor said.

"How do you like this dress, Mommy?" Cissie Burke asked.

Without the tranquilizers, Honor would have been annoyed by the interruption. But she just smiled and let Joanna admire the latest costume on Cissie's Barbie doll. Honor had brought the doll and a half dozen outfits from the States for her. The Barbie craze was unbelievable. Every girl under the age of eight seemed to own one.

Cissie was a chubby blonde with marvelous creamy skin, not one of Pete's freckles. She did not look like Joanna at all. Except for her hair color, she could easily have passed for Honor's daughter. A rueful thought. Pookie was so homely. But Honor was not letting that bother her either. Nothing was going to bother her from now on.

Cissie went back to her bedroom to try another outfit on Barbie. Before Honor could resume the adult conversation, Pookie and Tom Burke came charging up the stairs from the street and burst breathlessly in on them. "Tom showed me the exact spot in the street where the monk burned himself to a cinder," Pookie said. "It's right out front."

"Where's Matt?" Joanna said.

"He's coming. We ran up the stairs ahead of him. He's such a slowpoke," Pookie said.

A wail from the stairs revealed that Matt did not approve of this maneuver. Joanna hurried into the hall and returned with Matt, who was sobbing hysterically. "Oh, calm down," Honor said.

"That was mean, Pookie. You should be nicer to your brother," Joanna said. "He's still just a little boy. As for you, Thomas Burke, Matt is your guest, just as much as Pookie. You should be more considerate."

Honor pulled Matt onto her lap and soothed him down. He sobbed and clung to her. "They said the Viet Cong were going to get me," he said.

"Who said that?" Joanna cried, really angry now.

Pookie and Tom looked guilty. "I did," Tom said. He was the exact image of his father, except for his eyes. They were Joanna's, wide, dark brown and serious.

"It was my idea," Pookie said. "He's a pain. He's such a crybaby."

Joanna looked over at Honor, expecting some sort of reaction. But Honor was not going to let Pookie bother her either. "She's got a mean streak, like her father," Honor said. "Why don't you all go play now?"

"I think your dinner is ready," Joanna said. "Go ask Mrs. Truc."

Dinner was ready. Joanna had to drag Cissie away from another costume change for Barbie. Finally the adults were alone again. Honor resumed their conversation, even though she could tell Joanna was upset by it. One of these days she would have to tell Joanna how psychiatric advice and tranquilizers kept a wife nice and calm about a husband like Adam.

"Would you have any idea who Adam might be foolin' with?" Honor asked.

"No. Are you sure you're not jumping to a—a hasty conclusion, Honor?"

Could it be Joanna? Honor mused, behind her shield of chemical calm. She and Adam had always been kind of attracted to each other. But she was too sincere, too honest to steal her best friend's husband. No, it was out of the question.

"How do you know he's done it before?" Joanna asked.

"He wrote her a note on a pad. I was able to read the name, it came through on the page under it. Dear Priscilla. I've adjusted to it, like the psychiatrist told me to. But I am certainly not goin' to let him *repeat* the performance."

Smiling, a woman of the world, while Joanna stared wide-eyed.

Nothing was going to bother Honor, including Saigon. Ever since she arrived, she had heard nothing but terrifying rumors. The government of the man with the silly name—what was it?—Ngo Dinh Diem—was about to collapse. They seemed to be arresting everyone in sight, Buddhist priests, college—even high school students. The government also seemed to hate Americans. There were rumors that all the Americans in Saigon were going to be assassinated. Without the tranquilizers, Honor would have turned around and gone straight back to the good old U.S.A. with the children. Why, taxi drivers spit at Americans. When an American boarded a bus, all the Vietnamese passengers got off. Some restaurants turned them away.

"I don't know how you've stood this place so long," Honor said.

"I enjoyed Japan a lot more," Joanna admitted. "But Vietnam's quite an experience. It's probably the only war we've ever fought where you kiss your husband goodbye in the morning and know that by noon he'll be in a helicopter getting shot at by the enemy."

"You *like* that?"

"No," Joanna said. "But it makes you feel part of the whole thing—the Army—being a soldier—"

Honor saw that the denial was perfunctory, polite. Joanna really liked that side of being in Saigon. But she looked so haggard and sleepless, so unhealthy, it was obvious there were other things she did not like about being here. How could anyone like it? Honor wondered, glancing at the moisture oozing from the apartment walls. The humid air was stupefyingly hot. It made Virginia in August seem balmy.

"It's not going to work, Supe. It just won't work."

Pete Burke's deep voice echoed in the stairwell. He opened the door and strode into the room, looking like a one-man army as usual. Behind him came Adam, half his width, his green beret at the standard cocky angle.

"Well," Adam said. "The ladies are half sloshed already, I see."

"If you're looking for an excuse to get that way yourself, that's not it," Joanna said. "What won't work?"

"The plan this genius and his fellow guerrilla warfare experts have sold the President of the United States," Pete said. "To convert the war into a counterinsurgency operation."

"It'll work, if we have the patience," Adam said.

"Patience has nothing to do with it. The guys up North aren't going to sit around and let you do it. Our intelligence tells us they're ready to start operating at battalion strength. Then at regimental strength. Then come divisions. They'll eat you alive."

"They can't do that countrywide. We'll keep enough hardware around to fight them in the provinces where they try it. In the other provinces we'll start hunting them."

Pete came back from the kitchen with two bottles of beer, still shaking his head. "Adam," he said, "it might've worked three years ago. It's like hunting a tiger. When he was a cub, you might have been able to kill him with a twenty-two. But now he's damn near full grown and you need a heavy weapon."

"Whatever in the world are they talkin' about?" Honor said.

"It's the Regular Army versus the Special Forces," Joanna said.

478

"This bozo doesn't understand we're trying to *save* the Army from a fiasco out here," Adam said. "We've got Kennedy halfway on our side. But does that impress Peter the Great? No. He still fights for the standard solution, more firepower. He's so narrow-minded you could use his brain for a pencil sharpener."

"The Army, Adam, honestly, to hear you talk it's always in some kind of danger," Honor said. "And you're ridin' to the rescue of it."

"When are you going to learn to keep your mouth shut about things you don't understand?" Adam said.

The words made her blink like the crash of a gun or the sting of a slap. But there was no shock, no pain. Honor thanked God again for Librium. Tranquilizers were wonderful things. They kept her nerves so steady, no matter what Adam said or did. She would not have been able to stand Adam without them. He had not been very loving lately. At first he had been wonderful. He had felt sorry for her, when her nerves were so bad, after Hawaii. But as the Librium took hold, he went back to saying cruel things to her. She had tried to be forgiving. She realized she had hurt his career, forcing the Army to pull him out of Laos, abandoning his village of Meo tribesmen to the Communists. She could understand why Adam got angry every time he looked at her. For a while it seemed like he would be stuck permanently at Fort Bragg as an instructor. She would have been reasonably content with that—Bragg was a nice post, in spite of the integrated schools—if Adam hadn't been so unhappy.

Now he—or, more precisely, they—had talked his way back into the field. Swallowing her disappointment about his refusal to accept the Command and General Staff School offer, Honor had invited Adam's commanding officer at Bragg to dinner and put on a superb performance, lying about how much she'd love to go to Saigon, even dismissing the attack of nerves she'd had in Hawaii as if it were a thing of the past. She had done her part and Adam was still making nasty cracks.

"Does Pete talk to you that way?" Honor asked Joanna, smiling, letting the words just drawl out to show she was not really bothered. "Adam says people married thirteen years don't have to be polite anymore."

Joanna was not sympathetic. That was another thing Honor liked about being on Librium. You were able to look at people as if they were behind a glass wall in a separate room and did not know you were watching them. Joanna glanced at Adam in that distressed disapproving way of hers, then back at Honor as if she thought that her question was stupid.

"We—we argue sometimes," Joanna said.

"Ah, he doesn't mean it, Honor," Pete said. "He talks that way to everybody. Underneath he's still the same miserable bastard you decided to love in spite of his defects back in 1950."

"What if you're both wrong about the war? What if we can't win either way?" Joanna said.

They were off again, discussing the Diem government and its chances for survival. In her own way Joanna was as bad as Amy Rosser, with her perpetual desire to be *in* the Army. Honor only wanted to be *with* the Army. She saw no point in trying to understand what the men were thinking and doing. Soldiering was a complicated business. A woman's business was her family, her home, her husband's happiness when he was home with her. Honor hadn't wanted to come to Saigon for a dozen reasons and this was one of them. You could never get away from the war, the Army's worries and woes. It was all around you.

Adam was arguing that it was vital for President Diem to survive the coup that was coming. He might be needed as a figurehead in a coalition government. Pete was saying that he doubted if the President would survive. Kennedy was taking a very dangerous gamble. The Americans had given the South Vietnamese Army guns and tanks and told them they were independent. It was too late to change the signals and assert control of their trigger fingers. Overthrowing a government was a violent act and there was no way to limit the violence if the government fought back. Pete wasn't at all sure that Diem would accept an offer of asylum in the U. S. Embassy. He was a very stubborn man. And very brave. He might even defeat the coup. Then where were they?

"It's something I don't think the United States should do," Joanna said. "Overthrow a government we created and supported."

480

"Grow up," Adam told her. "This is 1963. We've got to be as tough as the other guys."

"What do you think of Mrs. Kennedy, off there in those Greek islands on that tycoon's yacht?" Honor asked Joanna. Jackie Kennedy was the only part of the Kennedy administration that Honor admired. She had brought style and good taste to the White House. But when Honor left California, the country was buzzing with disapproval of Jackie's vacation aboard the yacht of Aristotle Onassis, the Greek shipping magnate.

"I really haven't thought about it," Joanna said. "What are the papers saying about Madame Nhu's speaking tour?"

Honor drew a blank. "Who's she?" she asked. Joanna explained that she was President Diem's sister-in-law and was touring the United States, condemning the Kennedys for trying to sabotage Diem's government.

Pete said he almost agreed with Madame Nhu. He was having grave doubts about Kennedy's methods in Vietnam. "No, no," Adam said. "Kennedy's still our best hope. He may not be the idealist we thought he was. But he's open to new ideas. For the Army, for the country."

"If he isn't an idealist, what is he?" Joanna said. "A liar?"

"A neo-realist," Adam said. "That's someone who defends ideals by fighting dirty."

"The end justifies the means," Joanna said.

"Let's hope so," Adam said with a wry smile.

"I'm beginning to think he's just another politician. Which means he'll screw the Army if it suits him," Pete said.

"Sometimes I think you're a reincarnation of someone who got it in the head at Little Bighorn," Adam said. "One of Custer's Irish sergeants."

"Come to think of it, if George Armstrong was around today, he'd be wearing a green beanie," Pete mocked. "And if you try going it alone against the VC with your counterinsurgency act you may end up fighting your own Little Bighorn out here."

There was a knock on the door. A tall blond civilian with a scraggly mustache peered in. With him was a tiny, wraithlike Vietnamese girl. Joanna introduced Carl Springer and his girlfriend, Nhan. "What's the word from MACV?" Springer said. "To coup or not to coup?"

"General Harkins called a staff meeting today. He told us he had just sent a message to Washington, guaranteeing the President there wouldn't be a coup," Pete said. "It's all just a lot of talk."

Springer laughed and pulled a slip of paper out of his pocket. He handed it to Pete, who read it aloud. "Please buy me one bottle of whiskey at the PX."

"That's the password my contact at VJGS promised me. Tomorrow we sink the Penguin and start swimming."

"What's all that mean?" Honor asked.

"The VJGS is the Vietnamese Joint General Staff," Joanna said. "Their army headquarters. The Penguin is what some people call President Diem."

"Why do they hate that man so?" Honor asked.

"He's a dictator," Carl Springer said.

"Isn't the man in the North, Ho Chink whatever, a dictator too? Why don't they just have an election and see which one wins?" Honor said.

"Not a bad idea," Pete said, glowering at Carl Springer. "Ho wouldn't get ten percent of the vote down here. It would be like Henry Cabot Lodge running for governor of Georgia."

This was something Honor could comprehend. "You mean it's like the War between the States?" she said. "Except this time we're fightin' for the South?"

"Right," Carl Springer said. "And when we win we're going to reinstitute slavery. Then we'll export it back to the U.S.A. and end those damn freedom riders once and for all. That's what General Harkins and his friends at MACV would like to do."

"Carl, you're ridiculous," Pete Burke said.

Honor, studying Springer through the distancing glass of her tranquilizers, decided he was somewhat drunk.

"Won't go that far, Pete? Old true blue saluter? Don't want to face up to the god-awful truth about your goddamned Army?" Springer started to giggle. "You guys are pathetic. Beautiful but pathetic. Our brave heroic Fascists."

Springer's Vietnamese girl was distressed by his behavior. "He only had one cigarette. But he's very tired. He thought the coup would come last night. He waited near the palace until dawn."

"I don't care how many he's had," Pete said. "Get him out of here."

The girl took Springer's arm and led him to the door still giggling. He got control of himself and said, "I'm sorry. Excuse me. It's definite, Pete, for tonight. I thought you ought to know—I mean— for Joanna's sake—the kids. This city's going to go berserk."

"We'll handle things if it happens," Pete said. "Go sleep it off, Carl."

Springer and the girl departed. Honor looked after him, baffled. "One cigarette? What was she talking about?"

"Marijuana," Joanna said. "You can buy it everywhere. A lot of Americans have started using it."

"I tried it in Laos," Adam said. "It's harmless. Just gives you a mild feeling of elation. Perfect for fighting a losing war."

"I don't like this country," Honor said. "I really don't."

"You can go home anytime," Adam said.

Suddenly the Librium was not working. The dislike on Adam's face was so obvious. A strange darkness seemed to invade Honor's mind, then her body. She made an effort to summon her old feelings, the pride in being an officer's wife. But the Librium seemed to stand between her and those memories. As if the memories were outside her and she was inside an invisible glass booth.

"Excuse me."

She went into the bathroom and took another pill. She splashed water on her face and told herself it really did not matter. She was *not* bothered. Except she would like to find out who Adam was fooling around with.

When she came out Joanna was serving supper. It was baked chicken, for which she disclaimed all credit. Mrs. Truc, her amah, had cooked it. Honor was trying to find someone who could cook American food. Joanna said she would consult Mrs. Truc about it. They spent the supper talking about old times and old friends. Joanna kept in touch with a lot of people. Sam Hardin and Ruth were on their way to Berlin. Other classmates and their wives were scattered all over the world, Korea, the Middle East, Europe. Adam said they were the new Romans, fighting the barbarians all around the rim of the empire.

At Joanna's urging, Pete opened two bottles of some French wine. She was obviously trying to regain their feelings from happier days. But Adam kept going back to Vietnam, the importance of changing the way the Army was fighting the war. Pete got more and more annoyed with him. By the time they left the two lieutenant colonels were practically snarling at each other.

Back in their villa on Alexandre Dumas Street, after the children went to bed, Honor could not restrain a rebuke. "Honestly, Adam, why don't you ever quit? Couldn't you see Joanna and Pete just wanted to have a friendly get-together without all this strategy and tactics talk?"

"They're like you. They don't want to think."

"I want to think—about us. Why've you been ignoring me since I arrived? Have I said or done something?"

"No. I've just got a lot on my mind."

His tone was cold but the words sounded honest. The way he looked at her in that sorrowful-wise way he had. He knew so much. But he had trouble getting anyone to listen to him. She had tried to tell him a hundred times that he had to learn to be more patient, more persuasive with people. Instead of talking to them like they were stupid. The way he talked to her. She could tolerate it because she had learned to adjust to him and she loved him. But other people did not love him, they did not even like him after he tore them apart in an argument. Half the officers in the Special Forces School disliked Adam by the time they left.

She kissed him and said she understood. But she missed him. She missed having him in her arms. He looked at her and smiled in a way she thought—or hoped—was admiring. It was sort of rueful at the same time. "You're beautiful," he said, in that mocking way, as if she didn't know there were two meanings to the word.

They made love. It left her disappointed. It must have been the tranquilizers and the wine. It was like doing it half underwater, like she was underwater and Adam was on the surface. His face seemed to ripple in the heat and humidity. The watery air pressed down on her like the weight of his body multiplied by the weight of the house, of all Saigon.

The next morning Honor felt like her bones were made of lead. She dimly remembered Adam getting up. He said something about staying in the house. She drifted down into a shallow doze.

BLAM BLAM BLAM. A series of explosions rattled the windows of the house. Little Matt started screaming outside the bedroom door. Honor ran to him in her nightgown. "Mommy, it's the Viet Cong," he howled. "They're shooting in the street."

BLAM BLAM BLAM. More explosions. Cannon fire. Then the rattle of smaller guns. My God, it was the coup. They were shelling the presidential palace, only five or six blocks away. She reeled to a window. Heat waves shimmered in the moist air. The villa's gate was open and Pookie was out in the street. Was the child insane? Honor rushed downstairs to the front door. "Pookie," she screamed. "Are you tryin' to get killed? Get back in here."

Pookie paid no attention to her. She gazed down the street toward the boulevard. "Oh wow, tanks," she yelled. "They're throwing in tanks. This is terrific."

"Get in the house this instant."

The telephone rang. It was Amy Rosser, who lived four doors away. "Have you got a weapon?" she said.

"You mean a gun? No."

"You better come up here. I've got a forty-five and six hand grenades."

"I'll be there in two minutes."

"Don't use the street. There's a gate at the back of each garden. We leave them unlocked in case we have to fight from house to house."

Appalling. Adam had told her Alexandre Dumas was one of the safest streets in Saigon. Honor flung on a Hawaiian muumuu and a pair of go-aheads and shepherded Matt and Pookie through the four gates to the rear of the Rosser garden. Amy was waiting for her at the back door of the house, a big Army .45 in her hand. Honor felt frightened just by the sight of it. "Do you know how to shoot that?" she said.

"Of course," Amy said.

"Show us," Pookie said.

"Now is not the time to waste ammunition," Amy replied. "My God, she looks like Adam, doesn't she?"

"The very image. Do you think they'll come after us?"

"Not deliberately. But they're great looters. We might see a few of them."

On the boulevard the cannon and small arms rose to a new crescendo. Amy led them into the living room, where her chubby six-year-old, Grace, was peering out a window. "Would anyone like a drink?" Amy said. The children opted for Cokes. Honor said a bloody mary would help. Amy went out to the kitchen to get the refreshments. Some heavy guns started firing at the head of the street, less than a block away. The house rattled with the concussions. Matt started to cry again. Pookie and Grace held their ears.

The telephone rang. "Get that, will you, Honor?" Amy yelled from the kitchen. "It's probably George."

Honor picked up the phone, trying to keep the noise out of her free ear with her other hand. "Hello?" she said.

"Priscilla?" the voice on the other end of the line said. "Is that you? All I can hear is gunfire."

It was Adam. "This is Honor. Who are you callin'?"

"Oh—I—I just called our house. You weren't there and I was trying to find out if you were okay."

"I'm fine," she said. "We're all here because Amy's armed to the teeth."

"Tell her if there's any sign of trouble, to call this number." He gave Honor the number and she scribbled it on a pad. "We'll have a helicopter over the house in five minutes."

"All right."

Honor stared at the number on the white pad. *Priscilla*. Was it possible? Adam and Amy?

Amy came in with the drinks on a tray. "That was Adam," Honor said. "Callin' to tell us to use this number for help if we need it."

The phone rang again. This time it was George Rosser. Honor handed the receiver to Amy. "Hello, dear," she said. "No, I'm not scared. I think we'll be all right. I've got Honor and her two kids with us. Adam Thayer just called and offered to send a Special Forces helicopter over to increase our firepower.''

Amy served the drinks. "Adam stopped in this morning and told us that the coup was coming," she said. "George didn't believe him but I decided to keep Grace home from school just in case."

"He said something about it to me but I was half asleep," Honor said. "I was still asleep when the shootin' started. I'm just worn out from this heat."

"It took me two months to adjust to it," Amy said.

Honor looked at her, baffled, confused. Was she a friend or an enemy?

"Adam called you Priscilla just now," she said.

"I can't imagine why. Unless—" Amy smiled playfully. "You're bringing back an old memory. Thirteen years ago. Remember how he used to tease me about being descended from the Pilgrims? He called me Priscilla. You remember her? The one who married John Alden?"

"Oh yes," Honor said.

"Adam can't stop teasing people. Even in a crisis. He must be fun to live with. George has very little sense of humor."

Was she laughing in her face or was she completely innocent? Honor wondered. There was no way to tell. No way to prove anything. A name on a pad in Annandale, Virginia, six years ago. *Dear Priscilla.* Had Amy been living in Washington then? Yes. She had been in Washington. Alone. George had stayed in Turkey and Amy had come back to Washington alone.

The heavy gunfire continued for another hour, then faded away to an occasional sputter of small arms. George Rosser called to tell them it looked like President Diem was holding out, waiting for loyal Army units to rescue him. Amy drafted Pookie and Grace to play canasta. The .45 rested beside the scorepad as Amy dealt. She looked like a Wild West gambling queen. Honor found it impossible to concentrate on the cards. She could not stop thinking: *Dear Priscilla.* Grace could not get the rules for canasta straight and Pookie was bored. Matt stayed by the window, watching the gate. Amy had appointed him the sentry.

About four o'clock, the gunfire picked up again. A minute later, Matt yelled, "Viet Cong," and dove to the floor. Amy grabbed the .45 from the card table and snarled, "Upstairs." They scrambled for the stairs with Matt in the lead. Amy crouched on the landing, both hands aiming the gun at the front door, which swung open to reveal George Rosser carrying an automatic rifle.

"Jesus Christ," Amy gasped. She whirled on Matt. "Don't you know an American officer when you see one? You're not very bright for nine."

Matt burst into tears again. George reported that President Diem and his brother still refused to surrender. They had also rejected an offer of sanctuary in the American Embassy. But they had no hope of winning. Fourteen South Vietnamese generals and seven colonels had denounced them over the national radio.

George kept shaking his head. "I can't understand how Washington could treat us this way," he said. "We look like fools. The President, McNamara, the Ambassador, everyone's in on this thing but us."

"Us?" Honor said.

"MACV," Amy said bitterly. "The Army. The whole thing is disgraceful."

"Isn't Pete Burke on staff there? He knew about it last night," Honor said. "A reporter friend came in and told us just before we sat down to dinner."

Amy exchanged a grim look with George. "Do you still have doubts?"

"I guess not," George said.

Adam showed up about an hour later. He was in a very cheerful mood. He had been watching the fight around the palace. They were knocking out the President's tanks, one by one. It was only a question of time, he said. They started talking about the Vietnamese general in command of the coup. George said he was an idiot. Amy said his wife was a bigger idiot. George said Vietnam was going to be a mess if Adam and his friends thought a dodo like that could run the country. Adam said he would be good enough for the time being. They wanted somebody dumb, who would let them reorganize the war.

"If you want to stay out here, George, you ought to volunteer for the Special Forces," Adam said.

Honor could see that George Rosser regarded this as an insult. Adam did say it in a mocking obnoxious way.

"I'm not interested," George snapped.

"I don't think it suits George's talents," Amy said.

Sticking by her husband. Honor liked that. Maybe she was wrong about Priscilla. Maybe it was just a coincidence. They went home and Honor served canned spaghetti for supper. Pookie told Adam how Matt had thought George Rosser was a VC and Mrs. Rosser almost shot him. Adam looked disgusted and asked Matt when he was going to grow up and stop acting like an idiot. "It was her fault," Matt said, pointing at Pookie. "She said the VC might wear American uniforms. Major Rosser had a rifle in his hand."

Honor defended Matt. His mistake was not so stupid after all. But she was wasting her breath, as far as Adam was concerned. Adam had long ago decided the child was stupid, like her. And poor Matt had no tranquilizers to help him adjust to it.

After supper, the firing around the presidential palace picked up again. About nine o'clock, a tremendous explosion shook the whole city. They could see flames leaping in the air. Adam talked on the phone to someone, urging him to arrange a cease-fire so President Diem could surrender. They did not take his advice and the gunfire continued into the night. Sleep was impossible. Honor dozed and woke up, dozed and woke up, as the cannons crashed and the machine guns chattered. At 3 A.M. she got up and took a Librium. She noticed Adam's bed was empty. Maybe he was having a drink downstairs. She decided to join him. She could use one too.

He was not in the house. Very odd. She went back upstairs and found his uniform still neatly hung over a chair, his jump boots beside it. Where could he be? She checked the children's rooms; no sign of him. She peered out the front window and then out the back window. Nothing.

She poured herself some white wine and sat in the kitchen trying to think, while the distant gunfire continued. Suddenly she knew where he was. It all came together. He was with Priscilla. With

Amy. *The garden gates are all open*, Amy had said. Adam was with her on the lush grass in the back of her garden.

Instead of weeping, Honor got the black sensation she had experienced at the Burkes', the sense of darkness spilling from her brain down through her body, black ooze that slowly became a new feeling: rage. This time Adam would get the war they had almost started to fight back there in Virginia. This was the end of the truce she had signed with him, first because she felt sorry for him after the Pentagon disaster and then because she felt guilty about damaging his career after her breakdown in Hawaii. She was through letting him insult and humiliate her in public with his nasty cracks. Above all, she was through letting him fool around with other women. Especially when the other woman was a double-crossing hypocritical bitch named Amy Rosser.

She looked up and Adam was standing there in his pajamas and robe. In his hand was his .45 service revolver. "Where the hell have you been?" she said.

"I thought I heard someone prowling around the garden," he said.

"You sure you weren't doin' the prowlin'?"

"What are you talking about? I thought the guy might come back. I decided to wait for him. I sure as hell would rather shoot him out there than wait for him to get in here."

"You're a goddamn liar," Honor said. "Duty-honor-country. An officer never lies, cheats or steals. So far the only thing you haven't done is steal. When does that start? Come to think of it, you've already started. Your classmate George Rosser is having his wife stolen out of his bedroom by you every night. Or is it every other night? What's your schedule, hero?"

"You're out of your skull," Adam said. "Take another pill."

"I've taken my last pill," Honor said. "I'm goin' to make you regret what you've done to me. I am going to make you regret it for the rest of your life."

BLAM BLAM BLAM went the cannons. *Chig chig chig* went the machine guns. The war was going full blast.

IV

"Tong Thong fini," Mrs. Truc had said when she came to work on the morning of November 2, 1963. Translation: President Diem is finished. Mrs. Truc drew her finger across her throat and produced one of her rare smiles. Joanna did not reciprocate. She was too tired. A night of gunfire had not been conducive to sleep. By this time she had no faith whatsoever that removing Diem would improve American prospects in Vietnam.

Pete had departed for MACV headquarters at dawn, leaving Bruce Lindstrom in command of defending the apartment house. Pete was not foolish enough to entrust Lindstrom or anyone else with a gun. He had acquired a supply of tear-gas grenades and gas masks. If a mob attacked the building, they were to flood the lower floors with gas and retreat to the roof, where helicopters could rescue them.

But no mob attacked, although the firing had ceased around 6 A.M., and Saigon's streets slowly filled with people. About noon, Pete returned, accompanied by Carl Springer. Pete looked inordinately gloomy and Carl had lost much of his usual effervescence. "Diem and his brother are dead," Pete said. "They shot them after they surrendered. Pretty crummy."

"The jerks," Carl Springer said. "Don't they realize how bad that's going to look in the U.S.?"

Pete had been losing patience with Carl for several weeks. Their friendship, begun in Quang Ngai Province, had been rooted in the mutual admiration for the risks they were both ready to take, Pete to lead his men, Carl to get his story.

"This isn't a goddamn publicity contest, Carl. It's a war," Pete said.

Springer listened uneasily while Pete told Joanna and the Lindstroms that the President and his brother had escaped from the besieged palace through a secret tunnel and taken refuge in the house of a wealthy friend in Cholon, the Chinese section of Saigon. The rebel generals had discovered their hideout and the Ngos fled to a nearby church, where they surrendered. En route to Army headquarters in an armored car, they were shot at point-blank range.

"What a mess," Joanna said.

"They just murdered them in cold blood?" Karen Lindstrom asked, wide-eyed.

"They had it coming to them," Carl Springer said. "They murdered a lot of innocent people in the last ten years."

"They were fighting a war, Carl. Innocent people get killed in every war. Haven't you ever read a history book? Or a newspaper, when we were in Korea and you were what—twelve years old?"

"When are you going to stop trying to sell that Korea bullshit?" Springer said.

"When are you going to stop encouraging people to murder our friends?"

Joanna sympathized with Pete's anger but she recoiled from his ruthless assertion of war's brutality. She had been recoiling—even fleeing—from Vietnam for months now. Ever since she had looked out the window of her apartment and seen a man sitting in the lotus position, the traditional Buddhist posture for meditation, in the center of a whirling column of flame. From that moment, she had begun yearning for some way to escape the human cauldron of Vietnam. Throughout the blazing summer and fall, Saigon had been a maelstrom of riots and rumors. Pete had become more and more baffled and dismayed by the divided, indecisive policy of the American government, the drift toward persuading the ARVN generals to revolt against Diem, without taking the U. S. Army, the ARVN's advisers, into the plot. Now it had ended exactly the way Pete had predicted it would end, with Diem and his brother dead.

President Kennedy and Henry Cabot Lodge must have known it would end that way. Pete, a mere lieutenant colonel, had known it. Where did this knowledge leave those who were here to bear the burdens, meet the hardships, in defense of freedom? Were they accomplices or victims? Joanna tried not to think about it.

After lunch, Pete went back to MACV. About 3 P.M. Adam Thayer, his green beret so radically cocked that the Latin motto on his badge was almost unreadable, appeared at her door.

"You've heard the news?" he said.

Joanna nodded. "Pete told me."

"No doubt you, like the moralists at MACV, blame it on Lodge and Kennedy?"

"You don't?"

"Lodge offered Diem sanctuary in the Embassy. He refused."

"We've still got blood on our hands."

Adam shrugged. "Who is we? Can an abstraction known as the United States of America have blood on its nonexistent hands? Who's more responsible, the politicians or the generals at MACV who kept lying about the war to the President, McNamara, even poor Diem? Morality is out of place in Vietnam. I don't think there's been much of it around here for two thousand years or so."

"That's not entirely true, Adam," Joanna said, thinking of Thui Dat's insistence on her husband remaining loyal to Diem.

"Maybe. Anyway, it brings me to the point of my visit. Honor seems to be having a new kind of nervous breakdown. She's convinced I've been having an affair with Amy Rosser. She's threatening to tell COMMUSMACV Harkins himself about it. Accuse us both of moral perfidy and so forth. Harkins would love to bring a Special Forces officer up on that sort of charge. They're aching for any chance to discredit us. Would you mind trying to talk some sense into Honor's head?"

Joanna found it hard to focus on anything personal. She was discovering history's power to obliterate, trivialize individual lives. Her willingness to help was passive, automatic, a reflex of the private Joanna, a semi-stranger who seemed only remotely involved in what was happening around her.

She rode through Saigon with Adam. People were tearing down

pictures of Diem. Later she would read newspaper stories sent to her by her mother about huge crowds exulting in Diem's downfall. She did not see any huge crowds in Saigon that day. The city lay in its tent of heat like an enormous stunned animal. Adam told her why Honor suspected him of sleeping with Amy. It was a pathetically flimsy story, a name on a pad, a name that recalled the innocent fun of West Point hops in 1950, a patrol of their villa's garden on a night when it was all too possible that an armed prowler might have been in the bushes.

"Why would she suspect the worst?" Joanna said.

"It has something to do with not wanting to be here in the first place. I never thought when I married her that she could endanger my career. I thought I could tolerate her stupidity. She's already put one large hole in my record, with that performance in Hawaii. Do you realize I'd probably be running the Special Forces show out here if it wasn't for that fiasco?"

"Adam, I was there, in Hawaii. It wasn't Honor's fault. If anybody has to be blamed, I'm guilty. I let her drift into the wrong company."

"I didn't expect you to be her keeper."

"I know. But—it—the breakdown—was partly because she needed you—she loves you so much, Adam."

"You said the same thing to me in 1950. What does it mean? That I should become her keeper? Turn my back on four years at the Academy, three years at Harvard? Seven years of breaking my skull to get where I can make a contribution to the Army—the country. Because a woman I can barely talk to loves me?"

"No. No."

She was not capable of passing judgment on Adam's dilemma. Any more than she was prepared to judge Kennedy for the murder of Diem. She began to realize she was morally adrift.

They passed the Xa Loi pagoda, one of the headquarters of the Buddhist movement. A small crowd had gathered on the street around it. Someone hoisted a poster with Diem's face on it and set it on fire. The crowd cheered wildly. Several dozen shaven-headed monks stood in front of the big iron gate applauding and laughing.

Joanna shuddered. She saw a burning man in the column of fire. The memory reawakened a sense, a fear, that Vietnam was permeated by an evil stronger than any American good, an evil that transcended politics and idealism, that only people like Thui Dat, with her Catholic faith, could comprehend or confront.

Adam let her out of the taxi at the head of Alexandre Dumas Street. She walked its two brief blocks to the Thayer villa, the last house on the street. Honor answered the door. She looked bizarre, her hair unbrushed and uncombed, her face a ghastly white without makeup.

"Adam asked me to come," Joanna said.

"You're wasting your time," Honor said.

They sat in the kitchen. Joanna had never seen Honor angry—fiercely, wildly angry—before. "I've had it with that man. He is a sneakin' lyin' scum," she said. "He has treated me like trash for the last time. He is goin' to find out he can't drag me around the world with him and then ignore me, abandon me, make a fool of me, with that Philadelphia Main Line bitch. I'm goin' to get satisfaction, legal satisfaction, against both of them. Then Adam is goin' to find out he is dealin' with a woman. A woman that other men—"

She stopped. Perhaps she saw the dismay Joanna was feeling. Perhaps it was visible on her face. "But I don't want that. I don't want to be that kind of woman."

Joanna took her hand. "Honor," she said, "Adam swears it isn't true. Tell me why you think it is."

Between spasms of tears, Honor presented her evidence, the complicated bits and pieces of coincidence that had convinced her that Adam and Amy Rosser were guilty of adultery. Joanna held Honor's hand for another moment. Was it possible? The answer was yes. Anything was possible in Vietnam. She heard Adam saying: *I don't think there's been much morality around here for two thousand years*.

"Honor darling," Joanna said. "You couldn't convince anyone with that evidence. An old nickname. A disappearance in the middle of the night that Adam explained. But even if it were true—and I don't believe it is—even if it were true—what would you gain from exposing them? You'd ruin the Rossers' marriage. You'd ruin Adam's career. Probably George's career too. Adam would divorce you. George would divorce Amy. It would be a shambles.''

Honor began to crumple. She rubbed her sleepless eyes like a tired child. ''Jo, I'm so unhappy. Why doesn't he love me?''

''He does love you,'' Joanna lied. ''He told me he loved you on the way over here. You're very different people. Like most married couples. Pete and I—we've gone through a lot of bad feelings, serious misunderstandings. But love—real love—carries a marriage past those things. As long as there's trust. You've got to take Adam's word for—his love.''

Honor shook her head, clinging desperately to her anger. ''He's fooled you completely. You've always worshipped him, I wish you'd married him.''

For a moment Joanna wondered if the public madness of the last few weeks in Saigon was about to sweep her away. ''There's no point in thinking that way, Honor!'' she said, with superfluous vehemence. ''Adam's married to *you*. There's Pookie and Matt to consider.''

Honor nodded wearily. ''You're right, Jo. But in my heart I *know* I'm right about him and Amy. No one will ever change my mind about it. Unless I hear Adam swear before God himself that it isn't true.''

''He will, if you give him a chance. He'll tell you how much he loves you. But give him time—give yourself time to calm down. It's been a terrible twenty-four hours. Why don't you take a pill and go to bed for the rest of the day?''

''I won't take any more of those goddamn pills. They let Adam get away with treating me like dirt. That's what led to this other thing.'' She told Joanna how the tranquilizers made everything seem to happen behind glass. ''I'm not going to live that way,'' she said. ''I'll just take a good stiff drink when I need to steady my nerves.''

She proceeded to pour herself at least four ounces of bourbon and drink it down. Joanna led her upstairs to the bedroom. Suddenly, impulsively, Joanna put her arms around her old friend. Wordlessly. A moment of pure affection. While she wondered at the weakness, the helplessness of affection. Honor thanked her and they wept together for a moment. Then Honor lay down and fell asleep almost instantly.

Downstairs, Joanna phoned the Special Forces headquarters and asked for Lieutenant Colonel Thayer. "Can we have a drink?" she said.

He told her to meet him on the terrace of the Continental-Palace. It was a favorite rendezvous, just across the square from the Caravelle. Joanna arrived first and ordered "Ba-Me Ba"—33 brand beer from the black-trousered, white-jacketed waiter. She took a long deep swallow of it, even though she knew it was so strong it would make her face flush. Saigon had returned to business as usual. She looked around her. American soldiers of every rank were buying drinks for beautiful Vietnamese girls, journalists were conferring with Vietnamese contacts or with each other. Several tables of well-dressed Vietnamese were in a celebratory mood. Diem haters, no doubt, like most of the city's café society. Outside the low plaster balustrade that separated the terrace from the street was the usual swarm of street urchins, poking their hands at the nearest drinkers for loose change. A pocketbook left within their reach was certain to vanish.

Adam strolled toward her in his green beret, his face grim. Without his smile he looked menacing, almost cruel. Joanna wondered if she would still love him if she had accepted his June week dare in 1950.

He ordered a bottle of Tiger, another Vietnamese beer, and listened solemnly while she told him that she had persuaded Honor to relent. "I promised her you were going to solemnly swear it wasn't true about you and Amy."

Adam smiled mockingly, and raised his right hand. "I swear it."

"And you were going to tell her that you loved her. If you can't say that with some degree of sincerity, Adam, I think you should seriously consider divorcing Honor. If you go on this way, you're going to have her mental illness—or her death—on your conscience."

Adam drank his beer and studied her for a moment. "Can't go to confession anymore since you and the Church parted company on the pill. So to ease your guilty conscience you've got to reform everything in sight—is that it?"

"No," Joanna said, with a tentative smile. "Just the people I care about."

"What if you can't change them—any more than you can change the rest of the world? Do you stop loving them? Stop caring about them? For that matter, do you stop caring about the rest of the world, even when you find out how corrupt it is? Those street kids out there, ready to steal the watch right off your wrist—should you care about them? Are they worth risking your soul and body to save from Communism?"

"I'm not following you, Adam."

He studied her for another moment. The bony New England face, the mocking eyes, darkened. "You know what I'm out here to do?"

"What?"

"Set up assassination and sabotage teams. To kill suspected VC here in the South. And attack selected targets in the North."

"The American government is going to do that? Kennedy?"

"I briefed Bobby Kennedy on it. 'Good, good,' he said. 'Great.'"

"But what does that have to do with your marriage?"

She knew the answer to the question the moment she asked it. She almost flinched at the certain knowledge of what Adam would say.

"The government has licensed me to commit murder. I am under orders to lie to the press and everyone else about my murderous mission. Including Pete, my oldest friend. Why, in the light of the just stated facts, should I regard a little deception of my beautiful brainless boring wife as a heinous offense?"

"Then it's true—about you and Amy?"

"Sure."

Suddenly Joanna saw her relationship to Adam the way he saw it. She was still half adversary, half object of desire. It was not her body he wanted; she could not compare to Honor's beauty or Amy's trim elegance. It was her spirit that challenged and provoked him. He wanted to shape it in the image of his own reckless soul. Joanna felt a gust of fear. It was fitting, somehow—if there was a place where she could lose her soul it was this country, where images of peace and enlightenment became weapons of war, in whirling columns of flame. Part of the fear went beyond the personal. She saw that Adam also stood for something national, something that had fatal implications for her American faith, rooted in the soaring rhetoric of John F. Kennedy.

"Don't think I'm not grateful for the good advice. To be more kind, loving. Why not? Being a good husband is part of the game. I've been resisting it. I've been resisting the game from the start."

"That's horrible, Adam."

"No, it isn't," he said. "If I were married to you it might be. If I didn't share what I really thought with you, it would be an offense against the kind of love we might have had."

Joanna felt dazed, mechanical, as if Adam were wrenching her soul out of her body, shaping it to his own design, and shoving it back into her. She looked past him at the grimy undernourished Asian faces peering at them over the balustrade.

"Do you love Amy?"

"Not really. But I can talk to her. And she's a great fuck."

"What does that mean, exactly?"

"She does everything."

"Does she love you?"

"Not as much as she loves George's career."

He paid the check and they walked into the suffocating heat of the Saigon twilight. The street was jammed with cars and pedicabs and taxis. Vietnamese girls strolled past, exchanging glances with oglers at the outer tables of the Continental-Palace.

"I really appreciate what you've done with Honor," Adam said. "I'm sorry if I upset you just now. But I didn't want to—maybe I couldn't lie to you. I never have. It seemed the wrong time to start."

"I almost wish you did," Joanna said. "But—I'm glad you didn't."

For a moment she saw her life as a losing struggle to match Pete's unflinching physical courage, the pure white ferocity of Adam's commitment to the truth.

He kissed her on the lips, a brief, not quite brotherly embrace. "Thanks," he said.

Three weeks later. It is three weeks later. Three weeks of watching Pete argue with Carl Springer, with Adam, with Tony and

Clara Emerson, repeating to all of them his relentless soldier's conviction. "The coup was a mistake. We're all going to pay for it before this thing's over."

In memory the words hang there in the moist Saigon air like a swarm of deadly insects or death-bearing helicopters, descending on those optimistic young American faces. Not even Lieutenant Colonel Burke himself, a massive image of American military strength, realized how fearsome his prophecy was. He never dreamt it was not in his power to shield those he loved from the enemy that was waiting in the Iron Triangle, the A Shau Valley, War Zone C.

Cissie comes running out of her bedroom and climbs on Pete's lap to say good night. "Give me a bounce, Daddy," she says. Pete flips her a foot in the air with a flick of his leg and she giggles in glorious glee. He kisses her and gives her a squeeze that makes her squeal. She loves him to rough her up. Around them, drinks in hand, the other Americans in their apartment house continue their chatter.

"Big Minh is a leader. He just hasn't been given a chance."

"They should have elections and choose a civilian government."

"They won't do that until the generals make their fortunes."

"Root out corruption."

"Counterinsurgency."

"Meaningful negotiations."

"Liberation front."

"Military solution."

"Tran Van Huong."

"Tran Van Don."

What was happening? Time has stopped, fixed in that miasma of ideological and military platitudes and incomprehensible Vietnamese names, like the unreal stars of a planetarium. Names words emotions swirling around the father and daughter in the worn wing chair. The heart, that unstable organ, begins to fragment like an abandoned space capsule reentering the atmosphere of earth.

But time never really stops. Let us be precise about time. Let us admit its relentless supremacy. It is three weeks and one day later. It is three o'clock on the morning of November 24. President Diem and his brother have been in their graves for twenty-two days. For three weeks and one day the Americans have watched Saigon slide into sleazy sneering corruption while the Vietnamese generals, Diem's murderers, quarreled in the Gia Long Palace and Carl Springer and Tony Emerson pontificated and Pete grew more and more gloomy. The ARVN war effort had stopped, he said, fumbled to a halt, and the VC were building in strength everywhere.

At a dinner party earlier that night Adam told everyone President Kennedy would act to fill the vacuum, you could always depend on the Kennedys to act, they were men of action, they would carry the war North, they would make Ho Chi Minh squirm.

It is 3 A.M. and the telephone is ringing in the Burke apartment on Le Van Duyet Street and Lieutenant Colonel Burke is answering it in his usual style: "Burke here." Joanna lies awake beside him, staring into the night. Nothing unusual about it. Most Army wives had insomnia in Saigon. It was their heroism, their defiance of death's first cousin, darkness.

"What?" gasps Lieutenant Colonel Burke. "Are you sure?"

A pause while the voice of the duty officer at MACV replies.

"I'll be there in ten minutes."

"What's wrong?"

"The President's been shot."

That was when Joanna began distrusting time. For a moment she thought it had unreeled, they were back three weeks and any moment there would be a blast of gunfire from Tu Do Street as the tanks attacked the Gia Long Palace.

"What President?" she said.

"Jesus Christ. We've only got one. Kennedy."

"Who shot him?"

"I don't know. We're going to Condition One around the world. It could be World War III. They want us at headquarters. No matter what happens don't leave the apartment. If things go sour, I'll get you out of here."

"Where did it happen?"

"In Dallas."

He had his khakis on, he was lacing his shoes.

"Should I tell the kids?"

"Why not? He's dead. It's confirmed."

She really meant, should I tell myself? Can I admit this has happened? She was back on the beach at Mo Ka Lei hearing those star-shining words, feeling them reach across six thousand miles to illuminate her American heart, displacing her negative otherworldish Catholic faith with a nobler, more human credo. There was no other word for it, *credo*, in its root Latin meaning. *I pledge my heart*. She had pledged it, Pete had pledged it that night at Mo Ka Lei three years ago.

Here in Saigon she had watched the pledge become soiled, mutilated. Adam had appeared to tell her that the words were simply part of the Kennedy game, and they were all players willy-nilly, with winning the only meaning. But death, Adam had said nothing about death. Wasn't death the crucial difference between life and a game? Death and love. There were no games that could control them.

What if the game included God, after all? Did John F. Kennedy die because he was guilty of the murders of President Diem and his brother? It was hard for any American in Saigon on November 24, 1963, not to wonder, to at least try to read that possibility into history's blurred message. It became another ingredient in Joanna's growing demoralization.

The next morning, dazed from lack of sleep, Joanna tried to answer Tom's bewildered questions, only to be confused all over again by further events in Dallas, above all the murder of the assassin, Lee Harvey Oswald.

Joanna was almost grateful to be distracted from the macabre public theater of Dallas by a totally unexpected visitor: Thui Dat. She stood hesitantly in the doorway, her eyes red-rimmed, her lips trembling. The white ao-dai, the gleaming black hair, the perfect features of her delicate oval face, were consumed in grief. "I have come to seek Peter's—Colonel Burke's—help in saving my husband," she said.

"Pete should be home in an hour or so," Joanna said. "Come in. Let me get you some coffee."

Joanna made some instant coffee. When she returned to the living room, she found Thui weeping. "Excuse me," she said. "I am so miserable. My husband has been arrested by the generals who led the coup. He is here in Saigon awaiting trial. It is all my doing. I urged him to scorn the men who came to him with proposals to betray the President. Even though some were from your embassy. I told him I could not live with a man who dishonored his oath of loyalty. Now they are going to kill him.''

"No," Joanna said. The word was automatic, involuntary. After she said it she realized her utter helplessness, her ignorance of what was happening around her. She was as exposed as this woman to the history that was engulfing them.

"I am ashamed to burden you at such a time. When you are no doubt as shocked by the murder of your President as I was at the death of President Diem. Do you think Kennedy was the victim of traitorous generals in your American Army?''

"No!" Joanna said. "Such a thing is—really quite impossible."

Thui heard the words as a rebuke. She nodded sadly. "You mean such things occur only in wretched countries like Vietnam," she said. "You are no doubt correct."

A few minutes later, Pete arrived home for dinner. He listened with growing distress as Thui repeated her story of General Dat's arrest. He borrowed Joanna's typewriter and immediately began a long memorandum to COMMUSMACV General Harkins, asking him to intercede for Dat. Although Thui was staying at the Continental-Palace, Pete insisted on her eating dinner with them every night for the rest of the week. He explained to Joanna that they were her only friends in Saigon. People from Hue were considered virtually enemy aliens by the Saigonese. It was typical of the regional and ethnic hostility that permeated Vietnam.

When General Harkins did not reply to Pete's memorandum, Joanna joined the campaign. She took Thui to the Cercle Sportif and introduced her to Jane Skelton, who soon arranged a dinner party at which Thui met Brad Skelton and several other colonels on the MACV staff.

Thui rose to the occasion with sure feminine instinct. Her white silk ao-dai glowed in the candlelight. Her makeup remained subtle, understated. She seized that elegiac mode of Asian poetry Joanna had perceived in her parents and made it her theme. Around it she orchestrated a whole symphony of other effects, gentle courage, tearful resignation, plaintive need. She talked of the crude quarters in which she and her husband had lived in Quang Ngai while he was training the 25th Division, because he refused to take bribes and lived on his salary. She described two Viet Cong attempts to assassinate them and their two children, the first by firing a rocket at the house, the second using a bicycle loaded with plastic explosives. Both times the houses were destroyed but they were not at home. She relived the anguish with which she had advised her husband to remain loyal to President Diem.

By the time the dinner was over, there were a half dozen champions of General Dat at MACV besides Pete Burke. Several of the Americans knew one or two of the ruling Vietnamese generals or their aides. Within the week the charges against General Dat were dropped. He and Thui came to the apartment on a Sunday afternoon to thank Pete and Joanna. Thui was wearing the white silk ao-dai she had worn at the triumphant dinner party. "You have my gratitude forever," she said. She thanked Joanna and kissed Pete with considerable fervor. General Dat laughed and said something in Vietnamese. Thui smiled and said something tart in reply.

"What did I miss?" Joanna said.

"He says I am in love with your husband," Thui said. "He's right. But it is the kind of love I feel for Father Buu Dong. A noble love. Greater than one can have in marriage."

Glancing at Pete, Joanna saw a glaze of admiration on his face. When was the last time he had looked at her that way? During June week in 1950. She felt a twisting pang of loss, failure.

A noble love. Greater than one can have in marriage.

She thought about Adam and Honor, George and Amy. Was the Army the enemy of love? Or was it marriage itself?

Pete stood at the window watching the Dats get into a taxi. "Isn't she tremendous?" Pete said. "We've got to straighten out this country."

Joanna walked to the window as Thui's slim figure, shimmering in the violent sun, vanished into the taxi's darkness. "Are you sure you aren't being unduly influenced by the way her ao-dai clings to her figure?"

"What a hell of a thing to say."

Pete was glaring at her. The taxi made a U-turn, passing through the discolored concrete in the middle of the square where the Buddhist monk had died in his whirling column of flame.

Pete, I want to get out of here. I want to go home. The words trembled on Joanna's lips. She whirled and fled into the bedroom. She flung herself face down on the bed, pressing her face into the pillow. After about five minutes, Pete sat down on the bed and put his hand on her shoulder.

"I'm sorry. I guess we're all feeling uptight."

She said nothing.

"You're not jealous of Thui, are you? I mean—she's a beautiful woman. But—you're my wife."

Fundamentals. Pete Burke always dealt in fundamentals. The big hand rubbed her shoulder. "Listen. This thing with Thui has brought me a lot closer to Brad Skelton. He runs the planning group in the Army Support Command. That's the operations arm of MACV. I'd love to work for him. Maybe you could start telling Jane how miserable I am working for Hamburger. The war's practically come to a stop. There's nothing for me to do. I think I can get away with a minimum of damage."

Fundamentals. Lieutenant Colonel Burke always dealt in fundamentals. His wife. His career.

On the dais a Vietnamese band assaulted American songs with a heroism seldom displayed by the ARVN. On the dance floor of the Cercle Sportif, officers in dress blues, wives in evening dresses that showed signs of travel fatigue, tried to follow the erratic beat.

It was New Year's Eve. The Burkes were sitting at a table with Brad and Jane Skelton and two other colonels from MACV and their wives. Pete was telling them what the generals' junta was doing in Quang Ngai Province, from which he had recently returned. The junta had thrown out all the officials who had been loyal to President Diem. The province chief had been fired and the ARVN had permitted a mob to beat him so badly he was in the hospital. "He was one of the most effective anti-Communists in Vietnam," Pete said.

Adam strolled up to them with Honor on his arm. She was

wearing a tiered white silk chiffon gown with a blue sash. Her red hair was set in thick whorls over her ears. "Sorry we're late," Adam said. "Had trouble getting our pet cobra back into his cage."

Honor had called Joanna two weeks ago and asked if she and Adam could sit with them at the ball. None of the other Special Forces people were going. But Adam had agreed to go, if they sat with the Burkes. Honor had spent a half hour telling Joanna how nice Adam was trying to be, how glad she was that Joanna had stopped her from going berserk that day after Diem was killed. "It was all that shootin'—and those damn pills," she said. "Honestly, Jo, if I was any place but Saigon, I'd be happy."

Joanna had already arranged to go to the ball with the Skeltons. She had been spending a lot of time with Jane at the Cercle Sportif, doing her best to help Pete escape General Hamburger. Joanna asked Jane if they could add the Thayers to their table and she had cheerfully agreed. Introductions were quickly accomplished and the Thayers sat down. "Pete just got back from Quang Ngai," Joanna said. "He says the situation up there looks very bad."

"The war is lost," Adam said. "The only sensible thing we can do is get the hell out of here as expeditiously as possible."

Pete and the three MACV colonels stared in astonishment. "Do you know something we don't know?" Brad Skelton said.

Honor smiled brightly at Adam, as if he had just told a very successful joke. Joanna wondered if she was drunk. And Adam too.

"Of course not," Adam said. "Nothing you can't find out by reading the papers. But don't worry, friends, we're not going to do anything sensible. Our new President, Lyndon Johnson, is a virtual guarantee against that. He's sending us a new commander, a man who knows exactly how to refight World War II and Korea. General William Westmoreland."

"Is that bad?" Brad Skelton asked. Joanna noticed that Pete was looking appalled.

One of the other colonels, a swarthy man named Taliferro, said: "I served under Westy in Korea. He's a can-do guy. One of the best."

"He would be, if we were still fighting in Korea. Unfortunately the name of this country is Vietnam. In case you haven't noticed."

506

Colonel Taliferro's jaw tightened. He turned to his wife and said: "Would you like to dance?"

Adam began denouncing the part Westmoreland had played in smashing the Coordinating Group in 1956. He had been secretary of the general staff at the time.

"I don't see anything wrong with what he did," Brad Skelton said. "His job was to protect his boss, the chief of staff. Those guys were publicly embarrassing him. Loyalty in the Army runs up, not down, Adam."

"I think it should run both ways," Adam said.

"Adam, they're playin' 'Cheek to Cheek.' One of my favorites. Let's dance," Honor said.

Jane Skelton watched Adam and Honor until they reached the dance floor. "Brad told me the Green Beanies were strange. Now I'm convinced," she said to Joanna.

"He's brilliant but—"

What could she say? That the Army had inflicted a deadly wound on Adam's spirit? Or was it wounded long before the Army challenged and aroused his idealism at West Point? Joanna realized Pete was staring at her. She stopped and let him finish the remark.

"He was my roommate at the Academy. One of the brightest people I've ever met. But I've never thought much of his judgment."

Joanna knew that was the worst thing an officer could say about another officer.

"The sooner we got rid of those jungle jocks, the better," Brad Skelton said.

Pete led Joanna out on the dance floor. "Talk to that nut," he said. "You invited him to join the table."

"I didn't invite him. Honor asked me. They're our oldest friends."

"Okay. Talk to him. If I try it, I'm afraid I'll hit him."

Joanna obeyed when Adam asked her for the next dance. "Don't pick a fight with Brad Skelton," she said. "Pete's hoping to get on his staff. He's feeling more and more desperate, working for that idiot Hamburger."

"That's all you think about now? Peter the Great's career? Amy Rosser has gotten to you?"

"It's not all I think about. But it's certainly no crime to try to help where you can. Pete's very unhappy, Adam."

"Maybe it's creative pain. It will give birth to doubts about the system. That's when he'll start to be a real soldier."

"Please, Adam. As a favor to me."

He led her off the dance floor through French doors to a balcony overlooking the swimming pool. He leaned on the stone railing and lit a cigarette. "I don't like what's happening out here," he said. "What it's liable to do to the Army. These can-do game players like Westmoreland are letting Johnson slide us into another stalemate war with a lot worse odds than we had in Korea. We'll be up against an enemy with more resilience, in a country where we can't use a third of our firepower. Doesn't that upset you? Don't you want to stop it?"

Adam was trying to tell her that they were all directly in the path of the immense historical beast that was blundering toward them. The ground was already trembling beneath their feet. But she had moved too far away from him, spiritually and psychologically, out of revulsion or perhaps fear of his scarifying truth. She still stood beside Pete although she was uneasily aware that the foundation of her commitment was being eroded day by day.

"I don't see what I can do. Or Pete. Anyone at our level."

"There's a lot you could do, if you're willing to take a few risks. The press is on the right side. If you feed them the right stories we can embarrass these game players right out of their jobs."

"Adam—that's so disloyal. And I don't think it would work. Reporters don't care about the Army."

"They're far from perfect allies, I agree. But it's an unavoidable risk. Pete's in a perfect position to do the game players a lot of damage right now. He has access to MACV's confidential files."

"You must know you're asking the wrong man to even consider such a thing."

"Am I asking the wrong woman to ask the wrong man?"

"Yes."

He stubbed out his cigarette and held up his arms. "Let's go back and play the game."

They glided onto the floor to "Dancing in the Dark."

• • •

During the first months of 1964, as the Viet Cong's strength rose in the countryside, casualties among the advisers leaped shockingly. There was a funeral service at Tan Son Nhut Air Base for "friends going home" almost every day. When General Hamburger learned that some of these coffins were prayed over by a lone chaplain, with no other American mourners to be seen, he decided that one of MACV's wives was henceforth to be on call to represent the Army and the women of America. Amy Rosser was made the secretary of this operation, and Joanna soon came to dread her brisk voice on the telephone. Usually she knew nothing about the man besides his name and place of birth and—if he was a West Pointer—the year he graduated. Nevertheless, Joanna felt she should write a letter to his wife or parents, trying to convince them that she and the other Americans in Vietnam truly regretted the death of their husband or son.

It was even more heartbreaking if the dead man was one of the young captains or lieutenants whom Pete was always inviting to dinner. Most of these impromptu guests had been cadets during the two years Pete had been a tactical officer at the Academy. Pete regarded them as younger brothers; Joanna's feeling for them was more maternal. So many of them, when talking to her, retained their boyish, earnest cadet manners. After dinner, they would spend hours discussing the problems they were having with their South Vietnamese counterparts. Pete patiently listened and gave advice. Afterward he would tell Joanna that the advice was worthless—the problem was the cowardice or stubbornness or corruption of the Vietnamese officer, which no one could change. But it helped to know there was someone at MACV who was willing to listen to their woes.

When one of these former dinner guests was killed, Pete would be depressed in a stoic bitter way that Joanna found disturbing. "We're building up quite a score to settle with Victor Charlie," he said after the third or fourth death. Joanna found the deaths demoralizing. Often she was unable to sleep for a whole night after a funeral at Tan Son Nhut for a boy they had known. She began to dread the sight of Pete in the doorway with a smiling young captain or lieutenant beside him. Sometimes during dinner she would be paralyzed by the sudden bursting question in her mind: *Will you be the next to die?* Her hand would freeze to the platter of steak or chicken. She would be unable to lift it, to speak, for a full minute. While Pete and the young man chatted about helicopter tactics, ambush warning signs, new VC heavy weaponry.

Then death invaded the apartment house, their vertical American village. He came casually, bowing his way among them during an offhand conversation at an Easter party. Bruce Lindstrom remarked to Pete that he had decided to take Karen and the two children for a week's vacation at the mountain resort of Dalat. Another Protestant missionary with whom they were friendly had a car. .

"If I were you, I'd fly," Pete said. "That highway isn't safe."

"Can't afford it," Bruce said. "From what I can find out, the VC haven't harmed any civilians on that road. If they stop you, it's just to give you a lecture from one of their agitprop teams."

As the Viet Cong grew bolder, they often blocked the highways to Dalat, Cap St. Jacques and other resort towns and forced travelers to pull over and listen to one of their specialists in agitation and propaganda (hence the term *agitprop*) explain why they were fighting the American imperialists and their South Vietnamese lackeys.

"I wouldn't trust any VC with my safety or my kids' safety for sixty seconds," Pete said. "Those agitprop teams are backed up by a squad of guys with automatic rifles."

"Jesus has brought us this far," Karen Lindstrom said. "Surely He'll get us to Dalat and back."

By this time the Lindstroms had long since opened their church. They were disappointed by the tepid response of most Saigonese to Protestantism. Their converts were largely "rice Christians," slum dwellers who came to partake of the free meals the Lindstroms served each evening. But the ministers' faith-fueled enthusiasm remained undimmed. Joanna still admired them for their dedication. She and Pete had gone to a service at the church, which was only a few blocks away on Pham Dinh Phung Street. She had been touched by the sweet simplicity of Bruce Lindstrom's sermon in which he tried to tell his congregation that Jesus loved each of them individually. It was far more inspiring than the bored French mumbles that Catholics got as sermons at the Saigon cathedral. Even Pete had admitted he was impressed, after initially resisting the idea of setting foot in a Protestant church.

The next morning, Joanna accepted for safekeeping two of the Lindstroms' pets, a parrot named Micah and a cat named Joshua. She watched them load their bags into the car, a ten-year-old black Chevrolet. The other missionary was a beefy, moon-faced man, an administrator at the Seventh-Day Adventist hospital in Saigon. Karen waved goodbye and Cissie said she wished that she was going to Dalat with three-year-old Donny Lindstrom, who had become a favorite playmate.

Joanna took her for a swim at the Cercle Sportif and she and Cissie soon forgot about the Lindstroms. There the gossip concentrated on rumors of another coup to unseat the current Vietnamese general in power—and the date when William Westmoreland would take command of MACV. He had been in town since late January but spent most of his time flying around South Vietnam, studying the military situation. He was still officially listed as deputy to General Harkins. Everyone agreed that the signal for imminent succession would be the arrival of Mrs. Westmoreland and their three children. Jane Skelton was the dispenser of most of this wisdom. In her offhand way, she was as astute if not as intense an Army politician as Amy Rosser and her friend Florence Eberle. Jane told Joanna there was a good chance that Westy would make Brad Skelton commander of an expanded Army Support Command, and the first man Brad intended to ask for was Lieutenant Colonel Pete Burke.

"Mommy—there's Daddy!" Cissie cried.

The lieutenant colonel himself was striding toward them, threading his way among the scampering children and chaises asprawl with sunbathing American wives, his face very grim. Cissie ran toward him, her arms wide, and clasped him around the knees. He hoisted her above his head for a moment, gave her a kiss and told her to go play in the pool with her rubber raft. He resumed his glowering advance on Joanna and Jane Skelton.

"Hello, Jane," he said, and turned to Joanna. "I think you better come home right away."

For a moment Joanna was too weak to get up. "Is it Tom? Did they attack the school bus?"

He shook his head. "We just got a report from the chief adviser of Binh Tuy Province," he said. "The Lindstroms and their friends got stopped on Highway One by an agitprop team. There was a helicopter patrolling nearby and the pilot dropped down to try to scare the VC away. They shot Lindstrom and the other minister."

"Are they dead?"

"I'm afraid so."

We're all going to pay for it before this thing is over.

Two hours later, Joanna sat beside Karen Lindstrom on the couch in her apartment. Karen clutched a picture of her husband in his white ordination robes. "How could it happen?" Karen whispered to Joanna. "You go to church. You're a Christian. We trusted in Jesus. How could such a thing happen?"

Pete came in to tell Karen that the arrangements for her flight home tomorrow were completed. Karen did not seem to hear him. She was pursuing answers to why Jesus had failed them. "Maybe it wouldn't have happened if you didn't come out here with your guns and helicopters. If you just came as Christians."

Pete looked bewildered. Karen had always treated him with awed respect. She once told Joanna that Pete was her idea of what a Christian soldier should be. "Karen," he said, "I've seen a lot of men who believed in Jesus die in action. We don't understand those things. You just have to remember that Jesus died too—on the cross."

Karen Lindstrom was beyond theology. She began weeping again. "I wish they'd killed me too. I wish they'd killed all of us."

"Where are the kids?" Pete asked.

"In the bedroom," Karen said. "I can't face them. What am I going to do? I have no money."

Pete left Joanna with Karen and went into the bedroom. When Joanna looked into the room ten minutes later, she found Pete sitting on the bed with the two little boys on his lap, one big arm around each of them. "I hope you'll always be proud of your dad. I hope you'll always remember why he came to Vietnam—to help poor people. The men who killed him didn't know that. But you mustn't forget it, ever," Pete said.

512

The older boy, Bruce, Jr., six, seemed to understand. He nodded mournfully. His younger brother, Donny, simply looked dazed.

In years to come, Joanna returned to this image of the huge American officer with his arms around the two fatherless boys. It would become a kind of talisman. But now she only felt the futility of all forms of comfort. The dread that had haunted her after the first Buddhist monk immolated himself outside the apartment returned to stalk her nights. How could anyone shoot down unarmed men with their wives and children watching? How could God permit it? She had no answer, only the mounting fear that in Vietnam, anything, everything was permitted.

Then came death from another direction, equally brutal and unexpected. Brad Skelton and an AID official went out to inspect a strategic hamlet in Long An Province on the outskirts of Saigon. As they drove back to the city in the twilight, a VC hiding in the bushes exploded an electrically wired mine beneath their jeep. Skelton and the AID official were killed instantly. Their driver lost both legs below the knees.

The funeral service at the airport was the most disheartening yet. Everyone stood around inside the metal quonset hut, staring at the two flag-draped coffins, the Army people in one group, the AID people in a separate group, as if their griefs could not mingle. In a way, the appearance corresponded to reality. The AID official had been twenty-seven, a young man making a brief, undoubtedly praiseworthy contribution to the American effort overseas. Brad Skelton was forty-five, just reaching the point of maximum reward for his twenty-two years in the Army. *Career* was the word Joanna heard again and again as she stood beside Pete and listened to him talk to his fellow lieutenant colonels and colonels. Terrible to see such a promising career cut short. Suddenly she found herself gritting her teeth. Old hostilities stirred. Was career the foundation of duty-honor-country, the real motivation behind the readiness to bear any burden?

She walked beside Pete in the line of friends moving past Jane Skelton to say goodbye. "Even the score for him, Pete," Jane said as he gripped her hand. Joanna recoiled from the idea. Was that what she would say if she stood in Jane's place? She thought of Jane, dustcloth in hand, telling her the gossip at Leavenworth, confessing her anxiety when Brad was overseas. Joanna struggled to fix Jane in her feelings; she felt death required the effort. Jane was like an older sister with whom she had never become intimate; at least an older friend.

"It's God's will, Jo," Jane said as Joanna held both her hands for a moment. She could only nod and wonder what the words meant, in the context of what Jane had said to Pete. Suddenly Jane became a stranger to her, the whole scene part of a waking nightmare. Joanna thought of the other memorial services beside the lonely coffins, the meaningless medals from the commander of the South Vietnamese honor guard, the young advisers smiling at her across the table a week, a day, before their deaths. Adam's words about can-do game players, his declaration that the war was lost. *I don't know what to feel*, she thought. *I don't know what to think or feel.*

Driving back to their apartment they passed the presidential palace. A mob of Buddhists were chanting slogans in front of it. Their leaders were as hostile to the new government as they had been to Diem. A few blocks away, another mob came toward them. Their driver had to slow the car to a crawl. They chanted another set of slogans. "Catholics," Pete said. "I hope the riot police are ready for them." The Catholics were carrying clubs, chains, machetes. They were obviously on their way to attack the Buddhists.

The new government, anxious to show the Americans and the world that they were more liberal than President Diem's regime, permitted demonstrations anywhere and anytime in Saigon. The Buddhists were the most active at first. But the Catholics, bitter at Diem's murder, which they blamed on the Buddhists, opposed them with demonstrations of their own. Soon angry mobs were swirling through the streets, fighting each other with deadly weapons. At least nine people had been stabbed, beaten or hacked to death. Saigon was spiraling down toward anarchy.

A week later, a bomb exploded in a bar frequented by American enlisted men. Five sergeants were killed. One was a man who had served under Pete in Korea. Another funeral service at the airport, this one without wives. Enlisted men were not authorized to bring their families to Saigon. Their women wept at home.

"I'm afraid we're going to see a lot more bombing like that," Pete said. "Diem's secret police kept the VC in Saigon under pretty good control. After the coup the whole apparatus fell apart. The current government is trying to put together another one with our help. But it's a slow process. The VC can come and go as they please. From now on I don't want you or the kids to go near a restaurant. Don't even risk a drink at the Continental-Palace."

We're all going to pay for it before this thing is over.

The meaning of the words kept changing in Joanna's mind. What was *it?* Being American? Being a career-minded lieutenant colonel? What was *this thing?* Being an Army wife? When would that be over? Other words, still unspoken, crowded her throat. *I want to get out of here. I want to go home.*

Then came a shock that made those words impossible to speak. General Hamburger departed for a cushy berth in NATO. Behind him he left an Officer Efficiency Report on, among others, Lieutenant Colonel Peter M. Burke. It was devastating. He rated Pete in the mediocre middle range on everything, and added a postscript in which he said Lieutenant Colonel Burke had "a dangerous appetite for intrigue. It was difficult to tell whether he was working for me or the Central Intelligence Agency."

Pete was numb. He sat in the apartment for an entire weekend, contemplating the ruins of his career. "Can't you do something about it?" Joanna asked. "Can he just slander you with impunity?" She telephoned Adam, who came over and scoffed at the theory that one bad OER could ruin a man. "Hell, you should have seen what Eberle wrote about me after the Coordinating Group crashed," he said. Pete shook his head. Joanna saw how differently they regarded their careers. As differently as they regarded their lives. Pete had relied on steady, perfectionistic performance, Adam on seizing attention with a starring role.

On Monday Pete roused himself. He went to see Arnold Coulter. Only with the greatest difficulty did Pete persuade him to write a letter, stating that at no time had Pete ever worked for him in a CIA capacity. Pete had this statement added to his file. Then he went to Joe Taliferro, who had taken Brad Skelton's job at the Army Support Command, and asked him for a slot. "I told him I wanted the toughest assignment in the place, the one nobody else wanted. He gave me Long An Province. Where they're kicking the hell out of us," Pete told Joanna.

Joanna listened, nodded, murmured phrases like "great" and "you can do it"—saying words she no longer believed, not saying what she really thought: *I want to get out of here. I want to go home.* The new assignment meant they would be in Saigon for another six months, at least. She could not object. She could not ask Pete Burke to take her home, to leave Vietnam a beaten man— beaten by his own Army. She had to let him try to add a touch of Adam to his style, pull off something spectacular.

Other wives went home—or elsewhere. Amy and George Rosser left for England, where George was to spend a year as an exchange officer. Amy gave a series of spectacular dinner parties in her last week in Saigon, to one of which she invited Joanna and Pete. "I'm going to miss Saigon," she told Joanna. She sounded like she meant it. Joanna wondered if it had anything to do with Adam living four doors away. Other members of the Harkins-Hamburger entourage departed with similar éclat; not a hint that they were members of a losing team. Willard Eberle moved up to brigadier general and went back to the Pentagon. Joanna was outraged at the skill with which these military politicians made their exits, leaving Pete and others to fight the rising VC tide. Pete, who was spending half of his days and nights in Long An Province, in the Mekong Delta, only shrugged and reminded her of General Coulter's old adage. "The Army's like getting married. It's for better or for worse."

It was the wrong metaphor to give a poet who had not finished a poem in two years, whose secret self was beginning to accumulate a dangerous mixture of disillusion, rage and fear. Wrong was the order of the day, in the late spring of 1964 in Saigon. The Viet Cong tore apart two ARVN battalions in Long An before Pete could get the province reorganized. They rampaged through Quang Ngai, the northern province where Pete had advised the 25th Division, chewing up whole battalions there too, killing a captain of whom Pete was especially fond, a West Pointer named Christopher Sullivan. In Saigon scarcely a day passed without some sort of terrorist attack. More bars and restaurants were bombed. A warrant officer's wife was hideously wounded by a grenade flung into the taxi in which she was riding. Honor was in a state of near hysteria, afraid to leave her villa. A half dozen Army wives cracked and went home. There were rumors that they were going to evacuate all the wives and children. But President Johnson, Ambassador Lodge, the Joint Chiefs of Staff, one or all of them together decided it would be a humiliating loss of face that might panic the already shaken South Vietnamese.

On a Sunday evening early in May, a huge bomb exploded in the lobby of the Capital Kinh Do Theater in downtown Saigon. The theater was reserved for the American community and showed first-run movies every night. Dozens of wives and children were cut by flying glass, suffered concussions, punctured eardrums, from the blast. Honor and her two children were among the victims. She got a nasty cut on her chin and a broken arm. Joanna visited her almost daily as she convalesced. She was moody and tearful about the scar on her chin. The doctors assured her that plastic surgery would remove it and scheduled her to fly to Honolulu in July. Honor remained inconsolable. In outbursts of rage she blamed Adam for the whole thing. "I never wanted to come to this crazy place," she sobbed. After two weeks of this kind of behavior, Joanna began to feel somewhat sorry for Adam.

Joanna's own morale was buoyed by the arrival in Saigon of an old friend, Martha Kinsolving. Lover MacKenzie's widow was now a happily remarried mother of four—two girls and two boys. She and her husband, Vic, had spent the previous year at Fort Thompson, Arkansas, where the Army was devising new helicopter tactics for the latest innovation, an air-assault division. Vic had been sent out to Vietnam to study the helicopter tactics MACV was using with the ARVN. The commander of the Army Support Command designated Pete to work with him, and the two lieutenant colonels were soon flying all over Vietnam to talk to U.S. advisers and their Vietnamese counterparts. Martha and Joanna had lots of time to spend together.

As cheerful and unflappable as ever, Martha restored to Joanna's consciousness all the good memories of Army life. She was a living, laughing antidote to Saigon's nightmare.

Hindsight, that destroyer of remembered happiness, that devourer of consolation, whispers that it was the wrong time to laugh at Martha's stories of dogs that strayed onto the parade ground during a Fourth of July review, of the general who tried to tell her how to discipline her son when he was caught draping a sheet over an equestrian statue of Robert E. Lee to turn him into a member of the Ku Klux Klan. It was the wrong time to lounge beside the pool at the Cercle Sportif. But a prod of ambition made Joanna laugh all the harder at Martha's stories. Pete was tremendously interested in Vic Kinsolving's experience with the new air-assault division. He said it was going to replace the paratroopers as the elite division of the future.

On the last Saturday in May, Martha called Joanna to suggest they take the children to a softball game. A team from a Marine helicopter unit had challenged the Army Support Command to a game. Pete and Vic were spending the weekend in some muddy provincial town in the Mekong Delta watching an ARVN division and their advisers plan a major helicopter assault. Joanna readily agreed. Surrounded by a chain-link fence, Pershing Field was certainly one of the safest places in Saigon.

They sat in open bleachers, wearing wide-brimmed straw beach hats against the tropic sun. There were at least two hundred spectators, many of them officers' wives and children. The game was rather boring. The two pitchers were much too good for the hitters. It was still 0–0 in the fifth inning. The younger children, Cissie and Martha's three-year-old, Sally, grew restless and asked if they could go down on the grass in front of the bleachers. They found two or three other girls their age in a similar state of boredom and began playing tag.

As the last batter on the Army team struck out to end the sixth inning, Joanna saw Cissie, out of the corner of her eye, running along the bottom row of the bleachers to escape Sally Kinsolving, who was trying to tag her. That could lead to a bad fall, she thought, and was about to go down and order them to stay on the grass.

But she never moved. She never spoke. She still sits there, the dutiful mother, watching her chunky pig-tailed laughing four-year-old. She sits there forever in her memory, the jungle theater of regret.

There was an explosion of unbelievable force. Joanna felt herself flung forward by the blast and simultaneously sucked down as the bleachers collapsed. As she fell she saw Cissie hurled sideways off the bottom row toward the playing field. Then Joanna was on her back in the smoky debris, surrounded by moaning, screaming women and children. Her son Tom was pulling her to her feet, crying: "Mom. Mom. Are you all right?" Military policemen and the baseball players swarmed among the wreckage pulling out bodies. "A pipe bomb," someone said. "A pipe bomb."

"The no good sons of bitches," someone else said.

Then Joanna remembered. "Cissie,"-she said. "Where's Cissie?" She stumbled past the rescuers, the victims, to the grass. A white-helmeted military policeman was kneeling beside a small figure in green cotton overalls. "Mommy, it hurts," Cissie said. "My tummy hurts."

Blood was soaking the front of the green overalls. Martha Kinsolving appeared beside them. She was leaning on Tom's shoulder. Blood oozed from a cut over her eye. "We'll take her in my car," she said. "We won't wait for an ambulance."

"What about your kids?"

"They're all right. Just banged up."

Clutching Cissie to her breasts, Joanna ran to the parking lot. With Martha's hand glued to the horn, they careened through Saigon to the Navy Dispensary. At one intersection they almost hit an ambulance that was clanging toward Pershing Field. By the time they reached the dispensary Cissie's head was lolling like a rag doll on Joanna's shoulder. Was she breathing? Joanna could not, she would not answer that question. The corpsman at the reception desk took one look, seized Cissie from Joanna and ran down the corridor. The last glimpse Joanna had was of one chubby arm dangling.

Joanna sat there, brushing mechanically at the blood on the front of her sundress. Martha sat beside her. "Where are your kids?" Joanna asked.

"Tom's taking care of them."

"You don't have to stay."

"I'll stay."

Ambulances clanged to the door bearing the other victims. Nurses and Navy corpsmen administered morphine, set up a triage system to get the most seriously hurt to the operating rooms. Over the next hour there was a steady flow of frantic mothers and fathers arriving, faces numbed against the worst. Joanna knew most of them. She had sat with them around the pool at the Cercle Sportif, she had taken Cissie or Tom to their apartments or villas for birthday parties.

Hours later, so it seemed, a young doctor walked toward her. He was wearing an operating-room gown. A uniform. Logical. Death and uniforms went together, Joanna thought. She knew from the expression on his face that Cissie was dead.

"We lost her, Mrs. Burke," he said. "She died on the operating table. A piece of the bomb tore her intestines apart. Ruptured the spleen, the liver."

Martha MacKenzie Kinsolving took her hand. "Don't hold it back, Jo. Don't try to be brave."

Joanna shook her head. She could not weep. She was too amazed, too dazed, too disbelieving. Americans, especially well-educated Americans, people who live in the world of books and ideas, are insulated against such events. Even when they walked through Army hospitals and faced their own husbands riddled by bullets, saw a thousand other men with murderous wounds, they groped their way to some glimmer of purpose in the suffering, some vague sense of choice, of accepted risk. But the suffering of the innocent, the experience of being a victim? How could such a thing happen to the beloved daughter of Joanna Welsh Burke of Cincinnati, Ohio? Joanna the earnest striver to do or say the right the dutiful the moral thing. All Joanna could do was cry: *"No!"*

No. No. No.

They thought she was refusing to believe that Cissie was dead. What she was refusing was her assent to the fact of her death. She remembered Pete, sitting beside Karen Lindstrom, saying: *We don't understand*. But Joanna understood and refused to accept it. Do you hear me, husband, mother, father, God? I refuse to accept it.

520

At home they found Mrs. Truc weeping, holding Cissie's Barbie doll. Tom was there with the Kinsolving children. He had told her. Martha sent Mrs. Truc home. Pete was somewhere in the Mekong Delta on a helicopter, watching the ARVN hunt the Viet Cong. Martha decided it would be wiser to get him back to Saigon before telling him. "He might do something crazy," she said.

Joanna nodded passively.

Honor and Adam came. Honor wept and held her. "We should never have come out here. It was crazy for them to bring us out here," she sobbed. Adam simply looked at her, stony-eyed. "We'll talk some other time," he said, and took Honor home. She was no help. Adam could see that Martha, the general's daughter, death's veteran, was the best person for Joanna now.

If there was a best person.

If there was any person.

Martha sent Tom to stay with her children at the Kinsolvings' villa. She made it into an important assignment, giving him all sorts of details about what time they were supposed to go to bed and what they liked to eat for dessert. She had an amah who was prepared to take care of these things, but she did not want Tom to feel she was just getting rid of him.

Martha talked about death, calmly, gently. It was not entirely cruel. "Right now, Jo, you don't believe you'll ever get over this: You just want to die. That's the way I felt when Lover was killed. Then you'll begin to realize Cissie isn't completely lost. As long as you live, you'll have her, the way she was today. Laughing. Innocent. It sounds crazy to you now, Jo. But that's not all bad."

The words sounded vaguely familiar. A memory stirred in Joanna's numbed brain. Suddenly she was back twelve years, standing in the bedroom of Blanche Coulter's mountaintop house in Yokoshima, listening to her tell Arnold Coulter that it was a consolation to think that her dead son would never change, never grow away from her now. Joanna shuddered. Martha could not know what she had just recalled. She listened and nodded as Martha talked of other Army families who had lost children to disease, accidents. She was a shrewd psychologist. She was trying to deflect Joanna's anger from the Army, from Pete. But Joanna's secret self was shrewder. She saw through the maneuver. She was not going to forgive anyone, ever.

About 10 P.M. Adam came back. Martha went home. Adam sat down on the couch and took Joanna's hands. "Tell me what you're thinking," he said. "The exact truth."

"I lost my faith today. Not just in God. I've been losing that for a long time. The other faith."

"Yes."

"Kennedy."

"Yes."

"Bear any burden, face any hardship. America's faith."

"Yes."

"Have you lost it too?"

"Yes."

"What should we do?"

"There's only one answer," Adam said. "I have no magic power; I make inward strength my magic."

Zen toughness. The Samurai's creed. They were back thirteen years, in the Doubting Hut in Japan. But the years had added a new idea.

"And play the game?"

"We're not playing the game now."

"What are we doing?"

"Hurting. Helping. Living."

"When do we go back to playing the game?"

"When you're ready. When you're strong enough."

She shook her head. "It won't work, Adam."

"There's nothing else. Absolutely nothing else."

Footsteps on the stairs. Thunderous footsteps. The stamping ascent of a giant in combat boots. Adam's last words were still hovering around them when the door burst open and Pete stood there in his battle dress. The peak of his field cap cast a shadow on his tormented face. His .45 dangled from a holster on his hip. A canteen bulged on his opposite hip. Other packets, probably ammunition, were clipped to his web gear belt. In his anguish he had not even removed four grenades from the bandoliers on his chest. He was an image from a whirlwind, a paradigm of war.

"They told me at the airport," he said. "I went to the dispensary. I had to see her. Kiss her one last time."

Joanna fled, before Adam's eyes, or from Adam's eyes, from his therapeutic, dangerous philosophy, to the arms of the man she had chosen or more precisely the man who had chosen her. She plunged into his world of metal and sweat, mud and grief, and simultaneously opened her arms to his wounded courage. They clung together and she wept and he wept. She had seen him weep over his dead. Now she was joining him, becoming part of his grief, his fate, in a way she had never imagined.

In the darkness of the stairwell she saw Victor Kinsolving, also in his battle dress. His wide brow was furrowed, creating a quizzical baffled expression. If Vic had left, if Adam had left, perhaps Joanna could have stripped away the gun and grenades, the paraphernalia of war. Perhaps she and Pete could have been what eventually they had to become, parents, alone with their grief. But she was fatally outnumbered by the soldiers.

They slumped in chairs. Pete asked for a drink. Joanna found some bourbon in the kitchen. As she poured double shots into the glasses, a flare rose into the night on the outskirts of the city. Moments later brilliant red tracer bullets crisscrossed from a half dozen directions. The war had not stopped. History continued its blind thrashing.

In the living room she heard Vic Kinsolving say: "There's only one answer to this mess. Bring in our own guys."

Joanna did not pour a drink for herself. No one noticed. She distributed the glasses, each a former jelly jar. What was Cissie's favorite jelly? Strawberry. She would have to remember those things. She would have to start remembering everything about Cissie.

Pete held up his glass like a chalice. "I see a lot of dead VC in here," he said. "I hope you guys do too."

"In spades," Vic Kinsolving said.

"Amen," Adam said.

Was that an evil wish? Joanna was surprised to discover that without God she still believed in evil.

No, she told herself. Killing people was their profession. Adam was there, saying Amen. No different, really. The Army was still his satori.

She remembered Blanche Coulter's words: *They don't know how to comfort us.*

V

HOME they came, Lieutenant Colonel and Mrs. George Rosser, that love-dovish, fortyish pair, hand in hand on the foredeck of the S.S. *United States*. Dinner at the captain's table last night, George in his dress blues, Amy in a Balenciaga gown, George talking largely about NATO's strength, the reality of a Russian threat. A Midwest congressman and his wife had listened, enthralled.

"Aren't you worried about Vietnam?" the congressman's wife had asked.

"Only that it won't last long enough to give me a shot at commanding a battalion out there."

The congressman had liked that. It was the way Army officers were supposed to talk. The trouble was, George meant it. But Amy felt confident that she could cope with George now.

A year in England had been the perfect restorative after their near disaster in Saigon. It had been almost possible to forget Vietnam, while George toiled on staff studies for NATO, and they enjoyed the company of the officers and ladies of the Royal South Oxfordshire Regiment, with whom they were billeted. It was fascinating to see how another army operated. To a British officer, the regiment was his home. Most of them stayed in it for decades. Only a handful moved up and out to larger things. There was none of the whirlwind shuffling from assignment to assignment that was the standard policy of the American Army. The English problem was boredom. Amy decided she preferred the American system.

The Rossers were going home to an exciting job in the Pentagon. Their old friends the Eberles had not forgotten them. Willard was now secretary of the general staff, a man who could twist arms throughout the Pentagon to get what he wanted. George was going to be on Willard's staff. Yes, dear, Amy had explained to Georgianna, the secretary of the general staff had his own staff. There was simply no end to staff jobs in the U. S. Army.

Lieutenant General Henry Hamburger was also coming home to become deputy chief of staff for personnel, a job that had no small potential for helping his friends. Amy and George had kept in close touch with Henry and Millicent while they were in London and the Hamburgers were in Brussels. Amy had reserved hotel suites, bought theater tickets, trudged through Harrod's and Selfridge's with Millicent, who loved to shop but could never make up her mind about anything. Amy did some research on Staffordshire china and helped Millicent launch a collection of antique platters that would make marvelous conversation pieces on her dining-room wall. Amy never did figure out what Henry was doing at NATO that brought him to London so often. He seemed to have a big staff and was studying troop morale in all the NATO countries. He also made a lot of visits to Spain, where he had had several talks with General Franco.

Breathing the salt air, feeling George's muscular arm around her waist, Amy was amazed by how happy she was. It had been a difficult tour at first, loaded with potential disaster. It had not been easy to abandon her affair with Adam Thayer. They had continued it to the very day she left Saigon, in spite of Honor's angry suspicions. Joanna Burke had done a beautiful job of quashing those, thank God.

At first, Amy thought Joanna had quashed Adam too. Amy heard nothing from him for a week. She had been relieved. The thing had been too wild, too dangerous, meeting him in the garden at 3 A.M., playing every kind of game in the lush grass, with George, her daughter Grace, sleeping only a hundred yards away. It had also been fantastically exciting, especially the last night, when the machine guns and tanks were blasting the presidential palace.

The following week, when she got a telephone call that began: "Hello, Priscilla?" she had been amazed by the intensity of her desire. It suffused her like one of those hot flashes her mother complained about during change of life. Was she that hungry for him? She had insisted to herself that her desire for him, his desire for her, was strictly sexual. She had abandoned the comradeship of their first encounter in Washington with only a twinge of regret. Meeting him in the darkness had made it easier. They were simply bodies, accompanied by detached whispers, gasps, sighs.

When Adam again arranged for afternoon meetings on the junk in the Saigon River, Amy was forced to recognize her previous theory as deception. There was something between them—not comradeship, because neither trusted the other anymore, but something more than sex. She gradually realized it was the Army, the complex way they both loved it, while their spouses merely tolerated it.

Adam knew so much. His mind was a honeycomb of projects, trends, struggles in the Pentagon, Congress, the White House. He kept in touch with the ongoing probably eternal feuds between the Army and the Air Force, the Army and the CIA. He made her laugh describing the dozens of intelligence men from each branch, including the Navy, tripping over each other's leads in Saigon. He told her in horrific detail about the assassination program he and a certain general were running, the Army's attempt to show they could be just as tough as the CIA. He foresaw the downward spiral of the ARVN, the fatal mistakes in training and doctrine made ten years ago. He gave her a viewpoint on the Army, the war, that was as tough and contemptuous—and as quietly impassioned—as his own. It was absurd, ridiculous, to care about the Army, the doddering dinosaur that did not seem to care about anything, above all its own disciples who toiled inside its belly, its bowels, its small brain. That was why it was also necessary to play the game, to mock caring even while deep within the heart caring, or at least its shadow, fascination, survived.

There was also sex, which was more offhand, ironic, delicious;

two pilgrims worshipping at the shrine of the cock. They never used their real names, it was always Miles, Priscilla, amusing references to "ye Christian soldier" (George) and "ye shrew" (Honor). But on the last day it had been difficult to be amusing. Adam told her he was getting out of the assassination business; he was going up to the highlands to work with a tribe called the Rhade, deep in VC territory.

"Is that playing the game?" she asked.

He shrugged.

"Don't get killed on me, will you?"

He grinned. "I would love to get killed on you. Perhaps we could arrange for ye Christian soldier to do it. What a finale. I like big endings. As you may have noticed."

He rolled her over and bit her on the behind.

"You know what I mean, you bastard," she said, face down.

Suddenly they were back to the comradeship of the Pentagon wars. She wanted to cling to him, to weep a little and tell him she really meant that. To show him she knew that in the Army there was always a line where the game ended and the real meaning of it, the necessary killing, the possible dying, began.

Did he know it and avoid it, despising all emotion as weakness? Presuming (wrongly) that she shared this heritage too? She only knew that when she looked up, his green beret was on, he was buttoning his paratrooper's jacket. "Let's not say au revoir or goodbye," he said.

He lit a cigar. "Wait for the usual signal," he said. She lay face down on the bed until he stamped twice on the deck. It meant there were no obvious spooks or police in sight. She rose, put on her ao-dai, her hat and veil, and briskly departed, looking neither to the right nor to the left, in the style of someone above suspicion or at least indifferent to it.

England was what Amy had needed after veering so close to moral and marital chaos. Its casual order, its familiar dowdiness, restored her Philadelphia self. There was nothing in the least seductive about England. It was like a cold bath after a night of drinking, a shocking return to normality. At first the shock kept fading, and a yearning for Saigon's steamy dissolution, Vietnam's supine conquerability, for Adam, returned. With George's help, the wish gradually dimmed.

In the latter days of Saigon, when everyone in the Harkins' entourage seemed to be sliding toward oblivion, Amy had almost stopped thinking about George, except when she faced him at the dinner table. Exhausted from overwork, appalled by the violent gyrations of American and Vietnamese policy, George had barely touched her for weeks at a time. Amy had made no attempt to persuade him. In England, her Philadelphia self needed his dull but comfortable lovemaking. She regularly lured him to bed with invitations that even George could not ignore.

So the year had passed with its usual rapidity, and now they paced the deck of the S.S. *United States* beneath a starry September sky, discussing what 1966, the Pentagon tour, held in its impenetrable weeks and months. Ever since President Johnson sent the GIs into Vietnam to rescue what was left of the ARVN, George had been itching and fretting about getting out there in command of a battalion. He said it was the hot new item that everyone had to have in his file. Letters from Florence Eberle more or less confirmed this assertion. But Florence cautioned that it was very important to get a good battalion in a good division. The Pentagon was full of stories about promising careers wrecked by the chanciness of combat. The North Vietnamese had a *very* good Army, Florence said.

Other letters kept Amy in touch with the class of 1950. From Honor she had gotten vivid, if somewhat hysterical descriptions of the final days of the officers' wives in Saigon, as VC terrorists rampaged and the ARVN collapsed. Honor included the shocking news about Cissie Burke's death. Amy had written Pete and Joanna a sympathy note, which was never answered. The Burkes had left Vietnam after Cissie's death and spent a year at Fort Thompson, Arkansas, where Pete got a battalion in the 11th Airmobile Division. When the division went to Vietnam, Joanna had done something completely unexpected—enrolled in a Ph.D. program at a state university in northern New York, where she had friends on the faculty who were admirers of her poetry. Honor, quoting Adam, said Joanna was trying to escape the Army—which made no sense for an officer's wife. Honor was afraid Joanna blamed the Army for Cissie's death.

A different version of Joanna's state of mind came from Ruth Hardin. She wrote that Joanna had recovered from the tragedy and was as "true blue" as ever. Ruth and Sam Hardin had spent the year at Fort Thompson with the Burkes. Sam was now in Vietnam with Pete, also commanding a maneuver battalion. Ruth was sure that Sam was going to get killed this time. Counting Korea, it was his fifth year of combat. Ruth sounded like she would relish his demise, just to prove she was right. Sam apparently made a policy of never accepting Ruth's advice on anything. He and Pete Burke were the combat stars of '50. But Pete would have to do something spectacular, like capturing an entire North Vietnamese division, to overcome the OER Henry Hamburger had given him in Saigon.

Adam Thayer had survived his Special Forces tour in the mountains with the Rhade tribe. The North Vietnamese had attacked his base camp and only the arrival of reinforcements from the 11th Airmobile had saved him. Adam got minor hand and leg wounds and went home with a Purple Heart and a Silver Star. He was in Washington now, working for General Newton Ingalls in congressional liaison. The Pentagon was mustering its best and brightest to cope with the political problems of Vietnam. For a few days, Amy was unsettled to discover that she would encounter Adam again in Washington. But her year in England had left her confident that she could cope with him, too. She was not going to get involved again; her Philadelphia self did not want or need Adam Thayer.

In New York, the Rossers went directly from the pier to the Metroliner to Washington. The house Amy had bought ten years ago was waiting for them in Alexandria. As they followed a redcap with their luggage through Union Station, a half dozen police cars roared up to the entrance, their sirens screaming. White-helmeted cops raced into the concourse. A hoarse voice came over the loudspeaker: "Ladies and gentlemen. There is no cause for panic. But we would like you to evacuate the station as soon as possible. We have just received a bomb threat. Please evacuate the station by the exit nearest you."

Grace started to cry. Georgianna started to tremble. "It's like Saigon," Grace wailed.

"Shut up," Amy said. "Just keep walking."

As they went out the swinging doors to the taxi stand, a policeman approached George. "Excuse me, Colonel. I wouldn't wear my uniform downtown today."

"Why?"

"Big anti-war demonstration. They're expecting forty thousand or so."

Amy had read about the anti-war movement in English newspapers. But she had always discounted the more vivid descriptions of it as typical English exaggerations. The British enjoyed portraying the Americans as chaotic bumblers, beset by insoluble problems. The Vietnam war was also unpopular because of the predominance of left-wingers in the British press corps. Now, as the Rossers drove to Alexandria, they saw the streets full of young people with long hair and outlandish costumes—like a bunch of rock music stars who had multiplied by some miraculous or diabolic process. Several were carrying red and white flags, with yellow stars on them. Georgie asked what country the flags came from.

"They're Viet Cong flags," George said.

Amy was breathless. Enemy flags in the capital of the United States of America? "Why doesn't somebody arrest them?" she asked.

"We're not legally at war with the Viet Cong. Congress hasn't declared war on anybody," George said.

At their house in Alexandria, they found their furniture, which they had sent ahead, dumped in usual Army mover fashion. A note from Florence Eberle was pinned to the mantel, telling Amy she had supervised the arrival and hoped that the "Huns" had not broken anything irreplaceable.

A wild scream from the kitchen. Amy rushed out to find Grace with her hands over her ears, standing before the open refrigerator. Inside was a dead cat with its belly ripped open. Pinned to it was a note: "Welcome home, killers. Remind you of Vietnam?"

A howl from upstairs drew Amy in that direction, while George comforted Grace. Dangling from a rope in Georgianna's closet was a woolly white dog, its tongue protruding. On the rope was another note: "This is what war criminals deserve." A revolting stench filled the room. The temperature was in the eighties and the creature had apparently been hanging there for days. Amy felt ill. She went into the bathroom and lifted the lid of the toilet. The head of another dog, a puppy, stared up at her. On the inside of the toilet seat was another note: "Feel sick? You should."

George told Georgie and Grace to go outside while he searched the rest of the house. There were no other corpses. George buried the remains in the backyard and Amy tried to control her rage and talk calmly to the girls. "The country seems to be going a little crazy," she said. "There are some very vicious people loose. We didn't let the VC scare us in Saigon. We're not going to let them scare us here."

"Why do they hate us?" Grace asked, a puzzled pout on her fat ten-year-old face. "Daddy didn't kill any VC. He worked in an office."

"Other people in the Army did, stupid," Georgianna said. "The Army did a lot of lousy things. They used napalm on villages, burned women, kids to cinders."

"That is not true," Amy snarled. "Where did you hear that?"

"From kids in my class in England. Army kids. They heard their parents talking about it."

"You shouldn't believe what foreigners say about your country. They envy us. The whole world envies us. While we risk our lives and spend our money defending them. It's sickening. I won't stand for enemy propaganda in my own house."

"You just got a dose of it," Georgie said. "What are you going to do about it?"

At fourteen, Georgie was harder than ever to love. Her taste in music was atrocious, nothing but clanging rock. In England she had spent most of her time pursuing rock stars like the Beatles and the repulsive Rolling Stones. She had spread a four-by-four picture of their satanic leader, Mick Jagger, on the wall of her bedroom. Amy had forced her to take it down. They had had another battle over Amy's refusal to let her wear miniskirts. Georgie had retaliated by wearing nothing but blue jeans. She now seemed determined to be as unfeminine as possible. Yet she was maturing physically. She was menstruating, her breasts were developing. This only made Amy feel her denial of her femininity was even more reprehensible.

George returned from his burial chore. Amy wanted him to call the police and demand the arrest of the vandals who had desecrated their house. George shook his head. "In the first place, they won't catch them. In the second place, it'll get in the papers and we'll get even more harassment."

"That's the way to catch them. Lure them out of hiding. I refuse to believe the forces of law and order are helpless. Get Army Intelligence to work on it. You're not a second lieutenant anymore."

George argued for a while but Amy was adamant. He gave up and called the police. Two detectives appeared and George had to dig up the corpses to prove they were not imagining things. The detectives took down statements from everyone, while the furniture and trunks sat there, unmoved, unpacked. Amy telephoned Florence Eberle, more from a need to tell someone who would identify with her outrage than for any practical reason. Florence agreed it was horrible and swore that she had locked the house. The detectives meanwhile searched the premises and found a push-in cellar window through which the perpetrators could easily have entered.

A *Washington Post* woman reporter called Amy about the incident the next day. She wanted to know if George had been returning from Vietnam and seemed confused when Amy said no, from England. The reporter asked if George had ever served in Vietnam. Amy angrily asked what difference that made. Too late she realized this sounded like she had something to hide. "We were in Saigon for seventeen months," Amy said. Ah, said the reporter. And what had Colonel Rosser done in Saigon? He was SGS to General Hamburger. And what did General Hamburger do? He was deputy to General Harkins, the commander-in-chief of the Military Assistance Command. And what did they do? "They ran the war, you idiot," Amy said. "What do any of these questions have to do with what's been done to me and my family? Both my children had nightmares last night. I couldn't sleep." Coolly, the reporter replied that she was only trying to find out if Colonel Rosser might have been involved in some "reprehensible actions" in Vietnam. Amy slammed down the phone, too stunned to answer her. She looked around her disordered house and burst into tears of rage.

Goddamn them, Amy muttered, as her head began to throb ominously. She would show them. She would put her house in order. She would not let them invade her home. The Army would help her; they had to help her. She called Florence Eberle, who heard the hysteria in her voice. Within the hour, Florence, who was living at nearby Fort Halleck, arrived with a swarthy master sergeant named Riggio and three privates. "You remember Sergeant Riggio, don't you? He was with us in Germany," Florence said. "I told him what happened to you and he and these three young men volunteered to help." Amy said of course she remembered Sergeant Riggio, although she did not have the faintest recollection of him. They went to work.

In four hours of furious effort they put down the rugs, positioned the furniture, hung pictures, while Amy and Florence decided where to display the Chinese scrolls and ivory carvings Amy had bought in Saigon. By four o'clock the job was done. Sergeant Riggio and his assistants sat in the kitchen, sweaty and exhausted, sipping beer from cans. Amy felt triumphant, exalted.

"I can't tell you men how much I appreciate this," Amy said. "If I had to wait until Colonel Rosser got gack from the Pentagon and then spent the next week putting this place together I would have felt those—those peace freaks were winning—"

"Sure, ma'am," Sergeant Riggio said, wiping sweat from his dark forehead.

"We'll catch them. Willard said he'd get the FBI to work on it," Florence said. "We can't allow these people to attack our officers' families. We'll make an example of them."

Amy noticed that the privates said nothing. They just drank their beer. "Have any of you been in Vietnam?" she asked.

Sergeant Riggio glowered at the privates. "These guys are all training to be dog robbers, ma'am."

"What?"

"Orderlies, dear," Florence said. "The Army has an excellent school for them at Halleck."

Amy gave the sergeant twenty dollars and the orderlies five each.

When George and the girls came home—from the Pentagon and from school—they exclaimed with surprise at the scrubbed and shining house, its furniture and works of art in splendid array. Amy felt ready for anything. Later that night she tried to entice George into bed to celebrate. But he said he had a ton of work in his briefcase. Between the war and the protesters, the Pentagon was in overdrive.

The animal story appeared in the *Washington Post* the next day, a tiny item on page 16. It simply stated that Lieutenant Colonel Rosser and his family, moving into their Alexandria home after a tour abroad, found bodies of dead dogs and cats apparently planted by anti-war activists. The police were investigating. Amy felt vaguely disappointed. She had half hoped the snippy reporter would slander them in some way, so she could write a scorching letter of protest to the paper.

That night, around midnight, just as she was drifting down into sleep, the telephone rang. George answered it, snarled something and hung up. A half hour later it rang again. It continued to ring at half-hour intervals all night. Around 4 A.M. George was too tired to wake up and Amy crawled over him to answer it. "Oink oink oink," said a voice. "Oink oink oink."

Bleary-eyed in the dawn, George reminded her that he had predicted the newspaper story would make trouble. At 9 A.M. Amy called the telephone company and told them to change her number. They said it would take several days. She called George at the Pentagon, hysterical again. Amy could not believe this was happening to her, an officer's wife, in the United States. At lunch with Florence Eberle at the Fort Halleck Officers' Club, Amy learned that officers and their families were being harassed all over the country. Worse, the Army had decided to do nothing about it. They just reported the cases to the local police and let them investigate in their halfhearted way.

At dinner that night, Amy raged to George about the situation. He shrugged wearily and said there was nothing else to do. The Army had no authority over civilians. They could not arrest a civilian, even on an Army base. "Then what's the point of being in the Army?" Georgianna said. "It seems like a lousy deal to me." Amy was asking the same question but she was groping for a different answer. Something fundamental in her life was being violated. A contract she had signed with God, the United States, some sovereign power, was being abrogated. And George just sat there, shrugging, blinking sleepily into his soup.

"Oink oink," went the voice on the telephone, for the first half of the night. They finally took the phone off the hook and lay there listening to Ma Bell's computer whine its eerie complaint. In theory, George was violating orders. He was supposed to be available twenty-four hours a day like all officers on duty at the Pentagon.

The phone company finally changed the number and semi-peace returned. It was semi because a day seldom passed without news on television of a protest march, a campus demonstration somewhere. Each was a scrape on Amy's ever more exposed nerves. Adding to the strain was the way Georgianna took an almost feverish interest in the protests. When she talked about them at dinner, Amy invariably told her to shut up. They were sending Georgie to a private school in Alexandria, Posey Hall, where she could get special tutoring and psychological counseling, to the tune of five thousand dollars a year. It was filled with misfit offspring of bureaucrats from the State Department and other civilian branches of the government. At Parents' Day, Amy sat next to a thin febrile woman whose husband was something in Far Eastern affairs at State. Her name was Wax. The first thing she said, after she learned Amy was an Army wife, was: "Do you think Johnson should stop the bombing?"

"On the contrary," Amy said. "I think he should flatten North Vietnam from the panhandle to the Chinese border."

Amy soon learned that Georgie and the Wax woman's daughter, Pandora, an equally mangy-looking fourteen-year-old, who specialized in wearing cut-down Army fatigues, were best friends. Pandora regularly showed up on Saturday with new records from groups with impossible names like the Jefferson Airplane and the Grateful Dead. When Amy refused to let them turn the stereo up as loud as they wanted it, they made Pandora's house their rendezvous and Georgie was scarcely seen for most of each weekend—a relief to Amy.

George occasionally asked where she was. But he was too tired and too busy to think about her very much. He did not think about anything very much except his latest action report. Brigadier General Willard Eberle had turned into a Simon Legree. Not even George was exempt from the lash of his tongue or the pressure of his ever escalating demands for more work from his staff. They called him Willard the Wizard because he seemed to think that action officers could produce reports by saying "Shazam!" He was fond of putting an action on a man's desk at 5 P.M. and telling him he wanted a report on it by 8 A.M. the next day. Frequently this meant the man did not go home that night. One new man, whom the general seemed to dislike on sight, was given two five-o'clockers in a row, and Willard threw the results in the wastebasket. It was just his way of maintaining staff readiness, he said.

George found it hard to repress the urge to call Willard a son of a bitch. Even Florence admitted to Amy at lunch that Willard had undergone a startling change of personality since he became a brigadier general. "The Army sends them to a charm school for three weeks, you know, where they learn how to act like generals," Florence said. "I don't know what they tell them, exactly, but I'm not thrilled with the results. He expects to get his own way on everything."

When the Rossers were invited to dinner at the Eberles' quarters, Amy studied Willard throughout the evening. There was a definite change, an obvious escalation of self-confidence, even a jump in the volume of his voice. He walked with a kind of swagger and pontificated freely, without repeating himself. Since everyone at the party was on his staff, no one contradicted him, as he prophesied that the war in Vietnam would last another ten years. In his opinion, there was only one way to win it. Build a network of highways throughout the country, defoliating the jungle for a half mile on each side of every road, making it difficult for the VC to blow it up. This would solve the supply problems that inhibited major operations, unite the country politically and enable the Army to bring its mechanized equipment and tanks into combat.

"I thought the helicopter had solved the mobility problem in Vietnam," Florence said.

"I'm talking about logistics, not mobility," Willard snapped. "I sometimes think that mentally you're still in Arizona in 1910 watching your old man chase the Apaches."

Everyone looked at the ceiling or their plates while Florence almost strangled with indignation. Willard continued orating on the war. When he paused for breath, the other husbands and wives fled, no doubt thinking they could get a decent night's sleep for a change. George began stifling yawns when Willard launched a diatribe against Lyndon Johnson's interference with the Army's conduct of the war. After a half hour of vituperation, Willard paused to freshen his scotch and soda. "Time to go, don't you think, Ame?" George said.

Willard looked at his watch and reluctantly agreed. It was after midnight. Outside, mid-December rain poured down. George said he would get the car, which he had parked down the street, and drive it to the front door. Florence went out in the kitchen to make sure the orderlies who had served the dinner were doing a 4.0 dishwashing job.

Willard helped Amy into her caracul coat. "Nice to see you again, Priscilla," he said. "Do you still like to fuck?"

He might have been asking her if she still played tennis. His voice was that casual. Amy tried to button her coat. She could not control her fingers. The buttonholes seemed sewed shut.

"Why don't we meet Wednesday at the Howard Johnson's motel on I-95 to talk it over?"

"No," she said.

"Too bad. I have this dossier I wanted to show you. About this officer's wife who had an affair with one of his West Point class-mates. It would upset the hell out of George if he saw it."

"All right. What time?"

"Three? The room will be reserved by Mr. Willard."

The next four days were the worst of Amy's life. What to do? Let him? The idea revolted her. Maybe she was not a virtuous woman. But she was not Willard Eberle's whore. What if she simply failed to show up? Willard was mean enough, tough enough, to make good on his threat. He was also smart enough to arrange for George to discover the dossier accidentally. It would be easy to drop it on his desk at 9 P.M. when the SGS office was empty.

By Tuesday, she could think of only one solution: Adam. His silence for the past four months indicated that he too had decided it was time to stop playing dangerous games. She telephoned him at the Pentagon's congressional liaison office. "Hello, Miles. This is Priscilla," she said. "Priscilla with a problem. Can you call me from outside?"

He was on the line in fifteen minutes. She told him what was happening. To her amazement, she wept. She had told herself she would be empty and cool. Just hearing his voice brought back Saigon.

"Here's what you're going to do. Call him and tell him you want that intelligence dossier. The file copy. Go to the motel. To his room. I'll be there."

"What will you do?"

"Kill him, maybe."

"Adam!"

"Just be there."

On Wednesday, she called Willard and insisted on getting the dossier. She forced herself to eat some lunch and at 2 P.M. drove numbly through Alexandria's suburban streets and joined the whizzing cars and rumbling trucks on I-95. In a half hour, the ugly orange roof of the Howard Johnson's motel appeared on the right. A faggy blond clerk, who was either sneering at her or had a permanent smirk on his face, said Mr. Willard's room was number 26 in B wing. Amy walked toward it on the bright green rug, feeling like she was sloshing through ankle-deep mud.

General Eberle was sitting in a chair, reading a thick pile of papers in a manila folder on the desk in front of him. He was wearing a dark blue civilian suit. "Ah," he said. "On time. Let us all praise Army training."

There was no sign of Adam. Had he deserted her? Had he thought it over and asked himself what was in it for him? Why should he make an enemy of a general as influential as Willard Eberle? She had betrayed him to Florence; wouldn't it be perfect revenge to betray her to Willard?

General Eberle took off his coat and tie. "Let's have a drink," he said. He gestured to a bottle of scotch on the dresser. "I'm in no hurry. I hope you aren't."

Amy shook her head.

"Why don't you take off your dress?" Willard said. "No point in mussing anything. All you've got to do is relax, Priscilla. I guarantee you a good time. A very good time."

The old Willard, repeating himself. Adam, where are you?

The door clicked open and Adam stepped into the room, smiling broadly. He was wearing his Green Beret uniform. "First time I've loided a lock since training days. Remember me, General? Adam Thayer."

Willard Eberle rose to his feet. He was taller and heavier than Adam. But his sedentary jobs, his fondness for scotch, had created sags in the jowls, chest, gut. Adam was lean and far more menacing.

"What the hell are you trying to pull?" Willard growled.

"I might try pulling out your intestines, inch by inch. How's that for openers? I've got murder on my mind, General. I've been trained to commit it in a lot of gruesome ways."

"You go looking for trouble, don't you, Thayer," Willard said. He did not show a flicker of fear. For a moment Amy's confidence in Adam's reckless courage wavered.

"A basic character defect, no doubt about it," Adam said. "Let me make it clear that this lady had no idea I was going to stage this scene. She called me up and asked me what she should do about your proposal. I pretended to be the world's biggest coward and told her she should cooperate."

"I believe you. About the lady's relative innocence. She would never be guilty of such deplorable judgment."

"Yeah," Adam said. "My judgment is deplorable, all right. If you and your fellow insider assholes could read, we wouldn't be losing a war in Vietnam. I spelled it all out in words of relatively few syllables back in 1955, General. All about coercive war and why we shouldn't fight another one. I can see from the blank expression on your face that you've never even heard the term. There's a lot to deplore, General, including that star on your shoulder and your scheme to rape this woman. Do you know something? She cares more about the goddamn Army than you ever will. That's why I'm here. So you don't ruin that thing in her, that caring. It's fucked up, like mine is. But it's there.''

That was not really true, Amy thought. She wanted to care that way. She remembered wanting to do it when Adam had asked her, ten years ago in Washington, *Jesus, Amy, don't you care?* But she had been afraid of the cost, the pain. Now that she saw how much Adam was prepared to risk for her, in the name of that caring, she would try again. She would wait for a chance to make his words come true.

"Why don't you go into politics? You make great speeches," Willard Eberle said.

Adam moved so swiftly, for a moment Amy thought Willard had lunged at him. With a snarl and a grunt, they coalesced and Willard hurtled across the room with Adam's hand on his throat. The two of them slammed into the wall so hard the bottle of scotch flew off the dresser and crashed onto the floor. They were both against the wall and Adam had a long curving knife at Willard's throat. Fumes from the splattered scotch made Amy's eyes water.

"How's this for a little action, General? Does it speak louder than words? If you ever go after this woman again, I'll kill you. Maybe this way, with the knife some dark night. Or maybe some morning with plastique in the engine of your car. Or maybe with a high-powered rifle when you're strolling down a Washington street with one of the several dozen Pentagon secretaries you've been fucking. No matter where I am I'll get on a plane and come back here and do it.''

Willard Eberle said nothing. His eyes revolved down toward the knife. But he still did not show any fear.

"Do you read me, General?"

"I read you," Willard said.

"Okay." Adam let go of Willard's throat. "Now get the hell out of here. Let's go back to trying to win the war."

Willard seized his coat and tie and made a rapid exit. Adam scuffed at the smashed scotch bottle; the fumes were now engulfing the room. "Too bad he didn't leave us the booze. But we'd better get out of here. He's the sort that might call the cops and get them to raid the place."

He scooped up the intelligence file and glanced through it. "Good news," he said. "Nothing in here about Saigon. I thought he might have had us tailed there, too. You should excuse the expression."

Amy clung to him, weeping. For a scary moment she felt more married to him than to George. "Stop," Adam said, hands at his sides. "We'll never get out of here. There'll be a headline in the Metro section of the *Post*. Green Beret officer gets medical discharge after week in hotel room with mystery woman. Unable to pass minimum physical fitness tests, shrunk from six feet one to five feet seven, Lieutenant Colonel Thayer had no comment as doctors fought for his life at Walter Reed Hospital . . ."

They walked out to their cars. "He'll hate you forever," Amy said as they stood beside her Buick.

"It's worth it."

"I love you—in a certain way. You know that."

"No, I didn't. I'll try to remember it."

"Where are you living?"

"I've got an apartment in Washington. Honor's staying down in Charlesville with her mother. I go down there on weekends, when I can stand it."

"I—deliberately didn't call you. I thought it was best. I gather you felt the same way."

Adam nodded. "I'm trying to make it with Honor. As much for the sake of the kids as for anything else. It's bad enough for them, watching the country come apart."

"Yes," Amy said.

"But some night, when he can't sleep, Miles may give you a call."

He kissed her this time. She was swept by an intense, almost humbling desire for him. He was not afraid. That was the heart of it. He was like John Stapleton, afraid of nothing. Would he die the same way? She stepped back, impaled by the memory of that old pain. "I really better go. The kids will be home from school."

"Yes. I'll get rid of this."

As she drove away, he was ripping the Army's file on their love into small pieces and throwing them into a green barrel marked TRASH.

It should have lasted for years, perhaps for a lifetime, the memory of that afternoon. But everything seemed to conspire against it. The war churned on in Vietnam, with no end in sight. George began getting five-o'clockers, night after night, sometimes sleeping most of the week on a cot in his office. He looked hangdog and became sullen, distant. Willard was giving him the business. What could she do about it? In Washington, it was protest time. A spring offensive by the anti-war movement culminated in a massive assault on the Pentagon, the most frightening thing Amy had ever seen on television. An army of berserk young Americans hurling insults and excrement at American soldiers. But the most demoralizing thing Amy saw in that river of marchers was her daughter Georgianna beside her friend Pandora Wax, who was carrying a Viet Cong flag.

Georgie did not deny it. She defiantly informed her mother that they had had a teach-in at school and decided the war was immoral and unjust.

"How can you say such a thing when your own father will have to go out there next year and risk his life fighting in it?" Amy screamed.

"That isn't the only thing wrong she's done, Mommy," Grace said. "You should see what she's got in her closet."

"What?"

"Go see."

As Amy charged upstairs, she heard Georgie say: "Just wait, you little fucker. I'll get you yet."

In Georgie's closet, on a shelf, like a set of objets d'art, were a dozen plaster casts of male genitals. Each had the name of a prominent rock star on the base. Georgie had joined a Chicago rock fan club, the Plaster Casters, which specialized in such mementos.

"You will not play another note of that music in my house," Amy shouted. "You will not see your friend Pandora again under any circumstances. You will *never* go near another anti-war parade. Do you hear me?"

"Yes," Georgie said. "But that doesn't mean I'm going to do it."

Amy slapped her in the face. Georgie slapped her back; no, it was more than a slap, it was a punch, followed by a kick. "If you hit me like that again I'll kill you," Georgie screamed. "You rotten goddamn bitch you made Daddy what he is you made him a killer he wouldn't be in the Army if it wasn't for you he told me he wanted to quit years ago but you like killing and hurting people."

"Get out of my house," Amy said. She no longer saw her daughter Georgianna. This foul-mouthed blue-jeaned slattern with the unwashed hair and obscene mouth was the enemy, invading her house, her fortress. Georgie stalked out snarling.

When George came home, twelve hours later, he was appalled. "Jesus Christ," he said. "Haven't I got enough on my mind? Can't you handle the kid? You don't seem to do anything right these days."

"I can't do anything right? What about you? Telling Georgie you wanted to quit the Army but I wouldn't let you."

"It's more or less the truth, goddamnit," George snarled. "I wish to hell I didn't listen to you. Have you had a fight with Florence Eberle too? Something's got Willard's back up. He's after my ass day and night. Nothing I do satisfies him. I've got to rewrite everything three times."

"I haven't seen Florence for two months," Amy said.

"Maybe that's it. Why don't you invite them to dinner, for Christ's sake? We owe them, don't we? Willard's like an old lady about that sort of thing."

Wrong. Amy's whole world seemed wrong, and there was no way she could right it. She could not invite the Eberles to dinner. She did not have the nervous stamina to endure it. It was unbelievable. The United States of America was undermining her will to persist, survive in the life she had chosen. She had to talk to someone who could explain what was happening to her, who would understand her feelings of outrage and betrayal.

Who else but Adam? But she could not bring herself to call him. She sensed—and feared—that this time there would be no hope of resisting him. Her Philadelphia self, which she had considered her bulwark against him, had been battered, even shattered. She waited a day, a second day, while George sulked and Georgianna defiantly sought refuge with her friend Pandora Wax and Amy had to listen to Mrs. Wax tell her on the telephone that she ought to stop treating her daughter as if she was a private in the Army.

A few mornings later, the telephone rang as Amy paced her spotless house. She had just spent four hours furiously cleaning it, making it perfect. Everything gleamed, from the living-room baseboards to the stainless-steel kitchen sink, from the breakfront displaying her Meissen china to the sideboard containing the Kemble silver. "Hello, Priscilla?" said a low voice.

Adam? She almost cried his name. But the voice continued. "This is your admirer from the Pentagon. I'm about to make out John Alden's efficiency report. He deserves a good one, Priscilla. But that doesn't mean he'll get one. He tries hard and he has a fair amount of talent and brainpower. But this is a cold cruel world, Priscilla. We raters have to be tough, to guarantee that only the best get to the top of our Army."

"Yes," Amy said.

"The last time we met, your protector hurt my pride. A man with hurt pride finds it hard to write an enthusiastic OER. He also finds it hard not to be suspicious of pleas of innocence when they come from third parties. There's only one way you can speak for yourself, Priscilla, and prove you didn't invite that Green Beanie to our little rendezvous. Do you read me, Priscilla?"

"Yes."

"Good. I'll meet you at the Howard Johnson's motel this afternoon at three. Don't worry about George. He won't be home for dinner."

"Yes."

General Eberle was waiting for her when she arrived. He had another bottle of scotch. Amy drank quite a lot of it. She let him take off her clothes and fuck her in various ways, while he told her she had a hell of a body for a woman of forty. Afterward she drank some more scotch and fell asleep. When she awoke it was dark outside. The general was gone. Her watch said eight o'clock. She called home and told Grace to fix a TV dinner. Grace said Georgie had still not returned. Amy lay there on the disordered bed, thinking about what she had let Willard do to her. Wasn't it a kind of expiation, a sacrifice, to redeem herself with George? Yes, she thought. Yes. She tried to think of it that way.

But it was impossible. Behind the thought lay the fear, swelling to a certainty, that something in her had died, an idea, an emotion, a hope, that she would never be able to regain. Suddenly she wanted to get out of America. She wanted to go anywhere, Korea, Bangkok, even Saigon, if they let her. Any place but the ruinous United States of America.

VI

COUNTY highway 659 from Danville ran through mile after mile of fields lined with delicate green tobacco leaves baking in the spring sun. Honor preferred 659 to the new interstate. In a few minutes, up ahead, she saw the white majesty of Story Hill, one of the great houses of old Virginia. The Greek-revival building, with its two-hundred-foot long colonnade, had been inspired by the Parthenon in Athens. She had taken Pookie and Matt out to see Story Hill when they first came down to Charlesville a year ago. She had told them how she used to go to dances there when she was a teen-ager and the house was still owned by the descendants of the original builder, Rowan Story. Once it had been the biggest plantation in the South, with over three thousand slaves. Now the house was owned by the state; it was a museum. Her high school classmate Felicia Story lived in New York, designing children's clothes.

The kids had been bored. The same thing happened when they drove to Danville to visit the Sutherlin Mansion, where Jefferson Davis and his cabinet met for a few despairing days in 1865, enabling Danville to claim it was the "last capital of the Confederacy." Honor did not blame Pookie and Matt for their yawns and impatient "Let's go, Mom." It was all too far back, the War between the States, the Old South. The kids had another war on their minds. That was one of the reasons Honor had let Adam talk her into moving to Charlesville, 250 miles from Washington, D.C. She wanted to get Pookie and Matt away from the anti-war crazies, who were infecting the minds of so many Army children. Amy Rosser's older daughter, Georgianna, had run away from home. No one knew where she was. Pookie said the war did not have anything to do with it. Georgianna just hated her mother. Honor found that hard to believe. Lately she found almost everything hard to believe.

Honor slowed her mother's new Chrysler as highway 659 entered Charlesville, where the speed limit was thirty-five. She did not want to get a ticket. It would upset her mother, who seemed to think she was not competent to drive alone. Mother was always offering to get someone to chauffeur her here or there. You would think a daughter who had come back alive from Japan and Hawaii and Vietnam could be expected to survive on the American highway. But Mother had always specialized in fearing the worst. Now she had a perfect illness for a worrier, a heart condition. Mother's heart attack was the other reason Honor had decided to live in Charlesville while Adam toiled the usual Pentagon hours for Major General Newton Ingalls, head of the Army's congressional liaison staff.

Passing the stately red brick houses on the outskirts of Charlesville's business district, Honor ticked off the names of each one: Woodburn, the Columns, Ardmore. Most had been converted into apartments. In one or two a widow lived with a few black servants and her memories. Honor had spent happy hours at birthday parties, pajama parties in those houses. Most had been built in the decade before World War I, when tobacco profits boomed. The original families had clung to them through the hard times of the twenties and thirties, and the more prosperous forties. But fewer children or none at all, the rising cost of everything, had made them more and more foolish as single-family residences. Throughout the fifties her mother's letters had been a litany of the deaths of patriarchs and matriarchs, houses sold, children vanishing into larger worlds, Washington, D.C., or New York.

546

In the business district, Honor parked in one of the angled slots before the three-story brick building where her father had practiced dentistry for twenty years. She went into Prince's Market next door to get some ice cream for tomorrow night's dessert. Ashby Prince, gray-haired now, with a big potbelly, stood at the check-out counter. "Honor," he said in his gravel voice, "how you?"

"Just fine," she said.

"How's your momma?"

"Good as you can expect at her age."

"Now wait a sec—she ain't no more'n four years older'n me. I can remember her as queen of the prom when I was a freshman. I 'member wonderin' why there wasn't a girl in my class with them kind of looks."

Honor forced a smile. She had heard too many stories about her mother's triumphs as queen of various local balls. With no warning Ash Prince turned serious. "See the paper today? Lost another boy."

"Oh no," Honor said. "Who this time?"

"Cal Randolph's boy. Didn't you date him sort of?"

Honor nodded. Calvin Randolph, star quarterback of Charlesville Central High School. In her junior year he'd made more passes at her than he attempted on the football field. But no completions. Even then, before she tried for the title of Miss Virginia, she was an artist at avoiding completions. Cal Randolph had married Sally Stuart, as blond and pretty as he was blond and handsome. They had gotten married right out of high school. Now they had a son, dead in Vietnam.

"Where do they live?"

"Down toward Danville, I believe. In one of the developments. He's a foreman at the mill."

"I'd like to see them—to tell them—how sorry I am."

"Terrible thing. Boy dyin' in a place like that. Seems so far away. I sure hope we know what we're doin' out there."

"So do I," Honor said, seized her ice cream and fled.

People seemed to think she had a personal interest in every local casualty in Vietnam. Damn that country, Honor thought as she drove home. It was driving everyone crazy. Especially Adam.

She headed west on 659 out the other end of Charlesville. After about four miles, she flipped her blinker and swung off the highway and up a circular drive to an antiquated red brick house, like the ones in town. Behind it stretched five hundred acres of rolling pastures, half in tobacco, half in grass for cattle. As she got out of the car, she could hear her father saying: *Sell it, let's sell the whole damn dumb place.* And her mother crying: *It's my land. It's in my blood.*

In those days, Honor had sided with her mother. The farm gave her the privilege of stabling a succession of ponies and horses only a few steps from her door. By jumping a few fences she could ride four or five miles in almost any direction. Now she understood her father's exasperation. Her parents had inherited the place when Mother's brother Estin died going eighty miles an hour down highway 659 on New Year's Eve, 1929. Her father had kept things going with the income from his dental practice. The old house practically ate money. There was always something—a roof, a chimney—that needed repairing. The farm had never made a profit, even during World War II. The tenant farmer who did the mowing and milking and tobacco curing ate up most of the surplus cash, literally. Mother would have had to sell the house and farm years ago, if it were not for the good investments her lawyer had made with the $250,000 in insurance money she had gotten when her husband died.

In the house, Honor found her mother sitting in the cool dim kitchen talking to Rachel Carter, her aging black cook, who came in only two days a week now. Her mother was wearing a flowery mostly purple silk dress. She had on her pearls and her silver bracelets. Her face had a pinched, birdy look beneath her dyed blond hair, which she insisted on wearing in a mass of girlish ringlets. "Finally," she said. "I thought sure you were goin' to be late."

"Hot enough in Danville to make you think it was July," Honor said, shoving the ice cream into the refrigerator's freezer. "But I got some beautiful shrimp for dinner tomorrow night."

She opened the bag and showed them the fat shrimp, still in their shells. "Seems an awful long way to go for a first course," her mother said.

"Adam loves shrimp," she said. "Loves it more than lobster."

"Awful lot of work to get'm ready," Rachel Carter said.

"I don't have enough to do around here, anyway," Honor said. "Half the time I'm just heatin' up what you left in the icebox."

"I never thought you'd be so much in the kitchen, Miz Honor," Rachel said.

"I don't know where she gets it," her mother said. "I never was. Still can barely boil an egg."

"You either learn to cook or starve when you're in the Army," Honor said.

"I can't get over the way she's lived," her mother said. "I always thought an officer's wife lived like a lady. Don't they have orderlies, that sort of thing?"

"Generals do," Honor said. "I'm goin' to take a bath. I smell like somethin' straight from a Saigon back alley."

Ten minutes later, Honor lay in the tub, ruefully regarding her long-limbed body. There were twenty pounds of fat around her waist. What was wrong with her? Why couldn't she stop eating? Why couldn't she diet? She knew the answer to both questions. It ached in her throat. Last Tuesday, April 7, had been her birthday. Not a word from Adam. Not even a telegram. He had forgotten her birthday last year too. What made the ache especially sharp was the feeling that he had tried to love her again. He had tried to make a new start.

After that terrible night in Saigon, when she had cursed him and called him a liar and a thief, and Joanna Burke had come the next day to talk sense to her, Adam had changed. He had become considerate, loving in small, everyday ways. He had stopped making those cutting remarks to her. He even treated Matt more like a father should. He did not make love to her nearly as often as she wanted him. But she blamed that on Saigon, the god-awful heat and humidity, the strain he was under, trying to stop the Viet Cong terrorists.

That year, he had brought her two dozen beautiful lilies on her birthday. God knows he owed her flowers, with her arm in a cast, her face scarred because the U. S. Army insisted on keeping women and children in a war zone to shore up its prestige. Honor's hand went to the place on her chin where the plastic surgeons had repaired her wound. Everyone told her it was a marvelous job. There wasn't a trace of that damnable scar. But she still saw it every time she looked in the mirror. She still thought the doctors had left a waxy unnatural shine to the skin there.

When they came back to the States, and Adam went to work for General Ingalls in congressional liaison, that was when the trouble started. They couldn't find a house near Washington that they could afford. Adam jammed them into a two-bedroom apartment on Connecticut Avenue and started working the usual Pentagon hours. Little by little the bad feelings crept into their lives again. Questions were answered with snarls. Complaints were answered with insults. Honor was convinced that it wasn't her fault or even Adam's fault. It was the war in Vietnam. He had explained the whole thing in his Harvard thesis, why the Army should never get into that kind of a war in Asia. But no one had listened to him. Now he had to go up to Capitol Hill and defend the war to congressmen and senators, defend the Army's policy, try to get more troops. He was being forced to lie, or at least come awfully close to lying.

Tomorrow night, Adam was coming down for a weekend. It was his first visit in a month. She had called him up and practically demanded an appearance. Her mother was making all sorts of remarks (which she carefully avoided telling Adam) about how *amazin'* it was that Honor let Adam neglect her so. Was she married to him or wasn't she? Bad enough that he rambled off to Laos and Vietnam, leaving her with two children and practically no money. Now here he was in Washington, D.C., treating her like she was living in Nome, Alaska.

Mother was making Honor wish she had never written her a single letter about her troubles or borrowed a single dollar from her. But it was hard to defend Adam. She had to face it, at the moment they were only about half married to each other. Even on the weekends he visited, he sometimes did not make love to her. Which gave her all sorts of ideas about what he might be doing in his one-room apartment on Wisconsin Avenue. When he was here, he spent more time talking to Pookie than to her. The child was so damn precocious. Honor had all she could do not to feel jealous. Adam spent money they could not spare to have *The New York Times* delivered every day so Pookie could read it. Then he told her not to believe more than 20 percent of what was in it.

Her mother rapped on the bathroom door. "Honor, what *are* you doin' in there?" she called. "Father Rausch is goin' to be here any minute."

Was she right? Honor had lost all track of time. She dried herself and applied plenty of powder, bottom and top. She stood in front of the full-length mirror and felt her breasts. Last Tuesday had been her fortieth birthday. Time to start doing those old-lady things. She studied the breasts for a brief moment. They did not look forty. Snapping on a brassiere, she dressed in gray slacks and a tailored pink shirt and went down the back stairs to the kitchen. The old wall clock said it was only 3:15. Her mother just liked to nag, that's all there was to it. No wonder her father had jumped at the chance to escape to the Army.

By 3:30 Honor had the tea and cucumber sandwiches on the coffee table in the high-ceilinged parlor. She tried talking to her mother but all she heard was another list of her friends' illnesses. Pookie and Matt got off the school bus and trudged up the path. Honor watched them, fretting over Pookie's inability to gain weight, admiring Matt's good looks. He had the red hair and creamy skin she had inherited from her father.

"Hey, cut that out," Matt yelled as they came in the door.

"What's going on?" Honor called.

"She goosed me," Matt said as he appeared in the doorway of the living room.

"Pookie, that is not a ladylike thing to do," Honor said.

"Everybody does it to him at school," Pookie said. "I told him to bust one of those rednecks in the mouth but he's nonviolent."

"Rednecks?" her mother said. "There are no rednecks in Charlesville. That's a Yankee slur word."

"Well shut my mouf, Grandma," Pookie said. "Their necks look mighty red to me."

"Honor, you have a very impertinent daughter," her mother said.

Father Rausch arrived to rescue Honor from having to decide how to deal with Pookie. He was the new pastor of St. George's

Episcopal Church. He was young—not more than thirty—and did not like to be called Father. He preferred Vince. Tall and rather homely, with curly hair and a narrow face, he visited her mother once a week. She insisted that she was not strong enough to attend church. Father Rausch was very understanding about it.

Honor had begun to suspect that Father Rausch had another reason for visiting so regularly. After conversing with her mother for a few minutes about her arthritis and her fluttery heart, he invariably talked to Honor about the war. He said she was the only person in Charlesville who knew anything about Vietnam. It was difficult to discuss the war in Charlesville—really discuss it. Everyone talked about it but no one discussed it. Everyone expected Father Rausch to be a superpatriot, to praise the heroic sacrifices Americans were making in Vietnam. But he was worried about the war, about the way Americans were fighting it.

That was the way he talked, hesitantly, cautiously. Honor's mother had been shocked to find Father Rausch had such doubts. Mother's solution to the war was simple. Drop a few atomic bombs on Hanoi and other parts of North Vietnam. Honor had also responded pretty vehemently to Father Rausch's doubts, at first. She had told him about the bombing of the Kinh Do Theater, her broken arm and gashed face, Pookie's concussion. She described Cissie Burke's death. Father Rausch admitted VC terrorism was terrible but he wanted to learn more about how the Americans were fighting the war. He asked what Adam had been doing in Saigon when she was there with him. Honor was embarrassed to admit she did not really know. It was secret stuff, something to do with counter-guerrilla warfare. She told Father Rausch that she had once heard Adam snarling on the telephone: "How do we *know* he's a VC? Christ, I've got to have better evidence than that before I kill someone."

Father Rausch wondered if that sort of thing was moral. Honor loved the way he used that word. He was from Baltimore and he had just the slightest touch of a southern accent. He seemed to breathe the word, more than say it. He was beginning to wonder if the whole war was moral. He was particularly worried about the bombing. Honor tried to explain what she understood about that. The United

States had started it while she was in Saigon. They had had to do something to encourage the South Vietnamese. They were getting so panicky. Father Rausch did not think that was a moral reason. Honor was embarrassed and saddened that she could not resolve his doubts. It reminded her of how little of Adam's Army life he permitted her to share. She began thinking about some way to bring Adam and Father Rausch together. Maybe Adam would respect her a bit more, if he knew she was discussing such serious topics. And she was sure Adam would be able to answer all of Father Rausch's questions about the war.

Handing Honor his hat, Father Rausch greeted everyone in his easy smiling way. He urged Matt to join St. George's Teen Club and teased Pookie for refusing to go to church. To Honor's relief, Pookie withdrew without giving him a snippy answer and Matt, as he followed her, promised to consider the Teen Club. Matt and Honor were the churchgoers. Honor had started going to be polite to Father Rausch. She had been surprised by his sermons. Instead of the boring stuff about immorality she had heard from his predecessors in the 1930s and 1940s, he talked about Jesus, what He meant in each person's everyday life. After one especially fervent sermon Honor said he sounded like a Baptist. Father Rausch said he considered that a compliment. The Baptists were in touch with the spirit of early Christianity, in their singing and shouting and stomping. A lot of his classmates in the seminary felt the Episcopalians needed some of that spirit.

"Father—I mean Vince—I got some good news in the mail," Honor said. "Adam'll be down this weekend. I do hope you can come to dinner Saturday night."

"I'll be delighted."

"I'm goin' to invite Bobby and Trudy Southworth."

"I know them well. Bobby's father is our head vestryman."

"Old Bobby, as we call him, is my lawyer," Mother said. "If it wasn't for him, this beautiful old house would be torn down. I never had the faintest notion he was a shrewd investor until seven or eight years after the war, when all the stocks he told me to put my husband's insurance money into just went up and up."

"He's a solid citizen," Father Rausch said. Honor sensed that he did not like Old Bobby, who had a real mean streak. Just about everybody in Charlesville, including his son, disliked him.

"I'm pouring today, Father," her mother said, hefting the silver teapot. "I'm feeling much better. Not a speck of pain in my arm. Do you want milk and sugar as usual?"

"Adam may call at the last minute and say he has to work up some testimony for the general," Honor said as they sat down. "It's gettin' so the general won't say a word before a committee in Congress without havin' Adam read it first."

"Really?" Father Rausch asked. "Why?"

"That's the way generals are. They always have someone like Adam to do their thinkin' for them."

"You mean generals are basically rather stupid?" Father Rausch asked.

"Just careful," Honor said. "Actually, this one, Newton Ingalls, Adam's boss, is a real brain. Has a collection of Chopin records and reads Marx and Clausewitz and those other Germans Adam always talks about. He's crazy about Adam. We went to dinner at his house a month or two before I came down here, and you'd never believe the conversation. Ingalls quotin' some Chinese general and Adam quotin' the Duke of Wellington. They had two congressmen and a senator there."

Honor's voice trailed off. It was not a happy memory. Adam had snarled at her on the way home because she had distracted one of the congressmen that the general was trying to get to vote for more troops in Vietnam. Was it her fault that the old fool was more interested in talking about horses to a pretty woman? "I told you his vote was crucial," Adam had raged.

"I'll be fascinated to hear what your husband thinks of the recent demonstrations against the war in New York and San Francisco. They had three hundred and fifty thousand marchers in New York," Father Rausch said.

"Yes."

"It's a moral voice, a moral shout, if you will, that the President, the Army, can't ignore."

"Yes. I do so love your idealism, Father—I mean, Vince. Adam used to be that way. But seventeen years in the Army has—I don't know—"

"Destroyed it?"

"I hope not. But it's sort of—invisible, now. I just have to hope it's there."

"Human idealism is a fragile thing. It needs divine support. It needs Jesus," Father Rausch said.

Honor barely heard him. She was too bemused by her own words. If Adam's idealism was really gone, what would she do? Already only half married, she could see the whole thing veering off the road, tumbling, burning, a movie wreck, into some ravine. It wouldn't happen. She would not let it happen. But what could she do to prevent it? Dinner the following night became very important.

"I see in the paper we had another death in Vietnam. The Randolph boy," Father Rausch said.

"Yes," her mother said. "His father used to date Honor, didn't he, dear?"

"What? Oh—Cal Randolph. Yes."

"I still say we ought to drop some atom bombs. Like we did on the Japs," her mother said.

"I'm afraid there are some serious moral problems involved in that alternative, Mrs. Prescott," Father Rausch said.

The next day Adam arrived in their battered Volkswagen about noon. Honor did not like the gray circles under his eyes. Pookie kissed him with her usual fervor and Matt extended a limp hand. "Good Christ," Adam said. "Haven't you learned to shake hands like a man yet?" Honor got a perfunctory kiss. She followed him upstairs and told him about the dinner. His mouth twisted with disapproval. "I'm so tired I can hardly see," he said.

"Take a nap," she said.

He slept most of the afternoon and arose to announce he was going to wear civilian clothes to dinner. Honor was upset. She hated the way he looked in civilian clothes. Like most officers, he bought cheap suits and had them tailored too tight. When he ignored her objections, she got somewhat hysterical. "I want you to look like an

Army officer," she said. "Not some—some salesman. I told you, two of my oldest and dearest friends, Trudy and Bobby Southworth are comin'. And Father Rausch—"

"You're unique," Adam said. "No one wants to see an Army uniform these days. Have you stopped watching TV? Don't you know everyone considers the Army a bunch of freaks, sadistic killers? I went to the last peace march they had in Washington. I never thought I'd hear Americans talk that way about the Army."

He was hurt, genuinely hurt. It surprised her. She had grown to think that Adam never let anything hurt him. He always had a fast answer to every attack on him or his arguments.

"I'm still proud of it," she said. "Even though—"

"What?"

"Nothing." She had been going to tell him some of the things Father Rausch had asked her about Vietnam.

Adam relented and agreed to put on a uniform. He lay on the bed in his undershirt and chatted with her as she dressed.

"I had a call from Joanna yesterday," he said. "Big Peter's been assigned to the ROTC command. She wanted to know if anyone could arrange to get him ordered to that school she's going to—Seward State."

"Were you able to do it?"

"I had Ingalls call personnel. Pete worked for him in Hawaii. I think the fix is in."

"Is that a good deal—the ROTC? It doesn't sound so hot to me."

Adam shrugged. "It's not bad for Pete Burke. Gotta do something in between combat tours. When you're fighting a twenty-year war."

"Is it really gonna last that long, Adam?"

"Longer."

"I had a letter from Joanna last week. She's worried about Tom. He's gotten into a couple of fights with anti-war kids on the campus."

"They've got a pretty hot anti-war movement up there. Our old friend Annette Haines is running it. I don't envy Big Peter, going up against that bitch."

"Joanna says she tries to stay out of it. Just study."

"Easier said than done from the way she sounded on the phone. What's the point of this dinner tonight?"

"No point. Just some people who wanted to meet you."

"What are you doing, prancing around telling the rednecks about your hero husband, the guy who kills VC with his bare hands?"

"No. I don't say a word about you. Nothin' so heroic about what you're doin' these days, anyway."

"How true," Adam said.

The Southworths arrived first. Trudy wore a shimmering silvery cocktail dress, Bobby a blue blazer with the country club's crest in gold, a monogrammed blue shirt, a red tie with the same tiny gold initials on it. Trudy was wearing her blond hair in a bouffant style, which seemed to shrink her small face. At twenty, when she had snagged Bobby, she had been cute, but never pretty. The cuteness was gone now. Lumpy was the best word to describe her face.

Bobby had followed in his father's footsteps and was now Charlesville's leading lawyer. He and Honor had gone steady during her senior year in high school. She could have had him for a husband, just by crooking her little finger. But he would never be Ashley. He was still handsome in a fleshy, square-jawed, down-home manner. And still athletic, the way he moved and smiled in a confident physical way. But all he had ever talked about in senior year was cars and how much money he was going to make. The gray Mercedes parked in their driveway proved it had not been all talk.

Trudy Southworth was a gabber. They had scarcely sat down in the living room when she had Honor's mother wide-eyed with a list of the latest marital collapses. "It's practically an epidemic around here," she said. "Is there a lot of divorce in the Army, Honor?"

"I don't know of one," Honor said, looking at Adam.

"I can think of a few marriages that should have broken up," Adam said. "But the Army frowns on an officer who gets a divorce. They think it reflects on his judgment."

"Lawyer'd never make any money in an Army town, I guess," Bobby Southworth said. "I'm makin' half my money from divorces these days."

Honor's mother blamed it all on television. "It's taught people to act like movie stars," she said.

The bell rang. Rachel answered it and Father Rausch joined them in his sober gray. He shook hands all around, accepted a bourbon and water and sat down, smiling.

"I've been anxious to meet you, Colonel Thayer," Father Rausch said. "Honor's told me you've spent a lot of time in Vietnam."

"Enough," Adam said.

"Boy, I'd love to be out there huntin' VC in those choppers," Bobby Southworth said. "Must be real excitin'."

"Oh, I don't know," Adam said. "I find pillaging and rapine much more to my taste. But I'm old-fashioned."

"Seriously," Father Rausch said. "I've gotten somewhat worried about our—moral stance in this war."

"Why?"

"For the reasons that have brought so many young people into the streets," Father Rausch said. "Don't they trouble you?"

That was pretty neat, Honor thought. But it was also a little unfair. Adam was troubled. All she had to do was look at him to see how troubled he was.

"I'm worried about something more important than our moral stance, Vince. I'm worried about the war itself. I think the most immoral thing you can do is fight the wrong war."

"Then you think we should get out—withdraw?"

Adam shook his head. "Too late. As an officer and a gentleman and a Harvard man, I can't recommend that my country commit geopolitical suicide. We could have lost gracefully in 1963, if Jack Kennedy had had the political guts to withdraw then. But he decided to run a stalemate machine over there until he got reelected. Lee Harvey Oswald nullified that idea, leaving lackluster Lyndon to flounder into an all-out war. Which we can't afford to lose."

"That strikes me as the most shallow pragmatism," Father Rausch said.

"My personal opinion is we ought to let loose a few regiments of Marines on those protesters," Bobby Southworth said.

"I agree with you, Bobby," her mother said.

"Now there's shallow pragmatism," Adam said.

Honor could see that Bobby did not exactly know what pragmatism was. Neither did Honor. But Bobby didn't like to be called shallow.

For the next hour Mother and the Southworths sulked while Adam and Father Rausch debated the war. But it did not go the way Honor had imagined it, with Adam explaining or excusing the things Father Rausch thought were immoral. Adam took the offensive, and attacked Father Rausch for what Adam called "the fundamental immorality" of the way America was allowing the war to drag on endlessly. "You and your fellow peace marchers have forced the gutless wonder in the White House and his hollow men in Congress to fight the war halfway your way, which will eventually cause tens of thousands to die unnecessarily."

"I'm not a peace marcher," Father Rausch said, glancing somewhat nervously at Bobby Southworth. He was undoubtedly thinking of what Bobby Southworth, Sr., might say at the next meeting of St. George's vestry. "I'm simply asking questions."

They went in to dinner. Honor served the fresh shrimp that she'd spent hours peeling and deveining last night, followed by chicken divan. No one so much as noticed the food. Father Rausch kept asking Adam about free fire zones, napalm, defoliants, poison gas—all the things the anti-war people complained about. Adam answered him patiently at first. But he kept drinking bourbon and giving Honor angry looks. His answers became more and more curt. Finally he said he wasn't interested in "minor immoralities."

"I'm shocked by your moral indifference, Adam," Father Rausch said.

Adam stood up. He was trembling. Her mother and the Southworths were wide-eyed. They thought he was going to attack Father Rausch. So did Honor. Instead, Adam walked over to the sideboard and poured himself almost a full glass of bourbon. "If you knew how hard I've been trying to resist moral indifference, Vince. Resist it and pretend to have it at the same time. A certain amount of pretense is necessary in this world, Vince. In the Army we call it playing the game. But there's a limit to it, Vince. A limit to the soul's tolerance of pretense."

"Have you reached it, Adam?" Father Rausch said in a softer, gentler voice.

Adam ignored him. He drank the entire glass of bourbon. Slowly, deliberately. Then he turned to Honor and said: "Is this your idea of rest and relaxation? I spend my days and night answering idiots like this who happen to have gotten elected to Congress. Why should I come down here to get more of it—and put up with you in the bargain?"

Honor looked at his contorted face and thought: Ashley's dying or dead. What will become of Melanie?

Adam took the bottle of bourbon and went upstairs without another word. Honor stumbled through excuses about how hard he had been working, while her guests nodded and said of course they understood. Father Rausch said he was sorry he had talked about the war. "I had no idea that it was affecting men in the Army, men at Adam's level—so deeply. I guess I thought of soldiers in the usual clichés—tough, ruthless, unemotional."

"I don't think that justifies such ungentlemanly behavior," her mother said.

Honor scarcely heard them. She was hearing Trudy Southworth on the phone tomorrow morning telling everyone in Charlesville what Adam Thayer had said to his wife. The Southworths departed immediately after coffee. Father Rausch tried to assure Honor that his feelings were not hurt in the least by the way Adam had talked to him. "Taking a little punishment now and then is part of my job," he said. "A lot of people abused Jesus, you know. In a way I'm glad it happened—because it gave me a chance to see, to understand a little more, why you're so unhappy, Honor."

Honor was stunned. She had not realized her unhappiness was so visible. "I can also see why you're reluctant to open your heart to Jesus. You're afraid it will draw you farther away from Adam. But it won't, Honor. It will draw you closer to him. Jesus's love will heal the kind of hurt Adam gave you tonight. I'm sure it's not the first time he's spoken that way to you."

"I—I don't even know how to ask—how to pray, anymore," Honor said.

"Just close your eyes and let Jesus come into your heart. Talk to him the way you want to talk to Adam. Tell him the loving things you want to say, how much you want to help him."

Father Rausch reached across the table and touched her hand. He said good night to her mother and departed. Honor sat there facing the wreckage of her dinner party. "He can talk all night about Jesus. I don't think you should tolerate those kinds of insults from that man," her mother said.

"Go to bed, Momma," Honor said.

In the kitchen Rachel Carter finished doing the dishes and went home. Honor turned out the lights and slowly climbed the wide worn stairs to the second floor. She heard voices coming from her bedroom and stopped at the head of the stairs to listen.

"Maybe Ingalls will do it differently," Pookie said.

"He won't. It's too late. Such a goddamn mess, Pook. I don't think I can take any more of it," Adam said.

"Dad—I can't stand thinking of you—as a quitter."

A silence. "You're right. Thayers don't quit. They fight to the last brain cell."

"I love you."

"I love you too, Pook."

Pookie came bursting out of the bedroom, tears on her cheeks. "He's going back to Nam again," she said, running down the hall to her bedroom.

Honor went into the bedroom. Adam was sitting in a barrel chair by the window. The bourbon bottle was on the sill, sporadically outlined against the headlights of cars on highway 659. "Is it true—what Pookie just said? You're going back to Nam?"

"Yeah. Ingalls is going out there. He wants me to come with him."

"When are you leavin'?"

"Next Friday."

"Why didn't you tell me? I wouldn't have had anyone to dinner. Our last weekend till God knows when."

"You didn't give me a chance to tell you."

Pookie's words, *I love you,* seemed to be reverberating around the room. Along with Adam's words, *I love you too.* When was the last time Honor and Adam had exchanged those words? *Adam,* she wanted to ask him, *why are things so wrong between us? Why are we only half married? Why don't you, why can't you say I love you to me?* But she was afraid of that searing tongue. Afraid of his answer.

"Come to bed," she said, trying to sound affectionate. "Let's say goodbye the way soldiers say it."

"Too drunk," he said. He took the bottle and went downstairs, leaving her there, staring into the darkness.

The next morning he was gone. He must have driven back to Washington, in spite of the bourbon. Honor and Matt went to church. Father Rausch preached a sermon asking the question: What would Jesus think about the war in Vietnam? He said that Jesus would have compassion, forgiveness, for everyone. The Viet Cong and the GIs and the war protesters and the professional soldiers who were obeying orders even when they thought the war was being fought the wrong way. He said that he felt Jesus would feel especially sorry for them. He reminded them of the story of Jesus and the centurion—how Jesus had praised his faith. Jesus did not call him a killer, a warmonger. He treated him as a man of honor. Father Rausch urged them to pray that the healing power of Jesus's love would find its way into everyone's heart. Honor felt he was looking right at her as he said these last words.

She closed her eyes and tried to think about Jesus. But all she could feel was an empty space, all she could hear were those echoing words, *I love you,* that Adam had spoken to Pookie, not to her. All she could think of was the way Adam had talked to her in front of her oldest friends. Did Jesus have to deal with *bastards* like that? She struggled to control her rage. Did Melanie believe in Jesus? Probably. But Honor was feeling more more like Scarlett.

On Monday, about noon, Honor got a call from Bobby Southworth. "You know, I really felt sorry for you Saturday night," he said. "You and the colonel don't seem to be gettin' along."

"Oh?" Honor said.

"I kind of know how you feel. Trudy and I don't get along much better. When you get right down to it, Honor, I'm just plain sick of that woman. I don't think I've ever gotten over you, Honor, I don't think I ever have. I swear it. Could we meet somewhere and talk about it?"

"I don't think that would be a good idea, Bobby. It would only lead to a lot of trouble for both of us."

"Not if we do it the right way. I'm not suggesting anythin' that could get either of us into court for alienation of affection, Honor. I'm talkin' about you visitin' me in my office, maybe discussin' what kind of case you might have against the colonel. A man can't talk to a woman that way, these days, Honor, without it costin' him a lot of money. That's mental cruelty, Honor."

"No, Bobby."

That night, Honor dreamt she was in Bobby Southworth's office. Only it seemed to be more of a bedroom, and they were not discussing mental cruelty. He was kissing her and whispering that he'd always wanted her. It was a very upsetting dream. Bobby called again two days later, about eight in the evening. Honor took the call in her bedroom. Bobby said he had to go up to Richmond on some legal business. She could go up there to do some shopping. They could have a whole day to talk. Honor said no again. That night she had another dream. She was in Bobby's Mercedes. He pulled off the highway and started kissing her.

Honor spent the next two days praying for Adam to telephone. She wanted to say goodbye to him, she wanted him to say something, anything, that sounded loving before he left for Vietnam. But Friday dribbled to a close without a call. The next day Pookie showed her a story in *The New York Times* about Major General Newton Ingalls going to Vietnam as the probable successor to General Westmoreland.

"Wow," Pookie said. "If Dad keeps cool, he could wind up with a star or two. Westmoreland's coming back to become chief of staff. That means Ingalls may do the same thing."

Honor was barely listening. She closed her eyes and tried to think about Jesus. The phone rang. She heard her mother answer it in the hall. Someone's arthritis had probably flared up. For the rest of the day, Honor felt like a sleepwalker. She asked God, Jesus, not to let Bobby Southworth call again.

That night, as she trudged up the stairs to bed, her mother called: "Honor? Honor dear? Could you come here for a minute?"

Her mother was sitting up in bed rubbing cold cream on her hand and face. She had her hair in rollers. Who did the woman think she was going to snag at seventy? Honor looked around the room. Nothing had changed in here since 1944, the same dull white curtains and faded brown wallpaper and canopy bed past which Mother had paced while she told Honor that her father was dead, murdered in a whorehouse in Quillen, Texas.

"Honor," she said, "Bobby Southworth called earlier today. He asked me to speak to you. His marriage to Trudy is breaking up. He's asked her for a divorce."

Honor walked out of the room. "Honor?" her mother called. "Honor? I'm only trying to give you some good advice."

Honor lay awake most of the night, trying to think about Adam. Trying to pray to Jesus. But nothing happened. She could not think. She could not pray. She could only remember Adam's insult in the dining room. *And put up with you in the bargain.* Was Bobby telling her the truth? Was that mental cruelty? Was her mother's advice any good? She remembered Father Rausch's sermon about forgiveness. Especially for Army officers. His words about idealism. *A fragile thing. It needs Jesus.* But Adam did not believe in Jesus. He would never believe in Jesus.

The next day, about noon, Bobby Southworth called again. "Honor," he said. "I just want you to know, Trudy's givin' me a divorce. It's goin' to cost me a lot of money. But it'll be worth it, Honor, if I can convince you it's for your sake. Your momma tells me the colonel flew off to Vietnam without even callin' to tell you goodbye. Don't you think you ought to give it right back to him by doin' a little flyin' of your own? I'm sittin' here with two plane tickets to Nassau—"

She hung up on him again. He called back. "Nassau, Honor, beautiful blue water, fantastic beaches. Just the two of us, Honor, findin' out where we went wrong. Findin' our way back to each other."

She hung up again. After lunch, her mother took a nap. When she awoke she summoned Honor to her bedroom for another talk. On the stairs, Honor stopped and closed her eyes. She prayed to Jesus. *It's up to you,* she said, *what happens is up to you. Just let me tell you one thing. I would love to go to Nassau.*

In the bedroom, her mother was sitting at her dressing table, combing her hair. "Honor," she said. "We've really got to talk. Woman to woman."

"Yes, we do, Momma. Maybe for the first time. You walked out on your man, when he went to war. Maybe he would have gone to that whorehouse no matter what you did. But when you turned your back on him, you made a certainty of it. I'm not blamin' you, Momma. You were born and raised in this house, you weren't meant to live in some backwoods Texas or Alabama Army town. But I'm not you, Momma. I've gone everywhere with Adam. He's real unhappy right now about a lot of things, including me. And he makes me unhappy. But if I divorced him now, I'd feel like I wasted all the years I've spent—sixteen of them—tryin' to love him and tryin' to keep him lovin' me, no matter where he went. I'm not goin' to do it, Momma. I'm not goin' to make your mistake. So stop talkin' to me about Bobby Southworth."

"HOW CAN YOU SAY THOSE THINGS TO ME—YOUR MOTHER? WHEN YOU KNOW WHAT I'VE SUFFERED? HOW CAN YOU SAY IT? I WANT YOU OUT OF THIS HOUSE. I WANT YOU OUT OF MY HOUSE BY SUNDOWN."

Honor stood in the hall while the tantrum raged. Hairbrushes cracked against the closed bedroom door. She wondered where and how she had found those words. Who had said them, Honor or some other creature, a spirit braver than her own? Jesus?

Pookie raced up the stairs from the living room. "What's going on?" she said.

"Momma and I just sort of fought the War Between the States and a little of World War II," Honor said. "I think we're goin' to be movin' soon, Pook."

"Suits me. I've learned everything this dink high school can teach me. Where are we going? Hawaii?"

"No. One of the towns around West Point. Maybe Cornwall. I need—I need to feel close to the Army—to Daddy."

Pookie fixed her with those wide gray eyes, Adam's eyes. "I understand," she said.

565

VII

It was just like the Korean War, Joanna thought as she sat in Kennedy International Airport and watched the tourists pouring in from Europe, the Caribbean, with bragging labels on their luggage, smug world-traveler smiles on their faces. No one cared about Vietnam, no one thought about it until they turned on their televisions at night and gunfire erupted in their faces. No one in the real world thought about the war. Only on the campuses and Army bases, those two oddly contrasting unreal worlds, was it thought about obsessively.

While she waited for Pete's plane to arrive from California, Joanna read a letter from Martha Kinsolving. She and Vic were down at Fort Cullum, in the broiling Texas panhandle, where Vic and other Vietnam veterans were turning two more divisions into airmobile outfits. The letter was full of bewildered exclamations about the anti-war movement and groans of distress about the problems it was causing with draftees. AWOL rates were soaring and acts of insubordination, even sabotage of equipment, were becoming common. Martha had never seen anything like it in all the years she had spent in the Army.

"There's Dad," Tom said, and rocketed out of his seat to go racing through the crowd like a broken-field runner. Joanna still could not see Pete. She waited, wondering what she would feel. She was hoping for a burst, a surge of love that would obliterate all the

566

doubts, the guilt she had been feeling about maneuvering Pete into becoming head of the ROTC at William Seward State University. For the tenth time she told herself that the Army had made the primary decision, to commit some of their best officers to the embattled ROTC program. The anti-war movement at Seward State was no worse than it was at most schools and a lot less violent than it was at places like the University of Wisconsin. She may have done Pete a favor, getting him Seward. It was the biggest ROTC unit in New York State. If all went well, it would be white points in the record.

The crowd parted just in time for Joanna to see her husky fifteen-year-old crash into the big soldier with the chest full of battle ribbons. She found envy mingling with pleasure. Tom Burke would never love her with that unique blend of admiration and affection. She was Mom, an okay cook, an adequate companion, but off base a lot of the time. Joanna put Martha's letter in her purse and walked toward Pete's embrace. He was smiling. There was not a trace of the flickering mixture of anger and sadness with which they had parted a year ago.

Let's have another baby, Pete had said, *as soon as they got to Fort Thompson, Arkansas, after burying Cissie at Punchbowl, the military cemetery in the Hawaiian hills above Honolulu.*

No, she had said. No. No. No.

And each morning thrust another Enovid in her mouth, while the big soldier clumped helplessly outside the bathroom door.

No, she had said. I will not forgive God for what He has done. I will not forgive the Army. I will not incidentally forgive you.

Now she had spent a year trying to escape that answer, that tormenting mixture of rage and despair. She had fled it down the nights and days of papers on the seventeenth-century lyric, characterization in Chaucer, form in the modern novel, the abracadabra of graduate English studies. It was a logical refuge for a failed poet, incapable of finding an objective correlative for her savagely conflicted emotions. She had hoped at the end of a year she would have the worst feelings under control, she would be able to return to the Army and resume playing the game.

Now Blind Chance, the eyeless mindless ruler of the world, in a spasm of benevolence, which was as meaningless as his malevolence, had delayed her return to duty for another year. A good thing because she seriously doubted her ability to resume the performance.

Pete kissed her gently, firmly on the mouth. He flung a mighty arm around his wife and son. "You two look great," he said.

"You look tired," she said. Gaunt was a better, blunter word. He had lost a lot of flesh.

"I got a bad case of dysentery my last month in Thua Thien," he said. "Couldn't do anything for it. Polymagma, Enteromycin, nothing worked. I still get it, about once a week. It's one of the reasons personnel suggested this ROTC deal. The docs thought I could use an extended R and R."

Tom looked uneasily at his mother. "I don't know whether you'll find Seward State so restful, Dad. Didn't Mom warn you about the peace freaks?"

"I told you not to call them that," Joanna said.

"All the colleges have them," Pete said. "I'm not worried. We're going to have a great year."

"Then what? Back to Nam again?" Tom asked.

"Maybe," Pete said. "Maybe the Pentagon. It depends on how the war's going."

"How are General Dat and Thui?" Joanna asked.

In several letters Pete had mentioned seeing the Dats. After six months as a battalion commander in the 11th Airmobile, he had been assigned to Hue, the capital of Thua Thien Province, as adviser to the province chief.

"He's dead. KIA," Pete said.

"My God, I thought he didn't have a command," Joanna said.

"I got him one. I went down to Saigon and talked them into giving him command of a new division they were putting together. The new head of state, Thieu, went to military school with Dat. He liked him and went along with it. On his first operation, Dat's helicopter was hit and exploded in midair."

"I'll write to Thui."

Pete nodded glumly. "It happened two weeks ago."

Pete had a thirty-day leave. They spent the first week in New York, showing Tom the standard sights, the Statue of Liberty, the

Empire State Building, Radio City Music Hall. Joanna also insisted on the Metropolitan Museum of Art. It did not win an A rating from either of her companions. But it was soon obvious that New York was incidental. Wherever they went, Pete and Tom talked about the war. It was Tom's fault, mostly. He wanted to know all about the new M-16 automatic rifle, the late-model helicopters, the flareships and infrared sights for night fighting.

At dinner on the fourth night they went to the Lobster, a seafood restaurant on Forty-fifth Street, where Pete had taken her after the Army-Notre Dame football game in 1949. Before they opened their menus, Tom was asking Pete about casualties on Long Range Reconnaissance Patrols. "For God's sake," Joanna said. "Can't we talk about something besides Vietnam? We're on vacation."

Suddenly the two faces confronting her, so familiar, so similar, were frowning accusers. "Sure," Pete said. "What do you want to talk about?"

"I—I don't know. The pennant race. Anything."

Patches of silence dominated the rest of the meal. Pete and Tom talked sporadically about school, his favorite subject, American history, his hopes of making the junior varsity football team this fall. She answered awkward questions about her English courses.

That night, in their hotel room, Pete said that Tom had told him about going with her to an anti-war teach-in. "Why would you go to one of those things, much less take him?"

She was in her nightgown, sitting on the edge of the double bed. He was in the bathroom, brushing his teeth. "I thought he should hear both sides of the argument," she said.

"He says it wasn't an argument. No one spoke for the other side. Our side. If you'd done that, I could understand it, Jo. If you stood up and told them what the VC did to Cissie."

"I haven't told anyone about her. I made Tom promise not to mention her. I want you to do the same thing."

"Why?"

"I can't stand the pity. I had all of it I could take at Fort Thompson. Pity won't bring her back."

For a year at Fort Thompson, where Pete had helped train the 11th Airmobile for Vietnam, Joanna had almost drowned in the Army's sympathy. Even Ruth Hardin had softened her usual abrasive style to tell her how sorry she was. The general's wife had invited her to dinner a half dozen times and ordered the chaplain to confer with her. The president of the Women's Club had been anxious to excuse her from doing anything arduous. But Joanna had played the game. She accepted Adam's challenge. She had played the noble Army wife, smiling through her tears. She had toiled on a half dozen Women's Club committees, she had given sit-down dinners, she had deceived them all, except her husband. Pete had heard that savage *no, I won't have another baby* and suspected the icy rage behind the words.

Now, in another bedroom, he was hearing an echo of that subterranean revolt. Joanna turned her head. Pete was standing in the bathroom door studying her. He is not stupid. Remember, he is not stupid, she told herself. But there was still something boyish, innocent about him, whispered the secret self. At forty, after sixteen years of killing people, of studying how to do it better and better.

What was happening to her?

Pete did not touch her that night. The first three nights they had made love. But the burst, the surge of feeling she had hoped would obliterate her secret self did not come. She did not come. The game player told herself it was a year's abstinence. She had taught her body to forget this desire, this wish to be held, engulfed, subdued. The secret self replied with a mocking question: Why? Did she resent, perhaps even hate, that version of love? Did she accuse it, her submission, her surrender, of Cissie's death?

The next day they drove over to New Jersey to visit Pete's mother. A widowed sister had moved in with her. They lamented the fall of Monsignor Clancy, whom both obviously regarded as more important in their lives than their late husbands. The monsignor was in a nursing home, paralyzed by a stroke. Mrs. Burke held forth on the anti-war movement. "The Commies are behind it," she said. "What a shame Senator McCarthy's dead. We need him now more than ever."

They drove north for another week's vacation among New York's Finger Lakes. The days were hot, the nights deliciously cool. They took long mostly wordless walks along the shores of the lakes while twilight's purple haze gathered around them. The landscape was so bare, so pure, Joanna felt they were being purged of something foul that she had been unable to escape in New York. Was it Vietnam? The word seemed unreal in this world of crystal water and geometric farms and placid orchards. Only a few hundred miles away was her home state, Ohio, the beginning of the prairies. Suddenly their lovemaking had some of the tenderness, if not the richness, of other days. She was able to tell Pete how happy she was to have him home again, and half mean it.

The last two days were spoiled by an attack of dysentery. Pete lay in bed, taking pills, his face bleak with pain. It passed and they drove east, toward the headwaters of the Hudson, where William Seward State University crowded its guardian hills. Army style, Joanna gave Pete an orientation tour. As they drove past the new poured-concrete social sciences building, with its round tower and winglike roof, Tom pointed to a sign painted on successive windows in yellow letters.

STOP THE WAR MACHINE

"There's the opposition, Dad," Tom said.

At the apartment, Joanna found a letter from Carleton Haines welcoming her back to the campus and asking her to read several dozen poems submitted to *Antithesis*. She had become the magazine's unpaid associate editor. Pete went to Washington for a two-week course on ROTC procedures and Tom went out for the high school's junior varsity football team. It was all very normal. Even Annette Haines's dinner invitation was normal. They chatted like old friends. Annette said she had spent the summer in Washington, working for the anti-war movement. Nothing wrong with that. Protest was as American as apple pie.

Later, of course, Joanna realized that she had always known what was going to happen. Half knowing was really not much different from knowing, when guilt came stalking, sneering on the midnight trade wind. But that alienated September Joanna was listening to other voices, whispering excuses, pleas, challenges to guilt, to love.

"So you're just back from Vietnam," Annette Haines said, almost the moment drinks were served, while Jay Morrison, of the shark's smile, and Emerson Mather with his frozen glare, a half dozen other hostile faculty faces formed a circle around the beribboned, bemedaled victim. It was a kind of unholy rite, improvised, like the execution in Shirley Jackson's short story "The Lottery." But this jury did not throw stones. They threw words, ideas, insults.

Joanna had briefed Pete like a well-trained Army wife. He knew the background of each of them. Annette Haines, Ph.D. from Harvard in international affairs, Marxist head of the Political Science Department, leader of the campus anti-war movement. Historian Jay Morrison, Ph.D. from Columbia, son of New York socialists, father of a loud-mouthed teen-ager whom Tom had punched in the mouth for calling Lieutenant Colonel Burke a fascist killer. Emerson Mather, chairman of the English Department, Ph.D. from Ohio State, Quaker parents, conscientious objector in World War II, kicked out of a job in Ohio for supposed leftist leanings during the McCarthy era. The lieutenant colonel had all the information he needed to understand why each of these people regarded him with hatred and/or contempt. It did him no good whatsoever.

Gradually Joanna began to think of the evening as something else, the killing of the bull. Pete was doggedly brave, infallibly polite. They slashed at him from right, left, rear. He sat there, stubbornly shaking his head. Of course civilians got killed in Vietnam. Civilians got killed in World War II and Korea. The bombing was necessary as long as the enemy insisted on reinforcing and supplying their army in the South from their bases in the North. Defoliation was necessary; nothing wrong with it if it did not get out of hand. The Army was doing its best to fight a war in a populated country with reasonable humanity; the Communists, not the Americans, had chosen the battleground.

"How many Vietnamese have you killed, personally?" Emerson Mather asked.

"I have no idea," Pete said. "In the U. S. Army there is no reporting of personal kills."

"No psychopaths wandering around with notches on their carbines?" Annette Haines said. "Get off it, Colonel. We're getting to know a lot about your Army. You're all in love with killing people."

Pete's big hands opened and closed in his lap, a sign that he was struggling to keep his temper. "I'm in love with defending my country. That's my profession," he said.

"Since when is that a profession?" Emerson Mather said. "Every citizen is ready to defend his country. There isn't a man here—or a woman—who wouldn't fight if he saw an enemy tank coming down the street toward his house."

Pete proved he was a gentleman by not laughing in Dr. Mather's face. The professor was a skeletonic five feet one, with sallow skin and eyes blinking behind thick steel-rimmed glasses. The idea of him doing battle with a tank was ludicrous.

"When enemy tanks come down our streets, it'll be too late to fight," Pete said. "We're trying to prevent that from ever happening, by fighting in Vietnam. I can see you've never heard of our Forward Strategy."

He started trying to explain it to them, straight from the agreed doctrine of the Command and General Staff School. Jay Morrison told him the Forward Strategy was nothing but a cover for American economic imperialism. "Sweatshops, that's what you're fighting for in Vietnam, Colonel," Annette Haines said. "That's all you've done in Korea—given our flag-waving capitalists a reservoir of cheap labor."

Joanna sat mute. What did she want to happen? she wondered later. What was she trying to do, see, discover? Hurt Pete as much as he (personifying the Army) had hurt her? Or play an Adamesque game with him, inflict "creative pain"—to stimulate new thoughts, attitudes? Or discover a limit to his patience, his strength, his love? All three, or none of the above? A new kind of multiple-choice test.

Annette was measuring the enemy. The dinner was a reconnaissance in force. Joanna had known it. Except that she knew nothing. She was innocent, a game player, a failed poet listening to voices. She was trying to sleepwalk through history.

"We're going to stop your war machine, Colonel," Annette Haines was saying. "We're going to take away your cannon fodder. We're going to change the allegiance of the true believers, the middle Americans, the kids here at Seward State. We tried appealing to their intellects at our teach-ins. Now we're going to work on their emotions. We're going to teach you a few lessons in leadership,

Colonel. We're going to make you realize you can't get away with killing peasants in a country seven thousand miles away.''

Walking home in the cool darkness, Pete was silent. Joanna could not read his mood. He only spoke once, and he seemed to be talking to himself. "I can't believe I'm in the United States of America."

In the apartment, Joanna did not know what to expect, once they had shut off the TV and shooed Tom to bed. Pete showered, got into his pajamas and lay down on the bed, his hands behind his head. She followed him, and when he showed no interest in talking, began to doze off. When he finally put his arm around her she was half asleep. A dangerous state of consciousness for a game player.

"Why didn't you talk back to them, Jo? Why did you just sit there?" Pete asked.

"Dr. Mather is chairman of the English Department. He's my mentor—the man who decides whether or not I get a Ph.D. Would you talk back to some general who was sounding off—no matter how much you disagreed with him?"

"That depends on whether it's a matter of conscience. I talked back to Henry Hamburger."

The game player was wide awake now. He was after her, the way he stalked the VC in the jungle, step by methodical step, encircling them on the right and the left with his death-bearing helicopters. He wanted her to surrender Cissie, to give up her proof of his perfidy. He wanted her to let him take Cissie out of her arms, in the name of his God, his country, his Army. But he would not catch her. She was as clever as the VC. She would fade away into the foliage of half-truths.

"I don't see why this is a matter of conscience to me. If you want my—my honest opinion, I want the war to stop. Not for their reasons. But I want it to stop."

"So do I. But there's only one way to stop it. By winning it."

"Of course," she said. While the secret self whispered: *Liar, liar, he wants it to go on forever.*

She lay awake for hours. He was awake too, beside her. Was he watching, waiting for her to collapse, confess her guilt? That was the night Joanna began to fear the future.

Pete had no such qualms. Fear was foreign to his nature, his training. He tackled the ROTC command with the same thoroughness and intensity he had brought to all his previous assignments. He began by personally interviewing each of the five hundred students in the program. He wanted to get a handle on their motivation, their attitude toward the Army and the war. Most of them were in the ROTC for the money. Not a few were shaken when he told them that the war was not going to end very soon. He wanted them to understand that this was not a game they were playing. It was very serious business.

Those who showed the strongest interest in the Army, he began inviting home for dinner. He also told Joanna to extend invitations to his two junior officers, Captain Carl Peterson and Lieutenant David Hanley. Joanna found herself confronting five dinner invitations in the next ten days. "I'm sorry," she said. "I just can't do it."

"What do you mean?"

"I don't have the time. I have to spend three hours a day, minimum, on my thesis. I have papers to write for three courses, at least a dozen books to read."

"Jo—I'm trying to create a sense of Army community here. I think we're going to need it."

"I know what you're trying to do. I wish I could help. But I have to get this work done."

What was she telling him? *We're not a team, we'll never be a team again?* Memories of old quarrels flickered dangerously around them. But Pete avoided a two-front war.

"Okay," he said. "I'll do the cooking."

"And the cleaning up," she said.

He chose simple dishes, steaks and chops, and recruited Tom to do the shopping and dishwashing. Joanna was amazed—and then envious—at how deftly he persuaded their son to do these chores. She had trouble getting Tom to pick up his dirty underwear and socks. The dinner with Captain Peterson and Lieutenant Hanley went smoothly. Hanley had just completed a tour in Vietnam and his wife, Connie, was complaining in muted tones about the year-long separation. Peterson was just back from two years in Germany and his wife, Pat, apparently could talk about nothing but skiing in the Alps, which they seemed to have done every weekend. It was no worse—and no better—than a hundred other Army dinners Joanna had known. The officers quickly left the women to themselves and got into an intense discussion of morale and leadership problems in the Seward ROTC.

Joanna was surprised to discover that dinner with the students was much more difficult. The first group of three did not seem much older than Tom. Farmers' sons from upper New York State, they called her ma'am and asked her primer questions about the Army. One of them brought his girl, a pony-tailed blonde with plaintive blue eyes. All were graduating in June and were interested in the Army as a career. The girl wanted to know if Army wives liked the life.

"Some do, some don't," Joanna said. "It's impossible to generalize."

"Do you?" the girl said. "I mean—like it."

Joanna realized her tone had raised doubts. She had been curt, dismissive. "Sometimes I've liked it. Other times I've hated it," she said.

"What did you hate?"

Joanna became aware that all conversation at the table had stopped. Her husband, her son, the three ROTC cadets were waiting for her answer. *All of it. I hated all of it,* she suddenly wanted to say. Instead, she said: "When I was ill, in the fifties, I had to sit in dispensaries for hours. Most wives dislike the medical program. It's so crowded."

"Jo had unusual problems," Pete said. "Three miscarriages in a row. If you're healthy, you don't have to fight the dispensary line too often."

Tom started talking about his boyish adventures in Hawaii, Saigon, West Point. Joanna looked at his glowing face, and realized her son was a hopeless Army brat. He loved the military life. Nothing wrong with that, she told herself, groping to hold on to her affection for him. Nothing wrong with entertaining these slightly older adolescents with stories about crabby colonels and dyspeptic generals, misunderstandings created by foreign languages. Except for the war. The boy who had brought the pony-tailed girl looked a lot like Ben

Shaughnessy. Were the Burkes luring him from this table, with its easy laughter and juicy American steak, to a flag-covered coffin at Tan Son Nhut Air Base?

Meanwhile, there was Dr. Emerson Mather to cope with. Joanna had come to Seward State thinking she would write her Ph.D. thesis on the poetry of William Carlos Williams, on whom she had almost completed her Master's thesis at the University of Hawaii. She had also expected to have Carleton Haines for a mentor. She discovered neither idea pleased Chairman Mather. His specialty was nineteenth-century American poetry. He dismissed the draft of her Williams thesis as "Hawaiian moonshine" and told her that she would write her doctoral thesis on Jones Very, a New England poet and friend of Ralph Waldo Emerson. Carleton Haines, whose specialty was modern poetry, meekly abandoned Joanna to Dr. Mather's mentorship. That was when Joanna began comparing academia to the Army. Few generals ruled their divisions more absolutely than Dr. Mather ruled the English Department of William Seward State University.

Annette Haines began the semester's anti-war campaign with a now kind of mass meeting, called a mobilization. Dr. Mather asked Joanna if she was going, and answered his own question. "I suppose your husband wouldn't stand for it."

"I haven't discussed it with him."

"It was fascinating, the other evening, listening to the way his mind works. I've never met an Army officer before. Isn't he rather terrifying to live with?"

"Not at all. Why do you say that?"

"He looks so formidable. Like something out of Homer. I'm not surprised that you're afraid of him."

"But I'm not. Not in the least."

"Well, I am," Mather said, and strode stiffly away.

Joanna did not go to the mobilization. But its roars of rage and rancor drifted down from the football stadium, where it was taking place, making it difficult for her to concentrate on a paper analyzing Longfellow's prosody. Dr. Mather always required a rigorously analytic paper on someone's prosody from each of his doctoral students. *Rigorous, rigor* were Dr. Mather's favorite words. He frequently found the drafts of Joanna's doctoral thesis on Jones Very lacking in rigor. This was not entirely surprising. She detested Very's murky mystic poetry.

A few days later, Dr. Mather asked Joanna if she had gone to the mobilization. She said no and playfully tried to blame him. "I was too busy working on Mr. Longfellow's prosody for you."

Dr. Mather declined to be amused. "You told me you weren't afraid of your husband," he said. "Who are you lying to, me—or yourself?"

The Mobilization for Peace was a theatrical success, but it seemed to have no appreciable impact on the ROTC at first. Pete continued to make substantial progress in his campaign to improve the regiment's performance and morale. Attendance at drill climbed to 98 percent. He instituted a physical-training program that had the future lieutenants galloping over the nearby hills for two- and three-mile runs behind Lieutenant Colonel Burke or one of the other officers. An ROTC touch-football team had issued a challenge to dorm and department teams and was currently undefeated.

One sunny October afternoon, a cadre of blue-jeaned protesters came down to the ROTC drill field with broomsticks on their shoulders and performed a parody manual of arms and marching maneuvers while the regiment was performing various evolutions under Lieutenant Colonel Burke's critical eye. When the ROTC ignored them, the protesters started marching into the regiment's formations. Pete asked them to leave. They told him to go fuck himself. Pete ordered his troops to escort them from the drill field. There was some scuffling but it was not widespread. Most of the protesters retreated peacefully. Pete stationed a few dozen guards along the perimeter of the field and resumed drilling.

ROTC ATTACKS PROTESTERS, screamed the headline in the campus newspaper the next day. A totally distorted version of the story, making the ROTC look like German storm troopers, told how the peaceful protesters had been assaulted without warning by the uniformed representatives of the U. S. Army, under the orders of their commander, Lieutenant Colonel Peter MacArthur Burke. Pete wrote a letter attempting to correct the newspaper story. It went unprinted and unanswered. The faculty senate passed a resolution condemning the incident and calling on the president of Seward State to discipline the ROTC.

In the midst of this furor, Joanna handed in her paper on Longfellow's prosody. Dr. Mather gave her a C and told her, with his usual offhand savagery, that she deserved a D but he felt sorry for her no doubt disturbed state of mind. Since Mather was rotten to all his students, it was impossible for Joanna to tell whether he was singling her out for special attack. She might even assume he was sincere in his sympathy.

There was something disturbing her mind. It was not Pete's troubles at Seward State. It was the war. Before Pete's return, Joanna had been able to block it out of her consciousness most of the time. She seldom read a paper or looked at television; she told herself she was too busy. She had told Tom she did not want to talk about it and he had respected her refusal. All this changed when Pete arrived. Each night at the dinner table Pete and Tom discussed the war in obsessive detail. She could no longer stop them by claiming they were on vacation. There were exhaustive analyses of Operation Cedar Falls, Junction City and other large-scale assaults on the enemy. Special attention was paid to the 11th Airmobile, which was fighting again in the Ia Drang Valley, where Pete had led a battalion last year. The 11th had battered two North Vietnamese divisions which had been planning to slash across central South Vietnam and cut the country in half. Listening to Pete explain it, the war sounded rational. Now that the Americans had a real army in the country, they were methodically attacking the enemy's strongholds, defeating his large units wherever they tried to operate.

But the irrational war, the one the rest of the country saw and experienced, refused to go away. Night after night on television there were films of helmeted flak-jacketed Americans assaulting another nameless mud-walled village, helicopters swirling meaninglessly above the same jungles or rice paddies. At least once a week, the local newspaper had a picture of a home-town boy killed in the fighting. Just before Thanksgiving, one of the ROTC graduates of last year, a boy named Charles Harding, was killed in a helicopter crash in the Mekong Delta. The boy had a younger brother and many friends in the regiment. Pete decided to hold a memorial service for him on the drill field. He saw it as the ROTC's answer to the Mobilization for Peace. He invited the president of the university and a dozen other members of the administration. He asked the boy's parents, who lived a few miles away, to attend. The boy had been awarded a posthumous Silver Star. Pete asked the Pentagon to send a brigadier general up to Seward to present it.

Joanna knew the memorial service was a mistake the moment she heard about it. She knew how profoundly Annette Haines and her cohorts had changed the minds and hearts of the majority of Seward's students. She knew how aggressive Annette was, how certain she was to respond to this challenge to her power. But Joanna said nothing to warn her husband, who still refused to believe that his beloved U. S. Army could be hated by young idealistic Americans. His wife knew just how much the Army could be hated every time she encountered the icy rage in the depths of her soul. So far she had kept these encounters to a minimum by silence, averted eyes. Lieutenant Colonel Burke was making it more and more difficult for her to maintain this policy. Let the hero learn the hard way, whispered the secret self, who bathed daily in the icy pool in the center of her body.

Annette Haines announced that the Mobilization for Peace would hold a counter memorial service. Two days before the date set for both events, the brother of the dead lieutenant resigned from the ROTC and announced he was going to the Mobilization service. He persuaded his mother to join him. His father stayed with the ROTC service, which did not draw a large crowd. The ROTC regiment, the university president and a handful of older faculty constituted the audience.

The general from the Pentagon turned out to be Willard Eberle, a name that conjured unpleasant Saigon memories for Pete. Eberle had just completed eighteen months as secretary to the general staff and was on his way to Vietnam to become deputy commander of a division. He flew to Slater Air Base, about ten miles away, and helicoptered to the campus. His aide, a West Pointer from the class of 1966, spent a half hour on the phone with Pete discussing where the general should land. He decided to come down on the drill field, just before the ceremony began. Although the helicopter landed at the far end of the field, the whirling blades blew off ROTC hats and frightened several women in the crowd.

The president of the university talked in his usual orotund style about Purpose, Tragedy, Democratic Faith. General Eberle made an equally sonorous speech. He said he was on his way to Vietnam. He intended to visit the place in the Mekong Delta where the dead lieutenant's helicopter had crashed. Hopefully, he would imbibe some of the spirit of self-sacrifice, of national purpose, that had drawn America to Vietnam.

Bullshit, Joanna thought, it was all bullshit. Eberle and the president of Seward State were expert spiritual frauds, shoveling bullshit into the crisp November air.

As Eberle handed the Silver Star to the boy's father, a stumpy man with a farmer's weatherbeaten face, a chant drifted across the drill field. "FEE FI FO FUM. FEE FI FO FUM." Over the brow of the hill came the Mobilization memorial service. At its head were six pallbearers carrying a coffin. Behind them came a column of at least a thousand students, carrying candles. Girls—or were they boys?—with streaming hair whirled in and out of the line of march. It was a clash of religions, Joanna thought, watching, curiously, dangerously unaffected by it all. "FEE FI FO FUM," chanted the voices. "WE WANT THE BLOOD OF SOME ARMY SCUM."

General Eberle stared, amazed. He whirled to say something to Pete. Later Joanna learned it was: "What the fuck is this?" Pete tried to explain about the alternate service, and simultaneously explain that he had no idea they were going to attack him. "Haven't you ever heard of intelligence?" Eberle said, as if Pete were a general with a G-2 on his staff.

Onto the field the mobilized marched. The boy's father, seeing his wife and surviving son walking on either side of the black coffin, began to weep. "FEE FI FO FUM. WE'VE GOT SOME BLOOD FOR THE ARMY SCUM," boomed the chant. Neither Joanna nor anyone else noticed the change in emphasis. The pallbearers stopped in front of the small platform, no more than two or three feet high, on which the ceremony's principal participants stood.

The pallbearers opened the coffin. Three of them took out pails. Before anyone on the platform could move, they flung the contents

581

of the pails in the faces of Pete, General Eberle and the president of the university. It was, Joanna learned later, a mixture of blood and guts which they had procured from a nearby slaughterhouse. "FEE FI FO FUM. DO YOU LIKE THE SMELL OF BLOOD, YOU ARMY SCUM?" chanted the marchers.

"Arrest them," gasped the president. A half dozen campus police, who had been as paralyzed as the rest of the onlookers, raced from the sidelines. The pallbearers ran down opposite sides of the line of march. General Eberle's aide was frantically wiping slop off his face with an inadequate handkerchief.

"The chopper," someone yelled. "Let's trash the war machine." The marchers stampeded for the helicopter. The crew, who had been standing outside it watching the ceremony, leaped into their seats and started the motor. The huge blades whirled menacingly. The would-be trashers stumbled back, shielding their eyes from the air blast. Some were so frightened they flung themselves face down on the ground. The helicopter rose and flew down the field to hover over the ceremonial platform. What to do? They obviously could not land anywhere else on this crazed campus. General Eberle was their responsibility. Some hand signals were exchanged, and a rope ladder dropped from the helicopter's belly. The Pentagon's representative and his aide made an ignominious retreat from the battle, while below their antagonists hooted triumphantly.

Back at their apartment, two hours later, Joanna listened to Pete on the telephone trying to apologize to Eberle. "General, if I had the slightest idea they were going to do such a thing I would have taken every precaution—

"Yes, sir.

"No, sir. Of course I understand you have to make a report, sir. I hope you'll emphasize the seriousness of the situation. We're not the only ROTC unit under attack, as I'm sure you know.

"Yes. Yes, sir."

Pete hung up and paced the bedroom. He was wearing his gray cadet bathrobe, still in good condition after twenty-one years. His befouled uniform was in the deep sink in the kitchen. "He's going to take me apart. It's unbelievable," he said.

Joanna knew what he was omitting. It was unbelievable to have his career damaged, perhaps ruined, on the campus of William Seward State University. Eberle's report would question his judgment, a worse black mark than the unproven accusations General Hamburger had made against him in Saigon. It was unbelievable to have this happen to him in his own country. After winning a Distinguished Service Cross, after leading a company, commanding a battalion in battle with continuous success, after advising whole divisions of our Asian allies. His wife, his supposed ally, his secret enemy, said nothing.

The Seward ROTC never recovered from General Eberle's retreat. Morale sank, drill absences soared. Upstate New York's rotten winter weather did not help. But the ongoing offensive of the Mobilization for Peace was the main reason for the decline. The faculty senate, dominated as usual by Annette Haines, passed a resolution condemning the supposedly reckless way the Army operated the helicopter, declaring it was a miracle that dozens of students were not killed. They also resolved that the president should apologize to the student body for participating in a pro-war propaganda ceremony.

Simultaneously, Annette Haines's student cadres went to work on individual ROTC members. They harassed them in their rooms, they ridiculed their girlfriends into dropping them, they jeered them as they walked to class, they ostracized them in the dining halls. Soon scarcely a day passed without Pete coming home to report another resignation. Worse, recruitment among the freshman class was the lowest in the history of the ROTC at Seward.

Pete grew more and more discouraged and bewildered. "What's wrong with these people?" he would ask. His wife said nothing. She toiled on her papers, she devoured monographs and special studies, she struggled to satisfy the demands of the people who were destroying her husband. She actually made that melancholy probability a reason for working harder. If Pete's Army career collapsed, her Ph.D. might be their only means of support. How could he make a living in the civilian world? No one else was likely to offer him a million-dollar Cadillac dealership.

Originally the Ph.D. had been an island, a refuge, toward which the wounded swimmer struggled mindlessly, her only strength a blind will to survive. Now it was a hilltop bristling with bunkers and weapons, her own personal Heartbreak Ridge, which Joanna assaulted with mounting frenzy. The enemy commander was Dr. Emerson Mather. Day by day, week by week, he fought a coercive war against her, steadily weakening her will with remorseless attrition. Her papers, her oral contributions to his seminar in nineteenth-century American poetry, which every candidate for a Ph.D. in English at Seward State had to survive, were never good enough. But her thesis was his favorite target of opportunity. In January he summoned her to his office and told her that her draft of the second half, done in faithful accordance with the outline she had submitted and he had approved, was "almost hopelessly" inferior.

"I think you should consider withdrawing from the program," Dr. Mather said. "Your place could be filled by a young man who otherwise might be drafted and sent to Vietnam."

"I'd like an opportunity to rewrite the thesis," Joanna said.

"I will give you one more chance."

She piled the revision on top of her ordinary course work. It meant staying up until 2 and 3 A.M., ignoring most of Pete's overtures to lovemaking, insisting with mounting irritation that he and Tom take charge of all the housework, turn down the television, leave her alone alone alone. But she could not stop them from talking about the war at the dinner table. She could not prevent them from occasionally opening the bedroom door, permitting a bland TV voice to inform her that a hundred Viet Cong were killed near Phu Loi, an ARVN battalion was decimated on the Minh Thanh Plantation.

Then there were Adam's letters. They began to arrive in January, addressed, as always, to "Dear Pete and Joanna," the now established subterfuge. They were written to her. Pete almost acknowledged it by neglecting to read several of them. Adam was on the staff of Lieutenant General Newton Ingalls. His main task was "lying to congressmen." His view of the war was unrelentingly gloomy. The North Vietnamese and the Viet Cong were taking horrendous losses. But they kept fighting, kept killing Americans, because they were convinced that they were winning the coercion game. The anti-war movement made them certain that time and will were on their side.

Then came a letter that went beyond pessimism. It was a cry of pure pain.

> My Rhade. They've slaughtered my Rhade at Bong Son. The NVA attacked them with flame throwers. They broke through the outer perimeter and the Rhade retreated to their bunkers to defend their families. The NVA went through the whole camp, firing flame into each bunker. They incinerated everyone, men, women, children. It took them six hours to break through the perimeter. In all that time, no one from the ARVN or our Big Army responded to their calls for help. We'd turned the camp over to ARVN Special Forces. They did an E & E (Evacuate and Evade) at the first barrage. Excuse me for being incoherent but this is the worst thing that's happened to me in my seventeen years in the Army. I'm responsible, directly responsible for their deaths. I talked them into fighting this war. Ingalls is getting command of I and II Corps. I told him we can't let this happen again. We've got to get people like Pete out here, people who can make the ARVN fight.

That was when Joanna began to think there had to be a way to escape history, this maelstrom that was whirling them all toward some unspeakable immolation, death in all its meanings, of the body, the spirit, death of love, death of hope. Struggling against a growing sense of collapse, she found herself hating the apartment with its rented furniture. A stranger in a strange house, she was stripped, isolated, a creature without a refuge. But it was too late to retreat, regroup her depleted forces. By the end of April, she was teetering on the edge of rout. She sat dazedly at her dinner table listening to her husband and son discuss Con Thien, Ben Tre, Ban Me Thuot, Task Force Oregon, body counts, defoliation, free-fire zones. Each battle name, each technical term with its implied harvest of death, left an invisible wound in her flesh.

The day, the hour of rout was undramatic. It ended, as many battles end, with a request for capitulation. "Are you going to sign our petition?" Emerson Mather asked.

"What petition?" Joanna said as she sat down beside his desk to hear another analysis of her failure to penetrate the abstraction-thick poems of Jones Very with sufficient rigor.

Dr. Mather put the piece of paper in front of her. Joanna had been up the previous night until 4 A.M. writing a paper on the novels of George Eliot. She read the statement once, twice, and failed to comprehend it.

> *We the undersigned, graduate students at William Seward State University, hereby call on the president and trustees of the university to terminate the university's immoral and intolerable contract with the U.S. government which permits innocent students to be seduced into becoming servants of the war machine. We demand the immediate end of the ROTC on our campus.*

The words finally penetrated her exhausted mind. She stared at Dr. Mather. Could the man be serious? Did he have any ability to feel, to imagine human relationships? She shook her head, answering her own question. He was as dry, as inert as a volume of one of the forgotten nineteenth-century poets in which he specialized. His fury over the war was a way of deceiving himself into thinking he was alive.

"I've been waiting," Dr. Mather said. "Waiting for you to prove to me that you're not afraid of your husband. Here's your chance."

Joanna shook her head again. She was not refusing him. She was trying to fit Dr. Mather into the world as she now understood it. She decided he was not responsible for what was happening here, any more than she was responsible. They were both pieces of flotsam whirling in history's maelstrom.

"Even your husband must admit that the ROTC no longer serves a purpose on this campus," Dr. Mather said. "It is nothing but a sign of contradiction, a disturber of the peace."

Joanna was not listening to him. She was hearing the voice of her secret self, telling her to sign it and say it was all part of the historical process, she was not responsible, she was a victim of necessity, that iron law that sends napalm down on Vietnamese villages and bomb fragments into the intestines of four-year-olds.

She signed it. Firmly, clearly, boldly. *Joanna W. Burke*, she wrote. She stared at the signature. Was that her real name now? Borrowed from a man she had just repudiated? Should she have signed Joanna Welsh? No, that name was even more irretrievably lost. She was in danger of becoming nothing, a creature without a name.

"Well," Emerson Mather said. "Well. Allow me to congratulate you, my dear woman. You have proven the power of conscience, the strength of the moral voice within each of us, even when brute force tries to stifle it."

He slid the petition across the desk and sheltered it within his hands, as if he thought she might try to snatch it back. "You have proven you are a woman of courage. You have earned an apology from me for expressing some skepticism on that point. I do apologize, most sincerely. You have demonstrated you are not afraid of the U. S. Army, even in its most formidable manifestation."

This creature of dust and inertia, this echoing repository of forgotten poets and poems, thought he had defeated the U. S. Army. He saw himself as a general who had outmaneuvered the Homeric dunderhead, Lieutenant Colonel Peter M. Burke, by attacking him at his most vulnerable point—his weak-willed passive wife. He did not know what this wife had seen and heard in her time. He did not know that she had walked the wards of an Army hospital in Japan and stood beside lonely coffins at Tan Son Nhut Airbase. He did not know that she had heard her husband weep for his dead men, his incinerated comrades.

"As for the latest draft of the thesis," Dr. Mather said, "I think it shows some improvement."

"Burn it," Joanna said.

"I beg your pardon?"

"Burn the goddamn thing. I'm going home and burn my copy."

She reeled across the campus in the May sunshine, a refugee with no place to hide. In the apartment Pete was on the telephone.

"Sure," he said. "Sure I want it. If I'm needed out there, that's all I want to hear. The Pentagon tour can wait."

He walked into the kitchen, so excited he did not notice the dazed condition of his wife, sitting at the red-topped table. "That was personnel," Pete said. "Adam's put the fix in. Ingalls is going to command everything north of Saigon. He wants me as adviser to the ARVN in Eye Corps. It's a terrific assignment. If we can get the little guys to stand up to the North Vietnamese along the DMZ, half our worries are over."

He sat down on the other side of the table. "It's a two-year tour," he said, in a more tentative voice. "You'll be entitled to quarters at Clark Air Base in the Philippines. I'll get a weekend off a month."

"I think you should resign from the Army before you go anywhere near that war again," Joanna said.

He took her hand. "Are you all right?" he said.

She withdrew her hand. "I'm fine."

The telephone rang. Pete answered it. "Yes, this is Colonel Burke." There was a half minute of silence. "I have no comment. No comment," Pete said.

He came back into the kitchen. "That was the student newspaper. They said you've signed a petition demanding the withdrawal of the ROTC from the campus. Is that true?"

"Yes," she said.

"You've joined them, is that it?"

"No. I told them I was resigning from the English Department. I'm going to burn that goddamn thesis. I hate them. But I hate the war too. I hate the thought of you going out there again. This time they'll kill you. Or the Army will make you do something that will turn you into a monster. Something subhuman. Something I hate."

"This is beautiful," Pete said. "This is really very neat."

"What?"

"The job you're doing on me. They've really thought it all out for you."

"No one's thought it out for me. I can't even think about it myself. I can only tell you what I feel."

"You can think about it. You will think about it. I'm a professional soldier. You're my wife. You've just made me look like a fool.

That goddamn story will get back to Washington. That will look great in my file, won't it? As for leadership ability, Lieutenant Colonel Burke has had trouble controlling his wife. Words to that effect. You've cut my throat, get the point?''

"There are things more important than your career. Adam said—"

"Forget Adam. Once and for all, forget that son of a bitch. You don't see him resigning, do you? You don't see him letting his wife sign petitions that make him look like a fool. He stashed that dum-dum Honor with her mother in Charlesville. Maybe I should have done the same thing with you. Stashed you somewhere and loved a real woman. Someone with the courage to stand by me no matter what happened."

"You mean Thui, don't you?"

"Yeah. I love her more than I've ever loved you. After Dat was killed, I couldn't sleep, thinking about her."

"I don't have courage? I followed you to Kansas, Japan, Hawaii, Saigon."

"Whining all the way."

She had hurt him and he was hurting her. He was using half-truths to hurt her the way her half-truths had hurt him. He was succeeding, precisely because the truth, even a 50 percent solution, scorched like lye in the face, sent rage surging to the brain.

"Away down deep, you're a bastard, aren't you? I can see why you like to kill people. You'd like to kill me now, wouldn't you?"

His big hands opened and closed on the red tabletop. For a moment she thought she might be close to death. But that iron self-control he had acquired at West Point transformed his rage into contempt. "You want me to beat you up, I can see it. You'd go straight to the phone and tell that kid reporter all about it. Admit it. This whole thing is a ploy cooked up by that bitch Annette Haines. You're working on me the same way the coeds've worked on the ROTC kids. But you decided you needed a little more pressure on me. It wouldn't be enough to stop sleeping with me. You hardly ever do that anyway. So you resign from the department and give up your wonderful dream of being an English professor. I'm supposed to roll over and say, 'Oh, Joanna, that's wonderful, I'll resign too.' ''

"None of that's true. I just want to get us away from it. The war.

I want to go someplace where we won't have to think about it. Where we can forget it.''

"Where's that? On the moon? It's too late for me to apply for the space program. Anyway, I'm not a pilot, I'm an infantryman. Christ, you're not even a good liar. You're not a good anything. Wife, mother. You drag my son to those teach-ins where he gets his head filled with lies. In spite of everything that's happened I'm still glad I came here because you would have turned that boy into a peace freak without me around.''

"Not a chance. He's just like you. A totally closed mind.''

"If that's what it takes to be a patriot, to care about my country, my Army, to stay loyal to the oath I took at West Point, so be it. I've got a closed mind. How does that tie in with that bullshit you fed me at Leavenworth about loving me, even though we had different minds? I bought that idea, I really tried to love you.''

"You don't think I tried to love you?''

"I don't know what you tried to do. You're a liar. That's your basic problem. You lie to yourself, to me. You've done it from the start. You never meant one word of that crap you fed me about poverty and the spiritual life when we were engaged. You bugged out on the only real challenge you ever had, reached for those lousy birth control pills—''

"Jesus, you haven't forgiven me for anything," she said. "It's all there in Joanna's efficiency reports, year by year. Everything she ever did wrong. Every table she forgot to dust. Every dinner she burned. Is that it?''

"Remember at Leavenworth—you told me you were going to make me happy? How would you rate yourself in that department now?''

"I tried," she said, looking past him as he was looking past her, staring at blank spots on the wall. As if neither could bear to see on the once-beloved face the death of their marriage.

"You tried," he said. The big hands opened and closed on the table. "I guess you did, now and then. When you were in the mood. When you wanted to play Joanna the noble wife. But most of the time you were feeling sorry for yourself and blaming me, the Army for it. I think you even blame me for Cissie.''

"I do," she screamed. "I do blame you and your rotten fucking Army. Your shitty duty-honor-country. She died for the only thing you care about—your goddamn marvelous career. Your next promotion. So someday you can walk around with a couple of phony stars on your shoulders."

The secret self had finally spoken. Pete nodded slowly, once, twice. She had confirmed his suspicions. Words were now superfluous. Hatred emanated from his glaring eyes, filling the room with a weird darkness. At the same time Joanna saw it all in its sad stark bare-bulb humility. They were sitting in another cheap kitchen but now they were exchanging declarations of detestation, departure, instead of lifelong commitment.

Footsteps on the stairs, a door opening and closing. It was Tom. "Hi, Mom, Dad," he said, zooming past them to the refrigerator. "What's for supper?" he asked, guzzling milk from a carton.

"Hot dogs and beans."

"Listen," Pete said. "Your mother and I were just having a—a talk. I'm going out to Nam again. ARVN adviser for Eye Corps. I was hoping she'd come out to Clark Field in the Philippines. But she's not buying it."

"Hey, why not, Mom? The Philippines would be cool."

"I—I want to stay in Hawaii. I was thinking of renting our old house on the beach at Mo Ka Lei."

She glared at Pete, half challenging him, half sullenly confessing that she could not tell their son that his parents' marriage had collapsed. Hawaii was the perfect refuge from the truth—and from the lieutenant colonel. The Army flew husbands from Vietnam to Honolulu once every six months for five days of Rest and Relaxation. Let corps adviser Burke explain why he would never make the trip. *You're the one with the courage, hero. You tell him*, she thought.

"If—if that's what your mother wants, it's okay with me," Pete said. "But I don't think you should go along. I don't think the schools are good enough in Hawaii. I'd like to see you go to that school in Cornwall-on-Hudson that we talked about—where they concentrate on getting you ready to take the entrance examinations for the Academy."

"What do you think, Mom?"

"I didn't know you were going to the Academy."

"I made up my mind a couple of weeks ago. I've been waiting for a chance to tell you. I mean—you've been so busy."

She nodded and glanced at Pete. Was there triumph on the lieutenant colonel's saturnine face? No. For Tom's sake he was going to play the marriage game for a few more days. She would try to match his parental poise.

"I think the Academy is a great idea—for you," she said.

"Do you have time to cook dinner tonight?" Pete asked.

"Yes," she said.

"Let's catch the news," Pete said to Tom.

They retreated to the living room. In a few moments the television voice filled the kitchen, where Joanna stood alone, trying to understand what was happening to her.

"HEAVY FIGHTING ERUPTED TODAY AROUND THE TOWN OF CON THIEN, TWO MILES SOUTH OF THE DEMILITARIZED ZONE. THE NORTH VIETNAMESE ALSO ATTACKED AN AMERICAN SPECIAL FORCES BASE IN THE MOUNTAINS EAST OF HUE. THE CITY OF HUE ITSELF WAS STRUCK BY ENEMY ROCKETS."

Hue, on the poetically named Perfume River. Hue was in I Corps. The corps adviser would undoubtedly visit it often. Joanna saw Thui Dat in her shimmering white ao-dai, smiling up at Pete. *A noble love*, she said, *greater than one can have in marriage*.

BOOK
FIVE

I

"JESUS Christ, they ought to spell the name of this place a new way. B-a-n-g C-o-c-k."

Amy Rosser laughed. The speaker was James McKelway French. He was about six feet two, with a Jimmy Stewart drawl and hooded eyes that assayed the world and found it wanting. Which was perfectly all right, even delightful, at twenty-five. Which was also perfectly understandable, considering the world he was assaying. They were standing on Bangkok's New Road in front of a neon-trimmed bar named the OK Corral. Past them streamed a fair number of the 37,000 American servicemen who poured into Bangkok each week for Rest and Relaxation. Seven days off from shooting and getting shot at in the jungles of the Ia Drang Valley or the rice paddies of the Mekong Delta. Most of the Americans were with Thai girls wearing cheap Western dresses. Only a handful wore the traditional Thai panung, wrapped tightly around the hips and falling in a soft drape to the feet. Few of the Americans were heeding the recent protest of one of Thailand's top officials that the GIs were offending the custom of the country by indulging in Public Displays of Affection.

James McKelway French of Butte, Montana, was a captain in the Air Force. Each day he drove to a base outside Bangkok and climbed into the seat of an F-100 Supersabre fighter-bomber and flew it at 1,200 miles per hour into Vietnam. A Forward Air Controller in a small prop plane hovering over the watery green checkerboard of the Mekong Delta told him where to drop his two bombs. Down streaked James McKelway French to unleash 1,500 pounds of death on the enemy. Around whipped Captain French for a second run, perhaps on another target, where he dropped his canister of napalm. With the earth churning and shuddering and burning behind him, he flew back to Bangkok and the arms of his forty-one-year-old mistress.

Amy would be waiting for him in her California ranch house on Soi Lumpini, within sight of the five tall towers of the monastery of the dawn, Wat Arun. Across the street was a traditional Thai house, a two-story unstained teak gem that she could have rented for half the price. But Amy knew when she came to Bangkok and saw its garish gorgeous marriage of East and West that she would remain American. Her emptiness was American, her loneliness was American. She could not, she would not have it any other way. It was a kind of revenge on someone or something. Also a punishment.

Her younger daughter, Grace, was reliving Amy's adolescent purgatory in a Connecticut boarding school. She wrote mushy, self-pitying letters about how unhappy she was. Amy wrote back telling her how much she hated Bangkok. Grace's sister, Georgianna, was gone, no one knew where. At this very moment she might be sidling along New York's Eighth Avenue, selling herself for a cafeteria meal. More likely, the sullen bitch was in San Francisco's Haight-Ashbury, stoned on hashish or insane on the latest craze, LSD. Whatever happened to her, Amy grimly told herself, she deserved it.

Georgianna and her friend Pandora Wax had run away a month after they had marched in another anti-war protest. Mrs. Wax blamed the whole thing on Amy, who, she said, had overreacted by forbidding Georgie to leave the house at night or on weekends for the rest of the year. Amy had responded by telling Mrs. Bureaucrat that Pandora had the morals of a prostitute. What really infuriated Amy was George's reaction. He had been distraught, sleepless for weeks after Georgie disappeared. He spent his spare time on the telephone with Missing Persons Bureaus in half the cities of the nation. They could only tell him there was an epidemic of runaways, as the cry "Never trust anyone over thirty" penetrated the rock-numbed consciousness of American youth. When he wasn't ignoring Amy, George was hinting that she ought to pursue their flower child to New York, Boston, San Francisco, or at least feel guilty about her disappearance.

When Amy refused to do either, he told her she was a cold woman. Her rage, which she totally concealed, was immense. Cold? She could still hear Willard Eberle grunting on top of her. She could still smell that heavy after-shave lotion he wore. She could still feel his hands, somehow leathery. For a moment, behind her closed eyes, she saw him as an alligator, drool pouring from one corner of his jaw. Cold? When her migraines came once a week now, like a cleaning woman, scouring her nerves, casting an unreal halo around George, Grace, everyone. Cold? When George Rosser, who had never commanded so much as a squad in action, was getting command of one of the fifty available maneuver battalions in Vietnam?

Later, as the date for his departure to Saigon drew close, George had apologized. Sentimental as usual, he wanted to leave a loving wife behind. When Amy told him she was not staying behind, she was following him to Asia and would await him in Bangkok, he tepidly acquiesced. He wanted her to stay in the United States and devote her year of celibacy to hunting their runaway daughter. Amy had sidestepped the question and George had departed, leaving it unsettled. Amy settled it. Within a month she was in Bangkok.

There was a Military Assistance Group operating in Thailand, with a dozen or so wives of field-grade officers living in Bangkok. Amy ignored them. She who had once treasured the company of other Army wives. Letters came from Florence Eberle, who toyed with joining her. Perhaps she thought her presence in the same part of the globe would make Willard behave while he was in Vietnam. Amy described Bangkok as a giant porno amusement park for enlisted men and frightened Florence into staying home.

She wandered the city alone for a month, like a tourist. She visited the gold-roofed, three-tiered Chapel of the Emerald Buddha in Wat Phrakaeo and contemplated the ancient thirty-one-inch-high figure, carved out of green jasper. She looked with equal interest (or disinterest) at the 160-foot statue of the Reclining Buddha in nearby

Wat Jetubon. Equally awesome (or boring) was the huge bronze Buddha in Wat Saket and the 25,000-pound golden Buddha in Wat Tramitr. She drifted in the early-morning coolness along the city's canals, called *klongs*, to the floating market; she rode in a three-wheeled taxi along Yawarad Road, Bangkok's Chinatown.

She spent her nights reading mystery stories, which she bought by the dozen at the airport. She almost always figured out the plot before she was halfway through. Suspense stories were better, especially Ian Fleming; there was no necessity to care about his characters. She listened to the Armed Forces Radio report heavy fighting in the Delta, in Quang Tri. She got hurried, dutiful letters from George, telling her he had a good battalion, except for one company commander, whom he had had to relieve. The anti-war movement seemed to have no effect on morale. She answered him briefly; Bankok was a bore, she said.

Then Amy met James McKelway French. She had taken a day trip on the steamer *Oriental Queen*, which included a visit to the King of Thailand's summer palace, and the ancient ruined city of Ayudhya. Little was left of this former capital of Thailand, which was sacked by the Burmese in 1767. At the height of its power, its rulers had controlled most of Burma, Malaysia, Laos and Cambodia. As Amy pondered the crumbling reddish walls of the royal palace, the ruins of the royal chapel, which once contained a standing Buddha forty-two feet high covered with gold, she heard a voice beside her: "Doesn't pay to lose a war, does it?"

Captain French was also touring (touristing, he called it). "Just tired of the native women," he said. They sat together on the boat back to Bangkok and watched the sun set above the wide fertile plain whose rice paddies reminded Amy of Vietnam. He was a pilot. Flying was all he wanted to talk about. How things looked coming at you at 1,200 miles an hour. How it felt to pull out of a dive at that speed, your chin suddenly connected to your chest, what it was like to fly an F-100 all the way from California to Thailand, refueling at the waving tit of a big silvery tanker plane above the empty Pacific, knowing you had only three tries and then it was up to you to find an island before your gauge hit empty. What it was like to bomb, the sudden wild freedom of being 1,500 pounds lighter. What it was like to fly through a monsoon storm, with nothing visible except the deadly tip of your wingmate's plane, dancing in the same turbulence.

They had dinner together at Piman, a theater-restaurant in a fourteenth-century Thai house. They ate *tom yam gung,* the native soup made from makroot leaves, lemon grass and water, and *gant pete,* pork cooked in coconut milk and a dozen spices. A mistress of ceremonies explained in English and French the meaning of the classical dances performed by a troupe of impassive gold-robed actors and actresses. Amy talked about Saigon, about the war protesters at home. Captain French was not interested. He talked about his wingman, who had gone down over the delta a week ago. One moment he was there, laughing over the radio about how close he had come to a tree line. Then he was a streak of brown-and-orange flame slashing across a quarter of a mile of rice paddies. That was when Amy knew she would sleep with him. She knew he was going to die the same way. It would mean nothing, then, whatever she had felt for him, love or disgust or comradeship.

It was the persistence of everything, everyone, that depressed her: husbands who went on being husbands, daughters who would not stop daughtering even when they told Mother to go fuck herself, old lovers who would not stop pursuing her (Adam, tracking her down with his usual skill, wrote long amusing letters about life on General Newton Ingalls' staff), an Army that continued to fight a war for a government that did not want to win it. A government, a people, so cowardly, so moronic, she sometimes wished she could shed her skin, forget she had once exulted to be part of a country that had made the name America synonymous with pride, triumph.

More than once, when Amy awoke in the morning and heard the hum of her American air conditioner attacking the scummy humidity enveloping Soi Lumpini, and looked at the sleeping boy beside her (always with a smile on his face, dreaming of flying, she was sure), Amy would say no, no, better this way, better to stay American, accept the emptiness. Those were the days when her migraine would torment her. When she imagined James McKelway French laughing into the slash of orange flame. How would she find out? She would not let him introduce her to any of his friends. She had not even told him her real name. When he had asked her, she had told him to make up a name for her. "Mary Ann," he said.

Captain French was puzzled by the way she gave herself to him so persistently; at times he felt the balance of taking and giving had shifted in the wrong direction, making his masculine ego uneasy.

"What are you thinking, when I'm in there?" he asked her once, after they made love in the usual acrobatic fashion.

"Nothing. It's when I stop thinking," Amy said. "The only time."

"I remind you of someone, is that it?" he asked another night.

"Yes," she said.

He was a metaphor of Adam. His daring, his obsessive love of one thing. Eventually he began to talk about sharing it with her. He wanted her to fly with him. Literally. She said she was willing; but how? That would take a little thought, he replied. She listened while he told her what it would be like. She would sit behind him in "the bathtub," as they called the second seat in the F-100. She would see, hear, feel everything, exactly as he did. She would know why nothing else really mattered, as long as you could fly.

"I'd love it," Amy said.

She did not tell him it was the danger she wanted; how it would feel to risk becoming an orange slash of flame.

A few days later, Captain French appeared at the house with a complete flight suit—gray leather gloves, black leather boots, a big white plastic helmet, a parachute, an oxygen mask and zip-on tight canvas chaps, known as a G suit, which automatically inflated to keep the blood from rushing out of the top of the body when a jet pulled out of a dive. He made Amy practice sitting in a chair with her knees hunched up, the position you take if you have to eject.

"Why?" she asked.

"If you don't, the instrument panel takes off your kneecaps," he said.

"Fun," Amy said.

"I think you can handle it," Captain French said.

The next day Captain French brought home a new identity, readily purchased in Bangkok. Amy became Mary Ann Mercer, reporter for the Philadelphia *Inquirer*. Official-looking documents accredited her as a foreign correspondent. Her passport even proved she had spent a year reporting from Saigon. The following day Captain French drove her out to the air base and introduced her to the wing's public information officer. "This is the newshen I told you about. Crazy about planes. Air Force all the way. Says she wants to write something about the guys who're really winning this war. Tired of goin' by chopper bus."

The PIO officer, a chunky peppery Southerner, was delighted. He asked Mary Ann Mercer to sign a paper, holding the Air Force blameless for any injuries she might sustain. That done, it was simply a question of choosing a mission. "The sooner, the better," Mary Ann Mercer said.

Two days later, Amy put on her flight suit in Captain French's quarters and drove with him to a briefing in a long tin quonset hut. She sat in the back row, the peak of a field cap pulled down low to reduce the chance of later identification. She listened to the briefing officers outline the mission and talk about the number of VC that had been KBA (killed by air) the day before. Amy studied the boyish faces of the pilots and wondered if she should get up and run for her life. It was insane. If she were caught, she would be disgraced, George's career ruined. She did not move. She did not care about George's career anymore.

She fell in step beside James McKelway French and he led her and two other pilots to a square blue truck, of the sort that had delivered bread and laundry in Bala-Cynwyd. The flight leader, a redhead with an incredible amount of freckles on his face, said: "You know he's the worst pilot in the squadron?"

"Likes to bomb upside down," said the other pilot, who sported an unreal walrus mustache.

The driver of the truck called off the numbers of the planes and the other pilots got out. Captain French and Amy were alone. "Four four five," the driver said. She took off her field cap and put on her flight helmet and stepped down onto the concrete runway. Captain French led her toward a ridiculously slim plane camouflaged gray and brown and olive. Under each wing was a 750-pound bomb, greenish brown with a yellow ring on its nose. Next to one of the bombs was an aluminum canister full of napalm. Amy climbed up a yellow ladder, positioned her parachute on the seat and let Captain French strap her in. He dropped into the seat in front of her and said, "Canopy coming down." The heavy plastic bubble clonked over them. Orange flame gushed from the tails of the planes to their right and left; they pivoted and taxied onto the runway. With a roar that shook the plane, Captain French started their engine. In a moment they were on the runway, rolling faster and faster, for what seemed an eternity.

Then they were up, free, climbing toward a bank of gray monsoon clouds. "Dig Bangkok," Captain French said, and stood the plane on its wing, displacing Amy's stomach. Below them white hotels and golden temple spires flashed in the sun. Ribbons of toy cars and people-ants crept along the tree-lined streets. All this vanished a moment later as they plunged into a cloud layer. They burst through it to emerge into a stark white sky, blazing with the tropic sun. The other two members of the wing positioned themselves only inches away, a tactic Amy thought was limited to air shows.

"How about a little roll for our guest?" Captain French said.

Over they went, all three of them, bombs and napalm gleaming in their bellies while the earth and sky revolved. "Do it again," Amy said.

"That sounds familiar," Captain French said.

Once, twice more they rolled while Amy's heart stopped beating and her body became tissue paper. Then the flight leader started talking to someone on the radio. Amy heard something about Seven Mountains and Victor Charlie. Down they dove through the cloud layer to emerge above monsoon-haunted Vietnam. The rice paddies were a dull green beneath the metallic sky. Ants toiled in the paddies. Occasionally one followed a larger ant, a water buffalo. Ahead Amy saw a small plane circling above a series of humpbacked hills.

The flight leader was talking to the small plane, a Forward Air Controller. "Let's make sure these guys never get back to the U Minh Forest," the FAC said.

"That's what we're here to do," the flight leader said.

"I'm going to mark," said the FAC.

Amy watched the small plane bank and fire a rocket into the trees at the base of the mountain. A white puff rose above the greenery. "They're scattering. Hit fifty meters east."

"Lead is from the west," the flight leader said. Amy watched him hurtle toward the ground in a long steep arc, then bound up over the flat crest of the mountain. Behind him a red flash erupted, followed by lightning-swift explosions of gold, red and brown.

"Good bomb," said the FAC. "Put the next one fifty meters west. They're running in that direction."

The other wingmate repeated the flight leader's performance.

"Some ground fire. Looks like fifty-millimeter stuff," someone said.

"Here we go," Captain French said.

Down down they plunged, rolling over as they dropped until they were upside down, part of the plane now, part of the whole machine of war, plugged into its G-suit lifeline to keep their unreliable human blood under control, the green earth rushing up and a glimpse through shattered trees of little men, not ants now, running, and one of them aiming some kind of gun up at them. Amy's head seemed to float from her body as the F-100 snapped over at the last possible second and the two bombs went *thunk* and they were rocketing up the slope of the mountain so close to the trees it was not possible they could clear the crest; the altimeter was at zero; there would be a flash and a crash; her head was crushed now beneath her flight helmet, her whole body was being squashed by a thousand pounds of gravity. Then they were climbing straight into the sun and the Forward Air Controller was estimating at least 200 KBA's

The FAC muttered a curse. In the same matter-of-face voice he said: "I just took a bullet through my fuel line. Can you guys stay around to cover me?"

"Only for another ten minutes," the flight leader said.

The small single-engine plane spiraled slowly down to land in a rice paddy about a mile from where they had bombed. The flight leader called someone for a helicopter to get the pilot out. Figures in black emerged from the trees and began running down a long dike through the paddies to attack the FAC. Down swept the flight leader, his twenty-millimeter cannon pumping death at the attackers. Geysers of water and mud erupted around them. In a flash, the dike was swept clean. Then the wingman hurtled in from the left, and Captain French came in from the opposite direction to pump more shells into the figures floundering in the dark green water. For several minutes there was no movement in the water or on the dike as the three jets circled and the FAC stood on the wing of his plane waving his thanks.

"Where the fuck is that helicopter?" the flight leader asked. A calm radio voice said the helicopter could not possibly get there for another twenty minutes.

"We've only got five more minutes of fuel time," the flight leader said.

"Sorry about that," the radio voice said.

"Let's use our napalm. Lead is from the east again."

Down went the flight leader. This time Amy saw the silvery bomblike canister float into the trees and watched an enormous *whoosh* of flame leap like a thousand beseeching arms above the shriveling greenery. The wingman bombed fifty meters to the left. Captain French went after the attackers along the dike, to make sure none of them were still alive. Again he rolled over, snapped upright, and Amy felt the torment of gravity tearing at her flesh. This time with bombs gone and fuel low, they pulled up with miraculous swiftness. Amy looked back and saw a man stumble out of the sea of fire on both sides of the dike and run along it, his arms out, a human flaming cross.

For another two minutes they circled. Finally they swooped low, waggling their wings over the FAC to wish him luck. Then they were soaring up up into the clouds and the FAC was only an ant on a strip of silver.

"Will they save him?" Amy asked.

"Not a chance, unless we got every VC in those woods," Captain French said. "Which is unlikely."

They did roll after roll as they went home. They sang a song, a fighter pilot's favorite, she later learned, about a girl named Mary Ann, who did everything. Amy barely noticed. She realized she had stopped thinking about her own death. She was thinking about the death of the FAC, alone on his silver wing, the surviving VC methodically surrounding the paddy, murderous for revenge. She had flown into Vietnam in search of more meaninglessness, even hoping for the final meaninglessness, her own useless death. Instead, she had found courage. Why did one man's death somehow reestablish a sense of linkage with the Army, the war, in a way that she thought she had lost forever? The death of a stranger, a man she would never know?

Adam would die that way. He almost did, at Bong Son, gunning down Vietnamese at point-blank range in the trenches. John Stapleton died that way on the frozen banks of the Chongchon River. George? She could not imagine it. Was that the root of her despair? Not merely becoming Willard Eberle's whore. But selling herself, betraying Adam, for nothing. For love, marriage that was a lie. Was that the primary sin she had committed, in the private religion which she had unknowingly joined, the church of the brave?

At the air base, they rode back to Captain French's quarters, where she became female again. His two wingmates joined them for a drink.

"Mary Ann," they said, raising their dark brown glasses. "Anyone crazy enough to fly with Frenchie has more guts than brains. Which maybe explains why you love him."

I love you all, Amy thought. It was too ridiculous to say. But she felt it again, the link, that might as well be called love. It was shocking to contemplate, but she would have cheerfully gone to bed with any one of them.

That night, she found herself curiously unenthused for the acrobatics her private fly-boy enjoyed so much. She let him take her from behind, she let him go down on her for a half hour, she gave him an exquisite blow job. But the performances aroused her only in an automatic way. She felt tender; she could not summon her cold whoriness. He of course noticed nothing. He kept telling her how he thought about having her while they were bombing. He almost came, he said.

He never said a word about the Forward Air Controller.

The Army and the Air Force were different, Amy thought, as she drifted down into sleep. Different kinds of courage. She liked the Army's better. Maybe it was simply older. She was older. She had lived long enough to lose the ruthless uncaring of youth.

The next morning James MacKelway French gave her a playful pussy rub and drove out to the air base for another run over Vietnam. Around five, Amy mixed martinis. Five o'clock, six o'clock passed without his staccato jazz knock. Seven o'clock. Bangkok's neon began to glow against the darkening sky. Amy slowly drank the martinis for both of them.

At 9 P.M. she called the air base and asked for his flight leader, the redhead. His name was Weldon. "Frenchie went in," he said. "We were working on some VC in the U Minh Forest. No parachute, couldn't have been a parachute. We were right down on the treetops when it happened. Lizen, you want to talk about it? I'll take you to dinner or something."

She realized he was drunk. "No," she said. "Thank you. No."

She was through with twenty-five-year-olds. For the next three weeks, the closing days of 1967, Amy lived like a nun. Instead of praying, she followed the war. She wrote dutiful letters to George. She read, without flinching, stories of the ever more violent protests against the war at home. Finally she called the wife of the commanding general of MAAG in Thailand and introduced herself, implying that she had just arrived in Bangkok and wanted to associate with Army wives. Mrs. General, whose name was Marge Kennerly, could not have been more friendly. Which meant, Amy concluded, that she had survived with her reputation intact. She was glad, for George's sake. That was all the feeling she could muster for George. Polite, tepid good wishes.

Amy was soon a member of the small officers' wives club that met for bridge and gossip once a week at the Officers' Club of the air base outside Bangkok. The gossip was all about the war, the way the U.S. government was fighting it. Marge Kennerly, a broad-beamed woman with an aggressive jaw, said Lyndon Johnson was a disgrace, and the State Department was filled with no-win cowards Each week, at least one leading Thai official asked her husband why the United States did nothing to prevent tens of thousands of tons of rice and ammunition and weapons from pouring into Vietnam through Cambodia. Amy found herself joining this growing sense of outrage. Part of her, at least, could identify with the Army again.

George flew into Bangkok for a Christmas–New Year's leave. He looked tired, in a lean taut interesting way. Amy almost felt hopeful the first night, as they drank martinis and discussed the desultory fighting George's battalion had been doing around the provincial capital of Ban Me Thuot in the highlands. George talked somewhat ruefully about Pete Burke, who was a senior adviser for I Corps, and Adam, who was a favorite of Newton Ingalls, the general who was likely to take command of MACV sometime in 1968. The war was going fairly well. They'd thrown the VC and the North Vietnamese on the defensive, almost everywhere. If they could hold the momentum, the big war might be mostly over in a year or two. There might be sporadic guerrilla warfare for another ten years. He would know more about future plans when his tour as a battalion commander ended in January. He would go on staff at MACV. Willard Eberle was there already, looking for a slot for him. Willard had run up a surprisingly good record as a brigade commander of the 18th Division. He had had one of the lowest casualty rates and highest body counts in Vietnam.

Willard Eberle's name ruined everything. Amy could feel her flesh congeal, her migraine stir. That night she let George have her, dutiful, prone in the missionary position. If he noticed her lack of enthusiasm, he did not mention it. The next day her migraine was murderous. She wandered Bangkok with him seeing a white halo of anguish around all the temple spires and Buddhas. She groped her way through the next four days in the same condition. George went back to the war looking glum. On the last day he had compounded her despair by asking what she had done to find Georgie. When she said nothing, he almost exploded. Amy saw him off at the airport feeling her marriage was barely breathing. She tried to care. Nothing happened.

Three empty weeks later, three weeks of spiraling down into meaninglessness again, instead of a letter from her husband, there was a letter from Adam.

• • •

Is it true? What I just heard? That you let Willard have you? He didn't say when. I don't care when. I just want to know if it happened. I want to know if that walking fraud is lying or telling the truth for once in his life. It will reveal something decisive about the nature of things. Of women, above all. I was writing a year-end report on the fighting in I Corps for Ingalls, loading it up with all the stats that the whizkidiots in the Pentagon love, body counts by division, brigade, battalion, when I noticed that the count for Eberle's brigade was incredibly high. The figures had to be inflated. I pointed it out to Ingalls. Eberle had transferred to MACV for the last six months of his tour. Ingalls had no control over him. He told me to forget it. But I went up to the brigade outside Phu Bai and started interviewing junior officers and sergeants. They all admitted inflating their figures. It was an order from brigade. They figured everyone else in the Army was doing it. Why not? Some ass kisser wrote to Eberle, telling him what I was doing. When I got back to headquarters, Eberle was in Ingalls' office having a heart to heart. After he left, Ingalls tore me apart. I'd disobeyed an order, he said. For the good of the Army, I told him. He blew up and told me that he'd decide what was good for the Army, that's what he got paid to do. He demanded all copies of my interviews and warned me against leaking anything to the press. I gave him everything and went over to the Officers' Club to have a double scotch and forget the whole damn thing. There was Willard at the bar with a couple of full colonels on the make. I sat down at the opposite end. "Goddamnit," Willard said. "I didn't know they let pissheads into this club." He walked over to me and said: "Thayer, I'm going to even the score with you before you get out of this Army. If you're smart, you'll quit at twenty."

"I'm in for at least thirty, General," I said. "Ready for trouble all the way."

"You've got me wrong, Thayer. I don't scare. You

thought you shook me the last time. I just waited a little while and got what I wanted. She was a great fuck. Definitely worth the wait. You don't know how to wait, Thayer. That's the secret of success in the Army. Waiting."

He left me sitting there, a shambles. Is it true?

Adam

Amy replied with a telegram. I WILL BE IN SAIGON ON JANUARY 30-31 AT THE ROYALE. It was the only hotel room she could find, after hours of phone calls. January 30 and 31 was Tet, the Vietnamese New Year, usually a time of truce and leaves for troops in Vietnam. Amy thought this would be the most convenient time to see Adam.

What would it be like? she wondered as the Pan Am 707 landed at Tan Son Nuht Airport. Would Vietnam infest her blood and nerves again? Taxiing from the airport in the thick blanket of exhaust fumes from dozens of Army jeeps, trucks and the usual tangle of civilian traffic, Amy stared at the tin-roofed shacks lining the muddy alleys of the Bui Phat refugee quarter, which had grown enormously in three years. Across the river lay the wide boulevards and comfortable villas of French Saigon. No, she thought. It was going to be just like Bangkok. Another foreign city, a bit more full of accidental Americans. She had no desire to possess or be possessed by it. She had no desire. She was inert, moving toward an explanation that could not be explained, a sin that could not be forgiven. But the attempt had to be made.

She sat in the hot, high-ceilinged room of the old hotel, watching the Casablanca fan go around and around. That was the way the world went, around and around, clock hands, the body's sluggish blood. About noon, Adam appeared. He was drunk. "I've been sitting downstairs in the bar all morning, trying to decide whether to come up. If it wasn't true, you would have said so in the telegram. Why did you come all this way? So I can beat you up? Maybe kill you?"

"I had to see you. To tell you how much I—I regret it. How sorry I am that you found out."

"Why did you do it?"

"He said he was going to ruin George. It seemed so—so awful—to let that happen. Oh, Adam, I thought I could do it and forget it. No one would know but Willard and me. I thought I could bear the disgust for George's sake. But something happened inside me. Something got lost or broken, something we had together that helped me stay with George, with everyone. It's gone and I don't know what to do."

"Neither do I," Adam said.

"What was it? What did we have? It would help if I could even name it."

"It doesn't have a name. It would be a mistake to try to name it."

"It was love. Neither of us can admit that. We've both been afraid to admit it from the start."

"A kind of love."

"I still have it—for you," Amy said. She was sitting in a straight-back chair like a student giving a recitation. Or a confession to this priestlike, hungry-hawkish, inflexible New England face. The face of her blood, ancestral. They had played at Priscilla and Miles, but beneath every joke there is always a reality.

"I could have it again. I love what you are. Even though I know it's wrong, what you're doing, fighting with generals. Trying to reform the Army single-handed is crazy. I'd love you anyway. I'd rather be your wife than a general's wife."

"You don't love me," Adam said. "You love the Army. Or to be more precise, your idea of the Army. You're like me, you love ideas of things more than the things themselves, more than people."

"I *love* you. I've never said that to anyone before. Not this way. Not—offering. How much lower can I crawl?"

He was still standing just inside the door. He walked toward her and stopped an arm's length away. He ran his fingers down her cheek. "My Army wife," he said.

It was not reconciliation. It was farewell.

"We'd end up hating each other. Every time I looked at you I'd remember that son of a bitch Willard Eberle was sitting behind a desk somewhere, polishing his stars. Every time you looked at me you'd see that thought on my face.''

She shook her head.

"Yes, you would. Because it would be there."

"You can't forgive me?''

"I forgive you. But I can't forgive the Army. For making someone like Willard Eberle a general.''

For a moment she wanted to tell him about flying into Vietnam with James McKelway French. The Forward Air Controller alone on his silver wing. The community of the brave. But it was too inward, too difficult. And of course he would despise her for sleeping with Captain French. For the first time she glimpsed the passionate chastity of his mind, his intolerance of sin, failure, imperfection. She did not share it. Was it essentially male, this refusal to compromise, to surrender in any way?

"There are five hundred generals. Only a few are as detestable as Willard.''

"He's a symbol, a symptom.''

He raged about the way the Army was fighting the war. The one-year tour, with only six months in combat for officers, the ticket-punching get-ahead cover your-ass psychology that destroyed all sense of commitment to Vietnam as a nation or the Vietnamese as a people. She had read most of it before in his letters, but he always spiced it with delicious gossip about who was getting promoted and who was getting the business and what the latest reorganization at the Pentagon really meant. Now she saw (or heard) his rage turning *against* the Army.

"We deserve to lose this war," Adam said.

Amy realized she would never say that, never believe it. Not as long as she could still see that nameless American, waving farewell to the last hope of safety, alone on his silver wing. Somewhere at the core of the Army there was still a community of the brave and she would find it. That was all she needed. She did not demand this impossible perfection that was destroying Adam.

Should she try to tell him that as a final gesture of comradeship? No, better to make the farewell as simple and as plain as possible.

"I'm glad we did this. Talk. I always loved it as much as—the rest of it. The talk."

"Yes," Adam said. For a moment he looked puzzled, as if he sensed that she had found a source of strength, endurance that had eluded him.

"Goodbye," she said.

She kissed him gently on the lips, like a sister kissing a brother. After he left, she sat there beneath the rotating fan, wondering what to do. Telegraph George? Some kind of explanation would be necessary. *I came to Saigon because I sensed our marriage was falling apart.* She could not muster the strength to say it. Eventually it grew dark. She went downstairs to the hotel restaurant, ate some bouillabaisse and went back to her room. About ten o'clock she took a shower and went to sleep.

She was awakened by a tremendous explosion that sent bits of plaster raining into her face. She stumbled to the window, which now had a big crack in it. Below in the street, some kind of Army vehicle was burning. Men in black pajamas were running past it. One stopped, hoisted a bazooka to his shoulder, and the man beside him shoved a rocket into it. The rocket whizzed down the street and another explosion made the old hotel shudder. On the outskirts of the city a Fourth of July display of red tracers and white flares filled the sky. What in God's name was happening? Another coup? The government of Vietnam had been fairly stable for the past two years.

Amy called the desk. "What's going on?" she said.

"Beaucoup VC," gasped the operator. "Stay in room."

VC in Saigon? Amy stayed in her room. There was nothing else to do. Outside, a full-fledged battle was raging. Tanks and armored personnel carriers rumbled past, blasting the now unseen enemy. The tinkling sound of ambulance bells drifted through the dawn. Across the Saigon River in the Bui Phat slum a half dozen fires were raging.

About 7 A.M. Adam called. "Are you all right?" he asked.

"Yes. What's happening?"

"An all-out VC offensive. They're attacking every provincial capital from Quang Tri to Ca Mau."

"Where are you?"

"At Phoenix City BOQ. They just blew out all the windows."

"Is there fighting at Ban Me Thuot?"

"Heavy. It's heavy almost everywhere."

"I thought we were winning this war."

"It's a desperation gesture. We've been praying for them to come out and fight. I still can't believe they're doing anything so crazy. They must be factoring in the political value of it."

Amy tried to get some news on the radio in her room. All she heard at first was a confusing mixture of Viennese waltzes and Vietnamese popular songs. She learned later that the VC had captured the radio station in downtown Saigon but the South Vietnamese had cut off the transmitters and switched the station to an alternate unit outside Saigon, where the operators had nothing but tired music tapes to play. Eventually, as the day progressed, news began to come in from Armed Forces Radio. The Viet Cong had penetrated an amazing number of cities. At Qui Nhon they were ranting revolutionary appeals over the captured radio station. At Ban Me Thuot, the headquarters of George's brigade, the town was a chaos of gunfire and explosions. Outside, Saigon continued to reverberate with small-arms and cannon fire. A squad of sappers had attacked the U. S. Embassy but all had been killed by midmorning.

Adam called every hour or two. He was trying to get back to Phu Bai, but nothing was flying out of Tan Son Nhut. The airport was under attack by several battalions of Viet Cong. Not until the following day did he get a flight back to General Ingalls' headquarters. Amy meanwhile abandoned the hotel and wandered around Saigon, watching (along with crowds of Vietnamese) furious fire tights across the river in Bui Phat and other sections of the city, as government troops attacked isolated pockets of Viet Cong.

At one of these street scenes, she heard a gravel voice calling her name. "Mrs. Rosser? Amy?" She turned to blink up at the toothy face of Brooks Turner, her reporter friend and neighbor from Alexandre Dumas Street. "What the hell are you doing here?"

"I flew in to spend Tet with my husband. He's up at Ban Me Thuot. Probably fighting for his life."

"I think it's the other way around. The Great General Offensive and People's Uprising, as they call it in Hanoi, seems to have failed miserably. There was no uprising. In most places the people just hid in their cellars. The ARVN is fighting like they've never fought before."

"How nice."

"You worried about George? I've got a guy in Ban Me Thuot. Let's go back to the villa. We may have some copy from him."

Brooks hustled her into his Renault and drove rapidly across Saigon to Alexandre Dumas Street. It was as peacefully suburban as it had been in 1963. Brooks said that her old villa was occupied by one of the twenty-seven generals now in Saigon. "A pompous asshole named Eberle. You know him?"

"Slightly," Amy said.

In the house, three exotic Eurasian secretaries, any one of whom could have posed for a *Playboy* centerfold, greeted Brooks with giddy smiles and simultaneously managed to frown at Amy. They thought she was competition. They relaxed somewhat when Brooks introduced her as the wife of his old friend Lieutenant Colonel Rosser. Brooks began shuffling through pages of copy that the secretaries had typed from correspondents elsewhere in Vietnam. "Holy shit," he said. "Listen to this."

He began to read from the middle of his stringer's story.

"The situation at Ban Me Thuot was critical. The Communists were roaming at will throughout the city, shooting South Vietnamese officials and Americans. Attempts by ARVN units to fight their way into the city were stalled by heavy resistance. I was at the airport, a fiercely contested site. The VC had heavy machine guns on two sides of it. Suddenly over the nearby jungle ridges, like the cavalry of old to the rescue, came the helicopters of the 1/3 Maneuver Battalion of the 1st Brigade of the 5th Airmobile Division, commanded by Lieutenant Colonel George Rosser. Down onto the bullet-swept airstrip they came, their armored helicopters pounding the dug-in VC with rockets and machine guns. One helicopter was hit by a shell from a recoilless rifle. It spun into a crumpled mass of smoldering metal; injured men could be seen crawling out of it. Colonel Rosser, whose command of the 1/3 was supposed to end today, instantly organized a rescue operation. Leaping into an ARVN armored personnel carrier, he ordered his radioman and a dozen troopers aboard it and roared across the airfield into a deathstorm of VC automatic-weapons fire. While his gunships worked on the enemy from above, Rosser and his squad leaped from the personnel carrier and dragged wounded men back to the vehicle. Five of his men were hit, none of them seriously. As they went back for the last man in the downed chopper, another recoilless rifle round struck home and the gas tank exploded. Lieutenant Colonel Rosser plunged into the flaming interior to drag the unconscious pilot to safety. Rosser was badly burned on the face, hands and chest but he refused evacuation and organized his battalion for an immediate attack on VC positions around the airport. In two hours, the airport was cleared and the 1/3 was moving through Ban Me Thuot. As I write this, they are heavily engaged. Lieutenant Colonel Rosser is still in command."

George? Amy thought. *George?*

She had to sit down. Brooks Turner thought it was normal feminine fragility. He had no idea that Mrs. Rosser was weak-kneed because she had just discovered that all these years she had been living with a real soldier but had never given him a chance to prove it.

George. *One of the brave. George.*

"It was his last day in command?" Brooks Turner was asking her. "That's one hell of a story."

If you only knew the whole truth, Amy thought. *That* is one hell of a story.

II

"Pook, you look just wonderful. You truly do," Honor said.

"Ask him about My Lai," her brother Matt yelled through the bedroom door.

"Matt, you shut up!" Honor said.

Pookie was dressing for her first West Point dance, the plebe

Christmas hop. She did look wonderful; not beautiful, she would never look beautiful, but wonderful in a delicate, fairylike way, which her gauzy dress emphasized. Her hair, still so fine and wispy Honor sometimes thought you could blow it off her head in a single puff, was cut in gamine style. Honor had sprayed it to keep it down on her forehead. Oddly, Pookie's tomboy figure was fashionable these days. But Honor was still hoping *some* curves would develop. She didn't care what the fashion was, she still believed men, real men, liked flesh in the right places.

Honor wanted 1969 to end peacefully, happily. So much of the previous twelve months had been turmoil of one kind or another. Adam had come back from Vietnam with almost no warning at the beginning of the year. He had told her that he was assigned to West Point, which made her ecstatic, at first. She had been living in a rented house in Cornwall-on-Hudson that cost a fortune to heat. Now they could get quarters on the post and the move would be painless, only a few miles. Not even the Army's movers could do much damage in that distance.

When they moved, it soon became apparent that something was very wrong. Instead of getting a lieutenant colonel's quarters, they were stuck in an attached house with a leaky roof and a furnace that broke down twice a month. Their next-door neighbor was a major who had graduated in 1956. Adam taught one course in the Social Sciences Department. Otherwise he had nothing to do. He avoided her questions about why he had left General Ingalls' staff so suddenly. Instead of talking to her he drank. Almost every night he went to bed drunk. Honor finally demanded to know what was happening—what had happened in Vietnam.

Adam told her. When General Ingalls replaced Westmoreland as COMMUSMACV, Adam went with him to Saigon. He was supposed to do what he had done so well in Washington, sell the Army's point of view to congressmen. But Adam started telling the congressmen who visited Vietnam in droves that President Nixon's Vietnamization program—replacing the Americans with ARVN troops—was not going to work, it was really surrender in disguise. General Ingalls called him on the carpet and Adam told him that he should resign in protest against the President's policy, which was going to demoralize and disgrace the Army. Ingalls exploded into one of his famous rages and Adam was on his way home from Vietnam.

Honor was bewildered. "Adam, I just had a letter from Amy Rosser, practically green with envy because you were so close to the man who's goin' to be chief of staff after Westmoreland, who could have gotten you anythin' in the Army."

"I don't want anythin' in the Army," he said, mimicking her. "First, I want an Army that stands for something. That doesn't collaborate with the political cowards and liars that run this country."

"Adam, you can't change the country. You can't even change the Army. It's too big. You—we're—too small. We've got to live our own lives."

"I don't accept any of that. Get it through your head once and for all. I don't accept it. I've tried to play the game. I can't do it."

He meant it. She saw, with a kind of bewildered awe, that Ashley was not dead. But he had grown older, and was in danger of becoming a bitter, defeated man. Honor tried to turn him away from the disaster he seemed determined to bring upon himself. But Adam would not listen to her, even though she prayed desperately to Jesus for help. In the year since she had left her mother in Charlesville, Honor had learned to talk quietly to Jesus in her heart, the way she wanted to talk to Adam. The ability had come to her just the way Father Rausch had promised it would. She told Jesus how glad she was that Adam was still Ashley, that he still had his ideals. But she did not see why this meant he had to destroy his career.

As soon as he arrived at West Point, Adam started working on a book, *Resignation in Protest*. Using General Ridgway's resignation in 1955 to protest the Eisenhower administration's budget cuts, and other examples from history, Adam argued that the failure of even one general to resign in protest against the U.S. government's conduct of the war in Vietnam was an indictment of the Army's moral bankruptcy. Working fourteen hours a day, Adam wrote the book in three months and sent it to the Pentagon for clearance. It was denied. Adam asked permission to give a lecture on the subject at West Point. It was denied. He sought support in the Academy's

Social Sciences Department. No one dared to agree with him in public. Adam Xeroxed the manuscript and circulated it to a select group of first-class cadets, to whom he was giving a course called "The Politics of Coercive War." Inevitably the faculty and Superintendent heard about it, and many of them, especially the Superintendent, were furious. They accused Adam of damaging the loyalty of the cadets at a crucial time in the school's history. The Superintendent called him in for a verbal reprimand.

Honor tried to talk to Adam. He retreated to his "bunker," as he called it, an old coal bin in the cellar which he had fitted out as a study. He spent as much time down there drinking as he did writing. Pookie, who was in her first year at Vassar (on a full scholarship), was seldom home. When she was around, Adam paced his drinking so that he never staggered, never made less than perfect sense. On most other nights he got smashed.

A lot of people were drinking hard at West Point in 1969. Politicians, writers, professors were saying such terrible things about the Army. It drove some wives half crazy. Their next-door neighbor, the major's wife, was a sad example. She was drunk by noon almost every day. When the major pulled a second tour in Vietnam, she wouldn't believe he hadn't volunteered for it. Even when he showed her his orders, her head was so scrambled she thought the standard language, "Request for Orders," proved he'd volunteered. When they stopped fighting over that they fought about the Army. She wanted him to resign. By the time he left, she was having crying jags and filing for divorce.

Ruth Hardin was even worse. Sam had become a full colonel and was deputy commandant of the Tactical Department. Honor invited Ruth and Sam to dinner and Ruth got smashed. After two drinks Ruth bad-mouthed the Army with staggering virulence. She said she did not know a general who wasn't a girl chaser. She agreed with all the dirty things the anti-war people were saying. "They ought to court-martial a few generals as war criminals. That's the answer," she said.

"Hear, hear," Adam said, pleasing Ruth, although they meant completely different things. Adam wanted to court-martial generals for failing the Army, Honor understood that much. Sam got into a terrific argument with Adam about his attitude. Sam said a lot of things Honor agreed with—about Adam expecting the real Army to be too perfect, too much like West Point. Adam got furious and said he was sick of combat meatheads like Sam and Pete Burke putting him down because he could read a book. Sam said he could read a book too, he'd even read Adam's thesis. Ruth fought a sort of guerrilla war against Sam on the fringes of the brawl, calling him "Colonel Straight Arrow" and sneering at his combat record in Korea and Vietnam.

In an odd way the evening made Honor feel better about Adam's craziness. She was able to tell herself it was part of the general craziness that was infecting the Army and the country.

About a month after this argumentative dinner party, news of My Lai, the incredibly ugly massacre of an entire Vietnamese village by a berserk lieutenant and his company, swept the country. For West Point it was a special embarrassment. The company was in the division that the Academy's current Superintendent had commanded in Vietnam. At first no one at West Point knew what to say or do. Don Marble, Adam's old friend from Harvard, was back at *The New York Times* as an editor. He called Adam and persuaded him to talk to a reporter. Adam said the "moral stench" was so strong he was afraid it would blow the windows out of the place. He said the Academy had no alternative but to fully and frankly discuss My Lai, and help the cadets understand how such a thing could happen in the Army. More important, far more important, was the story of why and how it was covered up. Adam's name was not mentioned in the interview, but few people at the Academy had any doubt who gave it. A few days later the Superintendent made an emotional speech to the cadets, denying there had ever been a cover-up, and asking the Corps to rally behind him. The cadets had responded with cheers and applause. The next day, in the course he was teaching on coercive war, Adam had told his first-class students that the Superintendent was a fraud who had abused the confidence of the Corps. The accusation flashed through the cadet barracks like electricity. A lot of people on the faculty stopped speaking to Adam.

● ● ●

A knock on the door. Pookie's date was arriving. Honor opened it and Cadet Thomas Adam Burke became a gray presence in her front hall. He looked so much like his father, Honor was momentarily speechless. The same red hair, freckled forehead, wide nose, thick-lipped smiling mouth. They had had Tom to dinner several times, but the effect was still the same, every time Honor saw him. "I swear, I feel like it's 1950 again," she said, giggling. "And it's your father comin' to meet your mother at the Hotel Thayer."

"I'm afraid Dad outweighs me by about forty pounds, ma'am," Tom said.

"You'll catch up to him."

"I sure hope so."

Adam emerged from his basement study. Honor could see he was drunk, by the shine in his eyes. But he was in perfect control of himself. "Hello, Mr. Ducrot," he said, using the old-fashioned name for plebes. "How do the lower orders like the new system?"

"What new system?" Pookie asked.

"Thanks to the criticism of certain people about our antiquated ways"—Tom looked at Adam with such an admiring smile Honor's heart overflowed with affection for him—"plebes are no longer required to recite nonsense like how many gallons of water there are in Lake Poplopen. Now we have to know something useful, like the exact fuel capacity of an M-60 tank or the precise horsepower of the engine of a CH-54 helicopter."

"I'm having second thoughts," Adam said. "The old system may have been better. It trained you to perform the numerous meaningless tasks you will have handed to you as an officer of the U. S. Army."

"Adam," Honor said, "will you *ever* stop arguin' on both sides of every question?"

"Sir," Tom said, "maybe we can change that part of the system too."

His idealism was so beautiful Honor almost wept.

"Know how many people got killed at My Lai?" Matt asked.

"Pay no attention to the peace freak," Pookie said.

"I believe the body count was one hundred seventy-five," Tom said. "Do you know how many people the VC murdered at Hue?"

"No," Matt said.

"Four thousand two hundred and six," Tom said. "That's confirmed by the corps adviser on the spot."

"He means his father, freak," Pookie said.

"That only convinces me all over again that the whole thing stinks," Matt said.

"We're agreed on that, Matty," Tom said. "But we've got to sweat it out and win it somehow. Which reminds me, sir," he said to Adam. "I've rounded up a dozen guys who said they'd love to drop by on Saturday mornings for that informal seminar we discussed."

"We'll start right after the New Year," Adam said. "A new Army for a new decade. That'll be our motto."

The last time Tom came to dinner, he and Adam had retired to the basement bunker for a private conversation. From Adam's cryptic comments, Honor gathered he had a lot of doubts about an Army career, doubts that My Lai had intensified.

"How do you like your drag?" Honor said. "Isn't that the prettiest dress?"

"Great," Tom said.

"Oh, stop making him break his cadet oath, Mom," Pookie said. "I look like something left over from the 1950's. If this place wasn't so encrusted with tradition, I'd be wearing blue jeans and so would Tom. We're not on duty."

"I think there's still room in the world for some tradition," Honor said. "Good Lord, do you people want to change everything?"

"Probably," Pookie said.

Tom laughed. "A lot of people in the Corps are talking like that these days. A lot more since we've realized how the Superintendent used us to improve his public relations."

"How's your mother, Tom?" Honor asked, to change the subject.

"Still soaking up the Hawaiian sunshine," Tom said. "She says she likes teaching high school English. Makes her feel young."

"Wonderful," Honor asked. "Well, you two better get on to the hop."

It was clear to all their friends that something disastrous had happened to the Burke marriage. Joanna lived alone on the beach at Mo Ka Lei. Pete, as far as anyone knew, never took the week of R & R he had coming to him every six months. Honor still corresponded, but Joanna's letters were strangely vague and brief. She was having some gynecological problems, which took her to the Tripler Army Medical Center once or twice a month. Otherwise, there was practically nothing in her letters about the Army. She did not even seem that enthused about Tom going to the Academy.

Honor waited up for Tom and Pookie. She watched a Fred Astaire movie on TV. Then came the news with the latest figures on American withdrawals from Vietnam. Casualty figures next. Two hundred and ten Americans killed last week. Heavy fighting in the A Shau Valley and at some place called Qui Nhon. The names meant nothing to Honor. She made no attempt to follow the war.

As the news ended, Tom brought Pookie home. Honor heard the conversation in the hall. "Listen, I really had a good time. I'm amazed," Pookie said.

"I know what you mean. I did too."

"I like your friends. I thought they'd all be hard-core. I thought you'd be too. You were the last time I saw you in Nam. All you wanted to do then was kill Cong."

"I've grown up a little. Especially since I came here and started talking to your father."

There was quite a long silence. Pookie strolled into the living room as the front door closed. Since she never wore lipstick, Honor could not tell for sure whether she had kissed Tom good night. But the silence had been promising.

"How was the hop?" Honor asked.

"Tolerable," Pookie said, flopping into a chair. "Tom's not the horror I thought he'd be."

"Why should he be a horror?"

"Oh, you know how it is. Friends of babyhood, that sort of thing. You always turn out to hate them. I thought he'd be pretty square. He's not. That whole plebe class is pretty hip. Surprising. I can just see me trying to explain that at Vassar. When they heard I was going to a West Point hop, at least six people stopped speaking to me."

"That's terrible!" Honor cried. "Amy Rosser, a half dozen other Vassar girls married class of '50 boys."

"It's a different scene, Mom." Pookie lit a cigarette and offered one to Honor. She felt bewildered, somehow younger than this casual seventeen-year-old. "Tom's really cool about the Army. He thinks Dad's terrific."

"I hope he's got more common sense. Like his own father. Pete's goin' to be a general one of these days. You watch."

"Not a chance," Pookie said. "Tom knows it. Colonel Burke's passed up a Pentagon tour—twice. To stay in Nam."

"I don't see why one silly tour at that dreadful place is so important."

"Got to punch the ticket, Mom. Dad's got a better shot at a star, even now. General Ingalls could change his mind about him. He's got a conscience. That's what Dad is trying to do. Give the Army a political conscience. Tom thinks it's terrific."

Pookie went back to Vassar, which was seething with anti-war agitation. Tom Burke and about a dozen of his friends began coming to the Thayer quarters each Saturday to discuss the Army and the war with Adam. Honor served coffee and Danish pastry, which the cadets wolfed down as if they lived on bread and water all week. They spent most of their time talking about My Lai and the cover-up that enabled it to go unreported for so long. They also discussed other scandals that were wracking the Army. Major General Carl Turner, the Provost Marshal General, the head of the military police, was convicted of selling government rifles for his private profit. The Sergeant Major of the Army, the highest-ranking enlisted man in the service, was caught stealing thousands of dollars from service clubs in Vietnam. The investigation revealed that a brigadier general was heavily involved in the same scheme.

What upset Honor was Adam's reaction to these horror stories. He was gleeful. He said they proved that the Army had lost its soul. He traced it all to what he called "the greed for promotion." He told the cadets the officer corps had substituted the management psychology of big business for the old idea that the Army was a calling, a special vocation like the priesthood. It was this greed which led the generals into a no-win war in Vietnam. Honor heard Tom Burke urging Adam to write a book on this subject. He said it would be a perfect follow-up to Adam's book on resignation in protest, which he and his friends had all obviously read. Adam seemed to like the idea.

"Adam," Honor said when the cadets had left. "They're not going to let you publish that book, any more than they let you publish the other one."

"I'll circulate it in the same way," Adam said, "Xeroxed copies."

"They'll throw you out of the Army, Adam," Honor said.

"No they won't. If they did I could publish anything I wanted. And I know a lot of things they'd rather not see in print."

"They'll throw you out of the Academy. Half the people on the faculty won't be seen speakin' to you now. Their wives are even wary of talkin' to me."

"Look on it as a price you have to pay for marrying a man with a conscience."

"Katherine White says you're goin' about it the wrong way. You've got to be patient when you try to change the Army."

"Katherine White is an idiot, and so is her husband."

"She's not, Adam. She's a lovely woman. And her husband is a great admirer of yours. He says you're the smartest cadet he ever taught."

"Did he really say that?"

"Yes."

"I guess Horace isn't all bad."

Honor had met Katherine White at the West Point Women's Club. They both sang in the Choraliers, a glee club that performed at post parties and dances. Being of similar height and both second sopranos, they stood side by side at performances and rehearsals, and grew friendly. One day after a rehearsal Katherine invited Honor back to her quarters on Colonels' Row, overlooking the Hudson, for a cocktail. Her husband, Colonel Horace White, who was a professor of mathematics, joined them. He was a bluff, good-natured man, who pleased Honor by saying nice things about Adam's brilliance as a student.

Honor writhed at the sight of the Whites' beautifully appointed house, full of pieces of furniture that Mrs. White had inherited from her parents. Her father had been a major general. She listened wistfully as Mrs. White told stories of her girlhood in Panama, when her father was the military commander of the Canal Zone. Colonel White chimed in with reminiscences of his boyhood on Army posts in the Far West. His father had been a graduate of the class of 1886. Colonel White had become a member of the faculty in 1945. This was their twenty-fifth anniversary year at West Point. They had a son, Robert, in the yearling class and a daughter, Susan, who was married to a captain from the class of 1963.

If only Adam had listened to her, Honor thought, he could have had an appointment to the Academy faculty. They could be living in one of these lovely old houses, entertaining friends when they came to West Point for reunions. Katherine White also sang in the West Point chapel choir. Honor volunteered to join her there, and their friendship deepened. Katherine White was so serene, so satisfied with her years as an Army wife. Honor found herself swamped with regret and longing when she thought of her own experience. She shared some of her feelings with Mrs. White, and little by little told her about her problems with Adam. Katherine White was wide-eyed when Honor told her about the book Adam was planning to write, attacking the Army's promotion system. She said Adam had apparently failed to learn the first principle of Army loyalty. "You never let the public into the Army's quarrels. You have to be patient in the Army. If something's wrong the Army will fix it, though it may take time."

They also discussed the current outburst of criticism and denunciation of the Army. Honor was surprised to discover Mrs. White was not particularly bothered by it. She said it was only a little worse than the attitude civilians had had toward the Army before World War II. Then, the Army had to rely on its own spiritual resources. It would—and could—learn to do it again.

"That's where the wives come into the picture," Katherine White said. "They help supply that spiritual dimension. We wives have our own tradition, you know. I must give you some books to read."

She gave Honor the memoirs of Elizabeth Custer and other nineteenth-century Army wives who followed their officer husbands onto the western plains and in several cases died beside them in forgotten battles with rampaging Indians. She gave her diaries that Colonel White's mother had kept of her Army travels, full of gritty details of life in China and the Philippines before World War I.

Honor was fascinated. She admired the courage, the endurance of these women. But she found it hard to apply their moral example to her situation at West Point during the year 1970. The war and ever wilder protests against it churned at her in the newspapers and on television. Her son Matt got more and more involved in "the movement," as he called it. Adam encouraged him. "If I were eighteen, I wouldn't go to Vietnam," he said. "The day Lyndon Johnson announced he wasn't going to run for reelection, every officer in the Army should have resigned, and every draft-age male in America should have burned his draft card." Honor asked Adam why he was putting such ideas in Matt's head. He would do him a lot more good if he tutored him in history and math, both of which he was flunking at James Wilson High School in Highland Falls.

"I have better things to do with my time," Adam said, and retreated to his bunker in the cellar. When the typewriter clacked, he was working on his book. When there was silence, he was getting drunk. He spent about half the nights getting drunk.

Early in March, Honor was sitting in the living room, reading the saga of Colonel White's mother on Mindanao in 1909. The place was worse than the Wild West. No one knew when one of the native Moros would go amok and attack an American with a kris, one of their huge swords. Once they went amok they kept killing people until someone shot them.

The doorbell rang. Honor answered it. There stood Tom Burke, in his gray cadet overcoat. "What a nice surprise," she said.

"Is Colonel Thayer home?" he asked.

"He's in the basement. I'll call him."

She led Tom into the living room. "Can I get you somethin' to eat?"

"No, thanks ma'am. We had good chow tonight. Pork chops."

"How about a Coke?"

"That'd be fine."

Honor went out in the kitchen and called down the cellar stairs to Adam, in his bunker. He came upstairs and strolled into the living room to greet Tom. Honor was relieved to see Adam was not drunk. She got out the ice, poured the Coke and walked down the short hall to the living room. She heard Tom saying: "—and we've been thinking a lot about what you've told us about the Army's moral dilemma. Particularly about My. Lai. Twelve of us have decided to sign a statement saying we're prepared to resign in protest if the Superintendent refuses to explain, immediately, how he allowed My Lai to be covered up while he was in command of the division."

"That's a pretty serious step," Adam said. "You realize, no matter what happens, you're putting your career in the Army in jeopardy?"

"Sir, after listening to you, we're not sure we want careers in the Army."

Adam was upset by this remark. He paced the living room rubbing his hands up and down his sides, as if he were in pain. "That's not what I intended to do. Damage your enthusiasm for the Army. I thought—I presumed—that was a fixed fact. I only want to channel it in the right direction."

"Can you arrange with your friend at *The New York Times* to get our statement published?"

"I think so. But maybe you should wait a few days, before you act."

"Sir, you've been telling us the Army should have more openness, more honesty in the chain of command. We've got to start somewhere, why not here?"

It was wonderful, his idealism. But Honor also saw his innocence, his naïveté. She watched while Adam twisted on the horns of his self-created dilemma. In his heart he knew it was a pointless gesture that would only ruin twelve young men's Army careers before they even began. But he could not resist the temptation. It appealed to his innate recklessness. Honor listened, more and more horrified, as he slid into semi-agreement with the plan. He ended by saying he was 99 percent certain he was ready to work with Tom and his friends. But he still thought they should all think it over for twenty-four hours.

Honor came in with the Coke. Tom drank it and joked about a letter he'd gotten from Pookie, reporting on a Vassar plan to invade

627

West Point some weekend soon and embarrass the cadets into admitting that the war in Vietnam was immoral. "She says she expects to get paid the going rate for secret agents."

By the time Tom said good night, Honor could scarcely control herself. "Adam," she said, the moment the front door closed, "you can't let those boys do such a thing. They'll ruin their careers—and yours too—for all time."

"Mine's ruined already," Adam said. "Maybe a good cause needs some sacrificial lambs."

"Doesn't the Army have enough trouble without you makin' more for it?"

"The Army deserves all the trouble it gets," Adam said.

"I don't agree with that," Honor said. "The *Army?* Maybe some generals do. But the whole Army? That's *us*. Our friends. Pete Burke deserves trouble? Haven't he and Joanna got enough of their own? Sam Hardin? He's got to put up with Ruth, for God's sake. Adam, if Tom got himself dismissed from the Academy, it would break Pete Burke's heart. You know it would."

"Maybe the heart has to be broken, before the brain starts to think."

"Adam, I'm sick of your brilliant sayin's. *Nothin'* can change the fact that Pete is your best friend. And Joanna is my best friend. If you want to know another bit of truth, I've got more respect for Pete than I've got for you. God knows he's got more reason to hate the Army than you've ever had, losin' little Cissie out there in Saigon. But he didn't creep home to write books. He's stayed out there, tryin' to win this miserable war."

"Ah. Now we're getting down to it. I'm the same coward who shook all over when he went into combat in Korea and I can't do this to my hero friend's son."

"You're not a coward. I just said that once when I was mad at you. But you know what I think?"

"What? For the sheer novelty of it, I'd like to hear what you think. About something besides what's good on TV."

He was mocking her as usual. She felt her old fear of him, of his cruel tongue, her old feelings of inferiority. But she was not afraid of losing his love anymore. She had Jesus in her heart to console her.

He helped her see what was wrong with Adam—his inability to love anyone, anything.

"I think you've lost your way, Adam. I think deep inside you something has gone wrong. You're almost to the point where you'd like to destroy the Army to change it."

"Jesus Christ," Adam said, "Jesus Christ."

"What's that mean?"

"I've been living all these years with wisdom's child. And didn't know it."

He was mocking her again. Honor was filled with a terrible resolution. She asked Jesus to give her the strength to stop Adam. She would do it for Joanna and Pete. She would do it for the Army, that idea revered by women she admired, women like Katherine White. She would also do it for Honor Prescott, to prove to herself that she had not lost touch with Melanie, with that girl who had walked into Grant Hall and fallen in love with the idealism on Cadet Thayer's face, with the idealism and innocence on all their faces, repeated now on Cadet Thomas A. Burke's face. And lost, so terribly lost, forever gone, from Lieutenant Colonel Thayer's face.

The next day, when Adam departed to teach his course, Honor telephoned Sam Hardin and asked if he would come up to their quarters. "It's personal business. But it's Army business too," she said. As deputy commandant of cadets, Sam was directly involved in discipline problems. He listened, grim-faced, while Honor told him about Tom Burke's visit, what she had overheard. "I think the boys'll be all right. If you talk some sense to them. But not while Adam's here. You've got to separate them from Adam."

Sam Hardin nodded. "I agree, completely."

"I hope it can be done—without him findin' out anything about this talk. I—I still love him, Sam."

"Why?" Sam said with sudden startling vehemence. "Don't you ever want to put a gun to his goddamn head? That's the way I feel toward Ruth, about three times a week."

"I—it's been hard, Sam. Praying—praying to Jesus—is the only thing I've found."

He shook his head. "That isn't my style."

At 3 P.M. Adam returned home looking strange. Honor had been braced for rage, resentment, perhaps even a refusal to obey the orders transferring him—and her—God only knew where. Instead, he was elated. "I've got orders to report to Saigon in forty-eight hours," he said.

"Oh, Adam," Honor said. "That's terrible."

"Maybe. Maybe not. Maybe Ingalls has finally decided to change the system out there. Why else would he want me back? He knows what I stand for."

For a moment Honor almost told him the truth. She could not bear the hope on his face. Ashley was not dead. But he was about to be humiliated, and she, Melanie, had arranged it. Fighting back tears, she asked Jesus to help her love Adam no matter how bad, how sad, he became.

Adam thought her teariness was caused by his abrupt departure. "I'm sorry this is happening so fast," he said. "I'm sure they'll give you a month or so to move. Maybe you ought to go back to Charlesville."

"No," she said. "I think I'll look for a house around here again. That way I can still use the post, see friends."

"Okay."

That night, Honor drove Adam to Stewart Air Base, where a plane was leaving for Hawaii. "What about Tom Burke and those other cadets?" Honor asked. "You can't let them do anything so reckless now, without you around to advise them. They'll just get expelled."

"You're right," Adam said. "I'll write him a letter."

"I think it'd be better if I talked to him," Honor said. "He might not wait for a letter."

"Okay," Adam said. "Tell him I decided it would be the wrong war in the wrong place at the wrong time."

That night, Honor invited Tom to dinner. Matt was off at some anti-war rally in Peekskill. She told Tom that Adam had just left for Saigon on a secret assignment. "He asked me to tell you to give up that idea about threatenin' to resign in protest," she said. "He realized it would break your father's heart."

Tom nodded glumly. "That's what Colonel Hardin said. I spent an hour with him this afternoon. One of the other guys must have talked to him about it. I guess you're both right. It just seems so—so wrong that Dad's still out there getting shot at and the Superintendent is enjoying that beautiful house with something like My Lai on his conscience."

"Tom honey," Honor said, "You've got to be patient in the Army. If somethin's wrong, they set it right eventually."

Did she really believe that? Honor wondered. It was faith, a kind of religion. Maybe it was better to believe she was lying for the sake of Pete and Joanna.

No, she decided. She believed in the Army. She believed because of all the sacrifices and heartbreak the Army exacted from its followers. Jesus would not allow so much idealism to be wasted. He would make sure it added up to something, somewhere.

III

NAKED after a long swim, Joanna stood in the bedroom of her cottage at Mo Ka Lei, combing her hair before the full-length mirror on the door. The perpetual trade wind hummed through the screens. She had swum far out toward the blank horizon, savoring the sea's cool fingers on her breasts and thighs, a metaphor of freedom—and danger, which somehow made the freedom more real. In the house after a swim she often remained naked, letting the trade wind dry her flesh.

Sometimes she stood before the mirror contemplating her body. Was she trying to escape this reality? Was she some kind of anchorite, hoping to deny the pleasure of male hands on rounded breasts, male fingers probing the silken hair beneath her belly? No, she still knew that wanting, she still welcomed it. Sometimes it was harsh and metallic in her throat, the taste of rust, sometimes it was as sweet and yielding as a mango's flesh. She was married. To the world. To a man. To men. She was still part of their grief and their pleasure, their defeats and victories.

> *Though we are born of the same parents*
> *We don't die of the same parents.*

In the lotus position, she contemplated this koan and opened her body and mind to wisdom. But wisdom still refused to come. She could not shed her skin. She could not achieve the one true reality of the sages. Other realities were more compelling; lesser realities, in the scale of the sages, but not lesser to Joanna Welsh Burke.

"Joanna? Mrs. Burke?"

The male voice, followed by a very masculine knock, slowly penetrated her consciousness.

"Official visitors," the voice said.

Throwing on a muumuu, she padded through the windswept house to the porch. There, in dark outline against the glare of the sun on the ocean, stood a short burly colonel in khaki and a slightly taller young man in cadet gray.

"By order of the commandment of the U. S. Military Academy," Sam Hardin said, "I am hereby consigning to your authority one recognized plebe. If he doesn't behave himself, give me a call at Schofield Barracks."

"Oh," Joanna cried. She burst open the screen door and threw her arms around Tom, then stepped back for a maternal examination. "My God, you've grown, gained—what?"

"Twenty pounds," he said. "I'll make that football team yet."

"I told him to try for cornerback. His father always wanted to play in the backfield," Sam Hardin said.

"It's awfully nice of you to drive him down, Sam. I would have been glad to meet him at the airport."

"We hopped an Air Force plane together," Sam said. "We had a good talk. I found out what's wrong with the whole Tactical Department."

"Sir—was I that bad?" Tom asked.

"I'm just kidding." Sam smiled at Joanna. "What do you hear from Pete?"

"Oh—Tom hears more from him than I do—about the war."

She could not tell this old friend, in front of her son, that she had not had a letter from her husband for three years. Tom looked uncomfortable. "It's like I told you, sir—Dad says Vietnamization is bull. We're dumping all sorts of stuff on the ARVN that they'll never learn to use."

Sam nodded glumly. Joanna strove to change the subject. "Will either of your boys be going to Leilehua? I'm teaching senior English there, you know."

"Bob'll be a senior, I hope. It depends on how benevolent they are about his grades. You've got my sympathy, trying to teach him anything."

"He won't be any worse than his classmates. The war's got them all distracted. I've tried everything to get them interested in reading—science fiction, Tolkien—nothing works. As for Hawthorne and Longfellow—"

Sam shook his head. "It sure isn't your fault. You've got proof of your educational prowess right here," he said, smiling at Tom. "Have you heard about his class standing? Nineteenth. That's pretty damn good."

Joanna clapped her hands. She was genuinely delighted. "His father will be so proud of him."

"I wish I could get at least one of my boys interested in studying," Sam said.

"You must bring them—and Ruth of course—down for a swim while Tom is here."

"The invitation is accepted, unconditionally. I'll give you a ring."

Sam shook hands with Tom, gave Joanna a kiss on the cheek and strolled to his car. Joanna noticed he had the same springy walk he had had as a cadet; he still held his head in the same cocky, confident way. A fighter's strut.

"He's a terrific guy," Tom said.

"Yes," Joanna said. "I've always liked him. I wish I could say the same for his wife."

"Another great Army marriage?" Tom said.

"They're still together."

"No word from Dad."

She shook her head.

Tom stared past her at the surf breaking on the reef. "This war," he said. "If we could win it—he'd come home. Maybe then you could—"

"Maybe."

She was determined to treat him like an adult; no false hopes. She was treating herself the same way.

"But we're not going to win the damn war. People at the Academy say it's as good as lost. Colonel Thayer says we deserve to lose it."

"I know. I don't agree with him."

"Did he stop by here on his way out to Nam?"

"Yes. We had quite an argument."

"Have you heard from him since? Pookie says he was really excited when he left the Academy. He thought Ingalls might have something hot for him to do."

"I haven't heard a word. Listen. You're not out here to discuss the war or worry about other things that can't be changed. You're here to have a good time. There's a teen club at Schofield with squadrons of pretty girls who will probably maim each other to get at you. The car is yours any time you want it. School's over for me, too. I'm on ninety-day leave."

Tom forced a smile. "I'm ready to swing a little. Plebe year was rough."

Tom was simply too intelligent to deceive indefinitely. When Pete did not come to Hawaii for the first five-day leave, Tom had begun to wonder. That Christmas, when he visited Joanna for two weeks between his cram courses for the entrance exams to the Academy, he asked her what was wrong. She told him, calmly, sadly, about the quarrel at Seward State after she signed the petition to withdraw the ROTC from the campus. "Your father thought I was betraying him. I was, in a way. I have to live with that. I can only hope that eventually he'll forgive me."

"Why did you sign it?" Tom asked.

"I told myself I was against the war. But I really blamed him for Cissie. I wanted to hurt him as much as—I thought he'd hurt me."

"That doesn't make sense, Mom."

"I know, Tom. Not when you hear it from the outside. When you work on it—I mean think hard about it—and live with it from the inside, it connects. It involves the kind of person I am, the kind of man your father is. I was never able to love him for what he was—is. That kind of love—between two very different people—is hard. I never managed it. I failed.''

The whole truth. She had spent a year painfully acquiring it. Her journey toward it had begun the night she arrived at Mo Ka Lei and realized it was her seventeenth wedding anniversary. She looked around her. The house was almost exactly the same. The rattan rugs, the bamboo furniture. For a moment she was profoundly frightened. She was afraid she was going to see the ghost of herself emerging from the kitchen where she had told her husband: *I've never been so proud of you in my life*.

She had sat in the dark empty house, the trade wind sighing sentimentally through the windows, and tried to think about her life. She had spent seventeen years trying to love a man, a husband, seventeen years that were ending in failure. How could she prevent, deny, that last word from entering her flesh, from becoming Joanna? She heard Pete's savage indictment. *You're not a good anything. Wife, mother. You're a liar, that's your basic problem. You lie to yourself, to me.* She saw Joanna the bride gliding dreamily through West Point's June week, confidently proclaiming the supremacy of love. She hated that stupid girl, that spiritual fraud, that self-deceiver.

Pacing the dark empty rooms and the windswept beach for the next three months, Joanna slowly accepted the reality of her failure. She decided it was too late for excuses. It was no consolation to tell herself that she was the victim of a second-rate education, an upper-middle-class childhood. Not even history, Vietnam, Cissie's brutal death, could exculpate her. The game player had come to the end of the game. She had sinned against her marriage, against the commitment she had made to Pete, to the Army, here on Mo Ka Lei, with the same trade wind sighing past them in the night.

By September she was past half knowing, past sleepwalking through history. She stalked the beach in the noon glare, the harsh white sunlight of knowing. Because of her sin, Pete would stay in Vietnam until it ended, one way or another. He would stay until he was killed or some kind of victory was won so he could prove to her and to himself that he was not fighting for the next promotion, that Cissie's death meant something. All the deaths meant something.

What if she still denied it? The possibility froze her, there, on the blazing noon beach. What if she still refused to pay history, God, the Army, that price? What if she refused to surrender Cissie to duty-honor-country? Her failure would be absolute, eternal. At that moment, standing there on the white sand with the sea, the rustling palm fronds, and all the other clichés of Hawaii's paradise around her, she realized that she still clutched Cissie to her heart. She would run from them all, from Pete with his cry of duty done, honor vindicated, from Martha Kinsolving with her consolation of memory, from Adam with his heartless game playing. She would hide somewhere, anywhere, in madness or in malice with that small body in her arms.

To escape that nightmare at the end of the tunnel, Joanna wrestled with the darkest angel, forgiveness. He sat against the wall of her bedroom in the night. He met her on the beach in the noon glare. They never spoke. They exchanged a wordless paradox. You cannot forgive until you have been forgiven. You cannot be forgiven until you forgive. Week after week the deadlock continued.

She sought help from Zen, that long-neglected toughener of the mind and spirit. She bent her head over koans night and morning. But she could not get past the obvious wisdom of one koan, on which she meditated for a week. *It can't be swallowed, it can't be spit out.*

Meanwhile, her life had to be led. Her body had to be fed. Her days had to be filled. She got a job teaching English at Leilehua High School in Wahiawa, near Schofield Barracks. Over half the teen-agers in her class were Army children. She hurled herself into the task of making words, language, interesting, of creating enthusiasm for reading as an adventure. The Army children were as hard to reach as the Filipinos and Japanese and mixed-bloods who constituted the other half of the class. It was a losing struggle, particularly with the boys. Vietnam and the turmoil it was causing absorbed them.

At home, Joanna let the war absorb her too. Each night she sat in front of her television set and watched the bombs fall on North

Vietnam, the helicopters whirl down on thatch-roofed villages. She welcomed the pain, the revulsion. She was through running away from history. She paid particular attention to the war in I Corps. It seemed to be going well, if the Army was telling the truth—which Adam's letters had long since caused her to doubt. But there were other truths to think about in I Corps. Often she lay awake at night, imagining the province adviser in the garden of the Dat villa in Hue, sweeping Thui into his arms, lifting her mouth to his mournful lips. Dry-eyed, Joanna permitted it, she wished Pete the happiness she had denied him with her lies, her game playing.

In January, the war began coming to her in an unexpected way. Tom sent her the long letters Pete wrote to him, describing his difficulties with the ARVN, his occasional successes, the real state of the war in I Corps. That was how she came to learn, long before the rest of America, about the massacre of the innocents at Hue.

She had been as amazed as her students, as the rest of the nation, by the astonishing explosion dubbed the Tet Offensive. She noted with particular anxiety that Hue was the one city the North Vietnamese and Viet Cong successfully seized and held, being driven out only after weeks of street fighting. From Hue via Tom's prep school in Cornwall-on-Hudson came the story of what had happened inside the city.

> . . . We were trapped in our compound for the next four days. The VC and the NVA had complete control of the city. They rounded up all the Catholics they could find. They dragged Thui and Sa and Le and her parents, Mr. and Mrs. Nguyen, out of their houses and herded them out of Hue into the jungle and machine-gunned them all, and threw their bodies into a creek. Other VC took Father Buu Dong down to the beach and buried him alive. . . .

That night Joanna lay awake again, trying to feel Pete's grief, trying to share his pain. She saw with her poet's eyes the AK-47 bullets riddling Thui Dat's shimmering white ao-dai, watched that exquisite face sink beneath the waters of the creek. All Joanna could hear was Pete's cry to heaven: *Why her? Why not the lying, whining bitch I married?* Joanna tried to understand for Pete, tried to accept for him God's indifference to human love. In the darkest corner of the bedroom, the angel of forgiveness stirred uneasily.

Other letters from the ARVN adviser in I Corps told her more about the inner story of the war.

> . . . People coming out here say the newspapers are making the Tet Offensive sound like a victory for the VC. I can't believe it. Are the reporters' minds that poisoned against us? We beat hell out of the murdering bastards everywhere. If Washington gave us three, maybe four more divisions, we'd clean this thing up for good. . . .

> . . . Everybody out here feels pretty let down about President Johnson's decision not to run again. The troops feel he's bugged out on them. I can't blame them. I only hope he knows what he's doing. It looks like he's more or less admitted the protesters are right. It makes it pretty hard to ask men to keep on fighting when the commander-in-chief takes a walk. He's really left the officer corps between a rock and a hard place. But I still think we can do the job. It's just going to take longer and be a lot more difficult. . . .

The old can-do Army spirit. Mocked by Adam Thayer. Abused by Presidents. But not scorned by Joanna, who had tried to love a man who personified it. Gradually Joanna began to think of the Army in a new way. As an organism, an entity, a family, bound together by suffering. Why did she refuse to yield Cissie to the priesthood into which she had married? Why did she refuse to let them lay that little body on their godless altar, on which the word DUTY explained and demanded everything? She could only reply like the quintessential Protestant she had become: *God helping me I can do no other.*

She watched the Army's suffering intensify as the American will weakened after Lyndon Johnson bugged-out and the anti-war movement grew in ferocity. Joanna received an almost hysterical letter from Martha Kinsolving, telling her what the peace marchers had done when Vic Kinsolving returned to Vietnam for another tour. A month after he went into action in the Mekong Delta, Martha received a telegram telling her that he was dead. After an hour of

638

agony, she read it again and realized it was a fraud. Martha told of other women, authentic widows, receiving obscene phone calls gloating over their husbands' deaths. Army children were being insulted in public schools by anti-war teachers, urged to revolt against their parents.

Thinking of these things in the small hours of the night, Joanna was tempted to speak to the angel in the darkest corner. But she did not write the pleading letter to Pete that this required. Part of it was the fear that Pete would not believe his liar wife. Part of it was the dread that he would tell her that nothing, not the most abject apology, would bring him home now, until he avenged Thui.

Tom discovered three classmates at the first Schofield teen club dance. Their fathers were stationed at Fort Shafter, the Army's other major base in Hawaii. The almost-yearlings acquired girls and made the Burke cottage at Mo Ka Lei their headquarters. They liked it, one of the boys, a husky blond named Marvin, told Joanna, because it was far away from "the damn Army." She heard a disillusion, even a mild cynicism in their talk that did not surprise her. She suspected it was a healthy thing.

She was more surprised to discover that Tom was the leader of the group. She realized that the diffident personality he had displayed to her in recent years was really wariness. With his fellow males a mysterious natural dominance he had inherited from his father emerged. He made most of the decisions about where to go, what to do—not without vociferous objections from his cohorts, of course. Even more surprising was the way he dominated their bull sessions about the Army.

She noticed they called him "Marshal." One day she asked him what the nickname meant. "My future rank," he said with a grin. "The guys claim I won't be satisfied with five stars. They'll have to create a new rank for me—field marshal."

"You're in for thirty, as Dad used to say?"

He nodded. "Does that bother you?"

"No."

With or without the girls, the cadets snorkeled and bodysurfed, and played touch football by the hour. When the game got rough, male epithets would drift up to Joanna on the porch, which they thought was out of earshot. They were better spoken, but not much better behaved, when Sam Hardin and Ruth came down to the beach with their two boys. Tom instantly organized a mini-squad and they performed a mock drill for the former deputy commandant of the Corps. They reversed every order, crashed into and knocked each other flat, and finally doubled-timed backward into the ocean, where, with a final salute, they sank from sight.

"They're a lot more rambunctious than we were," Sam said. "Which explains some of the gray I've got in my hair."

When the cadets emerged from the water they invited the Hardin boys to join them for a touch-football game. "No, thanks," the elder boy, Robert, said, giving his brother David a wry look.

"Come on," Tom said. "We'll take it easy on you. We won't hold a single demerit against you. Even Marvin. He collected about two hundred from your father. But he's been born again here in Hawaii. He forgives everybody. Even Kincaid, who stole the only decent-looking girl he danced with last night."

"Go ahead, Bob. The exercise will do you good," Sam said.

"I think you roughnecks just want to pound them around," Ruth Hardin said to Tom.

"I'd rather go for a swim," Robert Hardin said. "Come on, Dave."

They sauntered down to the water together. They were built like Ruth, thin and tall. They did not look athletic. Joanna could almost hear the ache of Sam Hardin's frustration as he stared after them. "Think I'll take a dip too," he said.

The cadets went back to their football. Joanna was left alone on the porch with Ruth. She shook her head gloomily. "I can't imagine why you let Tom go to the Academy, Joanna. When you think of the way the Army's gone to pieces in the last ten years. Do you think the next ten or twenty will be any better?"

"I didn't have much to say about it. He's been fascinated by things military since the age of four."

"I made damn sure that didn't happen to my kids," Ruth said. "I told them the real story. They know the score about the Army. What a rotten lousy stinking deal it is."

Joanna sighed. Ruth had not changed. It was clear by now that

Ruth was never going to change. Joanna remembered the year she had spent with Ruth at Fort Thompson, Arkansas, when Joanna was playing the game. She had made Ruth a kind of litmus test. If she deceived her, she was safe. No one else had a sharper, more savage eye for Army frauds and phonies.

The sharp eye was still at work. Ruth asked Joanna why she was not living in the Philippines, with the wives of other corps and province advisers. Joanna said she could not stand the boredom. She preferred Hawaii, where she was able to hold a job. "I like teaching," she said.

"You see Pete every six months?"

"He couldn't get away—for his last leave."

"Just like my hero," Ruth said. "Colonel Straight Arrow. That's what the boys and I call him. He loves hardship tours. I told him if he went back to Nam again, we were through. He's been out there three times, '62 to '63, '65 to '66, and '68 to '69. Always in the field, too. Getting shot at. You know who he reminds me of? Arnold Coulter. Remember him? Everyone who ever went near that nut got a bullet in the head before they were through. He never even got scratched. That's the way Sammy is. Everyone around him gets hit and he walks away."

"How are your mother and father?" Joanna said. She had long since given Ruth a carefully neutralized version of her relationship with Betty Parrott in Japan.

"They split up about five years ago. He got drunk and beat the old girl up once too often. I don't know where he is now. On skid row, probably. My mother's working as a waitress in California. God, what a rotten life she's had. What do you think of the war these days?"

"I—I'm beginning to think it'll never end."

"I'm against it. If it wasn't for Colonel Straight Arrow, I'd be out there marching with the peaceniks. He told me if I did it, and messed up his beautiful career, he'd kill me. Pete ever threaten you that way?"

Joanna shook her head. She saw that Ruth had changed. She had acquired a new dimension to her dislike of the Army. The rhetoric of the anti-war movement had jibed perfectly with her inherited resentments and hatreds. "Colonel Straight Arrow punched his fist right through the bathroom door one night last spring at West Point. I thought he was going to kill me that night. Because I agreed with Adam Thayer about the goddamn Army. He's got the right idea, Adam has. Court-martial a half dozen generals for this mess. Maybe shoot a few."

Ruth ranted on about the war. Sam emerged from the water and strolled down the beach with his sons. He put his arms around their shoulders. Joanna noticed that the older boy, Robert, slipped away from his embrace. The younger boy tolerated it. She realized that she was glimpsing a family in anguish.

At the end of the month Tom went back to West Point. In September, Joanna returned to her classroom, where she was pleased to discover Robert Hardin among her pupils. After their first class, she gave him a warm hello. "How are your mother and father?" she asked.

"Okay," he said in a listless voice.

"Give them my best. I hope we'll have a nice time together this year. We're going to read some interesting books."

The class was the usual collection of self-starting bright kids, sluggish mediocrities and stalled dullards. Joanna was distressed to find that Robert Hardin was among the dullards. He never said a word in class. His compositions were atrocious. He failed his first test catastrophically. He had obviously not read even one of the assigned short stories and poems.

Joanna tried some after-class counseling. "What's wrong, Bob?" she asked. "Why didn't you study for that test?"

"What's the point?"

"What do you mean?"

"I'll be in Vietnam next year. Unless I take off for Canada."

"Why would you do a thing like that?"

"Matt Thayer did it. His old man practically told him to do it."

"Wait a minute, Bob. Not everyone who gets drafted goes to Vietnam these days. The Army's withdrawing thousands of men each month. Anyway, not everybody eighteen gets drafted. Aren't you going to college?"

"Marks aren't good enough."

"If you do some work this year, maybe they will be good enough. I know some people at the University of Hawaii. I might be able to help— if you let me."

He shrugged, muttered something about English being boring and left with a vague promise to do some studying. When Bob's drift continued, Joanna called Sam and suggested a conference with him and Ruth. Sam came alone one afternoon and told her, clench-fisted and scowling, the story of his losing struggle to make a student of Bob. "Ruth does nothing," he said. "When I'm not there, she lets them look at TV till their eyes fall out of their heads. She can barely read a book herself."

"We have a lot of kids with Bob's problem," Joanna said, bypassing the reference to Ruth. "Not all Army kids, either."

"Not much consolation," Sam said.

"I think he's a pretty unhappy boy, Sam. He doesn't see a very bright future for himself."

She summarized her conversation with Bob about Vietnam.

"That's Ruth again," he growled. "She has absolutely poisoned that kid's mind about the war, the Army. Dave's not so bad. I can talk to him. Bob just tunes me out. What can I do about it?"

"I have no magic answer, Sam. Maybe— try something unorthodox. Let up the pressure. Try to talk to him about the war—his future—without telling him what to do."

He grimaced. "That's a bad habit among Army fathers, I guess."

"Almost all fathers," Joanna said. "Working here's been an education for me, Sam. It's made me remember something Martha Kinsolving told me about the Army twenty years ago. She said it wasn't much different from the rest of middle America—except when it's fighting a war."

Sam nodded glumly. "And this Army's been fighting a war for nine years now. With no end in sight."

The year, Joanna's life continued. Bob Hardin showed no improvement. Letters from the I Corps adviser in Vietnam drifted into the house at Mo Ka Lei, now sent via West Point. Nixon's Vietnamization program was continuing, with more and more thousands of American troops withdrawn each month, leaving officers like Pete deeply pessimistic as they watched the South Vietnamese try to take over the war. Tom's letters were resolutely cheerful; she suspected he wanted to make sure she did not worry about him. Other letters from friends around the globe reported on their varying fortunes. The Kinsolvings were enjoying a year at the Army War College in Carlisle Barracks, Pennsylvania. Amy Rosser was pushing George ahead at her usual brisk pace in Germany. Honor wrote troubled letters asking Joanna if she had heard from Adam.

After another conference with Sam Hardin, Joanna gave Bob an F for the first term. This produced a nasty telephone call from Ruth. "Don't you know Army people stick together?" she snarled. "Haven't you learned anything? You always were a snob, you and Amy Rosser, you think you're better than the Army. No wonder Pete walked out on you. Everybody knows that, by the way. You haven't fooled anyone with your beach cottage act all these years. Everybody knows you had a real man, the best soldier in his class, and you screwed him up so bad he's going to stay out there in Vietnam until he dies."

"You're going to screw up your man too, Ruth," Joanna said.

"I'm sure as hell going to try," Ruth said. "It's exactly what the bastard deserves."

Joanna decided not to take that last threat seriously. Ruth was like her mother, when it came to saying one thing and doing another. Watching her in action at Fort Thompson, Arkansas, Joanna had noted that Ruth was infallibly obsequious to higher ranks, ten minutes after bad-mouthing them to one of her friends. Nevertheless, the first part of the call was a serious matter in itself. Joanna decided to tell Sam about it. She informed him she was having Bob transferred from her class. Given Ruth's attitude, it was unrealistic to expect the boy to do any work for Joanna Burke. Sam grimly agreed.

Joanna winced, thinking about the conversation that probably took place in the Hardin bedroom that night. Obviously, Sam was having more and more trouble concealing the depths of his marriage's malaise. It had been possible, even relatively easy, at a lower rank, when Ruth's griping could be passed off as comedy. Even at the lieutenant colonel level, when Joanna saw a lot of Ruth at Fort Thompson, her game playing instincts remained intact. But now that

the anti-war movement's rhetoric had infected her, it was difficult to see how Sam could continue the subterfuge much longer.
Ruth was almost out of control. She was clearly ready to insult a
general or do something else with malice aforethought to embarrass
Sam.

One day after lunch in late March, Joanna opened a newspaper
and saw words that could not fail to attract an Army wife's eye: TWO
AT SCHOFIELD MADE BRIGADIERS. One of the two was Sam Hardin.
Farther down in the story, which summed up the latest appointments
to brigadier general, Joanna saw another familiar name: George A.
Rosser. They were the first two men in '50 to become generals.
Joanna instantly thought of Pete, reading this story in the *Army
Times* or hearing it from a classmate over the telephone from
headquarters. Sam Hardin's career had paralleled Pete's in so many
ways; how could he avoid thinking: *There but for my traitor wife, go
I?* The possibility filled Joanna with almost unbearable sadness. She
felt the pain of Pete's ambition, that gnawing combination of hope
and desire, endured over so many years.

She decided there was only one thing to do: face the fact that
other men were inheriting Pete's dream. She had been forcing
herself to face everything else in her life since she returned to Mo
Ka Lei. After school that afternoon she drove over to Schofield and
found the Hardin quarters in the field officers' section of the huge
post.

She rang the bell. A harried-looking Filipino maid answered the
door. "Is General or Mrs. Hardin in?" Joanna asked.

The maid nodded, her eyes wide and tense. "I'm an old friend.
Mrs. Burke. Are they receiving visitors?"

The maid shook her head.

A hand jerked the door wide open. Sam Hardin stood there behind
the maid, wearing tan slacks and a T-shirt. He was unshaven, his
hair uncombed. "Joanna?" he said. "Come on in."

She stepped cautiously into the house. The living room looked
like a regiment of AWOL's had had a drunken brawl in it. Lamps
were overturned, their shades crushed, their bulbs smashed. The
white walls were covered with orange and yellow anti-war slogans,
in which the word *fuck* was used repeatedly.

"Beautiful, isn't it?" Sam Hardin said. "Isn't this the perfect present to give a man the day he gets promoted?"

"Who—who did it?" Joanna asked.

"Ruth and the boys. She told me she was leaving me last night, when I came home with the news. The boys said they were going too. I—I got the hell out of here. I was afraid I'd hurt somebody."

"And they left this?"

"Right. Isn't it great? Doesn't it make you want to laugh? Admit it. You always thought I was a jerk, all these years—putting up with her."

Joanna shook her head. She saw the same pain on the lined but still youthful face that she had seen in Korea. "I—knew you weren't happy, Sam. Everybody knew that."

"But I didn't have the guts to get rid of her, right? My goddamn career was more important. That's what you thought? I'd sacrifice anything, my private life, my sons—to the career, to these, right?"

He held up a pair of general's stars in a plastic envelope. Joanna wondered how many hours he had been pacing up and down the wrecked house, clutching them.

"Sam, nobody thought any such thing. Everyone's been so wrapped up in their own careers, their own marriages. You're the one who's saying that—to yourself."

He stopped pacing and glared at her with such ferocity she remembered Ruth's claim that he had threatened to kill her. "Guilty conscience needs no accuser?" he said.

"Sam—you've got to calm down. Your promotion is in the paper. People will be dropping by. You can't let them see you—the house—this way."

He looked contemptuously around him. "Why the hell not? Let it all hang out, like the kids say. Maybe they'll take back these goddamn stars."

"You're being ridiculous. You earned those stars. You know damn well you earned them."

That stopped him. He stood there in the middle of the wrecked room, blinking blearily at her.

"Did you get any sleep last night?"

He shook his head.

"I did. On that basis alone, listen to me. You can't let Ruth destroy you. That's what she's trying to do. I think I know why. You remember that I knew her mother and father in Japan. The thought of being a general's wife terrifies Ruth. She was taught to hate generals."

He nodded slowly. The uncombed hair, the day-old beard, still gave him a berserk look.

"I don't think you should see anyone today. Call the division public affairs officer. Tell him to handle the congratulations. Say you've got a flare-up of Saigon belly. Come down to Mo Ka Lei with me. Take twenty-four hours to pull yourself together."

He looked wary. Did he think she was trying to seduce him? "The cottage has two bedrooms. And in spite of appearances to the contrary, I'm still married to Pete."

"Okay," he said. He went out to the patio and rinsed his face in water from the fountain. He called the public affairs officer and gave him the excuse she had suggested. Meanwhile Joanna inspected the rest of the house. Ruth and her sons had spray-painted their anti-war slogans in every room. They had smashed every dish in the kitchen.

Sam sent the maid home, locked the house, and Joanna drove him swiftly away from the scene of his humiliation, over Kolekole Pass to Mo Ka Lei. They said nothing all the way down. It was dusk when she shut off the motor in the carport.

"Are you hungry?"

"No," he said.

"Why don't you just have a slug of bourbon and go to bed?"

"You're full of good ideas."

In a half hour he was asleep in Tom's bed. She studied the face on the pillow for a moment. Now she saw how much it had changed since West Point, the day in the hospital in Japan. It was not merely lines of age. That hard mouth belonged to a man who had given difficult orders to other men and to himself. Those grim lines running from the edge of the mouth to the jaw were scars of harsh, fiercely willed control. *Three thousand blows in the morning, eight hundred blows in the evening*, said the koan. Sam Hardin had endured them all.

The next morning she arose early, put on a muumuu and tried to meditate. She sat on the porch in the lotus position and chose the koan:

> *I meet him but know not who he is*
> *I converse with him but do not know his name.*

About an hour later, she heard the door open behind her. "So this is where you get your power," Sam Hardin said.

"What power?"

"Whatever you want to call it."

"Loyalty, maybe. Friendship." She stood up. "Let me cook you some breakfast."

"Can I take a swim first?"

"I don't think there's a man's bathing suit in the house."

"That's proof of your virtue, anyway. I'll wear a towel to the water's edge."

She nodded. "I swim that way every morning. Nobody but retirees down here now. They tend to sleep late."

He came back as she was frying bacon and eggs and asked for a razor. She found one that she used to shave her legs. "I'm not so virtuous after all," she said, handing it to him.

"You'll never convince me of that," he said with a smile.

Sam sat down to breakfast looking reborn. His skin glowed, his eyes were clear and bright. "I really appreciate this," he said.

"It's what friends are for."

"I could have parted with Ruth without a tear. It's the boys that tore me apart. What can I do about them?"

"Keep trying to prove you care about them. That's all you can do. Make sure you have the right to visit them—if you and Ruth get divorced."

"We are divorced," Sam said. "I'll just hire a lawyer to make it legal. I don't care if it stalls me at brigadier. I never thought I'd get even one star, anyway. I can think of a dozen guys—Pete's one of them—who deserve it a lot more."

Joanna nodded mournfully. Sam ate his bacon and eggs and studied her in quick hard glances. "Pete have some problems somewhere along the line I never heard about?"

She told him about the OER Pete had received from Henry

648

Hamburger in Saigon, the disaster at Seward State with Willard Eberle.

"Two bad men to cross," Sam said. "The Army's like life, I'm afraid—unfair. But Pete's sort of compounded things, hasn't he? Staying out in Nam one tour after another, turning down the Pentagon, the War College."

Everybody knows, Ruth had sneered over the telephone. What was the point in lying to this man? "I'm afraid that's my fault, Sam."

She told him, briefly, quietly, what had happened between her and Pete. "Christ," Sam said. That was all. She was relieved that he did not try to tell her that she had a right to go slightly crazy after Cissie's death, that some of the disaster was Pete's fault. She preferred his silence—and sympathy.

She changed the subject to George Rosser, Sam's former roommate and his fellow brigadier. "Amy must be in ecstasy," Joanna said.

Sam laughed. "I never thought George would stick it out. I always said he was too smart to put up with the Army. He almost resigned about six times during plebe year. He kept telling me, 'None of this makes sense.' I just told him, 'George, have faith.' I didn't realize he was a Methodist and that meant something to him."

"Speaking of '50's brainpower," Joanna said, "do you know what's happened to Adam Thayer? He stopped by here on his way out to Vietnam, all excited about some big job General Ingalls had lined up for him. I never heard another word from him. Neither, I gather, has Honor. Has he gone back into the mountains to work with those tribesmen—"

Sam's face began darkening as Joanna talked. By the time she stopped, his good humor had vanished. "I don't think Adam would write anybody about what he's been doing in Saigon."

"What do you mean?"

"Adam's through. I wrote the report. I did it to protect Tom."

Curtly, angrily, he told her what Adam had almost persuaded Tom to do.

"How—did you find out about it?" Joanna asked.

"Honor told me. She wasn't going to let Adam ruin Tom's career. That's what she said."

For a moment Joanna wondered whose side she was on. The answer was unavoidable. Honor was right, Adam was wrong, no matter how good his abstract principles. She recognized the ambivalence of her feelings about Tom's military career but she did not want to see Pete hurt any more. Almost as important were her feelings about Honor. Joanna understood what a difficult thing she had done. It was an act of love, a reaffirmation of their friendship.

"What—are they doing to Adam in Vietnam?" she asked.

"Making it very, very clear to him that he is no longer wanted in this Army," Sam said.

Suffering. Joanna felt Adam's pain too. She remembered the excitement, the hope on his face when he sat on the porch last year speculating about his assignment. She remembered the hope and faith of other years, particularly the day they sat side by side on the shore of Lake Poplopen and she urged him not to let the disillusion with his first Pentagon tour destroy his idealism.

Joanna looked up to find Brigadier General Hardin studying her, those hard eyes penetrating her distress. "I—I've always admired Adam," she said.

"So did I. He was right about this war. I wish a couple of generals had read his Ph.D. thesis. And a couple of Presidents. But being a failed prophet doesn't give him the right to ruin a boy like Tom—and eleven other boys almost as promising."

Promising for what, to whom? That altar with DUTY engraved on it? The altar where the dead are offered up to history's god, Blind Chance?

Joanna only nodded, while this voice whispered within her. She sensed that something stronger than admiration was dragging her back to the pool of icy rage in the center of her body. The pool was empty now; desolation had replaced the rage. There was only a cavern haunted by the ghost of her secret self.

Brigadier General Hardin said he felt ready to return to Schofield Barracks. He thanked Joanna again for her act of friendship. She gave him a formal smile and said she was glad to have been able to help. He took the keys to her car, promising that a driver would return it before the end of the day. "I'm going out to Nam for another tour," he said. "I'll talk to Pete."

It was not Pete about whom Joanna dreamed and thought for the next few weeks. It was Adam. His humiliation infected her soul in a new way, more depleting, more demoralizing. She had been humbled by Pete's pain, by the stubborn silence with which he endured it. She suspected that Adam did not have that capacity, that will. Trapped between two kinds of suffering, she could only wait, wondering which would claim her, fearing that she already knew.

It was almost a year since Adam had gone to Saigon. His DEROS—Date of Estimated Return from Overseas—was approaching. She could not—would not—run away from him. She must face him—as she had faced everything else since her marriage collapsed. She continued her daily routine on Mo Ka Lie. A morning swim followed by meditation, followed by school, or—on weekends—by poetry. She had begun writing again last year. She thought some of the poems were moderately good. She had not tried to publish any of them. As part of her struggle with the angel of forgiveness, she had made a promise not to publish another poem until Pete returned from Vietnam.

On a Saturday late in April, she lay on the beach and worked all morning on a poem she called "Eggs." After lunch she took her usual nap. She left the poem on the coffee table in the living room. She awoke to hear a voice reciting the first stanza.

> "The poet stands with the egg in her hand
> She squeezes too hard.
> Life runs through her fingers."

She put on a muumuu and strolled into the living room. Adam lay on the bamboo couch, reading the poem at arm's length. He smiled at her. "I like it," he said.

"Thank you," she said.

She sat down carefully, warily, in a chair opposite him. "How are you?" she said.

"How do I look?"

"The same. Only older."

"You don't. You look more and more like Mrs. Robinson Crusoe."

He was referring to the deep tan she had acquired.

"Thank you."

"You're writing poetry again."

"Yes."

"Publishing any?"

"No. It's strictly for my own amusement. Or therapy."

He nodded. "Too many poets anyway. Like the Army's surplus of lieutenant colonels and colonels."

"You've been reassigned?"

"Back to the Pentagon to work as an action officer for the Deputy Chief of Nothing in Particular. With my luck it will probably turn out to be Willard Eberle, the one general I really want to kill."

"What were you doing—in Vietnam?"

"My dear girl. My duties were not limited to Vietnam. The Army found my services necessary not only in that pesthole but in Thailand and Korea. Let's begin with Vietnam. There I was deputy chief of staff of the Capital Military Assistance Command. I had a desk in the hall next to a sergeant. Mainly we seemed to be in charge of supplying chauffeurs and drivers for visiting VIP's and friends of the forty-one generals and their staffs in Saigon. In Thailand I was in charge of arranging for the rental of bungalows for officers who wanted to cohabit with their wives or with one or several of the local females. My commander there, a full colonel, liked to brag that he never worked more than an hour a day. His favorite sport was playing dead bug. Do you know the game? You go to a bar, any bar, and yell, 'Dead bug.' Everyone falls to the ground and wiggles his arms and legs. The last man down has to pay for the next round of drinks. In Korea I was in charge of negotiating with the head of the local businesswomen's society at Camp Howard, fifty miles west of Seoul. The local businesswomen are better described as prostitutes. The big problem was their refusal to sleep with black servicemen. Until I got there I wondered how I could make a living when I left the Army. What, after all, have they trained me to do in the civilian world? Now I know. I will make a very successful madam."

"I don't believe you're going to leave the Army."

"I'm afraid the Army is leaving me. Frequent reassignments to trivial jobs is one way that the big shots tell you they don't want you around. They'd rather have me leave quietly. If I don't, they'll go for the regulation that says, 'Retention of officers substandard in performance of duty or conduct, deficient in character, or otherwise unsuited for military service cannot be justified in peace or in war.' "

"You're not any of those things."

"Please say that again. It's one of the reasons I came here. Somehow, I told myself, somehow Joanna will have rediscovered the secret of hope, affirmation. Somehow she will still believe in Adam. Even if no one else does."

"I hate to see you so unhappy."

"Why? If I were a happy lieutenant colonel in this Army, I'd be despicable. Any officer who is happy in this Army has got to be either a crook or a moron. He has to have the soul of a traveling salesman or a helot."

"Is that really true, Adam?"

"Yes. Take my word for it. But I didn't come here to talk about the goddamn Army. I came here to see you. Are you still on hold, waiting for Big Pete to forgive you, for you to forgive him, the Army, God?"

"Yes," she said, disliking the mockery in his voice until she realized it was a sympton of his demoralization.

"It hasn't happened yet?"

"No."

"Why not?"

"I don't know. I can't stop being Joanna, I suppose. I can't accept those Zen ideas about everything and nothing being the same. I may be the monkey reaching for the moon in the water. But I'd rather reach for it."

"As soon as there are plum flowers, it becomes a different moon," Adam said. He got up and went to the window to look out at the sea. "I haven't thought about that koan for ten years."

"Remember how we used to try to find ones that meant something for each other?"

"Yes. What was the one you liked best for me?"

> *"Fearsome and solitary*
> *He does not boast*
> *He dwells gravely within himself*
> *Deciding who is snake, who is dragon."*

"I remember the one I liked best for you. But you denied it."

"What?"

> *"The golden bracelet on her arm*
> *Is too loose by an inch*
> *Yet on meeting someone she merely says*
> *'No, I'm not in love.' "*

A tremor passed over her flesh watching him there in the window, profiled against the open sea. She saw all the wounds that time, the Army, his own pride, had inflicted on him.

"Would you like a drink?" she asked.

"I'd like several drinks. Then I'm going to take you to dinner."

She made Polynesian punch. Adam drank an ominous amount of it. Contrary to his previous dismissal of the subject, he began talking about the Army, not with his old mocking humor, but with a bitterness that could only be despair. He described the ridiculous surplus of officers. "Since World War II, the ratio of generals to enlisted men has gone up 152 percent, lieutenant colonels, 257 percent. This means you've got talented men, dedicated men, leaders who are supposed to be able to handle a battalion of two thousand in combat, working as area beautification officers, accountable sensitive forms officers, vector control officers."

"What's a vector?"

"Anything that carries germs. Rats, bugs, ticks."

He talked about the luxurious base camps the Army had built in Vietnam, with swimming pools and air-conditioned officers' and enlisted men's clubs. "That's why morale is zero-minus. The troops come in from the field, from getting shot at and killed, and see eighty-five percent of the officers and seventy percent of the men sitting around these tropical resorts, eating steak and ice cream every night. No wonder they're fragging and assassinating us. We deserve it. Do you know what the percentage of officer deaths in Vietnam has been for the last three years? Two percent. Versus seven to ten percent in other wars. Do you know how many actual combat troops we had in Vietnam at the height of the buildup? Eighty thousand. Out of an army of five hundred and forty thousand. All the rest of

them sitting around those base camps or on staffs in Saigon, Nha Trang, you name it.''

She saw what he was doing. He was trying to destroy her opposition to the statement he had made on his way to Saigon—the Army deserved to lose the war. The country, perhaps, the bumbling chickenhearted politicians in Washington, Lyndon Johnson and his crew, deserved it, she had told him, but not the Army. She was thinking of Pete and Adam knew it. He had retreated, silenced by his ambivalent but nonetheless real loyalty to Pete, by his own hope, so cruelly illusory, for a new beginning in Vietnam. Now he was back, asking her to share his despair, his total loss of faith in duty-honor-country. He wanted to destroy the fragile link that held her to the Army—Pete's stubborn dedication and courage—by convincing her that it was meaningless, the product of a mind that refused to face reality.

What he did not know—what she did not tell him—was how this clashed with her attempt to feel Pete's anguish, the Army's suffering. The more he talked, the more she began to see Adam as part of this suffering. Listening to him, she felt her old awe, her spiritual desire for him, fuse with a wish to console him, sustain him somehow.

They went to Fisherman's Wharf above Kewalo Basin and drank more rum-filled punch and ate poached opakapaka and planked mahimahi. Around them sat dozens of middle-aged American tourists, the men wearing newly bought aloha shirts, the women with plum blossoms in their hair. They all looked so self-satisfied, so contented with the success that had enabled them to fly the Pacific to this American-owned paradise. They chatted about the view from the Pali, about shopping at the Ala Moana Center or the Kahala Mall. It was impossible to believe that any of them knew or cared about soldiers dying in Vietnam.

Adam became more and more depressed. ''It isn't just the Army, it's the whole goddamn country,'' he muttered. ''I've been doing some research on my second alma mater, the one I share with the Kennedys, fair Harvard. Do you know how many of those intellectual heroes died in Korea and Vietnam? Thirty out of thirty-three thousand graduates, so far. How's that for being ready to go anywhere, bear any burden, take any risk for freedom? The other Ivy League schools aren't much better."

"How's Honor?" she asked. "And the kids?"

"Honor is playing Army wife in Cornwall. Pookie is upholding the family reputation at the top of her class at Vassar. Matthew Ridgway Thayer has bugged out to Canada to make sure his moral purity remains unsullied by service in the U. S. Army. I can't blame the kid. Honor's more upset about it than I am."

He drank some of the Riesling he had ordered with dinner. "So here we are, without honor, without country, without any particular reason for duty."

"You want to take everything away, don't you?"

"It's gone. I'm not taking it away. I'm informing you that it's gone."

Suffering. The Army's suffering. She saw it again on his tormented face. The chattering room, the nautical decor of Fisherman's Wharf, began to dissolve in tears. Sympathy, a dangerous compound of grief and pity, flooded her withered heart. "What happens now that we've both stopped playing the game?" she asked.

"That's what I'm here to find out."

An hour later Joanna sat beside Adam in his rented car, rolling down the windward coast beneath a huge riding moon. Enormous white waves rose out of the golden water. At first, Adam had driven slowly along the curving road. Then he began to go faster and faster, daring the shoulder above foaming coves. Past Kahuku Point they roared, beneath the human-shaped stone that supposedly had once been an ancient Hawaiian prince who had been unfaithful to his beloved. Soon they were far down the southern coast, rolling along the deserted palm-lined byroad to the empty beach of Camp Erdman, just above Kaena Point.

Adam took her hand and they walked for a half mile along the beach without meeting a soul. For the first time, the trade wind made Joanna shiver. Was it possible, was she going to let Adam do what he wanted, needed, with her? Did she have the power to console, restore this tormented man? Or would he overwhelm the fragile barriers she had struggled to erect against her own despair?

Echoes of her Catholic past welled up, old sermons excoriating the sins of the flesh. How absurd the ~~idity~~ of that discarded faith. She was being drawn to this man by a force ~~s~~ persistent and enormous as this oceanic wind, sweeping across the s~~ reaches~~ from distant America, drawn by shared knowledge and share~~.~~

"I loved you in 1950," he said. "I should have ~~dropped~~ you—that day in the car."

"No," she said. "We did the right thing that day, Adam. You couldn't have lived with betraying your best friend. You would have ended up hating me—for letting you do it."

A hundred yards out, a wave mounted, a dark, heaving mountain. White spray blossomed at its tip and the wind sheared a veil of mist into the moonlight. On it came, more and more irresistible, huge. She remembered a line from a recent poem. *None but the wind's lips, the wind's fingers have explored me.* It was true. There had been nothing of the explorer in Pete Burke. Nothing of the searcher into the hollows and recesses of her body or her spirit. That was what she had wanted, to explore and be explored. The wave broke, a long churning line.

"I can't touch you, Joanna—unless—"

She would have to accept the first, the worst guilt. So be it. "I've always wanted you and needed you, Adam. Now we have this time together. Don't waste it."

He unbuttoned the jacket of her suit, and slowly, between long deep kisses, undressed her. They were like ghosts, she thought, pale ghosts in the coppery moonlight, assaulted by the charging Pacific combers, while the palm fronds clashed above them in the eternal wind. Ghosts on the tan sand as he knelt beside her naked and she ran her hands down his long lean body, ghosts blown here by history's wind, ghosts of their old wished selves, lost somewhere in the long journey from Sconnet, Cincinnati, West Point, to this pagan island in a distant sea.

Water and wind ransacked her body while his hands, his mouth explored her. Water and wind and beneath her back the primary sand, the gritty earth. Water and wind and earth, three of the four primary elements. But not fire. She was still numb, dry, dead with unconfessed guilt, regret. That she should be the first to fail, the first to betray. Peter MacArthur Burke leaped from the darkness beneath the palm trees to stand between her and Adam, between her and happiness, a warrior with a mouth of bronze, an Achilles figure blind with raging accusation.

And Honor beside him with her wounded mouth, a feathered thing, croaking sorrowfully. She flaps her wingless arms. She raises a claw to tear out Joanna's treacherous poetic eyes. Did Adam see them? Yes, in his stark New England soul he saw them with far more clarity. Dark rage against a snowbound landscape, guerrillas racing across time and space to fling their murderous satchel charges at these pseudo-innocents, these poseurs of regret and sorrow, pretending to escape the iron grasp of history, time.

Oh, Adam, can we do it? The words were on her lips when he entered her. She was dry; with fear, denial; there was none, not a trace of the soft mucus of desire. But he was there, within her. She felt the pulse of his flesh. He did not move. He held her in the vise of his arms, his tongue deep in her mouth for minutes, more minutes, until time began to blur, disconnect, and there was only wind and water, sounds of the sentinel palms, the guardian moon. They were not Adam and Joanna, they were anyone, ancient lovers from the legends of Hawaii. Kama and Ha-le-ma-no, who saw each other first in their dreams, and fled from their warring fathers to the grove of Ke-a-kui.

"Love me, Joanna. Jesus, love me."

He felt the dryness, the deadness of his own flesh, sensed his ghostness, in spite of the physical fact, the bony machinery of love that responded automatically to her nakedness. Still without stroking her, he plunged his tongue deep in her mouth again and consumed her in an absolute embrace. Slowly, she began to move against him, to escape the voices and faces that owned Joanna Welsh Burke, to blend with those ancient lovers who chanted their passion with such heartbreaking innocence and sweetness.

> *Alas, O my love*
> *My love from the land of the Kau-mu-ku wind*
> *My love of the home where we were friendless*
> *Our only friend being our love for one another.*

When he came it was like a breaking, more loss than gift, more a sigh of sadness than a cry of ecstasy. She sighed with him, acknowledging at last their long grievous infidelity. But with a riding spume of joy, like the whiteness at the very tip of a wave. "I've always loved you," she whispered. "Always."

They lay clasped in each other's arms for a long time, listening to the waves. They walked to the point and sat there, watching them mount, mount, and break on the jagged coral. The sea was speaking to them. The sea with all its meanings. The track of history. The face of God. She shivered in the wind. The air was damp with spray. "Let's go," she said.

They put on their clothes and drove slowly back along the coast to Mo Ka Lei. The moon was sinking into the black glowing water. At the cottage, they undressed and made love again. This time she was more reflective, more in possession of her self beneath their touches and kisses. This was the bed in which her husband had held her in his arms the night he turned down his chance to make a million dollars selling Cadillacs. A few steps away was the unlikely kitchen where they had renewed their marriage. It was necessary to face these things, even as Adam aroused her again, this time not in the name of their innocent selves, those romantic June week lovers of 1950, but as the man who was claiming Joanna now, Joanna-the-no-longer-good, Joanna the not very celibate-poet-of-Mo-Ka-Lei. Joanna-the-some-time-Army-wife.

It was not like being with Pete. He was always other, essential maleness. Adam was male, she knew that perfectly well from what was moving within her. But it was a different dimension of maleness, closer to an emanation of her own mind. She could give herself, enter him in spirit as he entered her in flesh. Not taken, consumed, as she had thought of him when the passivity of their first meeting possessed her. That was time, history, speaking then. Now she gave herself freely, deliciously, without the weight, the sense of being taken, conquered.

But there are many kinds of conquests. Adam poured rum and water and they went out on the porch. "I want to tell you everything," he said.

A mistake. She did not want to know everything. She wanted, for the moment at least, to avoid knowing, to linger in half knowing between the mythic love of Kaena Point and the realistic love in her husband's bedroom. She wanted to live between those two realities for a while. But Adam wanted her to join him where he was living, to become his wounded and wounding self. So he talked.

He described the failure of his love for Honor, which began after the rape in Korea. He acknowledged it as a failure. "I know now I was looking for a reason to stop loving her. Something about the submission, the desire that she extracted from me, almost against my will, rankled my soul. Call it New England pride. The refusal to admit that the body has its reasons, its seasons. The insistence on the supremacy of the mind."

He told her about his affairs. First with Annette Haines in Cambridge. He described it as an experiment to see if desire could be abstracted from its usual context and survive in an atmosphere of mutual dislike. Then in more detail, his complex relationship with Amy Rosser. He even admitted continuing the affair with Amy in Vietnam after he had promised Joanna to end it. After she had destroyed Honor's anger, ruined the moment when Honor might have become capable of dealing with Adam.

No, she was translating her own life-wife experience into Honor's life. Honor had dealt with Adam in her own way.

Joanna listened as Adam told her what had happened to him in Vietnam. "When they incinerated my Rhade at Bong Son, it was over for me. I knew we couldn't win and didn't deserve to win. That's when I decided to become outrageous, to take on guys like Eberle. To blow as many whistles as I could on all the goddamn generals and crummy cowardly Vietnamese buzzing around in their planes and helicopters cooking up phony body counts. I realize now it was my first step on my way out of this Army."

"You really mean it. You're getting out?"

"I want you to come with me, Joanna."

For the first time she saw what she meant to Adam. She was not, she had never been his Army wife. She had been part of the deep ambivalence he had felt toward an Army career from the beginning. Now she was his escape from the Army, his civilian wife. And something more important—his spiritual judge, his confessor. This was a religious rite they were performing, as close to faith as a late-twentieth-century soul could come. *Love me, Joanna. Jesus, love me,* he had whispered on Kaena Point. That was not the cry of the anguished soldier. It was personal loneliness, sadness, speaking. It was an ex-soldier, a fugitive from a defeated demoralized Army.

This realization did not evoke the expected response. Joanna was not with him anymore, as he told her what he had almost perpetrated at West Point with her son, Tom. He expected her to approve it. All Joanna could see was Honor's anguished decision to stop Adam in the name of friendship. No, a better word: love. All she began to know, as they sat in silence, was the impossibility of what Adam was trying to do.

She saw how difficult it was going to be, when they made love again in the dawn. It was exquisitely gentle yet stunningly sensual in a way she had never known. He kissed her and she kissed him everywhere without shame, without hesitation. She felt for the first time the thrust of maleness in the deepest most inward place, felt the shell of her innermost heart break, revealing the wish she had denied, replaced, evaded all her life, for a love that consumed every part of her being, a love in which giving and taking, conquest and submission, vanished with all the other words, a love that became reality.

Another koan burned like a tracer bullet through her brain and down her body. *Not to take what Heaven gives is to incur Heaven's calamity; not to act when the moment comes is to incur Heaven's misfortune.*

She had refused to take what Heaven gave. Now would she be unable to act when the moment leaped like a god from the depths of the sea? No. She could not, she would not let him go. She clung to him in the dawn, wild, passionate, free. But there were tears on her cheeks. He licked their salty knowledge and whispered: "Why?"

"Nothing. It doesn't matter," she said.

They slept.

Joanna awoke to a radio voice announcing: "TODAY THE U.S. COMMAND IN VIETNAM ANNOUNCED A MAJOR OFFENSIVE, THE LARGEST OPERATION IN TWO YEARS, AN INVASION OF ENEMY SANCTUARIES IN

CAMBODIA." She was hurtled back to her post-honeymoon days at Fort Ripley. Putting on a muumuu, she found Adam ransacking her bookshelves for an atlas with a map of Indochina. In a trunk, she found Pete's old map, the one he had spread across their bed during their first days in Saigon. She said nothing to Adam about its history. He spent the next several hours drawing lines on the map, simultaneously cursing the radio reporters for not giving him enough information. By late afternoon he was dismissing the supposed seriousness of the offensive. "It's a spoiling attack, to throw the NVA off balance while we continue our withdrawal," he said. But he kept the radio on until they sat down to dinner. It was obvious that Lieutenant Colonel Adam Thayer was still part of the U. S. Army.

That should have made it easier for her to tell him. Instead, it only became more difficult. After dinner, they sat on the porch talking about poets and novelists, comparing opinions about the new writers they had not had a chance to discuss in the last five years. They did not always agree. Adam liked the austere intellectual poets such as William Burford, the apocalyptic novelists such as Pynchon. Joanna was more enthusiastic about Sylvia Plath and Anne Secton, who made poetry out of the very flesh of their lives. But agreement was hardly important. It was the exchange of feeling, the mutual exploration of their loneliness that counted.

Again they made love with haunting, haunted delicacy and grace. At the end of it, there were tears on her cheeks again. He kissed them away. "Why?" he whispered.

"Nothing. It doesn't matter," she said.

The next morning a letter arrived from West Point. From Cadet Thomas Adam Burke.

Dear Mom:

The year of the yearling is almost over. Will I be glad to kiss it goodbye. I've gained another twenty pounds and think I've got a fighting chance to make the football team. They need a good cornerback. Had a letter from Dad yesterday. Is he proud of the way the ARVN 1st Division is fighting around Kontum! They're shifting him to be

adviser to the new 3rd Division. He's got to be the best the Army's got in that business now. Who can touch his experience?

Still not a word about his coming home.

Isn't that great news about Colonel Hardin making general? Everyone here is really pleased about it. I get a thirty-day leave starting July 1. Are you ready for some company at good old Mo Ka Lei? All I want to do is veg out on the beach and not think about anything, especially differential equations, for a couple of weeks.

Love

Tom

She showed the letter to Adam. He read it and dropped it on the dining-room table. "He's an interesting blend of you and Pete," he said. "I wish I'd managed that. Instead of getting one like me and one like Honor."

"Pookie may be like you. But she's a woman."

"What does that mean?"

"A lot," she said.

They went for a walk on the beach, past the retirees working in their gardens or sitting on the porches staring vacantly at the sea. Returning, the radio told them of the upheaval caused by the invasion of Cambodia. Riots had erupted on a hundred campuses. At Kent State in Ohio, National Guardsmen had killed or wounded almost a dozen students. President Nixon hurriedly announced a timetable for American withdrawal from Cambodia. "If that doesn't prove we've lost this war, nothing does," Adam said.

"And you're glad?"

"Sure," he said. "Why not? I told you a year ago why we deserved to lose it."

"Even if that's true—and I don't think it is—should you be glad?"

"Jesus Christ. Believe it or not, you sound like Honor."

"I don't consider that an insult."

Suddenly she could not bear the meaning of her own words. She fled past him out on the beach. He followed her. The sun was incredibly bright. It glared off the sea and sand, enveloping them, almost obliterating them in its noon ferocity. "I think there's something I don't understand here," Adam said.

"I respect Honor. I love her."

"Then it really is impossible. Us."

"Yes."

"What did it mean? What we've been doing?"

They were shouting at each other through the noon glare. They were eyeless, faceless in its brutal illumination. Their blinded words swung through its emptiness and drifted across the indifferent sea.

"Adam—I can't face it any more than you can. Let's wait. A little longer."

He strode back into the house. She walked the beach alone. Eventually she reached a deserted stretch of sand, where a huge ridge of brown and purple coral stopped her progress. Its innumerable hollows and edges were like the face of God. She flung herself face down, grasping the gritty earth with both her hands. Words spoke in her mind. *I take blindness as vision, deafness as hearing. I do not esteem my own spirit.*

She lay there, dry-eyed, for a long time, feeling the earth slowly shift beneath her. At twilight she arose and trudged back to the cottage. As she came in the door the radio was announcing: "U. S. ARMY SPOKESMEN ARE CALLING THE INVASION OF CAMBODIA A MAJOR SUCCESS. ENEMY CASUALTIES ARE ESTIMATED AT TEN THOUSAND. IMMENSE QUANTITIES OF RICE AND OTHER PROVISIONS HAVE BEEN CAPTURED." Adam sat before his map of Indochina. Without a word, she got out of the trunk her old Japanese tea service that Mrs. Togo had given her in Yokoshima. From the same trunk she took her tea mats and spread them on the porch. Then came a red kimono she had given Pete for Christmas and he had refused to wear, a blue-and-white kimono that Honor had given her. She handed the red one to Adam and put on the blue-and-white one.

He sensed her seriousness and put on the kimono. Boiling the water on the stove, she remembered the great rule of the tea master, Sen Rikyu. *To become expert one needs first love, second dexterity, and then perseverance.*

664

"Welcome to my little hut," she said as she poured the tea. "When you hear the splash of the water drops that fall into the stone bowl, you will feel that all the dust of your mind is washed away."

Adam recognized the words. He smiled. "I believe it was Sen Rikyu who said: 'If you have one pot and can make your tea in it that will do quite well. How much does he lack himself who must have a lot of things.' "

"Precisely," Joanna replied. "Many though there be who with words or even hands know the Way of Tea, few there are or none at all who can serve it from the heart."

Adam nodded. "Was it Sen Rikyu who also said: 'Though you wipe your hands and brush off the dust and dirt from the tea vessels, what's the use of all this fuss if the heart is still impure'?"

"Yes," Joanna said, and tears ran down her cheeks. Yet she managed to take the tea in three scoops, first a little, then a little more and then at last the largest amount.

She waited the required time and poured the tea, carefully wiped the pot and replaced it according to the ancient ritual. "When you take a sip from the bowl of powder tea, there within it lies reflected in its depths blue of sky and gray of sea," she said.

Adam smiled again. "What a lot of things just as though by sleight of hand can be done with you."

"I believe those words were directed by Sen Rikyu to his tea shelf."

"His double shelf, I think he called it. My words can also be applied to your double self."

She wiped away her tears and, after a few moments, served more tea. "In the winding path and the tearoom's calm retreat host and guest have met. Not an inharmonious note should disturb their quiet joy."

"Yes," he said.

She was calling him back to that moment in the Doubting Hut in Japan when he had recited for her—and her alone—the Samurai's creed. Calling him back to those dangerous, perhaps ruinous, but also magnificent ideals. Reminding him that this was the man she had loved.

The tears streamed down her cheeks. As a well-trained guest, he, of course, did not notice them. Calmly, he reached across the old kettle and bowls and kissed her hands. "You're right," he said. "You've always been right."

She closed her weeping eyes, unable to bear it. When she opened them he was gone. The kimono lay crumpled on the floor. She was alone again.

IV

THE Army car, with the single star of a brigadier general on the license plate, rolled down the main street of Quillen, Texas. Shop-windows full of the shine-in-the-dark civilian suits favored by the enlisted men glistened in the fierce noon sun. Other windows had dust-covered ads for Schlitz beer or Pabst Blue Ribbon surrounded by crinkled photos of the strippers on duty that night. Amy Rosser sat in the back seat of the car beside Nancy Edmiston, wife of Lieutenant Colonel Walter Edmiston, a battalion commander in the 1st Brigade of the 6th Armored Division, Lucius Carbondale, Major General, commanding, George Rosser, Brigadier General, assistant commander, support.

In front of the Left Face Café stood a bunch of T-shirted nineteen-year-olds, all with hair that came within millimeters of defying the regulation length. Their blue T-shirts had FTA printed on them in large yellow letters.

"What does FTA mean?" Nancy asked.

"Fuck the Army," Amy said.

"The GI movement," Nancy said. "We had them in Germany too."

"That bar is their headquarters. They publish a paper, also called *Left Face*. They profiled George in it last week. They called him a model fascist general. He's suing them for libel. They're finding out officers have rights too."

"God," Nancy said. "The Army is a mess, isn't it?"

"We're going to shape it up," Amy said. "We can do it, if we don't lose our nerve."

"It used to be fun," Nancy said. She began talking about their days at Fort McConnell, when Walter had been Henry Hamburger's aide and all they had to worry about was how to decorate the Officers' Club for parties. Like everyone in the Army these days, Nancy coated the past with nostalgia. She was conveniently forgetting what a pain in the ass Henry had been and what a bitchy little busybody she had been. Now Nancy seemed to be at the opposite extreme—limp.

"Do you ever hear from Helen Palladino?" Amy asked, acting on the axiom that a strong offense was the best defense.

"I got a Christmas card from her," Nancy said. "Jerry retired last year, at twenty. They're staying in Alaska, where they spent their last tour."

The loungers in front of the Left Face Café noticed the general's star on the car's license plate. They snapped to attention. But instead of saluting, they thumbed their noses.

"Aren't they charming?" Amy said. "Thank God we'll be getting rid of them in six months. The VOLAR is going to be a lot better, believe me," Amy said, using the acronym for the all-Volunteer Army which was soon to replace the draftees whose resentments and defiance fueled the GI movement.

"I hope so," Nancy said.

The listless tone of Nancy's voice was a sure sign that she was suffering from depression, the biggest bugaboo of the 1972 Army's wives. Amy had become an expert on depression since George got his brigadier's star and was assigned to Fort Cullum as assistant commander of the 6th Armored. She had organized a discussion group among the wives of the division's battalion commanders and urged them to organize similar groups with the wives of their junior officers. Most wives were desperate for a chance to ventilate the confusion and dismay everyone felt since the anti-war movement invaded the Army's ranks. Amy christened the discussion groups Can-Do Clubs. They had been a big success. The *Army Times* had done a feature article on them. The paper had run a picture of Amy accepting a commendation from Major General Carbondale.

A white-helmeted MP waved them through the gate of Fort Cullum. The huge base stretched ahead of them, group after group of old-fashioned boxlike barracks and drill fields, and beyond them, firing ranges for the 6th Armored and 11th Infantry Divisions.

"My God, it's big, isn't it?" Nancy said.

"Forty thousand men. Except for the weather, I like it. You can't get more Army than this. I prefer it that way. No civilian slobs around to point fingers and blat about the Army's way of doing things."

Nancy Edmiston nodded. She did not seem to be listening. Another bad sign. Her husband had arrived two months ago with their two children. He said Nancy was staying with her mother, who had had a stroke. Amy had suspected the story. She knew that an eager beaver like Walter Edmiston would go to great lengths to conceal any mental problems Nancy might be having.

"I'm surprised Walter didn't re-up for another tour in Germany," Amy said. "It's where the power curve is moving these days. George is going over there next month to become G-4 for the Seventh Army."

"It's my fault, I'm afraid," Nancy said. "I begged him to come home. The Army over there is a nightmare. The GI movement plus race riots. Drugs—"

"We've got all those charming problems at Cullum," Amy said. "You can't escape them."

Amy realized this sounded like a reproach. She began telling Nancy about the Can-Do Clubs. "I hope you'll join one," she said.

"Is it—required?" Nancy said.

"Of course not. But General Carbondale is very enthusiastic about them. I don't know any battalion commander's wife who hasn't joined."

"I need—a little peace and quite for a while," Nancy said. "Seeing my mother—got me down, I guess."

"Can-Do helps you ventilate down feelings," Amy said.

The driver stopped in front of Quarters 26, on Elm Street. It was no more than a bungalow, lying flat on the ground without a cellar or an attic. Paint peeled from the sides. "The housing is strictly World War II, I'm afraid," Amy said.

Nancy smiled wanly. "Walter warned me," she said.

The driver got her suitcase out of the car and opened the door. "Thanks so much," she said. "I really appreciate the welcome."

"Part of the job," Amy said, smiling into Nancy's bleached, sagging face.

Amy drove home looking forward to getting Nancy into a Can-Do Club. She would shape her up, and her husband Walter too, if necessary. There was no room for nostalgia in an Army wife's mental household. To be a successful Army wife, you had to learn to put the past behind you. Positive thinking was an absolute necessity. You had to stop blaming yourself for mistakes you may have made in the past. You had to accept the fact that everybody had limitations. The Army wasn't perfect, but was General Motors, General Electric perfect? By the time Amy reached her quarters on Peach Street, she had recited to herself practically every precept in the Can-Do Club credo.

In the living room, she found her overweight daughter Grace on the couch, letting a sallow-cheeked adolescent with a mouth like a dead fish nuzzle her breasts. Her blouse was open to the waist. Amy curtly ordered her to her room. She turned on the terrified suitor. "What is your name?" she snarled.

"Ronny—Ronny Flach," he said.

"What is your father's rank?"

"Sergeant. Master sergeant, ma'am."

"If I catch you anywhere near this house again, Ronny, your father will find himself in Korea twenty-four hours later. Do you understand?"

"Yes, ma'am."

Ronny vanished into the August glare. Amy stormed upstairs to tongue-lash her pudgy daughter. "It's bad enough to do that sort of thing in your own living room," she said. "But with a sergeant's son. Are you some kind of idiot? Are you trying to embarrass your father, like your sister?"

"He said if I didn't let him he'd get another girl. I don't have that many boyfriends, Mom. I'm not exactly Marilyn Monroe," Grace sobbed.

"You could be very attractive if you only stopped eating," Amy said. "You don't have the will power of a one-year-old. Do you want to wind up like your sister, sleeping with a half dozen different men each week? She calls it communal living. I call it prostitution."

"At least it's not as boring as Fort Cullum," Grace said.

After making a career out of being her mother's favorite, Grace was starting to talk back to Amy. It was a very unpleasant development.

"You'll be out of here in a month," Amy said. "You'll enjoy Norwood, even if it isn't the greatest college in the world. The social life is excellent. Mrs. Thayer—Pookie's mother—went there. Every year at least twenty or thirty girls still marry West Pointers. But you won't marry anybody—if you don't start losing weight."

"I'm not so sure I want to marry a West Pointer," Grace said with a pout. "Sometimes I think Georgie did the right thing, getting far away from the Army."

"She did *not*," Amy shouted. "She did not do the right thing. She has ruined her life. I've cut her out of my will. She'll get nothing from me. She'll be stuck in that commune forever. We'll see how she likes it in ten years."

This was not the first time Grace had made such ominous remarks. She knew that the threat to join Georgie always threw Amy on the defensive. Amy knew that the mention of the word *will* restored the balance of power.

Goddamn the kid, Amy muttered as she went back downstairs to inspect her living room. They were having another retirement ceremony this afternoon, the third this month. A colonel on the brigade staff. Amy was having a cocktail party for the man and his wife, after the parade. She ran her finger over every table and lamp base for dust. Teresa, her Mexican maid, did not have that English word in her vocabulary. Amy contemplated her Louis Quinze chairs, her Saigon lacquerware, her Bangkok figurines, her German porcelain and told herself she felt fine. She was secure in the fortress, the world she had created from her travels and adventures.

Goddamn the kid, Amy muttered again, as her head throbbed ominously. She did not want to think about Georgie. She did not want to remember those three months she had spent flying around the country conferring with police and private detectives, trying to find her runaway daughter. Calling Colonel Rosser long-distance in Saigon, telling him, humbly, no, nothing yet. Lying awake in miserable motel and hotel rooms, sleepless with sexual frustration and worry, wondering if she could hold her life together. It was amazing, the way George had changed after six months in combat. He had ordered her around like she was his servant. Or his child, who had disappointed and irritated him. At first she had loved it; awash in guilt, in loss of Adam, in the discovery that George was one of the brave.

During those three harrowing months of her search for Georgianna, Amy had begun reading every book on psychology she could find. She had decided to adjust, adapt to the new George that had emerged from Vietnam, to make a new beginning and forget the Amy who had been unfaithful and despairing in Bangkok, Saigon. She wiped the slate of the past clean with an act of the will. When she finally found Georgianna in the commune in San Francisco's Haight-Ashbury section, and the little bitch treated her with total contempt, Amy reacted with even fiercer resolve to ignore the implied accusation in her daughter's hatred. She even managed to convince George that the child was hopeless; it was fairly easy, since Georgianna unwisely mingled denunciations of the Army with her diatribes against her mother. George paid his namesake a visit on his way back from Saigon and came away sadly agreeing that Amy was right, Georgie was a casualty of the sixties, a captive of the anti-war crazies.

This victory, combined with the immolation of her old self, had enabled Amy to welcome George with genuine fervor. But something—she was not sure what—slowly dissipated her élan. Perhaps it was the difficulty of thinking of George as one of the brave when he trudged off to the National War College classrooms each morning and spent endless evening hours practicing the art of briefing. She must have listened to his spiel on the M-60 tank program twenty-five times before he gave it to his assembled classmates. Perhaps it was the dolorous fact that George may have learned to act like a general in Vietnam, but he was the same old humdrum George in the bedroom. Amy struggled fiercely to convince herself that this was all right. She was not an adolescent. She did not need or want kicks. By the end of the year she had that disappointment under control too.

She also heard the unbelievable story of Adam's banishment from West Point to a series of meaningless desk jobs in Asia. Florence Eberle was the tale bearer. Willard apparently had something to do with arranging this long-running long-range auto-de-fé. Florence said that only the tidal wave of bad publicity already engulfing the Army saved Adam from a court-martial. Willard in his wisdom had decided on another form of "elimination."

Amy stifled her sympathy, suppressed the regret, banished the thought that she could have saved Adam from this final blunder. She shook her head and tsked-tsked along with Florence. She told herself that this time she was finally through with Adam. He had talked about playing the game, he had hailed it as the only Army philosophy, but he had failed to play it. It made Amy concentrate with even greater intensity on her program to make George a general. By now, her card file contained over a thousand names. She was Florence Eberle's equal. In fact, Florence called her to get some names of "hot young colonels" for the series of dinners she gave as part of her campaign to get Willard his third star. Amy cheerfully supplied them, with George's name at the head of the list, of course.

Amy had even managed to stifle her revulsion for Willard Eberle. The thought of confronting Willard in Washington, D.C., had tormented her as she roamed the country in search of Georgie. She made a private vow that if he made another pass at her, she would invoke Adam's promise to come from the other side of the world, if necessary, to kill him. In spite of their farewell in Saigon, she was sure Adam would do it. But Willard displayed no further interest in her. Amy decided he was a scorer, a collector, always in search of new conquests. He was also too shrewd to have an affair with someone as clever and potentially dangerous as Amy Rosser. This did not stop Amy from experiencing a veritable efflorescence of hatred the first time she saw him. She concealed it behind a charming smile and a cheerful inquiry into his tennis game. She and George were soon playing doubles with the Eberles and Florence and Amy were having lunch once a week. She listened intently as Florence told her the inside story of the "high hurdles," as she called them, the really difficult jump from major general to lieutenant general. It depended almost totally on your friendships, your value to the people at the very top.

Amy also did not neglect Henry Hamburger, who was still deputy chief of staff for personnel. Milly Hamburger was delighted to hear from Amy; "a worker," she called her. Milly was head of the Washington Chapter of the Army Relief Society. They were planning a benefit and she was surrounded by people who called her with excuses about sick children and ailing mothers-in-law. Within a week, Amy was Millicent's mainstay. On the big night at the Kennedy Center (it was a performance of Leonard Bernstein's *Mass*) Amy had the exquisite satisfaction of being introduced by Millicent to the chief of staff at that time, General William Westmoreland, as *"my* chief of staff." George was introduced too, of course. Even he was impressed by that coup. Westmoreland, glancing at George's ribbons, asked him where he had won his DSC. George told him, with becoming modesty, and they had a five-minute discussion of the battle of Ban Me Thuot. Unfortunately Westmoreland retired three months later.

It was from Millicent Hamburger and Florence Eberle that Amy got the word that Vietnam was unpleasant ancient history, and Europe was where the power curve was moving. In fact, Milly, who was as shrewd as Florence behind her dithery southern-woman façade, suggested to Amy the perfect assignment for George after he left the National War College—command of the big Army firing range in Graffenwehr, Germany. "It seems like a nothing job," Milly said. "But I heard Henry say the other day that the last three colonels who had it became generals. Just about every general in the Army stops by there in the course of a year, and the commander gets to meet them and have them for drinks or dinner."

George had been dubious. He obviously did not like Amy resuming her management of his career. In fact, he practically demoralized her by wondering whether he ought to retire with twenty years' service. His older brother, now president of his own electronics firm, was urging George to join him in California. They would be closer to Georgie, and might be able to help her if she asked them. Amy had gotten somewhat hysterical and asked George to choose between "that tramp" and her. She got out the private detective's report on the sex habits of the commune and read it aloud to George. In the tender phase of their reunion, she had made only a general reference to it, and George had not asked to see it.

George accepted the assignment at Graffenwehr. It worked beautifully. They entertained no less than thirty general officers in the course of the year. George used his management talent to reorganize the logistics setup, saving about a million dollars by stockpiling ammunition on a more realistic schedule. That June, he got his star and away they whizzed to Fort Cullum.

Everything was going beautifully, Amy insisted, as she dressed for the retirement parade. A year from now, with the tour as the Seventh Army's G-4 under his belt, George would be in line for his second star. Henry Hamburger was retiring but Willard Eberle was still going to be around. He had gotten his third star and had recently completed a tour as commander of the Fifth Army in Chicago, a largely paper outfit. He and Florence were back in the Pentagon, where Willard was now deputy chief of staff for research and development. Just the sort of slot where George could make things go as Willard's deputy. R & D would keep George happy too. It would point him toward the civilian world. R & D people usually walked into cushy corporate jobs on retirement. Amy wanted to keep George happy. She wanted to make her marriage work. It was part of her job as an Army wife.

On the way to the parade, Amy checked the mail. An airmail envelope caught her eye. It was from Joanna Burke, still in that godforsaken cottage in Hawaii, according to the return address, teaching Army brats and mixed-blood morons in that public high school while Pete Burke went on trying to rescue the Republic of South Vietnam. Incredible how the boneheads like Pete and Sam Hardin remained involved in that mess, oblivious to the power curve. Amy had stopped off in Hawaii to see Joanna on the way back from Vietnam. It was fairly obvious that she and Pete had broken up—something else Amy had foreseen. In her Can-Do discussions, Amy often cited Joanna—without mentioning her name, of course—as the perfect example of what an Army wife should *not* be—perpetually brooding on life's wrongs, the Army's defects. God knows, she had some reason to be depressed, losing little Cissie in Saigon. But she had been that way before Cissie. Moreover, Amy had lost a daughter in Saigon too. Georgie might as well be dead. To hear George moan about her sometimes, she was worse than dead. But Amy did not let that depress her either. Not for one moment.

Amy glanced hastily through Joanna's letter. No personal news of any significance, just some stuff about how well Tom was doing at West Point—until the postscript. "I just had a letter from Honor. Adam's still at the Pentagon. He seems to be having problems with General Eberle. I remember Adam saying that he hated him. Do you know why?"

The retirement ceremony, with its review and blaring band music, seemed to last forever. The Texas sun bored into Amy's skull, in spite of the wide-brimmed straw hat she wore. Hank O'Connell, the retiring colonel, a big man, built like Pete Burke, stood at attention and accepted the dipping flags, the swiftly turned heads, of the final salute. His graying wife, Mary, stood beside Amy, dabbing at her eyes. O'Connell was class of 1943. A tough year to graduate. He had gone directly into combat in Europe, then more combat in Korea. Up until then, his career had looked promising. But he had refused duty at the Pentagon because he had five children and could not afford to live in the Washington area. His career had spiraled off into obscure assignments like the Rock Island Arsenal and Fort McCoy, Wisconsin. For the past year, he had been the 1st Brigade's inspector general.

Bland, Amy thought. O'Connell and his wife were both bland. But happy, in their simple way. At dances or dinners at the Officers' Club, they always arrived holding hands. George had not held her hand for a long time.

At the house, Amy discovered her Mexican cook, Rosalie, had burned the cheese hors d'ouevres. The house smelled like a fast-food joint. She ran around turning off the air conditioners, rigging exhaust fans at open windows. She was just getting things back in shape when George arrived with Major General Lucius Carbondale, the division commander. She apologized for the odor and Carbondale laughed. "Hell, we're used to it. Smells like a stripped gear in an old Sherman, don't you think, George?"

675

Amy did not think this was funny but she laughed very hard. Carbondale was one of the two-gun tanker types. His wife, Lorraine, was old Army, like Florence Eberle, cold as a gun barrel on the DEW Line. She commiserated with Amy about Mexican help. "They're on a par with Panamanians," she said. "I remember a cook we had in Panama—"

She launched an interminable story about a cook who could not tell fish from fowl. Other guests arrived. Amy smiled at them. The guests of honor appeared and George and Major General Carbondale greeted them. Amy was still stuck with Lorraine Carbondale, who was now telling her about an Eskimo cook they had had in Alaska. Amy noticed George slip away from Major General Carbondale and the O'Connells and head for Peggy Finch, the dark-haired, shapely wife of one of the 1st Brigade's battalion commanders. Memories of Helen Palladino crawled along Amy's nerves.

Smiling at Lorraine Carbondale's saga of horror in the kitchen, Amy felt a surge of almost uncontrollable jealousy. She told herself that she was being ridiculous. But the green demon still beat in her. She could not stop suspecting that George was liable to do to her what Willard Eberle had done to Florence: wait until he got his star and then start playing around. Once that first hurdle was cleared, generals did not need their wives in the way Amy wanted to be needed, as comrade, collaborator. The generals had access to each other, fellow members of a very exclusive club. They were still competing, of course, and a stupid wife could hurt them. But the need to be submissive, appreciative, affectionate to wifey, was no longer acute.

Amy happened to know that Peggy Finch was in a mood to fool around. She was having problems with her husband, who was dead-ending here at Cullum and was depressed about it. He wasn't a bad officer. It had something to do with a low OER he'd gotten on a previous tour. At the last retirement party, Peggy had spent a half hour in earnest, eye-batting conversation with George.

It was not just Peggy. Every time George went off to Houston or Oklahoma City to address an Association of the U. S. Army meeting on the Army's tank program or to some management seminar on computer technology, Amy pictured him in a motel with a stewardess or a bar girl. She told herself to stop, to go to sleep. George was not Willard Eberle. He went to church almost every Sunday. He was still his Methodist mother's dutiful son. But that too could be an act. He could be playing the game.

After the party the Rossers had a cold chicken and tomato salad supper with a surly silent Grace. George did not notice her mood. He retired to his den for the usual two or three hours of paper work and reading in his specialty, logistics management. The Army expected him to keep abreast of his professional field. Amy wondered uneasily if personnel had permanently slotted George for a staff man. If he was considered Willard Eberle's protégé, it was all too possible. That meant he would probably never get to command a division or an army—where a wife had responsibility, power.

She would not worry about it. She recited another line from the Can-Do Club credo. Let the future take care of itself. She tried to stifle all mental activity by watching a movie on television, a cops-and-robbers thing. Unfortunately, as a devotee of mystery stories, she had the plot figured out in ten minutes.

Going to bed, Amy felt sexy. Lately she had found herself wanting George whenever anxiety prowled her flesh. She needed some reassurance that she was reasonably happy with him. In the bathtub she stared down at her slim compact body and fought an overwhelming wish to be elsewhere, anywhere, in Bangkok, Saigon, with Adam or a twenty-five-year-old fly-boy.

No.

No.

No.

She was here, in Fort Cullum, and she had something to talk to her husband about. George was already in bed, reading a journal called *Computerology*. "That was quite a chat you had with Peggy Finch tonight," she said.

"Yeah. She's pretty upset," George said.

"The second long chat I've seen, in the past week. Any others?"

"What the hell are you talking about? She wants to know whether Jack should retire. He doesn't think he can make it on the outside. The Army hasn't taught him to do much but drive a tank."

She dropped it, satisfied that she had gotten another warning on the record. "I drove Nancy Edmiston in from the airport today," she said. "She's in pretty bad shape."

"I know," George said. "Walter told me about it. She couldn't handle Germany."

Amy was annoyed and found it difficult to conceal. "Why didn't you tell me?"

"Walter came to me as a friend. He's trying to keep it out of the files."

"I wouldn't put it in any file."

"I know. But—"

Amy felt even more irked. Her dislike of being excluded from the male world gnawed at her nerves.

"Wouldn't it be helpful—to get her into a Can-Do Club?"

George looked edgy. "I think it would do more good if I told Walter to stop trying so hard for his goddamn star."

"We wouldn't be living in a brigadier general's quarters if you took that kind of advice."

George looked even more uneasy. Amy realized that he had already given Edmiston the advice. "Worse things could have happened to us," he said.

How can you say that, you son of a bitch? Amy almost screamed. He was telling her that he didn't really care that she had made him a general. He was saying that all her years of migraines, of scheming, worrying, of listening to bores like Lorraine Carbondale, of swallowing her disgust every time she heard or thought of the name Willard Eberle, all that pain and shame and grief, meant nothing to him.

But she did not say a word. She went back into the bathroom and closed the door and stood there, shaking with rage, telling herself to be a well-adjusted wife. She did not sleep very well for the next several nights. But she remained a cheerful, smiling helpmate, the model Can-Do spouse.

A month later, Amy still seethed every time she remembered the conversation. She kept remembering it while she coped with another team of moronic packers and movers, all of them intent on destroying as much of Mrs. General's furniture and objets d'art as they could manage on the safe side of a court-martial. Amy's personal turmoil had made it difficult to do much for Nancy Edmiston. The troops in

Walter's battalion did nothing to contribute to Nancy's or Walter's equilibrium. Various companies tried to burn down their barracks four nights in a row. The most Amy could manage was a dinner invitation, at which Nancy and Walter looked equally haggard. Amy began to suspect that none of the battalion commanders in the 6th Armored were ever going to see a star. These nightly upheavals, the appalling desertion and AWOL rates, were all going in their records. It made her glad she and George were leaving for Germany at the end of the month. Even an assistant commander for support might end up getting tarred with some of those negative statistics.

After a raucous farewell party at the Carbondales', Amy and George and Grace flew to Andrews Air Force Base in Washington, D.C., and drove to the guest house at Fort Halleck. George had to confer with several senior logistics specialists at the Pentagon about plans to stockpile enough war matériel in Germany to equip divisions airlifted from the United States. Amy put Grace on a train for Norwood College and slipped her an extra fifty dollars to ease her through the first difficult weeks. She drove back to Virginia in her rented car. For no particular reason she could discover except a desire to kill some time, she found herself in Alexandria, on the street where the Rossers had lived in 1956. Little had changed, except the addition of a dozen or so shade trees.

She drove back to the impersonal room in the Fort Halleck guest house, remembering the conversation with George and the letter from Joanna. *Worse things could have happened to us. Adam was having problems with General Eberle*. In the room, Amy got out her address book, a condensed version of her card file, and yielded to a very impure impulse to dial Adam's number at the Pentagon. *Hello, Miles*, she was going to say. *Guess who's in town?*

A secretary answered the phone. "Is Colonel Thayer there?" Amy asked.

The girl started to cry. "No," she said. "He's in the hospital. He had a heart attack last night. I hope the bastards are happy now."

Amy hung up and dialed Honor. She got more tears and the whole story. Adam had persisted in being Adam. When his old boss, Newton Ingalls, returned from Vietnam to become chief of staff, Adam had sent him a memorandum, suggesting a study of body-count reporting in Vietnam. He said it would be a way of identifying a lot of liars and frauds in the Army, who should be forced to retire immediately. Ingalls did not even bother to answer him. But Willard Eberle regarded it as a personal insult and got Adam transferred to his R & D staff. Every day Adam got an action that would have taken three men a week to complete. He was told to have it on General Eberle's desk at 0800 hours the next morning. Adam would stay in the Pentagon all night, for a full week sometimes, getting no more than an hour or two of sleep at night.

"I begged him to go see General Ingalls or even Eberle and tell them that he'd keep quiet from now on," Honor sobbed. "He said some terrible things to me for givin' him that advice. So I told him to resign. We'd live on his pension somehow, no matter how little they gave him for his twenty-three years. He said he wasn't goin' to let anyone run him out of the Army. Now he's down in Walter Reed more dead than alive. But he says he's goin' right back to work as soon as the doctors let him. I was goin' to call you, Amy. I remember George worked for General Eberle. I was hopin' and prayin' you or George could do somethin'—anything'—he's goin' to kill Adam if he goes back there, I know he will."

"Honor, it's so—so—terrible," Amy gasped, tears streaming down her cheeks.

"Is there anything you can do?" Honor said.

"I'm not sure. I'll have to think about it. I'll talk to George. Willard Eberle is a very difficult, arrogant man."

"Bastard," Honor said. "He's the world's biggest bastard."

"Yes," Amy said.

She hung up and walked around the bare concrete-walled guest house room for a while. *Worse things could have happened,* George said. Amy got out her address book again and dialed Florence Eberle's number. She put a handkerchief over the mouthpiece and waited while the phone rang three times. On the fourth ring, Florence picked it up.

"Mrs. Eberle," Amy said. "This is a secretary from the Pentagon. I'm calling you to tell you that your husband is fucking me and every other woman in his office. You either fuck for General Eberle or you lose your job. In case you don't believe me, go out to the

Howard Johnson's on I-95. Pretend you're a private detective and ask the desk clerk how often a Mr. Willard comes there. Slip him five dollars and he'll tell you. He'll show you the signatures in the register.''

George returned from the Pentagon in time for cocktails. "I dropped in to see Willard," he said, sipping his martini. "He says he's got something very nice lined up for me when I finish this job in Germany.''

"Marvelous," Amy said.

George was in the mood that night, after they came back from dinner at the Fort Halleck Officers' Club. They were both a little drunk from martinis and a full bottle of Beaujolais. Amy felt tender in a new way. There was only so much a person could care about in a single life. When there were conflicts in caring, choices had to be made. She felt sad, but simultaneously exalted, not by George's lovemaking, but by the choice she had made. She told herself it was for the Army—the Army Adam wanted and would never get. Not for revenge. For the Army that she cared about in the right way now.

But not for George. Definitely not for poor George. She tried to make amends with love.

"Wow," George said as he washed up. "I'm going to give you a bottle of Beaujolais with dinner every night.''

The story was in the newspaper the next morning, a single column on the lower half of the front page. GENERAL DIES IN GUN ACCIDENT. It told how Lieutenant General Willard Eberle had been killed by a single bullet, apparently discharged when he was cleaning his .45. The bullet had struck him in the forehead. George almost cried when he read it. Not for Willard. But for George. Amy managed to make appropriate noises.

She let George call Florence and explain that they were booked on a flight to Europe that morning. Otherwise they would be with her for the funeral. Florence said she understood and there was no need to apologize. Willard's aides were taking care of everything. If there was one thing you learned to handle in the Army, Florence said, it was sudden death.

V

"Jo," said Sam Hardin's blurred voice, crackling and sputtering across four thousand Pacific miles. "I've got some bad news. Pete's missing. He may be dead."

Why was she so calm? Joanna wondered. Perhaps she had been expecting the call. That was simply not true. Everything she had been thinking and doing for the past four years was based on the premise that she would not receive this call. Pete Burke, survivor of Korean bug-outs, No Name Pass, the ambush-thick roads of Quang Ngai Province, the forests of Ia Drang Valley, Pete Burke was immortal. Others died of bullets and shells, other wives received these calls or telegrams from the impersonal bureaucrats at the Pentagon. But not Joanna Burke. After twenty-three years it was impossible.

But she had been expecting the call. A dread had prowled her nerves for three days, ever since the North Vietnamese had launched a massive attack across the demilitarized zone with their Main Force Army. The ARVN 3rd Division, which Pete was advising, collapsed and the entire province of Quang Tri fell to the enemy. The TV reporters had remarked, as a casual postscript, that a number of American advisers were missing in action.

It was not big news. Nothing about the war was big news anymore. There were no more American infantry, no draftees, left in South Vietnam. Only a relative handful of pilots and advisers—officers—which meant they were there because they wanted to be.

Joanna listened as Brigadier General Hardin, deputy commander of the First Region Assistance Command, the new name for the northern zone that included Quang Tri, told her what had happened. After the division's collapse, Pete had rounded up a few hundred men and made a stand on a hill south of Quang Tri city. For three days they held out against attacks by a full regiment of NVA regulars. Sam and the rest of the Region Command had used every Army helicopter and Air Force plane they could find to get him out of the trap. But heavy ground fire made it impossible. "They took to the bush, the last of them, including Pete, as the NVA poured into the perimeter from all sides. It was dark by then. If there's one guy in the U.S. Army who could fight his way out of that spot, it's Pete. But we haven't heard a radio signal from him for twenty-four hours."

"I appreciate the call, Sam."

"I had a long talk with him about you, Jo. Did he write you a letter? He said he was going to."

"No."

"He still loved you, Jo. He—I'll send you something to prove it."

The following day a slim boyish lieutenant from CINCPAC, the Pacific Command's headquarters in Honolulu, handed Joanna a transcript of the last radio contact with Pete. "General Hardin wanted you to have this, ma'am," he said. He explained the code words. General Hardin was Two-Fiver. Colonel Burke was Eight-Three. Joanna thanked him and he departed. She sat on the porch in the noon silence and read the laconic sentences, imagining them spoken over the roar of helicopter motors, the crash of shells, the chatter of machine guns.

"THIS IS TWO-FIVER, EIGHT-THREE. I'M COMING PRETTY GOOD. I'M STILL FIGHTING AND CHECKING. I'VE BEEN PROMISED A RESCUE CHOPPER IN TEN MINUTES, DON'T GO ANYWHERE."

HEAVY FIRING.

"THIS IS EIGHT-THREE. IT'S GETTING DARK DOWN HERE. THEY'LL OVERRUN US IN ABOUT TEN MINUTES."

"I'M WORKING AS FAST AS I CAN, EIGHT-THREE. HOLD OUT NINE MORE

MINUTES. KEEP THE LITTLE PEOPLE TOGETHER. WE'LL GET YOU ALL OUT. JUST HOLD WITH IT FOR NINE MINUTES. EVERYTHING'S AIRBORNE. I'M SENDING A LOW BIRD IN FOR A LOOK RIGHT NOW."

VERY HEAVY FIRING.

"WHERE'S THAT LOW BIRD? I DIDN'T SEE HIM."

"HE GOT SHOT UP BAD WITH .50-CAL. WE'RE PUTTING MORE ORDNANCE ON THE GODDAMNED STUFF. F-A-C, DO YOU READ ME? THIS IS TWO-FIVER. GET THAT STUFF WORKING IN THERE."

"THIS IS EIGHT-THREE. I'M LETTING THE LITTLE GUYS WHO AREN'T WOUNDED TAKE TO THE BUSH. SOME OF THEM MIGHT MAKE IT OUT."

"ROGER, EIGHT-THREE. YOU'RE THE BOSS DOWN THERE. BUT IF YOU CAN HANG ON FOR ANOTHER FIVE MINUTES, WE'VE GOT TWO MORE FLIGHTS COMING IN FROM DANANG. WE'LL STAY UP HERE ALL NIGHT LONG. DON'T GIVE UP HOPE. JUST PRAY AS I'VE BEEN DOING FOR YOU FOR THE LAST THREE DAYS—"

"THANKS. THEY'RE COMING INTO OUR TRENCH LINE. TELL JOANNA I LOVE HER."

"EIGHT-THREE? IT'S TWO-FIVER. OVER.

"EIGHT-THREE? IT'S TWO-FIVER. OVER.

"EIGHT-THREE? TWO-FIVER. OVER.

"NO CONTACT WITH EIGHT-THREE AS OF THIS HOUR. TWO-FIVER, OUT."

The war had ended. She remembered the earnest cadet begging her to understand the impossibility of a second lieutenant owning a Cadillac convertible, the gaunt soldier in the hospital bed in Japan, mourning his lost company, the bitter confused husband at Fort Leavenworth, the murderous soldier, holding up the glass of bourbon in the Saigon apartment, saying: *I see a lot of dead VC*. The husband whose trust she had betrayed at Seward State. She had known him as a boy, before history made him a serious dangerous man. He had known her as a girl, before she became an equally dangerous woman.

For the next week, Joanna ate and slept very little. She walked miles along the beach each day, and lay face down before the huge coral face of God. She did not pray for Pete's survival. She no longer believed in that kind of prayer. She simply recited over and over again the same koan that had appeared in her mind the day she had said goodbye to Adam. *I take blindness as vision, deafness as hearing. I do not esteem my own spirit.*

At times, in her lonely bed, grief shook her like a rattle. She died Pete's death in the jungle, the giant American surrounded by the small brown men who had miraculously survived his helicopters and artillery. Then grief would ebb and the whole thing would become mythic, a tale out of the Bronze Age. It had nothing to do with personal love, doomed children, lost ideals. The soldiers fought and died around her like figures in an ancient frieze, magnificent puppets in history's iron grip.

Toward the end of the second week, she glanced at herself in the mirror. She looked like a ghost. She had lost at least ten pounds. Through the center of her hair had appeared a two-inch-wide strand of gray. As she stood there, wondering if she were dying, she heard a helicopter clattering over the house. She was used to the noise. Helicopters and planes frequently flew over Mo Ka Lei on their way to various Army and Air Force installations on Oahu. But this helicopter was very low, and getting lower. She walked to the door and watched it land on the beach in front of the cottage. Sam Hardin, wearing summer khakis, a star gleaming dully on each shoulder, bent low to walk beneath the whirling blades. He carried a duffel bag in his hand.

Joanna sat on the porch and heard the end of the story. "Two of Pete's little guys made it back to Danang. They said Pete and about six others shot their way out of the perimeter the night they were overrun. They made it into the jungle but the next day they ran into an NVA patrol that outnumbered them ten to one. Pete told his guys to take off. The last thing they saw was Pete behind a log firing an M-16. There's no way he could have done more than buy time—"

"If he had to die, that was the way he would have wanted to do it," Joanna said.

"Officially he's listed as missing," Sam said. "We sent a patrol into the area to look for him. There was practically no chance of finding anything. The ARVN guys had no idea where it happened. I just felt it was something we should do."

685

"I don't need official statements. He's dead, isn't he, Sam?"

General Hardin nodded. "I brought his personal stuff from his hooch. Mostly letters from Tom, other people. None from you."

"I didn't write him any."

"Oh."

"I'm not a nice woman, Sam."

"I've got my own opinion on that one," he said, with a brief smile. "Could I—would you want me to see you again? I'd like to try to return some of that favor you did for me."

"I'd be glad to see you—anytime, Sam."

He touched her hand. "I'll call you."

As he walked toward the helicopter, she called: "Sam. Would you phone Tom at the Academy? I'd like him to hear the story from you. He can reach me here, anytime."

"Sure."

General Hardin boarded his helicopter. It clattered into the blue sky. Joanna sat on the porch and went through Pete's letters. The ones from Tom were full of war talk and Academy gossip—what she expected. But there was one from an unexpected correspondent that made her cry out with pain. It was dated January 25, 1968, five days before the writer was murdered by the Viet Cong.

January 25, 1968

Dearest Peter:

I understand why you spoke such loving words to me last night. I too feel the force of natural desire, urging me to express my love for you. But the respect I have for your excellent wife, the knowledge that we all act beneath the eye of God, makes this impossible. I hope you can bear this refusal. Now that I know how strong your feelings are for me, I find it immensely difficult to write these words. But I would like to believe that a love as noble as ours may become even stronger through denial—not cravenly chosen out of fear but because we are loath to soil its purity. There are worse things under heaven than unfulfilled desire. To die in dishonor, in sin. I could not let you face our murderous, treacherous enemy in that condition. . . .

The page shook in Joanna's hand. Tears streamed down her cheeks. There it was, proof that she had forfeited Pete's love. She could never hope to match this other woman, who embodied his supreme virtue—courage.

What had he meant by those farewell words as darkness closed in on his perimeter? *Tell Joanna I love her.* She found the answer in an unfinished letter, at the bottom of the duffel bag.

Dear Joanna:

This must be the twentieth time I've tried to write you this letter. This time I hope I finish it. I may not get a chance to write another one. We've got a lot of evidence that the North Vietnamese are coming across the DMZ with all the heavy stuff they can find. It's too much for my 3rd Division guys to handle. I asked Saigon for reinforcements but they turned me down. They're under too much pressure everywhere, in the highlands, the delta. It's only a matter of time before they collapse.

I saw Sam Hardin. He told me what you did for him. It made me realize you still cared about the Army. That meant maybe you cared—somehow—about me. In spite of what we said to each other that last night at Seward. I began to think maybe you were waiting at Mo Ka Lei because that was where we got it together for the last time, before Vietnam. Is that true? I hope so.

After the VC murdered Thui and her kids at Hue, I went sort of crazy. I swore I'd never come back until we won. I loved her. That's been mixed up with our argument. But you're still my wife, Jo. Tom's mother. I'd like to try to love you again, if you're willing—

Heavy shellfire. Looks like the NVA has moved up their schedule.

The letter ended with those last hastily scribbled words.

She wept for hours. Toward dawn she drifted down into a semi-sleep. Suddenly she was both awake and dreaming. She stood beside the bed, looking down at her sleeping body. A voice was calling her name. *Joanna. Joanna.* The sound mingled with the perpetual rush of the trade wind. Her dream self walked through the dawn-gray house to the front porch. About twenty feet from the beach, with the cold water swirling around her knees, stood Blanche Coulter in her black lace nightgown. *Joanna,* her drowned mouth called. *Joanna. Put on your mourning gown. Join me, Joanna. Death is so peaceful, Joanna. Everything stops, the blaming, regretting, forgiving, it all stops.*

She awoke trembling. Wasn't it the best way? whispered her own voice. She got up and dragged her trunk out of a closet and flung clothes out of it until she found it, near the bottom—the nightgown Blanche had given her. She sat down on the bed, the filigree black lace across her knees, shuddering now. Why was she doing this? Was it like Pete with the gun at Leavenworth? She had to look at it, face the possibility? She paced the house all day, with the nightgown on the unmade bed, defending herself against Blanche's voice. She had not sent Pete to his death in Vietnam. He had chosen it, he was no child, he knew the risks. She had been waiting here at Mo Ka Lei for him to return and renew their love. But the contrary was equally true. She had stayed here like the lying game-playing bitch she had become after Cissie's death, determined to make him crawl to her. Their broken love was not the whole reason he had stayed in Vietnam. But he had stayed as long as he thought the alternative was yielding to her obnoxious challenge.

Truths—human truths—don't cancel each other. They can coexist in the heart, like good and evil.

As darkness fell she found herself standing beside the bed, fingering the black lace. Lines from the poem about Blanche Coulter she had written long ago drifted through her mind.

> *Her eyes blot out*
> *Sorrow and remorse, faith and hope*
> *Death becomes a servant whom she casually summons.*

The telephone rang. Again and again and again. She finally answered it. "Mom?" Tom said. "General Hardin just called and told me about Dad."

She could see him in his gray cadet uniform. Around him loomed the stony comfortless battlements of West Point. "I thought it would be better—if you heard it—talked about it—one soldier to another," she said.

"He said some things about Dad I'll never forget."

He started to cry. She could not join him. She was a husk. "I knew he couldn't stay lucky forever," Tom said.

"No."

"I just wish—he'd come back to see you before it happened. I hate the thought of you and him—you know."

She told him what Sam Hardin had done to restore communications. She read him Pete's unfinished letter. "Mom," Tom said. "I can't tell you how much that means to me."

And I can't tell you, Joanna thought, how much this phone call means to me.

Tom wanted to come to Hawaii. But it was the middle of the term. He would miss precious class time. She told him it was not necessary. She was fine. He could call her anytime he wanted to talk.

When they hung up, she returned to the bedroom and put Blanche Coulter's nightgown back in the trunk. She shoved the trunk back in the closet and went for a long walk on the beach. The next day Sam Hardin called and asked her to dinner. She accepted. He drove down—helicopters were for official business only—and took her to a Japanese restaurant on Kahana Bay where they dined on sushi and shrimp tempura. Sam talked about Ruth and his sons. She had divorced him in California, and gotten half his salary for support. Ruth was drinking heavily and he had borrowed money to send the boys away to school. Sam discussed the war in Vietnam—what was left of it. He was bitter about the way Congress, yielding to the claque of the peace-at-any-price lobby, had slashed appropriations for the ARVN. "They've put a limit on how many shells their artillery can fire. That means they've got to use up men to take a hill." He told her about his boss in Vietnam, a major general, who had called a press conference to blast Congress's policy. "He knew he wasn't getting another star, so he figured what the hell. He sent me home before he made the statement. No point in ruining two careers, he told me. I think he got ten lines in *The New York Times*."

They drove back along the windward coast to Mo Ka Lei. There was no moon. At the house, she invited Sam to stay for a nightcap. They sat on the porch in the trade wind. "What are you going to do?" he asked.

"I don't know," she said. She told him about Pete's letter, what it made her realize. "I'm not quite as bad as I thought I was," she said. "But I'm still a long way from four point oh."

"Don't be so hard on yourself. I wasn't exactly a saint while I was married to Ruth." He hesitated, a little embarrassed by what he had just said. "I mean—when a marriage breaks up, there's always blame on both sides. You have to learn to live with your mistakes."

The next thing he said was obviously a logical step in his mind. "I know it's too soon to answer this, Jo. But someday—maybe six months from now—I'd like to marry you."

"No, Sam," Joanna said. "This time you deserve a woman who'll make you happy. I'm not that woman."

"I'm not asking you to make me happy," he said. "I can handle that on my own. I want you to be my wife because I think it'd be good for you—and good for me."

He was telling her, in his blunt Texas way, that they were too old for romance. He was also telling her a few other valuable truths. To stay here, clutching her memories, was futile and ultimately dangerous. She could not be sure what she would do if Blanche Coulter emerged from the sea with her siren song of peace again. He was also saying that he needed a wife who understood the Army.

"Think about it," General Hardin said. He touched her hand again. "Would it be all right if I called you for dinner next week?"

"Of course," Joanna said.

She thought about it, walking the beach in sunlight and starlight. *Suffering*, she thought. She was part of that now, the Army's suffering. From the darkness Pete had reached out to take Cissie from her arms. He had proved how much he cared, proved he fought for something larger than the next promotion. She had to respond to that caring, somehow. She began to think her response might include accepting Sam Hardin's offer. What was the alternative? To stay here on Mo Ka Lei, contemplating the scraps of wisdom, the shreds of humility, she had acquired? Zen told her there was no point to wisdom unless it was practiced in the everyday world. *How wondrously supernatural and how miraculous this! I draw water, and I carry wood!*

While she hesitated, the Army reached out to her with messages of regret for Pete's death. Amy Rosser, Martha Kinsolving, Honor Thayer, all wrote letters that Joanna read through tears. Honor said Adam was too devastated to write. George Rosser wrote a letter of his own, which surprised her with the intensity of its emotion. General Ingalls, the chief of staff, wrote another surprising letter, very personal, recalling the night they had met in Japan twenty years ago when he was an aide to General Stratton, declaring Pete the finest soldier he had seen in three wars, the personification of the West Point motto.

From Adam came not a word for a month. Then a night letter with only a two-line koan:

When the mouth wants to speak about it, words fail.
When the mind seeks affinity with it, thought vanishes.

Meanwhile, Brigadier General Hardin quietly, persistently pursued her. He took her to dinner at the Schofield Barracks Officers' Club. They talked about their children. Sam's two sons were doing better in school. Their anti-war frenzy was easing, along with the hysteria of the rest of the country. Through friends at West Point, he was keeping in close touch with how Tom was taking his father's death. They discussed Sam's career. Newton Ingalls wanted Sam to be secretary to the general staff, a job that had launched others toward multiple stars.

A burst of feminine laughter in the foyer of the club distracted them. They both looked toward the door. A tall fortyish brunette in a black chiffon evening dress appeared in the doorway. Joanna shivered.

"What's wrong?"

"That woman reminds me of Blanche Coulter. Arnold Coulter's wife."

General Hardin studied her for a silent moment. He knew what had happened to Blanche Coulter. He had been a company commander in Task Force Delta.

"That's Bud Callahan's wife, Lucille. He's my deputy at CINCPAC. You'd like her."

Reality, Sam was telling Joanna, was different from—and preferable to—dangerous dreams. Slowly, week after cautious week, he drew her into the Army world of Hawaii. He brought her to dinner at the Callahans' quarters. Lucille Callahan turned out to be an easygoing ingenuous joker, almost a total opposite to imperious Blanche Coulter. Shy Colonel Bud Callahan was equally different from flamboyant Arnie Coulter. They went to a luau at Fort De Russey beach with other members of Sam's staff and their wives. They went sailing off Diamond Head. On the water—and elsewhere, when they were alone—Sam let her talk—or say nothing—as she pleased. He was not a talkative man; life had excised the ebullience of his cadet days. But there was nothing gloomy about him. He seemed strangely—considering his personal past—undaunted. Part of it was his rank; being selected as a general does things for a man's ego. Part of it was inward, a determination, a resolution, to *be* undaunted, which undoubtedly had a lot to do with making him a general. This circular reasoning did nothing to solve the mystery of generalship. Joanna was not interested in solving it. For the moment she was content to absorb some of this quiet man's strength.

Toward the end of the second month, Joanna received a letter from West Point.

Dear Mom:

General Hardin called me the other day from CINCPAC. He said that he thought I should know that he'd asked you to marry him. He wanted to know how I felt about it. It isn't often that a mere cadet has a chance to tell a general that he can't do something. I was tempted to kid him a little, just to see what he'd say. But he was too serious about it. Anyway, I just thought you'd like to know that I told him I thought it was a great idea. I think it's something Dad would have wanted you to consider. That's all I'm going to say. I know a woman has a mind of her own on such matters.

Love,
Tom

About a month later, she returned from a dinner dance at Schofield and had a nightcap with Sam on the porch at Mo Ka Lei. He lingered, obviously hoping she would answer his question. He finally departed with the usual promise to call her for dinner later in the week. Joanna felt vaguely irritated at him, at his patience, at the pristine white world of Schofield Barracks. For the next three nights she slept badly. The spring term was ending and her restless pupils at Lcilchua did nothing to soothe her nerves. On the fourth night she did not sleep at all. At 4 A.M., after hours of pacing the dark windswept house, she lay in bed remembering Pete bouncing Cissie on his lap in Saigon, telling the Lindstrom boys not to blame anyone for their father's death.

Suddenly she found an alternative voice asking questions she could not answer. Why had the dark angel of forgiveness vanished? Was she forgiven? Or was she too despicable for forgiveness? Perhaps it no longer mattered who or what she in her desperation was now ready to forgive. Perhaps the question now was: What does she deserve?

Toward dawn the trade wind began to whisper *Joanna*. She began to regret the call from Tom that had rescued her from Blanche Coulter. Wasn't she being ridiculous, letting his distant love dissuade her from Blanche's invitation? All he had really done was make her realize the black lace nightgown was inappropriate, that it was necessary to make it look accidental. She would leave her towel on the beach and swim naked, as she did almost every morning. She would swim straight out, mile after mile, until her body became weary dross and she slipped down down into the ocean's silence.

No. She reached out on the magical wire to the same voice that had brought Pete's death and Pete's forlorn but undeniable love to her. She called Brigadier General Samuel Hardin at Schofield Barracks.

"What's wrong?" he asked.

"I—I can't sleep. I just thought—we might talk."

"Sure. What about?"

"Anything. What's the latest news from Vietnam?"

"Let's stick to good news. I just heard Tom's been made colonel of the 1st Regiment. Pete's old rank."

"Oh. I haven't had a letter from him this week."

"I read your poems."

"And—"

"I liked some of them. Some I didn't understand. You'll have to explain them to me."

"Sam—let me go. Find someone else."

"Just when I thought I was making progress? Why?"

"I told you I couldn't make you happy. I'm afraid I'll make you unhappy."

"What's wrong?"

"I remember too much, Sam."

"Who doesn't?"

He talked to her for a half hour about memories they had in common—some good, some bad. When she hung up the voice had vanished from the trade wind.

An hour later he was knocking on the front door. She met him on the porch in her muumuu, her uncombed, unwashed hair flying in the wind.

"Don't you know a woman my age needs some warning time to look decent?" she said.

"I'm worried about you. It's too damn lonely down here."

"I'm used to it."

"Jo. Before, you had a good reason to be here. Now it's gone."

"Which means I'm stupid? Or—"

"Just human, Jo. We hate to give up habits. Even bad ones. This place was a habit for you. A good one for a while. Now it's a bad one."

They stood there on the porch in the rush of the trade wind, the Pacific sun blazing on the beach and water. He was asking her to leave this refuge, to go back to the Army, to the world that had inflicted so many wounds, telling her, in his terse, authoritative way: *It'd be good for you.* The idea was laughable. The Army as healer of wounds? The Army as respite, refuge for the sleepless, the weary? Laughable.

But this man, with the bulky burly fighter's body, the chipped-from-stone face, was not laughable. His concern, his caring, was too visible.

694

"Why don't you set a date, Jo? I think that would—stabilize things."

"A date?"

"For the wedding."

She chose early September, a month away, a few days before the academic year started at West Point and other schools. Tom, and Sam's two sons, Bob and Dave, flew out for the ceremony, which took place in the Schofield Barracks chapel, with two chaplains, a Protestant and a Catholic, officiating. After a small wedding supper at the Officers' Club, they spent the night at Sam's quarters. She had vetoed a honeymoon. She knew Sam could not afford one. She said just being in Hawaii was a honeymoon.

He let her bathe first, then showered and joined her in bed. She was tense, uncertain how she would react to this decisive moment. Was she capable of loving this man—of loving anyone? Had memory turned her into an unfeeling zombie? She stopped worrying a moment after he kissed her and lifted the nightgown over her head. The general knew exactly what he was doing. The remark he had made, about not being a saint while he was married to Ruth, took on considerable specificity. He was a very skillful lover.

Swiftly his hands, his lips, created desire in her body. She welcomed it as a woman, returning to the real world of male and female. She welcomed it as Joanna-the-fugitive, glad that her flight was ending. As he entered her, she gave a sad-sweet sigh, almost a shudder. She was being entered by, she was reentering time, history, she was regaining her life, the one she had chosen, the one that had in so many mysterious ways chosen her. She was engulfed by a flood of gratitude, affection for this tactiturn soldier.

Just before they went to sleep, Sam drew her to him again for a long tender kiss. "Why in hell were you worried about making me happy?" he said.

VI

Mrs. Adam Thayer and daughter. Signing the register of the Hotel Thayer, the former Honor Prescott almost smiled. Right in the faces of her solemn mourning daughter and the solemn evening clerk.

Honor was thinking of Adam, what he had whispered to her one of the first times he escorted her into this looming stone pile just inside the grounds of the United States Military Academy. "Someday, when the old man goes, all this will belong to us."

Good memories. Honor had asked Jesus to help her concentrate on the good memories. Not the bad memories of the middle years or the sad memories of the last years with Adam. It was all for the best, she was sure of it. Adam was at peace now. The country was at peace and Adam was at peace.

Honor had tried to tell this to Pookie coming up from Washington. But she was not listening. She sat beside her mother, staring at the hearse on the highway ahead of them. Pookie was taking her father's death very hard. Honor understood the feeling. She remembered her own father's death.

At the West Point gate, an MP car, summoned by the white-gloved sentry, had met them, its dome light flashing. The MP's had led the hearse up Thayer Road beside the gloomy mist-shrouded Hudson. West Point weather. Just right for a soldier from Maine. The sergeant in the MP car had given her a poop sheet, telling her exactly when the funeral would begin, where to rendezvous. Very

696

Army. All laid on, spelled out. The Army laid it on for Adam, for their own.

They unpacked and went down to dinner. "I remember the first time your father took me to eat here," Honor said, looking around the almost empty room on the hotel's first floor. "It cost him a dollar more than he expected and I had to lend him the money. For the rest of the weekend he pretended I'd bought him as my slave. He kept callin' me mistress and then he started introducin' me to people usin' that name. You should have seen the expressions on their faces!"

"He was a real joker," Pookie said, but she did not even smile at the story.

Pookie ordered a martini on the rocks to start. Honor ordered a 7-Up. She had stopped drinking alcohol. Father Rausch did not think a person who believed in Jesus had to stop drinking. He was no Baptist. But liquor was no longer necessary. With Adam drinking so much in the last years, Honor stopped, trying to show him a person did not need alcohol to face life. Alas, Adam had kept right on drinking.

Honor ordered filet of sole for dinner. She was on another diet. But she weakened and chose Boston cream pie for dessert. "I had it that first dinner here. Your father teased me into it. He said it was the pie of his people. I'd never had it before. I think he was tryin' to get me fat, even then."

Pookie had a piece too. She would not gain an ounce. They were finishing the last creamy chocolatey bites when a red-bereted paratroop lieutenant appeared in the doorway of the dining room.

"There's Tom Burke. I didn't know he was coming," Honor said.

Tom walked toward them, smiling. Honor almost wept. He looked so much like his father. Pete and Adam, both gone. She remembered Adam saying: *When Burke here becomes general of the armies and I'm his chief of staff.* Honor asked Jesus for strength, courage to smile, not to weep. She would have years to weep.

"Hello," Tom said. It was Pete's deep voice. He kissed Honor on the cheek and Pookie on the lips. "How are you?" he said. As he sat down he reached across the table and took Pookie's hand.

"All right," Pookie said.

"We're fine," Honor said. "We're ready for the last salute."

Tom nodded. He looked terribly down. "I feel as bad as I did when Dad died," he said.

"It's for the best, Tom," Honor said. "You know how unhappy Adam was."

"If he'd taken better care of himself—I can't understand why he couldn't or wouldn't take more interest in writing the history of the war."

"He always said he wanted to do, not teach," Honor said. "I guess he thought of writin' as another kind of teaching."

"The Army needed that book," Tom said.

"I'm going to finish it for him," Pookie said.

"Your mother and—and Sam are having dinner at the commandant's," Honor said. "They wanted us to join them but I didn't feel up to it. The Rossers are comin' up from Washington later tonight. Isn't that nice? I mean—two generals droppin' everything and comin' up here to pay their respects—"

"It's the least they could do," Pookie said.

Tom nodded. Honor wasn't sure whether he agreed with her or Pookie.

"Have you had anything to eat?" Pookie asked Tom.

He shook his head. "Want to walk into town with me? All I need's a sandwich."

"Sure," Pookie said. "Do you mind, Mom?"

"Of couse I don't mind," Honor said. "Go ahead right now. You can have coffee with Tom, Pook."

They departed instantly. Honor noticed that Tom took Pookie's hand as they went out the door. If ever she'd seen a boy who was in love, it was Tom Burke. But Pookie was terribly unresponsive to him, it seemed to Honor. When she tried to talk to her about it, Pookie cut her off, Adam style.

Alone, Honor ordered another piece of Boston cream pie with her coffee. She admitted to Jesus that it was absolutely unforgivable but it tasted so good—and it reminded her again of Cadet Thayer, sitting across the table from her, declaiming: *I knew the South was culturally deprived. But I never realized they hadn't heard of Boston cream pie. One of my ancestors, Old Blubber Thayer, we used to call him, invented it.*

Honor went upstairs, took a bath and read a few pages of a small New Testament Father Fausch had sent her. It fit in her purse. It was easy to read on trains and buses. Her favorite passage was the story of the centurion who told Jesus: "Lord, I am not worthy to have you come under my roof." She had read it to Adam one night when he was too drunk to stop her. He suddenly recited the whole thing to her. His memory was amazing. "For I am a man under authority, with soldiers under me; and I say to one 'Go' and he goes and to another 'Come' and he comes." Then Adam had sat there and said over and over to himself, "I am not worthy, I am not worthy," until he started crying and she started crying and she had held him in her arms for a long time.

The telephone rang. "Hello, Mom?" Matthew Ridgway Thayer said.

"Matty, how are you?"

"Great, Mom. Things are going good in school. I got past my midterms. How are you feeling? I thought I ought to call and let you know I'm thinking about you—and Dad."

"I'm fine, Matty," Honor said. "Do you need any money?"

"I could use an extra fifty. I'm dating an expensive girl."

"Which one is this, now?" She could not keep track of Matt's numerous girls. He had run off to Canada with a Vassar dropout he had met at a peace march. Since that time he had had a half dozen other girls. Fortunately Honor was able to support his expensive habits. Her mother had died in 1971 and Bobby Southworth, Sr., had sold the family farm to a developer for $300,000.

Matt began explaining that his latest girl was French-Canadian, the daughter of a politician. Honor only half listened. Matt's refusal to serve in the Army for even two years had changed her feeling for him. He was still her son, she sent him money, but the sympathy, the caring that she had lavished on him when he was struggling to cope with Adam's dislike of him had vanished.

"What are you going to do, Mom?" Matt asked.

"I don't know. I'm in no hurry to make up my mind," Honor said.

"Why not come up here? Canada's a great country, Mom. No wars. They haven't fought a war for thirty years."

"Too cold for my southern blood, Matt."

Matt sounded a little hurt. So be it, Honor thought. "Well—I just thought I'd call," he said. "It must be a tough time for you."

"I'm fine, Matt. In some ways I feel closer to your father than I've felt for a long time."

"Praise the Lord," Matt said wryly. He had lost his religious feelings.

"Jesus has been a real help, Matt."

"Yeah. Well, so long, Mom. Send that money, okay? Fifty?"

"Yes. Keep studyin' hard now."

Honor hung up and sat there for a long moment. Did she really mean that, about feeling close to Adam? A sudden awful emptiness seemed to surround her. She thought of Adam silent in his coffin somewhere on the post, in a dark basement. Alone. Adam was alone and she was alone now. Without a man. *Jesus,* she prayed, *I really need you now.*

Pookie came in about ten o'clock. Honor took one look at her flushed cheeks and shiny eyes and knew she had had more to drink. With Adam's history, Honor worried about Pookie. When she graduated from Vassar and went to work at the Pentagon, Pookie started drinking with Adam at night until Honor stopped it. She told her either to stop drinking with her father or to move out. Pookie had stopped, but the tendency was there. Honor was tempted to scold her. But she did not want to risk an argument.

"You look like you had a good time," she said.

"Yeah," Pookie said, walking past her to stare out at the fog-shrouded river. "I always have a good time with Tom."

"Is he staying at the Thayer?"

"No. He and a couple of other ATG's are staying in a motel on the highway."

It took Honor a moment to remember that ATG stood for the Adam Thayer Group. Tom was the leader of this dozen or so cadets from the class of '73. They had created this unofficial organization as a sign of their admiration for Adam. They often visited him in

Washington. They discussed the history of the war in Vietnam that Adam had been trying to write.

"Tom's a wonderful boy," Honor said.

"Yeah."

"You don't agree?"

"I do agree. He wants me to marry him."

"Why can't you put it the other way? He wants to marry you?"

"I mean—I like sleeping with him. He's terrific in bed. But I'm not sure I can handle the Army."

Honor tried to absorb that double shock. She decided to say nothing about the sleeping remark. It was Pookie's business. Honor did not approve but it was her generation's style. "Why—why can't you handle the Army?" she said.

Pookie whirled, her narrow face twisted with grief. "Look at yourself, Mom. Look in the goddamn mirror. Did you handle it?"

"I—I did my best," Honor said. She tried to ask Jesus for help, for a better answer, but no words came. "It isn't an easy life. But I think you'd be happier with Tom than I was with your father."

"You mean you're encouraging me?" Pookie said. "You can sit there and encourage me? Knowing what the Army did to Dad? How they screwed him, destroyed him, because he had principles, ideals? Because he wouldn't kiss anyone's ass, no matter how many stars were tattooed on it? Why don't you hate it? What's wrong with you?"

Wrong? She could tell Pookie a lot of wrongs. A whole column of them, marching over the horizon, crying out Honor's wrongs. But she was not going to think of wrongs now. Not when she was trying to feel close to Adam, not when she had come to West Point for a final reunion before farewell.

"Honey," she said. "You don't understand. You're too young. You don't understand how it all happened. It's complicated. It's part us—and part history now. We lived through it, and it did things to us. But what we were before it started—that was important too. What Adam was. He never could have been a general. It wasn't in him. He didn't—really love the Army enough."

Pookie was shaking her head back and forth, back and forth like the rag doll that Honor remembered from her childhood. The rag doll for whom Pookie was named. *She looks like a rag doll I had when I was five,* Honor had said in the Boston hospital. *A rag doll named Pookie.* And Pookie she became. Now the poor blind doll, knowing only how to wag her head, was alive before her.

"Pookie, stop, please," Honor said, feeling the hysteria surging in her throat.

"The goddamn Army's got you," Pookie said. "Duty-honor-country. It's got you just like it's got everyone, even Joanna. Even—me."

Would Adam smile at those words? Honor would not be surprised if he was listening somewhere, somehow. Suddenly she was very calm. She knew the answer. As if Jesus—or Adam—had whispered it in her heart.

"Honey," she said, "that's not as bad as it sounds. In spite of everything I'm proud to have been—to be—an Army wife."

VII

WALKING along Thayer Road in the dawn, Joanna felt curiously free; perhaps she was simply light-headed from lack of sleep. West Point was shrouded in November mist again. The Hudson was a gray blank. She found herself thinking not of the past but of the present, of the problems she had finding volunteers to staff the Army Community Service Center at Fort Bellin, South Carolina, where Major General Hardin was the current commander of the 106th Airborne Division. Another worry was a symposium on career possibilities for Army wives that she was organizing. At the end of the week loomed a dinner for three congressmen from the Armed Services Committee. She and Sam had yet to decide whom to invite from the division staff.

In her room at the Hotel Thayer, Amy Rosser stared out at the fog-bound river. She had sat up most of the night reading a mystery story. George snored peacefully in his bed; an odd snore, a steady purr that reminded Amy of one of his computers whirring. Around 7 A.M. Amy's head began to ache. By 7:30 she had an unreal migraine. The headaches had become almost daily events since South Vietnam collapsed six months ago. Watching that last humiliating scramble for helicopters and boats had stirred memories of that other American defeat on the Chongchon River in North Korea, of Adam in Saigon mordantly predicting what she saw on the television screen. Being in Germany made it worse, not only for the memory it evoked; the obsequious losers she had known in 1950 seemed to be smirking at her from their sports cars and Mercedeses. George was no help. He blatted the Pentagon line that it was the South Vietnamese Army, not the American Army, that was losing and went to work each day at Seventh Army headquarters in Augsburg as if nothing had happened. Amy found herself yearning for the rage, the contempt, Adam would have showered on this national disgrace.

By eight o'clock Amy was seeing halos around lights and around George's drowsy face as he sat on the edge of the bed, scratching his balding head and yawning cavernously. She decided to risk an ergotamine, the drug of choice for migraine. They worked quickly, but if you took too many of them, you could become addicted, and the withdrawal headaches were worse than the migraines. A choice of difficulties, like everything else in life, Amy thought, as she gulped the pill.

Honor slept fairly well until she was troubled by a dream in the dawn. She and Adam were in some sort of camp on a jungly hill in Vietnam. Black smoke billowed from huts and holes in the side of the hill. Adam's face was smeared with soot. He was crying. "My Rhade," he kept saying. "My Rhade." She put her arms around him but he did not seem to notice her. Then out of one of the holes came a soldier with a flame thrower. He aimed it at them and there was a great *whoosh* of flame. Adam shoved her away just in time but he was struck by it. He danced in the flame, crying, "Yes, yes." Trembling in the gray light, Honor realized it was a dream Adam had often had in the last years. He had told her about it once.

When Joanna returned to her room, Sam's travel alarm was just going off. He sat up, instantly wide awake, as usual. "How'd you sleep?" he asked.

"I didn't," she said.

"Not at all?" he said, getting up and putting his arm around her.

"I'm all right. I really am."

He looked into her eyes for a moment. "I think maybe you are," he said.

At the end of Sam's year at the Pentagon as secretary of the general staff, they had journeyed to West Point to watch Thomas Adam Burke graduate. A week later, Joanna had spiraled into nights of bleak exhausted sleeplessness. She sat in her room and wept by the hour. At Sam's insistence, she had retreated to Walter Reed Hospital, where anti-depressant pills and daily talks with a gifted woman psychiatrist enabled her to see that she was suppressing her fear that Tom might die at the head of an infantry company, like Rod Coulter. In two months she had been ready to join Sam in Germany, where he was struggling to cope with an infantry division wracked by the backwash of Vietnam.

Amy dialed the desk and got the room numbers of the Hardins and the Thayers. She called them and suggested they have breakfast together. Honor was agreeable. Joanna said they would have to wait a half hour. Sam was out jogging. "He's trying to keep up with his twenty-five-year-old airborne lieutenants," Joanna said. Amy agreed to wait but she hung up, irked. George emerged from the bathroom in his undershorts. Amy glowered at the spare tire around his waist. It would never occur to him to go jogging. He was turning into a slug. Then her eyes found the pale skin on his arms and chest, relics of his burns at Ban Me Thuot. He was still one of the brave. A little overweight, but one of the brave.

"Sam's out jogging," she said. "You ought to take that up."

"I should," George said. For some time now, George had adopted the policy of agreeing with what Amy said, but not necessarily doing it.

"You could organize the whole computer center into a jogging club. It would make good copy."

"It would," George said, donning his T-shirt.

Honor spent the extra half hour before the mirror combing her hair and putting on her makeup. Pookie, already dressed, paced the room impatiently. She had wanted to wear a pantsuit to the funeral service, one of several she regularly wore to her job at the Pentagon. But Honor had insisted on a skirt. Pookie had retaliated by wearing it with a plain white shirt and a small black tie.

Honor told Pookie about her dream. "Bong Son," Pookie said. "I'm going to open the book with that story."

"Are you really going to write that book?" Honor asked.

"You bet I am," Pookie said.

"Wouldn't it get Tom in trouble, if you marry him?"

"Who says I'm going to do that?" Pookie paced the room for a while. "Whether I marry him or not, he's going to write it with me."

"How long will it take?"

"Years."

Pookie paced while Honor did her eyes. "Come on, Mom, for God's sake, you look okay," she finally said.

"I'll decide that," Honor said. "While we're on the subject, I think you should start to use a *little* makeup. Pretty soon you'll be too old to get away without it, Pook."

"You really think so?" Pookie said, studying herself in the mirror. "What do you think I should use?"

Stepping into the elevator beside Sam, Joanna found herself face to face with Honor. She felt her throat fill with tears. She was glad that Honor had declined the invitation to join them for dinner at the commandant's quarters with Martha and Vic Kinsolving last night. She was ready to face her now. They hugged each other for a moment and Joanna said: "I don't have to tell you how I feel."

Pookie stood beside her mother, expressionless, her wide gray eyes blank shards in her narrow face. "How are you, darling?" Joanna said, kissing her too.

"I'm fine," Pookie said in that toneless voice that Joanna suspected was reserved for the older generation. She could not imagine why her son Tom liked this girl so much, if she really was the dry stick figure she seemed intent on personifying.

"How is everything down at Bellin?" Honor asked.

"Hectic," Joanna said. "Not as bad as Germany, though. That was a real nightmare."

"Not as many discipline problems at Bellin," Sam said. "More fun jumping out of planes. Except for guys my age."

Amy and George were in the lobby when the Hardins and the Thayers emerged from the elevator. Amy gave everyone heartfelt kisses, really heartfelt. Joanna smiled at her with that same fuzzy disconcerting look she had had at twenty-two; Amy was still tempted to suggest she get her eyes checked. Why didn't she dye that gray streak? For some reason it struck Amy as a reproach. Or did she envy it because it was a sort of decoration? God knows, the girl—woman—was entitled to wear it. But others had been through some *Sturm und Drang* too.

Joanna did not look like she had slept very well, Amy decided. The only one who seemed rested was Honor. Still beautiful, even if she was thirty pounds overweight. That indestructible face; what she could have done with that face, Amy thought.

While George was politely kissing and condoling, Sam Hardin pecked Amy on the cheek and added a muscular squeeze that came naturally to him. He looked as trim and tough as the jungle fighter she had invited to her dinner table in Saigon in 1963. She wondered if he still chased girls. Amy could not imagine Joanna being very exciting in bed. At least she had no more worries with George in that department.

The two generals, ex-roommates, shook hands, while Amy winced. She had braced herself for pain. It still hurt, to see two stars on Sam Hardin's shoulders and only one on George's. At the rate Sam was going, those two stars would soon be three. Only the comers got command of airborne divisions.

"Keeping track of my assets, hotshot?" Sam said with a grin.

As the commander of the Army Logistics Commander Computer Center, George was responsible for the whereabouts of all the Army's far-flung equipment.

"Got a couple of crutches reserved for you," George said. "Anyone who jumps out of planes at your age is going to need some."

"You may be right," Sam said. "I ache all over after every landing."

They strolled to the dining room. Honor thanked George and Sam for coming, as everyone sat down. "I'm sure you're overwhelmed with work, like most generals," she said.

"This is more important than anything short of Condition One," Sam Hardin said.

"What happens then?" George said. "You guys down in Bellin start to get organized?"

"No. You line up your computers and attack. You'll be immortal, George. You and the guy who led the Charge of the Light Brigade."

Joanna smiled tolerantly at Amy. "They're just like Adam and Pete used to be. I wonder if anyone's ever done a psychological study of West Point roommates."

George grinned amiably. Amy forced a smile. It was hard for her to admit, but George did not mind being passed over for promotion to major general. In Europe, after Willard's demise, she had begun planning dinner parties at a frantic rate, ransacking her card file for politically potent names. George had sat her down in that calm firm way he had acquired since Ban Me Thuot and told her to cool it. He said that Willard's death had convinced him it was silly to work so frantically at the career game. Promotion was mostly luck, fate. He had held her hand in his sentimental way and told her that he wanted her to relax and enjoy this tour in Germany. He wanted it to be a second honeymoon. Amy had been touched—and then gradually rueful, as she realized how much she missed the thrust and parry, the maneuvering and politicking of the career game.

"I'm going to suggest it to General Ingalls," Joanna was saying in a jocular tone. "I'll write it. The title will be 'Should West Point Roommates be Allowed in the Same Army?'"

Amy winced inwardly again, this time at the name Ingalls. She was convinced that not a little of Sam Hardin's astonishing rise had to do with Joanna's friendship with the chief of staff. Two years ago Florence Eberle, still industriously collecting and distributing high-level Pentagon gossip, had written Amy that half the Army wives in Washington were turning green at the way Ingalls fussed over Joanna at dinners and cocktail parties. Apparently it was a combination of guilt over Pete Burke's death and Ingalls' pretensions to being an intellectual. Half the time he and Joanna discussed poetry. Incredible.

"Where are your daughters living these days, Mrs. Rosser?" Pookie Thayer asked.

Honor could see that Amy did not want to answer the question. "Georgianna is still living in San Francisco," she said in an edgy way.

"In a commune," George Rosser said. "It's not as bad as it sounds. They don't use drugs. They weave rugs, make pottery. She sent us a pot last Christmas. It was a nice job."

"Grace is a junior at Norwood," Amy said.

"My alma mater," Honor said. "Is she dating a cadet?"

"She's been to some of the hops," Amy said.

"Still as fat as ever?" Pookie asked.

"Yes," Amy said, discomfited again. "This year she's on a diet that's going to work or else."

"Or else we'll try another one next year," George said.

"What are you doing, dear?" Amy asked Pookie.

"Working at the Pentagon. In the Office of Defense Analysis."

"As a secretary?"

"No. As a special assistant to the Undersecretary of the Army."

"My God," Amy said. "They're robbing the cradle. You don't look old enough for that job. Really, Joanna, don't you agree she doesn't look a day over sixteen?"

Your turn to squirm, Amy thought. Wishing, at the same time, that the girl did not look so much like Adam. Why did Pookie dislike her? Amy wondered. Probably because she considered her a friend—and George a protégé—of Willard Eberle, her father's enemy. She suddenly wanted to take the girl aside and tell her the truth. *I loved Adam. I tried to help him.* But it was impossible.

Sam and George began telling stories from their cadet days about the wacky things Adam said and did. Joanna recalled the time he visited her in Japan and did a marvelous imitation of a French legionnaire. Amy recalled the day of the coup against Diem in Saigon, when Adam had tried to talk George into joining the Green

Berets. She made it sound funny, describing how George's eyes had almost popped out of his head. Honor found herself wishing the breakfast could last forever. It was so sweet, so comforting, to be surrounded by these old friends, talking about Adam with so much affection.

But it had to end, like all things good and bad. Generals Hardin and Rosser tussled for the bill. Sam won. "Let the airborne handle it, George," he said. In the same take-charge style, Sam insisted that Honor and Pookie ride to the chapel with him and Joanna. Honor agreed, although she thought Amy looked disappointed. George had a car and driver too.

As they drove along Thayer Road, Honor looked mournfully up at the houses of the faculty colonels. "There's where I always wanted to live. I always thought Adam would have been happier if he just stayed here and wrote books."

"No doubt about it," Sam Hardin said.

Passing Trophy Point, Honor remembered Ruth Parrott on the cannon, singing that crazy song about becoming officers' wives for the rest of their lives. She wanted to mention it, but she was afraid it would upset Sam Hardin. He probably wanted to forget Ruth. To Honor's surprise, Joanna recalled it. "She was right for all of us, except herself," she said.

"Do you ever hear from Ruth?" Honor asked.

Sam shook his head. "My oldest boy keeps in touch with her," he said. "She's living with her mother in California."

Classes were changing as the Rossers' car rolled past the Academy's barracks and classroom area. Dozens of cadets saluted the star on the license plate. Amy found herself renewing her determination to diet Grace down to marriageable size and make sure she went to every hop for the next two years. Grace rather liked the Army. There were bound to be one or two shrewd cadets who could see the advantage of marrying a girl with a general for a father and a trust fund in her future. It would be interesting to guide an officer son-in-law through the career labyrinth. Amy pictured him as major, lieutenant colonel, writing his gray-haired indomitable mother-in-law for advice.

Near Trophy Point the cars wound down the hill to the old cadet chapel beside the West Point cemetery. With its four Doric pillars and classic pediment, the building was more like a Greek temple than a church. Honor remembered Adam telling her how he used to come down here on Sunday afternoons at twilight and meditate on the great names that had worshipped in this building in their cadet days. Now it was only used for funerals. The interior, with its white pillars and heroic painting, "Peace and War," over the chancel, was as chaste and severe as the outside. It matched her grief, Honor felt. It evoked the Ashley she had loved.

Inside, before the altar, lay Adam's coffin, covered with the American flag. Joanna thought of the coffins at Tan Son Nhut Air Base. She was distracted by a smiling face, looking directly at her from one of the center pews. It was her son Tom, with four or five other second lieutenants. Hot tears leaped into her eyes. He looked so much like Pete. For a panicky moment she felt time unreeling. Why hadn't Tom warned her that he was coming?

Amy felt her whole body recoil when she saw Adam's flag-draped coffin before the chapel altar. She reproached herself. It was wrong to be a general's wife and be so incapable of accepting death. But it was not the death of life that grieved her. It was the death of love. The community of the brave was not enough. It was too difficult to believe in it when the Army persisted in its habit of overstaffing everyone and everything and promoting the usual mixture of geniuses and fools. She suddenly found herself trembling, fighting tears. She was like Adam. She wanted perfection, honor, courage. But she knew it was impossible. So she lived with the compromise. *Why didn't you?* Amy whispered to the coffin. *Why wouldn't you?*

Honor had seen the coffin before. She was not threatened by it. She felt warm, comforted by the flag concealing its rigid finality. Halfway up the aisle she saw Tom Burke half turned in a pew, looking at them. He looked so sad, and yet so soldierly in his paratrooper's uniform, so strong and so caring, she knew he was the right man for Pookie. The sudden flaring certainty was another comfort, another reassurance that she would survive her journey across this no-man's-land of grief.

The Army band played several hymns, including "Alma Mater"

710

and "The Corps." The chaplain, a slight, serious man in black, came out on the altar and read the 121st and 132nd Psalms.

"Now," said the chaplain, "Colonel Thayer's daughter has asked me to read a code of honor he attempted to follow throughout his life.

"I have no parents; I make heaven and earth my parents.

"I have no magic power; I make inward strength my magic.

"I have no armor; I make righteousness my armor.

"I have no body; I make fortitude my body.

"I have no design; I make opportunity my design.

"I have no friends; I make immovable mind my friend.

"I have neither life nor death; I make the Eternal my life and death."

Joanna found the words wonderfully calming and consoling. She was glad that she had not allowed Adam to abandon them. Even if her decision had led to this final farewell. Her love for Honor had left her no other choice. Even if there had been a choice, she would have despised herself for being a partner to Adam's desertion of those ideals. She would never have been able to forget the day in the Doubting Hut in Japan when she saw them shining on his youthful face.

For a moment she recoiled from her own harshness. Who had put such iron in her soul? Adam himself was partly responsible. The man who sat beside her had given her strength of a different kind. She found herself remembering what Sam had said, when Honor called with the news of Adam's death. For a moment Joanna had wept, then the words burst out: "I loved him, Sam." He had paused to absorb the possible meanings. "We all did," he replied. "He was our anger—and our pride. Out of control. But still ours."

"Let us sing 'Rock of Ages,'" the chaplain said.

They stood and sang this hymn to primary faith. Joanna listened, musing on a strange fact. In the last three years, Adam had been the only person for whom she felt any desire to pray. It was not prayer as she had known it in her Catholic youth. It was a reaching out in the night to a different God, a being of mystery and darkness, asking Him to give Adam peace.

Amy flinched when pallbearers from the Regular Army detachment stationed at West Point carried the coffin to a hearse, which drove slowly into the nearby cemetery. The mourners followed on foot. The sight of the open grave was almost unbearable to her. The earth swallowing that daring body, that reckless smile. But the sight of so many silent witnesses, the headstones of the Army's dead, steadied her. Here was the ultimate proof of the community of the brave. She would try again to be content with being part of it. She joined mechanically in the Lord's Prayer. As far as Amy was concerned, the farewell that mattered was the three volleys fired by a squad of white-helmeted soldiers, to the crisp commands of a sergeant. The last serious words she and Adam had spoken had been drowned in the gunfire of Tet. *I love you*, she had said. She had struggled to regain that difficult confession, to restate it to George, for George, with only partial success. She would try again. This moment told her she had no other choice now.

The bugler played Taps. A tall, angular major, representing the Superintendent of the Academy, took the flag off the coffin, solemnly folded it and handed it to Honor. It was over, Honor thought. Twenty-five years were ending where they began. The sun was coming out. It was going to be a lovely fall day. She felt she ought to weep a little. But her eyes were dry. She had given Adam her best years, her best love. At least once, perhaps more than once, she had saved him from his worst self, that angry spirit that wanted to hurt more than help, destroy more than build. She had helped him remain Ashley.

A half hour later, Joanna, Amy and Honor sat in one of the parlors of Cullum Hall drinking coffee. The generals had left them with the second lieutenants. The Old Grads were downstairs in the Alumni Office discussing the publication of a twenty-fifth reunion yearbook for the class of 1950. Joanna felt dazed as she contemplated the circle of young faces around her. Adam was a hero to them. To her son Tom he was a second father.

She had scarcely absorbed this discovery when she got a second shock. Tom told her that he and Pookie Thayer were getting married. For a moment she was filled with resentment and alarm. Did she really want Adam's spirit infecting Tom's life? Would this thin, intense creature be woman enough to satisfy her handsome muscular son?

Suddenly she heard Adam laughing. He whispered an old koan to her. *After years of dreams in the forest. Now on the river's edge laughing. Laughing a new laugh.* She could not control these young lives. She had not been able to control her own life. They had to live out their histories, public and personal, and learn to accept what Heaven sent them. Perhaps they would profit by their parents' experience. But she doubted it.

Amy eyed the lieutenants wistfully as they said goodbye. "If any of you are in Washington over Christmas, give us a call," she said. "My daughter Grace will be home for two weeks." They all politely assured her that they would keep the invitation in mind. Pookie Thayer departed with them, telling her mother she would wait for her at the Hotel Thayer. Amy could see from the expression on Pookie's face that she would warn the lieutenants that Grace was a fat slob.

"Let's wander around," Amy said. "The D.O.G.'s are obviously going to take forever downstairs."

On Cullum Hall's marble stairway, they stopped to gaze up at the huge plaques containing the names of the graduates killed in Korea and Vietnam. Amy's eyes found John K. Stapleton, '49. Joanna pondered Peter M. Burke, '50.

"Adam's name should be there," Honor said.

"Yes," Joanna said.

They went up the last flight of stairs to the ballroom. Their footsteps echoed hollowly as they walked to the center of the dance floor. The small gallery windows, the closed balcony doors reduced the daylight to dimness. The white and gold walls, the rich red upholstery were lost without the multiple ceiling lights. The room seemed austere, forlorn, Joanna thought. Then she heard the golden alto saxophones and satiny trumpets of the bands of 1950. Around them swayed ghosts of radiant girls and smiling cadets. The dancers joked about Public Displays of Affection and kidded about home states and cities and who was going to be a general. Joanna faced them without fear. Her long night's struggle with memory had not been wasted.

Amy shivered. She had forgotten that Cullum Hall was designed as a memorial to the Academy's dead. The names of famous battles were engraved on the frieze above them. The walls were dotted with plaques memorializing individual professors and graduates. They wandered aimlessly, looking for a familiar name.

"No plaques for the wives," Amy said.

"We didn't die," Honor said.

"We're walking wounded," Joanna said.

"Where's the aid station?" Amy said.

Each seemed to know, to feel, the need at the same moment. They opened their arms and clung to each other, weeping. The words from "The Corps" blazed in Joanna's mind.

> *Grip hands with us now though we see not.*
> *Grip hands with us, strengthen our hearts.*

It lasted about a minute. They blew their noses and wiped their eyes. But their faces were still wet with tears when they came down the marble stairs to the lobby. The generals were waiting for them. "What were you doing up there?" Sam Hardin asked, an edge of concern in his voice, as he noticed the tears.

"Remembering," Joanna said.

Amy reached for George's hand. He seemed mildly surprised but he let her take it. Sam Hardin took Joanna's hand. She put her arm around Honor. They went out into the fall sunshine together.

About The Author

A SENSE of history, an awareness of the impact of the past on every level of life from the experience of the individual to the travails of a city to the crises of the nation, makes Thomas Fleming's fiction and nonfiction consistently interesting and important. From such popular and prize-winning books of biography and history as *The Man from Monticello*, *West Point*, and *1776: Year of Illusions* to his cycle of ten novels, spanning two centuries, Fleming has created a body of work that is winning him a reputation as a major interpreter of the American experience.

A graduate of Fordham University and a Navy veteran, Fleming was a magazine editor before becoming a writer in 1961. He lives in New York City with his wife, Alice, also a writer.

BEST OF BESTSELLERS
FROM WARNER BOOKS

THE BOYS IN THE MAIL ROOM
by Iris Rainer   (93-676, $2.95)

They were at the bottom rung of the ladder, but not so far down that they couldn't see the top, lust for the glamor, covet the power, hunger for the dolls and the dollars. They were four guys with a future—baby moguls on the make in Hollywood.

SCRUPLES
by Judith Krantz   (96-743, $3.50)

The ultimate romance! The spellbinding story of the rise of a fascinating woman from fat, unhappy "poor relative" of an aristocratic Boston family to a unique position among the super-beautiful and super-rich, a woman who got everything she wanted —fame, wealth, power and love.

LOVERS & GAMBLERS
by Jackie Collins   (83-973, $2.95)

LOVERS & GAMBLERS is the bestseller whose foray into the world of the beautiful people has left its scorch marks on night tables across two continents. In Al King, Jackie Collins has created a rock-and-roll superstud who is everything any sex-crazed groupie ever imagined her hero to be. In Dallas, she designed "Miss Coast-to-Coast" whose sky-high ambitions stem from a secret sordid past—the type that tabloids tingle to tell. Jackie Collins "writes bestsellers like a female Harold Robbins."

—Penthouse

THE WORLD IS FULL OF DIVORCED WOMEN
by Jackie Collins   (83-183, $2.95)

The world is their bedroom . . . Cleo James, British journalist who joined the thrill seekers when she found her husband coupling with her best friend. Muffin, a centerfold with a little girl charm and a big girl body. Mike James, the record promoter who adores Cleo but whose addiction to women is insatiable. Jon Clapton who took a little English girl from Wimbledon and made her into Britain's top model. Daniel Ornel, an actor grown older, wiser and hungrier for Cleo. And Butch Kaufman, all-American, all-man who loves to live and lives to love.

THE LOVE KILLERS
by Jackie Collins   (92-842, $2.25)

Margaret Lawrence Brown has the voice of the liberated woman who called to the prostitutes to give up selling their bodies. She offered them hope for a new future, and they began to listen, but was silenced with a bullet. It was a killing that would not go unavenged. In Los Angeles, New York, and London, three women schemed to use their beauty and their sex to destroy the man who ordered the hit, Enzio Bassolino, and he has three sons who were all he valued in life. They were to be the victims of sexual destruction.

THE BEST OF BESTSELLERS FROM WARNER BOOKS

CALIFORNIA GENERATION
by Jacqueline Briskin   (A95-146, $2.75)
They're the CALIFORNIA GENERATION: the kids who go to L.A.'s California High, where the stars come out at night to see and be seen, where life imitates art, where everyone's planning to ride off into the sunset and make every dream come true.

PALOVERDE
by Jacqueline Briskin   (A83-845, $2.95)
The love story of Amelie—the sensitive, ardent, young girl whose uncompromising code of honor leads her to choices that will reverberate for generations, plus the chronicle of a unique city, Los Angeles, wrestling with the power of railroads, discovery of oil, and growing into the fabulous capital of filmdom, makes this one of the most talked about novels of the year.

DAZZLE
by Elinor Klein & Dora Landey   (A93-476, $2.95)
Only one man can make every fantasy come true—entertainers, industrialists, politicians, and society leaders all need Costigan. Costigan, the man with the power of PR, whose past is a mystery, whose present is hidden in hype, and whose future may be out of his own hands. In a few hours, a marriage will end, a love affair begin, a new star will be created, and an old score settled. And Costigan will know whether or not he has won or lost in the gamble of his life.

THE BEST OF BESTSELLERS
FROM WARNER BOOKS

A STRANGER IN THE MIRROR
by Sidney Sheldon   *(A36-492, $3.95)*

Toby Temple—super star and super bastard, adored by his
vast TV and movie public yet isolated from real, human
contact by his own suspicion and distrust. Jill Castle—she
came to Hollywood to be a star and discovered she had to
buy her way with her body. In a world of predators, they are
bound to each other by a love so ruthless and strong, that is
more than human—and less.

BLOODLINE
by Sidney Sheldon   *(A36-491, $3.95)*

When the daughter of one of the world's richest men
inherits his multi-billion-dollar business, she inherits his
position at the top of the company and at the top of the
victim's list of his murderer! "An intriguing and entertaining tale."

—Publishers Weekly

RAGE OF ANGELS
by Sidney Sheldon   *(A36-214, $3.95)*

A breath-taking novel that takes you behind the doors of
the law and inside the heart and mind of Jennifer Parker.
She rises from the ashes of her own courtroom disaster to
become one of America's most brilliant attorneys. Her
story is interwoven with that of two very different men of
enormous power. As Jennifer inspires both men to passion,
each is determined to destroy the other—and Jennifer,
caught in the crossfire, becomes the ultimate victim.

BEST OF BESTSELLERS
FROM WARNER BOOKS

DARLING, NO REGRETS
by Davidyne Saxon Mayleas (A90-558, $3.50)

A tale of glamour and wealth—of the worlds of fashion and advertising—and of a remarkable woman's climb to success. Franciejean arrived in New York with nothing and nowhere was where she was headed—until she met Jamie who taught her about culture, society, and love. All of life's glittering prizes came to her—but nothing could save her from herself and past.

THE LAST LOVER
by Tish Martinson (A93-023, $2.95)

Rosalie La Farge was the girl who had everything—an adoring father, wealth, social connections, and beauty—and a devoted, handsome Egyptian prince whom she would wed. But after her eighteenth birthday, the emerald-eyed beauty would be shadowed by tragedy—someone evil was hiding behind the mask of friendship to poison her life.

BELLEFLEUR
by Joyce Carol Oates (A96-924, $3.75)

A swirl of fantasy, history, family feuds, love affairs and dreams, this is the saga of the Bellefleurs who live like feudal barons in a mythical place that might perhaps be the Adirondacks. A strange curse, it is said, hovers over the family, causing magical and horrible events to occur. Past and present appear to live side-by-side, as the fantastic reality of the Bellefleurs unfolds.

To order, use the coupon below. If you prefer to use your own stationery, please include complete title as well as book number and price. Allow 4 weeks for delivery.